"Pyper upends genre conventions once again . . . a high-concept dark fantasy novel . . . Lily's journey with a monster who inspired the very literary tradition Pyper so skillfully exploits provides . . . a satisfying confrontation with darkness, both personal and mythological, that readers expect from the best horror."

Toronto Star

"A darkly entrancing tale that sweeps you off your feet from its first pages. Filled with deliriously clever nods to the grand Gothic tradition, *The Only Child* is also fiercely original, wildly provocative, and utterly satisfying, beginning to end."

Megan Abbott, bestselling author of *You Will Know Me*

Praise for

THE DEMONOLOGIST

"Smart, thrilling, and utterly unnerving. Pyper's gift is that he deeply respects his readers, yet still insists on reducing them to quivering children. I like that in a writer."

Gillian Flynn, #1 *New York Times* bestselling author of *Gone Girl*

THE
HOMECOMING

ALSO BY ANDREW PYPER

The Only Child

The Damned

The Demonologist

The Guardians

The Killing Circle

The Wildfire Season

The Trade Mission

Lost Girls

Kiss Me (Stories)

THE
HOMECOMING
ANDREW PYPER

**SIMON &
SCHUSTER**

London · New York · Sydney · Toronto · New Delhi

A CBS COMPANY

First published in Canada by Simon & Schuster Canada, 2019
A division of Simon & Schuster, Inc.

First published in Great Britain by Simon & Schuster UK Ltd, 2019
A CBS COMPANY

3 5 7 9 10 8 6 4 2

Simon & Schuster UK Ltd
1st Floor
222 Gray's Inn Road
London WC1X 8HB

Simon & Schuster Australia, Sydney
Simon & Schuster India, New Delhi

www.simonandschuster.co.uk
www.simonandschuster.com.au
www.simonandschuster.co.in

A CIP catalogue record for this book is available from the British Library

Paperback ISBN: 978-1-4711-7839-9
eBook ISBN: 978-1-4711-7840-5

Printed and bound by CPI Group (UK) Ltd, Croydon, CR0 4YY

MIX
Paper from
responsible sources
FSC® C020471

Simon & Schuster UK Ltd are committed to sourcing paper that is made
from wood grown in sustainable forests and support the Forest Stewardship
Council, the leading international forest certification organisation. Our books
displaying the FSC logo are printed on FSC certified paper.

For Ford

Aaron?

Yeah?

Where do you think he's taking us?

I don't know.

Isn't it—

It's weird. But Dad was weird.

You think Mom's gonna be okay?

She sent you over to pick me up so she could get her own ride, right?

Right.

So she's fine. She likes being alone. Sometimes I think she likes it better than being—

Aaron?

Yeah?

Have you ever been on this road before?

Nope. And I've never been driven anywhere by someone who won't even look at you either.

Aren't you scared?

Why would I be scared?

It's such a big forest. No houses or anything. It's like we've been driving through it since—before we woke up, before—

It's a big forest all right.

And spooky. Look at the trees. All crowded together. Like they're whispering. Or—

Listen to me, Bridge. This whole routine—it's just the old man setting the scene before the lawyer tells us what's what.

I know. But did you notice? Back there?

What?

The fence. The gate we drove through.

So?

That means all this is private property.

Okay. I've never told you this before, but when I was a kid, Dad would tell me these stories. Fairy tales, I guess. Children walking off the path and meeting up with creatures, doppelgängers, phantoms. They'd always take place in the woods around a castle called Belfountain. I never guessed it was real. That it was his.

I remember.

Really? So I already told you about—

No. Not you. Daddy told me the same stories. Except I'm not sure they were things he made up.

Why do you say that?

Because I've been here before. Because he brought me.

BELFOUNTAIN

1

WHEN MOM CALLED TO TELL ME THE NEWS, I WAS SURPRISED AT FIRST THAT Raymond Quinlan was capable of something so human as dying. We were given to understand that Dad was a man of many talents, but none we knew of was so great as his gift for disappearing. All our lives he would leave without saying when he would be back. It could be days or weeks or months. Long enough that just when you thought this time he wouldn't return, he did. Without warning, unburdened by guilt or explanations. But now he'd gone somewhere there was no coming back from, and it was almost disappointing, the end of his mysterious life coming not by way of stunning revelations or secret agents knocking at the door but the inevitable way it comes for all of us.

Less than an hour after I got off the phone with Mom, a woman called saying she was "a representative of your father's estate" and that a car would come first thing in the morning to pick me up. When I asked where this car would take me, I was told it would be a journey requiring a day away, the destination "necessarily confidential."

That "necessarily" irked me. A word my father would use to answer why he couldn't say where he went. It implied we should appreciate the complicated circumstances behind things having to be this way, his importance, the triviality of our need to understand.

You'll never tell us where you go, will you? I asked him once, though what I really wanted to know was if he ever missed us when he was gone.

No, Aaron. I'm afraid I won't.

Because it's a secret?

Yes, he answered sadly. A sadness for me, his tone made clear, not something he felt himself. *Necessarily so.*

The limo stops before I can ask Bridge more about her being here before. The driver pulls open the back door and speaks for the first time since we started out this morning, asking for our cell phones.

"Why do you want them?"

"Protocol," he mumbles, the accent hinting at Russian, his fat palm thrust a little too close to my face.

"What do we do?" Bridge asks me.

"You expecting any important calls in the next hour?"

"No."

"Me neither. So let's humor them and play by the rules."

We hand our phones over to the driver, who sticks them in the pocket of his blazer and, without another word, returns to sit in the front seat, leaving us to get out. He eases the limo away to park next to another just like it at the edge of a circular gravel area outside what must be the castle Dad spoke of in his stories.

What's the best word to describe it? Not "castle," certainly. Not "mansion" either, or "home" or "cabin" or "hotel." My mind can't stop thinking of it as a lodge, despite its enormity, the stateliness of its clean-lined, modernist construction. It's the walls made from whole redwood logs that does it. Flat-roofed and maybe a little more than a hundred and fifty feet wide, with a facade that consists of a single floor with few windows, the structure's main features are the oversized front door with its polished brass knob and Frank Lloyd Wright–inspired metalwork of the railings. It's a building that communicates its expense through its extraordinary natural materials in place of ostentatious grandeur.

"Do we go inside?" Bridge asks.

"I don't really want to."

This is out before I can prevent it, and I can see how it troubles Bridge. How she doesn't want to enter either. She's fourteen, and I'm twenty-two years older. A gap so wide you might assume we aren't close, but we are. We've made a point of it. My job is to be her dad-in-place-of-a-dad, offering advice on the rare occasions she asks for it, and her job is to make me feel like I'm not alone in the world.

"Let's explore a bit," I add, as casually as I can.

"Which way?"

"You're the one who's been here before. You pick."

Bridge looks around. We both do. There's a utility building off to the right at the edge of the trees where I assume the tools and maintenance machinery is kept, though there are no windows to look through to confirm this. I also note how its single door is padlocked.

On either side of the parking area are a number of trailheads leading off into the trees in different directions. Four in total, each with a small sign on a metal post. I have to squint to read the words: Red, Green, Yellow, Orange. The kind of generic route names you'd find on a corporate campus. I try to peer along the trails to see where they lead, but each of them, after a couple dozen yards, takes a turn and disappears into the uninterrupted woods.

"How about Green?" Bridge says.

We start toward the closest trailhead to our right. The trees seem to grow closer together as we approach, forcing our lines of sight to press

into the spaces between their trunks only to be stopped by the trees behind them, again and again. It makes me think of looking into a mirror
reflected in a second mirror, so that the image within the glass repeats
itself into a bending, infinite curve.

"You first," Bridge tells me, nudging my back with her elbow.

It's meant to be funny, and we both force out a laugh, but neither of
us move.

A memory has come at me so hard I feel it as a punch to the top of
my chest, a fist that passes through skin, grasping and cold.

There seems to be little pattern to what brings it back. The forest, in
this case. One that makes me remember a different forest. The men who
emerged out of it, whooping and calling out names in a language I didn't
understand. The blades they swung over their heads, catching winks of
the sun.

A buried piece of a different life.

Overseas.

I force myself to go forward. Two steps into the trees.

"You hear that?"

Bridge doesn't answer, only pivots to look in the direction the sound
came from. Movement through the trees. Sleek and dark and coming fast.

"Another car," she says.

We watch it ease to a stop in front of the lodge, the driver opening
the back door and extending his hand for the passenger's phone just as
ours had done. A second later our mother steps out.

"Hey!" Bridge shouts, and runs off. There's a strange dawning of recognition on Mom's face as she watches her daughter come and throw
her arms around her as if they'd been separated by an absence of years
instead of hours.

I'm about to make my way to join them when the hushed woods are
interrupted by another sound. Not a car this time. A shuffling approach
on the trail we were about to start on.

There's a temptation to pretend I hadn't heard it and run off as Bridge had. But my mother and little sister are here, and I'm the eldest son. Despite my fear, despite the memory of *overseas*, there is this—what I am in the family: the surgeon, stable and mature, committed to helping others. I can't run even if it's what I want to do more than anything else.

I have to tell myself all this in order to turn and look.

A figure makes its way toward me. Coming up a slope so that first its head, then its shoulders and legs become visible like a body rising up out of the ground. A woman. Gangly and slight, her arms flapping birdishly out from her sides.

"Aaron!"

She sounds different from when I last spoke to her, though that was almost a year ago, at Nate's funeral. Her son. Yet I can still recognize the scratchy, sarcastic tone as Franny's. My other sister, though the truth is I've never really thought of her that way. She was always something else before that. A phone call from the emergency room or police station in the middle of the night. A poisonous fog I tried to stay ahead of. Most of the time growing up it was like Franny was only waiting until she could move out and get into truly serious trouble.

Now here she is, a year younger than me but looking a dozen years older, half jogging my way in the ungainly, loping manner of someone whose legs are asleep.

"You beat us here," I say.

"I went for a walk. But I got spooked out there all on my own. That's a lot of *trees*. Too much nothing for this city girl." She glances over my shoulder. "Is that Mom?"

"She just pulled in."

"Well, the gang's all here then."

"Some gang."

Franny stands a few feet farther from me than she ought to. Taking me in. Comparing the man in front of her to the profile of me she'd framed in her mind. How long would she have to go back into her years of hustling and needles to find a picture she could recall in any detail?

"I'd say 'Sorry about Dad,' but I'm not sure what that really means," I say.

"It means he's gone. Even more than he was when he was alive."

"That pretty much nails it."

She takes a half step closer to me. "Before we go inside, it's important for me— I want you to know something, Aaron."

"Sure."

"I'm different now."

She searches my face for doubt. And I try to hide it. To not show, through some involuntary grimace or narrowed eyes, how many times I've heard this before from her. Sometimes through tears, sometimes in furious accusation, though mostly conveyed with the same stony conviction she speaks with now. It's convincing. As convincing as it was five years ago when she told me she was pregnant, and during the days in and out of rehab after Nate was born.

For almost her entire adult life, being an addict has been Franny's sole occupation. I'm sure she'd correct me about the past tense. Even recovered addicts are still addicts, the disease in remission but never wholly erased. I'm a doctor; I know I'm supposed to embrace this understanding of why people—why my sister—would devote herself to her own destruction from the first day she sneaked a twenty from our mother's purse. It wasn't a lack of will, not a flaw of character, but the bad luck of having contracted a virus. And as a disease is never asked for, it has the power to excuse all cruelties and neglect committed along the way.

But the truth is, I can't talk myself out of seeing Franny the same way I see myself. An escape artist. I ran from my life, and she did too, if only figuratively, following a trail of fixes instead of twenty-six-mile courses through the streets of different cities.

In both cases, you collapse at the end.

In both cases, you finish where you started.

And now here Franny is telling me she's broken the cycle. Underweight and with a twitchy uncertainty to the way she shapes her face, as if constantly adjusting an emotional dial between dead and insane, searching for the human midpoint. But not stoned. Her words clear and firm even if the rest of her isn't. And as for making a change, I should know it's possible. I did it for Bridge. Maybe Franny has done it as a memorial to her own child.

"I'm on a new path," she says. "And I'm not talking about all the stuff that's happened with the government and the police and the camps—that's made it different for *all* of us. I'm talking about me. A new direction."

"I can see that."

"No, you can't. Because it's not on the outside, not something you can see. It's not just that I'm sober now. And it's not only about losing Nate. It's *me*. I've turned things around. I work in a shelter now, did you know that?"

"I think Mom mentioned something."

"Doing good work in a bad place."

"That's great, Franny. Really."

But she doesn't want to hear my words of support. This, it's clear by her rigid jaw and hands gripped into pale-knuckled fists, is a prepared speech that must be spoken aloud, regardless of the audience. She's doing it to hold herself together, to prove that she is inching beyond the range of grief, that she can exist here in what remains of our father's shadow.

"Whatever happens today—whatever Dad left for us—I'm giving it to the shelter. That's the only reason I've come. I'm going to pick up my check, get right back into that limo, and do something positive with what I have."

"I believe you," I say. And I do.

I can't attest to whether or not my sister will go back to using once she returns to the city, but I'm certain she will do this. I know what it's like to make a sharp turn, to give shape to life by way of one big move. After that, however, all bets are off.

"It's good to see you, big brother," she says, and surprises me by wrapping her scrawny arms around my neck and pulling in close. She smells of lemony soap and coconut hair conditioner and lilac body spray. She smells clean.

2

I EXPECT MOM TO BE CRYING WHEN FRANNY AND I WALK OVER TO JOIN HER AND Bridge. From the bereavement of losing her husband, yes, but also the image of seeing her three children around her, opening their arms to take her in. Normally this would be more than enough to shatter her into spare parts. But while she appears underslept and a little shaky on her feet, her face is dry, the permanently etched, meek downturns of brow and mouth hardened into determined lines.

"My babies," she says, and I'm startled to find that I'm the one fighting tears.

We stay like that for a while. The surviving Quinlans. Linked in an awkward group hug, none of us able to find words to fit the moment.

Bridge is the first to pull away.

"Something's coming out," she says.

We all turn to find the brass handle of the lodge's front door glinting as it moves in a slow rotation. It allows the additional second required to register the word Bridge had used. *Something*.

The door slides inward. It's too dark to see much of anything, so that it seems it's opened on its own like the doors to cobwebbed manors did in the Saturday-morning Halloween spoofs I grew up with.

After a pause an elderly man steps out, as if assuring himself that all eyes are on the threshold before stepping through into the wan light.

"Hello, Quinlans!"

It's probably nerves, a reflexive response to the unintentionally comic tenor of the old man's Bela Lugosi–like welcome, the strangeness of being in this place together after so long being in other places apart—whatever it is, all of us burst into laughter.

For a moment, we're a little less worried, a little less brittle. The trees themselves lend us space, leaning away as if confirming the harmless humor intended by every detail of this performance. Limos! Silent drivers who take your phones! A funny stranger beckoning to us!

Eventually we quiet, returning to politeness with cleared throats.

"Please, come in. Come *in*," the man at the door says again.

The laughter is over. Nothing of it remains. The forest has swallowed it whole. The man at the door waits, waxy, preposterous. Yet despite all this, the signs of things sliding from strange to wrong, we have no choice but to carry ourselves up the steps and slouch inside.

3

IT TAKES A MOMENT FOR OUR EYES TO ADJUST ONCE THE DOOR IS CLOSED. THERE
are lights on—multiple bulbs set into a chandelier overhead, one that's
made of what looks like animal bones fused together into an ornate, alien
rib cage—but they're dimmed. For a time, all we can focus on with certainty is the man standing before us, a canine smile stretched tight above
his chin. He's got to be the lawyer. It's the boastful accessories that give
him away. The monogrammed cuff links, Ivy alumni tie, chunky Rolex.
Evidence of decades spent tallying up the top-end billable hours.

He introduces himself as Mr. Fogarty. A caricaturizing surname like
a minor character out of Dickens. In fact, he *looks* like a minor character
out of Dickens: silver reading glasses balanced on the end of his beakish
nose, small yellow teeth, the navy three-piece suit with a vest he keeps
adjusting but never unbuttons despite the humidity.

He looks at each of us in turn.

"This is all of you?"

"Who else were you expecting?" Franny says.

The lawyer spins on the heels of his leather oxfords to face her. "No one in particular."

"Okay. I know it's not your fault or anything, Mr. Fogarty. But I think I can speak for all of us when I say we're not totally comfortable with being dragged out here for something we could have done far more easily downtown," I say, backing Franny up while attempting businesslike civility. "So can I suggest we get started?"

He purses his lips as if sucking on a lemon. *Let's get started* was supposed to be his line and I stepped on it.

"You're the surgeon," he says. "I understand. Eager to return to work."

"I just don't want to be here," I say, and as soon as I do, I realize how deeply I feel it—a claustrophobic's urge to escape despite the abundant space of the front hall we stand in.

"Of course. It's a difficult time," the lawyer says vaguely, and starts off around a corner, leaving the rest of us to follow.

From the front the lodge was impressive in its dimensions, but as we enter at one end of the great room, the building reveals its true magnificence. Across from us stands what must be an almost twenty-foot-high wall of floor-to-ceiling windows that frame the dappled woods, deepening as the trees rise up a gentle slope so that there is no sky to be seen, only variations of green leaves and brown deadfall. We traverse a raised walkway of varnished oak opposite the glass with steps down to a sunken living room of modular leather sofas and Turkish rugs laid over the wide floorboards, a stone hearth big enough to stand in, and finally, looking over it all at the opposite end from where we first entered, a banquet dining table made of recovered barn planks.

This is where Fogarty stands behind a chair at the head, gesturing for each of us to sit. I stay close to Bridge, taking a place between her and the old lawyer as if to fend off a potential assault. Franny takes the spot across from us, and Mom sits directly to Fogarty's left, her instinct for good manners and hospitality active even now, despite this not being her home nor the lawyer a guest.

"Let me first express my condolences," Fogarty begins, the last to pull his chair back and lower himself into it, fussily touching the papers and files laid out before him as if practicing a complicated piece on a piano keyboard. "I didn't know Mr. Quinlan well—he was exact in his directions but a fierce defender of his time, as perhaps you're already aware—but if I may say, he struck me as a remarkable individual. One of the privileges of my work is meeting highly varied people of accomplishment, and your husband and father had a way about him that will remain with me. I struggle to pinpoint the precise nature of his uniqueness, the *aspect*, in addition to his obvious intelligence, that I found so—"

"He was a remarkable man," Mom interrupts him. Her hand flutters to her mouth as if in an attempt to retrieve the bitterness of her words.

"Indeed," Fogarty says. He likes this scene—the Reading of the Will—and its demonstrations of emotion like this that he's obliged to at least appear to subdue while allowing himself to savor at the same time.

"Do you know what he did for a living, Mr. Fogarty?" Franny asks.

"You didn't?"

"We took guesses sometimes. Thought he might have been a scientist. Sometimes we wondered if he was a spy. But he wasn't really the double-oh-seven type. And do spies or scientists own places like this?"

"I couldn't speak to that," Fogarty says, "and as for my knowledge of his occupation, I haven't a clue, I'm afraid. I handled his legal affairs—well, some of them—but it wasn't necessary to know the specifics of his business."

"That's interesting. Because we all came to the same conclusion."

"Oh?"

"It wasn't necessary to know who he was," Franny says. "Because, for us, there was nobody *to* know."

Fogarty waits for more of this, but when Franny sits back, fighting the new twitch at the top of her cheek, we all look to him.

"Shall we pause a moment?" he asks, lifting an expensive-looking pen from the table and waving it in slow, hypnotizing circles. "Do we need a break?"

"No break," Mom says, her voice now froggy and thick. "Please continue, Mr. Fogarty."

"Very well. Now, the way this works is quite straightforward," he says brightly. "You've been asked here to attend the reading of Raymond Quinlan's last will and testament, and as executor of that will, I am responsible for its administration. There are a number of what might be considered unconventional codicils here, but at its heart, the document is—"

"How much?"

This question takes all of us by surprise not only by its abruptness, but by who asks it. Mom. Leaning forward so heavily her elbows rest on bloodless white pads of skin.

"Mrs. Quinlan, a proper valuation would only be accurate once the assets have been liquidated, if and when that occurs."

"How much did he have?" she asks again, then looks around the table at the faces watching her, and only now hears the brusque tone of her voice.

"Forgive me, Mr. Fogarty," she continues, softer now. "My husband kept many secrets from me during his life, an arrangement I accepted, more or less. Even when we were young and first dating, he told me there were things about him I could never know. What did I care? There was love to make up for knowledge. I signed an extensive prenuptial agreement before they were common, or so I was later told. But now that he's gone, I don't want to live with secrets anymore. I couldn't care less about the money—I have little use for it, God knows—but until today I was unaware this place existed. Quite something to keep from your wife of forty-two years, wouldn't you say?"

Fogarty replies with a lawyerly shrug.

"So now there's someone who is possessed of information sitting in front of me," Mom goes on. "Now there's *you*, Mr. Fogarty. So you can understand my eagerness to learn as much as I can, and in as specific terms as it's known."

"Yes, I can see all that. I certainly can," the lawyer says sympathetically. "Well, let me jump to the bottom line then. Mr. Quinlan's holdings weren't complicated. He had transferred his financial instruments—stocks, funds, etcetera—into a cash account only months before his death. The amount"—Fogarty glances down at his papers before looking up again—"is presently just over three million dollars."

"But that's not all of it," Mom says.

"No."

"Because there's this place. What did he call it?"

"Belfountain," Bridge says.

"Quite right," Fogarty says, glancing at Bridge with theatrical astonishment.

"Belfountain," Mom repeats distastefully, as if it's the name of her husband's mistress. "How much of it is his?"

"All of it. No partners, no mortgage."

"What's it worth?"

"Forgive the cliché, but a property of this kind is only worth what someone is willing to pay for it."

"My mother might, but I don't forgive the cliché," I say. "You know the ballpark. So tell her."

I expect a dirty look from Fogarty, but he merely casts a cool smile my way. That's when I see it. The reason I feel such hostility toward this man, and maybe why Mom and Franny feel it too: he reminds me of Dad. Not in his looks or attire, but the superiority, the withholding of information, the way he'd make you ask for everything and in the asking reveal your neediness. It's a game I told myself I'd never play again, and yet here I am, perspiring with frustration, trying to intimidate this older man whose very posture confirms his control, the compiling of every weakness he'd detected in me.

"It's six hundred acres of pristine rain forest. One of the finest undivided tracts of its kind in the Pacific Northwest," he answers at an unhurried pace. "The sleeping cabins are modest but well-built, and in entirely good repair. And of course there's the main building we sit in now, an exceptional piece of contemporary architecture. So while the assessed value of the estate for tax purposes stands at twenty-seven million dollars, I expect it would attract offers significantly higher than that if listed on the open market."

No one replies to this, not right away. It is a Life-Changing Moment in the same way, I suppose, that hearing a terminal diagnosis or your newborn's first cry is. Of course, in this case, it's only money. But that can do it too if there's enough of it. An amount that, even without doing the math, each of us hears for what it is. Safety. Freedom. Transformation.

Mom is the first to eventually speak. A woman who is close to tears at the best of times, a four-decade state of weepy readiness, awaiting the triggers of nostalgia or affection or joy, but more often reminders of the long-buried disappointment in herself.

"Why did he need it to be so big?" she asks nobody in particular. "Six hundred acres! Guest cabins. And this place, the size of a small hotel. What did he *do* here?"

Fogarty tents his fingers and sets them on the table.

"I appreciate how eccentric this must appear to you, Mrs. Quinlan," he says. "But I was his attorney, not his valet. I'm not aware of—"

"Did he have—were there *friends* who would come to stay? Were there *parties*? I mean, what kind of parties would they *be*?" she laughs, no longer addressing the lawyer, merely speaking her confusion aloud, questions that echoed up to the room's timber rafters. "He didn't have friends.

We didn't have friends! Not the kind who would come to a—to a private resort in the woods to—to *what*? Do *what*?"

"These are undoubtedly legitimate questions, but they fall outside my—"

"Seven and a half million."

All of us turn to Franny. And she looks back at us with the expression of someone who has spoken aloud without intending to.

"I'm just saying," she says. "Assuming the minimum sale price of the property, and the proceeds equally divided among the four of us." She looks at Fogarty. "Am I right?"

"I won't hazard an estimation on the math," he says, "but you are correct in your assumption of the will's stipulating an equal division of assets. As I said, despite the specific nature of the holdings coming as a surprise to you, your father provided clear legal directions, if also some rather unusual conditions."

He lets this last part hang in the air, waiting for it to snag in our minds, a tightness to his lips that I read as a tell of excitement. He's not just an arrogant old-school dandy, I see now. Fogarty is a closet sadist.

"What conditions?" I say, and make a point of squeaking my chair closer to him. I'd like to make him uncomfortable if I can. But I also want to physically buffer Bridge from the strangeness I can sense is about to be unleashed upon us.

"Your father assigns all his assets, in equal terms, to his wife and all of his children," Fogarty pretends to read from the papers in front of him, then raises his head to speak directly to me. "On satisfaction of a single request that all of you stay on here at Belfountain for thirty days."

"What are you talking about?"

"Which piece is giving you difficulty?"

"Having to stay here for a month. Why don't we start with that?"

Fogarty takes in a long breath and billows it over the table in my direction, a hot gust carrying the scents of mustard and butterscotch candy.

"Wills are expressions of wishes," he says. "And your father wished for you, your siblings, and your mother to live here together for a period of time after his passing. I can only assume it was for the purposes of collective grieving, or perhaps reconciliation. Families are families, yes? In any case, to participate in the division of funds, each of you must remain on the property for the duration of the term. Naturally, the delivery of food and supplies has been arranged for, and you'll find comfortable bedding has been—"

"What if we leave?"

This is Franny. Fogarty takes his time shifting around to face her.

"You forfeit your share of the estate," he says.

"Even for a day? I mean, there's things that need to be taken care of. We all have *lives*."

"The instructions are clear. The perimeter of the estate marks the extent to which you may travel."

"I'd like my phone back."

"That would violate the conditions. No phones, no internet. No outside contact of any kind."

"Is this for real?" Franny says, starting to stand and then sitting again as if against a swirl of dizziness. "You're talking about a prison!"

"Not at all. You're free to go at any time."

"At a cost."

"A forfeiture."

"When does the clock start?" I ask.

This provides Fogarty with the moment he's been waiting for. He pinches up the sleeve of his shirt an inch to reveal the Rolex on his wrist and clicks a button at the side, starting the timer.

"Now," he says.

4

IT GETS NOISY AFTER THAT.

Franny shrieking about calling the police, Bridge crying and me trying to comfort her while telling Fogarty where he could shove his gold watch. Most troubling of all is Mom. The unhinged sound of her hatecackling at the last trick her husband had played on their marriage.

Maybe it is the haunting amplification of our voices through the cavernous interior of the lodge or the long drive here only now taking its toll, or the questions in our minds jostling and demanding to be asked first. Whatever it is, we all go quiet at the same time. Blustering and aflame moments ago, now exhausted, leaning into the table's edge or the backs of our chairs to hold ourselves upright.

Fogarty lowers his voice to little more than a whisper.

We listen.

He tells us that he's drafted notices to be sent to our respective schools or workplaces explaining our absences as a "family emergency." If any of us have partners or companions requiring similar explanation, he's prepared to do the same for them, but he believes none of us have significant others at present, and seeing how none of us correct him, it appears he's correct. No one will contact the authorities. No one will come looking for us.

In addition to regular deliveries of food, he's arranged for clothes in our sizes and a pair of sneakers for each of us in duffel bags he deposited in the front closet. There is no television or radio or computer anywhere on the estate's grounds, and no books or magazines to speak of, but we're assured of an "impressive collection of jigsaw puzzles" for our entertainment.

"You make it sound like a game," Franny says.

The old lawyer looks heavenward for an alternative phrase. "It's merely a request of the deceased. It lacks the competition of a game. Although, I suppose, there is an element of endurance. A test, then?"

"What happens if we all walk?" I ask.

"In that instance, Mr. Quinlan has arranged for his estate to be assigned to his alma mater."

"He'd give it all to his *college*?" Mom says.

"They'd probably name a dorm after him," Franny says.

"The amount is more than sufficient for that," Fogarty replies, taking Franny's point in earnest. "But Raymond's directions were for the donation to be anonymous."

"Of course," Franny says. "The invisible man."

Fogarty informs us that while there is technically no reason to make a final decision now—we can leave anytime and use the satellite phone in a metal box just on the other side of the gate to arrange for a ride—he will linger a short while in case any of us wants a ride back this afternoon.

"Hold on. Just *hold* on," I say, keeping him there as he seems about to slip out of the room. It takes a second to catch my breath, and I realize how exasperated I am, a helplessness that has led me to the edge of vertigo, my toes and fingertips tingling.

"Yes?"

"I don't think you understand. I'm a *surgeon*."

"I understand perfectly, Dr. Quinlan."

"There's patients—there's people counting on me."

"As I've already mentioned, your absence will be explained. You have colleagues who can cover your case list in such instances, do you not?"

"That's not the point."

"What is the point?"

I'm important. This is what I want to say. I'm a medical specialist, and these are difficult times. Some are calling it a national crisis, and who would argue otherwise? Emergency rooms across the country are over capacity with those who need to be patched, stitched, reassembled. But I say nothing. Partly because Franny speaks for me first.

"The point is he's a big deal," she says. "He's worked so hard to be one, to show his daddy what a good boy he could be, and he thinks he should be entitled to an exemption."

My sister looks at me without particular malice, only the fixed *Am I wrong?* expression of the aggrieved.

"Maybe this isn't the best time for a family therapy session," I say.

"No? When *would* have been a good time, Aaron? When I was in trouble taking care of Nate on my own and you were barely able to force yourself to return my calls? Or how about when he died? Even *then* you showed up late to the service and left early because you couldn't wait to disappear back to the hospital, where you could be everybody's savior." She cracks a wincing smile. "You know something? You're more like Dad than I thought."

Most of this strikes me as unfair. I *had* tried with Franny, taken dozens of runs at being a brother and a friend. But once she'd decided on her course, there was nothing I could do to coax her back, other than running my own life aground in the process. She might be cured now, she might be clean. But that doesn't mean she gets to rewrite the story.

Where she may not be entirely off is the disappearing act I've culti-vated over the years. *I have to go.* My refrain the same as Dad's.

"I'll give you a little privacy to discuss amongst yourselves," Fogarty says, only half suppressing his pleasure at all this as he starts toward the walkway to the entry hall. But Mom stops him.

"We're staying," she says, and shifts her gaze around the table, taking her children in one by one. "All of us."

"We don't have to do this, Mom. We could challenge it. In court, I mean," I say, with a confidence I don't actually possess. "There's no way this is enforceable."

"He wanted us to stay, Aaron," she says. "Which means he wanted it for a reason."

"What reason?"

"To show us something. Reveal his secrets. Or maybe just one of them. That's enough for me."

"I don't understand."

"I've devoted my life to a stranger," Mom starts, measuring her words, "and it's left something missing in me. Just as the three of you—it's *dam-aged* you. So I need to see the truth. Don't you?"

It strikes me how close Mom's words are to what I told Bridge when we first got into the limo. *Some part of me felt empty before you came along. A corner the light couldn't reach.* I meant it as a consolation for her losing Dad, the comfort that might come with knowing that although she'd lost a life in the past two days, she'd saved mine over the years before this.

But now here was Mom saying the same thing. *Something missing in me.* It's fairly obvious Franny has felt the same from the very beginning. Was it true for Bridge as well? Always a note about her "perfectionism" on report cards, and worryingly friendless outside of school hours.

"Bridge?" I say, turning to her.

"I'm not going."

"Me neither," Franny says.

"Okay. Looks like we're all in," I say, checking to see Fogarty's reaction. The lawyer is already starting away with a flapping wave of his fingers, clapping down the walkway in his hard-soled shoes. We all wait for him to call back with final instructions or wish us good luck. But a moment later we hear the front door swing closed, and there's nothing more.

5

WE PRETEND TO BE LESS FREAKED OUT THAN WE ACTUALLY ARE FOR MAYBE three or four minutes before Franny goes to check out front. When she returns, she looks even skinnier than before. The limbs she'd held straight through force of will are now rolling and loose, her gait wobbly as a baby giraffe's.

"He's gone," she says. "The cars too."

"So this is real," I say.

"Yeah. I pinched myself to make sure. Like, *hard*."

There's a sense all of us share of having a lot of important things we should be doing right now, rules and assignments to be written up. But none of us move.

"He wasn't lying about the duffel bags," Franny says. "And there's a bicycle outside the door that wasn't there before. One with a wagon attached to the back."

"I'm guessing that's for the deliveries," I say. "It's up to us to go to the gate and bring back whatever gets left there."

"Why a bike? Why not a pickup truck or golf cart or something?"

"Dad wanted us to get more exercise?"

The fact is I have an immediate idea about the bike. Nonmotorized. Our phones are already gone. Fogarty was careful to mention no TV or computers or radio. It may be less about denying us connection to the outside world than it is about limiting our options. Dad wanted to leave us with everything except an easy way out. He wanted to leave us with us.

"Anyone hungry?" This is Mom. Abruptly standing and clearing away her previous displays of emotion with a sharp sniff. "Where do you think the kitchen is in this place?"

She starts off, and our eyes follow her around a partition at the end of the dining area, up a few steps to another platform that looks down not only on the great room but the walkway that runs the length of it.

"It's up here!" she calls. There's a rubbery sucking sound as she opens the fridge. "Well, look at that. Something for everyone!"

She's working so hard at restoring her role as mother, chief children feeder and normalizer, it would be heartbreaking if the three of us didn't need it so badly. That, and judging by the way we wordlessly move away from the table and closer to her voice, we actually could use something to eat.

We come up the steps to find that the kitchen is just as impressive as the lodge's other spaces. Rectangular like the great room, it runs for perhaps forty feet from the dining area to the pantry, with an industrial gas range and a butcher block of the kind you'd find in a restaurant kitchen and steel shelves holding enough stacked plates and bowls to serve a wedding. A series of three long windows look out the front where I confirm that the limos are in fact no longer there.

There's a tinted mirror at a corner of the ceiling opposite the sink, one that's angled downward to reflect whoever stands at the butcher block like the ones they have on cooking shows. I catch a glimpse of myself in it when I turn, a more lost-looking version than my usual confident self as I scrub in or do rounds with a pack of interns following behind me.

By the time we gather around Mom, she's laid out open Tupperware containers of cold roast chicken, broccoli salad, spinach dip. Picnic food. We set to spooning it onto plates, eating as we stand there together, not wanting to return to the unprotected expanse of the dining room's banquet table.

"That shit'll kill you," Franny says as I drop a handful of potato chips onto the side of my plate. "And didn't you used to run four times a week or something? No offense, Aaron, but don't you think you could lose a few pounds?"

I'm not especially tall, but despite the couple extra inches around the waist added over the last few years, I remain slight in the limb-stretched way tall people generally do. Even in my marathoner days, I would often look like someone suffering a nutritional deficiency. Back then it was because I ran too much. Now it's because I work too much.

"Don't you think you could gain a few ounces?" I say, pouring some chips onto her plate before scouring the cupboards. "Oh no. This is *bad*. No booze."

"It's for the best, believe me. Think of this as rehab."

"If you start twelve stepping me, Franny, I swear I'm out of here."

"Great! The rest of us will split your share. So, first step: admit you are powerless and your life is unmanageable."

"Now that I think of it, as of today, both are officially true."

It's teasing banter, brother and sister giving each other harmless jabs like old times. Except I don't remember us ever being this open and easy in the old times.

A family eating a meal together. For a moment we're relaxed, relieved of all the questions that demand replies. Then I look over at Bridge, and, watching her chew and swallow, the moment of ease instantly passes.

The scar along her throat reminds me how close we can come to losing everything.

For me, that's her.

From time to time, I've thought it was odd—maybe even a little pathetic—to not have any real social life other than my Tuesday get-togethers with Bridge. Should I be living a fuller life than this? Is even asking this question an obvious sign that I'm not? Then again, the people I know with spouses or kids—most of them feel the same way. There could be dozens who cared about you, or only one, and in both cases you were left to wonder if it was enough.

Bridge looks over at me. Sees—as she can always see—how I'm muscling through these kind of thoughts. She gives me a kick in the shins.

"Save any chips for me?" she says.

"Really? Now *you're* giving me flak about the damn Pringles? Here, have mine."

I offer her a chip, holding it like a communion wafer, and she comes at it, teeth bared. I pull my fingers away a quarter second before she bites the chip out of the air.

6

AS WE TIDY UP AFTER DINNER, I CATCH MYSELF WATCHING MY MOTHER AS IF SHE were someone I'd only seen pictures of, a washed-up celebrity in a checkout counter magazine, but now had the opportunity to observe up close. She would have been beautiful when my father first met her. A sophisticated face, but one from a different era. An aging screen star from the old studio system, Olivia de Havilland, say, or Joan Fontaine. It makes her appear older than she is. Not necessarily in years but in her place in cultural time. Slightly lost in the way of a foreigner who doesn't understand the local slang.

In recent years, her face has been difficult to find, as she's taken to hiding it behind longish bangs, the collars of her coats raised to her jawline. Her body is increasingly hidden too. Mom entered the Shawl Age earlier than others, abandoning dresses in favor of layered wraps. For other women, these bundled fineries might be seen as a way of expressing yourself as one moves from a certain age to another. But I don't think my mother saw it that way. For her it was protection. A suit of armor composed of cashmere and silk.

As if feeling my eyes on her, Mom turns to face me. Smiles with a widow's exhausted pride.

"It's good you never got married, Aaron," she says.

"Never say never, Mom. I've still got time."

"Take all the time you want. It will still be someone you'll never really know."

Franny and Bridge pause to observe this exchange, but from a distance, like a show on TV in a dentist's waiting room.

"That's kind of negative, don't you think?" I say, offering a quick eye roll in Bridge's direction. "You're talking about Dad. Not everyone's like him."

"It doesn't matter who it is. They'll be someone with thoughts and plans they won't share—even when they're sharing their thoughts and plans."

"Not if they love you," I say, and it sounds pitiful, even though I believe it to be true.

Mom comes over and touches my face with a hand covered in dish soap, leaving a trail of popping bubbles on my skin.

"I don't know about love," she says in her singular tone of cheerful defeat. "But marriage? It's a game. And people like us are built to lose every time."

"What do you mean, people like us?"

"The bad liars."

My parents never spoke of divorce, not in front of me anyway, yet it haunted their marriage like a missing child. They couldn't have been satisfied. They weren't together enough for that. Our family wasn't together enough for that.

Other kids at school had more outwardly objective reasons for being pushed off course in their lives. The captain of the swim team, Jake Envers, had a mother who committed suicide by idling her car in their closed garage while sitting in the back seat with a bottle of pinot grigio and all the Mother's Day cards Jake had ever given her. Mr. Illington, down the street from us, went to prison for fraud, and the rest of his family had to stand on their front lawn as they watched the bailiffs take the furniture out of their home. I could never say so, but part of me envied those kids. At least they had clear answers to "What *happened* to you?" The best I could come up with was that I had no memory of my father ever opening his arms to me.

I tried to make up for it. I clung to my mother as much as I could, for one thing. I told Franny I loved her so often she asked me to cut it out. I left letters for my father on the desk in his study, and when he came home, he would place them into a drawer, unopened.

Through high school, Franny busied herself by skidding into the slow-motion crash of her life. And dancing along with her was Mom, always a step behind, hopelessly trying to shield her daughter while, at the same time, denying there was any real problem at all.

It left me to keep us a unit. Keep us the Quinlans. That's how I saw it, anyway. Like the passenger with a fear of flying who believes she alone maintains the plane suspended in air by holding her breath, I thought I was preventing us from spiraling apart by being good. Good grades, good at sports. Avoiding trouble in all its forms. Not *too* good—I was conscious of not shaming Franny—but striking a balance between being the kind of son and brother you could be proud of while not having to think about him too much.

I declined acceptance to colleges back East and went to Washington State. Mom agreed it was a good idea. "Just in case," she said. It was what she would say every time I decided against taking a risk. *You should be here, Aaron. Just in case.* She never said what dire possibility she had in mind, but we both understood it to mean one of them dying. Franny, Dad, herself. If any of them dropped, I would come in and clean things up, make sure Bridge was taken care of. Until then, I would remain on standby.

Waiting for something terrible to happen can leave you with a lot of free time. That's why I started running. Marathons that wiped me clean. Provided the illusion of a fresh start.

I ran to get away.

But I could never get away.

There was no getting Dad back, even then. Mom was too swaddled in antianxiety pills and defense mechanisms to be fully reached. Franny was Franny. Which left Bridge. The only child in a home that felt under-populated even on the once-a-year-or-so occasions we all found our-selves in it.

I slipped into the role of surrogate father without much effort. Not just because Bridge's real dad had resigned from the post, but because the two of us got along so well. There was an ease between us you wouldn't necessarily expect across the awkward chasm that divides a five-year-old girl from an introvert grown man. I think part of it came from the fact that I saw something of myself in Bridge. The brave solidity that, if you looked close enough, was slightly askew.

But along with this, I was curious.

How did she see our home, our mother, our father of the top secret phone calls that yanked him away from birthday parties and dance recit-als and nine-tenths of the meals we'd eat? How did she seem to know him in a way the rest of us didn't?

Once the kitchen has been returned to design-magazine spotlessness, we all take a tour of the lodge. At the end of the walkway that acts as a spine for the whole building, dividing the kitchen on top from the living area below, we come to the bedrooms. There are three, each with its own en suite.

"Is it all right if I take this one?" Mom asks before sitting on the edge of the bed in the third bedroom we poke our heads into.

"Of course," Franny says. "I'll be right across the hall."

"What about you two?"

"I want to check out one of the cabins," Bridge answers before I do.

"You can't stay out there all on your own," Mom says, making a move to rise but finding she doesn't have the strength.

"I won't be alone," Bridge says, and elbows me in the side. "Aaron will be with me."

After I carry Mom's duffel bag to her room and tell her and Franny good night, Bridge and I head out the front door, each of us with our own bags strapped over our shoulders, to once again choose between the four trails into the woods.

"How about Orange," I say. "Anything but Green. I don't like Green."

"Orange it is."

What I hope will be enough dusky light to see by instantly snuffs out as soon as we start into the trees. There are LED headlamps included in each of our packs, and we stop to put them on, clicking the beams to their brightest setting. The light pushes back against the encroaching charcoal night like a yellow fist.

We walk along a trail that, after the first fifty yards, narrows so that we have to proceed single file. Me ahead and Bridge behind, both of us crunching over twigs and fallen leaves more loudly than I would have thought possible even if we were jumping up and down in steel-toed boots.

"Hard to believe we're the only four people on all this land," she says.

I prevent myself from saying it, because I don't want to frighten her and because I have nothing to back it up with. But the truth is it doesn't feel like we're the only ones here. It could be other people, waiting. Or not. Whatever it is, it doesn't feel hidden. It feels like everything around us. Belfountain. The trees themselves seem to observe us with an interest bordering on hunger. The ground softening under our steps, testing its hold on us with tiny grasps of our heels.

"The time you were here with Dad," I say. "What did the two of you do?"

Bridge likes to wear her hair in a ponytail. When she turns to look at you—as she looks at me now—the hair follows a half second later, perching atop her shoulders as if interested to hear what you're about to say for itself.

"Just hike around," she says.

"Did he say anything?"

"Not really. He was kind of rambling, y'know? I was only five or something like that. Everything he said sounded like philosophy."

"Or riddles."

"Same thing."

"Do you remember anything from what he was rambling about?"

"One thing, I guess," she says. "We were walking along a trail like this one and we came to the end. There wasn't a cabin or anything. It just stopped. Dad stopped too. Asks me this question. Looking at me, totally serious, y'know? Like he was searching for the answer himself."

"What was the question?"

" 'Where does the path lead after it ends?' "

I let the words tumble around in my head until I can't tell if they're familiar to me or I've just made them seem so.

"What do you think he meant?"

"It was Dad. How do I know?" Bridge says. "Something about coming to the end and deciding whether to go ahead and make a new trail or go back on the one already there."

"Sounds like a Hallmark card."

"The way I'm saying it, yeah. But the way *he* said it—it sounded like this Big Idea. Everything he said, especially that day—Me! Dad! Alone together!—seemed big." She pauses. "It's strange, but when I try to think of him, it's hard to even remember what he looked like."

I'd heard of this before. The way even the most significant people fade in the memory of those who live on after they die, the physical being of the person translated from photographic portraiture into a collection of feelings, words, scents, or touches. Yet no matter how normal I know it to be, as I try to summon a picture of my father's face to mind, there's little other than the thick-framed glasses, an on-again, off-again moustache, ears that revealed long filaments of hair when he stood with the sun behind him.

There's still the sound of his voice though. Still the sense there was something missing about him that went deeper than him being gone so much. Not just an absence. An erasure.

I stop walking, and Bridge, head down, bumps into me. I turn around and she's readying a laugh, as if I caught her off guard on purpose, but one look at my face and she sees I'm not joking.

"Geez, Aaron," she says. "What's up?"

"I want to ask you something. And I want you to know that whatever your answer is, it's between the two of us."

She crosses her arms. "Okay."

"Dad never hurt you or anything, did he?"

"Hurt?" she repeats, dwelling on the word, as if it belonged to a language she only partly spoke. "You mean like abuse?"

"Not violence. Not, you know, hitting. The other kind. Anything that was wrong."

I expect her to have to think about her answer, align her memory with her standards of certainty, but she replies right away.

"No," she says. "What about you?"

"I'm pretty sure not. But the *pretty sure* nags at me a little. More now that he's gone."

Bridge steps closer. Rises on tiptoes to press her finger to my temple. "What's going on in there?"

"That's what I'm not a hundred percent about. When I think of him sometimes, it's like I've hypnotized myself. Or maybe he hypnotized me. Isn't that the way some of the survivors of bad stuff describe it? Like it's a shape they can barely make out through a fog?"

Bridge lowers onto the flats of her feet again and looks out into the snarled curtains of forest as if scanning for something there, a visual puzzle that asked you to stare at a pattern until a second pattern showed itself. After half a minute, she shakes her head, looks back up at me.

"Just because there's a fog around us doesn't mean there's anything in it," she says, stepping around me and carrying on up the slope of the trail.

7

THE TRAIL THAT HAD BEEN LEVEL AT FIRST NOW SLOPES DOWNHILL, A CHANGE that makes it easier to walk with our packs but also pulls a deeper darkness over us. From out of the forest comes something new. A thrumming. Mostly unheard when vibrating at the bottom end of its range and prickly as static at the top. Insects. But something else too. Alive in ways that reach beyond the animal or vegetative kinds of life. An intelligence.

I don't ask Bridge if she hears it too. I don't want to make her afraid. And I don't want to make me more afraid if she doesn't.

It's hard to guess how far we've gone. Four hundred yards? Six hundred? I'm about to suggest heading back. Not just to sleep in the lodge for the night but to head back to the city at first light. The words are there, my lips shaped to speak them, and then our headlamps find the square outline of a cabin.

"Cozy," Bridge says, walking around me, opening the single door and disappearing inside.

Illuminated only by the swinging circles of our headlamps, the room looks merely unfamiliar: a scratchy-looking sofa, amateur forest land-scapes hanging crooked on the walls, a round pine table covered with black knots like worrisome moles. But once we find the light switch, a pair of tabletop lamps spill gold up the walls and I see that Bridge was right. It's cozy.

"I'll take this room," she announces, already having turned on the lights in the small but workable kitchen, the bathroom, and each of the two pan-eled bedrooms with windows the size of shoebox lids over the headboards.

I drop my bag in the room next to hers, and I'm about to see if there's toothpaste and soap in the bathroom when I notice the closet door is open an inch. Was it that way when we came in? Something about it strikes me as intentional. An invitation to see what's inside.

"Hey! Check this out!"

Bridge comes in holding something in the palm of her hand. A circu-lar, solid brass lid that she lets me click open.

"A compass," I say.

"Pretty cool, right?"

"Where'd you find it?"

"In a box in my closet. I'm actually really into geography and stuff like that at school, and we did orienteering last summer at my camp. Re-member? But the compasses we used were crap compared to this one."

"Like it was meant for you."

"I'm definitely *keeping* it, so yeah. Why don't you look in yours? Maybe you got something too."

I know before I step over and pull open the closet door, just as Bridge knew it too. There will be another box and inside of it will be something just for me.

"Yours is bigger than mine," Bridge says when she sees the cardboard box wrapped with a single white bow on the closet floor. "Why don't you open it?"

I bend and hold the box in my hands a moment, measuring it for movement from inside more than for its weight, before untying the bow and lifting its lid.

"Shiny," Bridge says.

A running shirt and matching shorts. The super-lightweight kind I used to buy when I was serious about races, every gram I reduced from what I wore resulting in a theoretically improved pace. The fabric bright neon orange, dazzlingly reflective even in the cabin's dull light. Beneath these, my brand of running shoes, and in my size.

"This one's mine all right," I say.

"Don't you like them? You look *scared* or something."

"It's just strange. Don't you think?"

"That Daddy left us gifts?"

"Not the gifts. But that they were in the right cabin, the right room, before we even decided where we were going to stay the night."

Bridge considers this blankly before frowning.

"Well, I *like* mine," she says, and scuffs back into her room, closing the door before I can explain how that's not what I meant at all.

Before we fall asleep, Bridge speaks to me through her door. Something I've heard a hundred times. A strange kind of lullaby that calms her just as it does the same for me.

"It was July up at the lake," she says, and pauses, as if this is the story's title. "So hot the waves were like syrup. You and I standing at the edge of the shore's highest boulder, doing that countdown we thought was so funny. *One-ah, two-ah, three-ah . . . diarrhea!* Airborne long enough to wonder if we'd ever come down. Then everything went dark."

"But I was there."

"You were there. My big brother. We pulled ourselves up onto the floating dock. Started on the picnic we'd floated over in the rowboat. Laughing and eating and jumping around. Playing Peter Pan."

"You were nine."

"I was Wendy. And you were Hook, slicing the air with a dill pickle. We were having fun—and then we weren't. I could tell something was wrong from the look on your face. Before I knew I couldn't breathe."

"You ate too fast."

"Or laughed too much. Either way, you did what they told you in med school."

"The Heimlich."

"But it doesn't always work. It *didn't* work. All I'm thinking is *I'm dying*. But I'm almost okay with it, you know? Almost accepting. I'm watching you jump into the rowboat and pop open the tackle box like it's happening in a movie. You flicking through the rusted hooks and lures and pulling out a silver X-Acto."

"Less than ideal."

"*Much* less than ideal. But even when I figured out what you were about to do, I was fine with it. I trusted you. Even as I laid down on the dock and you cut a line through my throat, you told me with your eyes that you were my brother, that I would be fine."

"That's what I was praying for."

"And I am. I *am* fine."

That's how it ends.

A true story of panic that's somehow more calming than any song, and soon everything is quiet.

I'm awakened by a voice.

It's not that—it's something animal, it must be—yet it arrives as a human utterance, however shattered and alien. Outside the walls of the cabin. Distant, but piercing. A shriek of alarm that comes with the first blaze of pain, as long as the breath I hold in my chest.

When I finally exhale, it's gone. The night and the bedroom's darkness are comingled, endless.

I try to tell myself it was only some small, wild thing in the woods calling out in its death, the soundtrack to the forest's nocturnal cycle of hunting and hiding, but then it comes again. Unmistakable now.

My sister Franny. Screaming into the trees.

8

THE NIGHT PASSES OVER ME LIKE A VEIL.

I remember this feeling. The sensation of running without looking at the ground, each stride a launch into the air, its molecules ready to break apart and admit me to whatever lay beyond. A bargain between myself and the universe that, if I was fast enough, I could put gravity behind me once and for all.

Back then, I ran to be free of being.

Now I run toward my sister's voice.

I'd gotten out of bed and put on the shoes and neon shirt and shorts that came in the gift box without thinking about it. My body is fully in charge for the first time in years and it feels right.

Before I left, I shouted at Bridge to stay inside and lock the door. Will she do as I told her?

She will or she won't, my heart tick-tocks in reply.

Every question in my mind is spoken through the swing of my legs.

There's time or there's not.

I'm aware of cresting the slope up from the cabin and speeding faster down the other side, following Franny's voice more than the trail. I haven't hit a sprint like this since I was training for real, and now my lungs catch fire at the same time I fly out of the trees.

She's nowhere to be seen.

I carry around the lodge's closest corner, the saplings snuggled up to the walls slashing my cheeks and taking bites from my hands like attacking, unseen birds.

The pain stops the same time I do. My body making one last decision—*Don't go any closer*—before handing control back to my mind.

My sister is alone.

Standing in the powdery rectangle of light that comes through the wall of windows at the rear of the lodge. Staring into the trees with the stillness of someone who's just been shown something whose existence they would have never thought possible. It occurs to me only now that she's not screaming anymore.

"Franny?"

She doesn't turn. It forces me to walk closer, my eyes jumping between her and the spot she's focused on in the darkness.

I touch her shoulder.

"Aaron?"

She doesn't jump, doesn't face me. Only this word.

"I'm here."

She throws herself into me and I hold her. I'd like to go inside, but I've forgotten how, at certain moments, being in a family is a performance. Right now I'm the older brother who must appear fearless, so we stay like this.

"There was a man," she says when she finally steps out of my arms.

"Where?"

"Out there." She sweeps her limp fingers across the line of trees. "He was *staring* at me."

"What did he look like?"

"Tall. I couldn't really see his face. But I could see his mouth. Made me think of Mrs. Grainger, my third-grade teacher. If she saw a kid with his mouth hanging open like that she'd say, 'Are you trying to catch flies?' That was funny. But whoever *this* was? He wasn't funny at all."

"Did he say anything?"

"No," Franny says. "Once he knew I saw him, he came closer. Not really walking. Sort of—so slow, like he was *floating*. Like he—"

"Shh."

I look and listen. Not expecting anyone to walk out toward us, but hoping to detect some evidence of retreat, the returning swing of a disturbed branch or thud of a boot on the hollow earth. We stay that way for perhaps a full minute. The only thing my eyes catch on is something glowing on the ground a few feet away. A tongue of gray curling out of its orange mouth.

"Shit, Franny. Were you smoking?"

"Why the hell else would I be out here?" Her face sours, and she's the teenaged Franny again, ready to fight or lie or threaten. Do whatever was required to get away with it. "Are you *judging* me?"

"No. I just don't want you to set the whole state on fire."

She laughs at this, one that turns into a cough. "Too late. Haven't you been watching the news? The whole country's on fire."

I step over and crush Franny's cigarette butt under the heel of my shoe. When I look up from making sure it's out, I catch a glimpse of motion through the trees. A figure—or parts suggestive of a figure—that's there and then, in no more than a stride or two, soundlessly gone.

"Aaron? What's wrong?"

"Nothing."

"You saw something, didn't you?"

I turn to my sister. "I didn't see anything."

It's impossible to say if Franny accepts this or not. I spend virtually all of my waking hours working with other doctors and surgeons and lab technicians whose jobs require the straightforward exchange of blunt opinions. I'm not used to withholding troubling news. Which maybe makes Mom right. Makes me a bad liar.

Franny starts back toward the glass rear door of the lodge without saying anything more.

"Mom isn't up?" I call after her.

"Thick walls and Zoloft. I guess they really do the trick."

"What do you think it was, Franny?"

She looks back at me.

"I don't know, big brother. I didn't like it. And I don't think it liked me either."

She lingers, so I go ahead and say it. It's meant only as a harmless consolation, but instead the words come out too loud, too sure, striking into the night as a provocation.

"There's nobody there."

Franny snorts.

I should have done more for my sister; I know this. We both do. It's why I forgive her the angry glaze she pours over most of the words she directs my way. I don't forgive myself so easily. Bridge says everybody has a "thing," a defining talent or passion or problem. If she's right, then mine is an allergy to witnessing people in pain. I think of it as that—an allergic reaction, itchy and stinging—because to see suffering triggers it in me. It's why I became a doctor. But while as a surgeon I can work to diminish my patients' discomfort, Franny's kind is different. It comes not from physical damage but as a reaction to invisible assaults, the sense of not being wholly loved, not entirely wished for. I know because it is the kind of pain that afflicts me too.

Franny slips inside. I watch her pass through the living room and turn off the dimmed pot lights. The windows turn to blackboards smudged with the chalk of a quarter moon.

There.

It's not a sound that makes me look up. My response is automatic in the way one turns to see whatever has snapped a branch underfoot.

Someone's there.

So far off it's only the irregularity of the human shape against the backdrop of branches and tree trunks that renders it visible. Not the figure I might have caught a glimpse of as I put out Franny's cigarette.

An old woman.

Hunched, arms hanging too low at her sides, the gray aura of frizzled hair. She wears what may be a hospital gown or frayed bathrobe open at the front so that, as she sways slightly from side to side, the material shifts to reveal the downturned points of her breasts.

I want to run back the way I came. To prove courage to myself, I walk instead. But as soon as I've turned my back on her, my legs stretch their stride without my being able to hold them back, and my body is in charge again, building speed, carrying me away on the instincts of retreat.

9

I DON'T RETURN TO BED THAT NIGHT.

After telling Bridge a muted version of the truth—Franny being Franny, she'd gone out for a smoke and scared herself silly all alone in the woods—I promised her she was safe here with me. Whether it was this assurance or the weight of her fatigue, she was snoring like a puppy by the time I pulled her door closed.

There's an overstuffed leather chair in the cabin's living room, and I stay there until dawn, dozing off only to be rewarded with a foul dream I can't recall that left me coughing for air.

The old woman in the trees. Not a dream because I can see her and I'm awake. Not a dream because she was there.

But she wasn't. There's another line of thought reminding me of this. At once calm and bullying. *No matter what you saw, it wasn't real.* Words spoken in my father's voice.

I push it away as best I can. Listen for footsteps outside the cabin's walls. Get up half a dozen times to check that the tab on the handle is turned up in the locked position. Each time I do, I put my ear to the wood and try to feel if something else does the same on the other side.

When the light finally grows from the color of weak tea to limestone against the window's curtains, I knock on Bridge's door.

"You up?"

A moan sounds from the other side. "You're *waking* me up to *ask* if I'm up?"

"That's a yes?"

Once Bridge has pulled on some fresh clothes—a pair of jeans and a Yale sweatshirt, Dad's college, another gift from the grave more thoughtful than any he'd given in life—we head out into the forest's mist in search of coffee.

She's a tough kid. Not quick to cry when she falls out of the trees she still loves to climb or takes a kick to the shins on the soccer pitch. But that's not the kind of toughness I'm thinking of as I look at Bridge now. Hair a shiny auburn, the elongated green eyes and gap-toothed smile that communicate how she sees the comical aspects behind even the most earnest gestures. The kind of person people will fall easily, if perilously, in love with. She's laughingly told me stories about boys at school who already have, though she admits she doesn't know why. I have an idea. It's not because of her looks, not really. It's because they want to know what she's thinking.

"How'd you sleep?" I ask as we make our way along the trail, a steeper climb toward the lodge than I remembered it being in the night.

"Okay, I guess."

"Better than nothing. So, remind me of your position on bacon. I noticed some—"

"Aaron? What really happened with Franny last night?"

"I told you. She thought she saw something, but there was nothing there."

"How do you know that?"

"I looked."

"And you don't believe her."

"It's not that." I work to find the words that might get me out of saying what I don't want to say. "Franny is in recovery, on top of a whole world of grief. You might be able to recover from addiction, but I don't think you ever recover from something like what happened with Nate."

"I guess not."

"It wouldn't be surprising if someone who'd gone through that might hallucinate a bit here and there."

Bridge stops. I carry on for another couple strides before stopping and turning myself.

"You don't believe that," she says.

"Really? How are you so sure?"

"Because you don't sound like you. You sound like Dad. And because you think you might have seen something out there too."

How do parents do it? How do they stay ahead of their kids, cut them off at the pass, shield them from whatever they need shielding from? Either I'm too inexperienced at it to know, or all parents fail the same way I'm failing now.

"You're right," I say. "I don't think Franny was hallucinating. But just because she saw something doesn't mean it was anything bad. We're in the middle of hundreds of square miles of rain forest. There's still bears and deer and I don't know what else out here. It could've been anything."

Bridge absorbs this, stone-faced, before catching up and taking my hand.

"Don't lie to me again," she says.

"I won't."

"What we're doing here—this whole thing—won't work if we can't believe each other."

I squeeze her hand three times. Our code. We haven't used it in a while—we haven't held hands in a while, as she's moved into the physical aversions of teenagerhood—but she understands.

One squeeze means *I'm here*.

Two squeezes mean *I love you*.

Three squeezes mean *It's just me and you*.

We developed the code over the time we spent sitting side by side in the backs of taxis during our Tuesday get-togethers. Sometimes we go to the movies; sometimes I take her to her soccer practice or ballet. But there's always time to grab dinner, time to talk. While we both enjoy these meetings, I've come to rely on them probably more than she does. Her calling me out on the lies I tell myself is of greater use than the counsel I can offer about how to handle boys or teachers or bullies.

I'm about to say something along these lines when we come to the top of the slope. There, in the distance, the rectangular outline of the lodge appears through the tangled mass of trees.

I start toward it, but Bridge remains where she is.

"My turn," she says.

"Your turn what?"

"To be honest about something."

"Okay," I say, turning back to face her.

"The last few Tuesdays I haven't been able to make it to our dinners. Right?"

"You had rehearsals. The school play."

"They weren't rehearsals, Aaron."

"Where were you?"

"At the doctor."

"Why would—"

"I was being treated. But it's over. They say it's—it's *over*."

She's trembling. But I don't go to her. Not yet.

"Treatment for what?"

"Childhood leukemia. You know what that means. You're—"

"Oh my God."

"The doctor. Chemo. Four rounds. The oncologist pretty much said I'm in full remission."

"Pretty much."

"Yeah."

She doesn't have to say the chances of recurrence are on the high side. She knows. We both know.

"Why didn't—you could have—"

I try to speak the one question that needs answering first, but I'm fighting against throwing up. So she answers it for me.

"That's why I wanted you to go. The whole Doctors Without Borders thing. I wanted you to get away from here and help overseas," she says, and it's so painful to hear the apology in her voice, but she shakes her head when I take a step closer. "You were always talking about *doing something*, Aaron. Well, that was something. Saving people who never thought anybody cared enough to save them. And I knew if you stayed here, you'd just be with me all the time. Waiting in the waiting rooms, waiting for results. Waiting to see if any of it worked."

"What's wrong with that?"

"Because I'm all you have. And if the treatment didn't—if I wasn't *here* anymore, I wanted you to have something else."

She puts her arms around me. I hold her and feel the life in her and imagine part of my own life transferring into her, strengthening her blood so it can better fight the alien cells drifting in it.

Because I'm all you have.

That this is true doesn't shock me. What leaves me standing there, empty and still, is the realization that she blames herself for injuries I suffered. *Overseas.* The changes in me that came after. The never being what I was before.

"It was nobody's fault," I manage to say, pulling away from her so I can see her face. "It sure as hell wasn't yours."

"I know that in my head. But it doesn't feel that way. I see what it's done to you, Aaron. And it—"

"No. *Please*—"

"It was me who made you go."

"You didn't make me. You were trying to shield me. And what happened over there happened *to me*, not as a consequence of anything you did. Promise me you'll try not to carry that, okay? Because it's bullshit if you do."

"Okay."

"And no more holding things back. The big things, anyway. It's like you said. This whole thing won't work if we can't believe each other. Right?"

Bridge nods. Uses the sleeve of her hoodie to dry my cheeks. Sniffs the air.

"Someone's up before us," she says.

"How do you know?"

"There's a fire."

10

MOM KNEW, OF COURSE.

She was the one to take Bridge to chemo treatments, sit with her in the doctor's offices, ask the questions phrased in ways that opened the door widest to optimistic interpretation. Mom kept all of it from me because Bridge asked her to.

"Don't get mad at her, okay?" she says.

"I'm not mad."

"Are you going to bring it up?"

"Can I?"

"I can't stop you. But it would be better if you didn't. Not *here*. I mean, what difference would it make?"

"Probably none."

"So. Breakfast?"

"To be honest, I don't know if I want to puke or eat."

"Start with eating. Then we'll just roll with it."

I can tell this is something Bridge told herself during her treatments, a way of summoning the will to move on to the next task, the next meal, the next endurance of discomfort. I decide to use it the same way.

We start for the lodge. Now I smell the fire too. The cherrywood smoke from the lodge's chimney.

And in the next second, both of us see that the front door is open.

Had it been this way moments ago when we'd come out of the trail? Had it been this way all night, for anyone to enter, or had Mom or Franny opened it this morning for us once they got out of bed? It's a question I mean to ask but slips away when Bridge and I come around the corner of the foyer to find Franny loping at us. Sliding on the walkway's smooth wood in fluffy pink slippers that must have been included in her duffel bag.

"Morning, *Brigitte*," she announces, saying Bridge's name in a French accent that has always annoyed her but Franny has never seemed to notice. "Mom's in the kitchen and there's orange juice and Lucky Charms. You like Irish cereal?"

Bridge recognizes that Franny is trying to get rid of her, but she decides to be obliging. Once Bridge is around the corner and out of sight, Franny leans in close.

"Don't tell Mom," she says, looking at me in a way that makes it clear she's referring to last night. Two sisters, two requests to not bring up upsetting things with our already upset mother within the last two minutes. All of which is fine with me. We're Quinlans. We might be bad liars. But all of us are good at keeping secrets.

"You're sure she didn't hear you?" I ask.

"I'm sure. She took a double dose of her bye-bye pills and she was zonked," Franny says. "This morning she's all 'I slept like a baby! Must be the fresh air!'"

"I already talked to Bridge about it."

"That's fine. She won't say anything to Mom either."

"How're you so sure?"

"Because she wants to protect her the same way we did when we were her age."

Once more I'm surprised by how one of my sisters knows so much more about the dynamics of my family than I do.

"You okay, Aaron?"

"Yeah," I say, rubbing at the itchiness of my face and feeling the new growth of beard there. "How about you?"

"Could use some sleep. Which is a hell of a thing to say first thing in the morning."

"Nothing that coffee can't fix."

"You're in luck then. I made a pot. Strong enough—"

"For a spoon to stand up in it."

It's a Dad line. One of the few jokes I can remember him making.

"This stuff? Forget the spoon. It would hold up a fucking knife," she says, and slips her arm around mine, guiding me along the walkway toward the smell of toast and Danishes being warmed in the oven. It's sweet enough and I'm hungry enough that it fills the cavernous space of the lodge with a passable simulation of home.

"Hey, I wanted to ask you something. What ever happened to your friend from high school?" she says. "The super-cute one with the dorky name?"

"Lorne?"

"That's it. Lorne Hetman."

"Huffman."

"Whatever. Where is he now?"

"I have no idea. We weren't exactly friends by the time we graduated. In fact, we never spoke to each other again after that party at the Chaplets' house."

"Why? What happened?"

"Seriously? You were *there*."

"That doesn't mean anything," she says, and stops. "Tell me."

Lorne was the only person I might have once described as a best friend. We were both jocks but discovered a shared love for old movies, particularly the drive-in monster flicks from a generation earlier. *The Blob. Creature from the Black Lagoon. Godzilla.* We'd work our way through the cheesiest corner of the classics section of Blockbuster, then start all over again, staying up until dawn for sleepovers at my house.

It gave us the chance to talk about girls, his parents splitting up, my mysterious dad. It also allowed Franny to "bump into" Lorne after she came out of the shower wrapped in a towel, or for Lorne to ask Franny to join us, patting the cushion on the sofa next to him, promising her that Vincent Price in *The Tingler* would forever change her mind about "that dumb horror crap."

I was aware they were flirting. But I took it as only the most harmless kind: training for Franny (she was two years younger, a tenth-grade kid) and time-killing for Lorne. That's why when that spring Franny came down the stairs into the Chaplets' crowded rec room, reeking of pot smoke and wearing a Led Zeppelin T-shirt and cutoffs, I was surprised when Lorne immediately got up to offer her a beer. He wasn't being nice. He was *acting* nice.

A few beers later, as I watched from across the room, I could see Franny turn from looking playful to looking like she was going to throw up. I figured Lorne would retreat. She was wasted. She was my kid sister. But when he whispered something in her ear and started down the hall toward one of the basement bedrooms, Franny followed.

I remind Franny of all this, and when I'm done, she says she can't remember any of it.

"Well, the party, maybe," she concedes. "The Chaplets' place. The smell of it. Like cinnamon apples or something. We were there a lot, weren't we? Like, did the parents even *exist*? But Lorne and me getting it on—no, not really."

"You weren't getting it on with him, Franny. You were almost unconscious. He was—you were being *assaulted*. Or about to be, anyway."

"How would you know?"

"Because I checked on you. You heard me come in and looked at me from a thousand miles away."

"What did you do?"

"I told Lorne to stop. He told me to mind my own business. 'This is private, man.' As if that made everything cool. As if I had to honor whatever he wanted to do because it was happening in a room with a door."

"Did you leave?"

"No, Franny. I didn't leave. I threw Lorne off you, and when he started to talk shit to me, I punched him in the ear."

She looks like she's about to cry. But she laughs instead. "Why the *ear*?"

"I was aiming for his nose. But he moved."

"He must've been pissed."

"Not as much as I was. I started whaling on him in the hallway and into the rec room with everybody cheering us on at first and then, when they saw how freaked I was—like Lorne's-teeth-on-the-shag-carpet freaked—they got as far away as they could. I nearly *killed* him."

"I knew you guys had a falling out. I figured it was over a girl," she says. "I just didn't think I was the girl."

She looks out the enormous windows at the trees. Each taking on their own personality as the morning light plays over them, mutant branches and patches where leaves failed to fill in their green coat. An audience we'd only become aware of in the last moment.

Franny loops her arm around mine and pulls herself close, still looking outside.

"You gotta admit. This place is beautiful," she says.

"It's kind of unbelievable, actually."

"You're going to think I'm crazy, but maybe it's good we're in this place. Maybe we can be together here in a way we never could back there."

It's what I've hoped too. And right now it feels like something approaching the possible.

"You're right," I say. "I *do* think you're crazy."

She pulls away the arm that was around mine and gives my shoulder a whack, which is Franny's way of saying you're all right. You might just stand a chance.

11

WHEN WE JOIN THE OTHERS IN THE KITCHEN, I ASSUME THE BACON DUTIES AS
Bridge works at her bowl of marshmallows and Mom looks in all the
drawers and cupboards, taking inventory. Franny hands me a mug of coffee as the strips of meat send up salty smoke from the pan.

"Why would he make us do this?"

This is Bridge. And she's asking it of Mom, who rises from where
she'd been rummaging through a stack of Tupperware under the counter.

"I was only his wife, baby," she says. "You're asking the wrong person."

"Whoever he worked for, did he do good things or bad things?"

"I always assumed they were good. Now? To be honest, I'm not so
certain there's *anything* good you could do where they'd pay you the kind
of money to buy a spread like this."

"But you have an idea," I say, and Mom turns to me.

"An idea about what?"

"Why we're here. You've got a theory."

Eleanor Quinlan is a woman who can say a hundred different things with a sigh. Right now, it's one of gathered strength. The resolve required to say the thing she'd rather dance around forever.

"Your father didn't have a very good family life growing up," she says. "I didn't know the details, but his own father left when he was young. His brother turned out to be a criminal of some kind. And his mother was unwell. Her nerves. That's all he would say about it. 'She had a nervous condition.' So he had to take care of her instead of the other way around."

"So what?" Franny says.

"I think he wanted something better than that for his own family, even if he didn't have the first clue how to achieve it. He approached you three, his marriage, his estate too, as it turns out—he managed all of it like chemicals in a beaker. And now that he's gone, he's hoping that by mixing us all together we'll grow."

"My guess is it's a challenge," I say. "Like rats finding their way out of a maze."

"More like rats making a home out of the maze," Mom says, and sits next to Bridge, picking a marshmallow star off the edge of her bowl and popping it in her mouth.

I've learned more about my father's history in the last three minutes than the preceding three decades, and I can only guess it's the same for Franny and Bridge. None of us, however, ask Mom for more. Maybe because we're absorbing what's just been shared; maybe we figure that's all Mom knows. In any case, there're only the pops of the bacon frying until Franny starts out in a new direction of her own.

"I had a weird dream last night," she says.

"So we're definitely not talking about anything real," I say, worried she's forgotten about our agreement not to speak of what she thought she might have seen in the woods.

"A dream, like I said. But so real *seeming*, you know? Like here I am, awake, and I can still feel it clinging to me."

"What happened?" Bridge asks.

"There was water," Franny says, squinting as if pulling her subconscious into clearer focus. "Salt water. I could *taste* it. Can you taste in a dream? Doesn't that mean you're insane or something?"

"That's if you see colors," Bridge says.

"Is darkness a color? Because the water I was in was blacker than night. I *really* didn't want to go down into it—not just because I was afraid of drowning; I was afraid of the water itself. But I was tired. Like I'd been fighting to stay above the surface for hours before the dream even started. And then comes the weird part. From out of the silence, from out of the ocean—"

"There was music."

I finish Franny's sentence without being aware of it.

"That's not what I was going to call it. But yes," she says. "How the hell did you know that?"

"Because I had the same dream," I say. "A version of it, anyway."

"Me too," Bridge says.

All of us look at her.

"I could hear it when my head was above water, but it was a lot louder once I went under," Bridge goes on. "Like horns or something. A bunch of trumpets and tubas tuning up before playing a song. Except the tuning up *was* the song. It was so beautiful it almost stopped me from being scared. I was so tired of fighting that I just went down. Swallowed up by this sound so big it felt like I wasn't in water anymore. Just the sound."

I don't want to ask this next part. But now that Franny looks at me to do it, I see that it's up to me.

"What happened then?"

"Nothing," Bridge says.

"You mean you woke up?"

"I mean *nothing*. It just ended. What about you?"

The way Franny and I don't reply to this confirms what we already know. The dream ends with darkness. It ends with the end.

"Mom?" Franny eventually asks. "Any of this ring a bell with you?"

"I don't remember my dreams," she says, and while I note that this isn't precisely an answer, I don't pursue anything more. It's the smell of smoke that pulls my attention away. The bacon burning in the pan.

"Hope you like it well done," I say, happy for the diversion of scooping the hardened rashers out of the pool of spitting fat.

"It's bacon," Bridge says, holding her plate out. "How bad can it be?"

12

AFTER BREAKFAST I GO FOR A RUN. NOT THE PANIC-DRIVEN DASH OF LAST NIGHT, but still a near-full pace of the kind I used to be able to maintain for several hours. My hope is I can keep it up for maybe a quarter of that. A fact-finding mission to discover how truly out of shape I've let myself become.

I'm only a few minutes along the drive we came in on when I realize I haven't worn my watch or brought any water with me. I could go back, but I'm feeling strong, flushed with that bloom of optimism that runners in their first mile share with alcoholics downing their first drink.

The day is a classic Pacific Northwest game of bait and switch: the sun promising clear skies ahead before being obscured behind tectonic plates of clouds. Soon, the possibility of rain, implausible minutes ago, becomes a certainty with the first cold drops on my cheeks.

I like it. The air stretching the billows of my lungs, the rivulets of water dripping off my lip and into my mouth. And then, before I feel it coming, I'm bent over with my hands on my knees, wondering if I'm about to puke.

When I stand straight again, I realize two things at the same time. One, I'm dehydrated and farther out than I should be. Two, the estate's fence is visible a couple hundred yards ahead around the next bend.

I tell myself that, now that I'm here, I might as well walk the rest of the way to the gate while hoping the dizziness sloshing inside my skull eases away. By the time I get there, it's almost worked.

The fence is higher than I would have guessed. Eighteen feet, maybe more. And I don't recall the tight bundle of barbed wire at the top. A look along the fence's length, left and right, shows it going on as far as I can see.

The gate itself is a section the same width as the lane that, when opened, slides along a track in the ground. On the other side is the lock-box that Fogarty mentioned, the one that contains the satellite phone we can use to call for a ride.

To the right of the gate, above a small concrete pad, is what must be the food and supplies delivery system. It's basically a metal plate that rotates through the fence on this side and the other side. In the space of the opening between the two—a bit more than a square foot—there are wires that hang down like the rubber flaps you pass through in a car wash. In this case the wires are probably electrified. A discouragement against trying to crawl through the opening (even if there's no body other than a toddler's that would have a chance of fitting).

Something about being here at the limit of the property, contained within miles of woven steel, reminds me again of the figures Franny and I thought we saw last night. The idea that they are here as well. Inside.

Until now, I'd assumed the fence was meant to protect Belfountain from those who might try to get in. I'd read about people who would illegally clear-cut entire acres of redwoods up here. And that was before the riots and curfews. Now this place would offer more than free wood. It would offer a refuge.

But what if it is the other way around? What if the fence's height, the razor wire—what if it is meant to keep the ones in the forest inside?

I step closer to the fence. Careful not to touch it in case the whole thing is electrified. Fogarty said we were free to go any time we wanted. If that's true, how do we get out? There must be something here at the gate. A button or lock. But I can't find anything.

Nothing other than the gate itself.

To try to move it will require me putting my bare hands on it. I should know better—I'm a physician who's seen all the ways people can injure themselves by way of dumb decisions—but I tell myself that if I'm quick enough, I can test it with a glancing touch.

I uncurl my fingers held in a fist. Swipe them over the steel.

There's a jolt. But it's not electricity. It's the scratch of the metal's surface on my skin.

This time I throw both of my hands against the fence. Find the best grip I can through the holes. Pull hard to the right. The gate's frame shivers. So I yank it to the left. It moans before sliding a few inches out of position. With two more heaves I've opened it all the way.

It's only more forest on the far side. The same million dripping leaves as there are on this one. Yet there's a line between where I stand and the trees I stare at through the open gate that pulls them into sharper focus. *There* is more particular, more real, than *here*.

The instructions are clear.

Fogarty's voice returns to me so vividly I can imagine him speaking next to me, his polished shoes sinking into the rain-softened mud.

The perimeter of the estate marks the extent to which you may travel.

So here I am. I've finally achieved what I never could over all those marathons years ago. I've run all the way to the end of the world.

But I won't step off the edge.

It's not for the money. And I don't care what Dad wants us to learn. I'm here for Bridge. For her to discover whatever it is that makes her believe it's important to stay. For her to be safe.

I take in a full inhalation of air from the other side and hold it as if readying to dive underwater. Pull the gate closed. Walk back toward the lodge before ramping it into a cautious jog.

How far out *is* here? Other than being tired and thirsty and nauseated, there's no measure my mind can latch onto. The sun remains on sabbatical, so it's hard to say if it's still morning or if the grayness isn't the clouds but encroaching dusk.

The idea that I might pass out and not get up becomes more real with every stride. And if I go down, there's a good chance I'll lie here soaking wet through the night, a night that can drop twenty degrees between midnight and dawn.

I'd forgotten how, on long runs, thoughts at first multiply and compete for attention before filtering away to a single purpose.

Don't fall.

Everything reduced to this.

Just. Don't. Fall.

I figure I've got to be close when I hear something running up behind me. A rush of air, followed by the crunch of gravel.

Big. And faster than I am.

I could turn to look, but I know that would probably send me tumbling into the ditch. There's also the option of striking out into the woods and finding a place to hide. But if I can hear whatever it is, it's already seen me.

Don't stop. Don't fall.

All that's left is to do what I'm doing.

Except do it faster.

13

A BLAZE OF SOUND. SO LOUD IT TURNS MY MUSCLES RIGID, FORCING ME TO HOP TO
the side of the road and close my eyes against contact.

Then my mind recognizes the sound for what it was. A car horn.

One limo and then another roll past. The same models, possibly the
very same vehicles, that brought us here. I can't tell who the passengers
are through the tinted windows, but there are the outlines of heads looking at me, the man in the ridiculous neon outfit who doesn't seem able
to breathe properly.

The two cars pick up speed once I'm behind them and disappear
around the curve ahead.

Heading toward the lodge. Toward Bridge.

It heaves me forward again. A sensation like a hive of ants released
into my ears, carving their way inward.

Two more turns and I see that I was right: I was close. The limos
are both parked out front of the lodge, but no one—not the drivers, not
Bridge or Franny or Mom—stands outside. I weave toward the limo

closest to me and stop when, at the same time, all of the vehicles' rear doors open.

Four passengers get out. Two from the first limo and two from the second. The former is a set of adult identical twins. Blandly good-looking, slightly overweight. Not dressed exactly the same but close enough to be confusing, their hair home-dyed the color of hay.

The latter are a man and a woman, both looking at me. The woman is dressed in a professional skirt and blouse, her hair an aura of dark curls around her head. The man is a couple inches shorter than me but wider. His body is as purposeful as the woman's but more muscled than graceful, a guy who spends his gym time grunting with the weights. Yet his face is boyish, open. A wholesome assembly of features that used to be called "all-American."

Because she happens to be closer, or because she's been brought up to be polite (or is required to be for the job that bought her the tasteful jacket and skirt she wears), the woman approaches me.

"Sorry we didn't stop to offer you a lift back there, but our driver—"

"What are you doing here?" I gasp, a string of spit lashing onto the ground before my hand can reach my lip.

"I'm here—we're *all* here—to satisfy the legal terms," she says.

"I don't understand."

"Mr. Fogarty explained everything to us."

"Fogarty? Explained *what*?"

"You know who Mr. Fogarty is, don't you? I mean, I'm assuming you're a member of the staff or a caretaker of some kind?"

"I'm not staff. I'm not the damn caretaker either."

Her polite smile loosens. She's found herself standing too close to someone who's not of his right mind, someone breathing hard and now lurching in a dizzy circle, and she takes a long step back. It makes room for Mr. All-American to step into the space she's left.

"Everything okay?" he asks.

"You're trespassing."

"Really?"

"Yes. So unless you can tell me what the—"

His hands come up. So fast I only realize he's holding me back from coming closer after I press my weight against his palms. A defense of the woman behind him that proves the connection between them.

"Easy now. I don't know who you are," he says without threat, his eyes twinkly with what may be amusement. "There's no problem here. We just have to sort this out, okay?"

The wooziness instantly worsens, graduating into head spins that jolt my vision left to right and back again, over and over. Yet I manage to ask the man what I should have asked at the beginning.

"Who are you?"

"Jerry Quinlan. Raymond Quinlan was my father. What about you?"

He doesn't push me. He doesn't have to. He just brings his hands down, and it's not only his face that's spinning, it's the well-dressed woman, the dyed-hair twins. Mom and Franny and Bridge rush out of the lodge, all of them shrinking into a pinhole of light I try to hold on to, but when they're gone, there's only darkness.

14

THEY'RE STANDING AROUND ME. NONE OF THEM CLOSE EXCEPT FOR BRIDGE, wringing out a cloth from a bowl of ice water and folding it onto my brow.

"Hey," I croak.

She offers me a coffee mug of orange juice. "You need some sugar."

I drink it down and within seconds I'm feeling halfway human again.

"Welcome back. You passed out," the guy who'd introduced himself as Jerry Quinlan says. He stands the farthest away, silhouetted against the great room's windows. "I carried you in."

I scan the faces of the others. There's the brown-eyed woman who's come to stand behind Bridge, the paunchy twins, along with Franny and Mom between the sofa and the raised dining area, standing close together as if for warmth.

"We haven't really talked about anything yet," the woman says. "I guess we were waiting for you to come around."

"That's very kind," I say, intending a bite of sarcasm; but it eludes me, so it comes out sounding prim instead. "Maybe I can start?"

"Sure."

"Who are you people?"

"My name is Lauren. That's my brother Jerry," she says, pointing at the man by the window, then switches to the twins. "And these are my other brothers, Ezra and Elias."

"You're related."

"That's how brothers and sisters work."

"But outside your brother Jerry told me his surname too."

"Quinlan."

"Quinlan," I say immediately after she does.

"That's right. We're Ray Quinlan's children. This was his property, and the directions of his will brought us here."

Mom pulls away from Franny and comes to sit on the edge of the sofa next to me, drawing Bridge protectively against her legs.

"Is your mother with you?" she asks Lauren.

"Our mother passed away two years ago."

"I see."

"And you? May I ask—"

"Eleanor."

"Eleanor," Lauren repeats, her face brightening as she makes a connection in her mind. "Yes! I think I get it now."

"I'm sorry?"

"My father's secretary. Eleanor. He mentioned you sometimes. You're here as part of the division of the estate as well?"

Lauren smiles at my mother with kindly certainty, the look of someone who's unknotted a shoelace for a child. But the smile doesn't last long. It's the twisting of my mother's face that does it. I'm sure it's heading in the direction of the wailing sobs I've been expecting since we first got here, but it comes out in wracking laughter instead.

"His *secretary*? *That's* what he called me?"

Jerry comes to stand directly over Mom, over the three of us on the sofa. Close enough for us to read the sympathetic setting of his face.

"Forgive me, Eleanor," he says. "But if you weren't his secretary, who *are* you?"

My mother assesses the man standing over her as if for the first time. The kind of nice, clean-cut boy she'd call a "nice, clean-cut boy" and chastise Franny for failing to have found. But instead of being charmed, she hardens. Not from anything she detects in him, but who he represents, the evidence of the deception she's been victim to that he asserts just by standing in front of her.

"I'm Eleanor Quinlan. Raymond Quinlan's wife."

Jerry pauses. Then, as if internally deciding on a program and waiting for the software to boot up inside him, he softens. Shows us his solid, milk-hardened teeth, and brings his hands together in a single clap.

"That is *something*!" He lets out a whoop. "That is most *definitely* something!"

"Hold on," one of the twins says. It's the first one Lauren pointed at, which would make him Ezra.

"You're his family?" the other twin, Elias, says.

"His second family, it appears. Or his first, and *you're* his second, depending where you start counting," Mom says, once more suppressing a fit of giggles that's more disturbing to me than anything else going on at the moment.

"So you and you and you," Ezra says, pointing at Bridge, then me, then Franny. "You're our half sisters and half brother?"

"It would follow," Mom says.

This appears to be all the twins need to know for now, the two of them retreating to murmur between themselves. I can't hear what they say but I lip-read it as numbers. Calculating what our existence means to their diminished cut of the pie.

Franny comes to sit on the arm of the sofa as if to complete the arrangement of the four of us for a family portrait.

"Lauren? Do you mind if I ask you a question?" she asks. "Do you have any children?"

Lauren is momentarily startled by the question, and it's not what I was expecting Franny to say either.

"No, I don't. You?"

"Yes. A boy. But he died."

"I'm sorry to hear that—"

"Franny."

"I'm very sorry, Franny."

"You're a therapist or social worker. Something like that, right?"

"A psychologist. That a guess?"

"I'm an addict. Been all over the rehab map. I can tell the professional listeners from civilians right away."

"You're good."

"Nah. I'm bad, actually," Franny says, and while it's meant as a self-deprecating joke, it comes out so crushingly sad all of us are struck by it, even the twins, who stop their murmuring.

"My name is Brigit, but I like Bridge," Bridge says after a quick suck of air.

"Okay, Bridge," Lauren says.

"Can I ask you something else?"

"I think we've all got a lot of questions, so fire away."

"Are you related to me? Like, genetically?"

"I understand," Lauren hedges, and now I can see the psychologist in her now too. "You're asking because we look different."

"Yes."

"Different from my brothers. From you. You're asking because I'm black."

"I guess."

"Fair enough. I'm adopted. Me and you? No genetic relation. But your dad is *our* dad," she says. "So for better or worse, I'm a Quinlan from the ground up."

Bridge nods at this, and so does Lauren. We all do.

"I'd like to know who you *are*," Mom says finally with the willed composure of a hostess attempting to recover a dinner party conversation from difficult terrain. "Not just your names."

"We'll go first," Ezra and Elias say at the same time, not seeming to notice their shared words and mirrored facial expressions, the consistent oddness of their twinship.

They don't wear the exact same color clothes, but the same style, same brand. Preppily rumpled shirts with frayed collars, the galloping horses and mallet-waving jockeys faded and curled over their hearts. They look like golfers. Like men who never resist the opportunity to tell jokes to dental hygienists and flight attendants.

As it turns out, they're actors. Mostly commercials now, some guest spots on police procedurals ("Every show eventually has twins that murder their parents"), though it's been rough the past few years. While their identical appearance was their main selling feature, it put them in competition with the three other sets of twins of the same age in LA up for the same parts—parts that now mostly went to the Ludmarks, a pair of broad-shouldered brothers from Nebraska who sold themselves as "decent Mormon types," but were in fact "coke-snorting dicks."

They've tried getting out of the business. They almost made a go selling real estate, investing in ads on bus stop benches that played up the twin angle (*Most Agents Can't Be in Two Places at Once . . . But the Quinlans Can!*). The phone rang for a time. But they soon discovered that while they were good at *acting* like real estate agents, they were terrible at actually selling real estate. And to live in LA was to be constantly reminded that they were semi-famous once. Ezra and Elias were on the cast of *Better Together*, a family sitcom that ran for two seasons in the '80s.

"I don't remember that show," Franny says.

"We get that a lot," Ezra says.

"I remember. You two played the same part," Mom says. "I read an article about it ages ago. You weren't twins on the show; you traded in and out playing the same child."

"There are laws about on-screen time for kids," Ezra explains, pleased to be recognized. "So they'd hire twins to put one on set in case the other one was sleeping or had to get his diapers changed."

"Yes, that's right," my mom says, tapping the side of her chin. "You were the youngest. They gave you all the best lines."

"'Ah poop,'" Ezra quotes.

"That's it. 'Ah poop.' You were the cute one."

"We were adorable," Elias confirms dismally.

Lauren is next. A private practice in Spokane. Trauma recovery. Victims of violence, soldiers returned from service, survivors. She chooses to take only the ones she can assist in making measurable improvements, instead of the "midlife crisis cases and suburban melancholics" that bring home the bacon for the majority of her colleagues.

"You got any openings?" Franny asks, in her joking-but-not-joking way.

"Are you a survivor?"

"I was actually thinking about my brother."

"Franny. Don't—"

"What? Aaron is a doctor. But definitely a physician who won't heal thy self. Because despite the stoic exterior, he's a shitshow on the inside. Not that it's his fault. He went over to Africa, see, to do the savior act *there* instead of *here*, but he—"

"*Don't.*"

"Got caught up in more than he signed up for. An ambush. The real shit. And the good doctor couldn't do anything to—"

"*Stop* it, Franny!"

Overseas.

I close my eyes against seeing it, but see it just the same.

The rust- and blood-speckled blades of machetes thudding into bodies. The dying at my feet, writhing and choking. So many of them it appeared as if the earth itself was fighting for air.

"Aaron?"

Bridge's voice brings me back. Not entirely, but enough to nod as if I'm fine.

Lauren looks between the two of us. When it's clear we aren't going to offer anything more, Franny starts to tell us who she is. Which is, for her, the telling of how she lost Nate.

She speaks matter-of-factly, so that the story of how she was a crackhead who left her four-year-old with a group of other addicts she was squatting with in Rainier Beach one night is conveyed with the same evenness as an account of how she forgot her purse after heading out for groceries.

While she went out to score, Nate suffered an asthma attack. His mostly comatose caretakers later claimed they didn't notice the boy clutching his throat in the room they were sitting in, "But they were all liars, so they probably closed their eyes so they wouldn't have to get up off the floor." What's known is that none of them went to find the boy's inhaler. By the time Franny returned, it was too late.

"I found my rock," she says, "but I lost everything."

It would be a difficult, if not impossible, story for anyone to follow. But Jerry does a remarkable thing. Wearing a look of empathetic loss, he comes over to place his hand atop Franny's shoulder. A simple gesture, one that might otherwise risk the appearance of insincerity. Not from him. There's a directness about Jerry that marks him as the only one in the room who seems able to fully register the horror that Franny has just confessed to.

"I'm a gym teacher in Portland," he announces after withdrawing his hand, as if there were no other imaginable outcome to his life.

After a football scholarship to Wisconsin that ended with a thwarted attempt at a career in the pros ("Got dinged going up for a catch one time too many," he says, tapping his skull to lightheartedly indicate repeated concussions), he pursued the next best thing. Teaching.

"Those who can, do," he says. "Those who can't, join a union."

He laughs at his own expense, good-natured and mildly heartbroken. Over to me.

I swiftly hit the bullet points of my medical training, the surgery post at Swedish First Hill Hospital in Seattle. The truth is I love what I do: repairing bodies, taking out the bad parts, fusing and cleaning their interiors. So much simpler to fix people than understand them.

I don't talk about *overseas*.

But a quick glance at Lauren makes me feel certain that she knows. Not the details. The damage it left me with.

None of us, aside from Franny, mention children. None of us speak of a spouse, boyfriend, or girlfriend. It may be that they don't rate as figures of sufficient importance. It may be that, as Quinlans, we've all been similarly injured in ways that have conspired to see us live alone.

When we're finished going around the circle, Elias addresses us all.

"Excuse me for pointing out the pregnant elephant in the room, but does anyone else think this is fucked up?"

"I do," his twin brother answers.

The fact that no one else speaks to this suggests unanimous agreement.

"This may seem weird to ask at a time like this, so please don't think I'm too much of a jerk," Jerry says, addressing us with a bashful apology that I can sense Mom and Franny responding to. Me too. Perhaps it's impossible to respond any other way. He's my brother. There's some of me in him, and at the same time I recognize I want him to see something of value, something of himself, in me.

"Is there anything to eat?" he asks.

15

A FULL-ON FRIDGE RAIDING. THE SAME EMOTIONAL HUNGER TRANSLATING TO THE physical appears to be as true for the second Quinlans as much as the first, judging by the way they divide up what's left of the roast chicken and zap a pair of frozen pizzas in the microwave. Still feeling weak from my run, I make grilled cheeses for Bridge and myself. All of us carry our plates to the banquet dining table and take seats—accidentally or otherwise—alternating a member of the first Quinlans with a member of the second. There's a moment when all of us look across at one another, acknowledging the way we would appear as one family, not two.

"Did you guys say grace before dinner in your house?" Jerry asks me.

"No. You?"

"Not even at Christmas."

"Have at it then."

Me, Mom, Franny, and Bridge watch as the others destroy what's on their plates. It makes me tentative at first when I pick up my sandwich, but after the first mouthful my body responds, and I eat as ravenously as they do.

When we're done, we look up at one another and are plunged into a deeper awkwardness. The twins reddening. Lauren can't stop shaking her head. Franny, I can tell, is on the verge of telling one of her pitch-dark tales from her years in the gutter. As for Mom, she casts her eyes over the four newcomers and squeezes her lips tight.

Eventually Jerry pushes his chair back and pulls a silver flask from the inside pocket of his jacket.

"Those limo assholes took my phone," he says. "But they didn't take this."

He unscrews the flask's top and takes a drink. Then he offers it to Mom, who surprises all of us, or certainly the first Quinlans, by accepting it. She swallows a dainty sip before passing the flask to Lauren.

It goes around to all of us wordlessly, Bridge and Franny passing it on without drinking each time. Yet they too seem to be warming to the liquor's effects, the animosity and shock gradually giving way to an acknowledgment of the absurdity we've found ourselves sharing.

When the flask returns to him for the third time, Jerry frowns, shakes it, proving it's empty before returning it to his pocket.

"Well, what do you all think?" he says. "You figure we could talk for real now?"

We take it in small steps. The whisky helps. Chatter about where we grew up, the possibility that we'd unknowingly crossed paths at Mariners games or during childhood trips up the Space Needle. It's as if we're people who've found instant camaraderie with another group waiting to board a flight, and now we were working to discover the extent of the shared ground between us, plotting out the dots of coincidence between our lives.

The second Quinlans lived in Kirkland, while we, the first Quinlans, lived on Mercer Island. Similar suburbs on different compass points from downtown and far enough apart that we attended different high schools, dated boys and girls whose names we don't recognize, never played on a team that met the other in an all-city tournament. Yet there must have been close calls. So many, in fact, it's stranger that we aren't able to find a direct hit between us than if we did.

Our conversation is buoyed by full stomachs and Ballantine's and the mutual experience of the peculiar. Confronting one another and the secret that's now been exposed could have gone one of two ways, the traumatic or the humorous, and for now at least we've opted for the latter. We relate anecdotes of our father's behavior. Funny stories about how he never remembered our birthdays or would present random gifts bought exclusively at airport souvenir gifts shops, handing invisible ink pens to toddlers or electric razors to Jerry and me five years before puberty. Also hilarious were the times he would assure us that he'd join us on a holiday only to invariably bail at the last minute, waving at us as we reversed the station wagon out of the drive on our way to a golf resort (nobody played except him) or drive north to Canada only to be quizzed by customs agents suspicious about a mother, husbandless, driving her children over the border.

Mom is the only one who doesn't join us in the performance of One Big Happy Dysfunctional Family. She listens and pretends to recall the details as bittersweetly as we do, but it's obvious there's something she can't shift her mind from.

"How did they meet?" she says finally. "Your mother and Raymond."

Mom's curiosity leaves her so vulnerable all of us lean toward her to participate in it, a communal attempt to bear some of her pain so that she won't be crushed, as she appears she may be.

"It's a little bizarre, actually. But Mother thought it was romantic," Lauren says gently. "She was a nurse and Dad was one of her patients."

"Go on," Mom says.

"'He had a way of talking.' That's what she'd say when I asked how an older man in a hospital bed could charm a young woman into being his wife. 'He had a way with words.' She said it like it was a spell that had been put on her. Like she'd been fooled."

"Pleurisy," Mom says.

"Yes," Lauren says. "That's what he was in for. Lung infection."

"We were married then," Mom says. "I was pregnant with Aaron, but there wasn't a day I didn't visit him. I must have spoken with your mother. To think I was witness to it! My ill husband falling in love with one of his nurses right before my eyes while I was carrying his child."

It's not me or Franny who reaches out to Mom. It's Jerry. Cupping her hand under his as if to warm it.

"What was she like?" Mom says, looking to Jerry.

"She was a good mom," he answers. "Kind, a little fragile. A good cook, in a tuna casserole sort of way. She looked after us fine, but mostly her job was covering for Dad. 'He'd like to be here for your game, but work called him in.' 'Don't be angry at him, he's doing important work for the good of the country.' She was really good at deflecting blame. But she blamed him the whole time, like she was the only one who was allowed to."

He squeezes Mom's hand under his.

"She was probably a lot like you," he says.

Mom hasn't had much experience with honesty from men. Now that she's hearing it from Jerry, she sits up straighter to absorb it, weigh it. Eventually she draws her hand away and rises, leaving the table and going down the steps into the great room to stand at the windows with her hands on her hips, a homemaker's pose, as if discouraged at all the work ahead of her in raking up six hundred acres of leaves.

Bridge is about to go after her, but I shake my head, signaling Mom's need to be alone, but as soon as I've done this, I wonder if I'm right. I've been brought up to manage hurt by retreating, and to manage others' hurt by standing back from it, just as I kept away from Franny when she cried out watching them lower Nate into the ground and said nothing more than *It's over now* when Mom called to say Dad was gone.

"So other than doing the dishes—" Ezra starts.

"What happens now?" Elias finishes.

"Well, that depends on us," Jerry says. "It looks like we've got to make some decisions."

He pushes his chair back from the table, and I notice again how this man conveys physical strength built for practical purposes yet remains so boyish, almost cherubic. He's athletic, but he's only playing tough. This is what his rounded cheeks and over-long eyelashes say. The muscles and willfully deepened voice parts of an unsuccessful effort to disguise his prettiness.

"Before we get to that, tell me about the lawyer," I say.

"Fogarty?"

"That's the one."

"Lauren? You want to field that? I'm going to scare up some coffee."

"There's some in the kitchen," Mom calls at us, automatically shifting back into hospitality mode and then, hearing herself, returning her gaze out the window.

It leaves Lauren to explain how the four second Quinlans were awakened early this morning by drivers who told them they were to be taken to a meeting. The drivers could say nothing more about it, other than it concerned the administration of their father's estate. They were given no time to pack, and once they were in the cars, they had to surrender their phones. Fogarty addressed them over the limos' speakers on their drive to Belfountain, telling them their father had a considerable fortune, the primary piece of which was a property in the forest. The will instructed him, as executor, to distribute the assets among all the surviving members of his immediate family upon the satisfaction of a condition.

"To stay here for a month," Franny says.

"Without leaving," Ezra says.

"Or TV," Elias adds bitterly.

"All of which was twisted enough," Lauren goes on. "But then we arrive and find you."

"What about this place?" I glance over at Bridge, then back at Jerry. "Did he—did Dad—ever mention it?"

"Not directly," he answers, squinting. "But there were the stories."

"Stories?"

"The ones he'd tell us when we were kids," Lauren explains. "All about this magical place called Belfountain. I never liked them much myself. Made me think of that one about the witch and Hansel and Gretel."

"Well, here you are," I say, sweeping my arm around. "Welcome to the gingerbread house."

Jerry sits in the empty chair next to me. Takes a delicate sip of his coffee.

"Seems we're the eldest of our clans now," he says. "What do you think of that?"

"I think Ray Quinlan was one messed up son of a bitch."

"I'm figuring we've got a majority vote on that."

"And I think you're right. Each of us has to make a decision."

"About what exactly?"

"Whether we stay or go."

Jerry puts the coffee down. "This is a lot to take in. A lot of confusion. A lot of hurt. But I agree with Aaron. We have to put that aside as best we can to think about the core issue here."

"You're talking about money," Franny says, sniffing.

He turns to her. "Sure. Yes, I am. Because it's what's owed to us, what we deserve. Think of it as just money if you want. Me? I'm inclined to think of it as a second chance. I mean, if you do the math on—"

"Math? I thought you taught gym."

Jerry grins as if Franny is trying to flirt with him, even though it's fairly clear he represents something she can't stand. One of those outwardly flawless guys she never knew how to start with, the kind she saw the world handing over everything to just for showing up.

"I think even I can sort it out," he says, sustaining the grin. "Thirty days here to claim one-eighth of what? Thirty million? Forty? It's a weird ask, no doubt about it. But still, not much of a decision if you ask me." He looks from me to Lauren before landing on the twins. "What do you say?"

"If it means not having to say 'Ah poop!' a hundred times while getting our picture taken at a fan convention in Des Moines, I'm in," Ezra says, and Elias winces his agreement.

"Lauren?"

"I'm a psychologist," she says. "I'm in it for the research paper."

"There you have it," Jerry says. "The Quinlans of Kirkland are all signed up. How about the Mercer Islanders? Any of you looking to thumb a ride home?"

I look to Bridge.

"I'm not going anywhere," she says, and squeezes my hand three times. *It's just me and you.*

"Franny?"

"Thirty days? Shit. I've done half a dozen rehabs longer than that."

I consider shouting out to Mom to ask how she'd like to vote, but considering what she's already said on the matter, I don't see the need.

"We're in," I say.

"There it is! A full ship!"

Jerry grins his football-hero grin at me, an invitation to friendship. It decides something for me.

I want our side to win.

16

IT'S THE TWINS' IDEA TO HAVE A "CAMPFIRE" OUTSIDE TO MARK THE SECOND
Quinlans' arrival at Belfountain. Jerry seconds the motion so fast I don't
have time to suggest otherwise. It's not that I'm concerned about the
things we may or may not have seen in the woods. After all, Franny and I
had stood unarmed, and they hadn't approached, let alone threatened us.
And that's assuming there was anyone there in the first place.

My hesitation has to do with letting ourselves see our time here as
fun. Mom sent all of us to summer camp growing up, and while I loved
the swimming and hiking, I preferred the quieter, solitary activities
over the stories told around bonfires that ended with collective screams
when the guy with a hook for a hand showed up. It cheapened the experience somehow. Things that weren't funny that we were all expected
to laugh our heads off at.

I help Jerry and the twins carry out some of the firewood from next
to the hearth and foldout chairs Lauren finds in the front hall closet
along with those jigsaw puzzles Fogarty had mentioned. Soon we're

sitting around a blaze in the circular driveway out front, sending our laughter out into the dark, sparks rising like fireflies to tame the night.

The twins in particular are the stars of the show. Their give-and-take is practiced, yet it doesn't come across that way. A series of comic routines that culminate in an epic tale about swapping dates in the middle of their prom without the girls being able to tell the difference between them.

"Until, you know, the big reveal," Ezra says with a lewd smirk.

"Or, in your case, the little peep show," Elias replies.

"We're identical twins!"

"Not *that* identical."

"I don't know if I'm comfortable with this."

We turn to Lauren, who in fact looks a little queasy.

"You've heard these gags a thousand times," Jerry says. "You always thought they were funny."

"There's just a lot for me to wrap my head around." She looks at me and Franny and Mom and Bridge. "We all had our problems with Dad. But he's *gone*. It's why we're here."

"That may not be totally accurate for some of us," Franny says, not unkindly. "We're here because the will forced us to be."

"He's not forcing us," Lauren says, her voice shriveling.

"None of this was our idea. It was *him*, it—"

"He was my father!"

Lauren gets up and heads off into the lodge. I consider going after her, but she's not my sister, and I wait for Jerry or one of the twins to fulfill their role. But none of them move.

"We all have different takes on Dad," Jerry explains, shifting to squint at us through the licks of flame. "It's probably the same with you guys."

"Yes," Bridge answers.

"Well, in our case, Lauren is the soft touch," Jerry says. "The benefit-of-the-doubter."

"She has a point," Elias says.

"Maybe we should think of Dad in ways we can—" Ezra says, searching his mind. "What's the word?"

"Memorialize."

"Yeah. Maybe we should *memorialize* him."

"Okay," Franny says, clapping her hands together. "I've got one."

I didn't expect there to be as many Dad stories as we come up with. Through it all the tone remains light, almost affectionate. The edge of hostility, lurking beneath every anecdote, only increases the deliciousness.

"There was nobody worse at carving a turkey," Ezra announces.

"Nobody in the turkey-carving world," Elias agrees.

"To be fair, that's because he always got called away before he could finish the job," Mom says, automatically defending him before she can prevent herself.

"Remember the Thanksgiving when he had a cast on his arm?" Jerry says. "He was fighting with that big old bird, hacking at it with one hand. When I offered to help he said, 'Why would I need any help, Gerald?' and kept whacking at it until the carving board looked like a crime scene."

"Wait, I remember the year he had that cast on too," Franny says. "He chopped up our turkey the same way. But if Dad was at your house for Thanksgiving dinner, how could he be at our house too?"

"Maybe it was a different night," Elias says.

"We always had holiday dinner on Thursday," Bridge says.

"Us too," Jerry says.

"It's because he was at both houses," I say. "He started at yours and got a call. Then he came to ours, got another call—"

"And he was gone," Jerry says.

The fire makes a sound like snapped fingers.

"All those years, those times we thought he was ours," Mom says, "he was yours too."

In the quiet, there's a sound all of us hear. Somewhere a great distance away, well beyond the estate's fence, comes the repeated boom of a shotgun. It's followed by a gun of a different kind. A tat-tat-tattling of an automatic. Then it stops too. We've grown used to these noises over the past months. They happen, and we move on, pretending they hadn't.

"It's getting bad out there," Bridge says.

"It was always bad out there," Ezra says.

"He's right. We only caught glimpses of it before," Franny says. "Now all the ugliness is breaking through."

Franny's words make me think of hands punching up from the soil of freshly covered graves, of shark fins rising out of the water, of spiders skittering and spreading from nested holes in the ground. Buried things finding a way to the air.

"We better put this baby to bed," Jerry says, meaning the fire.

The whisky has left us dry-mouthed and headachy. We throw handfuls of dirt onto the fire until it's a sputtering mound of embers. Before going back inside, we pause to listen for gunfire again but there's nothing. It makes me wonder if we ever heard it at all.

17

FAMILIES TEACH US WHO WE ARE. THAT'S WHAT THE KIDS' MOVIES I WATCHED
growing up and the sappy commercials they air over the holidays tell us.
Family binds us. It's the download for our politics and faith software. The
way to see yourself more truly than any mirror.

And maybe it is all that. But I would define it as something else.

A family is a group of people who have different versions of the same
experience.

What I remember of our years in the Mercer Island Cape Cod with
a red-brick chimney and the Stars and Stripes hanging limp from a pole
out front isn't what Franny remembers, and is probably further still from
what Bridge took from living under the same roof.

Not that it was *bad*. There was a station wagon that puttered us to
practices and birthday parties, a rec room where we played the music
loud, a living room where we'd prop a fresh-cut spruce in the corner
and hang strings of popcorn from its branches once a year. But there
was something distinct about our house compared to the homes of our

friends. It was like we were acting at being a family instead of living as one.

I may be alone in this.

Or maybe I'm not.

Sometimes I think something happened to me growing up. A harm of the suppressed kind. I've wondered, if I went to one of those therapists who puts you under and takes you to the place you least want to return to, what I might find way back there. Would I know it was real if such a moment came to mind? How is a story distinguishable from history?

Chances are there's nothing there. What I am only reflects my particular scars from growing up as Ray and Eleanor Quinlan's son.

But they did nothing wrong.

They did nothing.

Once the fire is quieted, the second Quinlans collect the duffel bags the limo drivers had dropped outside and go off to find their quarters. It's decided that the twins will take the Red cabin, Jerry the Green, and Lauren the Yellow while me and Bridge remain in Orange and Franny and Mom in the lodge. I leave Bridge with Mom and offer to accompany Lauren along the trail to her cabin, throwing her bag over my shoulder and immediately regretting it, my legs still wobbly.

"I can manage," she says at the trailhead, pulling the bag off my shoulder. "But I appreciate the company."

"Are you a runner?" I ask as we start off into the trees.

"I try to get out a few times a week. Why do you ask?"

"I can just tell. Skiers know skiers, hunters know hunters. Or so I'm told."

"So runners know runners."

"That's it."

The trail narrows, forcing Lauren to proceed a step ahead. There's only the sound of our breathing, the dull clumping of our feet, the swing-ing light of our headlamps.

"It's bizarre, isn't it, to think about Dad making the drive up and down the I-405 between our two houses," I say, "and none of us having a clue about it until today."

"There's a lot none of us had a clue about until today."

"I can't stop imagining him in his car, heading a few miles north from dinner at our place so he could tuck you in for bed. What could he have been thinking?"

"I couldn't say. But I'm pretty sure he wasn't worried about getting caught."

"Why not?"

"Because someone who would keep two separate families, with two wives, two homes—those kind of men never are."

The trail takes an abrupt turn to the right and starts a switchback down a slope much steeper than the one that leads to the Orange cabin. It takes us a while to work our way left and right and back again, tackling the degree of descent in small servings. Once the trail levels out again, there's still no sign of any clearing or cabin ahead. The darkness is thicker here. Seamless.

"Did you get along? You and Dad?" I ask Lauren, genuinely curious. What if Dad loved her and Jerry and the twins more than us? What if *we* were the real second Quinlans and they the first?

"We didn't fight, if that's what you mean," she says. "I don't think he cared enough to get involved like that."

"That's not exactly what I meant."

"He was benign. As in *not there*. But when you're in my field, you know that that can leave its own kind of scars."

"Do you think it was harder for you being adopted?"

Lauren stops to look at me, and I wonder if I've offended her and then realize all the ways she'd have a right to be.

"I'm sorry," I say. "That was an incredibly stupid thing to—"

She raises her hand, the index finger up to show my apology isn't necessary.

"We're all adopted, if you think about it. At least it's how *I* think about it," she says. "None of us choose our family. We just *arrive*, one way or another."

"And make the best of it."

"Or the worst."

She starts on again and it takes a moment to catch up.

"So what's your theory?"

"Theory?"

"On Dad," I say. "What he did for a living. Who he really was."

"Well," she says, and comes to a stop again, turning to scan the endless green around us. "It certainly paid well."

"And was classified."

"He didn't tell my mother, as far as I know. And he certainly never told me. So maybe secrecy was required of him. Or maybe it was something he chose. Either way, he practiced it to perfection."

"Franny and I have wondered if he was maybe involved in espionage in some way."

"No chance."

"Why?"

"He was too interested in his own project, whatever it was, to work for some institutional bureaucracy."

"Something on the corporate side then."

"Could be. Likely a branch of the sciences or engineering. If you've discovered something useful, there's somebody who'll pay you enough to buy your own national park."

"It must have been good."

"I'd say bad, more likely. Think about it. If he parented his children and conducted his marriages the way he did, what do you think he was capable of in his professional life?"

"You think it was illegal?"

"I'm not saying that. But it's a professional hazard of mine to profile people, even the ones closest to me," she says, and grimaces, what I take to be a hint at the failed relationships in her past. "I see Dad as a more extreme case than my brothers do."

"An obsessive."

"A sociopath."

"Which would mean he didn't ask us here to hold hands around the campfire and promise to get together at Thanksgiving."

"I don't see that, no."

"So what do you see?"

"This? This is a humiliation," Lauren says, bitterness sharpening an edge to her words. "He couldn't feel, but he was interested in managing how other people felt. So here we are."

I'm not sure I agree with her but it's clear that her anger is not something to be tested. I also see now that it wasn't love for Dad that made her storm away from the fire earlier. It was her finding it wrong to be acting normal when none of this is normal. When Dad wasn't normal.

Lauren carries on ahead. I've got my foot raised to follow after her when my body goes still.

The sensation of being watched.

When I turn to look, I see that I'm right.

A tree that's not a tree at the top of the slope we've just made our way down. A quarter of the height of those around it and unnaturally shaped, its limbs hanging downward, a bulbous squirrel nest at the top. And moving. Weaving side to side in a way that has nothing to do with the direction of the wind.

These are the tricks the brain tries to play to prevent me from seeing what it knows is there.

The Tall Man Franny saw last night. Now revealed in more detail. Each announcing its unforgettability in the instant I notice it.

The mouth hanging open like his jaw's been broken. Arms at his sides. His hands lost inside what appear to be a pair of construction gloves that are too big for him, fattened and leathery. The look of something that's lost and has been that way for a long while. Unreachable.

Even though we'd covered a hundred yards of trail from where he is now, only a quarter of that distance separates us in a line up or down the slope.

As if reading my thoughts, he starts forward.

Not on the trail, but coming straight at us. Plowing through the brush, a controlled fall that his legs are able to negotiate, he is advancing at a seemingly impossible pace.

Trying not to trigger him into an outright run by seeing me do the same, I speed-walk up to Lauren.

"Don't stop. Don't turn around, okay?"

"Why?"

"Just drop your duffel bag and keep going."

"What are you—"

"Do it now."

She drops the bag.

Then she does what I asked her not to and turns around.

"Jesus Christ," she whispers, her fear lowering her voice into the tenor of an actual prayer.

The Tall Man breaks through the last of the brush to emerge onto the trail at the base of the hill. Unobscured by the forest, in the electric flash of our lights, he shows more of himself now—glaring and gut flipping and real—so that it's difficult to stitch all of him together. He can't be taken in as whole but only as a loose collection of particulars you see and move your eyes from only to see something else, something worse than the thing before.

A patchwork of a man. One who's no longer a man. An undead scarecrow who leapt from his post.

Clothes so stained—by dirt, by blood—they cling to him like plastic wrap.

A boot on one foot, the other uncovered, the skin swollen to the point of rupture.

The mouth. A black oval ready to bellow an announcement or bite or suck in all the air of the forest for himself.

"My God, my *God*," Lauren whispers in her prayer voice again.

She is spellbound by her terror, just as I was by mine. But watching her take in the Tall Man pulls me out of it.

"We have to run," I say, and the sound of the word offers a counterspell of its own. *Run*.

With his bare, torn-up foot the Tall Man shouldn't be able to match our pace. I try to listen for him—his step on an unearthed tree root, his wet breath, whatever words he might want us to hear—but there's only the tidal rush of panic in my ears.

A moment later another sound joins it. Hissing. When it stops, I realize it was a scream that failed to make it out of Lauren's throat. She gasps and swallows a new breath.

She's looked back. Just as I do now. Sees that he's faster than us.

The cabin comes into view.

Lauren bolts ahead of me. I try to make up the ground between us and realize I can't. My legs, already burning from the run this morning, harden into planks. No matter what I do I can't manage more than a toe-dragging shuffle.

It's not far to the cabin door. If it's unlocked and Lauren opens it, I should be able to throw myself inside right after her.

Her fingers are around the handle. Is it turning? Or is it only her hand sliding over the brass? A second later I see it's neither. She's looked back and seen the Tall Man behind me.

"Open it!"

I don't sound like myself. I sound like a child. A little boy witnessing his house burn down with his family inside.

"Don't look at him! Open the *door*!"

I don't see her do it, but she must turn the handle—or lean her weight into the already opened door—because one second she's there and the next she's swallowed into the cabin's interior darkness. Then I'm there too. Slamming into the door and crashing into the murk.

Lauren is on the floor. I almost come down on her but skid on one foot instead, holding an unlikely balance.

I watch as the door swings hard against the wall and starts its return. But slower than when it opened. Long enough to see the Tall Man launch himself forward.

I do the same.

Elbows, thumb, cheeks, teeth—random parts of me landing against the wood and propelling it closed. I don't lock it. I can't. Not from where I am after I slide down to the floor.

I wait for him to make contact. But there's nothing.

I bring myself up onto my knees, searching for the handle. When my fingers find it, I click it locked.

"Is he there?" Lauren whispers.

"Yes."

"Why isn't he trying to get in?"

"I don't know."

"Oh shit. *Shit*—"

Scratching.

A slow stroking over the outside of the door from the hinges to the handle. Growing louder as it goes. Harder.

His gloves. The ones so big his hands must be glued into them. Now dragging over the outside of the door, side to side.

"What do we do?" Lauren asks, though it's unclear whether it's a question addressed to me or herself.

"Find something to fight with."

"Like what?"

"The kitchen. Maybe there's something we could—"

"Stop."

I listen for what Lauren has heard. It takes a moment to realize there's nothing to hear.

"He's still out there," she says.

"How do you know?"

"I can feel it."

Time itself can be painful. There is nothing other than time that touches us as we wait on the cabin's floor for the Tall Man to find a way in. Time burning against our skin, inside and out.

"He's gone," Lauren says finally.

How does she know? It would be impossible to hear him leave. It can only be wishful thinking on her part. And yet, as soon as she says it, I join her in the same wish.

"You sure?"

"No," she says. "I just—"

"You feel it."

"Yeah."

I start to crawl over toward the sofa set against the wall under the nearest window facing out front.

"What are you doing?"

"Taking a look."

The Tall Man can look in at me more easily than I can look up at him, given the way I have to climb up onto the cushions and nudge the curtains apart with my nose before I can cast my light through the glass.

"Is he there?" Lauren asks.

"Not that I can see."

I walk back from the window, stepping over where Lauren still lies on the floor, into the kitchen. Pull a cheese knife with a decoratively curled point from the drawer. Come back into the living room and grip my hand on the locked handle.

"What are you *doing*?"

"Testing those feelings of yours," I say, and pull the door open wide.

18

IT'S STUNNING.

For the first time since coming to Belfountain, the rain forest—now, in the night interrupted only by my headlamp's bulbs—presents itself not as an enclosure but as a beautiful garden, magnificent and wild. The trees reaching out to each other, swaying to an undetectable music.

"He's not out here," I say.

Lauren comes to stand behind me. Scans what can be seen from over my shoulder.

"Okay," she says. "What're our choices?"

"Stay or go."

"You think we should wait until morning?"

"No," I say, thinking only of Bridge. Of the Tall Man making his way to the lodge. "We should go back."

"Now?"

"Now."

"Let me get a knife first."

"Take mine."

Lauren grips the cheese knife and frowns at its stubby length, the tip curved up like an elf's slipper. "Really?"

"It's the best there is."

"Aren't you bringing one?"

"This will come down to running, not fighting," I say, and it sounds like something imported from the outside, a logic that may not be applicable in this world. Here, it may be that running takes you where you least want to go.

We don't see the Tall Man on the hike back to the lodge. More than this, it's as if the return from the cabin peels away the memory of him, diluting his reality, so that when we step out of the trees and approach the front door, we're both clearing our throats with embarrassment. What will we say?

A skinny, homeless-looking man followed us in the woods.

So what? There were two of you, one of him.

He didn't seem right.

Did he say anything?

No.

So how do you know he wasn't right?

It's reassuring. But then we come inside and I see Bridge and Franny and Mom huddled together on the sofa as if clinging to a raft adrift in the great room, and the fear returns. The idea of them seeing what we've already seen.

We tell them what happened. I try not to dwell on the Tall Man's physical details, but they keep asking about him, and my hesitation ends up making him sound even worse. What did he want? This is what they demand to know next, but it's the one thing we can't answer. He came at us. He stroked his gloved hand against the door. But he didn't touch us, didn't attempt to force his way in.

"Was it him?" Franny asks me.

"I'm guessing it was, yeah."

"Was it *who*?"

This is Bridge. When I'm done telling her the full story of what Franny says she saw in the woods the night before, Bridge weighs the options in her head. It doesn't take her long. She decides to forgive me.

"We said no more secrets," she says.

"I know. But I told you I saw something."

"You didn't tell me *everything*."

"Full disclosure from now on. I promise," I say, and though the four of them are all present to hear it, it's one I make to Bridge alone.

Mom takes the report of the Tall Man the hardest. There aren't the nervous tears or blank-faced shock that would be consistent with her repertoire, only coldness. She removes herself to a corner of the room. Her lips moving noiselessly, as if teasing out a set of possibilities.

"You okay?" Franny asks, putting her arm around Mom's shoulder and pulling her close.

"I just thought, after today, there couldn't be anything new under the sun," she says with one of her feeble laughs. She looks at me. "What do you propose, Aaron?"

I'd hoped it would be enough to disclose, to share our disturbing experience with others and have them say it's over, we're all awake, there's nothing to be afraid of. But now I see it doesn't stop with that. It's not a dream that concludes with its telling.

Lauren asks if we should go warn Jerry and the twins. All of us look at the solid darkness outside the windows.

"First of all, there's probably nothing they need to be warned about," I say, sounding calm, which goes some way to actually calming me. "We should wait until morning. At first light, I'll head out to the Green cabin where Jerry is. Come up with a plan. How's that sound?"

Vague. Improvised. But nobody suggests anything else.

I offer to sleep on one of the sofas; Lauren will take the unoccupied room, Franny another, and Bridge will huddle in with Mom. These are the decisions we make out loud. But none of us move. In the end we stay where we are, sleeping in chairs with Mom and Bridge on a sofa. I tell them I'll keep watch through the night, that nothing will get in without me stopping it. This time it's a promise I make to all of them.

19

THERE ARE ASPECTS OF IT THAT REMIND ME OF A SLUMBER PARTY. THE DISCOMFORT of sitting tense and alert, for instance. The unfamiliar sounds and smells of a night spent in a strange house, the snoring bodies all around and me the only one awake.

Except this isn't some Mercer Island high school kid's birthday party.

Except the man wandering around outside, his face a portrait of emptiness, is the opposite of the bogeyman we told stories about and pulled the sheets up to our chins to protect ourselves against. Because we knew those monsters weren't real. And I know the Tall Man is.

I make myself some toast, and by the time I return to the great room, the rest of them are stretching and asking what time it is.

"Early," I say.

"You want me to come with you?" Lauren asks when she sees the chef's knife, an upgrade from the cheese thingy, in my hand.

"No, I'm good. Stay here. Someone will send word."

I'm hoping for something from Mom, an emboldening gesture for the walk ahead. But she only looks my way with a combination of pity and dread, as if an aura of disaster surrounds me and she doesn't want to come close enough to enter it.

Bridge follows me to the door.

"You're going to be okay," she says. But as I step outside, she locks the door behind me before I can reply.

Was it a better idea to do this in daylight?

I walk across the parking area toward the Green trailhead feeling exposed, even if the relative brightness reveals nothing waiting for me. But how would I know? Judging from the way the Tall Man had come down the hill, ignoring the course of the switchbacking trail, he knows how to travel through the forest, how to hide and track and survive in it. This is his element, not mine.

I make a point of not pausing before starting down the path to avoid running back and banging on the door to be let in. If I'm not capable of genuine courage, then the appearance of courage will have to do. Maybe this is all there is anyway. The soldiers storming out of their foxholes, the child promising her mom that today she'll find a friend at her new school. All of them finding bravery by faking it.

You pretend to not be afraid for this step, then the next. In time, you come to the Green cabin's door.

I'm about to knock but Jerry's voice sounds through the wood first.

"What are you doing out here?"

"We've got to talk."

"Why are you holding a knife?"

"That's what we've got to talk about."

He's not going to let me in. The doorknob doesn't turn, there's no call of *Just gimme a sec*. There's nothing.

"Jerry. This is serious. Open the goddamn—"

The door is pulled open a third of the way so I have to edge in sideways before it's shut again.

"Was it you?"

It takes a moment for me to find Jerry in the gloom. Standing off to my right and also holding a chef's blade in his hand, though his appears rustier than mine.

"Was it me *what*?"

"Walking around outside last night."

"No."

"But you know who was."

"A man I've never seen before. He followed Lauren and me on our way to her cabin."

Jerry lowers his knife, and I realize mine has also been held out in front of me, so I do the same.

"She okay?" he asks.

"She's fine. She's at the lodge."

"What do you mean he followed you?"

"One minute he wasn't there, and then he was."

"Could he have just been an employee? A maintenance guy or something?"

"I don't think so."

"Why not?"

Because he looked like the most lost thing I've ever seen.

"Because he wasn't," I say.

Jerry's eyes dance between the cabin's front window and the door, and back to me.

"Okay," he says. "So. What did he look like?"

"Tall. Dressed like he dug his way out of his own grave. His *face*. Mouth open like a shotgun wound. This stunned expression, as if he were searching for something but he didn't know what it was." I hear myself say this last part and it comes at me fresh, as if it were somebody else's thought altogether.

Jerry takes a step back and bumps his legs into the sofa. Instead of moving away from it, he lets himself fall back into its cushions.

"What's going on here, Aaron?"

"I don't know. He could have tried to break into the cabin, but he didn't. He could've hung around until we came out, but didn't do that either."

"You think it's all a game? Something Dad put together?"

"I guess it's possible. Being made to stay out here for a month—it's a game in itself, right? And then—surprise!—a second family he didn't tell any of us about. Why not throw another curveball into the mix?"

I don't know what I'm expecting. Some more pondering, probably. But without anything more to say, Jerry is up.

"You coming with me?" he says as he passes me and opens the door without checking to see if there's anyone on the other side.

"Where are we going?"

"To find this guy."

Unlike mine, Jerry's bravery performance is convincing. It's possible that, for him, it isn't a performance at all.

Jerry heads out and I follow him. My hand grips the knife so tight my fingers lose all feeling, and somewhere along the trail, it falls to the ground without my noticing.

20

JERRY HAS THE AIR OF A HUNTER ABOUT HIM. AN AUTHORITY AS HE PAUSES TO STUDY a print in the mud or a bent branch that suggests he knows more about searching for a predator in the woods than I ever will. Then again, given the twins' vocation, acting could run in his family in a way it doesn't in ours. It could be that Jerry is nothing more than a gym teacher who's used to ordering teenaged boys around and applies this confidence to every aspect of his life.

We work our way closer to the lodge at a tiptoed pace for fifteen minutes or so before Jerry detects a side trail I hadn't noticed on the way in. At first it doesn't look like much of anything. But twenty feet or so deeper, there's an evident pattern of pushed aside branches and indented grass underfoot that indicates a repeated course of travel for a large animal or man.

"There's another game Dad might have wanted us to play," Jerry says out of nowhere, as if we'd been conversing about the same topic without interruption since leaving the cabin.

"What's that?"

"Family Feud."

"Sorry?"

"Us against you. The two Quinlan teams. Only the strongest and smartest make it to the end and win the prize."

"You're not being serious," I say, even though it's pretty much what I was thinking.

"Look at us. This is some pretty crazy shit. And no offense or anything, but I don't even *know* you."

"Sure you do. I'm your long-lost half brother."

I try to keep my tone light. What Jerry is saying could be suspicious, or he could simply be explaining how unnatural this is. It's impossible to tell which is his intention, as he maintains a tone as half-jokey as mine.

He turns to face me. Smiling apologetically, but standing with his feet wide apart, rooted to the ground.

"How can I be sure of that, Aaron? How can I really know who you are?"

"You can't. We can either trust each other or not. Do you think I'm lying?"

"No. I don't."

"So I say we work together. We're family. It's an advantage we have."

"I agree. Believe me, I'm not accusing you of anything," he says with a sigh. "I'm trying to sort this out, that's all. I'm thinking how Dad might have thought."

"And how's that?"

"What?"

"I'm curious how you understand Dad's way of thinking."

It's a harmless query. But because we're out in the woods, possibly being watched—because we're invoking the presence of Raymond Quinlan—it comes out sounding loaded.

"If he's had a hand in this, it's going to be a jack-in-the-box," he says eventually. "We keep turning the handle until something pops out."

"That's an interesting way of looking at him."

"Is there another way?"

"Well, your sister's the shrink, not me. But seeing Dad as wanting each of us to open him up—I don't know, it speaks to a certain kind of experience."

Jerry cocks his head. Shakes an apparent stiffness from his legs. "You seem to be aiming at something here."

"We were both his sons, Jerry. Odds are, whatever contact you had with Dad was of the same kind I had with him," I start. "I just think, now that he's gone, we might compare notes. Maybe help each other see stuff that maybe we'd rather not see."

"I think I know where you're going here. And I'm going to ask you to stop."

"Don't you ever think about how Dad is kind of *blocked* from us? If something happened to me, maybe to all—"

"I'm asking you to shut your mouth."

Jerry looks more wounded than angry.

"I'm sorry. This is difficult for me to even bring up. And I didn't mean to—"

He holds his hand up. I figure it's to cut this conversation off, but then both of us hear something in the trees off to the right. At least, that's the direction I turn, though Jerry looks in the opposite direction.

He doesn't say anything. Not *Stay here* or *Get down* or *Circle back around*. He just bends low and starts into the bush to the left.

If he's wrong about the direction, whatever made the dull whump on the forest floor is closer to me than it is to Jerry. But he sure as hell seems certain. If I've learned anything over the last forty-eight hours, it's that noises can bounce around in the forest in a way that makes it hard to figure their distance or position. He may be going straight at the Tall Man. He may be leaving me behind.

I move in the same manner he did—crouching low and striking into the bush—except to the right. Hoping I'm wrong. Looking for a place to find cover and wait.

There's lots of potential camouflage out here if you happen to be wearing any shade of green. But if, like me, you're dressed in blue jeans and a blue Seahawks T-shirt and matching windbreaker (Dad getting all our favorites right in his duffel bag clothing purchases), there isn't anything but tree trunks to use as shields. None of them quite wide enough to be sure something on the other side couldn't spot you.

I keep moving as quietly as I can. Not looking for anything in particular now, not even a place to disappear, only advancing into the forest because the idea of waiting to be found is worse than the slow chicken walk I'm doing now.

When I look up after a minute or so, I find that the underbrush has thinned around me, the thistle and ferns only recently reclaiming the cleared soil. I wonder if it's an old burn site, maybe a lightning strike, a bald anomaly in the otherwise ceaseless thicket. But a few steps on and the growth only thins more and more before opening into a broader clearing.

That's not what stops me.

It's not much of anything now, but I recognize what it was. A single L-shaped wood structure the length of two tractor trailers fused together. Here and there on the flat ground around it are wood platforms that once acted as the foundation for wall tents. A circle of stones bordering a black mound of cinders. The two iron spikes of a horseshoe pit.

A summer camp.

It's not a place I've ever been to before. In fact, it's hard to imagine any parent sending their kid here, even when it was in good repair. The space of the site slightly too small, as if the effort of cutting its grounds out of the forest proved too difficult and what resulted was a cramped compromise. Hard to find even if you were looking for it.

Abandoned places are always a little sad, especially ones where children once played, sang songs by the fire, ran laughing. Yet this place feels more ghostly than sad. Maybe it's because I can't imagine what laughter would sound like here, what music would be allowed.

I think of turning back but convince myself there's a reason I'm here, push away the immediate counterquestions—*Why? Who says there's anything here for you?*—and start toward the sagging building I'm guessing was once the dining hall. Looking for something. A piece of my father. Something to convince myself that he'd intended I be the one to find it.

The windows along the walls and in the main entrance doors are boarded up, but carelessly so, leaving gaps at the corners and between the two-by-fours. On the ground, there are stray tent pegs and opened tins of food, the labels melted away on most but only faded on a couple others. Baked beans. Beefaroni.

There's a sign over the door I hadn't noticed when I first entered the clearing. Letters gouged into a slab of tree trunk and nailed into the pine so that, as all of it succumbed to the sun and mold, the words looked like they were becoming something else. A retraction.

BELFOUNTAIN

For as many times as I'd heard my father say the name, this may be the first time I've seen it written out. Pretty to hear and to speak, but it looks different to me now, the obese *B* followed by a jumble of letters. Over-voweled, inviting misreadings. *Elf* and *bell* and *mountain*.

Inside, I'm met by long-past odors: fried margarine and boiled bones for the making of soup. But these are only phantom smells. There couldn't be any of that left in the air after the years of neglect that have passed in this place. The watery strands of light that seep through the cracks of the windows show a row of tables and benches, award plaques high on the walls with the names of past orientation and archery champions engraved on brass plates. There are squares paler than the rest of the wall where photos probably hung, but they must have been taken away when the place was left, apparently the only things that were.

I should go because Jerry might wonder where I am. Because there's nothing here. Because I'm afraid that there is.

One of the swinging doors to the kitchen has been ripped away, and the fact that I won't have to touch the other one to step inside brings me closer. I float forward, reading the painted sentences on the exposed roof beams as I go.

> MY LITTLE CHILDREN, LET US NOT LOVE IN WORD,
> NEITHER IN TONGUE; BUT IN DEED AND IN TRUTH.

On the floor, boot prints in the seedlings and dust. Comings and goings along the same aisle I walk down. Likely from years ago. Though they could be more recent than that.

> THE MEMORY OF THE RIGHTEOUS IS A BLESSING,
> BUT THE NAME OF THE WICKED WILL ROT.

Lines of Scripture. *Little children.* Stern, magical, ambiguous. Is all of the Bible like this? Or is it only me not wanting to be here yet having to be, like many of the campers who would have read these same lines as they looked up from their hamburgers and oatmeal.

> THE WICKED WILL ROT.

There's something on the floor. I can feel it before I see it, a series of cuts carved into the planks, the simple outline of a map. Then

I look down and see it's more like a compass—but no, that's not it either.

I recognize it from the movies we'd rent for those teenage slumber parties where I could never sleep. Something bad.

A pentagram. The circle with a star made of triangles inside it. Wider than the aisle, so that it reaches under the tables. I bend down to fit a finger into one of the grooves and it comes back blackened with soot. The lines not drawn. Burnt.

When I stand straight, I notice similarly made, smaller lines in the tables and on the walls. Messages. Summonings. A crude language in competition with the biblical quotations overhead.

SATAN HEAR OUR VOICE

The sort of thing stoned vandals leave behind, kids who've got their hands on those paperbacks about rituals and "true" accounts of devil worship, sacrifice, possession. Hard to find a picnic table in a park or wall of a public toilet without some version of it.

Knowing this doesn't make me any less afraid.

WE SING FOR YOU

I step out of the pentagram's circle in the floor. Before entering the kitchen, I cast my eyes up at the ceiling and catch the last line of scripture on the rafters, sounding through my head as something close to a threat.

UNLESS ONE IS BORN AGAIN, HE CANNOT SEE THE KINGDOM OF GOD.

In the kitchen's leaden light, the stainless steel counters shine greenish as a snake's skin. Some of the larger cooking pots are still here, sitting on the stove top, the lids on. I don't pull them off to see if there's anything inside.

It's the walk-in freezer that's captured my attention. The padlock hanging open through the latch.

The handle pulls back with a guttural *clunk*, and from there the door eases wide without my having to do a thing, as if wanting to show me its insides, wanting to breathe. It reminds me that I haven't taken a breath myself for a while. When I do, the sound I make is that of a child startled after being struck.

There hasn't been power here for a long time, which makes it even more unsettling to walk into the freezer's warm tomb. The insulation within the stained steel walls holds the airless humidity inside, as it would any sound or voice that might try to get out. There's more space than I was expecting. The shelving has been completely removed, leaving only rust-weeping holes in the walls. Room that had to be made for the trapdoor in the floor.

It's also made of steel except it's new, a square plate of dimpled silver the size of a compact pickup's flatbed. A handle on the left to lift it open. It would be heavy if I tried.

I try.

It sends a warning flare of pain up my back, from my hips to the back of my skull. But I manage it. Once I have it past the halfway point, I let it go and it rests against the wall with a single *nick*, like the touching of nails to a blackboard.

Stairs. Each step made of smooth cement, heading into the ground beyond the range of what I can see.

Why do I do it? I ask myself this as I start down, ducking my head and reaching my hands out blind. It may be raw curiosity, but if it is, I don't experience it as *wanting* to know what may be down here. If anything, it's the opposite. I wish only to be protected from discoveries, from any new layer of Belfountain's possibilities. It's like the patients I have

who demand surgery instead of the alternative therapies or pharmaceuticals or waiting and seeing, things they could do to avoid it. They don't
want to be opened up, but if they submit to it, they hope they can put the
entire matter of illness behind them.

The stairs are steeply sloped but remain straight so that once I get
used to it, just enough daylight filters in to see shapes and outlines by.
The equidistant seams in the ceiling. The irregularities in the cement's
cratered face.

The steel wall.

There's no way around it. The stairs come to an end and there it is,
no space to stand.

A moment of inspection shows it isn't a wall, but a door. One with
no handle, no markings. I smooth my hand over its cold surface, drawing lines through the condensation, and feel nothing interrupt its gray
surface but a single keyhole built into the metal.

I press my shoulder against it. It feels more than locked. Sealed tight.

As an object, as an incongruent *thing*, it makes no sense. And the longer I lean into it, feeling for a vibration or voice from within, its possible
meanings flee from my grasp. The door has a purpose and history distinct
from the forest, from the Christian kids' camp built on the ground fifteen
feet above my head. Beyond that there isn't a single guess I could make.

But I do know this: the door is special. My knowledge of it even
more so.

Which means I can't stay here.

For the first few steps I don't turn, backstepping my ascent and
keeping my eyes on the door as if in readiness for it to be pulled open.
Then the darkness reclaims it and not being able to see it frightens me
more than imagining the thing that might open it, and I spin around,
jumping the last few steps up into the walk-in freezer's airless space.

I don't drop the trapdoor closed. Don't touch the freezer's door. I
just get out.

WE SING FOR YOU

Through the dining hall, dancing over the lines of the pentagram in the floor, keeping my pace to a walk as if to do anything else would confirm how terrified I am, I bring out the childish moan I can feel swelling up my throat.

Only once the light makes visible the stones around the charred circle and the overgrown horseshoe pit, a verifiable place in the world where things not only happened but are happening now, do I feel like I'm being watched.

A sudden wind picks up, blowing fast against my face. That's what my mind interprets it as before it discovers my body has taken charge. Moving my legs. Throwing me forward.

Running.

21

I HAVE A SENSE OF THE WAY I'D COME AND WHERE THE MAIN TRAIL IS BUT I CAN'T
find any sign of either. I'm relying on the logic that if the trail is reasonably straight I'll meet up with it if I don't get turned around.

The sight of Jerry standing a hundred yards ahead proves it's a good guess.

He doesn't see me approach, but he hears me, judging by the way he searches the horizon of brush surrounding him. It gives me the strange feeling of being the Tall Man myself. Semi-visible, deciding what action I will take next.

"Hey!"

I call out to him as I step back onto the main trail and he approaches with deliberate steps.

"Where'd you go?" he asks.

"Back that way."

"See anything?"

"Nothing. You?"

"Not a goddamn thing."

He keeps his eyes on me.

"You look spooked," he says.

"It's a spooky place."

He studies me a moment longer. Measuring the hazards I could potentially pose. It's only after he starts back along the trail that I realize I'd been doing the same thing looking at him.

When we return to the lodge, Ezra and Elias are in the middle of reprising their roles in a recent Delta Airlines commercial. A tearjerker involving twins separated at birth reuniting at JFK Arrivals after a lifetime apart.

"You haven't changed a bit!" they both declare at the end, chins trembling with emotion, before throwing their arms around each other.

Mom, Bridge, Franny, and Lauren, seated on one of the great room's enormous sectional sofas, applaud in the restrained manner of a golf gallery.

"A single day's work," Ezra says.

"Paid the mortgage for two years," Elias says.

"Do you two live together?" I ask, and all of them swing around, startled to find me and Jerry standing there.

"No," Elias answers.

"That would be *weird*," Ezra adds.

Lauren is the first to get up. "Hold on," she says. "How'd you get in?"

"The door was open," Jerry says. "I'm assuming that the boys didn't lock it after they came in looking for breakfast?"

The twins look first accusingly, then guiltily, at each other.

"Sorry," they say at the same time.

"Did you find anything?" Lauren addresses this to me.

"No."

"So what's next?"

"Maybe your brothers could do a live performance of the first season of *Better Together* for us?"

It's meant as a tension reliever, but it comes out as unkind. Everyone hears it, none more acutely than the twins themselves, who take seats on opposite sides of the rug from each other, turtling their shoulders forward against further injury.

"I didn't mean—" I'm on my way to apologizing, but Jerry steps ahead of me to stand directly in front of Lauren.

"This man that Aaron saw," he says. "You saw him too?"

"Yes."

"You're certain?"

"*Jesus*, Jerry. *Yes*. I'm certain."

Jerry paces once between Lauren and the twins before stopping to look down at Mom, Franny, and Bridge on the sofa—one, then two, then three—counting them off in his head as if taking a head count.

"I say we all stay here until we can sort this out," he announces.

Franny snorts. "It's so funny," she says.

"What part?"

"You. Automatically assuming that you get to make the decisions."

"I'm offering my opinion, that's all."

"Please! *Look* at you. Standing in the center of the room with your arms crossed and all of us waiting to hear what the great leader is going to say. We're out here and there're no cops, no laws, and you see an opening. Grabbing power."

"First of all, what's going on here—this isn't *political*. And second—"

"You voted for *him*, didn't you?"

"What? Hold—"

"Thought it was time to build some walls, go back to the good old days when nobody *bothered* people like you."

Jerry pauses. "How do you think you know who I vote for?"

"When's the last time you looked in a mirror?"

I wonder if Jerry is going to hit her. Not that he looks like he will. Not a violent man in the compulsive sense, but one distilled in the culture of weight rooms and off-campus keggers and sports bars who proves his masculinity through the giving and taking of shots to the jaw. As a pretty boy, he's probably had to prove it more than most.

But Jerry doesn't hit Franny. He grins at her. As warm and genuine an expression as I've seen him or any of us make.

"Okay, you got me, Francine," he says. "Of *course* I voted for him."

"Bingo!"

"Here to help."

Fear doesn't always take the form you assume it will. It can be a scream into the darkness, paralysis, a hopeless sobbing. But it can also come out in a guffaw, hearty and loud, as it does now from my own throat. I'm not the only one either. The twins rouse from their sulk to giggle like a pair of school kids. And Bridge, uncertain at first, is soon laughing along with the rest of us.

It's a release. But soon it distorts in our ears, the hysteria rising up through the hilarity, twisting our voices into those that come from behind the closed doors of an asylum.

"We should leave."

Without any of us noticing, Mom has gotten up and watches us from the farthest edge of the room. She doesn't speak loudly but we hear her clearly all the same. One by one, the laughter dies and returns to ice in our chests.

"We should leave," she says again. "Now."

"Why do you say that, Eleanor?" Jerry asks, ready to be convinced.

"It's not safe."

"Well, with respect, we don't know that. If you consider the facts— the likelihood that it's just a vagrant that Aaron and Lauren saw. Some tent-city guy who hitched a ride up here and can't find his way out again."

"That's not what's happening."

Nobody denies this. Not even Jerry, who, whether out of deference to Mom's seniorhood or to avoid hearing the sharpness that may come out in his voice, shrugs and sits on the arm of the sofa.

"We're all free to go," Lauren says, moving closer to Mom. "It's just a matter of the will—"

"I *hate* that word!"

Because I'm still standing at the top of the steps down to the great room, I can see how all of us jolt back at the force of Mom's shout.

"It was *his* will that was the only important thing all his life, and it's still him telling us what to do," Mom goes on. "What about us? What about *our* will?"

"I understand what you're saying, I truly do," Lauren says. "But it seems you're making a more practical suggestion. Am I right?"

Mom calms herself before speaking. Whatever she's about to attempt to convince us of, this may be her only chance.

"If we all leave, we can be safe," she says. "If any of you are concerned about the estate, we can contest it. Legally. What's going on, what he's asked—it's not normal. I can't imagine it standing up in a court of law, especially not if it's all of us together."

"I dunno. That Fogarty guy seemed pretty legit," Ezra counters.

"And we can't get legal advice without a phone," Elias adds. "To walk out now—that's a hell of a risk to hope some judge sees it our way."

"Bridge?" I say, and it takes a moment for her to blink her eyes clear. "What do you think?"

"We're all here," she says. "There's a reason for that."

There's nothing in her delivery to suggest if she thinks this reason will work for us or against us. But her posture is firm. She's not going anywhere.

Mom looks to Franny. The most likely vote to go her way, under the circumstances. But Franny only sighs.

"It's millions of dollars, Mom," she says. "There's so much that could be done—so much good. So much change."

"It *is* a lot of change," Elias agrees.

"A good chunk of change," Ezra nods.

"Just because nothing awful has happened doesn't—"

Mom lets this sentence hang there, as if speaking aloud the words we know to logically follow would risk triggering some magic of fate.

"Shall we take a vote?"

I'm the one who asks this, and so it's me who my mother looks at with despair.

"Don't trouble yourselves. I know the count," she says, and starts away toward the kitchen with first Bridge, then Franny following after to console her. I consider doing the same, but Jerry is coming at me to deliver a clap to my shoulder.

"What do you say we fortify the castle, doc?" he says.

22

TURNS OUT THERE'S NOT MUCH WE CAN DO. ONCE WE CONFIRM THE BEDROOM AND bathroom windows are locked, we search the lodge for any other possible points of entry. There's the front door, the glass door built into the giant windows along the length of the great hall that Franny had used to slip out for her smoke, and a third one off the kitchen that leads to the garbage bins with metal lids to discourage animals and bears. All locked.

Which still leaves the giant windows. Jerry guesses they're more solid than the walls; the reinforced glass is of the kind used in skyscrapers. Yet as the afternoon fades and the dusk grows, what's worrying is what we might see outside as much as how it might find a way in.

Over dinner, there's a discussion about the threat the Tall Man poses that eases our minds somewhat. His appearance suggested mental illness of one kind or another, and as Lauren points out, the mentally ill are statistically no more inclined to violence than anyone else. Our best guess is that he found his way inside Belfountain's fence somehow and is trying to survive.

There's also some talk about ways we could get our hands on the satellite phone in the metal box on the other side of the gate. But the rules Fogarty laid out would disqualify whoever went to fetch it from participating in the will's proceeds. How would anyone know if someone did? Maybe they wouldn't. Then again, maybe there're cameras recording our movements all along the perimeter.

None of us volunteers to try. Partly this is because we actually don't need the phone. It's also partly because nobody wants to be the one eliminated from the will and have to trust the rest of us to voluntarily make up for their lost cut. I wouldn't say this latter thought indicates any deep distrust between the two Quinlan families. It's simply a consideration that all of us judge best left unspoken.

After we've eaten, Bridge, Mom, and Franny retire to their rooms, leaving Jerry, Lauren, me, and the twins to determine two-hour shifts for each of us to keep watch while the others doze in the leather chairs. I take the middle of the night. Two to four. An island of nervous wakefulness between two seas of insomnia.

Yet there must be some sleep for me before the morning, because when I wake, I remember the dream I had. The same one from the first night at Belfountain that I shared with Franny and Bridge.

Jerry is up already, as he isn't in the chair he slept in. Judging from the restless snorts and coughs from the twins, they're having nightmares too.

When they both open their eyes, I ask if they can remember their dreams.

"Not usually," Ezra says. "But the one just now was a doozy."

"Got that right," Elias says. "Like *nas*-ty."

"What were they about?"

"Water," Elias says.

"Dark water. *Salt* water," Ezra adds.

"And this weird music. Like singing."

"Alien singing."

Elias turns to his twin brother. "You were there," he says. "In the dream."

"You too."

"Treading water."

"Not a pool or pond or lake, nothing with a shore. The water all the way to the horizon."

"Except you couldn't even see the horizon."

"Or the bottom below us."

"Like it was deeper than the ocean."

"Like space."

"Yeah. Empty as outer space."

Lauren sits upright in the chair she slept in.

"I had the same dream. I had it the first night I was here too," she says.

"Me too," I say. "Except last night it was different from before."

"Different?" Elias asks.

"Different how?" Ezra adds.

"My sisters were in it. And so were you."

23

ONE OR TWO OF US WERE MISSING IN SOME OF THE RETELLINGS. OTHERS HAD A
small detail to add that the others lacked. But unless some of us were outright lying, everyone who slept in Belfountain's castle last night dreamed
the same dream.

Everyone except Mom.

She doesn't say she didn't, just avoids the topic when she shuffles into
the great room in her slippers and purple velour tracksuit that must have
come in her duffel bag. She listens to us talk about the dark water, the fear
of what lived beneath our kicking feet, the cosmic singing. When Franny
asks her directly about it, she shakes her head—what could be a *yes* or *no*
or *I can't think about this now* sort of gesture—and heads off to the kitchen
to get started on mixing pancake batter.

"You're the shrink," Franny says to Lauren. "What the hell is happening to us?"

"I've heard of shared dreams within families before, but nothing
this extensive," she says. "There are theories of how telepathy can be

explained—you know, how people claim to have jumped out of bed at the exact same time a relative died miles away. This is different. Psychology proceeds from an individual clinical basis, not a group. We work on the assumption that while we influence one another, our minds process these interactions in distinct ways."

"So, bottom line, you have no idea and you're as freaked as the rest of us."

"It sounds like you're after my job, Franny."

"To be the shrink to *this* crew? I don't want it."

After an assessment of the dwindling supplies that remain in the freezer and fridge, it's decided we ought to send someone out to the gate and see if any food has been left for us. On the basis that I'm the only one to have made the journey there and back, all eyes turn to me.

Before I go, I wait for an opportunity to speak with Bridge.

Ever since I returned from the forest after discovering the camp, I've hesitated in sharing it. Even with all the strangeness of this place, the tunnel leading down through the hole in the walk-in freezer radiated something different. A thing not meant to be seen.

The best course would be to keep it to myself. An underground staircase, a solid steel barrier—none of it is going to attack us all on its own. If we never come upon it again, whatever it may contain will stay below.

I wouldn't disclose it to anyone if it wasn't for the promise I made to Bridge.

Later that morning, as Lauren and the twins busy themselves making a couple trays of lasagna, Franny and Mom whisper to each other in a corner of the great room, and Jerry walks through the place checking on everyone and giving pats on the back and little pep talks like the high school coach he is, I pull Bridge aside. We close the door to the bedroom Mom and Franny are using, and I tell her about the camp.

I'm expecting her to voice the same questions troubling my own mind—Who built it? Why way out there?—but she makes a statement instead.

"Daddy took me there."

"Where?"

"To that old summer camp. The door at the bottom of the stairs," she says, nodding as she works to summon the details. "He didn't call it a door though. He just said, 'There's something I want you to see.'"

"What did he show you once you got there?"

"Nothing. We were walking through the trees for what felt like a long time, and then it was there. A couple old buildings, a swing set. We went into one place, into the kitchen. Inside the freezer there were stairs going down. When we got to the bottom, he seemed about to say something but then changed his mind, and we turned back."

"Did he have a key? Did he open it?"

"I don't remember a key. And like I said, I don't remember it as a door. It was just the *end*, y'know?"

The sound of footsteps creak over the floorboards in the hallway outside. There's a pause as whoever it is notes the closed bedroom door before turning and heading away again.

"What do you think it is?" Bridge whispers.

"My guess is a gate of some kind."

"Like the fence we drove through? A gate *inside* a gate?"

"Something like that."

I start for the door, seeing this as an opportunity to return to the others without rousing suspicion, but Bridge stops me.

"Why me, Aaron? Why would Dad bring me there?"

"I don't know. Maybe he had to show someone, and he thought you'd have the best chance of understanding."

"That might make sense if he told me. But he didn't."

She flinches. A blade within her twists with the effort of trying to grasp our father's intentions. That I know how these attempts will invariably prove useless only doubles my sympathy. She needs a theory to cling to, a narrative that indicates he was human. It's not about making excuses for him. It's about seeing a way of not being the child of a man who meant to break you.

"Secrets—the big ones—are hard to let go of," I say. "Even when you want to, even when they're too much to bear. It's like they hang on to you by a power of their own."

Bridge nods again.

"We should get out of here before someone asks what we're talking about," I say, pulling the door open.

"We're not telling anybody else about this?"

"I don't think so."

"Because if they knew, they might try to find the camp."

"They might."

"And that would be bad."

"I'm not sure it would be good."

Judging from the way Bridge walks past me without another word, she agrees.

24

AT THE LAST MINUTE BEFORE I SET OUT, LAUREN ANNOUNCES SHE'LL COME WITH me. It's a decision Jerry doesn't look too thrilled about but doesn't attempt to prevent.

We start out walking the bike but soon guess it will take us the better part of what remains of the morning to reach the gate at this pace. That's when I suggest Lauren ride in the wagon attached to the back.

"This is ridiculous," she says, correctly, as she curls herself up in the plywood box.

"You'd rather do the pedaling?"

"Are you kidding? I just hope nobody sees us."

It felt like we were about to break into laughter a moment ago, but the idea of the two of us being observed by something out here, out in the woods, chokes it off.

After I get us up to a speed I can maintain, I'm impressed by how well the contraption rolls along, the momentum of our weight combined with my pride in showing Lauren I can handle the physical challenge of getting us to the gate in what feels like not much more than forty-five minutes or so.

When I dismount, she's out of the trailer and heading straight toward the food-delivery opening in the fence.

"Looks like we got a drop-off," she says.

Two cardboard boxes sit on the half of the metal circle on the outside of the fence. There's no sign of a vehicle or anyone waiting to ensure the delivery gets into our hands. I squint to see if there are tire tracks in the road and there may be—snaking lines that could be tire treads—or all I'm seeing is the dried retreat of rain.

"So this thing just turns around, like this?" Lauren says, spinning the plate around and plucking the boxes off.

"Okay," I say. "Let's get out of here."

"Hold on. How do you think this works?"

She's looking at the dangling wires over the hole in the fence the boxes passed through.

"I'm guessing it's part of the security features."

"You think they're electrified?"

"I haven't touched them to find out. But I—"

She pinches one of the wires with her thumb and forefinger before I can stop her.

"Nope," she says.

I watch as she stacks the boxes in the bike's trailer and rips one of them open. Pulls out a loaf of bread and a jar of peanut butter.

"Picnic?" she says, holding them both in the air.

"If you can find some jam in there, I'm in," I say, happy to be with someone brave for a change, instead of pretending to be brave myself.

Lauren puts her hand into the box and brings out a jar of raspberry jelly without looking.

"Where there's the *pb*, there's got to be the *j*," she says, settling into a level circle of tall grass at the edge of the trees a dozen feet behind us.

It's mostly shady, but the light finds its way through the overhead branches in irregular shapes so that as I sit next to her, she is visible in blocks of gray and dazzling yellow. We open the jars and each roll up a slice of bread, dipping it into the peanut butter and then the jelly with each new bite.

"You're not afraid, being out here?" I ask her.

"I'm not afraid of you."

"I wasn't talking about me."

"I know what you're talking about. The *unknown*," she says, and takes another sticky bite.

"Yeah. I guess I am."

"Well, I try not to worry about that too much," she says once she's swallowed. "As a matter of fact, I go out of my way to face it down. It's helped me."

"I suppose your patients are like that. People just imagining things."

"*My* patients? No. *My* patients have been through the most real shit ever. They have no need to imagine anything except maybe a day of feeling close to normal or a good night's sleep. It's why I've never understood people who go to horror movies or read novels about dragons or demons or whatnot. Why go looking for scary stuff when there's plenty of that available all around us?"

"Unless you've been protected from it."

"Safe," she says, and pauses, as if the word was the name of a fabled island. "Safety is a privilege."

"But it's one you had, right? We both did. I mean, we're Quinlans."

I intend this as a kind of joke, an acknowledgment of how, despite our upper-middle-class circumstances, our upbringings were fundamentally less than picture perfect. Instead, it nudges Lauren into a cloud of thoughts that make her lower what's left of her bread onto her knee.

"I've never told anyone this," she says, "but I think I know what it is to be a Quinlan better than anyone."

Lauren looks up into the branches and the new angle of her face makes her look different. Sadder, angrier, less controlled. More beautiful too.

"After she had the twins, my mom wanted another child, but their birth was hard on her—she couldn't carry children on her own after that," she says, lowering her eyes to me again. "Adoption. She liked the idea of rescuing a kid from the wrong side of the tracks, someone she could use the Quinlan sandpaper on to smooth away the rough edges. Dad seemed okay with all of it. If anything, he paid more attention to me than my brothers. It was like he felt more comfortable with someone who wasn't biologically his than the ones who were. It's funny, but sometimes I got the impression that he saw himself as an outsider just like I was, someone dropped into this reality who had to bluff their way through it, find a way to fit in. As if we were both adopted. Know what I mean?"

"Maybe he never liked himself," I say, and hear the subtext so clearly I worry I actually said it aloud. *Maybe he never liked me.*

"Did he *like* himself? That would've been a question he'd see as beside the point," Lauren says. "He simply *was* himself. A narcissist so self-involved he couldn't even be bothered to look in the mirror."

"You really did understand him in a way none of the rest of us did. How did that make you feel?"

She blinks at me. "*How did that make you feel?* Really, Aaron? Who's the therapist here, anyway?"

"That was dumb. All I—"

"No, it's okay. Nobody's ever asked me that before. Not about Dad." She moves her hand through the grass but I can't see it. I imagine it as a snake slithering between us. "I was five when I was adopted, which is fairly old as those things go. So when I became a Quinlan, I had a chance at having a real father for the first time. I just wanted to love him and for him to love me too. But he couldn't do that. The best he could do was remind me that I would always be on my own. It started me on this journey toward seeing how everybody could be reduced to a profile, a set of tics and prejudices and fetishes. Everybody is a fake. That was his message. A fake like him. Like me. But because we came from outside, we had an advantage. We *knew* we were fakes."

"But you're not."

"How are you so sure?"

"You just told me that. And because you're trying to get to the bottom of who you are because you believe there's something real there. It's why we decided to stay here, isn't it?"

"It might have had something to do with the money."

"Not for us. Not for you."

I hear the sound like a snake in the grass but this time I don't see her hand move.

"No, not for me," she says.

We screw the lids onto the jars and stuff them along with the bread back into the box. I offer Lauren a ride back to the lodge and she pantomimes a curtsy before getting into the trailer.

"Why'd you come out here with me, anyway?" I ask after a time, pedaling up a slope and taking a break as we roll down the other side.

"I told you. I don't like letting myself be afraid." I think she's done, but then she adds something I'm not expecting. "I realize things are kind of tense between our families. I mean, how could they not be? But I want you to know that I think you're okay, Aaron. In fact, I kind of wish you'd been a big brother of mine."

"I'm touched," I say without irony.

"You know what I hope?"

"What?"

"I hope there's hot sauce at the bottom of one of these boxes."

"And a bottle of whisky."

"I wouldn't get your hopes up."

Lauren's right. In addition to the rules that won't allow us to leave, the absence of outside news or entertainment lends a monastic quality to Belfountain. It's something I took at first to be a denial of pleasure, part of the sacrifice that must be made to earn the prize Dad has dangled before us. But now I wonder if, like the monks who devote themselves to their enlightenment, it's more about staying focused.

"What if we're wrong?" I ask, thinking about the camp but not willing to share this yet.

"Wrong about what?"

"What if this isn't personal? Not about Dad messing with our heads one last time, but bigger than that."

"Bigger?"

"His work."

"What was his work?"

"Exactly. Whatever it was, like you said, it was enormously lucrative."

"Assuming he made his money from his work. He might have inherited it."

"From an ancestral line of Quinlans none of us ever knew?"

"I hear you," she says. "It doesn't fit."

"None of it does. But if you're right about Dad being a sociopath of some stripe, why would he go to all this trouble in the service of feelings? Your theory is he didn't really have any of those, right?"

Her silence communicates her agreement.

"Where are you going with this?" she asks finally.

"What if Belfountain isn't the fruit of his work, but his workplace?"

"Doubt it. There's no offices or desks. No computers. There isn't even a phone line. Nothing."

I'm about to say something about how the lodge may not be that kind of office when the old woman appears in the middle of the road.

She's dressed as she was when I saw her our first night here. The bare feet, the threadbare robe and exposed chest, the hair standing high and stiff with filth.

What's different is this time she moves. Spreads one arm wide from her side as if beckoning me into her embrace. The other arm slides behind her back. To hold her straight. Or grab hold of something.

We're still rolling down the hill, the fastest speed we've reached. The wind huffing in my ears.

I could try the brakes—the old-fashioned backpedaling kind—but I doubt they'd make much difference. And I don't want to stop. I want to hit the old woman, feel the impact of her body. Prove she's real.

Lauren doesn't see the woman because she's facing backward. The next moment will come at us whether two of us witness it or only one.

When the old woman is ten feet away, it's clear she's not going to get out of the way.

My arms twist the handlebars by reflex. The bike jolting to the right.

Behind me, Lauren's weight is thrown from one side of the trailer to the other but she stays inside it. Not that I look. All of my attention is on the old woman. Eyes milky with glaucoma. Tar-covered gums. The spiky whiskers of a beard.

Followed by the feel of her.

The burn of her fingernails that scratch my face as we pass.

"Aaron!"

I'm pedaling now. The slope has evened out and the bike's speed relaxes into the same steady pace as before. Could the old woman catch us if she ran? I look back, half expecting to see her flying over the road, a witch with her robe flapping behind her like rotted wings. But we're taking a curve and the trees obscure where she stood from view.

"What *happened*?"

Lauren is pulling herself up onto her knees.

"I thought I saw something," I say.

"Was it him?"

"No."

"So—"

"I don't know what it was."

I touch my hand to my face. It comes back thinly glazed with blood.

"You're bleeding," Lauren says.

"Must have got hit with a branch back there."

"It looks too neat for that. There's, like, three lines on your cheek."

"Hold on," I say, and stand up on the pedals, driving us faster and faster until the leaves become a solid tunnel of green.

25

ONCE WE'VE TAKEN THE BOXES INSIDE AND LOCKED THE LODGE'S DOOR, LAUREN busies herself restocking the fridge and pantry shelves, hoping these tasks will transport her back to the everyday world. I know because I try the same thing myself. Shave. Take a shower. Put a Band-Aid over the worst of the slices on my cheek and repeat my story about an errant branch to the others.

None of it works.

I decide to tell everyone at dinner. Not only about the encounter with the old woman, but about how I've changed my vote. Mom was right. We have to go. The will can be contested, and our case will either hold up in court or it won't. But we were wrong to see this as an eccentric's amusement park. Dad told us the stories about Belfountain not as flights of fancy, but as the truth. Possibly even a warning.

I never get the chance to say any of this.

We're sitting at the dining room table, the twins' lasagna steaming on plates in front of us, when there's a banging at the front door.

If Jerry hadn't jumped out of his seat and broken into a sprint toward the foyer, we might have waited to see how long it went on for. But watching Jerry respond the way he does prompts all of us to rush after him.

When we make it to the door, Jerry is peeking through the three-inch-wide windows set on either side of the entrance.

"What's out there?" Elias and Ezra ask at almost the same time.

"I can't see—"

Bang! Bang! BANG!

Not against the door this time. The great room's windows.

It only takes a few seconds to turn and rush to see what's there. But by the time we look across the living area there's nothing to see outside. Only the glass still visibly vibrating in its frame.

"There's two of them," Jerry says.

I'm ready to talk about what we ought to do. But there's no talk. There's only Jerry unlocking the front door and stepping out into the night.

"What the *hell* are you *doing*?" Lauren shouts after him.

"Oh shit, oh shit, oh *shit*," Elias moans.

I lock the door.

"Why'd you do that?" Ezra asks.

"I'm keeping us safe."

"Jerry's out there."

"That was his decision."

The twins shift their weight from foot to foot in the way of drunks readying to throw the first punch.

"What's going *on*?" Franny asks.

"They're out there," Lauren answers.

"Who?"

"The ones who live in the woods."

The ones. The choice of words, along with the way she says it, suggests Lauren believes there is not only more than one, but more than two.

"Let's sit down," I say.

"And do what?" Ezra says, now coming up close to me along with his twin.

"Talk about our childhoods?" Elias says.

"We need to work this out together. And we need to stay controlled. Whatever is happening—"

As if in response to a whistle sounding at a pitch none of the rest of us can hear, the twins stalk off down the hall at the same time.

"Aaron?" Bridge pulls away from Mom's hold to stand next to me. "We should find a smaller room. And tools. Sharp things. Anything to fight with."

"Those are good ideas," I say, but remain where I am.

"Aaron?"

"Yeah?"

"We should do it now."

We start to. All of us heading toward the kitchen, when Elias and Ezra return holding serrated, wood-handled steak knives.

There's a helpless moment when I think they're going to attack us. I push Bridge behind me, shielding her. But the twins pass by and unlock the door.

"Don't do this!" Lauren pleads, but only Ezra faces her.

"That's our brother out there," he says, an actor at his most convincing because he doesn't appear to be acting. Then he too walks out into the darkness.

"Close the door," Mom says.

When we're locked inside again, there's nothing to do but put Bridge's plan into action. Go through the kitchen drawers and find what may be useful as a weapon (even harder than before, as the larger knives have already disappeared). Then we cram ourselves into Mom's room only to discover that none of the bedrooms' doors lock.

It's still better than standing in the middle of the great room. Here at least we can conceal ourselves and, if found, mount a focused defense against anything that tries to come in.

"I'll be back in a second," I tell them. "Don't open the door for anyone until I get back. I need to check that all the entry points are still locked."

"You think someone left a way in?" Lauren asks, a note of defensiveness in her voice.

"I just think it's worth checking."

I circle the lodge's interior to confirm all the windows and doors are secure. When I'm at the great room's wall of glass, I squint outside. It's too dark to see much of anything, so I flick on the floodlights.

They're powerful but don't penetrate the forest, only pull it claustrophobically closer. Yet turning on the lights triggers something to be heard, not seen. What may be a voice from outside. A possibly human cry from not too far off.

"Turn off the lights," Lauren says behind me.

"I heard something."

"Me too. That's why we should turn them off."

26

"WE NEED TO BARRICADE OURSELVES IN," FRANNY SAYS AFTER LAUREN AND I
return to the bedroom and tell the others we heard something outside.

I bend down to grasp the end of the bed frame. "Someone help me
with this."

"That won't work," Bridge says. "It's too big."

"How about this?" Lauren asks, pulling a wooden chair away from
the desk against the wall. "We could jam it under the door handle like
they do on TV."

"Does that even *work*?"

"Hell if I know."

"Okay," I say. "We'll do the chair thing. Then push the desk in tight
behind it."

We're trying to figure out how to get the back of the chair in tight
under the handle when there's a new round of slams at the front door.

Boom! Boom! BOOM!

Vibrating through the log bones of the structure and up our legs through the floor.

Bridge comes to me. Her face held up to communicate something that words, even if she were to attempt to speak them, couldn't capture. She looks so young. Like the day on the floating dock after playing Peter Pan. Her fear expressed as a need to reach me, for someone she trusts to share in it, to not be alone with the sudden fact of death.

"Help! *Help* us!"

A voice from outside. Shouting through the front door.

"We need a doctor! Aaron! *Please*!"

It's one of the twins.

"I have to go," I say to Bridge. "Stay quiet. Hide in the closet, under the bed. Nobody knows you're here."

On the way to the front foyer, I try to tell myself there's some measure of safety in where I've left Bridge, but of course the truth is if anyone gets past me, it will be a matter of minutes or less for her and the others to be found.

So why do I go?

Because this is what doctors do.

What I've done on transatlantic flights, after coming upon car accidents at the side of the highway, at a Mariners game when a man fell sideways out of his seat from a coronary. Why I went overseas. They call for a doctor and, even when I'd rather be as useless as everyone else—the head-shakers watching the clips of faraway disasters on TV or the rubber-neckers rolling past the wreck—I go.

It's not bravery. Not goodness. It's like being the eldest child, the only son. It's an expectation.

"Move back from the door," I shout through the wood.

"Hurry. We need—"

"Move away!"

There's what may be a shuffling retreat from the other side. Then I unlock the door and pull it open.

It's Ezra. Standing at the bottom of the steps down to the gravel parking area, shaking so violently it's like I've caught him midway through the performance of an experimental dance.

"He's over here," he says.

27

I FOLLOW HIM BUT HANG BACK JUST OUT OF REACH. THERE'S NOTHING TO INDICATE this is a betrayal and yet the better part of my instincts believes it is. If not set by Ezra himself, then by the thing in the woods that has trapped us both.

Ezra stops at the corner of the lodge and looks around it to where I can't see. Perhaps the Tall Man stands there, making him do this. Or they've been working together from the beginning, an elaborate performance now coming to its end. The twins are actors, after all. Maybe all the second Quinlans are.

These thoughts don't stop me from joining him and looking around the corner.

There's no Tall Man. Only Elias on the ground. Lying on his back, a dark stain seeping through his shirt, widening from the place where the polished silver handle of a hatchet sticks out from his belly.

He looks like a clockwork toy.

My first thought. It's the smooth, glinting metal of the handle coming out of him. Maybe two feet long, the right size and color for the winding key you'd twist to make him come to life.

No, that's not part of him. Somebody put that there.

The blood has spread even within the couple seconds I've stood looking down at him. His eyes roll around before fixing on me. His breathing a series of oddly coquettish gasps of surprise.

"What happened?"

"We got separated," Ezra says. "There was a voice—Elias thought it might have been a woman, but I couldn't tell—and he went after it."

"Was it—"

"I don't *know* what it was! I just heard him struggling with something. When I found him—" Ezra shakes his head, freeing himself from everything that doesn't matter now. "Can you help him?"

I get down on my knees next to Elias, roll the shirtsleeves halfway up my arms.

And do nothing.

A man is bleeding out from a wound to his abdomen. That's all I know, all I see. I try to summon a chapter from a medical textbook that covers the treatment in a case like this, but nothing comes.

I should remove the hatchet. Or is that exactly the wrong thing to do?

I don't *want* to do it. That probably means I should. In moments like these, the things you don't want to do are the things you have to.

The silver handle is jittering as Elias's breathing becomes more labored. This makes it even more difficult for my hands to find the handle, grip hard. The little pulses of waning life traveling through the blade within him and into me.

I should warn him. Reassure him. *This might hurt a little. I'm going to sort this out, okay?* But there's no sentence that seems remotely utterable, remotely true, and so before I succumb to the dizziness prickling around my face like a cloud of gnats, I pull a snort of air through my nose and lift the handle up and away.

He makes a sound. Not one that comes from his voice, but his body, an exclamation from the momentarily open space the blade once occupied.

I drop the hatchet on the ground. The top half of me weaving over Elias, fatigue draining me so abruptly I'm worried I'm going to drape myself over him and not be able to roll off.

"Okay, okay," Ezra is saying somewhere off to the side of me. "Now the next thing."

The next thing? What could that possibly be?

Apply pressure.

It's not specialized knowledge. Just something recalled from movies and TV shows. But how is pressure applied? Where? What is *pressure* in a situation like this?

I try.

Kneel closer and place one palm over the wound, then lay my second hand over the first. Push down hard.

Elias screams. His body spasming inward then falling back again. The heat of his blood pushing up through my fingers.

"That's *wrong*! That's *wrong*!" Ezra is shouting inches away from me.

This isn't applying pressure. This is an amateur version of CPR. And that's for heart attacks, isn't it?

I pull away from Elias and his eyes follow me, pleading. A second later Ezra's fist meets my shoulder.

"Do something!"

"I don't—"

"For fuck's sake. He's *dying*—"

"I don't know what to do!"

Ezra looks at me and sees that it's true. He doesn't argue anymore, only bends closer to his brother and whispers looping phrases of comfort—"It's okay. I'm here. Don't be afraid."—until Elias's breathing becomes a half dozen shallow hiccups before stopping altogether.

I've never seen them as twins as much as now. Before this, I took them as a comical adaptation of a single man, one who carried a mirror with him wherever he went and mimicked his own accent. They were one in a way none of the rest of us were. But now they are divided.

Ezra rises. His hands held out from his sides as if he's a tightrope walker finding his balance. Then he walks, toe to heel, toward the lodge's door.

28

THE DOOR IS LOCKED.

Nobody comes when I knock. I wonder if Ezra and I will have to survive the night out here. Behind me, the forest feels alive with new movement. Some of it animal, some of it unimaginable.

I knock on the door again, pounding with both fists this time.

When it opens, it's Jerry standing there.

"You left them? Hiding in here *alone*?" he shouts at me. When he sees his brother's face, my bloodied hands, his anger drains instantly away. "Where's Elias?"

"He didn't make it," I say.

"Didn't make it from what?"

"He's dead, Jerry. He was murdered."

The words themselves taste strange in my mouth. *Dead. Murdered.*

"That was him—that was his voice in the woods," Jerry says.

"We heard it too."

"I thought it was Lauren or one of your sisters. A woman. That's why I came back here."

I believe him. If I hadn't known Mom, Bridge, Franny, and Lauren were all inside the lodge when I heard the cry through the great room's windows, I would've guessed it was a female voice too.

"Jerry?"

Both of us turn to Ezra as if surprised to find him still here.

"Yeah?"

"Is this happening?"

"Yes."

Ezra grimaces, as if he had one last attempt at making all the badness go away and it failed, as expected.

But then his brother is there. His other brother, one half of all the family he has left, pulling him close in an embrace that gives them both permission to weep.

Lauren takes the news even harder than Ezra. As she's held by her brothers at one end of the sofa, at the other end Mom and Franny and I console Bridge, whose fear has finally overwhelmed her. It's overwhelmed all of us, but lending support to the youngest lets us hide the worst of it from view.

When we've partway recovered, the first thing Ezra demands we talk about is me. How I failed to help Elias.

"I honestly don't know. I don't," I say. "I just—nothing came to me in the moment. I'm so sorry."

"You must have been in shock," Mom offers.

"I guess. But it didn't feel like that."

Lauren studies me, the psychologist within her performing an assessment. "I'm sure there wasn't anything you could have done. Not without equipment or facilities."

"Maybe if we were in a hospital, it all would've clicked in," I say. "But I'm—I'm not sure—"

"You're a fucking doctor!" Jerry is suddenly close to me, shouting. "You were supposed to *help* him!"

"I *tried*!" I look over at Ezra. "You were there."

Do they see that I'm telling the truth? Whether it's that or the recognition that this debate won't solve anything, everyone now turns to Ezra.

"What about the body?" he says.

"What do you mean?" Lauren asks.

"I mean do we bury him now? Or do we do it in the morning?"

"Hold on a sec. I'm not sure anybody should go out there to dig a *grave*," Franny says, as gently as she can, though her ingrained sarcasm can't be wholly veiled.

"Not until the morning, anyway," Lauren offers.

"In the morning we're getting out of here. I'm assuming we're all agreed on that," Franny says. "Once we're back, we can send people to get Elias."

"No. Nope. No," Ezra says, shaking his head. "We can't leave him out there."

"I'm sorry for your loss, I really am," Franny says. "But why not?"

"He'll get cold."

I send Franny a hard look, silently telling her not to point out that Elias is going to be cold no matter where we put him, and she lets it pass.

"This must be unbelievably hard for you," I say. "You lost your brother tonight. But we can't forget how he was lost. How we're all in danger now and we'll only make it worse if we don't make smart decisions."

Ezra faces me. Dry-eyed. His head still.

"I'm not leaving him out there," he says, and rises.

"I'll go with you," Jerry says, and looks to me. "We're going to need some help carrying him."

• • •

I'm almost surprised he's still there.

I imagined the Tall Man dragging him off. Doing something worse. Yet, other than the whole of his shirt now discolored by blood, nothing has changed from how he was left.

Except I'm wrong about that.

"Where is it?" Ezra says.

"Where's what?"

"The ax thing. The hatchet."

We both look around the body, kick at the grass with our shoes. It's not where I dropped it after pulling it out. It's nowhere.

"Somebody took it," Ezra says.

Somebody took it back.

I can see Jerry understand this at the same time I do.

"You two get the arms," he says. "I'll take the legs. Let's do this fast."

Elias is even heavier than he looks. It slows us to shuffled half steps through the high grass.

"What was that?" Ezra asks. I didn't hear anything, and can't decide if I want to stop to listen for whatever it was or keep going.

"Nothing," Jerry answers, opting for the latter.

When Lauren opens the door for us and we lay Elias down on the foyer floor, the violence of the attack becomes more vivid in the full light. We can see it in the breadth of the wound, but also in his frozen expression. The terror not from death, but the way it came.

"Cover him," Ezra says, and walks away as if, now that his brother is inside, the duties to the other part of himself have been forever satisfied.

29

WE START OUT FOR THE GATE AT DAWN.

Jerry managed to convince Ezra to give up on the idea of burying Elias before we left, which still left the awfulness of all of us having to walk around his body on the floor, the white bedsheet we laid over him soaked through over the course of the night.

There's some discussion about whether we should take the bike or not. Jerry doesn't see the point, but I argue that one of us might need a rest along the way, and they could sit in the wagon and I could pedal for a time. In the end he doesn't stop me from squeaking along behind the rest of the party.

We don't talk much. Once in a while someone will ask how much farther it is, and it's left to me to provide an estimate. The route doesn't have many landmarks, only the curves around boulders and berms that look like the other curves around boulders and berms, the endless undulations of wooded ground on either side. It both stretches time and shrinks it so that just when I think the fence will be there over the next rise, it isn't, and its not being there makes me think it's still miles off.

"Not far," I keep saying until they stop asking.

It's good that we brought the bike. After what feels like a half hour or more of trooping along like a defeated platoon, Mom starts to hang back farther and farther. When I invite her to ride in the wagon, she refuses at first, repeating what may as well be the motto of her life. *I don't want to be a bother.* But eventually even she acknowledges her weakness and climbs in.

This time, it really isn't far.

The fence comes into view as a gray lattice. As we move closer its height, the sharpness of the razor wire laid atop it, its purpose to repel and contain, becomes clearer.

"That's where they keep the phone?" Jerry asks, spotting the metal box next to the road on the other side.

"That's what the lawyer said."

"Okay. We're all decided then? We leave together, all of us, right now. Agreed?"

We show our votes of assent through small nods and kicks at the stones by our feet.

"Good," Jerry says. "How do we open it?"

He poses this question to himself as he inspects the outline of the gate just as I had done when I first encountered it.

That's when I notice the humming.

An ambient resonance, constant and low, as if the product of the air itself. An electric lullaby.

"Don't!"

Jerry looks around at me, puzzled, at the same time he grips his hand to the metal edge of the gate.

His body stiffens. As in a game of Simon Says, his posture, his facial expression, the way his back heel is lifted in midstep off the ground—all of it is frozen. You could think it was a brilliantly deadpan joke if it wasn't for the reddening flesh of his hand. The wisp of smoke that seems to push its way out through the skin.

Jerry is flying.

There is no visible effort on his part, no kicking away or rolling of arms, and he looks like a plastic action figure that's been arranged into an inhuman contortion and then tossed by a giant's invisible hand.

He hits the ground next to Bridge, and she kneels next to him, putting her hand to his cheek, asking if he's okay.

"Don't touch it," Jerry manages, locking eyes with Bridge. "Nobody touch it."

Ezra hurls himself to the ground next to his brother on the opposite side from Bridge. Mom releases one of her sob-laughs.

"You're kidding me," Franny says. "It's electrified?"

"Locked too, I'd guess," I say.

"All of it?"

"Unless there's another gate somewhere along the perimeter, I'd say yes."

No one says aloud what this means. No one needs to. The only one of us who speaks is Lauren, who is saying the same thing over and over. "Oh my God oh my God oh my God."

Eventually, she's quiet too.

From out of the forest, something howls.

LEGACY

30

EZRA GUESSES COYOTES. FRANNY THINKS IT TENDS MORE TO THE MOURNFULNESS
of a hound. I don't say it out loud, but to me the howling could only be
wolves.

It doesn't carry on for long. Distant, but not unreachably so. As likely
coming from a source within the fence as outside of it.

When the sound stops, we don't speculate on what it was or where it
came from any further than we already have. Every thought in our heads
is a threat. Every turn from that thought only confronts us with another.

"We have to go back," Bridge says.

Jerry rides in the wagon. He's conscious and not outwardly injured
aside from the burn on his hand, but his balance is shot. That means the
trip back takes a while. Jerry's extra pounds force me and Ezra to push
the bike along by the handlebars every time we come to a hill. But what
really deadens our legs is the recognition that everything has changed.
Even more now than after Elias's death. The cold fact is that was the end

for him but not necessarily for us. Now we slouch back into the heart of the woods, the air pressing down on us with the weight of our error.

Here's what we know. What each of us is working to order in our minds according to our own fears or outrage or calculations of survival:

The stay on Dad's estate wasn't intended to be a get-to-know-one-another therapy session. It wasn't a game. The gate may be opened after another twenty-seven days, or it may not. It won't take nearly that long to determine how this turns out. Belfountain was never a fairy-tale kingdom. It's a prison.

Once we return to the lodge, we're reluctant to go inside. All of us seem to remember Elias's body in the foyer at the same time.

"It's going to take shovels," I say.

The equipment shed. The only chance we have to find not just what we need to dig a grave with, but tools to barricade the lodge's doors and smaller windows. There may even be something we can use to fortify the great room's wall of glass, if not cover it altogether.

The problem is the padlock on the shed's door. We talk about taking a rock to it or even heating it to a temperature where it would melt off (Franny vaguely remembers her high school science teacher saying such a thing was possible). As the rest of us carry on the brainstorming, Ezra walks away. We watch him head into the lodge. A moment later he emerges carrying the poker from the fireplace, long and heavy as a knight's sword.

The loop of the padlock is just large enough for the first third of the poker to slip through. Ezra positions it flat against the shed, grips the handle tightly with both hands, hikes one foot against the door. He puffs his lungs full like a squatting weight lifter. Heaves back on the poker.

The lock snaps and falls to the ground.

"Leverage," he says.

We all go in at the same time, including Jerry, who rises from the trailer and shambles into the shed's gloom. I'm the first to spot the pair of spades leaning against the wall, but there are other items of interest we pull off shelves or discover lying under oil cloths on the floor. Eight or nine two-by-fours spotted green with mold. A Folger's can of finishing nails.

The things we can use right away we haul out, and the rest—mostly just gardening tools, a battery-powered weed whacker, a box of mouse-traps—we leave in the shed. For some reason I slip a pair of pruning shears into the pocket of my windbreaker. A butter knife would probably make a better weapon. But I like the weight of them bumping against me, another heartbeat held close as I walk.

"I'd help but—" Jerry offers once we're all outside again, indicating his dizziness with the same tapping to his head he used to show the effects of his football concussions.

"We got this," Ezra says, picking up one of the shovels and handing the other to me. "Don't we?"

"This would be a good spot for him," I say, pointing over to a shady patch next to a clutch of buckthorn saplings between the Orange and Green trailheads. "What do you think?"

Ezra nods his approval. Steps close to me and grips my elbow with his free hand.

"Okay," he says. "Let's do this."

It takes the rest of the day to dig a hole, carry Elias's body swinging between us like a roll of wet carpet, and drop him in.

For the first hour of shoveling, I blink through the sweat and stop to look around the lodge's cleared drive, expecting to see the Tall Man step out of the trees. Ezra must be plagued by similar thoughts, as he proposes taking shifts with one of us digging while the other stands watch.

Plunge the spade's edge down. Separate the soil from the ground. Launch it to the loose pile beside the hole.

Stab, divide, heave. Stab, divide, heave . . .

It dulls the urgency of wondering what we ought to do next. It also quiets my guilt over watching Elias die.

Stab, divide, heave.

When we return inside, Jerry shows us how he's hammered some of the two-by-fours over the bedroom and kitchen windows, and done the same to reinforce the door next to the pantry. The nails he had to use are too short to make them very secure. And as for the great room's windows, there's nothing to be done. Yet he seems as grateful for the tasks he was able to complete as Ezra and I are.

"Just have to keep an eye on it," Jerry says, as if all of us aren't doing that already, looking for the monster to step out of Belfountain's snarled mass of life.

31

I COME OUT OF THE BATHROOM AFTER A SHOWER AND FRANNY IS THERE TO CORNER me in the hallway.

"You were in there awhile," she says, and with these words she's a teenager again, complaining about me hogging the hot water.

"I had a lot to scrub off."

"That must have been rough. Having to drag—"

"I'd rather not go through a play-by-play, if that's okay with you."

She grimaces in apology. "I'm scared, Aaron."

"Me too."

"Not just about what's happening out there. But in here."

She looks at me as if expecting her meaning to be clear. I assume she's talking about suspicions she has about members of the second Quinlans. In the next second, another possibility arrives. The *in here* refers not to the lodge, but our heads.

"Help me out," I say.

"Do you ever have the feeling you're losing your memory?"

"Little bits here and there. Names, some words. That's what getting older is all about, right?"

"I'm talking about since coming here."

"It's hard to keep a grip on the outside world in this place."

"That's *not* what I mean." She squeezes her eyes shut. When she opens them, they're shining with tears. "It's like I never had a past to begin with."

Had a past.

That this is something close to the feeling I've had my whole life takes me by surprise, as I've always assumed Franny was shaped by more objective injuries. What's different is that she feels that coming to Belfountain has triggered it. Unlike me, who's felt this way for as long as I can recall.

What's important is that Franny is telling me this. Reliably unreliable Franny. What she's experiencing is a symptom of withdrawal, most likely. A warped perception of time triggered by the anxiety of being here. All of it bringing her back to the loss that pulled the ground out from under her.

"This is about Nate, isn't it?" I say. "Trauma like this—it can strand you from what you know, what you love. It's like losing yourself. But he'll always be with you."

"That's just it. All I *have* is my love for him."

"And once we're out of here, what you carry of him inside—"

"You don't understand, Aaron," she says, and steadies herself, pushes aside her frustration for one last try. "I love Nate. But the boy that love was for, the games we'd play together, his first words, the shape of his face—all the things a mother never lets go of—aren't where they should be."

There are at least two deaths that result from dying. I've seen it a thousand times. The first is the failure of the body. The second is the failure of the living to remember. I'd always assumed the impact of the latter was buffered by its gradual retreat, the pulling of images out of the mind's photo album, one by one. But maybe for some—for Franny—it can come faster than that. Maybe it can come all at once.

Never had a past to begin with.

"I meant to tell you this, was waiting for the right time—but you know how it is with right times."

"They never come."

"I didn't want to hurt you more than you already were. Maybe I was chickenshit, and just ran away," I say, and pull in a ragged breath. "No, it was that. Might as well admit it."

Franny looks up at me about as soberly as a person could. "Is this about Nate?"

"Yeah. After he died."

"Tell me."

So I do.

I tell her about coming back to my condo a few days after the funeral, looking around at the collection of furniture and unread magazines and unhealthy plants that made up my life, and deciding to clean the place. Top to bottom, floors, corners, the whole deal. I'd been doing it a lot after I'd come home from overseas. My therapist called it "mental cleansing."

What was different this time was that it wasn't the attack I was thinking of as I dusted and scrubbed. It was Nate. And as if these thoughts of him brought part of him back, I was moving the sofa to reach the vacuum behind it and found a balloon. Green. Still fully inflated, with streamers and fireworks stenciled on it. A leftover from the little birthday party I had for Nate a few weeks earlier.

"It felt light in my hands but warmer than it should have, as if a pair of other hands had been holding it before passing it to me," I tell Franny, and she watches me as I speak, her chin trembling. "I don't know why I did it, but I untied the knot and let the air out. Just stood there feeling it pass like a warm breeze over my face. Except it *wasn't* a breeze. It was the air from Nate's lungs. He was the one who blew up the balloon. And I'd helped him do it, holding it as he huffed and puffed, and then tying the end when he was done. It was *him*. This thing I could *feel*. This voice I could almost hear."

"What did it say?"

"Something like, 'This is me. I was here. I was alive, Uncle Aaron.' But not in words. Just breath."

Franny is crying, but her body is more still and solid than it's been the last twenty-four hours.

"Thank you for bringing him back," she says, and gets up on tiptoes to give my cheek a cold kiss.

For dinner, Mom pulls out the lasagna leftovers, but when Ezra spots the aluminum trays, it's as if he sees a portrait of his lost twin in the baked cheese and noodles they made together, and we all silently agree to return it to the fridge.

"Ham sandwiches?" Mom offers with the same brittleness as when she would sell us a menu for school lunches on a Monday morning.

As we eat, to avoid complete silence, I ask the others what gifts Dad left for them. In addition to a compass for Bridge and the neon running gear for me, Lauren found a magnetic chess set in the bottom of her duffel bag.

She tells us it was the only thing she and Dad ever did together, just the two of them. He never let her win. Something she appreciated, actually. It meant he took her seriously. His intent was to teach her to look three, four, five moves ahead. What she came to learn was that you saw the way the game would play out not by tactics alone, but by thinking the way your opponent thought.

"It was psychology. Getting past the rules and strategizing in order to reach into the motivations of the person across the board from you," she says, before putting her sandwich down on her plate. "Once I understood that, we never played again."

Ezra and Elias were meant to share their gift. Dad's watch. The vintage Bulova they were always asking to wear.

"I don't remember that watch," Lauren says. "Do you have it on now?"

Ezra pulls back his sleeve to show us his bare forearm. "I left it with Elias," he says, and we all involuntarily glance at the wall as if we have the X-ray vision to see the freshly covered grave thirty feet on the other side.

This wasn't where I wanted the conversation to go. I ask Franny what was left for her, and as soon as I do, I realize this was an even bigger mistake.

A baby rattle. She found it in a drawer in the bedroom she and Mom are staying in. A really beautiful one, hand painted with colorful birds flying over a lake with snowcapped mountains in the background. Japanese, she guesses. Something Dad brought back from one of his trips for Nate, his only grandchild.

When she finishes, Franny glances over at me, and I can tell she doesn't recall the rattle. It's something else that's been lost to the years of junk put in her veins or, if she's to be believed, stolen by Belfountain itself in the time she's been here.

"What about you, Jerry?" Lauren asks.

"Me?"

"You're the only one left. What souvenir did the old man leave for you from the great beyond?"

Jerry digs into his pocket and pulls something out. Brings his hand to his mouth and blows.

Tw-eeeeee-t!

So shrill it jolts all of us in our chairs. When he's done, Jerry drops the referee's whistle onto the table.

"What do you make of that?" he asks nobody in particular.

"You're a coach," Lauren says, reassuring. "It's what you do."

"I know! I *know* that! Wouldn't he also know I've already *got* a damned whistle?"

You don't have to be a psychologist to see it. Jerry hasn't yet let go of being a player, the guy on the field that people watch from the bleachers. He's a teacher now, but one still young enough, fit enough, to think he could get back into the game someday. The whistle tells him something different. It says there's only the sidelines left for him.

"Don't look at me like that," he says to Lauren.

"Like what?"

"Like you're assessing one of your clients."

"I'm actually on your side here, Jerry."

"My side? What does that mean, exactly?"

Lauren takes a steadying breath. The kind I imagine a therapist must make before venturing into a topic she'd prefer to avoid.

"It means we're family," she says.

Jerry stares at her, and I almost expect him to ask her to repeat what she's just said because he hadn't heard it.

"That's one of those things that depends on how you look at it, am I right? Family," he says. "Consider us, for instance. Consider you. The twins had each other from birth. I had Mom to hold up. And you, Lauren? The special little gift who arrived late in the game? You were the observer. Watching us like you were the director of the psych ward. And this was when you were eight years old! You found your calling early, I'll give you that."

All of Lauren remains still except for the pooling tears in her eyes, thickening but not yet falling. She won't let them.

"That's not fair, Jerry."

"Maybe not. But it's true."

He rises with his plate in his hand.

"Thanks for the sandwich, Eleanor," Jerry says, and with his free hand picks up the whistle, weighs it in his palm, the plastic marble rolling around inside, then stuffs it back into his pocket.

There's more howling that night.

It comes through the wall of glass and reaches me in the chair I've almost fallen asleep in, which makes it hard to guess its distance, though I'd say it's closer to the lodge than it was when we were at the gate.

Not coyotes. A single animal. Throaty and hoarse.

I can't tell if Ezra or Jerry, the ones who've chosen the sofa and other chair, hear it too. They don't move. They don't ask in a whisper if anyone else is awake.

Which probably means they are.

32

WE DON'T ASK IF WE ALL HAD THE DREAM AGAIN. WE JUST START TO TALK ABOUT the ways last night's was different. The new details that, as Bridge puts it, make it like one of those invisible spy papers kids play with where the message is only revealed after shading with a pencil until the whole page is covered.

"So you go first," I say to Bridge in the kitchen as I spread peanut butter on her half of the bagel we're sharing. "What's your spy message?"

"My page isn't totally filled in yet," she corrects me. "But last night there was a boat."

The activity in the kitchen—Franny pouring Lucky Charms into her bowl, Jerry pulling hash browns from the toaster oven, Ezra cutting an apple, Mom frying up a storm—comes to a stop.

"It was sinking," Ezra says.

"Yes."

"The tallest part, where the captain steers, it went down last," Franny says.

"Yes."

"And then the outer space singing again," Jerry says.

"But it wasn't coming from space."

"It was coming from the water," I say.

That's not all that was different. This time, Bridge was in it too. Floating next to me but struggling, too tired to keep treading water, her arms slapping at the surface before she started going under.

I woke up then. Even in my dreams I can't tolerate the idea of anything bad happening to her.

"If we're all thinking what each other is thinking," Jerry says, "then you know what I think we ought to do this morning."

"Hypnosis therapy?" Franny suggests.

"No. How about you, Aaron? Take a guess."

"See if there's another way out through the fence."

"That'd be it."

"I'll go," Ezra says, popping the last of the apple in his mouth.

I would volunteer but I don't want to leave Bridge here on her own, not again. Jerry reads my hesitation, seems to understand it and approve as he looks my way with the smallest shake of his head.

"It's the two of us then, Ez," he says, and starts to pack his breakfast up in the plastic bag the bagels came in.

None of us can estimate how long it will take to hike around the entire perimeter of the estate. The terrain may be variable in the corners of the property we haven't seen. Whether the brush has been cleared away from the fence or allowed to grow thick against it will be a factor too.

What we're dancing around but not addressing directly is the thought that Jerry and Ezra may have to spend the night out there.

"What if there's another gate and it's wide open?" Franny asks before they go. "You won't just skip on out, right? You'll come back and let us know?"

"I will," Ezra says.

"We *both* will," Jerry says, and follows his brother out the door. "We're family, right? Leave no Quinlan behind."

33

FOR THE REMAINDER OF THE MORNING, MOM, FRANNY, AND LAUREN TAKE STOCK OF what's left in the kitchen so that we can ration it into portions if we have to. There's still enough to get us through the next couple days. More if we're careful. And there's no reason we can't expect further deliveries will be made to the main gate. Still, with the electrification of the fence and with it the removal of the option to leave, our dependence on supplies worries me almost as much as the Tall Man.

I'm sitting on the enormous slate slab that juts out from the base of the fireplace, a modernist plank of stone floating a foot off the floor, when Bridge joins me. She sits next to me, and I can feel the undercurrent of sorrow coming off her like heat from someone who's just finished a run, though she hides it with playfulness.

"You know what day it is?" she says.

"No idea."

"Tuesday. If we were back home, we'd be having one of our dinners tonight."

"God. You're right."

She looks up at me. "Tell me about them."

"Don't you remember?"

"Of course. I just want to hear you tell me."

"Well, we'd talk. I usually didn't have much to report, but you always had news."

"What was the news of my life?"

She's looking for a way out of this place. So I do my best to give her one.

When she was six and I first started taking her to a Chuck E. Cheese or a steakhouse (we took turns choosing), Bridge was still in the tail end of the Princess Era. This was a time when she'd happily spend an hour wearing the plastic tiara or white elbow-length gloves I'd buy for her, retelling the plotline from *Sleeping Beauty* or *The Little Mermaid*, which always ended with her eyes closed, imagining the scenes in her head.

Eight was the Age of Dance. Modern, ballet, hip-hop—her twice-a-week teacher singling Bridge out as her most promising student. Dance was the first career pursuit she ever declared, and based on my impressions when I attended her recitals, she actually had a shot. I was disappointed when she quit (a twisted ankle, then displacement as the teacher's favorite at the hands of a rival). But forever after I could detect the trace of sophistication she brought to the simplest movements as she returned a jar of pickles to the top shelf of the fridge, or waved goodbye and ran to the front door after exiting the taxi when I brought her home.

At ten came boys. Crushes. Jealous conflicts with classmates over the cute new kid (or the kid who everyone had ignored for years who'd returned from spring break with a haircut that elevated him to cuteness). Longing. Its reach swinging between the innocent to the worrying borderlands of grown-up desire.

During those dinners, what Bridge wanted to know about me above anything else was when I had my first date, first girlfriend, first kiss. The precise dates of these events were of crucial importance. She kept a literal calendar of when, based on my responses, she could expect these milestones to happen to her, and she would pelt me with questions when they didn't.

Our most recent meetings, from the age of twelve to the present, carried over many of the issues of romance but combined them in a newly curdled pubescent mixture of unpredictable moods, bodily alterations, ruthless girl politics. Bridge no longer looked to me for answers on any of these matters. What I offered was a dumping ground, a place to disgorge the self-contradictions I couldn't offer a prescription for even if I tried.

Tuesday dinners with Bridge are, by a wide margin, the event I look forward to most. They're not just a way of connecting with her, but with time. I told her this when we last got together. How following the stages of her life meant more to me than my own.

"That's because you haven't *had* stages, Aaron," she replied matter-of-factly. "You've always just been you."

Is this true? Did I enter the world feeling obligated and angry and alone?

"How're you doing?" I ask her now.

"I'm okay. We're getting out of here. I keep telling myself that. Seems to help."

"I was asking about you."

"I don't feel the cancer coming back, if that's what you mean."

"It's not," I say, though in truth it more or less was. "Just checking in."

Bridge gets to her feet, pats the top of my head. "Next Tuesday?"

"Wouldn't miss it."

34

I DON'T SLEEP THAT NIGHT. WANDERING THROUGH THE LODGE LIKE A GHOST LOOKING for other ghosts.

Everyone else is in their rooms at the end of the hall in the direction I think of as north even if there's no way of saying for sure, the direction of the sun these past days pursuing a random course through the clouds. The moon too. An angled crescent false as a clown's smile.

I'm trying to find the light of it through the trees, moving from the great room's glass to the small windows on either side of the front door, when I see it.

Not the moon. A figure standing outside. Watching.

There's not enough light to confirm it's the Tall Man. Whether it is or not isn't the right question anyway. It's about saving lives now. About Bridge. Is the best way to do that waiting to make sure a monster stands outside? If he moves back into the trees, this could be a lost opportunity. If he finds a way in, it could be a danger I won't have a chance of heading off.

"Aaron?"

Franny is in the foyer. One look at my face and she can see there's something outside.

"Lock the door behind me," I say.

I'm outside before Franny can demand I come back. Not that she does. There's only the *clunk* of the bolt sliding shut.

I hold a hammer in my hand. The one that Jerry used to nail the two-by-fours over the smaller windows. It felt heavy and decisive a moment ago. Now, in the cool night air, it shrinks to the size of a fork at the end of my arm.

The figure doesn't shift. Fifty feet away, maybe less. A distance that if crossed at a walk would give him the chance to square into position. But at a run, there might not be time for that.

I'm sprinting forward. The hammer raised over my head.

Feeling the weight of it, what it can do if I bring it down hard enough, takes me to a different moment. A different place. Something I'd forgotten from *overseas*.

The men emerging from the trees. Coming into the village with the machetes held at the level of their waists, swinging and slashing. And me doing the same thing. My hand gripped to a blade of my own. One that finds the arms and hips and throats of the men from the forest. Attacking the attackers. Cutting them down.

Stop!

It sounds like me. The part that wishes this wasn't happening, that would rather be running away from the bad thing than at it.

Aaron! Don't!

Hearing my own name is the first correction that brings me back to this forest, this night.

The second is seeing that it's not the Tall Man I'm about to bring the hammer down on, but Ezra.

He has his hands held up in front of him, and once I'm still, he brings them down to show how frightened he is. Not just by me about to attack him, but by whatever he's gone through, whatever he's seen.

"I'm sorry," I say.

"It's okay."

"I thought you—"

"I get it. But could you put that thing down?"

He means the hammer. It takes a moment to lower it, as if the metal and wood have interests of their own.

"How're we doing here?" Jerry asks, approaching with caution.

"We're good," I say. "Bridge, Franny, Mom, Lauren. Everybody's safe. What about you? You find anything?"

"Maybe we could talk about it inside," Jerry says. "I'm about done with this walking-around-all-night shit."

Jerry had told Ezra to wait out front while he walked around the lodge, making sure there were no signs of break-in before knocking at the door. By the time he returned, I was charging at his brother with a hammer.

"I wasn't going to wait for someone to get in," I explain in a whisper, the three of us along with Franny standing in the front foyer.

"It was a good plan," Jerry says.

"He nearly cracked my head open," Ezra says.

"But the *plan* was good."

"What about you two?" Franny asks. "You make it all the way around?"

"Every damn foot," Jerry says.

"Find anything?"

"There was an old lady," Ezra says. "We both saw her."

"What did she do?"

"Nothing. Just watch us."

"Did you try to get closer?"

"We figured she might be looking for us to do just that," Jerry answers. "And if that's what she wanted, it may not have been a good idea."

"You think the Tall Man was with her?" This is me, whispering again, not wanting Bridge to come around the corner to hear whatever the answer is.

"Is that what you're calling him?" Jerry says.

"You got a better name? Slim, maybe? Frederick?"

"The Tall Man it is. And no, we didn't see him."

"Anything else?" I ask.

"Three things," Ezra says. "There's nothing on the other side. No power lines, no roads, no buildings. Two, we took one of the shovels with us and tried to dig under the fence by the gate. Didn't work. It goes down *deep*. And the metal underground is charged just the same as aboveground."

"The third thing?"

"There's no way out."

"What about a ladder?" Franny asks.

"We don't have a ladder," Jerry answers.

"Maybe we could make one? With the tools in the shed?"

"It would need to be twenty-five feet high at least. To build that without lumber? Using a can of finishing nails? Not gonna happen."

Even though the four of us knew all of this, we were holding on to threads to the outside world. Now they've been cut once and for all.

"Not through the fence. Not over it either," I say, spinning a new thread. "But there might be another way. We'll just have to get a little lucky."

35

THE PLAN I PITCH AT THE FRONT DOOR IS SIMPLE: STAND BY THE FENCE'S GATE AND wait for whoever delivers the supplies to return. When they do, have them open the gate, and if they can't, ask them to call an ambulance to treat one of us at the lodge for emergency medical assistance.

"Why tell a story?" Jerry asks. "Why not just say we've been kidnapped or whatever is actually happening to us?"

"The truth could be something they already know about and have been instructed how to handle," I say. "But if we tell them there's a *problem*, it could push them off their game. Get them to act spontaneously."

This will either strike all of us as a good idea or we'll be too tired and shaken to come up with anything better. Franny and Ezra wait for Jerry's response.

"So who's going?" he asks.

I'm not planning to volunteer. But Jerry holds his gaze on me after asking his question, and it's clear he's not about to head out there again after walking around the entire estate in the night.

"Guess it's my turn," I say.

Jerry gives me a damn-right-it-is nod, but I don't read it as bitter. We're a team now and I've been tapped to take a shift.

"When're you heading out?" he asks.

"Now."

"In the dark?"

"Nobody said the deliveries would come during daylight."

Jerry pulls his headlamp off and hands it to me.

"Take some batteries with you," he says. "Believe me. You don't want this thing to go out."

I pull together a plastic bag of food, one of the steak knives from the drawer, the batteries Jerry suggested, an empty pickle jar of water. Tie the arms of a sweatshirt over my shoulders. When I'm back in the foyer after making Franny promise to keep Bridge safe until I return, Lauren is standing there.

"Ezra filled me in," she says.

"He woke you up just to give you bad news?"

"You think I was asleep? That's really funny."

She raises her arm to show me a plastic bag of her own.

"I'm coming too," she says.

"You don't have to."

"No. But if you go alone and we have to wait a long time for you to come back, it makes sense to have a messenger."

"You didn't mention how I might not come back at all."

"I didn't think I needed to mention that," she says, and clicks her headlamp on, blinding me.

●   ●   ●

It's still dark when we arrive at the gate. After a sip from the water in the pickle jar, we nestle down in the grass at the edge of the road. Lauren faces to the left and I to the right. We don't pull the steak knives out. It's as if doing so will risk materializing the danger that, for now, remains waiting just beyond the range of our headlamps.

Should we speak? Would that make sitting here, slapping mosquitos from our necks, any better? The dark decides it for me. There's too much of it to not attempt to push it back with conversation.

"Lauren?"

"Yeah?"

"I've got something I'd like to ask you."

"That makes two of us. You go first."

"How did Dad die?"

She pauses. Not upset by the nature of the question, only working to retrieve the answer.

"A cardiac event. That's what the lawyer said. Or did someone else say it? Jerry or one of the twins? I definitely remember that word, anyway. *Event*. Like it was an opera or wedding reception."

"Did you ask for any details?"

"I suppose I didn't need any. You?"

"Same."

"A man Dad's age—it happens."

"It's not how he died I'm stuck on. It's how little we know about it."

"He's a man of mystery."

"Yeah, but this time the mystery isn't him. It's us."

Around us, within the space of seconds, the plants, the trickling stream at the bottom of the ditch, the road's gravel, all of it gains a muted color. The dawn painting the forest.

"My turn," Lauren says, pulling her legs up and wrapping her arms around her knees.

"Okay."

"What was that about you forgetting how to be a doctor? After Elias was—after what happened?"

"That's not exactly how I'd put it. Forgetting. But I'm not lying, Lauren."

"I'm sorry. That sounded like an accusation. I was just laying out the logical problem—"

"I know what the logical problem is. And I don't have the answer to it."

"Then what do you have?"

A feeling of helplessness. Being an alien to myself. Angry without knowing who to be angry at.

These are all the things I consider saying but don't. They don't get at the larger thought I've been having, something I haven't arrived at fully in my own mind, so I take a run at it now.

"I wish I could have done something for Elias," I say. "But since coming here—there's been a change. That's the only way I can describe it. Which makes me wonder if you feel the same."

She doesn't answer this right away.

"Being here—" Lauren stops with a tiny gasp. "Let's just say it's made me question who I am."

The morning continues to color itself into existence. But instead of the different shades of the forest's green making it less formidable, it reveals its capacity for deception, to hide in plain view.

"I was thinking about our families," Lauren announces.

"What about them?"

"Don't you find it interesting that none of us have romantic relationships to speak of? That none of us, other than Franny, ever had kids?"

"I blamed Dad for that. It's kind of automatic for me now. You got trouble making friends? *Dad*. No girlfriend? *Dad*. Feel like only half a person most of the time? *Dad*."

"I came to the same conclusion myself for a long time," she says. "But now that I see all of us here together, the absences we share in our lives, the same dream we have at night—they're conditions I recognize from my practice."

"Trauma. That's your specialty, right?"

"So I'm wondering if we've all been through something. I'm wondering if that's why I was drawn to this area of therapy in the first place."

If Lauren is right, why don't any of us remember? She'd probably say this is precisely the way trauma works—it conceals its own scars; it masks, obliterates. But wouldn't *something* come through?

It's my powerlessness to grasp what might have been done to us that brings the outrage. If I knew what my trauma was—the one before what happened *overseas*, the one that feels like it might have involved Dad somehow—maybe I could have shielded Bridge from it. I could have stood up to whatever wanted to take part of our identities away (*Let's just say it's made me question who I am*) instead of filling the space with work or dope or whatever each of us put at the top of the daily to-do list that we pretended was a life.

"Shhh."

Lauren hears something. Then she sees it. Her eyes widening before she wills herself into composure, stands up, and walks toward the fence.

36

A WHITE PANEL VAN. NO WRITING ON THE SIDES, NO WINDOWS IN THE REAR, AS nondescript a vehicle as there exists. It seems to slow its approach when it spots us so that it rolls up to within twenty feet of the gate at a walking pace, the individual stones grinding and popping under the tires.

It stops. The engine cuts off. The audible ratchet of the emergency brake being set.

Nobody gets out.

It hadn't occurred to me that the driver would be under orders to have no contact with those on the other side, that he might turn around and no van, this one or any other, would ever come back. How do we appear to whoever considers us through the windshield that mirrors the patch of sky overhead so that we can't see who sits behind the wheel? A man and a woman. Respectable, intelligent sorts under normal conditions, but desperate now. People to avoid.

Lauren doesn't speak. I can only assume she fears what may happen if she does. The sound of our voices, calling for assistance, will be the end of it. It would be so easy to not help. Any additional nudge from us might decide the matter.

The door opens. The driver, a man, gets out. Slow as someone trying not to antagonize a bad back, though this may only be what suspicion looks like.

"Well, well," he says, louder than necessary as he comes a few steps closer but leaves the van's door open. The seat belt warning bell tolling from inside, but he doesn't go back to close the door. "Good day to you!"

The delivery man is middle-aged, portly, his bald head covered by a wool cap set at a comical angle atop his head. The fleshiness of his face welcoming in the way of a contented husband and father, a lover of simple pleasures: extra gravy on his potatoes and telling stories to the grandkids who climb onto his knees. A man who would not only provide you with directions if you asked, but offer to drive you where you're going.

"Can you help us?"

I ask this as plainly as possible. A reasonable man asking another reasonable man a question; there's no need to see it as anything but what it is. And while the delivery man mostly appears to hear it this way, his round face droops a little. His natural friendliness, the muscles used to hold his grin up loosening at the indication of something not quite right.

"You two don't work in there, do you?" he says.

"No, we don't."

"Then who are you?"

"My name is Aaron Quinlan, and this is my half sister, Lauren. We're being held prisoner. One of us—a child back at the main building—has been seriously injured—"

"Hold on now, *hold* on—"

"Needs medical attention. Could you open the gate?"

By the look on his face he hears this last part as if it was something to take offense at. An insult directed at his wife. His country.

"Open the gate?" he repeats.

"Let us out. Or if that's something you're not able to do, could you get on your phone and call for an ambulance?"

He scrutinizes me through the woven metal. Takes his time. The friendliness incrementally vacates from every aspect of him.

"Wait, wait, *wait*," he says finally, as if a number of options have cohered in his mind all at once. "Y'all refugees or something?"

"What?"

"The fence. All the hush-hush. This one of those detainment facilities?"

"No. It's not that—"

"You must be pretty special if you've got the whole place to yourselves," he says, too pleased by his internal detective work to pay any attention to me. "Most camps I've seen on TV are a lot more filled up with illegals than this here. How many *are* you, anyway? Half dozen? Dozen? Man, you've got to be bad news. You've got to be *spies*."

Lauren quiets me with a little back wave of her hand. This isn't working and now it's her turn.

"I understand what you're thinking, but we're not refugees or spies or anything like that," she says, her tone confiding, respectful. "We're the victims of a crime. Kidnapping. If you don't believe us, that's fine, just tell the police we're here. It won't be on your hands."

"But it *will*, lady. I've got instructions. 'Don't tell anybody what's going on up there.' Good thing is, I don't even know. *Boom!* Done."

"You're making a mistake. We're—"

"No. Uh-uh," he says, shaking his head so hard his jowls shudder. "*You* made a mistake. If you're in there? *You* made a big mistake, and I promise you, it's not touching *me*."

The delivery man starts toward the van.

"We'll die in here!"

Lauren's cry stops him. He looks back at her, then at me. He appeared so likable and open a moment ago. Now the hatred alters his features even as we watch, transforming him. He looks through the fence and doesn't see a man and woman. He sees the cause of every problem he's ever had. *Why me? Why hasn't it been easier? Why haven't I gotten all I wanted?* And the answer is us.

"I'm not helping you," he says. "I quit. What's more, I'm not *telling* them I'm quitting. And I'm the only one who drives these boxes up."

"Please. Don't—"

"Shut up! *Please, please, please.* That all you people do? Beg for hand-outs?"

He regards us with the same exasperation he would a pair of stray dogs who keep coming around scratching the paint off his door. It firms up the decision he'd only tried out seconds ago.

"Well, you can starve in there. Understand?" he says. "Because I sacrificed for my country. My family was *born* here. So it's what you deserve, far as I'm concerned."

A handful of sentences run through my mind, appeals I might voice aloud.

I can give you millions of dollars.

Do you have any children? You do? Because my little sister, my fourteen-year-old sister, is in here too.

I'm trying to decide between them when the delivery man hops up into the van and pulls the door shut.

It's the engine throat-clearing to life that starts us shouting for him to come back. There's no argument anymore, no attempt to reach his emotions or loyalties. Lauren and I wordlessly holler and wave the same as anyone standing on the wrong side of a fence.

The van reverses and goes forward twice, making sure not to slide into the ditch. When he's got himself straightened out, he rolls off down the road, the brake lights winking as he goes.

37

WE TRY TO TELL OURSELVES SOMEONE MAY STILL COME FOR US. THE DELIVERY man will have a change of heart. Even if he carries through with not bringing us the supplies he's supposed to, his employers will figure it out and replace him. There must be a system in charge of this operation, some kind of oversight.

The more Lauren and I work to buttress these arguments, the less convincing they sound. The forest itself seems to mock our attempts at hope. When we finally give up, the willow leaves applaud in a breeze too high up for us to feel.

When we make it back to the lodge, Franny is standing at the door. I assume she's waiting for us. But she's not looking our way, her gaze seemingly fixed on the mound where Elias is buried.

"Franny!"

She swings her head around and clasps her hands to the doorframe as if steadying herself on the deck of a rolling ship.

"She's gone, Aaron! She's *gone*!"

• • •

It's true that life can flash before your eyes.

It's also true that life may not be your own.

As I rush to the lodge's door, Franny's tear-puffed face coming into detail with each stride, I measure my existence through the Tuesday dinners I've had with Bridge. The "cocktails" with Shirley Temples (for her) and lager (for me). The comic books created on napkins to kill the time as we wait for our orders to arrive. The permission we'd give each other to be goofy, a pair of bratty kids out on the town.

Bridge is gone and she's taken both of us with her.

"Where'd she go?" I demand of Franny when I reach her, grabbing her hard by the knobs of her shoulders. "What *happened*?"

"She didn't say she was going. She didn't—"

"I told you to *stay* with her!"

"No, no, no," Franny says, stepping out of my grasp. "Not Bridge. *Mom*."

And she's there. My little sister approaching from behind Franny and squeezing into the space between us. Looking up at me.

"Mom left us," she says.

"Why?"

I'm not expecting an answer from her. But she offers one anyway.

"I'm not sure. But I think she went to look for Dad."

38

NOBODY SAW HER LEAVE. THE OTHERS WERE KEEPING TO THEMSELVES, WAITING for Lauren and me to return, and then Franny noticed the front door was unlocked and Mom was nowhere to be found inside. Jerry offered to go out and look for her but Franny begged him not to. There were forces trying to pull them apart—something the Tall Man and the old woman were part of, but more powerful than the two of them put together—and they had to resist.

"We have to find her!" Bridge shouts at me when I lean against the foyer's wall to avoid slumping to the floor.

"I know. I—"

"Aaron!"

"Just give me a second. Just—"

"*Please*! It's our *mother*—"

"Stop it!"

Franny's shout quiets both of us.

"It's scary that Mom's not here, Bridge," she goes on once all of us are looking at her. "I'm fucking scared too. But now is the time to work through things. Be smart. Wouldn't Mom want that? For you to do the right thing not just for her but for everybody?"

This reaches Bridge the same as it reaches me.

"Yes," she says.

Bridge sits cross-legged on the floor. A student who's made a presentation and now it's someone else's turn.

Jerry and Ezra take the opportunity to ask me and Lauren questions. When we're finished relating the exchange we had with the delivery man, Jerry speaks for us all.

"Nobody's coming for us."

Lauren attempts to reason how there must be people who know we're here, that they wouldn't just leave us like this.

"Nobody's coming," he says again. "Fogarty said thirty days. Maybe they'll open the gate, maybe not. But we're on our own until then."

Now that we hear someone say it all other possibilities dissolve.

We talk about whether or not we should look for Mom. Without referencing Franny's earlier mention of "forces" or what happened to Elias, it's decided it's too dangerous to just fan out into the woods calling her name like we're searching for a lost dog. We'll wait until late afternoon to see if she comes back on her own. If not, we'll consider our alternatives.

All I want is to rest. Talk with Bridge about anything other than what's happening so that the fear I can see in the way she's now breathing through her mouth instead of her nose might be quieted. But Franny won't let me. She pulls me into her room and closes the door.

"I saw him, Aaron."

She means Dad. I'm so sure of this I can see him too, waving at us through the great room's windows, laughing in the superior way he did when we'd tell him the bedtime stories he told were too scary, as if the only humor he responded to was seeing how unstoppably the seeds of irrationality could grow in inferior minds.

Which means Dad isn't dead.

Which means this really is only a game. Soon Elias will walk in wiping the dirt of his grave off his face. Fogarty will show himself too, ask if he can keep the silk Princeton tie as a souvenir. The limo drivers will arrive to return our phones and laugh as they pull corks from champagne bottles. It's over. We can go home, wherever that might be or how it might be changed after Belfountain.

Then again, it could be another kind of game altogether. One that was never intended for anyone to win.

"He was there, just outside the window. While you were gone," Franny goes on. "It was *him*. It was Nate."

Who's that? I almost say. A second of forgetting followed by a burning shame.

"You're under a lot of stress," I hear myself say, my voice as empty as the words it speaks.

"This wasn't stress. This was my son. This was Nate. He was there. Looking through the glass like a kid at the zoo. He was cold. He was *shivering*, Aaron."

"He wasn't there, Franny."

"Because he's dead."

"Yes."

"It doesn't feel that way."

"That's grief. That's denial."

"You're telling me about denial? About grief?"

"I was only—"

"I'm not arguing. I need you to understand."

"Understand what?"

Franny takes a moment to line up the words in her head.

"I'm not sure what dead or alive mean anymore," she manages finally, slow as someone reading a book aloud by candlelight. "This side of the fence or the other. All those lines, those boundaries. They're not what we thought they were."

"What are they then?"

"They're stories."

Franny doesn't look well. If anything, she's gained weight since coming here, but it's been added to parts of her that needed it least. Her jawline, her hands. She appears swollen instead of well nourished.

"Ghosts aren't real," I say.

"But in stories they can be. When Dad talked about this place, they were."

I'm back to where I've always found myself with Franny. Even during her good stretches, we'd come to the point where she revealed herself to be less strong than she proclaimed, less changed for the better. The circle always returned to the essential Franny: making empty assurances or spinning ridiculous narratives of conspiracy and victimhood. The only thing different about this time from all the others is that even as I see her as having lost her hold on reality, I don't entirely disagree with her.

"I miss him too, Franny," I say. "I miss Nate too."

They're magic words that achieve two things. The first is how they bring Franny to hold me close. The second is how they show me how much I do miss him, that my sister's not the only one who's been broken by the way her son was taken from the world.

39

I MUST HAVE FALLEN ASLEEP ON FRANNY'S BED. WHEN MY EYES OPEN, BRIDGE IS
there, sitting in a chair in the corner of the room.

"Hey there," I say.

"Hey."

"How're you doing?"

"Take a wild guess."

"Worried about Mom. About everything."

"Aren't you?"

I'm worried about you.

"Of course," I say.

Only then do I notice the box resting on Bridge's lap.

"Whatcha got there?"

"That's what I want to show you."

She pulls her chair closer into the circle of light from the lamp on
the table. I look at her to continue, but she says nothing, only glancing
down at the box.

"What's in it?" I ask.

"That part's interesting. But so is the box."

"How?"

"Look again."

So I do. As if new particulars have been added to it as we spoke, I see it for what it is. A tackle box. The same one I opened to pull out the silver X-Acto blade I used to cut a hole in Bridge's throat.

"How did you bring that in?"

"I didn't. I found it."

"Where?"

"In the shed. Yesterday, when the rest of you were looking for shovels and tools. I saw it right away and brought it inside."

She sets it on the bed. Its reality deepens without my touching it. An enhanced, hyperrealism to the bulbous handle, the scratches in its paint that show the steel beneath.

"How'd it get here?" I ask.

"Dad must have brought it."

"Why? There're no rivers or lakes I've seen to do any fishing."

"He wasn't using it to fish."

I'm supposed to open it. I think of those potato chip cans with springs inside that look like snakes that leap out when you pull off the lid. Then I think of worse things.

The lid is cold to the touch, as if Bridge had hidden it in the freezer. It requires one hand to grip the box and another to wrench the lid up, which comes away with grinding complaint.

I have to lean directly over its dark insides to see what's there.

A key. Different from any car or house key I've seen. The neck rounded and long, the jagged end cut more deeply and numerously, so that it looks like the mouth of a miniature creature, grinning.

"Was there anything else in here?"

"Nope."

"Does anyone know about this? Even Franny or Mom?"

"Just you." She's not looking at the key. She's looking at me. "You know what it opens, don't you?"

"I have an idea."

Bridge has aged in the last two days. I have a similar initial impression every Tuesday when we meet. She's growing up. But this is only what it is to be fourteen years old. Going around shocking the people who know you with all the ways you're not how they remember you or how they would prefer to hold you in time.

"It's not the fence we have to get over, Aaron," she says. "It's something else we have to find."

I've read a study about how married couples can read each other's minds. Not just anticipate the other's decisions and actions based on precedent, but complex webs of reasoning dictated almost word for word, picked up from the other like a radio signal. It's also true between brothers and sisters at least some of the time.

"Okay," I say. "I'll go."

"You're not leaving me behind again," she says, and slams the tackle box's lid closed so hard I'm worried someone will hear it all the way down the hall.

"It's not *safe*, Bridge. And I—"

"Why are you always *doing* that?"

"Doing what?"

"Pretending you're the brave big brother even when you're scared shitless. It's not an *act*, Aaron. Being the Good Guy isn't the same thing as being good. Being you."

She almost yells this, and what's far more alarming than any concern she's been heard outside the room is how acute her frustration is.

"You're right. I've got that mixed up my whole life," I say. "But here's the deal. I care about you. Mom and Franny too. My patients. I want everyone to be okay and I'll put on the Good Guy costume—no matter how bad it fits me, no matter how itchy it feels—if it helps make that happen."

"You *are* good, Aaron. But that doesn't mean you have to be alone."

This hits me harder than her raised voice of a moment ago. It's the simple truth of it that's so striking.

"Okay," I say. "Come with me."

She doesn't need to hear where I might take her. We're together in this now, no more leaving her hiding under beds pretending it will make a difference. I won't go without her, and she's prepared to wait for the next step.

"Take it," she says, and I pull the key out, half expecting it to be sharp enough to cut me.

"What about the box?"

Bridge has it under her arm as she goes to the door.

"This?" she says. "This doesn't mean anything to anyone but us."

We start a fire in the great room's hearth because it's something to do. Soon the heat from the blaze has all of us sweating, keeping as far back as the room allows, waiting for the flames to die down.

"Maybe Mom will smell the smoke and follow it back," Franny offers.

Nobody replies to this. I don't think any of us can picture Mom pushing through the underbrush, led home by her sniffing nose. And then there's the consideration of what else might be drawn out of the forest.

Once the fire has calmed, Jerry smothers it in ash, and it hisses and pops with demonic threats.

"There's about two hours of daylight left," he says when he turns to us. "Either we go out there now and try to find your mom, or we let her go it alone all night."

"She's not strong enough," Franny says to me, and I take her not to mean Mom's chances of surviving a meeting with the Tall Man, but the night itself. I can't say I disagree. The thought of our mother poking around somewhere out in Belfountain's hundreds of acres isn't sustainable for long before it collapses, dissolving like a sugar cube in a warm rain.

"So we do a search," I say. "Two groups, with somebody staying behind to man the fort."

Bridge comes to stand next to me, indicating her intentions. Lauren raises her hand.

"Could you use a third?" she asks.

I look to Bridge, who nods. "Sure. Jerry and Ezra, you good?"

"Good to go," Jerry says.

All of us separate to collect headlamps and water, but I stay where I am to speak to Franny.

"You okay with this?"

"What do I have to do? Not open the door? Yeah, I think I can handle that."

"It means you're going to be here on your own."

Franny slips her hand into the front pouch of the hoodie she wears. Pulls out the gift Dad left for her. Nate's baby rattle.

"I won't be alone," she says.

"Let's go! I want us back by dark," Jerry calls out, and I leave Franny where she stands, swaying from side to side as if rocking an infant to sleep.

40

BRIDGE STARTS FOR THE GREEN TRAILHEAD BEFORE ANYONE ELSE DECIDES which way they'll go. Lauren and I follow after her. Once the trees have obscured the lodge from view behind us and we're well out of earshot, I ask Bridge why we're going this way.

"This is where you found the way to the camp, right?"

"Yeah. But I'm not sure I can remember the exact direction I took."

Bridge turns to face us. Pulls her compass out. "You find the side trail that took you there. I'll take care of the coordinates."

"Hold up," Lauren interjects. "What camp? What's happening here?"

I look to Bridge. "Can I tell her?"

Bridge comes back to take Lauren's hand. "Lauren should know *every-thing*," she says. "But let's keep moving while you talk. We don't have a lot of time."

"So we're not looking for your mom anymore?" Lauren asks.

"We're looking for her," Bridge says. "We're *also* looking for a way out."

Bridge pulls on Lauren's hand, and the three of us march up the trail's steady grade, the forest's air heavy in our throats.

The born-again Christian camp. The underground gate. The key.

I bring Lauren up to speed as swiftly as I can, in part because I'm also keeping an eye out for the side trail, in part because it all sounds less unsettling with some of the details edited out. The claustrophobic darkness of the stairwell under the walk-in freezer. The sense that some living thing breathed on the other side of the door.

When I'm finished, she doesn't say anything, and I wonder if it was a mistake sharing any of it with her. Bridge and I have a history, a trust that goes without question. The two of us like Lauren, and based on that we brought her in, but we've overlooked that she belongs to a different family from ours. She's obliged to tell Jerry and Ezra about all this just as I was to tell Bridge, and now she'll turn and start back.

But that's not what she does.

"I'm assuming you don't want my brothers in on this?" she asks finally.

"This puts you in a difficult situation, and I'm sorry about—"

"Just tell me, Aaron."

"No. We'd like it kept between ourselves for now."

"Fine. I think that's the best way to go too," she says, putting her hand on Bridge's shoulder. "Let's see if that key works."

Just when I start to think there's no way I'm going to find the path I started off on before coming upon the camp, I stop at a divot in the soft ground off to the right. My shoe print. Already partly overgrown in a weaving of grass and clover.

"This way," I say.

"Wait," Bridge says, pulling a small notebook out. She scribbles down the readings, the estimated distance we've traveled from the lodge, the side trail's direction. When she's done, she signals for me to carry on and the two of them fall in line behind me.

I'm worried there won't be time to find the camp, discover we were wrong about the key opening the door, and get back before nightfall. I'm worried even more about what we'll find if the door can be opened. But I believe Bridge is right. The only possibility of escape isn't over the fence, or through it, but deeper into the ground beneath our feet. It makes me think of Elias. His body being dropped into the hole. How where he is now, in the cool soil, is closer to the outside than we are.

Wasn't that what Bridge had remembered Dad said to her when he brought her here as a child? The crucial decision on the direction we ought to take.

Where does the path lead after it ends?

He must have meant something more than encouraging his daughter to be courageous. It was about having to go so far in whatever you set out to do that you encountered a border. And once you did, what was important was to forge your own passage through it.

Lauren finds the camp before I do.

"There," she says, and goes forward into the clearing without pausing.

I take mental note of everything as if there were some chance that it had been folded up and taken away since I was here. The horseshoe pit, the shabby dining hall. And just as Bridge noted but that I hadn't seen last time, a swing set in the forest's lengthening shadow, lopsided and seatless, the chains swinging slightly as if someone had given them a push before disappearing into the trees.

Bridge leads us into the dining hall. She doesn't look up to read the Belfountain sign over the door, but Lauren does, glancing back at me. It feels essential that we make as little sound as possible, so I merely mouth the words *Just wait* and follow her inside.

I watch as Lauren takes in the scripture written on the rafters, along with the demonic messages on the tables and walls. *Satan hear our Voice.*

None of it slows her advance toward the kitchen. *WE Sing for YOU*. And then she finds herself standing in the center of the pentagram burned into the floor. It holds her in place like a magnet, pulling her earthward.

"What is this?" she says, raising her arms out to her sides, and for a moment, she actually appears to be sinking, her legs dissolving into darkness.

"Just kids, probably," I say.

"*What* kids?"

"I don't know."

"What kind of people would—I mean, Aaron, this is—"

"In here."

Bridge stands waiting for us at the kitchen entrance.

"It's in here," she repeats, and slips inside.

41

THE WALK-IN FREEZER'S DOOR IS OPEN. HAD I LEFT IT THAT WAY? OR DID BRIDGE pull it free herself, in silence, before Lauren and I joined her where she stands at its pitch-black threshold? I want to ask, but the words are too heavy to be spoken, their uselessness announced in advance.

We will enter the freezer no matter what. It's our fate. Our father's will.

Bridge flicks on her headlamp, and Lauren and I do the same. Gather around the open trapdoor leading into the ground, the three of us like mourners at a funeral.

"This isn't right," Lauren says. It isn't clear what she's referring to at first, but then I hear it as meaning everything. The hole. The camp. Us. We're not right to be doing any of this.

"I'll go first," I say, and step down into the stairwell.

The air is cooler beneath the surface, yet my skin feels hotter, an oily sweat that glues my shirt to the tops of my shoulders. The dark pushes back at the bluish spray of LED light, diluting it.

"Hey, Aaron?" Lauren says from what sounds like a hundred feet above and behind me. "Maybe we shouldn't be here?"

All of us hear the tremor in her voice. The fear of being the first to come into contact with whatever we might release. Whatever might already by waiting for us.

I don't answer her.

It's so much narrower than I remember from my first trip down, the walls almost bulging inward like an inflamed throat. At the bottom, the steel door holds me back at the deepest point. The moisture shining and nippled on the smooth surface.

"Here," I say, pushing my back against the wall so Bridge and Lauren can see it.

"Looks serious," Bridge says.

"Not a vault or anything like that," Lauren agrees. "Custom-built. And it would've been hell cutting and squaring it into the ground like that."

Nobody has to ask me to try the key but I hesitate as if it's a required step. When I pull the key out and come close to the door, I hear Bridge and Lauren move away. I wonder, if it opens, if whatever awaits on the other side will be slowed enough by what it will do with me that they will have time to make it out.

The key slides in and clicks into place.

It takes a little effort to turn it. There's an internal *thump*, a single, amplified heartbeat, when the key is rotated as far as it can go. I'm expecting I'll have to push or pull the door free, but it slides to the left, a smooth grating of metal against metal until it stops with a muffled crash.

The smell comes first.

Mold, primarily. Followed by the antiseptic sourness of a hospital waste bin, ammonia and soiled bandages, bodily discharges in paper bundles. Maybe something else. Something no longer alive.

A short hallway. I lean back again and let Lauren and Bridge look down the ten feet to its end.

"Another door," Bridge says.

This one is different from the sliding steel one. There's no keyhole for one thing, only a numerical pad on the wall next to it. For another, there's a porthole window, small and high, no more than a foot in diameter.

"We go back now, right?" Lauren says.

Bridge doesn't reply, just passes by me.

I hesitate, trying to think of a way to secure the steel door so that it doesn't slide shut on its own somehow—or can't be pulled shut by someone who waits behind us in the walk-in freezer—but there's nothing that will hold something so heavy as the door if it started to move. The thought of being closed in here almost hijacks my body completely, the urge to bolt overcome only by the idea of Bridge being trapped on the other side and me not able to get to her.

We approach the second door without asking what it might mean. It's the porthole window. The promise of the glass, the world within.

Bridge is there first, but because of the window's height she can't see through other than the glimpses she catches as she jumps up and down. The slap of her shoes on the cement floor resounding like smacks to exposed flesh.

"Let me," Lauren says.

She rises up on her toes. The reflected glare of her headlamp dazzles her, so she turns it off. She circles her face with her hands to shield the glow of our lights from her eyes.

"It's hard to see anything."

"Is there electricity?" I ask. "Lights?"

"There must have been at one time, but not now. The only light is coming from these—I don't know—these tubes on the ground here and there. Hold on. I can see a little better now."

"Is it a room?"

"A hallway. Chairs, desks, paper. It's all trashed. And there's—"

"Lauren?"

"Oh my *God*."

"What?"

"There's blood. *Lots* of it. Like something's—"

She stops again. I expect her to pull away but she only presses her face closer to the glass.

"What's going on?"

"There's something in there," she says, and only now does she pull away and look at us. "Something moving."

42

LAUREN TAKES A FULL STEP BACK FROM THE DOOR, A REFLEX OF FEAR AS MUCH AS to allow me to look inside. There's no choice but to slide closer. Draw my hands up the cold steel and stare into the darkness on the other side.

Not quite darkness.

There are half a dozen glowsticks, each of them radiating the greenish yellow of streetlights in fog. They reveal a wide corridor leading straight ahead through gaps of shadow to a wall at the far end, maybe sixty feet away. Doors on either side, most of them ajar but at least one still closed. Office furniture, leather-bound log books and files along with random metal equipment of some kind, boxes overflowing with spiraled wires, power cables, most of it overturned and scattered.

"I don't see any blood," I say.

And then I do.

So much of it I think at first it's part of the vandalism, cans of paint thrown against the walls and left to congeal in pools on the floor.

Something dragged through it, leaving a diminishing trail of lines. A kind of haphazard musical staff that approached the door before fading.

Not something. A body.

This comes instantly, certainly. It could be nothing other than a human body. Lying at the end of the hall.

"How about now?" Lauren asks from what sounds like a great distance behind me. "On the walls? Spread out—"

"I see it."

"What do you think went on in there?"

"Just a sec. I'm trying—"

The body moves.

A moment ago it had the jagged outline of a figure lying on its side—the jutting shoulder lowering to the elbow, the rounded hip—and now the line is bending. Rising up from the floor. Its head. Turning and locking into place when it finds me.

"Aaron?"

"There's someone in there."

"*Someone?*"

"Yeah."

"Okay," Bridge moans. "I want to go now."

The figure stands. A woman. The hair so long and straggled it appears like a hood around her face. A face that comes into greater detail as she takes her first step forward, then the next. Moving into the light from one of the glowsticks.

"It's her," I say, but it comes out sounding like someone else's voice entirely.

"*Please*, Aaron. Let's *go*."

The old woman from the woods. Now lengthening her stride the closer she gets to the door, a bare foot slipping as it touches down in a pool of blood but immediately recovering, leaving new prints behind her.

"Aaron?"

I'm already moving back from the window. Not triggered by Lauren or Bridge's demands but so as not to be close to the door when the old woman reaches it.

But we don't leave yet. The three of us watch the porthole, waiting. Telling ourselves we're safe and convincing ourselves just enough not to run.

"You said it's 'her,' " Bridge says. "Who's in there?"

I'm about to answer when the old woman's face appears against the glass.

Lauren utters a low exhalation in place of a scream. Yet even now the fear nudges me forward instead of turning me away. Compelled by a force stronger than curiosity, a need to know and see and feel so great it's as if my life turned on my experiencing all of it.

"Who are you?" I ask, and the old woman cocks her head as if she registered my voice but couldn't make out the words.

I try again, louder this time.

"What's your name?"

She closes her eyes. I take it as a flinch against pain. But the longer she stays that way I read it instead as an effort to concentrate, to remember. The eyes open. Her mouth stretched into an uncertain grin.

"Do you know who you are?"

She frowns, as if suspecting a trick.

"Are you alone?"

The old woman looks behind her, then back at me. Both what was left of the grin and the suspicious frown disappear. Replaced by wide-eyed worry, her arms hugging herself as she starts to rock slightly from side to side.

"Let me in," I say.

She might be shaking her head no. She might just be shaking.

"Maybe you can do it from your side. Put your hand on the handle and turn."

"What are you doing?" Lauren says.

"We need to get inside." I turn to her, then to Bridge. "Everything that's happening to us—it has to do with what's already happened in there."

"Already happened? I can make a guess," Lauren says. "Someone was *killed*, Aaron. That's human blood on the floor. And this woman wasn't the one who did it."

"So how is she still alive?"

Lauren doesn't answer. She looks at me as if I'm the one she should be scared of, and takes another step back.

But Bridge stays close to me. "You're right," she says before looking back at Lauren. "The only way out is in."

I look through the window at the old woman once more, her expression unreadable because it keeps changing, sliding from anxiety to confusion to suppressed mirth.

"Try the door," I tell her. "I'll make sure—I'll protect you from whoever else is in there with you."

She almost laughs at this.

"How do you get in and out?" I shout at her. "I've seen you. Out in the woods. Is there another way?"

She's afraid now. Her head looking over her shoulder as she backs away.

"Don't go!"

The old woman walks backward from the door. Her eyes held on mine in pity, as if I'm the one locked underground, not her. What did I say that made her go away? Nothing. It *wasn't* me. It's something she's heard. Inside. Something that's coming.

"What happened to you?" I shout into the glass, and the question blasts back at me, demanding the same explanation of myself.

The old woman is ten feet away, fifteen, walking through the same pool of blood as before, leaving a new line of footsteps.

As she goes, she does something odd. Every time she passes a glow-stick she bends to pick it up and tosses it into one of the open rooms. Each time she does the hallway darkens in grades, swallowing her.

"What's she doing?" Bridge asks.

"Putting out the lights."

"Why?"

"Because there's—"

"There's something she doesn't want you to see," Lauren finishes for me.

The old woman reaches the end of the hall. Only one glowstick remains on the floor, but she doesn't reach for it. Her head turned to the right, watching, as a new shadow plays over the wall.

A shadow that bends down and picks the glowstick up.

For a second, the two of them stare down the hall at me. The old woman and the Tall Man floating in a circle of underwater green. His one gloved hand on the glowstick and the other on the silver hatchet, the corner of its head notching into his thigh over and over without him seeming to feel it. The steel coming away shining and black.

"Oh no. Oh *Jesus*—"

He hides the glowstick behind his back and it turns them into outlines. Paper cutouts you'd see taped to school classroom windows at Halloween.

The two of them start forward. The bogeyman and the witch, coming for the door.

43

THE STAIRS HAVE MULTIPLIED SINCE WE CAME DOWN THEM. NOT ONLY MORE OF them in number but also stretched out like an accordion, so that each step demands something near a full leap.

Lauren reaches the top first, then Bridge. By the way they stand there, I assume the freezer door has been closed. *Entombed.* The word arrives like the name of an old girlfriend or childhood pet, intimate and particular.

Once I join them, I see that it's still open, and we start forward again. We rush out into the kitchen and, for the first time, one of us speaks.

"Wait," I say. "We should close this."

I throw the freezer's door into the latch and it locks shut with the loud *pop* of a pistol shot.

The three of us listen for a voice or pounding from the other side. There's nothing for long enough that I start to believe that we *are* hearing something. The Tall Man listening for us just as we listen for him.

• • •

When we're in the forest again I tell them what I saw. I'm as quick as I can be about it, because the falling dusk has me worried about the Tall Man coming after us and also because I want Lauren and Bridge to agree not to tell the others what we found.

"I don't think I can do that," Lauren says as we make our way along the trail. "And I don't understand why I should."

"Because they'll see it only as a threat. They'll go hunting. But they'll fail. And that place—it's not just where those—" I almost say *creatures* before correcting myself. "Where those people live. Whatever we need to know is in there."

"You want to keep this a secret so you can play detective? Satisfy your curiosity?"

"No. I want to keep this a secret so all of us have a chance to survive."

It doesn't make a lot of sense as I hear myself say it, but there's not another way I can come at what I believe. I can only hope that Lauren feels the same way Bridge and I do.

"If you're right, how do we get around the guy with the gloves?" she asks.

"We know he and the woman are out in the woods most of the time."

"So we go in when they're not there?"

"That's it. We have to find the other way in—because there has to be a second exit that—"

"Quiet."

Lauren and I look at Bridge. She nudges her chin, pointing along the trail. The lodge is now coming into view, the kitchen windows a band of yellow like a monobrow. It's not the structure itself she's alerting us to, but the figure standing at the bottom of the steps by the front door.

We turn off our headlamps. It makes it harder to not step on anything that might make a sound, but we crouch low and proceed closer.

"I think I heard something out there," the figure says to someone just inside the lodge's door.

"It's Ezra," Lauren says. "Ezra!"

"Lauren!"

The three of us come out of the trees, and Lauren runs to her brother, briefly inspecting him as if to make sure he's whole. Jerry joins them, his eyes on Bridge and me.

"Anything?" he asks.

"We didn't find her. You?"

"No. I'm so sorry."

Lauren looks back at us. She's going to tell them about the camp and she's silently apologizing. Then she looks at Bridge. I can't see my sister's face but whatever it conveys changes Lauren's mind.

"Let's get inside," she says, slides her arms around her brothers' waists, and guides them up the steps into the light.

We gather in the kitchen but none of us eat. There's the inspection of the last few apples and oranges in a bowl on the counter, the shaking of a bag of bread crusts—all the rituals of food inspection without the appetite. Jerry is the last to hold an apple in his palm and replace it before he speaks.

"I think we should talk about where things stand. Aaron, maybe Bridge shouldn't be here for this?"

"It's up to her. Bridge, you want to—"

"You don't think Mom is missing," Bridge says. "You think she's dead."

She stands on her own closest to the dining room. For a moment I'm worried that she's ill. Her cancer has returned and I'm seeing it before she can feel it. But I look at her a moment longer and recognize that I'm wrong. She's recharging. Her body folding inward. Readying.

"I don't know anything," Jerry says. "I'm just trying—"

"But that's what you *think*," Bridge says. "My mother is gone and isn't coming back."

Jerry glances at me, sees I'm not going to bail him out. "Yes, that's what I think."

"Because it's been too long?"

"And because we know there's someone out there who is—look, Elias was killed. It happened at night. And it's night now."

"So we shouldn't look for her anymore?"

"We should do what we need to for those of us still here." He reaches for an orange before pulling his hand back, seeing the emptiness of the gesture for what it is. "These search parties we're throwing together and arming with cutlery and flashlights—it's not going to work. If your mom knocks on the door tonight or tomorrow morning or whenever, great. But for the sake of all of us, we have to assume she's not going to."

"Fine. Okay, fine," Bridge says, her lower lip curling out.

I go to her. My pride in her so great it pushes back against the first plumes of grief blowing up from within, and when I open my arms and she steps into them, it's me drawing strength from her more than the other way around.

We talk about what our plan should be. Some radical options are put forward, including Franny's idea that we climb the fence while wearing oven mitts (nobody goes to the trouble of pointing out all the ways that wouldn't work). We hypothesize how we might go on the offensive and take down the Tall Man ourselves. But we don't know if he's alone. And there's no question that when it comes to killing, he's better at it than any of us.

The conclusions we eventually come to are the same we started with.

Everyone stays inside.

Keep all doors and windows secure.

Ezra, Lauren, Jerry, and I will keep watch in shifts through the night.

Only then, before going to our rooms, sofas, or chairs to attempt sleep, do we eat.

44

THE DREAM OF BLACK WATER.

Of all the ways it is unique and strange—how it's passed between us, how it enlarges in scope each night—the strangest and most unique is how it announces itself as the product of the subconscious and, at the same time, feels more acutely real than anything experienced in our waking hours.

Another odd thing: I have this thought even as I dream the dream.

I'm in the water, fighting to stay up. There's no boat in sight. Remembering the descriptions the others gave of a sinking vessel, I rotate and find it behind me.

Outlined against a sky pinholed with stars, nosing down so sharply the rotator blades poke up through the surface at its stern. A blink of electric light behind the windows of the bridge, brief as lightning. It shows I'm not alone. Other bodies riding the thick swells around me. Some treading water, chins up. Some facedown longer than a held breath would allow.

Bridge is one of them. Still swimming. I see her, try to go to her, but the water hardens into icy slush.

When a wave washes over my head, the world is muffled, replaced by the mute simplicity of the water. The alien singing rising up. The voice of the ocean itself.

Then I'm breaking through again, snapping at breath. The night shattered by screams. A voice that doesn't belong to the dream.

It belongs to Belfountain. To my sister.

45

IT'S COMING FROM THE KITCHEN, FRANNY.

I'm off the sofa and rounding the dining room corner when she crashes into me.

"It came in!" she shouts into my chest. "It came *inside*!"

Whatever she's referring to isn't visible in the kitchen. There are the broken plates and a saucepan I'd heard her fling off the counter as she came my way, but nothing else.

Franny breaks away from me and runs down the elevated walkway toward the bedrooms, where she huddles with Bridge at the far end. I signal to her to stay where she is as Jerry comes up from the great room to join me.

"What's going on?" he asks.

"I don't know. Franny thinks she saw—"

"Saw *what*? I thought it was your shift!"

"Is it?" I glance over at my watch on the coffee table, the timepiece we were using to designate our turns to be awake, but it's too far away to make out what it says. "I was—Ezra didn't wake me up. What time—"

"*Shit*, Aaron."

Jerry is about to curse me out, or maybe throw a fist my way, when he looks behind him. "Where's Ezra?"

He'd been on the other extension of the sofa from me before the start of his shift when I drifted off. Not there now.

Jerry and I turn to look at the far end of the kitchen at the same time. The pantry door is slightly ajar. I start toward it with Jerry at my shoulder, his breath whistling and catching in his throat.

"Hold up," he says. He looks in the drawers, the sink, opens the dishwasher. "All the knives are gone. Everything."

"Someone took them?"

He shakes his head. "There's sure as hell nothing here we can use."

"Oh my God."

Lauren stands at the entry to the kitchen. Her eyes held by something neither Jerry nor I have noticed.

And then we do.

Jerry's breath doesn't whistle or catch anymore. It just stops.

I lean my body over the blood on the floor. A wide line pushing out from under the door and around its edge, tonguing around the corner, coming faster along the grouted crevices in the floor than over the tiles.

My hand on the knob. Pulling the door open through the crimson pool.

Ezra's blood. Easing out from his stomach as it had his brother's. His body in a self-defensive posture, arms crossed over his front and knees curled up, a question mark on the pantry's concrete.

Jerry nudges me aside. "Oh, *shit*."

It came in. Franny's conclusion after finding the body. *It came inside*. Which means it might still be.

The kitchen door, the one that opens to the garbage bins outside. It's the most likely way the Tall Man would have gained entry. I start down the short hall and flick on the light.

The door is open. Not forced. Unlocked.

I shoulder it closed. Turn the bolt.

"Was it—"

"Yeah. I'll check the front door and make sure the others are safe," I tell Jerry. "You search the rest of the place."

Lauren has joined Franny and Bridge outside the bedrooms. None of them are speaking but it's clear Lauren has told them about Ezra. Even after I confirm the front door is secure and stand with them none of us say anything. None of us touch.

When Jerry returns, he comes at me.

"You were supposed to be on watch," he says, raising his index finger and jabbing the air inches from my chest.

"I know that. I—"

"It was up to *us*!"

"Jerry, listen. Ezra didn't wake me up. That was the way it was supposed to work."

"Or you don't remember him waking you up. Like you don't remember how to be a doctor."

"No, not like that."

"Oh for *fuck*—" He slides a hand over his face as if wiping a set of darker intentions away. "You've got so many excuses, you'll have to forgive me for not being able to keep up with the bullshit."

"What's just happened—you're hurting more than I could ever imagine. But everything's changed now, so we—"

"You're right about that, Dr. Quinlan. It's all changed." Jerry circles his hands in front of him, his body searching for something to do, something to strike at. "I don't have brothers anymore. It was *your* turn to make sure nobody got in, but they did. And unless that psycho has his own goddamn key, somebody opened the door for him."

I hear what Jerry is saying. We all do. His accusation isn't that I might have welcomed the Tall Man inside, but that I killed Ezra myself. I might suspect the same of me if I was in Jerry's position, reeling off the cocktail of his rage, his fear.

The thing is, I *am* feeling his fear. It's what allows me to see how all of us are standing at a point where everything will be decided. Yet I have no idea how to direct this moment, how to bring us back to a place where we can preserve the narrowing chance of saving ourselves.

"I would never hurt Ezra," I say.

"That's *wonderful*. What am I supposed to do with that, Aaron? Because here's the thing: you're not my family. I don't *know* you." He swings around to take in Franny and Bridge. "Any of you."

Jerry is bouncing on the balls of his feet. A boxer's dance.

"Don't hit him."

He looks over at Bridge, his fingers curling into fists.

"Please don't hit him," she says.

Her words add invisible sandbags to his legs. The hands stop circling the air and loosen, but only a little, his fists now opened to show their hollow cores.

"I'm not staying here," he says.

At first, I take him to mean in this spot, this chilly, slate-tiled foyer with the rib cage chandelier hanging above us. But he moves to the door and it's clear he means he won't stay in the lodge.

"Lauren?"

He pauses for her to join him. I'm anticipating his disappointment when she refuses. But as Jerry starts for the door, she goes after him. When I put my hand to her shoulder, she spins around.

"This is a mistake," I say.

"He's my brother."

She looks into me. It allows me to see something too.

This is how families operate. They forgive, they bail each other out. But they can't forget the walls that define them, how they decide who's allowed in and who must be kept out.

"He's my brother," Lauren says again, and is the first out when Jerry opens the door.

46

EZRA'S GRAVE ISN'T NEARLY AS DEEP AS HIS TWIN'S.

Franny and Bridge help as much as they can with the shoveling, but they're as tired and broken as I am. After singlehandedly pulling his body from the lodge to the spot next to where Elias lies, it's all I can do to fit him into the long groove in the ground and cover him with loose soil.

That night, we're putting away the dishes when Bridge points out that Jerry and Lauren didn't take any food with them.

"They'll be hungry," I say. "Which means they'll come back in the morning when it's light out."

This doesn't come out sounding particularly believable. But all we have is the performance of hope and we stick to the script.

• • •

I stay awake all night. It gives me time to form the lie I plan on telling Franny in the morning. The announcement that Bridge and I are going to the fence's gate to check for new supplies, when in fact we'll head into the woods to find another entrance to the underground hallway where we saw the Tall Man and the witch.

But at sunrise, when Franny shuffles into the great room and I tell her this, she does the opposite of what I thought she would. She insists on coming along.

"We can't leave the door open," I say. "Someone has to stay."

"It's not going to be me. I *won't* be left alone, Aaron. I won't."

"We should tell her," Bridge says, appearing in the bedroom hallway behind her.

"Tell me what?"

I step up onto the dining room's platform, pull out chairs for the two of them.

"Have a seat."

The story of the camp, the key, the murderous beings that live inside. How Bridge and I believe whatever was going on down there is connected to Dad. Franny listens to all of it with her head lowered so that I vacillate between thinking she's crying or sleeping.

"Our father," she announces when I'm done. "I'll be honest. I wasn't too blown back to find out about the secret second family thing. But this? Didn't see it. You got me there, Dad."

She slaps her knees. The only thing that's missing is actual laughter.

"It's why we're here," Bridge says.

"I don't doubt that, honey. But here's my one reservation. Why should we do what he wants us to?"

"Dad brought me here. Before."

Franny looks the way I probably did when Bridge told me the same thing.

"Why'd he do that?"

"I think it was to show me everything he'd done. Show me the truth."

"Couldn't he have just sent us postcards or something?" Franny asks, her exasperation reddening her face into an eraser atop a thin, yellowed pencil. "'So sorry for being evil and insane. Move on with your lives and don't look back. Love, Daddy'?"

"I didn't say he was *sorry*," Bridge says. "I think he just wanted us to *see*."

This stops Franny. Her body transformed to a wax figure in the first stage of its melting.

"It makes me crazy too," I say to her. "The idea of submitting to Dad's plan— whatever it is—it makes me sick. But this is his place, Franny. Belfountain is his brain. Which means we have to find out its language. We need—"

"We need to find out who he was," Franny says.

"We need to find Mom," Bridge says.

47

BRIDGE LEADS THE WAY ALONG THE GREEN TRAIL WITH ME AND FRANNY BEHIND her. I don't like having her exposed as the first in line but she's got the compass and she's the only one who can read it right.

"This way," Bridge says, striking out off the trail where I wouldn't have guessed we should.

I've been here twice before, yet this part of the forest feels particularly unfamiliar. The trees appear closer together than elsewhere, the trunks of the birches peeling and huddled. It prevents any view farther than twenty feet or so. It also throws every *crack* and *crunch* our feet make back at us.

When we reach the camp we stop to figure where the second underground entry point might be. Bridge thinks it's some distance beyond the clearing.

We walk through the high grass of the camp's grounds trying to imagine the children who would have run here, laughed, and played Capture the Flag, but nothing comes.

"It's like a cemetery," Bridge says. And even though it's not like a cemetery in any obvious way, it seems to me that she's right. A place of markers for the dead, stand-ins for lives of unguessable shape.

As we go, I estimate that if the hallway we saw through the porthole window runs more or less straight, we're passing over it now. If I'm right about that, the most likely second entrance will come at the opposite end.

We're into the forest again. I'm about to suggest we've gone too far when a ridge rises up from the ground like a partly collapsed wall. Fern covered and leaning away from us. A dozen feet to the top.

In the center of it, a gaping mouth. Nearly perfectly oval, perfectly dark, the stones on the visible part of its floor black as coal nuggets. A cave.

We climb up without a word between us. It takes longer than the modest slope of wild thyme and jutting limestone would lead you to believe. At the top we look back the way we've come, and I'm so ready to see the Tall Man at the base that for a moment he's there, starting after us, effortless and swift. And then, in the next instant, he evaporates like a shadow when the sun goes behind a cloud, and there's only the bunched trees that, from this elevation, look oozy and squat.

The entrance isn't large, only twice my body width and a foot shorter than I am when standing. I know because I'm upright now. Walking to the edge of the darkness and peering inside. A trickling rivulet of water rushing toward my shoe as if it recognizes something.

We turn our headlamps on, revealing circles of yellow on the damp stone floor. The illumination only works to make the walls feel closer than they were in darkness. The bulbs and joints of the rock wall. The sharp fins that jut down from the ceiling. As we advance, the motion of the beams lend the rock a lurching animation, its arrowhead edges and zigzagged cracks grabbing and retreating.

It's why we almost fall into the hole.

An opening in the cave floor that marks its farthest point. It appears to be a natural formation until we gather close to its edge. See the concrete steps heading steeply down into its depths.

"Doesn't look too stable," I say.

"And I don't feel too stable, so maybe I'll go first," Franny says, and starts down.

The stairs are so narrow and steep it requires us to descend in side steps. We have to hold our beams down at our feet to prevent slippage, as any of us falling would take out those below.

While clearly built by industrial means, these stairs are far more basic and hastily constructed than those that led to the door with the porthole window. I try to occupy my thoughts with how it was done, holding at bay the claustrophobia that sounds in my ears as a shrill ringing of tinnitus. A noise that hides, just beneath it, the breath and scratch of a human shriek.

"Wait," Franny says, farther below than I thought she was. "There's something here."

Bridge and I join her, and the three of us take up the entire breadth of the tunnel that is now level and starts away into a hallway with concrete floors, walls, and ceilings. But there's also something else. A barrier that separated where we are now from the rest of the hallway. A square of plate metal smashed off its hinges, now leaning up against the wall.

"Somebody fought their way in," Franny says.

We study the metal as if reading it. And in return it relates an episode of violence and desperation.

"All the dents and scratches are on the inside," I say. "It was a fight to get out."

Not that it makes a difference now. This is the page of Belfountain's story we least want to turn but have to. A trail of blood, not bread crumbs, has led us here. And inside is where the witch lives.

48

THE CEILINGS ARE LOW AND COMPOSED OF PERFORATED PARTICLEBOARD THAT looks like domino tiles. On the walls, randomly placed landscape paintings (some higher than eye level, some at the waist). Oils of frothing seashores and sunlit groves, all unsigned but probably the work of the same artist, considering the consistent palette of colors. The first rooms off the hallway are bedrooms of identical size, not quite prison cells but equipped with only the simplest comforts: single beds, corkboards spotted with thumbtacks over foldout desks. Put together, it suggests a place that's part bomb shelter, part Siberian hotel, part mental hospital.

"You think Dad did those paintings?"

You'd think that Franny would be more urgently interested in what might have gone on here. Yet her question is the one I'm most curious about too. There's the overwhelming sense that we are closer to our father now than we'd ever come in our lives under the same roof with him. No matter how awful or strange the things that occurred here, these halls were his true home.

"They're his," Bridge answers before I can.

"Why are you so sure?"

"Because he thought he was an artist. Just not the normal kind."

"So the paintings—"

"A hobby," she says. "His real work is what he made here."

Once we're past the bedrooms, the hallway meets another running off to the left. We shine our lights down its length and see that it's the same one where we'd seen the old woman when we'd come down from the walk-in freezer. There's the blood on the floor and walls, now dried into footprints like a choreography map. The metal rim around the porthole window where I'd pressed my nose glints sixty feet away. Which makes where we're standing now the exact spot where the Tall Man had appeared.

The hallway we'd entered through continues ahead before coming to a wall. The entire complex, from what we've discovered so far, is shaped like a T.

"Straight, or down that way?" I ask.

"This room looks bigger than the others," Bridge says, starting down the hallway to the left and slipping through the first doorframe.

"Bridge!" Franny calls out, but I'm ahead of her, almost tripping over a nest of wires and some kind of electronics component of black dials and knobs. I lurch through the doorframe and my headlamp flashes over Bridge's back, standing rigid, a few feet inside.

"You okay?"

I bend and pick up a steel strip of the kind that houses power cords and wield it in front of me. But as I stand and play my light over the space we're in, I can't spot the witch or the Tall Man. Yet what I can see stops me the same as it stopped Bridge.

"It happened here," she says.

The room is double the width of the ones with the beds but much longer, maybe forty feet from one end to the other. Aside from a few desks and toppled office chairs, the only furniture is a number of similarly shaped boxes set upon stainless steel platforms, each set waist-high, their legs on wheels like gurneys. The boxes themselves are made of brownish metal, with electric cables feeding out of their sides, some of which lead to outlets in the wall and others to computer terminals on the worktables (or used to, as most of the computers lie smashed on their sides on the floor).

The number of boxes, angled and body-sized, puts me in mind of a showroom in a discount funeral home.

"There're names on them," Bridge says, walking between the boxes and letting her hand stroke their curved metal lids.

Eight. The same number as the combined Quinlan families.

"This one says Jerry," Bridge says.

Franny passes me to join Bridge before she too stops at one of what, considering their metallic smoothness, I don't think of as boxes anymore, but pods.

"This one's yours," Franny says.

She's looking at me strangely. Her mouth hanging open in a consuming, skeletal way that reminds me of the Tall Man.

I can see my name on the pod even before I start to approach. *AARON*. Spelled out in those adhesive letters on a gold foil background you see stuck on roadside mailboxes.

My hands are on the edges of the lid before I'm aware of moving close enough to reach for it. The idea that, if I lift it open, I will find myself inside arrives with such force it holds me still. I'm here, breathing in the bunker's filtered air, my body at my command. Yet the unseen contents of the pod have overtaken these formerly reliable tests of reality. If the cool metal at the ends of my fingers is a coffin, the dead man within is more present and alive than the one who is about to look down on him.

"You have to," Bridge says.

The lid rises and it's me doing it. It's me, aware of how I'm about to be ruined like the child who nudges open the door to his parents' bedroom to witness who they truly are, the things they do that cannot be understood.

There is no body. Only water.

So lightless in its steel container that it appears black as bitumen, reflecting my headlamp without allowing any illumination to penetrate the surface. I place my palm on it and I feel its resistance, the whole weight of my hand held up as if it were no more than a sheet of paper. The lid falls fully open, and the vibration sends a half dozen silver ripples inward from the sides that blend and diminish within seconds, leaving the liquid smooth once more.

I've seen isolation tanks on TV, read magazine features on spas that feature individual tubs filled with saline water so that you rest on the surface and meditate or sleep or, as I'm sure I would, bang on the lid and demand to be let out. The pod in front of me is like those in some respects, but unlike them in others. The screen, for instance. How the whole interior side of the lid is transparent plastic, semicircular, glowing faintly blue.

"Here," Franny says, picking up a narrow console from the floor. Two cords run from it to the side of the pod. "Maybe these do something."

The console has three dials on its face and two switches. She tries the first of these. Nothing. When she flicks the second, it begins.

The pod's curved screen comes to life. Images—some moving, others still—sharpen into focus. The quality of the visuals is unlike anything I've ever seen: three-dimensional but without the cutout fakery of the effect when seen through the glasses they hand out in cinemas. This has a genuine suppleness and veracity. There's a soundtrack too. Speakers I can't see but must be located both in the pod's lid and beneath the water's surface, as it comes from all around, causing the water to tremble slightly so that the motion gives it the appearance of an oil slick sliding and spreading over its surface.

It takes longer than it should to recognize what it is. Once I do, I watch. Franny and Bridge come to stand on either side of me.

"What is it?" Bridge asks.

"It's the movie of my life," I say.

49

IN FACT, IT'S SOMETHING BETWEEN A SLIDESHOW AND A MOVIE. A COMBINATION OF images appearing for differing lengths of time—some remain on screen for close to a full minute, others flashing so quickly I can hardly make them out—and a similarly varied range of sounds. Phrases of music, effects both quiet and deafening (a shattered glass, crashing tide, orgasmic moan). Pieces of random-seeming facts conveyed in a neutral, androgynous voice, like excerpts from AM radio advertising. Together it's disconcerting, transfixing. Simultaneously unlike lived experience and an amplification of it. Like a dream. Like art.

Some of it is shaped as scenes with compressed beginnings and ends. Lisa Gerber breaking up with me at my locker in eleventh grade. Mom letting me hold Bridge for the first time in her maternity-ward room. A fistfight I lost to some guy who thought I was looking covetously at his girlfriend (I was) from the other side of a pool table.

Most of it, though, is vaguer, less coherent than a story. Snapshots. Pictures of faces (friends growing up, a favorite med school prof, ex-lovers) and buildings (the Cape Cod–style house where we grew up, my high school viewed from the parking lot). Younger versions of Franny and Mom. Images that are discernible but also muted in some way, blurred or fogged or bleached. The thudding machetes and gurgled screams from *overseas*. Places on bodies where surgical steel split skin but never the patients' faces. Close-ups that are too close up to take in the whole.

The picture that takes my breath away most is the fuzziest of all of them, but it remains on the screen longer than the others.

There are the tortoiseshell glasses set upon a small, bluish nose. The hair finger-combed to the side. The cheeks, round and smooth. Harmless.

His voice too. Subdued, slightly Southern flavored, polite. Speaking some of the words and sentences I remember best.

Strong enough for a spoon to stand up in it . . .
A castle in the middle of an endless wood named Belfountain . . .
Have to go, have to go. I'll see you when I see you.

"Daddy," Bridge says.

When his image is replaced by another, I'm finally able to pull my attention away from the screen. The other pods all have cords running out of them connected to consoles with dials and switches. All of them individual movie houses to float in. Each with their own show, their own life.

Franny scans her headlight over the other pods as Bridge and I do, as if measuring to see if any have moved on their own since we entered.

"What are they?" she asks.

"I don't know exactly."

"You think I—you think we were *made* in those things?"

"No. Not physically, anyway. But maybe in some other way."

"*What* way?"

"Our past. A version of it. The stuff we think makes us who we are.

It's all here." I point to the pod two over from us labeled *FRANNY*. "And that's you."

As Franny approaches the pod, horror reshapes her expression in a rictus of anticipated pain, but her body shuffles closer anyway. Her limbs advancing with the terrible need of the undead.

"Aaron?" Her hands grip the pod's lid as she looks back at me.

"You don't have to do this."

"I'm not sure that's true."

"We can wait. Come back later. We can walk away and—"

"I'm going to be *inside* here, aren't I?"

Franny stares at the pod and I honestly don't know what she will do next. I'm not sure she will ever move again.

"I always knew you could fit me in a box," she says finally. "I just never thought I'd be around to see mine."

She starts to shake with the same wracking, noiseless sobs as Bridge and me. As I watch her, I can see that, for all of us, it's equal parts confused emotion and panic.

She opens the lid.

Over Franny's shoulder I watch a few seconds of her slideshow-movie on the pod's screen before looking away. It feels like an invasion of privacy, or something even deeper than that, more perverse. There are things I know will be there that I don't want to see. All the years of doing whatever she had to do to buy a fix, the pornography of addiction. The long stretches of nothingness mistaken for bliss. Nate will be there too. The fragments of a brief life poorly recalled, a child loved and neglected and lost.

"None of this is real, is it?"

Based on her words alone it isn't clear whether Franny's question is asked of our being here or the authenticity of the images played out over the screen. I can only tell what she's referring to by how shattered she is.

The "real" is her. The Mr. Turtle pool she loved. Eli Einstein, her middle school crush. Nathaniel Quinlan, her son.

"He can't—he can't take my *baby* away from me! Not a second time. He wouldn't do that, would he? He wouldn't do that to his *daughter*?"

She closes the lid on her pod and backs away from it as if expecting something to push its way out from inside.

I open my arms to Franny. She enters my embrace as accidentally as a ghost ship floats sideways into harbor.

We only separate when we hear the soundtrack of Bridge's life.

One-ah, two-ah, three-ah . . . diarrhea!

Air rushing past ears, then the crash. Bubbles squirming up to the surface, followed by the density of the water, muffled as the grave.

The Day My Big Brother Saved My Life. More coherent than any of the other memories contained within my pod or Franny's. The movie playing on the screen looks and sounds more vivid, more simultaneously poetic and terrifying, than what I carry with me.

Tick-tock! Tick-tock! Tick-tock!

Jump to: Me and Bridge playing Hook and Wendy, dill pickles for swords.

Jump to: My face, twisting, at the realization that my sister can't breathe.

Jump to: The X-Acto blade in my hand. Bridge's point of view looking up at me, her breathing calm, and whatever she conveys through her eyes settles me, lets me bring the blade to her throat.

Jump to: Darkness.

The screen and speakers are lifeless for so long I assume the show's over, that this is how Bridge's story begins and ends for her. But then there's a voice that comes up out of the black water of the pod. Dad. Walking next to her through a breeze-cooled forest, speaking against a backgrounded concert of birdsong.

Where does the path lead after it ends?

Bridge closes the lid.

Both of us look around. Franny isn't here.

We scan the long room with our lights, both wishing for and dreading a glimpse of her rising up from behind one of the pods where she'd been hiding.

I can tell Bridge is holding herself back from calling out for her the same as I am.

We back away from Bridge's pod and turn to face the doorway where we came in. Stepping as quietly as we can over the scattered wires and equipment, our beams concentrated on the wall on the opposite side of the hallway like a spotlight awaiting the appearance of a stand-up comedian.

We're paused in the doorframe, stretching our necks forward to peek around the corner, when a figure steps into the spotlight.

"You need to see this," Franny says.

50

WE FOLLOW HER TO WHERE THE BLOODIED HALLWAY MEETS THE ONE WE CAME
in through. She heads to the left, the direction we didn't go, where
there are only two rooms. One is a kitchen: cupboards ripped from the
walls; a still-running fridge that emits a rank, meaty odor as I pass; a
table and floor littered with the empty packaging of frozen waffles and
corn dogs.

"Eggos and Pogos," Bridge whispers.

The other room is an office. Filing cabinets lining one wall, and on
the other side a wooden desk, heavy and broad as the kind school prin-
cipals sit behind. This is where Franny goes. Spreading out a number
of files over its surface like a magician showing a set of oversized cards
before impossibly revealing the one you'd selected while her back was
turned.

"I found these in that first filing cabinet," she says. "The one marked
'Subject Summaries.'"

She's been crying. But as before, her tears make no sound, as if her feelings come from a deeper place than that.

"We should go," Bridge says.

"She's right, Franny. We've been here too long. We can think this through and—"

"Read this," she says, picking up one of the files and offering it to me.

The file's blank cover opens on its own like the fairy-tale books at the beginning of the kids' movies of my youth. The narrator's voice-over reading aloud the opening words.

FRANNY QUINLAN

Subject Profile

Birthplace: Seattle.
Current residence: Seattle.

SUMMARY

Frances Quinlan ("FRANNY"), 31, sister to AARON and younger sister, BRIDGE. Middle child of the Eleanor Quinlan family. Troubled, restless childhood. Initially shoplifting, school truancy, allegiance to rebellious social groups. As early as middle school: drugs. Daily pot use escalating to heroin and crack cocaine after high school. Adulthood of severe addiction.

Son, Nathaniel ("Nate"), born five years earlier from START POINT. Father a fellow addict (unnamed), moved east, no contact since prior to birth. Nate is recalled only vaguely but powerfully: sweet-faced, angelic. Asthmatic.

Nate dies in rooming house while being overseen by fellow addicts as FRANNY was out seeking crack cocaine. Even after her return to the rooming house, it takes over two hours—following

a hit from her pipe—for FRANNY to remember the child and find
his body.

This latter fact is <u>KEPT SECRET</u> by the subject.

FRANNY employs various coping mechanisms that allow her to appear "recovered." In addition to her (so far) successful drug-
free life since Nate's death, she has resolved to devote her
remaining years to helping other addicts. She insists that
she's "changed." She sometimes believes this, but at other
times her inner weaknesses remind her—

Franny reaches over and turns the page, and the next one. When
she stops, she stabs her index finger into a page with the header "Origin
Identity."

"Now this," she says.

LYNN WEST

Origin Identity of FRANNY QUINLAN

Birthplace: Sacramento, CA
Current residence: Los Angeles

SUMMARY

Lynn West ("WEST"), homosexual, unmarried but since 2012 in
on-and-off relationship with Nadia Pender, San Diego high
school teacher. Long-distance relationship resulting in multiple breakups and jealousy. Currently works as sound editor in
film production, primarily animation. Non-drug user. No children.

Raised as one of four children in fundamentalist Christian
household. Only West child to remain committed to her faith.

Historically, WEST has dated exclusively using Christian social media apps. Seeks husband (see: Facebook feed)—a posture
presumably for the benefit of her parents/family (possibly
also employer?) to whom she has not "come out."

WEST recently purchased bungalow in Silver Lake. No pets.

Hobbies: hiking, reading, movie buff (mostly kids films,
foreign animation, Studio Ghibli, etc.). Fondness for out-
of-doors. Devotes vacation time on outings to—

Bridge pulls the file out of my hand. Replaces it with one she's picked up from the desk.

"Let's read this one together," she says.

BRIGIT QUINLAN

Subject Profile

Birthplace: Seattle
Current residence: Seattle

SUMMARY

Brigit (called BRIDGE by family and close friends), aged 14.
Emotionally intuitive. Academically average, athletically inclined (dance, soccer).

Keeper of a journal she believes no one but her father has
read. This is why he seems to understand her at a level more
precise than even her brother, AARON.

Father brought her alone to Belfountain when she was 5. This
leaves her with conflicting feelings of being CHOSEN as well
as CONFUSION about the event itself. She has the strong sense
that her father is not a good man. But she remains divided in
her theories on the possible NATURE OF HIS CORRUPTION.

Personality (and her physical self) marked by a previous episode of survival. Her brother, AARON, a medical student at
the time, performed an emergency tracheotomy on her using an
X-Acto blade from a fishing tackle box (see: IMAGE INVENTORY)
while on holiday at the Quinlan lakeside cabin. BRIDGE's feelings about this are complicated. She is grateful to AARON, but
blames her father's absence at the time of the event. Where
was he at the most frightening moment of her life?

Above defines her operating mode as one of DISTRUST.

It's my turn to flip ahead to the second set of paperclipped papers
in the file the same way Franny pushed me. This is what Bridge is most
terrified of. She reads with her cheek pressed against my arm, her lips
moving as they mouth the words.

OLIVIA GOLDSTEIN

Origin Identity of BRIDGE QUINLAN

Birthplace: Tacoma, WA
Current residence: Seattle

SUMMARY

Olivia Goldstein ("GOLDSTEIN") is the eldest of three daugh-
ters of Barry and Lee Goldstein. Father: Corporate finance.
Mother: Recent return to employment at private accounting
firm.

GOLDSTEIN deemed academically "gifted" according to school
assessments. Additional proficiency in athletics, primarily
track (state finals).

Accomplishments understood as particularly notable given GOLD-
STEIN's history of periodic, severe depression. Episodes of
self-harm, including hospitalization following suicide attempt

(scissor wound to throat). <u>Note:</u> This injury to be accounted
for by BRIDGE as the scar from the emergency tracheotomy performed by brother, AARON (see above).

Currently on daily dosage of Sarafem. Talk therapy has yielded
no previous trauma or sexual/physical abuse. Assumed chemical
imbalance by psychiatric evaluations.

Stated career goal: marine biology. Love of marine life—
whales, dolphins, sharks. Maintains extensive aquarium in home
bedroom.

Bridge closes the file. Looks up at me with her finger tracing the
outline of the scar on her neck.

"I did this?" she asks. "I did it to *myself*?"

"I don't know, Bridge. I don't—I can't put it together."

"There are two people," she says, the back of her hand slapping at her
file. "Two people! But which one is me?"

"I think we need to slow down—"

"One is me, and one is somebody else," she carries on, not listening
to me or anything other than her own thoughts. "Except I'm the fake.
The other person, the one I don't know—the one who is *so sad*—that's
who I really am."

I have no idea how it was done. I don't know what it means for us in
anything other than this moment. But the thing is, I feel certain that what
Bridge has just said is true. My little sister, the one person in the world
I would die for, have wanted to make proud, is a forgery. Franny too.
Which means I'm no more real than they are, no matter that the story
that played out on the screen of my pod is the only story I've ever known.

Franny staggers back from the desk. The paperclipped pages falling
from her hand and fluttering to the floor like a graceless, multi-winged
bird.

"Something was done here," I say. "Done to us. I'm not—"

"Dad was—he was *never* real?"

I reach out to Franny in case she's about to pass out, but she jumps back from contact.

"My *child*," she says. "Nate never *existed*?"

"I don't know. I don't know," I say, and would keep saying forever rather than tell her the thought that is gaining weight in my mind, in the very core of me, more certain than the face of the girl I lost my virginity to or my first day leading a procedure in the surgical theater.

No, you never had a son. Nate was never born. Never lived, never died. He's haunted you your entire life but he's even less than a ghost.

Franny sifts through the other files on the desk. I see Jerry's name on one, Lauren's on another. She pulls out the one with my name on it, but I don't touch it.

"Aren't you going to read yours?"

"Not now."

"What? Don't you—"

"Not *now*."

I fold the file in half and stuff it into my pocket. When Franny hands all the others to me, I do the same with them.

"He'll be coming back soon," Bridge says.

I start away but Franny grabs me by the arm.

"Why are we leaving if everything is here?" she says.

"We don't know what this is."

"It's us. It's all we have."

"That doesn't mean we have to stay."

"Then what *does* it mean, Aaron?"

We're flesh and blood. We feel and remember and love. Even if none of us are who we think we are.

"It means we have to go," I say.

51

WE MAKE OUR WAY BACK PAST THE AMATEUR LANDSCAPE PAINTINGS. FRANNY AND I keep our eyes ahead when we pass the other, bloodied hallway that leads to the room of pods. But Bridge flashes her light down its length.

"Mom?"

Franny doesn't go back but I do. And see the same thing Bridge does.

The old woman stands in front of the door with the porthole window. Then she steps closer. Her feet bulging and bare. The pale blue hospital gown open at the front, a peepshow of folds and moles and dried blood.

The witch.

I hear this. Think it's Bridge before realizing it's me.

Our lights brighten her features as she approaches. The pockets of yellow in the corners of her eyes. The pair of scissors held in her hand.

"Go," I say.

The skin of the old woman's feet meeting the cracked concrete floor like the slap of meat on the butcher's board.

"GO!"

52

THERE'S A CATEGORY OF FEAR THAT DENIES YOU THE AIR TO SCREAM.

It's why we're so quiet as we run through the steel portal that's been wrenched from its hinges. The only sound that reaches us is the old woman's breath. Rattling and semi-verbal, as if searching for names or curses that have slipped her mind.

The stairs were difficult to come down and are now almost impossible to ascend. I've situated myself at the end of the line so that I'm able to put my shoulder to Franny's back. We advance like a worm. Stretching thin and muscling tight, over and over.

The air reaches me before the light. A chestful of weightlessness. It doesn't last long. Once we've emerged from the cave, the effort we've made arrives in a thousand needlepoints of pain.

Franny is the only one to look back. Whatever she sees makes her jump.

Spilling and sliding but never quite crumbling altogether; she makes her way down the ridge like a skier losing and regaining control, over and over.

Bridge goes next. I'm about to follow when I feel the witch's touch.

The cold scratch of her hand on my cheek, the fingers hard as bone.

Falling down the ridge after leaping from its edge.

Getting up after blacking out.

Making it back to the gravel parking area outside the lodge.

I can only confirm the last of these because that's where I am now. Blinking away the light after being shielded by the forest's canopy, watching Bridge and Franny rush to the lodge's front door. My eyes catching on something on the edges of what they can see.

He's standing over the twins' graves. His height accentuated all the more by his head being lowered. The stillness of a ceremonial moment of silence.

Bridge seems to sense the Tall Man, not see him, as she slows even with her back to him.

"Get inside!"

It's my voice, but it comes out stronger than I am, more aware of what is happening and the things most likely to come next. It doesn't appear that Bridge hears me. But the Tall Man does.

He raises his head, and the silver hatchet, glinting and slick as if carved from ice, slides up his pant leg. His mouth hanging open as before, but now it reads as anguish instead of hunger. Or perhaps it was always this way. These two absences combined as one suffering.

"*Run!*"

I tell Bridge this. I tell myself.

I catch up to her at the same time we join Franny already pounding at the door.

"Open it!" I'm shouting even as I grasp the handle and find it locked.

"We *left* it open!" Franny says.

Bridge is the only one of us keeping up with the facts of the moment. The only one watching the Tall Man.

"He's coming," she says.

The pruning shears. The ones I took from the shed. Is there time to fish them out of my windbreaker pocket and—and what? The thought goes nowhere. I keep pounding at the door. Franny joins me with her brittle fists.

The door hears us. The wood gives way to the gray space behind it.

I let Franny and Bridge in first, bracing for the hatchet to swing into my back.

"Aaron!"

Bridge has my hand, pulls me in as the door clicks shut.

"Is it him?" Jerry asks. "*Aaron!* Is it—"

"Yes!"

"Does—"

CRACK.

All of us jump back as the silver line of the hatchet's blade cuts through the door. It stays there like the tip of a tongue, tasting the difference between inside and outside, before it's pulled away.

CRACK!

The second strike meets the first at an angle, slicing an X into the wood. Weakening it.

We'd been quiet until this. Now all of our voices come together in a chorus of pleading. I don't see her but Lauren's voice joins in too. Only Bridge maintains anything resembling a coherent thought.

"Leave us alone!" she shouts through the door.

The rest of our voices fall off, waiting for the next strike to come. It doesn't.

We don't hear him leave. There's no way to see him as none of us dare go close to the side windows to look, yet we feel him go as if we do.

"Why'd he stop?" Lauren asks nobody in particular, and nobody answers her.

It prompts me to reach into my pocket. Pull out the files we'd taken and hand Lauren and Jerry the ones with their names on them. They hold them without opening them.

"What's this?" Lauren asks.

"It's what Dad kept in the cellar of the gingerbread house," I say. "It's us."

53

"THIS IS BATSHIT," JERRY SAYS, SLAPPING HIS FILE ONTO THE COFFEE TABLE.

We've retreated to the great room, deciding that being away from the door is worth being visible to the forest outside the giant windows. Without being asked Lauren tells us how they came back to the lodge for something to eat. When they found us gone, they lingered, guessing something was wrong.

"So what is it? Other than that thing out there?" Lauren asked us. "What's wrong?"

Bridge and Franny did most of the talking. The discovery of the summer camp, the second cave entrance, the pods, the old woman with the scissors. As they traded the story back and forth between them, Jerry remained silent. Until now.

"Are you *listening* to this, Lauren?"

"Yes."

"So you agree it's bullshit."

"I don't think I do."

"Can I ask why the fuck not?"

"Because it explains so much."

"About why Dad locked us in here?"

"No. About me."

Jerry looks around for someone to return his exasperation. "How about you, doc? You think we're all clones or something?"

"Not clones," I say. "Just not ourselves."

"Because you saw a bunch of tanks with our names on them? That's a hell of a leap."

"I know it's hard to grasp. But think of the scale of this project, Jerry. They've gone to great lengths to keep it secret. So yes, what we're talking about is pretty far past the boundaries of what we know. Far past what's legal too. That's why it's been built way out here. Why there's a fence."

"Why we can't get out," Franny adds.

Jerry shakes his head at me but doesn't have an immediate reply. He's trying to not go where the rest of us have and it's draining him right before our eyes.

"So these isolation tanks," he says eventually. "They put ideas in our heads?"

"They put our whole lives in our heads," Franny says.

"Fake memories."

"Yes, but they don't just overlap with our real memories," I say. "The fake ones are all we have."

"How'd they *do* that? Kill us?" Jerry laughs uncomfortably. "Are we *dead* right now?"

"Maybe," Bridge says.

"So what's that make *this*? A dream?"

"It's not a dream," Franny says.

"One part of it is," Bridge says.

Jerry looks at her. "What part?"

"The dark water. The sinking boat," she says. "The music."

Jerry doesn't shake his head at her as he had at me. It's because he believes her, even if he doesn't believe the rest of it yet.

"How do I know you're not making this up?" he says, addressing this to me.

"You think we're in on this?"

"Could be."

"You're arguing with yourself," Lauren says.

"How's that?"

"You're trying to hold on to your disbelief but you don't have any. It *is* insane. It's also true."

This does it. Jerry has nothing left to fight with. He sits next to Lauren. Opens his mouth and closes it again.

"I didn't bring the twins' files, but I read some of it when we were underground," Franny says. "There was no Delta commercial. They weren't even actors."

"Who were they?" Lauren asks.

"Dentists. They had a practice together in Fort Lauderdale. Two kids each. They had *lives*."

"What about *Better Together*?" Bridge says. "We all saw them on TV. Well, you guys did. 'Ah poop.' That was their *thing*."

"There was no *Better Together*. They must have put that into our heads as part of the background to make Ezra and Elias fit in."

"I can only remember a couple scenes they were in anyway," I say.

"Me too," Franny says.

"No. Only one," Jerry says, and it's true. When I think of either of the twins as TV stars, I can only see them—or the one character they played—in a single sequence. A kid wearing pin-striped shorts, covered in chocolate ice cream, delivering his trademark line to his dad whose anger melted away at his son's overwhelming cuteness as the studio audience uttered a collective *awwwww*.

There's a moment as we take the measure of one another, trying to read who is having the toughest time of it. But we're all equally bewildered. We all look ill.

"I guess it's time to see who I really am," Lauren announces, and opens her file.

It's like watching someone sleep through a nightmare. There's the same twitches, stretches of stillness, winces. A whimper of recognition before she raises her glistening eyes to us.

"My name is Kayla Thomas," she says.

She was a pediatrician in Chicago. Her area of specialization was cancers of the blood. Work that meant everything to her, particularly following her divorce and the loss of her only child. A daughter, Addison, who died in a car accident with her grandfather—Lauren's dad—behind the wheel. She never remarried. Never spoke to her father again.

"I had a daughter," she says, drawing Bridge close against her. "I don't remember anything about her. Not her face, her laugh. Nothing."

Jerry is about to put his arms around her, but stops and pulls away.

"What about Dad?" he says. "The will, the lawyer, the estate. None of that is real either?"

"We can't be sure about that," I say. "There must be someone behind this. It might be him."

"What about the hatchet man? The old woman who came after you," Jerry says. "How do they fit?"

"I have no idea," I say.

"I do," Lauren says. "Belfountain. The haunted forest. It's a fairy tale."

"And every fairy tale needs monsters," Bridge says.

All at once Jerry stands as if discovering the sofa is smoldering under him. He grabs his file off the coffee table and opens it to the first page.

"This is a description of me," he says.

"Keep reading," Franny says. "The second section tells you who you were before."

He turns the page to the Origin Summary memo. Scans what might be the first paragraph or two before closing the file.

"I'm not doing this," he says.

"Who are you?" Franny asks him. "You saw, didn't you?"

"I'm Gerald Oliver Quinlan."

Franny reads his face as if it were the pages from the second part of Jerry's file. "You hurt someone."

"What are you talking about?"

"I thought I had a son who died, but I never did. You thought you were a wounded football hero, but you're not."

"Shut up."

"You did something awful."

"Shut the *fuck up*!"

Hatred. Decisive and boundless. Jerry is capable of it. He shows a flare of it now, directed not just at Franny but all of us.

That's not all I know now that I didn't ten seconds ago.

I carry the same rage in myself.

Whatever I was before this, I was a man familiar with violence. Not the controlled kind of surgery, nor the isolated episode of *overseas*. It happened in my life, gave shape to that life.

I don't know what side I was on, but I had a stomach for it.

More than that. I was good at it.

54

JERRY SWINGS HIS FIST AT ME AND MISSES. MY FIST DOES THE SAME. FINDS THE side of his face, his mouth, his ear.

Bridge and Lauren have to pull us apart. Then the shouting and taunts. The spitting of blood on the rug, the calls for a bandage that Jerry insists he doesn't need.

It all distracts everyone from the fact that I alone didn't read my file. It wasn't intentional. But now that we're all slumped in different chairs, catching our breath, I decide I don't want to know.

Franny is the first to speak.

"There's something more," she says, rising to pull what looks to be a folded, glossy brochure from her back pocket.

"What is it?" I ask.

"I'm not sure. I took it from the same room we got our files."

She unfolds the thick paper and smooths out its creases over the coffee table. The cover page has a diagonally stamped *DRAFT* over its front.

"Why don't you read it for all of us," Lauren says.

YOURSTORY

It's time to be free from history.

It's time for . . . YOURSTORY.

<u>PROSPECTUS</u>

Overview for Investors

Talk therapies. Meditation. Mood-altering pharmaceuticals.

The demand for a new self—a new future—has never been greater than today. But how do we get there?

The problem is that we always return to remembering who we are.

But what if you could change that past? What if you could trade the life you've led for one that's new?

Yourstory is a memory alteration therapy that can literally change the story of our lives.

And in these challenging times, the market for deleted pasts and new beginnings is unquestionably vast.

WHAT IS YOURSTORY?

FOUR STEPS TO A NEW PAST

STEP ONE: Erase

The first step of Yourstory's process is what we call Induced Endpoint, or IE. IE is achieved by a surprisingly simple exercise: physician-controlled euthanasia.

Our research has determined that termination of life, combined with a neural protein "bath" of our own patented devising, is the only method that fully erases our connection to the past. But don't think of it as the

End. Think of it as a light switch. *Flick!* You're gone. *Flick!* You're safely returned to life and ready for a new future.

STEP TWO: Introduce

There are generally two kinds of memories: semantic and episodic. Semantic memories are a baseline of common knowledge, including cultural and historical reference points (how a cell phone operates, who won last year's World Series, the outcome of the Second World War, etc.). These are preserved in the Yourstory process. Episodic memories are the details of personal recollection (your first love, family experiences, the inclinations and aversions created by emotional response). These are erased in IE.

In the second step of Yourstory, patients are introduced to the new lives they've chosen. The physical means by which we achieve this is a combination of cutting-edge technology and ancient meditative tools. Once IE is completed, clients are mildly sedated and placed in specially designed flotation tanks. In this embryonic state of blank—but waking—consciousness, they bear witness to their new lives. Our research has yielded a method of Memory Introduction (MI) that is completely seamless, convincing, and effective.

STEP THREE: Stimulate

The hippocampus. When it comes to memory, this is the control booth of the brain. It's here that our minds link new information together and encode it into memories. By using various techniques of optogenetics, the brain can be artificially stimulated in the same way it would be if experiencing something new or momentous in "real" life.

To make a memory a lasting one, our brains must be attentive to all the senses. That's why with Yourstory, while the MI program is underway, the brain is simultaneously stimulated by neural implants to excite our sense of smell or touch, even our emotions.

STEP FOUR: Implantation Erasure

Of course it's crucial that our clients not be aware that they've been the subjects of a therapeutic procedure (particularly one involving a death experience). The fourth and final step of Yourstory, therefore, erases the memory of the process itself.

Fortunately, this is the easiest part. During the IE, MI, and Stimulation stages, the client is kept in a state of semiconsciousness, so that whatever memory she may

"That's it?" Jerry says.

"There was more, but the pages have been ripped away."

"They *did* that to us?"

"Seems so," Franny says. "Though why I'd pay anybody to change me from a lesbian sound editor into a heroin addict is anyone's guess."

"We weren't clients," Lauren says. "This brochure or whatever—it was for a stock offering. They were planning to go public but still had trials to do. They had to prove it could work."

"Not public trials," I say.

"Experiments," Jerry says. "Us."

"Yourstory," Lauren repeats, weighing the viability of the word itself. "How much you figure people would pay to be someone else? Artificially reincarnated. To die and come back different?"

"A lot," I say.

"More," Jerry says. "Everything they have."

55

SHE TOLD ME SHE WASN'T HUNGRY, BUT I HEAT UP SOME FISH STICKS FOR BRIDGE
and me anyway. We take our plates to the farthest end of the dining table,
the others in the great hall so far off they appear as figures on the opposite shore of a lake.

"You want to talk about any of this?" I say, drawing a fish stick
through a pool of ketchup.

"I think I'm too freaked to talk about it."

"We're going to get out of here, okay?"

"Are you saying that as my big brother? Or just whoever you are?"

"It doesn't matter. I'm saying it. Me."

Bridge picks up a fish stick. Crams the whole thing into her mouth.

"I remember more than just the dark water from before," she says
after she swallows. "Not dreams. Memories."

"How can you tell the difference?"

She looks away at some point over my shoulder as if lip-reading
someone standing there speaking. "It's like meatballs," she says.

"Okay."

"So meatballs all look the same, right? But if you had two different people make them and put them into spaghetti sauce and you ate them, you could tell they didn't come from the same place. They'd *taste* different."

"You're saying these thoughts you have from before—they were made by someone else."

"They weren't made by *anyone*. The memories we have now—the cabin at the lake, our Tuesday dinners together—those were put in our heads. But the memories I'm talking about were lived."

"Homemade meatballs instead of frozen."

She laughs. A sound that's so good to hear I almost gasp.

"Yeah," she says. "Like that."

She clears her throat. The humor replaced by something she's summoning into words out of the darkness.

"There were soldiers. Police. Or men who used to be police," she says. "Men in uniforms who came to our school and took some of the kids away. I remember our teacher crying. Everybody was crying."

"Did they hurt you?"

"No. They asked us questions though."

"Like what?"

"Like 'Do you love your country?' and 'Where were you born?' None of it made sense. And they didn't *seem* mean. They smiled and called us 'buddy' and 'sweetheart.' But that just made them scarier."

For the second time I attempt to eat, but the ketchupped fish stick looks wounded with the others gathered around it in sympathy. I push my plate away.

"Me too," I say. "I remember the police too."

"What happened, Aaron? Was it a war? Were we invaded?"

"I think it was us. Us against ourselves."

"Did we win? The people on the good side?"

"I don't know. I'm pretty sure, whatever it is, it's still going on."

• • •

I'm awake.

I know because Bridge is kneeling next to the sofa. I know because I can smell her fish sticky breath.

"There's something outside," she whispers.

I'm on one of the sofas in the great room. All the lights are off, but I can see the outline of Jerry sitting up in the chair closest to the hearth, staring out the wall of glass. I take a quick scan outside but can't see anything other than the impenetrable tree line.

"What is it?" I ask him.

"I can't tell," he says, his hands whitening with his tightened grip at the edges of the armrests. "Something that wasn't there before."

As if his words enact an external reality, I look outside again and see something that wasn't there before.

It doesn't move. A limbless sapling. A halved flagpole. But those things don't transport themselves into a place where they didn't exist before. They don't watch.

"Go to the bedroom," I tell Bridge. "Lock the door."

"I'm not leaving."

"Bridge, I'm not asking, I'm—"

"It won't make a difference."

Now that she's said it, I hear it as something I've known all along. The lodge's open-concept layout, high ceilings, wall of glass. There's no hiding in Belfountain's castle.

"Okay," I say. "Be ready."

I get up and slide toward the windows. The shape outside detects my approach—I can sense this without it changing position—but even as it comes into clearer focus, it doesn't reveal itself, doesn't respond.

"What are you doing?"

Jerry has come up behind me.

"We can't just wait until there's nothing left," I say, and as I do, I realize that what I believe to be outside, the thing I fear most, isn't the thing standing there, but the forest itself. All of the estate, reaching out from here to its walls as a single organism.

I sidestep to the left, all the way to the wall. Feel for the light switch and turn it on.

The mouth. This comes first. The Tall Man's lips stretched over gray studs of teeth.

He comes at us.

There's an apron of grass between the trees and the window that's been untended long enough that some of it is patches of dirt, some of it grown to ankle height. The Tall Man passes over it soundlessly, a quiet that reaches out from him like an odor.

He comes into the stark illumination of the floodlights and shows himself to be more corpse than phantom, a marriage of decay and grace. And unlike a ghost, he doesn't pass through the wall of glass but stops at it. His eyes, white and bulbous, moving between me and Jerry.

They only stop when they find Bridge.

I back away from the glass and feel Jerry do the same, both of us seeing what he's going to do before he begins to do it. The silver hatchet gripped in both of his gloved hands. Its head rising up over the waxy snarl of his hair.

The sound of it comes a fraction before the impact, as if a glitch in the soundtrack. Not a crack but an impenetrable wash of noise. A wave that drives your head into the ocean's floor.

"Bridge!"

The wall of glass smashed into diamonds, falling over us, biting our skin. I try to find her but I'm blinking through darkness. I bring the back of my hand up to swipe something sharp from my face and it lets me see. The sharp thing was a shard embedded in my forehead. The darkness was blood.

Jerry is shouting. At once close by and in another world. Trying to ward off the Tall Man who is walking into the castle. I don't look back but I can hear him coming. The crunch of his feet over the glass.

Bridge is here. Backing away from the Tall Man, the cold air that blows in and brings the smell of the woods with it.

"Run!"

It's me telling her this, but it's only my grip around her forearm that makes her move. Pulling her over the shards that reach all the way to the stairs up from the great room.

The lodge's front door is already open.

Outside, Franny is there, urging us forward. Lauren is there too. Already running, already gone, a few strides ahead of Franny.

Bridge is out first, then me. The hardness of the air holding us back, a freezing weight in our lungs as if we'd taken a breath of lake water down the wrong way.

The last thing we hear before we throw ourselves into the trees is Jerry's voice. A wordless shrieking coming from inside the lodge. It wavers between a signal of bravery and agony, an unreadable human utterance, animal, prehistoric.

It goes on longer than you'd think a held breath would allow. And when it stops, it doesn't come again.

56

WE DON'T MAKE A CHOICE TO TAKE THE RED TRAIL AWAY FROM THE LODGE. IT'S THE one we start for because it's the one that none of the three of us have gone down so far.

The trail curves more than the others. A meandering through the trees that will play to the Tall Man's strengths. I ready myself for him to plow onto the trail ahead after taking a straight line from the lodge. What will I do when it happens? There must be an attack I could attempt, a self-sacrifice. But nothing occurs to me.

"There!"

Franny is ahead of the rest of us. Now she plunges off the trail, leaping like a deer, gangly and flailing. Bridge goes after her, then Lauren.

I hold my arms up against the thrashing branches, but it doesn't stop them from cutting into the side of my neck, the sharp ends stabbing at my eyes. Even after I've broken through and the cabin is there, I come to the door with my hands up as if in surrender.

Once I'm inside, Bridge locks the door.

The cabin is like the others in layout, though with slightly different furnishings. This one is more committed to a hunter's retreat theme. A camouflage-pattern blanket laid over the top of the sofa's back, oil paintings of ducks flying in formation over marshes with rifle barrels poking up from the reeds, the mounted head of a buck over the archway to the bedrooms.

Bridge follows me into the kitchen and watches as I go through the drawers and cabinets. All the utensils, if there ever were any, have been removed. There's nothing to defend ourselves with any more useful than a salad spinner.

When we return to the living room, Franny is stepping away from the front window. She turns to look at us.

"He's here," she says.

A shattering smash against the cabin door.

"Open up!"

It's Jerry.

"Open! The . . . *door*!"

I'm not going to. I'm thinking about seeing if Bridge could fit through one of the bedroom windows. I'm thinking about charging into whatever is outside and wrapping myself around it, buying some time. But none of this happens. Because Franny goes to the door and opens it.

"Sorry if I *disturbed* you," Jerry says as he strides in and kicks the door closed with the back of his heel.

"Is he after you?"

Jerry looks at Franny as if this is exactly the sort of question he'd expect her to ask. The contempt that comes from being surrounded by weakness, by an entire world of weakness.

"Why don't you take a look for yourself?"

Franny doesn't move.

"What happened back there?" I ask, and Jerry turns his attention to me.

"We had a *problem*. Which you left me to handle."

He opens his hands, stretching the fingers as if to crack their knuckles, but it's only to draw our eyes to his palms. The lines and creases a map of white lines drawn through blood.

"We need to *know*, Jerry," Lauren pleads. "Are you saying—"

"I'm saying you don't need to worry. It's just us now. Just family."

His right hand reaches behind his back and pulls something up from where it had been tucked into his belt. A knife. The chef's blade from the lodge that was among the ones we thought the Tall Man had taken away.

"Where'd you find that?" Franny asks him.

"Where I put it. Along with all the others."

"I don't—"

"You *wouldn't* understand."

He trades the knife from one hand to another. There's an audible click as the handle pulls away from the red glue of his skin.

"That's why when the shit hits the fan you turn to people like me," he goes on. "But God forbid if somebody breaks a nail or a skull, you forget that you were the ones who asked for help in the first place."

"I never asked you to do anything," Franny says.

"See, *that's* what I'm talking about! *That's* the kind of thing I've heard come out of the mouths of entitled bitches like you my whole goddamned life."

"You remember," I say, coming between the two of them as I use my hand at my side to signal Bridge to move away. "Who you were before."

Jerry sees what I'm trying to do, and he grins his toothy grin at me in mock congratulations.

"You're no doctor, Aaron," he says. "But you're not a total shithead either."

"The watch," I say, voicing my observation at the same time I take note of it. "The one Dad gave the twins."

"What about it?"

"You're wearing it."

Jerry looks cross-eyed at the Bulova on his wrist. "Nice, right?"

"Ezra left it with Elias when we buried him."

"And I dug it out," Jerry says. "No point leaving one of the only souvenirs from dear old Dad in the dirt like that."

Jerry shifts focus from the watch to us. Grips the knife in his right hand and waves it in front of him. It pushes the three of us back deeper into the cabin's living room. When the backs of our legs hit the sofa's edge, he holds up his hands for us to stop.

"Seeing as you're *curious*, I don't remember everything," he says. "But yeah, I've got some ideas."

"Who were you?" Lauren asks.

"A serviceman. Maybe a cop. But then I was given another assignment when the priorities got switched up. Domestic security."

"What did you do?"

"The *good* stuff. Illegals. We were given quite a bit of latitude. And what I mean by that is we could do absolutely whatever the fuck we wanted."

Jerry shakes his head as if at the recollection of a college stunt, an accomplishment that, while perhaps foolish, demonstrated the boldness and stamina of his younger self.

"I remember *them*, that's for sure," he says, his amusement now curdling with something else, poisonous even for him. "How terrified they were. Some of them saw us coming and literally shit their pants. And we hadn't even *done* anything yet."

"Why?"

This is Bridge. Her voice firm but without accusation. The steadiness of a prosecutor bringing a witness to the place they must go.

"Why what, sweetheart?"

"Why kill your brothers?"

Jerry shakes his head and gives Lauren a *Can you believe this?* look.

"Well, first off," he says, "they weren't my brothers."

"But you didn't know that when you did it."

"You got me there," he says, making a sucking pop with the inside of his cheek. "I guess I'm just exercising my rights and freedoms. It's what smart people do. So when we got driven up here and I saw there was thirty million on the table and that there was nobody to tell me what I could and couldn't do—well, I seized the day."

"By killing Elias."

"You got to start somewhere. And I started when I walked into that big house and saw that pretty little hatchet by the fireplace. All polished up like this designer feature. I figured I could put a few scratches in it. And I did. But then Ezra heard me working on Elias out in the woods, and I had to leave the blade in him. When we all came out and it was gone—that's when I was sure."

"Sure of what?"

"That the homeless guy—or whoever he is—he'd be my cover. That once he took the hatchet you'd all figure it was him. I mean, I would have done it all anyway most likely. But sometimes the breaks go your way, know what I'm saying?"

He shifts his hungry gaze from Lauren to Bridge, and for the first time I see the potential in him for actions worse than killing. Ways of hurting intended only for the pleasure in delivering the hurt, watching what it did.

"Why did you let us go to the fence?" I ask him, drawing his attention to me instead of them. "It looked like you wanted out as much as the rest of us."

"I couldn't take you all down at the same time. So I had to go with the flow. But even if that gate opened, I doubt any of you would have made it through."

Jerry straightens his knees, stands at his full height. A motion that is the precursor to something else.

"Listen to me," I say, and he does, but only partly. "There's no money. No estate. We didn't know that before. But we do now. Getting rid of them—of us—isn't going to make your cut any bigger."

"Maybe so. Maybe not."

"Jerry, please. We won't say anything—"

He comes at us as I speak and Franny sees it all before I do.

Sees the blade drive into her. Hears the screech of the steel as it grinds against the bottom rung of her ribs. Screams the second before it happens.

The knife is pulled away almost as quickly as it goes in.

Once it's out Franny goes quiet. As if her pain was activated by a circuit that's been broken, leaving her puzzled and then, when she looks down to see what comes out of her, astonished.

She sidesteps away. An attempt to recover her balance but she can't, and she slams against the wall and slides down the paneling to the floor. Nothing moves but her hands. Scrambling into the pouch sewn into the front of her hoodie like a pair of spiders trying to find shelter from the rain.

The four of us watch her.

"How's that?" Jerry says to himself. At first intrigued, then awestruck. "How's *that*?"

I'm moving as he speaks. Going at him. A good-sized man slamming into a smaller, thicker man who remembers how these things go.

But I remember too.

Something from my life before that is familiar with the shifts required to throw a body to the floor. The simultaneous struggles to get on top. To hold arms under the weight of knees. To push down with the thumbs into the cradles of bone that hold the eyes.

I remember this but forgot he has the knife.

He's under me, pinned at the shoulders. It allows him to bring the blade up but limits the arc to the length of his forearm. Still, it's a good enough reach to cut me.

The pain rolls me off him and I end up next to Franny against the wall. Her eyes frozen, mouth agape. Her characteristically mocking face.

I look up in time to see Lauren starting toward Jerry where he still lies on the floor, her leg pulling back to deliver a kick to his head. The knife stops her. Raised and warding her off like a crucifix holding a vampire at bay.

He takes his time getting to his feet. Blinking, rolling his shoulders.

"That shouldn't be too long," he says, referring to my wound. The slice he made to the soft flesh at the top of my chest.

He will make more cuts now.

There will be nothing I'll be able to do as he steps over and brings the knife down where I'm slumped, my legs jerking at the knees. He'll do it again and again.

What he actually does is worse.

"Let's go," he says, turning to Bridge and Lauren.

Lauren takes Bridge's hand and opens the door. The two of them wait there in the pale light that blinds me nonetheless.

Before she goes, Bridge looks back at me.

The dark is coming. It could be death, it could be one of the increments along the way. All I'm sure of is how the core of me has gone prickly and cold.

Jerry is nothing but a smudge of shadow in the doorframe, leering in and out of focus. But I can still see his teeth. The upper row of perfectly aligned slabs like a miniature, marble wall.

"You look like all the others," he says, an observation that provokes what sounds like pity in him, but it's not that.

There's a throbbing in my throat that wasn't there a second ago. Something trying to come up. Hard as stone, turning and scratching.

I open my mouth and what comes out is my sister's name but I'm the only one to hear it. And then even I'm not here anymore.

57

I REMEMBER EVERYTHING.

A July afternoon so hot it thickened the waves to syrup. Standing at the edge of the shore's highest boulder—

One-ah, two-ah—

Then everything went dark.

Thinking you'd been under too long—

My sister. My little sister.

Broken phrases. Coming to me out of the air. Trying to recall how they fit together, the precise wording, helps bring me back. Lifted into consciousness by threads of meaning.

The little sister is real, even if the memory isn't.

Bridge.

He took Bridge.

Moving hurts but not as much as I'm expecting. I'm able to sit up, straighten my legs. I've made the same mistake that Jerry had in overestimating the extent of the damage his knife did. He thought I would bleed out, but the cut isn't so deep. I slip my hand under my shirt and feel the skin below my shoulder. It's almost dried, the bleeding mostly slowed. If it opens up again, it may still bring me down. Just not now.

Before I attempt to rise, I notice how one of Franny's hands has slipped out of her hoodie's pouch. The fingers wrapped around the baby rattle Dad left for her. The hand-painted birds flying over a Japanese lake.

I stand up. Franny seems to congratulate me for this simple triumph with her look of mock amazement.

"I'll find her," I say.

A promise made to the dead. A stranger I've known my whole life.

I wonder if it's the lack of food or water or blood that makes the air feel so cool on my skin. In typical Pacific Northwest fashion, it has never been outright hot nor cold in Belfountain. But there's a damp weight to the place now, a pressure, like a drizzle of soil falling over me.

I'm curving back along the Red trail. That maddening switchback feels like it's only inching me closer to the lodge when I see something up ahead.

The witch laughs when I spot her.

"Where did they go?" I shout, my voice so hoarse it's on the verge of evaporating.

The old woman flaps her hands with the excitement of a child.

"Where did he take them?"

She plows away into the deeper bush.

It's all I can do to keep up with her. It's not her speed so much as the way she doesn't seem to feel the thrashings and bites of the branches and roots. I let them thrash and bite me too.

She's leading me nowhere. I see this too late.

We aren't going to Bridge or the lodge or a secret passage through the fence. She's a madwoman doing a mad thing and all it means is I've wasted time I don't have.

"Wait!" I call to her. "Wait!"

She keeps going as if she hadn't heard me. It makes me even more furious. Rushing up to her and, when I'm close enough, grabbing her arm so that she looks at me.

"Where is she?" I gasp at her. "Where's my sister?"

There isn't anything in her face to indicate comprehension. All that reaches me is the smell of her. Salty and mineral like a creature of the sea.

Her free arm lifts up. Points through the trees.

It can't be there. But it is.

The house I grew up in. The Cape Cod with a red-brick chimney and the Stars and Stripes hanging limp from a pole out front. Exactly as I remember it except it's here, gardenless, in the middle of Belfountain's woods.

The front door opens.

I back away, but now it's the old woman's turn to hold me by the arm, her grip strong. She knows who's opened the door. She wants me to see too.

A figure steps out. It takes a second to match its identity to a living person, because the person who's there isn't alive.

She waves.

My mother. Welcoming me home.

58

SHE KEEPS STANDING THERE. KEEPS WAVING.

I go to her and the old woman follows just behind me. When I reach the porch, Mom seems to give a signal, a half wink I'm not sure has even happened, and the witch stops at the bottom of the steps.

"Come in, Aaron," she says, backstepping deeper into the front hall.

It's my mother speaking. Telling me to do something, which means I do it. But this moment, one that ought to provide familiarity and comfort, delivers only the opposite. Walking over the threshold into my home to approach my mother in the hallway is the most frightening thing I've done.

"What happened to you?" I ask her.

"I was here," she says, not sounding like herself, not like she did before. A barely masked impatience, the hostility that comes with seeing others as standing in the way of where you alone can go. "And there."

"This is wrong."

"What is?"

"You." She backs away from me. A retreat that instead of making me feel safe communicates a threat. "Who are you?"

"Well, you know who I'm *not*."

It comes to me then. How Mom's file hadn't been among the others Franny found. How there hadn't been a pod with her name on it.

"Who are you?" I ask again.

"Aaron. Don't move, okay? Don't—"

"Where's Bridge?"

"There's no need—"

"*Tell me where she is!*"

She reaches for something around the corner behind her. A counter-top that, from memory, held the notepads and mug with pens and pencils. When her hand returns to view, it's holding a revolver.

"The living room," she says.

The interior here is as I remember it too. But I can also see the evidence of haste in its construction: nailheads poking out where they hadn't been entirely hammered in, sections of exposed plywood wall, the way the Laura Ashley wallpaper doesn't reach all the way to the ceiling. In the corners there are stray crates marked *'80s* and *'90s* and inside them random items: a rotary-dial phone, packs of Marlboros, a Rubik's Cube. On the glass coffee table a variety of magazines from different periods of the past: Michael Jackson on the cover of *Time*, a *Sports Illustrated* with the Blue Jays winning their second World Series in a row, a stack of yellow-spined *National Geographic*s.

"It's something, isn't it?"

"No," I say. "It's nothing."

She considers this, then nods in the manner of a teacher congratulating an unpromising student for his effort.

"In fact, it *was* rather unnecessary in the end," she says. "We built this place for the photo shoots, the home videos, but we could have done that in any studio. The idea to do it *here* was to have you and Bridge and

Franny spend a little time walking around the space, absorbing it all. But it didn't work. Even half out of it, each of you could tell it was fake. So we ended up having to erase *that* from you as well."

The gun looks alien in her hand, a thing of magic, as if she wields a hissing snake or glowing wand instead of a Beretta. How do I know what kind of gun it is? I feel sure it belongs to a set of knowledge not given to me in the pod. Another piece that's slipped through. More and more of it is returning. Held back for a time but now too powerful to be resisted, forcing its passage like the tide dissolving a wall of sand.

"Are you going to kill me?"

"What a question!" she exclaims, and flutters her free hand over her heart. Yet her expression doesn't match the horrified intent of her gesture. She remains detached, observing me.

"Are you going to tell me or not?"

"I'll confess to improvising at this point, Aaron," she says. "My current thinking is that I need to find the others, particularly that half brother of yours, once he's done with whatever he's up to. You may well be helpful in accomplishing that. You're *motivated*, aren't you? A surprise. Your profile didn't suggest that you'd be the most emotionally involved of the group, but I'm rather proud of the impact that the imprinting had on you."

She moves to stand with her back to the bay window so that to look at her leaves me squinting to see her through a corona of light.

"We have a little time," she says in the brisk tone of an executive heading up some marketing spitballing session. "I'd be curious to know how you're responding to all this."

I want you to suffer. I want to squeeze your throat closed and never let go. I want you to feel what it is to have not just one but two lives taken from you.

"Not well," I say.

"Do you have any specific queries?"

"Where's Bridge?"

She rolls her eyes. "Really? You're sticking with the devoted big brother arc?"

"Where *is* she?"

"With Jerry somewhere. Care for me to speculate?"

She's clearly bored by this—the concern of one doomed subject over the fate of another doomed subject—and there's a risk of losing her interest.

"Please don't," I say. "Tell me about Yourstory instead."

"You found your files, along with some of the promotional documents. Were they not clear?"

"What I don't understand—how all this—what do you call it? The business model. If you take this to market, how do you get away with destroying people like this?"

"*Destroying* doesn't strike me as remotely the right term, Aaron." She clears her throat to articulate a string of words she's said before so many times they come out by rote. "People *want* oblivion, Aaron. It allows them to carve something new out of the ashes. It's what will make Yourstory possibly the most important, transformative therapy since early humans devised their first god to pray to."

"And you own it," I say, the words prompting a wave of physical illness that almost silences me. "You're the 'Dad.' Ray Quinlan. The workaholic with all the secrets. You fashioned him after yourself."

"I gave him some of my best lines too."

"So this place—Belfountain—it's all yours."

"It's special, isn't it? There were a few parcels like it elsewhere—some I could have set up with more straightforward construction, to be honest—but it was the old summer camp that sold me. All those Bible-thumpy messages about forgiveness, new life. Born again! Not to mention the additional advantages of having Camp Belfountain already marked on the maps so all the excavation that had to be done could happen under existing structures. Dig a hole right under the old dining hall and connect it to a cave system. If you happened to be looking at the site from a satellite, you wouldn't think anything had gone on down there in thirty years."

"It must have cost a fortune," I say, and it comes out with unintended admiration.

"Fortunately, I was in *possession* of a fortune. I sold some neural implantation patents a few years ago—really interesting stuff, emotional variation, antidepressive stimulation, amazingly lucrative pharmacological alternatives. But making sad people less sad wasn't my real interest."

"That's killing people and giving them fake memories."

The hand holding the gun stiffens.

"What is a self other than a past?" she says.

In the pictures they showed me in the pod, the view outside the bay windows Mom stands in front of revealed a tiered garden leading up to a crabapple tree. Now there's only the rain forest, thick and close.

Along with the witch. Staring. She wants in but isn't allowed, and she holds her eyes on me, dark buttons, empty and shining.

"It gets rid of the bad things you've done—or have been done to you," I say, forcing my attention back to Mom. "A shame remover."

"That's clever! A stain remover for the conscience. Thank you. I'll have to remember that for the rollout." Something rueful passes over her features. "It was always going to be a self-improvement tool. But *now*, after what's happened—the clampdown, the internment programs, the whole unpleasant pageant—well, we *all* have so much we'd like to forget. The things we did. Didn't do. The things we stood and watched."

There's a creak in the floorboards upstairs. A single crunch from the shifting of weight. Mom (I can't stop myself from thinking of her as this) doesn't appear to hear it. Her mind elsewhere, reflecting, self-congratulating.

"I've learned so much these past few days, despite the many difficulties. I've learned so much *from* the difficulties," she says. "But what genuinely startled me was how few gaps Yourstory left in all of you. Next time I'll put even less into the MI. Turns out it's better when what we provide isn't much more than scant suggestions. And then, once you come out and start to be around other people again, you tell your stories and they tell theirs. Mix and match. The brain is so hungry for memories it'll take some from others if it has to. Make them up out of next to nothing."

"Jerry is the only one who doesn't know who he was before this," I say, wagering there's no way she'd have a way of detecting my lie. "Who was he?"

"You don't really want to know that. You want to know why he killed all of you."

I note the past tense as well as the inclusiveness—*killed all of you*—but push it away to pursue my first point.

"So it was him," I say. "It wasn't the man in the woods?"

"No, no," she says with what may be a note of sadness. "That's why I left the lodge. I knew he was out there, and that someone other than him was a murderer. Things were quite far off the rails at that point. That's when I turned on the fence. And when more of you started to die, I had to secure myself."

I'm tempted to ask more, but she's become distracted by the mention of the Tall Man in a way that threatens to pull her away.

"What about Jerry?"

She approaches a chair—a plaid upholstered La-Z-Boy I remember being Dad's favorite to sit in while hiding behind the newspaper—and I'm hoping she sits in it, perhaps putting herself at a disadvantage. She appears to have the same thought and merely leans against one of its arms.

"He was what, these days, they call a patriot," she begins. "Fearful, taste for violence. A deportation squad officer right from the early days. All of which made him a fascinating candidate. Could we cleanse him of not only what he'd witnessed of cruelty but being cruel himself? I honestly thought we'd been successful until—well, we don't need to be forthcoming about that in the research we release, do we? I mean, who's going to know?"

I'll know, I think of saying but stop myself. *I'm probably the only one alive who does, and soon there won't even be me.*

She studies me as if reading my thoughts. There's a flicker of something I mistake for pity, but when she speaks, I hear as only her curiosity.

"Do you know who you really are, Aaron?"

"No."

"Shall I tell you? You're not a doctor, as you've already discovered. Not a runner, either. You—"

"Stop."

"A leader of a kind. Defiance! One of the few who didn't get scared off even after—"

"*Stop!*"

She raises her eyebrows. The gun too. Aiming it at my head instead of my chest.

"All right," she says. "But would you like to know how you died?"

She takes my silence for acquiescence. Or maybe she doesn't care what I want to know or not.

"I was confident of Yourstory's methodology. But it was unproven. And I confess that some of the initial trials were, well, *less* than successful. Memories are stubborn. Pharmaceutical cleanses, protein sponges. The past came back no matter what chemical manipulation we applied. I knew, deep down, that only a total shutdown would do the trick. Death. But my financial backers were rather nervous about experiments involving, you know, the real thing. Even now. Even them. You should have seen their faces when I brought it up! I knew I would have to proceed on my own. And that called for human subjects."

There's the creaking in the floor upstairs again, directly over our heads. This time Mom definitely hears it too. Her eyes glance up at the ceiling as if it were glass and she's confirming what she knows to be there. But she doesn't mention it, only looks back down to the gun, and along its barrel at me.

"It was essential that all of you be taken at once," she goes on. "Hiring goons to drive around snatching people—a common sort of crime, but it offered patterns to be discovered. And in any case, it was important that I know *who* was being taken, to have an idea of their profiles so that I could evaluate the efficacy of their transformation."

As she speaks, I feel the cold water lapping against my chin, my lips, as I struggled to stay above the surface. The twins, Bridge, and the others around me doing the same. The alien song reaching up to us from the deep. Not a shared dream, not the sensation of floating in the pods. The last moments of our lives.

"We drowned," I say. "You drowned us."

"We could have done it a different way, of course. Something controlled in the lab. Lethal injection. But I felt it needed to be organic."

"Mass murder isn't organic."

"Really? How do you think you were *born*, Aaron?"

I try to think of the answer. Try to envision who my real mother might be, where she delivered me, the faces of those who first blanketed me, held me. Not even the vaguest guess comes to mind.

"In water!" my false mother exclaims in reply to herself. "The most intimate darkness. I recreated that as best I could. Do you see the circularity? Birth and death? Mother to ocean? No? Well. Perhaps the elegance of it is outside your grasp at the moment."

"Why a boat? Why not drown us in a tank here at Belfountain instead?"

"Missing at sea. One of the last ways to truly disappear. You've *already* been declared dead. A swift turnaround. With an abduction on land? It would take *years*."

Once again her words make my head swim. *Declared dead*. Which makes me what? An error. A monster. Nothing.

"How was it done?"

"The old-fashioned way. A bribe. I can tell you, the whale watching business isn't what it used to be," she says, her free hand picking at a thread in the chair's armrest. "So the captain of one such vessel was quite amenable to a new identity in a foreign country and more than enough money to see him through the rest of his days. Because you'd all booked your tickets in advance, we had time to find out who you were, the broad strokes of your personalities. Then, an hour out—an explosive charge below decks. Enough to sink the ship but *look* like the engine blew. Our boat recovered your bodies, then revived you on board—a successful process in all cases but one. We sedated you, brought you here. The Coast Guard's search for survivors was predictably brief and fruitless. And all the while I had you here, becoming something new."

"What was the music we all heard? Under the water?"

"I was interested in that too. I assumed it was some aural hallucination triggered by the compound we administered on the rescue boat. But my subsequent investigation suggests that it was something else altogether." She grins, a pause to lend emphasis to what comes next. "The whales," she says. "A choir of humpbacks, serenading you into the afterlife. Isn't that remarkable?"

I can hear them now. Another true memory, the last of my life. Sounding up from the endless dark.

"Well," she announces, straightening. "Perhaps we should proceed to—"

"What about Fogarty, the lawyer?"

"An actor. Apparently well regarded in the San Francisco theater community, but I personally thought he overcooked it a smidge."

"And the limo drivers? They were actors too?"

"They were *limo drivers*."

Through the window, the old woman steps closer. At first I think it's to press her face to the glass, but then she veers off toward the front door. A moment later I can't see her at all.

"Were you ever going to let us go?"

"You know, I hadn't decided on that. It was possible—well, I certainly *liked* the idea. A united family, getting together for Sunday dinners and summer holidays."

She flinches at this. A flare of discomfort that comes from a place she normally has safely contained. But only for a second. She arches her back in a yogic pose of strength.

But it lets me see something. We weren't the first prisoners at Belfountain. There had been others before us. Two of them.

"Who is the Tall Man?" I ask. "The old woman outside?"

"I admit that working mostly on my own, as I was forced to do, led to a number of mistakes. Not anticipating the danger Jerry brought, for instance," she says, nodding to indicate that she's heard my question but that the answer must be approached indirectly. "Also leaving the key to the lab in the shed—I'd simply forgotten about that one. So many *stages* to the construction, so much *Here, you'll need this*. And yes, the escapees. The ones you call the Tall Man and the old woman."

She sighs at the thought of them, wistful and strangely girlish, as if at the memory of some lost intimacy.

"You haven't told me who they are."

"Who are they *now*? Failed experiments," she says. "But *before* that? They were my only family. My mother. My son."

The sound of a foot coming down at the top of the stairs. From where I stand, I'll only be able to see who it is when they've completed the descent, but there's no question that it's a person up there, deliberate and slow.

"Over the time I was developing Yourstory I was losing them, bit by bit. My mother to Alzheimer's. My son to—well, they gave it a number of different diagnoses," she continues, louder than necessary, before pausing with a sigh. "Acute bipolar disorder. That's what most of them hung their hats on. But what's that *mean*? A defective mind. Faulty wiring. True for both of them. It's why I rushed my work so much at the end. I thought I could save them. Wipe their bad brains clean and reboot them. A second chance at sanity for my son, at memory for my mother."

"Your family," I say, catching up.

"Yes."

"We thought they might have been ghosts."

"*We're* the ghosts, Aaron. Sentimental hangers-on, wishing we could go back to the good old days. Ghosts are my prime market."

Another step on the stairs. If I turn my head, I might be able to see the legs of whoever it is, but I sense that to do so would be the end of the agreement I have with Mom to not shoot me dead here and now. She's pretending not to hear the person on the stairs. So I must do the same.

"Every obsessive is motivated for personal reasons, and I'm no exception," she says, as if in reply to a point I've made. "My father left when I was a child, which perhaps explains why the one I created for you was such a cold spot. But you must believe that I *wanted* you to have a father. Everything I've done here—it's always been about family. I tried to save my own because I loved them. And after they slipped away, I loved the memory of them. I still do. Because memory is all there is."

The weight on the stairs seems to be actively growing, now sounding great enough to crack them. To fall through the floor altogether.

"I *wanted* to be your mother," she says to me, blinking. "Wouldn't you agree that, in some sense, I always will be?"

The steps reach the base of the stairs and pause.

"Steven?" Mom says. "I'd like you to meet someone."

I look. The Tall Man doesn't appear to hear her or understand her words if he does. He doesn't move other than his heaving torso, as though he's drawing breath through a hole in his back. He's without the silver hatchet. Stooped and bleeding. His mouth pulled open in silent agony.

"Aaron, this is my son, Steven," she says, and steps closer to him.

Whether it is to embrace the Tall Man or guide him over to shake my hand or whisper her command for him to attack, I can't say, because in her approach she lowers the gun a few inches, momentarily forgetting it's there at the end of her arm, and I'm rushing at her, leaping into the space between us even after the crack of the shot.

59

SHE'S SO LIGHT. BIRD-BONED. AND LIKE A BIRD, SHE FLIES.

Her head hits the window behind her. At the impact, she utters a single grunt and lands on the floor, arms crossed over her chest as if a stubborn child refusing to play a game.

Seeing Mom there delivers two pieces of information I hadn't grasped the second before.

The bullet missed me.

She's not holding the gun anymore.

It's there on the floor where she dropped it when I connected with her, just beyond her right foot. I'm bending to pick it up when she sees it too. But instead of reaching for it she starts screaming.

"*Help* me*! Steven!*"

Her voice unlike any of her previous tones, frantic and shattering. The strangeness of it prevents me from understanding its meaning.

"*Steven!*"

I feel the Tall Man moving. The vibration of his bulging feet on the shoddy floorboards. One more step and he'll be on top of me. If I look, I can confirm it. If I look, I won't move before he's here.

The gun is there and it's the only thing in the world.

I fall onto my side next to it and pick it up at the same time that Mom pushes away from the wall and stretches out her leg, kicking my face. But it's something I'm barely aware of. There's only my hand slipping around the gun, lifting the gun, raising the gun to my right, and firing once, twice, a third time.

The Tall Man attempts to close his mouth. To speak? To spit? It doesn't work, whatever his intent. The gray lips shiver and fall open again, his eyes not on me, but on his mother. There's no recognition in them. There's nothing I would identify as emotion. It was her voice he responded to, not her, and now that he can't hear her, he topples onto his back, his spine and knees locked so that he comes down like a felled tree.

"What did you do? What did you do?"

She's getting up. I figured she'd broken something. Maybe she has. But it doesn't stop her from rolling onto her knees, reaching for the arm of the recliner, fighting her way to her feet.

"Don't move," I say, and point the gun at her face.

"You *hurt* him. You—"

"I didn't hurt him. I shot him. Now don't fucking move."

She stays where she is.

Her eyes dart over to see whoever walks in through the front door. Soft padding over the carpet, the steps tentative as a child's.

I try to find whoever is there in my peripheral vision but the angle won't allow it. It requires me to look away from Mom, though I keep the barrel trained on her.

The old woman. Peeking around the corner from the front hall, her eyes flicking from the body on the floor, to Mom, to me.

By reflex my arm swings the gun over and aims at her.

"Don't," Mom says.

Pleading. Not as startling as her shrieked appeal to the Tall Man yet it's the most genuine sound I've ever heard her make.

"She doesn't *know*. *She doesn't know*."

I don't understand what she means and for a moment I consider firing if for no other reason than she's asked me not to. Then I see how the old woman looks at me, confused but seeking approval, the wish to not cause any harm, to please. *She doesn't know.*

"I'll take you to them," Mom says.

60

MOM GOES FIRST.

As she passes the old woman, there's the briefest glance between them I worry might be some kind of secret signal, and I stay back another stride in case one of them comes at me.

Once Mom is out the front door and down the porch steps, I look back at the old woman. Through the semidarkness of the hallway, her eyes glint at me like black pinheads pushed into a dried apple.

"Don't come after us," I say.

Her head lowers an inch in the way of a dog disappointed to be told it won't be coming along for a walk. Other than this she doesn't protest, doesn't advance or retreat. I pull the door shut, and there's only the pinhead eyes, as empty of the future as they are of the past.

I tell her to take me to Bridge and Lauren first. Then she has to turn off the electrical charge to the fence and open the gate.

"This way," she says.

At first I think I can figure out where she's going, a backtrack toward the lodge that takes one variation, then another, each successive branching off the trail we're on more abrupt than the last. Soon I'm turned around so completely I'm free of even a guess at which way we're headed. Not that it matters. Either Mom is taking me to where I have to go or she's not. To be freed from choice is a liberation, and I can feel the lightness of it now the way I suppose it is with soldiers following orders.

"How far is it?" I call ahead to her.

"It's here."

And it is.

We come out of the cover of trees and into the shaggy yard around another suburban home in the middle of the woods, this one a boxy split-level with a rooster weather vane on the rooftop. The Kirkland house where the second Quinlans believed they grew up.

I expect Mom to head for the front door but instead she veers to the left, starting for the side.

"Aren't they in there?"

"Inside," she says. "But not in the house."

I don't like how she's in charge again, even with a gun pointed at her, but there doesn't seem to be a way to swing control back my way. She knows things, can do things. She is my mother and father rolled into one.

We pass around to the back where there's another structure, this one not trying to look like anything other than what it is: a cement block, flat topped and windowless. It frightens me.

"What's this?"

"It's sort of the control center of the whole place," she says. "You said you wanted the fence turned off, right?"

At the narrow end of the building, there's a steel door with an entry code pad next to it much like the one next to the underground porthole door. Mom places her hand onto the screen and the door latch clunks opens.

"You want me to—"

"What's the code?" I ask.

"What difference—"

"Tell me."

She barks out a laugh. "Your father's birthday," she says without turning around. "Do you remember?"

"July 4, 1951."

"Very good!"

"Open the door."

There's something to smell before there's something to see. Acrid urine, wet fur, animal waste.

"What's in there?"

"Your sister," Mom says, and steps into the dark before I tell her to.

61

I LIFT THE GUN HIGHER AS IF IT'S A FLASHLIGHT THAT WILL SHOW THE WAY. AS soon as the shadow of the structure's interior falls over me, the weapon feels all the more useless. A dead weight in my hand as meaningless as a bundle of keys.

It takes a moment to realize I'm not following Mom, but the whimpering.

"Is that a dog?"

"Poor thing," Mom says, dimly visible ten feet ahead of me, the light from the partly open door showing her working at the buttons and dials of a power board against the right wall. "Not my idea. The security contractor thought it would be sensible in case external conflicts reached all the way up here. A *guard dog*. And wouldn't you know it, I've completely forgotten to feed the creature. I'm frankly surprised it's still alive. I mean, *look* at it."

To her left, a fenced pen. Inside, pacing through mounds of its own filth, is a German shepherd mix of some kind, its hackles raised and head dipped so low it could be crossbred with a hyena. It never stops whimpering. Somehow the tenor of it makes it clear that it's not voicing its loneliness but its simulation, a bluff meant to get one of us to open its cage door. It looks at me when it comes my way, and when it turns, it swivels its head to keep staring at me.

"The howling," I say. "It was the dog."

"That was part of why I had to slip away. I was concerned that one of you might follow the noise it was making and find the house and this place and—well, you *did* find the lab, so my coming here to feed the beast was a waste of time, as it turns out."

I keep watching the dog as it watches me. It pulls me away from why I'm here, what Mom is doing.

"There were two originally, you know," she says.

"Two what?"

"Dogs. This one and one at the lab. When I left my mother and Steven down there after their unsuccessful therapies, the two of them decided to let the animal out. God knows why. Well, there wasn't food for all of them so—oh *dear*. Steven had to take care of it. That was all the mess on the floor you no doubt discovered. That *dog*. There was a fight. The dog lost."

Mom squeezes her chin as she works the keys on the board, recalls some sequence in her mind, starts clicking again.

"I suppose the smell of it got to him eventually," she goes on, "because Steven knocked that second door down, hammered it down with such—"

"You left them down there to die?"

She looks at me. "There was food."

"But you closed the doors on them. Your mother and son. You locked them down there."

"They *weren't* my mother and son anymore. Nevertheless, I didn't have the heart to—"

"Where's Bridge?"

I shake my head as if pulling myself out of an attempted hypnosis.

"She's close."

"You said she—"

"You wanted me to turn off the fence," she says, and punches a button on the board. "There. It's off."

She's counting on me to speak next. The back-and-forth rules of conversation are a powerful convention, as some study of hers has probably told her, because what she does is so straightforward it takes me completely by surprise. Instead of honoring the gun, instead of waiting for my words, she shifts away from the control board and slides back the bolt on the dog's cage.

It stops whimpering at the same time it comes at me.

I was right.

This occurs to me in the fragment of time of the dog's advance, its claws scratching on the hard floor, the show of its teeth like the raising of a pink curtain.

It was faking.

It's not the only thought I have either. The animal has been trained to not hurt Mom, only others.

Which means she was lying about having nothing to do with it.

Which means the dog was her idea.

"On!" she shouts, which makes no sense until the dog's teeth wrap around my ankle.

The gun cracks. A deafening noise inside the concrete crypt, so loud it comes to me with the same as the pain of the bite: a flash of brightness, sickening and yellow.

I manage not to fall. Yanking the dog forward and back at the end of my leg. All of which means the bullet didn't hit the animal.

A few feet away, I'm aware of Mom moving away. Her arms wheeling back, a hand slamming down on the control board.

"Oh . . . oh . . . *oh*."

An escalation of polite astonishment, as if she's pulled a soufflé out of the oven to discover that it's not only fallen, it's burnt.

The bullet found her. Her body folding under itself. I don't know if I aimed at her or the dog or if it was a stray shot that found the base of her throat. I don't know how it happened, but even through the searing pain, there's satisfaction that it did.

The dog releases me. Leaping straight up, jaw snapping, looking for the soft flesh of my inner thigh. Part of its training too.

I don't aim this time either. I just shoot down as the dog comes up.

It comes close enough that I can feel the rancid heat of its breath as it yips once before tumbling backward. The animal rolling onto its side, opening and closing its mouth as if testing to see if it still works.

I limp for the door at the same time I think I should shoot it again. But the gun isn't in my hand anymore. I must have dropped it after taking the shot. If I did, it must be next to the dog.

My ankle feels like there's an iron shackle that's been left in a fire for hours fused tight around it. That doesn't stop me from dragging it along at my side, learning how much weight it will take. It buckles when I'm not more than ten feet out.

I turn to find the dog having the same trouble I am.

The shot must have got some part of its hind leg. It comes out of the bunker and blinks against the light. Not a powerful animal, underfed and greasy, the head so low it appears shrunken with shame.

I've seen people like this before. Experiences from my previous life, breaking through now in a solid cluster. Despite their appearance, the weak, the desperate—they're the ones you ought to be afraid of. The ones who won't listen, won't reason. The ones with nothing to lose who'll come and keep coming.

62

A HOBBLED RACE BETWEEN MAN AND DOG.

If it was observed from the trees, it might appear comical, a Chaplin-esque dance of limps and hops. So long as you didn't see the terror on the man's face you might assume it was an act.

I make it to the house's back door, and when it opens, I scream for the first time. If it had been locked, I was so ready for the bite against the back of my good leg that another second's reprieve only doubles the panic.

It's not a good idea to go upstairs. I think this once I'm halfway up the stairs.

I can hear the dog throwing itself at the first step but scrabbling to lift itself to the next. I'm lucky there's no carpet on the varnished wood, leaving it slippery. Lucky too that the dog's leg is making it hard to bound up at me as it otherwise would.

I'm at the top of the stairs when my luck runs out.

The dog figures out how it's done. Lifting with its front legs and jumping with its uninjured back one. Once it's got this down, it rushes up, leaving a looping signature of blood over the steps behind it.

I look down a hallway with three open doors off it and throw myself through the closest one. Kicking the door closed at the same instant the dog slams into it.

A moment's pause before it starts scratching at the wood. The whole time it's whimpering just as it had in its cage.

I slide over and put my back to the door. It gives me the time to look around and see that it's Lauren's room.

Judging from the *Purple Rain* movie poster on the wall and the volleyball trophies lined up along the top of her dresser, it was designed to look the way it did when she was in high school. Aside from the rain forest crowding close to the window's glass it's the absence of any human scent that gives it away. It also makes the room feel unbearably lonesome.

The dog stops.

I can hear it panting, the wet smack of its chops. I wonder how the thing on the other side might be killed. Animal and man waiting for each other in the loneliest house in the world.

Eventually I hear it go away. The thump of its hindquarters down the stairs, the startled yips of suffering as it goes.

Bridge is out there. I need to find Bridge.

But that won't happen if the dog is at the bottom of the stairs or hidden in the living room, ready for when I come down. There's no way of knowing when the right time might be.

I open the door. Slide over to the stairs. Nothing there but trails of blood. The dog's coming and going, and one of my own.

At the back door, I look out over the tall grass, the trampled courses we'd made through it, the concrete outbuilding. I can't see the dog, though it could be anywhere. Would my chances be better if I reversed, walked the length of the house's interior and tried the front door? Maybe.

Maybe not, if the animal is also inside and can corner me as soon as I make the move.

I'm at the bottom of the back porch steps when I hear the growling.

Echoed and hollow, coming from inside the concrete bunker. I watch the dark rectangle of the open door but the animal doesn't come out. It's busy. I can tell from the ripping and tearing. The clack of its teeth as it eats.

I start away to the right and enter the woods. Straight for a time, then left, straight again, right. Trying to make myself difficult to follow. It would have left me totally lost, except I know where I have to go, even if it will be hard to find from where I am. But I'm starting to understand Belfountain now. If I just keep going, I will come to one of its trails. Once you've followed it to the end, take another step and you'll be there.

63

I HEAR THE HOWLING WITHIN MINUTES OF COMING UPON WHAT I'M PRETTY SURE is the Green trail.

It's on the move. Following my scent with greater certainty than me following the trail to the spot where I hope to head off and find the camp, the hole at the end of the cave beyond it that will take me down.

Jerry could have taken Bridge and Lauren back to the lodge or to one of the cabins or found a place in the woods it would take hours to discover. But I don't think he's in any of those places. For one thing, he assumes I'm dead. For another, he's not hiding. He's learning all he wants to learn, satisfying his wants, before leaving this place a grave behind him.

The place Mom called the lab would allow him to do all of these things. And Bridge could take him there.

• • •

I come to the camp sooner than I expected. Limp through the grounds, keeping my eyes straight on the trees on the far side. Then I'm into them. Keep going until the ridge.

The climb up is harder and higher than the last time. With my gnawed ankle it hurts a lot more too. When I reach the cave mouth, I roll over the ground and into the darkness. Eventually the tunnel's narrowing width forces me up.

At the hole I pause before descending, listening for voices below or howls from the woods, but everything is quiet. Even the moist breeze that I've been grateful to for cooling the sweat at the back of my neck has stopped, thickening the air into broth.

When I reach the bottom and step through the battered metal door I see how the Tall Man broke out. He used the heavy fire extinguisher that's missing from its box inset on the wall and now lies battered on the floor. Swung it into the steel door until it started to bend, pulling away from the bolts. Once he could get his hands through, he must have put on the oversized gloves and pulled until it came off altogether. And then the two of them had come up into the forest and wandered like spirits, drinking from rain puddles and eating leaves and roots without any way of knowing how they had come to be abandoned in this way.

I slide my back along the wall, careful with each step not to disturb any of the wires or files on the floor. When I'm at the T-junction where the other hallway runs left to the porthole door, I notice how there's the same kind of keypad on the wall next to it on the inside just as there is on the outside. Locked both ways.

There's something moving in the shadows straight ahead. But it's not something I can see. It's something I can hear.

A chair being dragged over the floor. A male voice. Coming from one of the rooms along the hallway to the left.

I come around the corner and freeze.

Lauren. Lying on her side in the hallway outside the pod room. Her body behind a console on the floor so that I didn't see her at first, one arm out in front of her like a swimmer stretching to touch the end of the pool.

The blood, her stillness, the frozen eyes. Then the eyes blink. Look up at me.

She whispers something and I bend close to hear.

I died.

I understand her to mean her life before this. That everything that happened at Belfountain doesn't count because she'd already lived, already passed.

She glances down. She wants me to check under her. I roll her halfway over as gently as I can and she stifles her pain. It's a steak knife. One she must have pocketed before Jerry took them all.

I tried.

Her lips say this, soundlessly. The same word she had whispered a moment ago. Telling me that she'd resisted as best she could, she'd been brave.

I pick up the knife. When I stand, her eyes remain open, but they are still now in a way they weren't before.

" . . . all the time in the world . . . "

In the pod room, Jerry is speaking and Bridge is sobbing, but even without seeing her, I can tell she's trying not to.

" . . . can be friends, or we can be something else. It all amounts to the same thing, so you might . . . "

His voice is drowned out by the blood in my ears. An escalating expression of force, what remains of me. The body telling the brain it will take it from here.

I come around the doorframe. Jerry is standing with his back to me ten feet away. He's holding the chef's blade in his right hand. A comma-shaped puddle of blood on the floor, the tip of it dripping, adding to its size. He's talking to Bridge, who sits in a metal desk chair—has been *told* to sit there, *told* not to move.

She sees me. The quickest dart of her eyes that she instantly corrects but Jerry detects it anyway. He starts to turn around. It lets me notice how his belt is unbuckled, the top button of his pants undone. Readying himself.

I'm thinking about all this as if it's already happened, already become the past, because it arrives from the mind and the mind is far away from things, as far as someone reading about a war compared to the ones fighting it.

The body is doing something else.

The body brings the steak knife into the top of Jerry's shoulder, pulling it out and doing the same to the middle of his back. When he spins around to defend himself, it goes into his side.

He drops to his knees, but his arm is moving, the one with the chef's blade at the end of it, a wide arc intended for the back of my knee. It's slow though—slower than me—and I'm able to kick the blade out of his grip before it gets close.

Jerry's mouth is moving.

Cursing me, showing me he's not afraid. I can see that without hearing the words. But he's in the past now too. His threats, the intimidating confidence and handsomeness. He's behind me. The body wants only to go to Bridge, help Bridge up, get her out.

She's out of the chair before I reach her. Taking me by the hand and pulling me past Jerry, who's weaving from side to side while remaining on his knees as if screwing his body into the ground.

"Leave him," Bridge says.

We're starting back toward the tunnel when both of us hear the click of claws on the concrete. Bridge and I back away from the corner, but we don't take our eyes from it, as if so long as we can't see the animal it isn't actually there.

"What is it?"

"A dog," I say.

"Will it—"

"Yes."

We've backed up far enough that the dog stands at an equal distance from the pod room door as we do. There's just the iron door to the cave behind us, the one with the porthole window.

"We run on three," I say. "You ready?"

"Ready."

"One. Two—"

Jerry comes out into the hallway.

For a second we watch him just as the dog does. Jerry's pants are undone and his belt buckle is clanking against his hip, a look of groggy irritation on his face. If it weren't for his wounds, he would appear hung-over, rising from a fitful rest to tell somebody to turn the music down or get him a coffee.

He looks one way and sees us. Looks the other way and sees the dog.

We never get to *three*.

64

JERRY COMES AT US FASTER THAN I WOULD HAVE THOUGHT HIS INJURIES WOULD allow. I get in front of Bridge and widen my stance, preparing myself for the blow, then see from where he's looking that he doesn't care about reaching me or Bridge. It's the door at the end of the hall he's going for.

Bridge is ahead of me. She would have made it to the door before any of us if Jerry hadn't shoved her against the wall as he passed. It doesn't take her down though. She regains her footing and has caught up to him by the time it takes me to reach my top hopping, jumping pace.

My target isn't the door. It's Jerry. I launch myself at him, grabbing for any part to hold on to. My fingers pull into fists, gripping the fabric of his untucked shirt along with folds of his skin, and throw him behind me.

Bridge slams into the door. Tries the handle.

"It's locked!"

I think of the different ways to numerically express Dad's birthdate. Month, day, year? Day, month, year?

"Enter 07041951. See the keypad?"

She presses some buttons. "Didn't work. What's the number?"

"July fourth, 1951. Dad's birthday." I say the numbers again.

Bridge finishes the sequence. Pulls on the door. It eases open with a depressurizing whoosh, popping my ears.

"Go!" I shout at her when she looks back.

She slips out the door and it seals shut again.

I suppose it's relief in knowing that Bridge is free, that at least she is out of Jerry's reach even if there's only the enormous forest waiting for her outside of the cave—whatever it is, the exhaustion hits me now, a few feet short of the door. I wouldn't move if I didn't hear the dog behind me. The animal paused, watching the three of us struggling against each other and now seeing the two wounded humans left behind.

It was the body that pushed me forward when I was in the pod room. But it's the mind that does it now.

You're so close.

I take a dainty skip with my good leg.

You can let all of it go on the other side.

Another skip. Another and another and I'm there.

The door sucks open with a blast of fresh air, hard as water. Something is behind me—the dog, a rush of motion, the sense of weight about to crash into me—and I squeeze myself through the gap. The door clicks shut.

"The number worked on this one too," Bridge says. She's standing by the external keypad, blinking the sweat from her eyes.

A soft *thump* against the door.

"Open it."

Jerry's face. Three inches from mine through the porthole window's glass. Not shouting, not reasoning. He's giving me an order.

"Open the *door*, Aaron."

I keep my shoulder to the metal surface. Stare at Jerry through the glass, his skin pallid and buttery.

"Let me the fuck out!"

There's no refusal other than my staying still. Jerry reads it in me before I'm certain of it myself. I won't open the door. There is no order or plea I will listen to. A realization that brings a nauseous smile to his lips.

"I read the file. I know who you were before. I *know*," he says through the glass.

I look past him and he turns to see the dog approaching. It holds its head higher than before, nourished and emboldened.

Jerry turns back to the window and I can see him consider begging me to help him, but he changes his mind. There's no way he can stop the fear from showing. But he can keep his mouth shut.

Even so, he appears about to say something when the dog scrambles forward and rips into the back of his leg. After that there are only his screams.

The door trembles. When I peer through the porthole again, Jerry is down on the floor, the animal upon him.

"Can you walk?" Bridge asks.

"I'll be faster if you hold my elbow."

She cradles my arm in both her hands and the two of us start up the concrete stairs. I came down the same stairs only two days ago but it feels like months. It makes me think how Belfountain, as with all fairy-tale places, is no more constrained by time than by geography. The characters in those stories—Hansel and Gretel, Rapunzel, Cinderella—the way they existed as only names on paper prevented us from feeling the horror they would have experienced as they were enslaved, imprisoned, baked into pies.

A whistle.

Not the kind made with pursed lips, but a sports whistle, loud and shrill. The one left for Jerry as a gift and that he'd put in his pocket.

I wait for the dog to growl or whine before silencing him, but there's only the abrupt interruption of the whistle, then nothing.

65

IF WE HAVE A CHANCE OF GETTING OUT, IT'S NOW. WE COULD TRY TO GO BACK TO THE fake house to find the gun. But I don't know how to get there. We could spend hours wandering around before we found it. There's a good chance we never would.

Eventually, the dog's hunger will return.

Eventually, it will come for us.

We stumble through the camp and into the forest to join the trail again, start back toward the lodge. When we get there, we see where Jerry had been digging at the twins' graves, a group of smaller piles of soil next to the two larger ones. We proceed into the lodge where I pull a quarter-full jug of orange juice from the fridge, and then the two of us walk out through the smashed wall of glass.

Bridge takes a drink. Hands the jug back to me. The juice is too sweet, too cold, too good. And then I remember that I'm still alive.

"You found Mom," Bridge says once we start out along the road.

"Yes."

"She wasn't who we thought she was. She knew."

"Yes."

"What about the Tall Man?"

"He's gone. They're all gone."

"The dog?"

"It'll come for us. But we've got a little time, I think."

When we reach the fence, I tell Bridge that if it's still electrified I might not get up again after I touch it. If that's how it goes, she shouldn't stay with me but go back to the lodge. Secure the food, barricade herself in one of the rooms. Wait for help.

"Sure," she says. But she's only agreeing because there's no point in arguing. She knows there's no help coming. Either we get out now or we never do.

I walk up and place both hands against the metal.

There's a tremor in my arms, but it's only me, anticipating the jolt that doesn't come. I slip my fingers through the holes. Then I pull back hard to the left.

"Still locked," I tell Bridge, looking up at the barbed wire. "There's one thing I want to try."

It's been a long time since I've climbed a fence. Not that I remember having ever done it; it's only how my body feels pulling itself up while negotiating the too-small footholds and finger locks that tells me I have. Once at the top, I use my free hand to pull the pruning shears from my pocket.

The wire isn't thick. Clamping the blades firmly around a point is half of the challenge, and pressing through the cut without the sharp burrs gouging into my face is the other.

I can only do it with my right hand. Soon my left is numb, and my bad ankle won't stay in the hole in the fence, so I have to choose between coming down again or falling. Whatever cuts I've managed so far will have to be enough.

"Watch out," I call down to Bridge before letting the shears drop to the ground.

I start dividing the wire to the sides. When it has yielded the widest gap I'm ever going to get—a couple of feet, no more—my hand is so bloodied it looks like I wear a single, shining glove.

I pull myself onto the top of the fence. Shimmy into the gap between the razor wire, the sharp ends snagging into my skin on both sides. When I'm halfway, I hold myself in position as firmly as I'm able.

"Climb up," I tell Bridge. "Up and over me."

"Are you crazy?"

"Do it."

I'm worried she's going to refuse. But then the fence is shaking, and I have to hold on hard as she makes it up to where I am.

"Put one leg over me so that you're sitting up on my back," I say.

"The wire—it's *in* you—"

"I'm all right. Can you do it?"

She doesn't answer. She's doing it.

"Ow!" The burrs find her on the way up and again at the top "*Ow!*"

"Now slide over to the other side."

"I'll fall!"

"Hold on to me with your one hand. Your foot will find the fence if you lean over far enough. I won't let you fall."

When her foot comes into view, I guide it into a hold in the fence. Bridge slides over my back until her other leg is free. Then she grips my jacket and lowers herself until she can hold the fence on her own. I watch her scramble down to the ground. Once she's there, she looks up at me.

"Now you," she says.

"It's going to be messy."

"You're already messy."

I try to climb down the other side head first. My hips are barely past the top bar and I'm tumbling through air.

The meeting of body and ground takes my breath away. For a good while all I do is try to find the air again, coax it down my throat until my lungs accept it.

"Does it hurt a lot?" Bridge says.

"Not much."

This is true. It may ultimately be a bad sign, but for now there isn't much more than a burning here and there on my skin that I keep waiting to dull but never does.

"Look," Bridge says.

The old woman stands on the other side of the fence. Maybe she followed us here and only now arrived. Maybe she was here the whole time, watching.

She makes no appeal to be released, doesn't speak. She remains more still than the trees around her. It's as if she had always been there. An object—pickup truck, corroded bed frame—you sometimes come upon in the woods and mistake for a living thing because it's halfway between the two, a piece of the human past losing its identity as the vines and branches pull it deeper and deeper into the green.

OCEAN

66

NEITHER OF US IS SURPRISED TO FIND THERE'S NO SATELLITE PHONE INSIDE THE metal box. Even if there was, we couldn't let whoever answered know where we were.

We walk all the way to the interstate. None of the few pickups or military vehicles that pass stop to check on us. Our hope is that we look like a problem. To inquire how we came to be shuffling along this remote road, a bloodied man and teenaged girl, would be to involve yourself in that problem. We're counting on the self-preserving calculations that go into minding your own business.

By the time we collapse in the prickly grass next to the on-ramp, it's almost nightfall. The highway groans behind us. We need help. We cannot ask for help. The paradox of prison escapees or refugees or wounded animals.

Bridge's questions reach me through the near dark, and somehow because she is only a graphite silhouette, it's easier to answer them directly. She wants to know about all the things Mom told me in the house-that-wasn't-our-house. Who Jerry was in the life before. How we were chosen, left to drown, returned from the dead.

She doesn't ask who I really am. She can tell I'm not ready for that, and like an actual friend, an actual sister, she lets it go.

When I'm finished, it's dark. The passing headlights almost touch us but not quite, so that with every passing vehicle Bridge is briefly stretched out, a shadow that bends and rushes over the grass.

"I think I know why the Tall Man came after us," she says.

"Tell me."

"He saw us and recognized something from before. He saw a family and he wanted to be closer to it. Part of it. He was *lonely*, Aaron."

I nod but I'm not sure she sees me do it. It makes me feel invisible. A spirit observing its final glimpses of the world and trying to memorize it, holding fast to the vague outline of this one person sitting next to me.

"My file," Bridge says. "Brigit and Olivia. Neither said anything about my cancer. What do you think that means?"

"It means it's not true."

"Is that what you think, or what you hope?"

"I'm doing my best to make them the same thing."

"But some of it you can't hope away. Like me cutting myself. That part was true."

I reach out for her but I can't find her in the darkness. "You're different now," I say, and imagine casting a spell toward her through my fingertips. "You can make yourself different."

At the earliest sky-bruising of dawn an older model Sunbird rattles onto the shoulder. An arm appears from out of the driver's-side window, waving us over. Bridge starts toward the car. A woman's arm, no other passengers.

"You going into the city?" the woman asks once we're stuffed into the back seat and she starts us rolling onto the blacktop.

"Yes," I say.

"Need a hospital?"

"Yes."

"Any preference?"

"A busy one, I guess."

None of us speak over the next couple hours until we reach the outerlands of the city, the sound barrier walls separating the lanes from the malls and housing developments and schools. Then the low-rise office buildings, the software developers and makers of parts that go into fighter jets and submarines.

"There're checkpoints along here sometimes," the woman says. "You two have ID?"

"Not me," Bridge answers.

"I do," I say, feeling the wallet in my back pocket but not pulling it out. "But I'm pretty sure it's fake."

The woman looks at me in the rearview mirror.

"Don't tell me anything more. The less I know the better," she says, returning her eyes to the traffic ahead. "Most days I wish I didn't know a goddamn thing about any of this."

A few minutes later we're downtown, stopping on the edge of the university campus, a block from the Swedish First Hill Hospital. When we thank her, she waves at us with her fingers as if shooing away the very concept of gratitude.

"We've got to stick together now, right?" she says.

Once she's driven off, I tell Bridge to wait under an elm on the Union Green. I warn her not to talk to anyone until I come back.

"Who am I going to talk to?" she says, trying a smile and getting it halfway right. "You're the only person I know."

• • •

In the emergency room the doctor doesn't ask any follow-up questions when I tell her I was injured in a dog attack. A neighbor's rottweiler that jumped the fence. She doesn't believe me, but decides the truth isn't necessary. There's an administrative nurse who asks for my insurance information, and when I assure her my roommate is bringing my health card from home, she laughs in my face.

It's a chaotic, bad-smelling place I've never been to before, yet this is the hospital where I worked as a surgeon. In the life I never lived I would have been treating these shouting, pain-twisted people around me, not been sitting among them, waiting my turn. I wish at least this one aspect of Mom's made-up story had been true.

When my wounds have been swabbed and bandaged, the doctor tells me an orderly will come soon to take me to get some X-rays done. Once she pulls the curtains closed, I count to thirty and slip through them, heading right and going straight the way someone who knows where they're going might.

There's the certainty that my doing this will trigger an alarm. But I make my way out a side door without any of that. I might have gotten lucky. They might have been aware of my leaving but happy to see a case like mine walk away, a number they could wipe from the board.

Bridge is waiting for me. I hoped she would be but figured there were a dozen good reasons why she'd be gone. Police spotting her and sweeping her up. Passersby noting her soiled appearance and offering help of either the genuine or false kind. There's also the possibility that she would leave on her own.

"You're still here," I say.

"I didn't stay the whole time."

"Where'd you go?"

"I borrowed a phone. Called the police."

"Bridge. Do you know what—"

"Not for us. And I didn't tell them who I was. Where we were."

I look at my sister and instead of telling me she waits for me to see it in her.

"You sent them to Belfountain," I say. "To find the old woman."

"Yes."

"Because you didn't want to leave her there."

"No."

Bridge starts to walk and I follow her. Part of me wants to ask her who she borrowed the phone from, if they could have reported us. Part of me knows it won't make any difference in where we have to go next even if they had.

"How are you?" Bridge asks after a stretch of silence between us as we make our way along Pike Street toward the waterfront, the mountains a watercolor in progress.

"Aside from feeling like a pincushion covered in duct tape, I'm fine. You?"

"Tired. But I think I'll always be tired, you know?"

We pass a group of National Guardsmen at a corner, then a similar clutch of men—not army, not cops, just uniformed militia, the official-looking patches and stripes down their pants stitched on at home—holding mismatched rifles. None of them question us. They're too occupied by striking the right pose, trying to find the balance between menacing and bored.

At the park by the waterfront we sit on a set of concrete steps and look out over the harbor. In the distance tankers slide over the horizon as if cleaning it.

"I don't know if I've ever been here before," I say. "But the water—it's so familiar."

"Maybe it is."

"Maybe. Or maybe I was born in St. Louis or Des Moines or Toronto. For all I know, this is the first time I've ever seen the ocean."

Bridge looks directly at me and waits until I turn to her.

"I have this idea," she says. "There're some things we're born remembering. The ones that are always there no matter what. The stars." She shifts her eyes back to scan the blue horizon again. "The ocean."

We remain like this, the tide distant and massive as a crowd marching in the streets.

"What about you?" Bridge asks after the sun slips behind a wayward cloud and a coolness returns us to wakefulness. "What do you remember from the beginning?"

"Just one thing," I say. "Just you."

67

IT TAKES A LITTLE OVER AN HOUR TO PANHANDLE THREE DOLLARS. ENOUGH TO PAY
for a half hour on a computer in an internet café, but it turns out we only
need five minutes to look up the news stories about the missing Olivia
Goldstein and figure out where she lives.

We share a chocolate bar with the leftover change and walk over the
course of the afternoon. Neither of us says much. Olivia has a mother and
a father and a brother who are about to have the dead returned to them.
The thought of this, the startling, frightening joy it will bring, takes hold
of our thoughts.

It's a fancy neighborhood, but in the Seattle manner. Which is to say
it's not about the grandeur of the house, but how well it's hidden, in this
case obscured by a wall of hedge and the junipers behind it.

The two of us stand at the end of the curving drive, peering up at
what we can glimpse of the Tudor facade: the basketball net over the
closed garage, the uncollected newspapers wrapped in plastic on the
front walk, the neglected lawn growing wild.

"They must be so sad," Bridge says. "You can feel it from way out here."

"Not for long. You've come back."

"Yeah. I've come back."

I wait for her to move but she only looks at the *GOLDSTEIN* stenciled on the mailbox and then back up at the house.

"They're strangers," she says.

"They're your family."

"But I don't remember them."

"It'll come back. And if it doesn't, you'll learn. They'll help you."

"What about you? What are you going to do now?"

"I don't know."

"Are you going to go away? Will I—"

"I'm not going anywhere. Nowhere far."

Later, I'll try to recall if she was crying when she put her arms around me, gentle as she could so as not to disturb the bandages over my cuts. It's because it was hard for me to see her face through my own tears, which came without warning and wouldn't stop.

When she pulls away, she squeezes my hand twice. Our code.

I squeeze hers back. One time. One more.

"See you Tuesday?"

She doesn't understand for a second, and then it comes back. Our standing dinner arrangement. The secrets shared over tables in Chuck E. Cheese or downtown oyster bars. She laughs without making a sound.

"Tuesday," she says before she turns and starts up the drive.

I stay there for a time. It's hard to say how long.

Piece by piece the world tells me. The spinning leaves of an oak in a neighbor's yard. The distressed yowl of a cat. The smell of the sea. All of it asking the same thing.

What now? What now? What now?

Maybe freedom always feels like this.

My file is still folded in my pocket. The answer to who I really am that, with each breath, feels more disposable.

Where does the path lead after it ends?

I take a step. And another. Each one a little faster than the one before, testing my strength. Nameless and unhistoried and light.

I'll go on.

I'll run.

ACKNOWLEDGMENTS

Thank you to Anne McDermid, Peter McGulgan, Chris Bucci, Jason Richman, Kevin Hanson, Laurie Grassi, Crissie Johnson Molina, Siobhan Doody, Nita Pronovost, Catherine Whiteside, Sarah St. Pierre, Randall Perry (and the whole team at Simon & Schuster Canada).

To my children, Maude and Ford, and to my wife, Heidi, thank you for listening to the idea early on and nudging me in the right directions.

ABOUT THE AUTHOR

ANDREW PYPER is the author of *The Only Child*, which was an instant national bestseller in Canada. He is also the author of seven previous novels, including *The Demonologist*, which won the International Thriller Writers award for best hardcover novel and was selected for *The Globe and Mail*'s best 100 books and Amazon's top twenty best books. *The Killing Circle* was a *New York Times* best crime novel of the year. Three of Pyper's novels, including *The Homecoming*, are in active development for feature film and television. He lives in Toronto. Visit **AndrewPyper.com** and follow him on Twitter **@andrewpyper**.

HEALTH EDUCATION IN SCHOOLS

Second Edition

Edited by

KENNETH DAVID *and* TREFOR WILLIAMS

Harper & Row, Publishers
London

Cambridge   San Francisco
Mexico City   São Paulo
New York   Singapore
Philadelphia Sydney

First published 1987, a second and fully revised and updated edition of *Health Education in Schools*, edited by James Cowley, Kenneth David and Trefor Williams, first published by Harper & Row, 1981

Harper & Row Ltd
28 Tavistock Street
London WC2E 7PN

British Library Cataloguing in Publication Data
Health education in schools.—2nd ed.
1. Health education—Great Britain
I. David, Kenneth II. Williams, Trefor
613'.07'1041 RA440.3.G7

ISBN 0-06-318376-5

Typeset by Katerprint Typesetting Services, Oxford
Printed and bound by Butler & Tanner Ltd, Frome and London

CONTENTS

Alysoun Moon MA, SRN. Research Fellow, HEC Project: Health Education in Primary Schools, Department of Education, University of Southampton.

Anne Moore JP, SRN, DHe. Senior Health Education Officer, Nottingham and Bassetlaw Health Education Unit.

William Rice MA(Hons), MIHE. Joint Executive Officer, Teachers' Advisory Council on Alcohol and Drug Education.

B. Keith Tones MA, MSc, PhD. Reader in Health Education, Leeds Polytechnic.

Noreen Wetton MA. Deputy Director, HEC Project: Health Education in Primary Schools, HEC Health Education Unit, Department of Education, University of Southampton.

Trefor Williams BA, DHe. Director, HEC Health Education Unit, Department of Education, University of Southampton.

Charles Wise MEd. Senior Area Adviser, Gloucestershire Local Education Authority.

CONTRIBUTORS

Len Almond MEd, DASE. Lecturer in Physical Education and Sports Science, Loughborough University.

Nancy Beecroft DHe. Senior Health Education Officer, Nottingham and Bassetlaw Health Education Unit.

Jill Coombs PhD Research Officer University of Bath.

Ann Craft BSc (Econ), SQSW. Research Officer, BEC Health Education for Slow Learners Project, University of Bath.

Kenneth David BA. Freelance Lecturer, formerly County Adviser for Schools, Lancashire, with special responsibility for personal relationships.

Fiona Dowling. Research Assistant in Physical Education and Sports Science, Loughborough University.

Peter Farley MA (Oxon). District Health Promotion Officer, Exeter Health Authority.

Gay Gray BA. Director, HEC Health Education Project 16–19, HEC Health Education Unit, Department of Education, University of Southampton.

Jean Hildreth Adv.DEd. Senior Health Education Officer, Nottingham and Bassetlaw Health Education Unit.

Tim Hull MSc, MIBiol. Senior Lecturer in Health Education, Essex Institute of Higher Education.

Ian McCafferty BA, MEd. District Health Education Officer, Nottingham and Bassetlaw Health Education Unit.

EDITORS' INTRODUCTION

In 1981 we edited Health Education in Schools and at that time James Cowley was one of the editors, and made a major contribution to the planning. We regret he was not able to join in editing the present revised edition as his work now lies in South Australia, where sadly we see that he has left health promotion for other fields of work. We miss his energy and imagination.

In preparing the present work there are very few chapters without major changes and revision in content. In six years we cannot only see better ways of presenting the topics in each chapter, but there have been many changes in direction and policy in health education which are now included. Compared with 1981, health education is more clearly identified as part of the increasingly important personal and social education programmes in schools.

In Part 1 we have limited our review of the bases of health education to one chapter by Keith Tones. We have in Part 2 – the school context – rectified an omission in the earlier work by including a chapter on education for special needs, and have major revisions of the work on health education in primary and secondary schools. In Part 3 – a co-ordinated approach – we have limited ourselves to the four topics of science, physical education, English and pastoral care. These illustrate our strong conviction that in 'the pastoral curriculum' and in co-ordination between subject departments in secondary schools and subject areas in primary schools we have the main keys to the successful presentation of personal and social education and health education.

In Part 4 – teaching approaches – we have a revised contribution on the importance of informal approaches and group work, and have added a chapter on sex education, not dealt with in the first edition. In Part 5 – further developments – we have added a necessary new contribution on the

-19 age group. We have consolidated and revised the appendix on resources, and have included a contribution on the European dimension in health education.

There remains part of our introduction to the earlier edition which still remains very relevant and still represents our firmly held views. We set out to survey the present position of health education in schools in the United Kingdom, and to provide evidence of possible future developments. The book is intended as a basic reader for this wide-ranging and diffuse area of education. We believe that health education is seldom nowadays seen as a narrow parade of physical matters; it is almost universally understood as an omnibus title for physical and mental attitudes to responsible health for the individual and the community, to well-being within a supportive family life, and to lives lived positively and with some contentment. Curriculum terms such as 'personal and social education' correlate closely with this view of health.

We hope that *Health Education in Schools* will, with this wide view in mind, provide support or legitimization for the endeavours of practitioners in health education working in and with schools, and will offer a framework for consideration by others who are facing the need to systematize work in this area.

We consider that the work surveyed here should be seen as part of the basic and in-service training of all teachers, not of specialists only. We also feel that it can be part of the reading of health staff who are associated with schools, and of many medical staff and perhaps parents.

Every educational approach needs to be supported by a philosophy and theory, and this is provided by some of our contributors. We believe, however, that there is a strong practical theme to the book, and many of the contributors are concerned with classroom practice as well as with curricular management and development.

This book cannot and should not be prescriptive; it is intended as a source book to provide ideas for those who plan for health education and those who teach it. All schools should have a plan for how they influence children in their health careers, in company with caring parents, but that plan has to be based on a particular school and the personalities within it. We have avoided too much emphasis on particular schemes, for curriculum planners will seek what their school needs from many sources. The formulation of health schemes should be attempted only when set within the specific context of a particular school with its own idiosyncracies and ethos. We hope that this book will support those who are responsible for such schemes.

Change is continuous in health education, and no text can ever be up to date. Since preparing this edition of *Health Education in Schools* we regretfully note the government decision to replace the Health Education Council by a National Health Service Special Health Authority. Schools owe a great debt to the HEC, for in recent years many useful curriculum developments have been encouraged and developed through the Council and its professional staff. We shall observe with interest the effect of a less independant NHS institution on health education in schools.

The new Authority is to assume responsibility for public education about AIDS. The present pamphlet, *Don't Die of Ignorance*, has probably been effective with the reading public. We shall now see how the approach to the non-reading public is directed, and whether schools are well supported in their never-ending and controversial task of preparing pupils for such aspects of life in modern society. The way homosexuality and promiscuity are dealt with will test the past safe blandness of many political and governmental approaches, as will the possible free provision of condoms and drug injection needles, which could be part of a programme for coping with an AIDS epidemic. Moral condemnation seldom changes human behaviour, and we foresee bitter debates about the practicalities of helping young people to face the sexual facts of life, as there will be on approved 'safe sex'. Schools have for years been faced with criticism in their efforts to help youngsters comprehend sexual behaviour; it is an interesting development to see our critics faced with new realities and bewildering new targets to challenge.

The Director of the United Kingdom AIDS Foundation is reported as saying: 'The aim must be to contain AIDS through straight communication, and buy time for research into this difficult disease. We need to communicate at two levels: a concentrated message to high risk groups, and frank information to the public at large.' There appears to be a major moral and health-education debate in that quotation alone.

We have been reflecting also that we could have dwelt more in this edition on multicultural aspects of health education. We have not so far seen this as a separate part of our theme, for we have considered our overall view of the philosophy, curricula and methodology of health education as being generally appropriate to all cultural and social groups. Reading recently of the Coronary Prevention Group's concern at the high incidence of heart disease among Britain's Asian community, and the possible link with social status, isolation and racial prejudice, makes us reflect on whether teachers are continuing to deal with the multicultural aspects of learning in health education, and in personal and social education. 'Work in health education can be enriched by opportunities to study the ethnic and cultural variety of modern Britain', as Her Majesty's Inspectors comment in *Curriculum Matters 6* (HMSO, 1986). We hope it is so in fact.

ach month our views on health education could be developed with
ifferent priorities. We seem at times to be dealing with the wider
problems of life in society today, rather than with what has in the past been
seen as a modest and minor subject area.

THE BASES OF HEALTH EDUCATION

INTRODUCTION TO PART 1

Health education may be very pragmatic in much of its content, for it is concerned with the everyday living of ordinary people, and there is a considerable practical and physical content to the health problems of people and communities. Increasingly, however, one discovers that health education is full of considerations of values and attitudes, and prejudices are often the enemies of positive health matters. So the apparent simplicities of health matters are often overshadowed by the controversies of feelings. As we further extend the limits of what we see as the boundaries of health education – the political dimensions of pollution, for example, and legal and economic aspects of family life – so we continually rediscover that health education, like any educational activity of worth, needs to be underpinned by a sound rationale or deeper philosophy if it is to be taken seriously by practitioners, and by politicians and their public.

Keith Tones offers in this opening chapter a viewpoint on some of the philosophical aspects of health education. It is wide ranging, as the title indicates, and provides an introductory survey of this subject area and its 'problematic nature' as he terms it. He gives attention to informed decision-making and the health-action model, and we value reinforcement of the view that health education is less about 'telling' than about 'feeling' and 'thinking'.

He is at present Reader in Health Education at Leeds Polytechnic, and for some years has been training health-education specialists, both in schools and in the National Health Service. After reading psychology at Cambridge, Keith Tones taught in a secondary modern school and then lectured in colleges of education until his present appointment. He is well known and respected in health education circles, and we again appreciate his revised opening chapter.

1

HEALTH PROMOTION, AFFECTIVE EDUCATION AND THE PERSONAL–SOCIAL DEVELOPMENT OF YOUNG PEOPLE

Keith Tones

All man wants is an absolutely *free* choice, however dear that freedom may cost him and wherever it may lead him.

(Dostoevsky)

THE PROBLEMATIC NATURE OF HEALTH EDUCATION

In 1974, an influential document produced by the Scottish Education Department commented on the marginal status of health education as follows:

> Health education occupies an indeterminate and ambivalent position; it has not yet been accepted as an essential part of the fabric of education. It tends to fall into the no-man's land between the school and the home, or within the school to be everyone's concern but no-one's responsibility.

(SED, 1974)

Since that time it has undoubtedly moved much closer to centre stage. Its importance and potential have received recognition in many quarters and government – through DHSS and DES – has lent its support. Moreover, it would appear that health education is valued in most schools. According to a recent survey of a $12\frac{1}{2}$ per cent sample of schools in England and Wales (Williams, 1985), some 87 per cent of primary schools were teaching about health and a further 4 per cent planned to do so in the near future. The comparable figures for secondary schools were 85 per cent and 9 per cent respectively.

However, despite these favourable indications, there are still many difficulties associated with health education. There are many barriers to be overcome before the 'approved' model is implemented, viz. an integrated, cross-curricular approach co-ordinated by teachers enjoying senior status.

Barriers to Implementation

The main obstacles to implementing a comprehensive and effective health-promoting curriculum are:

1. Health education is frequently accorded a low status – being considered an appropriate subject for girls and the less able! This is associated with the fact that it is not examined – with the rare exception of an occasional pioneering CSE Mode III.
2. There is no universally agreed definition of health education. It is therefore frequently confused with related subjects – particularly personal and social education (PSE). This in turn leads to territorial difficulties and may well cause confusion in the mind of head teachers who are faced with demands for precious timetable time from enthusiastic advocates for apparently different curricular subjects which nevertheless seem to be addressing very similar issues in very similar ways.
3. Irrespective of definition, health education is omnipretentious. It not only lays claim to relatively factual areas in, say, biology or home economics but also seeks to venture into the 'soft' areas of values and feelings. It invades areas which many see as the preserve of parents or psychiatrists; it seeks to change attitudes and modify behaviour. This is not surprising given the World Health Organization's (WHO, 1984) definition of health as not merely absence of disease but mental, physical and social well-being but, since this could well encompass the whole purpose of education and schooling, it hardly forms a sound basis for precise curriculum planning. As Goldstein (1975) remarked, 'if the study of health is the study of everything, it is the serious study of nothing'.
4. 'Mainstream' health education has strong medical connotations. The power and mystique of medicine is such that teachers may feel distinctly uneasy and apprehensive in dealing with such matters – and resort to invitations to visiting experts.
5. Because the approved model requires not only complete collaboration across subject boundaries but even seeks to lay bare the hidden curriculum and engineer institutional change, the prospect of what for most schools would be a major organizational and interpersonal upheaval is sufficient to deter even the most stouthearted!

6. The main concern of health education is not with knowledge and understanding but with decision-making, attitudes, values and social skills. It therefore requires a substantial shift towards less formal teaching methods: group work, role play and the like. This transition is inevitably threatening to many teachers – especially when preparation for teaching health education is sketchy or non-existent in initial teacher training and the opportunities for in-service training are limited.
7. Finally there is an increasing central pressure from government. At the time of writing, almost ten years of attempts to invade 'the secret garden of the curriculum' appears to bc bearing fruit (Holt, 1983). In so far as this central pressure favours the establishment of health education – and as indicated earlier, this does seem to be the case – then it is clearly not a barrier. However, there is some evidence that the 'official' interpretation of health education may not be entirely consonant with what many people see as its major purpose – the broad-based promotion of personal and social development.

Some of the problems listed are not readily solved. The status accorded health education must clearly depend on what we consider most worthwhile in the school curriculum. Recent HMI approval of PSE (DES, 1979) would certainly seem to indicate 'official' recognition of the broad-based definition of health although current concerns with narrower utilitarian goals may undermine this apparent commitment to health education and PSE. As for the issue of medical competence and teacher insecurity, wc should perhaps welcome the recent emphasis on demedicalization in WHO which points out that the health professions have only a relatively small part to play in health promotion – being concerned primarily with illness (WHO, 1984)! At a more practical level, it is worth reasserting the view that teachers should do the teaching while health personnel should be used as resources. Teachers are prepared to translate other specialisms into material suitable for their pupils and can well do the same for relevant medical matters. Admittedly factual errors in health matters might be more significant than mistakes about, say, Roman Britain, but there is a plentiful supply of resources and advice available to schools for health-education teaching. Indeed this subject area is especially favoured with a plethora of (readily accessible) free materials.

As for the remaining difficulties – these will only be addressed once a clear, pragmatic operational definition of health education is formulated. Nomenclature is not important; it does not matter what elements of the health promoting curriculum are called but it *is* important to avoid overlap and achieve meaningful and comprehensive coverage. Teachers need to know precisely how their own subject area contributes to the health promotion goal – and of course they need to have agreed beforehand that the goal is worth pursuing. The overlap between PSE and health education is considered to be a particular bone of contention and a proposal for mapping out respective territories appears at the end of this chapter.

The second factor at the heart of the problematical nature of health education is its central concern with values, attitudes, moral issues and social skills, in short its affective aspect – which will receive detailed appraisal after consideration of some different approaches to teaching about health.

APPROACHES TO HEALTH EDUCATION: SOME PHILOSOPHICAL ISSUES

Four separate identifiable approaches to health education may be used to describe the philosophical basis for practice. These are discussed in greater detail elsewhere (Tones, 1981, 1986a). The issue of 'voluntarism' is central to this discussion. In rather crude terms it is a question of whether you believe that an individual has a right to choose his or her lifestyle – including those behaviours which are manifestly self-destructive – or whether they should be persuaded or coerced into treading the straight and narrow path of health! The first approach to be considered implies the second course of action. It will be referred to here as a 'preventive medical model'. Its rationale is simple and its logic is compelling.

The Medical Model

The so-called *medical model* has reigned supreme for 50 years or so – although it has been subjected to increasing challenge in recent years (Vuori, 1980). The medical model offers a relatively narrow and partial interpretation of human health and illness. In brief – and rather simplisti-cally – people are viewed as machines; scant regard is paid to the environ-ment except as a source of pathogens which interfere with the smooth running of the organism. The reductionist approach of modern science has been strikingly successful in its analysis of the anatomy and physiology of the human robot. After several technological and pharmacological triumphs, modern medicine has prided itself on its capacity to repair the machine and even replace some of the worn parts in its attempts to prolong active life. In the process, the medical profession has gained a great deal of power and prestige.

Criticism of this process of 'medicalization' – the tendency of medicine to lay claim to and take over more and more aspects of everyday life – has taken several forms. Writers such as Illich (1977) argue that modern medicine tends to sap individual self-reliance and generate expectations of a pill for every ill. Holistic approaches to healthy living have attacked the narrow focus of modern medicine and prefer to see the individual in terms of traditional approaches to health, that is, as part of the ecosystem. However, the health-education approach which we are now considering offers a more muted but nonetheless substantial challenge to recent medical practice. It asserts that the more grandiose claims of curative medicine must be curtailed and argues that the focus of medical effort should be on prevention with health education playing a highly significant role. The argument may be summarized as:

1. After a long history of marginal effectiveness, doctors acquired some powerful weapons which they used to defeat the infectious diseases which were the major causes of death at the beginning of the present century. This halcyon period dates from the mid-1930s. There are, of course, those who insist that the improvements in living standards which were responsible for the substantial health gains prior to medicine's discovery of the 'magic bullets' would have eventually produced the same effects as those achieved by medical intervention (McKeown, 1976). It would, though, be churlish to deny the real benefits which new drugs and technology provided.

2. However, from the 1950s, medicine proved increasingly ineffectual in its attempts to deal with a new generation of diseases. These 'chronic degenerative diseases' (heart disease, cancers, stroke, arthritis and the like), which represented the effect of wear and tear on the machine, did not respond to wonder drugs or to surgery – despite the dramatically increasing cost to the health services of high technology. It was even suggested that the quality of life of patients might be suffering in the process with doctors undervaluing care in the constant attempt to cure the incurable.

3. Accordingly, it was argued that there should be a shift of emphasis from cure to prevention. Health education would have a star role in the new 'preventive medical model'; since people's lifestyle and behaviours seemed to be involved in causing or, at least, hastening the diseases of civilization, education should be used to persuade people to change their lifestyle. Where medicine had the facilities to cure disease or detect it at an early stage, education should be used to persuade people to use the services and follow the advice. Where disease had left permanent impairment – such as following a heart attack – education would be needed to help with rehabilitation and thus ensure that such a patient resumed as full a life as possible.

Within this new version of the medical model primary prevention (that is, preventing the onset of a disease) is clearly preferable and the school provides a captive audience for health education along with the possibility of influencing the population before they acquire the bad habits which might lead them to a premature death or an unhealthy old age. The logic of the argument is particularly appealing and dramatically expressed by the following extract from the Leverhulme Health Education Project (1978). It discusses the likely fate of children in a secondary school of 1,000 pupils.

> Thirty five of the children, more than one whole class, will die before they reach the age of 45; two hundred more, nearly 7 whole classes, will be dead before they reach the age of 65, that is before they have time to enjoy retirement. Of those who die before they reach 65, ten will be killed in road accidents – not to mention another hundred who will be seriously injured – sixteen will die from heart disease and another sixteen will die from cancer, mainly from lung cancer (which is now affecting a growing number of women). Approximately two hundred will have none of their own teeth when they reach their fortieth birthday. More than a hundred (nearly four whole classes) will seek treatment for a venereal disease within 5 years of leaving school. More than a hundred will, for a prolonged period of their adult life, consult their doctor concerning their mental health. Rather more than one in every four of the thousand will abandon, or be deserted by, or become separated from, their wives and husbands, or – what is perhaps worse – will become separated from their children.
>
> Leverhulme Health Education Project (1978)

Various government reports support this diagnosis in their assertions that the school has an important part to play in dealing with a range of social problems – including those of concern to preventive medicine. Moreover, as Reid and Massey (1986) have persuasively argued, it would seem that many of these preventive educational tactics have been successful. However, somewhat to the chagrin of those who view the school as a significant arm of preventive medicine, many teachers and educationists have reservations and consider that the school is above all an *educational* establishment!

Voluntarism and the 'Educational' Model

The philosophical basis of this second approach to health education rests on the view that education should primarily be concerned with rationality and freedom of choice. It has a long pedigree (Sutherland, 1979). This pursuit of rationality should be the school's main contribution to transmitting that which is most worthwhile in society. As Hirst (1969, p. 142) put it,

> If once the central objectives of rationality are submerged, or are given up so that . . . other pursuits take over, then I suggest that the school has betrayed its educational trust no matter how successful it may be in these other respects, and no matter how laudable these other ends may be in themselves.

The educational model of health promotion is, of course, not so naïve as to posit that merely providing information about health issues is sufficient to bring about behaviour change. Rather it considers that the primary goal of health education is to facilitate decision-making irrespective of the nature of the decision which might ultimately be made. People must be free to choose. This emphasis on voluntarism is not only the preserve of *school* health education: the Society for Public Health Education of America has adopted this principle in its code of ethics (1976). Indeed the importance of protecting free will and fostering informed health choices has consistently been supported by writers such as Green (Green *et al.*, 1980) who argues that health education must always be concerned with *voluntary* responses to the educator's messages.

The importance of fostering decision-making is quite clearly endorsed by many current health education curriculum projects. For instance the influential Schools Council Project: Health Education 5–13 (Schools Council, 1977) states that the major aim of health education 'should be to help children make considered choices or decisions related to their health behaviour'. Admittedly, the emphasis on decision-making probably reflects a concern to avoid the mere 'passing on of information' rather than a full-blooded commitment to freedom of choice. Indeed, analysis of subsequent statements about 'personal involvement' and 'responsibility' suggests that liberty is to be constrained by certain other overriding factors! In fact promoting informed decision-making is a goal which is emotionally satisfying but difficult to achieve in practice and, like the educational model itself, philosophically problematical. The criticism levelled at such approaches has to do with the illusory nature of genuine free choice which, at first sight, would appear to offer such a worthwhile goal for health education.

It is, of course, well-recognized that unbridled freedom of choice is rarely available and two justifications have been traditionally offered for imposing restrictions on such freedom: paternalism and utilitarianism (Wikler, 1978). It has, for instance, always been accepted that certain categories of individual are incapable of making rational decisions and must therefore have decisions made for them – for their own good. These include the severely mentally handicapped and, of course, children. Similarly individual freedom must always be limited by utilitarian considerations – for the good of society at large. It is indeed naïve in the extreme to expect very young children to make certain kinds of decision just as it is ingenuous to take individuals through a process of value-clarification and then happily condone subsequent decisions no matter how antisocial these might be. However, a rather more subtle and less obvious restriction is the sapping of will by any drug of addiction. This might be recognized in the stereotype of the 'junkie' pursuing his next shot of heroin but less so in the schoolchild whose social needs are met by the cigarette he or she has finally learned to tolerate. Even less apparent is the limit to choice imposed by the insidious process of socialization. Children who have been reared by parents who value independence and seek to equip their offspring with social skills and the confidence to use those skills will clearly be favourably placed in comparison with their less autonomous fellows who are handicapped by low self-esteem.

An even more important limitation to free choice is that imposed by social, environmental or economic constraints. It is plainly fatuous to exhort individuals to act responsibly when their environmental circumstances clearly make such a choice either impossible or difficult. For example, it is obviously not merely ineffectual but also unethical to expect someone living in poverty in an inner-city slum to have the same degree of choice as an individual living in privileged middle-class circumstances. Not only are there limitations imposed by the physical and social environment but barriers are also erected by poor self-image and the 'learned helplessness' created by the kinds of adverse socialization already mentioned. Any attempt, therefore, to educate people to make informed health choices in such circumstances is unethical: it is a new form of Social Darwinism – only the fittest make the healthy choices and survive! Paradoxically, recognition of the illusory nature of free choice may lead to the adoption of what at first sight appear to be two diametrically opposed approaches to health education. The first is the preventive model discussed earlier: if people cannot be expected to choose, then use persuasive skills to coerce them. Better still, manipulate the environment so that it is conducive to health choices – an approach adopted by some practitioners of the new 'health promotion' movement. The second approach adopts a more radical posture arguing that health education should be addressing the fundamental social issues underlying disadvantage and ill health.

The Radical Model

Irving Zola, in an address to the United Ostomy Association of America in 1970, explained what he saw as the major problem facing medical care in Western nations in terms of a river populated by drowning people (McKinlay, 1979). An overworked doctor lamented the fact that he spent all of his time rushing into the river, dragging the drowning people to shore and applying artificial respiration. The doctor barely had time to resuscitate the patient before he had to dash again into the torrent to rescue the next victim. He suddenly paused to ask himself the deeply significant question 'Who the hell is upstream pushing them all in?'! At first sight, this might appear to be just another argument for prevention rather than cure but the title of McKinlay's article (1979, op. cit.) – 'A Case for Refocussing Upstream: the *Political Economy* of Illness' (author's emphasis) – demonstrates the new radical concern. Health promotion should be 'refocussing upstream' and tackling the root cause of ill health. And the root cause is to be found in the social structure of nations and communities. For example, rather than considering individual behaviours such as smoking as the main cause of lung cancer and other associated diseases, attention should be directed to the antisocial activities of tobacco manufacturers and advertisers. Rather than 'blaming the victim' we should blame these commercial interests and government for failing to take adequate action. Again, a particular powerful contemporary issue is that of unemployment. Rather than try to deal with the demonstrable ill effects of unemployment by educating and treating individuals, should we not be more energetic in pressuring government to tackle unemployment? The 'Black Report' (Townsend and Davidson, 1982), which has been especially influential in recent years, argues for a major investment of resources and political will as the only means of dealing with the well-recognized inequalities in health prevailing in our society. In the words of a well-worn metaphor, to try to persuade individuals to modify their health behaviour in the face of overwhelming adverse social circumstances is like tidying the deckchairs on the *Titanic*.

What are the implications, then, for health education – especially school health education – of this radical approach? In short, the main function of education is considered to be that of 'critical consciousness raising' (a process which has an excellent educational pedigree – originally in the adult literacy field [Freire, 1972]). People should first be made aware of the existence of the social origins of ill health and then should be persuaded to take action. According to Freudenberg (1981) health educators should 'involve people in collective action to create health promoting environments' and should help people organize 'to change health-damaging institutions, policies and environments' (Freudenberg, 1984). This might, at first sight, seem far removed from the concerns of health education in school, but as we will see later, a combination of social education and lifeskills training as a precursor to 'mainstream' health education may well lay the foundations for such radical activities. However, before any such action is feasible, people must believe that they are capable of acting. In other words they must come to accept that they have the capacity to influence their destiny and acquire the social skills to do so. Such a goal is at the heart of the fourth model of health education to be considered here – that of self-empowerment. This approach has one especial advantage; it serves to reconcile the dilemma of choice mentioned and not only facilitates a radical approach to health promotion but helps an individual make the kinds of health choice which may prevent disease.

The Self-Empowerment Model

Before considering the self-empowerment approach in greater detail, it might be helpful to indicate how the four models interrelate since it would be misleading to suggest that these approaches to health education are inevitably exclusive or antagonistic. For instance, a self-empowerment model builds on an educational approach, and in some way potentiates it: informed decision-making becomes a more attainable goal when an individual becomes more self-empowered. Furthermore, a self-empowerment approach might well achieve preventive outcomes and lead to the adoption of a 'prudent' lifestyle rather than one that is health-damaging. Indeed, the rationale underlying certain *specific* health-related lifeskills programmes is that a self-empowered person would be better able to resist pressures to smoke or abuse alcohol or other substances (see for instance Botvin, Eng and Williams, 1980). Again, where a radical approach makes use of a community development strategy, its goal will be self-empowerment. Kindervatter (1979), for example, describes one of the main purposes of such 'non formal' education as helping people gain 'an understanding of and control over social, economic and/or political forces in order to improve their standing in society'.

The difference between the models is probably best illustrated by asking about what would be acceptable criteria of success. For the preventive model this would be the adoption of approved behaviours leading to a reduction in mortality or morbidity. For the radical model success would mean popular action leading to social change – for example, local initiatives resulting in the rehousing of tenants in damp housing. For those seeking to promote self-empowerment (a more sophisticated variant of the educational model), the capacity to choose freely is success enough.

The self-empowerment model, then, seeks to facilitate *genuine* informed decision-making. In essence, it aims to do this by not merely providing information on which decisions might be based, but rather by modifying aspects of personality. These attempts to foster personality growth involve changing the ways in which people view themselves and equipping them with a variety of skills which will help them interact more effectively with their environment. More particularly, the strategy adopted by the self-empowerment model is designed to enhance feelings of worth and self-esteem and to promote the development of a conviction that it is possible to be in charge of one's life. This latter belief is known technically as 'internal locus of control'.

Self-esteem is associated with health in a common-sense way; it could, by definition, be said to be one aspect of mental health. Similarly, it makes sense to assume that persons having little self-respect will not be motivated to 'look after themselves'. Less obviously perhaps, people enjoying high self-esteem will be more likely to form their own opinions and have the courage of their convictions (Coopersmith, 1967). As Aronson and Mettee (1968) show, individuals having high self-esteem will be more likely to experience high levels of dissonance when they 'act out of character' – for instance when they fail to take regular exercise while being persuaded that this measure would be beneficial to their health. At all events, the promotion of self-esteem appears to be an essential component in the up-to-date health education project!

Various steps have been proposed to develop self-esteem (for example, Hamachek, 1971 and Samuels, 1977). SCHEP 5–13 (op. cit.) deliberately sets out to develop a realistic self-concept in young people. Manifestly, such a step could be disastrous if the child's defence mechanisms were stripped away and he or she came to realize that he or she was in fact generally inadequate and unloved! For this reason teachers are asked to set attainable goals for children which will generate a feeling of self-satisfaction once achieved. Children are taught to be sensitive to the ways in which they can damage each other – and teachers too are asked to be especially sensitive to the sociometry of the classroom.

Perhaps more important still is the importance of recognizing the potentially damaging effect of the whole ethos and structure of the school and the process of labelling which Hargreaves (1967) captured so well in his identification of a 'delinquescent' subculture of recalcitrant 'drop-outs' in the secondary school. Again while the use of discussion, role play and 'social engineering' have an important part to play, a particularly valuable strategy involves equipping students with social skills – such as assertiveness – which makes them more effective and thus enhances not only their self-esteem but also their beliefs about their capacity to influence their lives or, in other words, their locus of control.

The notion of perceived locus of control (PLC) was developed by Rotter (1966) and is further discussed by Phares (1976). Those individuals having an 'external locus of control' will tend to believe that their scope for action is limited by fate, or by 'powerful others'. The concept has an obvious affinity with such ideas as Seligman's theory of 'learned helplessness' (1975) and fits into the broader theory of a self-perpetuating 'culture of poverty' – which is central to the radical critique of the victim-blaming approach discussed earlier.

The application of PLC to the health field has been extensively researched (Wallston and Wallston, 1978). External locus of control has been associated (as one factor from many) with sickness while 'internality' is correlated with non-smoking (James, Woodruff and Werner, 1965), reduction or cessation of smoking (Strickland, 1973), greater likelihood of contraceptive use (Lundy, 1972), weight loss (Jeffrey and Christensen, 1972), seat-belt usage (Williams, 1972) and inoculation against flu (Dabbs and Kirscht, 1971). Seeman and Evans (1962) also indicated that 'internals' knew more about medical conditions, were more inquisitive with doctors and nurses and indicated less satisfaction with the amount of information received in hospitals.

Interestingly, in the context of the Health Action Model, internality has been associated with the value of deferring immediate gratification for some greater future reward. As Phares (op. cit.) says, 'To attain control over one's environment, to achieve competence, or to reach positions of power and influence generally, all require that the individual eschew the lure of the present for the greater promise of the future.'

The self-empowerment model of health education, then, has obvious advantages; it seems to facilitate the kind of democratic political involvement, which is needed if the root causes of ill health are to be tackled, while facilitating individual choices in a way which will in all probability be congruent with a preventive medical approach. It is also clear that health education alone cannot provide the necessary teaching. Self-empowerment starts with parental and family influences and, ideally, should be developed during the entire 15,000 hours of schooling. This is clearly the prerogative of personal and social education; self-empowered health choices could be seen as the culmination of sound affective education which facilitates *all* decision-making throughout the individual's 'health career'. It involves, above all, values teaching and a kind of 'alliance' between social education and lifeskills teaching. However, before exploring this notion further, we need first to consider the factors which govern individual decision-making and the ways in which health-related values, attitudes, beliefs and behaviours develop over time. This requires some consideration of the useful health-career concept now to be described.

SOCIALIZATION AND
THE CONCEPT OF HEALTH CAREER

The school curriculum is much more than a timetable divided into little parcels of knowledge purveyed by different subject specialisms. The recent HMI *View of the Curriculum* (DES, 1980) reminds us of its scope and breath:

> The curriculum in its full sense comprises all the opportunities for learning provided by a school. It includes the formal programme of lessons in the timetable; the so-called 'extra-curricular' and 'out-of-school' activities deliberately promoted or supported by the school; and the climate of relationships, attitudes, styles of behaviour and the general quality of life established in the school programme.

The organic nature of this amalgam of learning experiences which make up the formal and 'hidden' curriculum of the school should help us recognize that its fundamental task is socialization. Socialization is a process of fitting individuals into an existing social structure; it is concerned with transmitting whatever a given culture considers is most worthwhile. The school is but one socialization agency and the individual is exposed to many influences as he or she progresses along a career from 'womb to tomb'. It would of course be wrong to think of people being passively moulded; the process is one of interaction. Nonetheless, as a result of this interaction, an individual develops values, beliefs, attitudes, knowledge and behaviours. Many of these are related directly or indirectly to health.

Primary Socialization and Family Influence

It is a truism to remark that parents and the home are critically important influences on the child and its future development. The Jesuits affirmed, 'Give me the child until he is seven and I will give you the man.' Proverbs (22:6) make a similar claim, 'Train up a child in the way that he should go: and when he is old, he will not depart from it.' The same wisdom is expressed, rather less poetically, in the Law of Primacy which claims that primary socialization is both more powerful and more enduring than later socializing influences. In other words, the influence of parents, family and home is potentially more powerful than any attempts which the school or other 'secondary' socializing agency might make in relation to values and attitudes. It is therefore apparent that where the primary socialization process has been thorough, attempts to 'resocialize' (change existing behaviours and their underlying values) will either meet with little success or require the use of behaviour change methods which would almost certainly be viewed as unethical! This is hardly surprising since primary socialization utilizes a particularly potent and insidious mix of persuasive tactics. Parents act as models for their children who imitate their actions and internalize their values. They reinforce this with a mixture of reward and punishment and thus shape behaviours and attitudes in a way entirely reminiscent of Skinner's operant conditioning techniques!

Secondary Socialization and the Influence of the School

Secondary socialization is less powerful than primary socialization. It is characterized by a lower level of emotional involvement and greater formality. However, as will be clear from earlier comments, those schools adopting a medical model of health education will be concerned to shape pupils' health behaviours and instil those values associated with responsible decision-making. Where the school's values promotion coincides with primary socialization, consolidation will result. Where it does not, the well-recognized phenomenon of 'culture clash' will occur.

Moreover the school's socialization efforts will meet with competition not only from the home but from peer groups. As any teacher knows only too well, the power of peer socialization is akin to primary socialization in the normative pressure it exerts. As research on smoking has clearly demonstrated (Tones, 1985), while parental smoking behaviour and attitudes are significant influences on future recruitment to smoking, peer-group pressure would seem to be even more powerful.

The Mass Media and Other Agencies

Once the young person has left school, further pressures are brought to bear and new influences are exerted on the health career. The workplace and, increasingly, quasi educational influences such as the Youth Training Scheme offer new health norms. Throughout life, of course, the health service and, particularly, the general practitioner and the primary health-care team, seek to provide a positive input into the health career – although as the individual moves into mature adulthood and old age, the concern is more and more with resocialization and a last-ditch attempt to change unhealthy practices!

Again, mass media constantly convey normative messages about health throughout the lifespan and their claimed harmful effects on children have been the subject of many a report. While these influences are far from benevolent, it would be wrong to assume that the power of, say, television is greater than that of the school. It would, of course, be misleading to deny the *indirect* albeit insidious impact of mass media's 'norm sending' function. Media convey mixed messages about sexuality; they extol the virtues of machismo and a superficially glamorous lifestyle which advertisers are delighted to associate with their products as part of a meretricious compensatory dream world. The popular press reports on cancer are frequently counter-productive and conflict with the goals of cancer education. Even the very process of news reporting – in the way it ignores prevention and glamorizes hi-tech curative medicine – can be construed as 'unhealthy'. However, it would be equally misleading to assume that the apparent power of mass media might easily be harnessed by the forces of good health! It is often argued, for instance, that if only health education had at its disposal sufficient funds to lavish on spectacular media advertising, the health product would be sold to its apathetic customers with the same degree of success as washing powder. Nothing could be further from the truth; where people are already motivated or ready for change, the mass media may indeed have a significant effect. However, the health 'product' typically involves expenditure of effort, deprives its consumer of pleasure or offers the prospect of some degree of suffering! In such cases mass media will achieve nothing. The teacher should rather look to the home or the peer group as sources of unhealthy influence rather than the mass media.

A Nutrition Career

The health-career concept is a useful way of identifying the influence of the various socialization agencies already mentioned on an individual's health throughout the lifespan. It is especially useful for those engaged in planning health education programmes – either globally or in the narrower confines of the school. It is a device which helps the planner take account of the many factors affecting health-related behaviours and attitudes both before and after the point in time when any particular health-education intervention is being planned. It may thus be used to explain present behaviours in terms of past influences or to predict future behaviours – together with their associated medical outcomes. For instance knowledge of a child's social background and its parents' smoking patterns makes it possible to guess at the possible effect of the child's exposure to a smoking peer group at adolescence. The designer of a programme of smoking education could therefore not only build in appropriate anticipatory guidance but also be in a position to plan an integrated and coherent set of educational activities for the whole community. The health-career concept will be illustrated here by examining some of the main factors affecting dietary choices. Since the 'input' of food and the 'output' of energy are complementary processes, a nutrition career would normally be considered alongside an 'exercise career'. However, for the sake of simplicity, only those factors affecting nutritional status will be considered here. These are represented diagramatically in Figure 1.1.

The importance of good nutrition for health is well-recognized and most nutritionists agree about the kinds of dietary change needed in the UK. For instance the programme for the 1980s proposed by the National Advisory Committee on Nutrition Education (NACNE Report, HEC, 1983b) recommends the following changes:

• Reduction of total fat by 10 per cent
• Reduction of saturated fat by 15 per cent
• Increase of polyunsaturated fat of 25 per cent
• Reduction in sugar of 10 per cent
• Increase in bread, potato, fruit and vegetable consumption by 25–30 per cent
• Increase in total dietary fibre by 25 per cent
• Reduction in salt by 10 per cent
• Reduction in average intake of alcohol by 10 per cent
• Increase in exercise

Translated from the clinical context, changes such as these represent a fairly dramatic change in human behaviour. They involve abandoning foods which give pleasure and adopting those which might be viewed with distaste. They may also signal an attack on values and attitudes having a deeper significance than the foodstuffs themselves. This will become clear when we examine the various socializing influences which cumulatively affect dietary choice.

The Social Context and the Local Community

It is important to remember that the individual's progress along the health career occurs within a physical and social environment. The kinds of shopping or sports facilities available in the neighbourhood will have an impact and food preferences will be affected by the nature and accessibility of local provision and the cost and quality of food supplies. Again, the social class of the community may have a dramatic effect on food choice and consumption – both directly and indirectly. Wilkinson (1977) shows that lower socioeconomic groups consumed about 40 per cent less fruit and

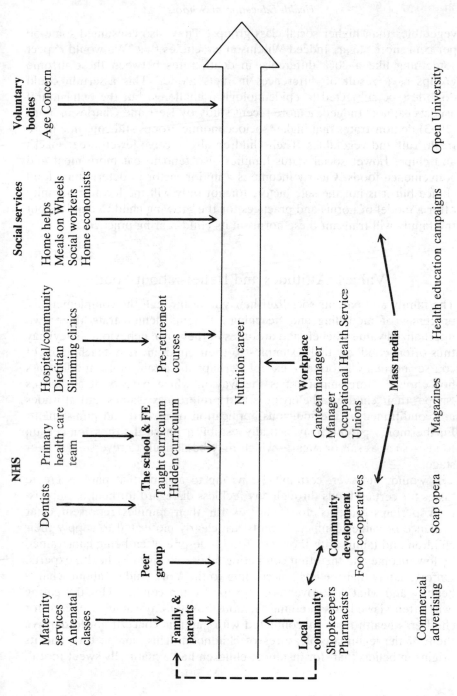

Figure 1.1 Educational influences on a nutrition career

vegetables than higher social class groups. They also consumed some 50 per cent more sugar. Indeed Wilkinson concludes that 'We would expect something like a 20% difference in death rates between these income groups as a result of differences in diets alone.' This assertion could doubtless be subjected to epidemiological challenge but the behavioural aspects cannot. Indeed, a more recent study by Kerr and Charles in York (1983) demonstrates that higher socioeconomic groups still consume more fresh fruit and vegetables. Their children also receive fewer sweet snacks and chips. Lower social status families also tend to eat more meat and convenience foods. Clearly income is a major factor in determining food choice but it is not the sole factor, for not only will the local community offer a model of norms and practices for the growing child to emulate but the family will transmit these norms in its child-rearing practices.

Values, Attitudes and Beliefs about Food

The family and parents socialize their young through the complementary processes of modelling and 'teaching'. Parents demonstrate their own internalized values, beliefs and attitudes in their own behaviour. They may thus offer 'good' or 'bad' examples to their children. Any teaching is, of course, normally informal – except perhaps in certain more middle-class households! More important is the way in which parents of all classes 'shape' their children's behaviours and preferences; values and attitudes are conditioned by the judicious application of reward and punishment. Furthermore, parents may actually establish physical tastes for certain foods – such as salt or sugar – which may be difficult to reverse at a later stage.

It would, however, certainly be wrong to assume that parents create tastes for certain foods through any feckless disregard for health. Surprisingly perhaps, parents' food choices for their families represent clear evidence of values conflict. Parents are clearly motivated to supply their children and family with the 'best' food – despite often being constrained by low income and the often conflicting advice received by health experts. Unfortunately their beliefs – according to the York study – about what is healthy and what is enjoyable or 'proper' often conflict. Healthy eating 'was often viewed as something virtuous but not enjoyable'. Concern for children's health typically conflicted with parental concern not to deprive them of the legitimate pleasures of childhood. This view in turn had its origins in beliefs that, for instance, children had a 'naturally sweet tooth', or needed sugar for energy. Moreover, dietary propriety was such that the mother might be seen to be failing in her duty if she did not serve at least one 'proper' meal a day – and proper meant with 'meat, vegetables and such like', a traditional Sunday dinner and 'food in separate little piles on the plate'. Retribution was anticipated for serving 'improper' foods: 'If I served him lasagne he'd throw it at me" (Kerr and Charles, 1983).

The symbolic nature of food is further illustrated by its role in child control and the expression of love. The sweet or biscuit is of course frequently used to keep the young child quiet or to reward him or her for achievements. Sweets and chocolates are seen as the entirely legitimate way for relatives – especially grandparents – to show their pride and affection in the grandchild. Teaching about food, then, cannot be divorced from 'parentcraft' teaching; the home economist not only must be a nutritionist but must also consider his or her role in teaching values.

Mass Media and National Norms

A detailed discussion of a nutrition career is beyond the scope of this chapter. However, even a cursory glance at Figure 1.1 reveals the considerable variety of socializing influences on the individual during the lifespan – and the equally wide variety of potential or actual health-education inputs. The mass media do of course supply a continuing background influence against which choices are made. Reference has already been made to the tendency to overestimate this influence compared with interpersonal education – even when the food industry spends several millions of pounds a year on advertising what NACNE would consider unhealthy foods. However, mass media do represent national norms which include social values which have at first sight little to do with nutrition but which are none the less important. The most striking example would have to be the association of food with female attractiveness and general worth. An absorbing piece of recent research (Tones, 1983) claims that in 1959 the average 'Playmate' in the centrefold of *Playboy* magazine weighed 91 per cent of the national average but by 1978 the models' dimensions had dropped to 83 per cent of that average figure. During the same period, women of all classes under the age of 30 had become heavier. The gap between the ideal norm and reality was thus larger and presumably resulted in higher levels of dissatisfaction among the majority of women who did not meet this artificial norm (Cataldo, 1985); as Orbach (1978) asserts, fat is indeed a feminist issue.

The Role of the School

The traditional role of the school in nutrition education centres on biology and home economics. From what has been said, food has values repercussions and relates to the broader area of PSE. Apart from implications for family-life education, food reflects aspects of gender role which is the concern of sex education. Perhaps, less obviously, nutrition education overlaps with political education since one of the most important environmental constraints on healthy diet is the EEC's Common Agricultural Policy. Moreover, the various pressures on government nationally from commercial organizations and the farming industry, whose profits may be threatened by the implementation of NACNE guidelines, represent classical political lobbying.

Equally political – albeit with a smaller 'p' – is the hidden curriculum. It is well-recognized that the tuck shop and the schools' meal service may well be conveying powerful messages about food which are dramatically at odds with the formal teaching about nutrition.

INFORMED DECISION-MAKING AND THE HEALTH ACTION MODEL

We have so far considered how social norms and the individual beliefs, values attitudes and health-related behaviours which they represent emerge during the lifespan of each individual in the form of a health career. A cross-sectional perspective will now be presented. This will seek to define the complex of factors which operate at any one point in time when an individual is faced with making a decision. An understanding of these factors is of particular importance given the current orthodoxy which states that the task of health education is primarily to equip young people with decision-making skills. It is not always clear what this actually means. Is teaching to be so structured that any kind of decision-making is acceptable – so long as it is efficient? Or does the term *'responsible* decision-making' – which is frequently seen in curricular statements – indicate that only certain 'approved' decisions are to be taught? As indicated earlier in this chapter the notion of decision-making was central to SCHEP 5–13. It also appears in the view of health education proposed by the 'My Body' Project (HEC, 1983a) which states,

> This project is based on the view that people are actively involved in shaping their own environment. To do this they must make choices. Therefore the aim of health education should be to increase children's ability to make choices about the things that affect their health.

However, since the major goal of the project is avowedly to reduce recruitment to smoking and teach children to avoid damaging their bodies, it is clear that only certain 'healthy' choices are acceptable. This kind of issue will receive further discussion when the nature of controversy and values clarification is examined. However, the apparent confusion points to the importance of understanding how decisions are made and the factors which influence health choices. These are illustrated in the context of a health action model (HAM) which is shown in Figure 1.2.

Three categories of health-related behaviour are shown in Figure 1.2. Routines are those behaviours which have become habitualized – frequently as a result of early socialization. For instance, brushing teeth, washing hands and patterns of eating are often established as a result of parental influence. Adults too will learn a variety of skilled behaviours which operate smoothly and automatically once they have been established. In the context of the present discussion, the significance of such

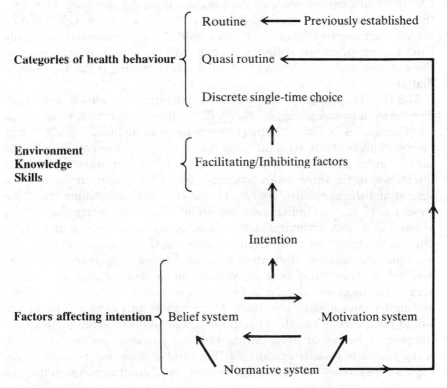

Figure 1.2 The health action model and categories of health behaviour

routines is that they do not require a conscious decision once they have become part of each individual's repertoire.

Quasi routines refer to categories of behaviour which at first sight appear to involve conscious decisions but on closer inspection require little conscious deliberation and deliberate choice. Consider Harfouche's (1965; 1970) description of a particular society's attitude to breast-feeding:

> Lactation management and breast-feeding as an act and way of life are acquired in the home. The pattern has a familiar transmission; girls usually identify with their mothers, and after marriage they try to comply with the wishes of their in-laws and husbands.

The mother's role is prescribed in unequivocal terms:

> Nursing is a duty; a mother who does not nurse denies her baby's right . . . she is stingy, lazy, negligent, lacks affection like a step-mother . . . no lactation no affection.

Clearly in this kind of instance the pressure from the 'normative system', that is, the influence of social norms and powerful people, is such that only the very self-empowered or foolhardy would dare to contemplate deviating from normal practices! Admittedly such extreme situations are rare, but the example serves to remind us that decision-making is rarely a simple matter.

The HAM is primarily concerned with deliberate discrete choices – such as a decision to accept heroin when offered it or, conversely, to refuse an additional drink in club or pub. This decision-making process – which may be conscious or, more typically, unconscious – results from an intention to act in a given situation. The intention to act is, in turn, influenced by the interaction of the three major 'systems': the belief system, the motivation system and the normative system. However, before examining these, we should note that an individual's intention may never materialize in the absence of certain 'facilitating factors' and/or in the presence of 'inhibiting' influences. Environmental circumstances must be appropriate if, for example, the pressing problem of unwanted teenage pregnancies is to be avoided; contraceptives must be available and accessible. Again, the teenager in question would need to *know* where to obtain the contraceptives and understand how to use them. More importantly perhaps, he or she would need certain social and communication skills to avoid unprotected intercourse before or even during the first romantic encounter. These social interaction skills would probably involve using assertiveness techniques either to say 'no' or to negotiate the use of contraceptives in the face of probable embarrassment.

The Health Action Model and Health Beliefs

A belief is a probability judgment. It defines the way in which an individual views the relationship between some object and its attribute – for example, the relationship between exercise and health or between smoking and heart disease. Beliefs are the foundation on which health decisions are built. The belief system forms the interface between knowledge and motivation: unless information is accepted as true and accurate, it is obvious that a person will not be motivated to act on that information. It is not surprising therefore that various theories and models have been designed to explain the relationship between beliefs, attitudes and behaviour. One of these has had a particular appeal at a common-sense level and demonstrates succinctly the ways in which beliefs govern preventive health actions. It is known as the health belief model (HBM) (Becker, 1974) and states that the following conditions must be fulfilled before any given preventive measure will be adopted:

1. The individual must believe that he or she is *susceptible* to the health hazard in question. For example, he or she must believe that pregnancy is a *real* possibility after the first occasion on which unprotected intercourse has taken place – otherwise there would seem no urgent need to insist on contraception.
2. The individual must also believe that the health hazard is *serious*. If tooth loss and artificial teeth are not viewed with concern, young people are hardly likely to respond to health education messages which urge dietary discretion and regular tooth-brushing.
3. The individual must in addition believe that the recommended health measure will be *beneficial*, that is, it must be *effective*. For instance, an experimental smoker will have to accept the dubious proposition that he or she will be more attractive to the opposite sex if he or she does not 'smell like an old ashtray'; otherwise there is no incentive to join the ranks of the non-smokers!
4. The individual must also believe that there are relatively few *costs* or disadvantages involved in adopting the 'healthy' behaviour or resisting the 'unhealthy' behaviour. For example, in the field of social and emotional well-being it is considered important to promote the 'considerate way of life'. A pupil must therefore not believe that being helpful and kind to other children will result in his or her being labelled 'soft' or 'teacher's pet' by his or her peers.

Apart from the key beliefs listed, the health belief model (HBM) argues that some 'trigger' or critical event might be needed (such as interpersonal pressure or a television programme) to tilt the balance in favour of the health choice. The later formulation of the HBM also recognized its lack of affective emphasis and stated that some kind of positive health motivation might also be needed to stimulate action – a point which will be developed later.

The Self-Concept and Health Actions

While the central HBM beliefs are undoubtedly important, there are other categories of belief which merit consideration and which might well be the focus of health-teaching. For instance beliefs about cause and effect will in turn generate beliefs about susceptibility, seriousness and the like. Consider cancer education. It is generally recognized that the major goal of cancer education is to reduce *cancerophobia* – the irrational fear of cancer. A major factor contributing to this fear is the general belief, associated with pessimism, that cancer is incurable, mysterious, and 'triggered' by a wide variety of events in unpredictable and uncontrollable ways. An important piece of research by the BBC (1983) suggests that one belief might be pivotal – the belief that cancer is a single undifferentiated disease. Those who believed that there were several varieties of cancer were more likely to hold an optimistic view about prevention and cure. The lesson is obvious: efficient teaching in the relatively cool and detached atmosphere of biology should create the sound understanding necessary for establishing an accurate belief about the nature of cancer. This in turn should have a knock-on effect on those beliefs associated with pessimism and finally make *one* significant contribution to counteract the unduly negative attitude to cancer which is at the core of cancerophobia.

Arguably more important than cause-effect beliefs is that cluster of beliefs about self which constitutes the self-concept. These include not only the HBM belief about susceptibility or personal vulnerability but, more importantly, those beliefs about personal effectiveness which relate to notions of locus of control and are central to the concept of self-empowerment discussed earlier. If we consider again the single most important issue in education for family planning, that of avoiding teenage pregnancies, the centrality of teaching related to the self-concept may be illustrated. It has been argued that at least some unwanted pregnancies may result not from ignorance about contraception but from a sense of futility and hopelessness associated with an oppressive environment and perhaps the prospect or reality of unemployment. Now, while this might rightly be seen as an argument for social change, it should also justify an emphasis on personal growth and development in the context of general and specific lifeskills education for self empowerment.

The Motivation System

The motivation system describes a complex of affective elements which ultimately determines the individual's attitude to any specific decision and his or her intention of carrying out any such specific action. An important part of this complex is an individual's value system, that is, those emotionally charged beliefs and elements of faith which make up what an individual considers most worthwhile in life and which are at the centre of moral education and religious teaching. They may relate to general codes of conduct, to feelings about family and friends, to career – and even to health!

Equally important components in the motivation system are those 'drives' which trigger powerful emotions and may override the less immediate influence provided by values. The term *drive* is used here to refer to basic instinctive urges such as sex or hunger and also to acquired motives such as addictions – the importance of which is often underemphasized when applying models such as HBM to activities like smoking or heavy consumption of alcohol. Other factors such as anxiety, guilt or embarrassment may also be ignored; yet these powerful emotions may also determine action or inaction even in the presence of generally favourable attitudes.

Again, just as each individual has a cluster of beliefs about self, he or she also values himself or herself to a greater or lesser extent – something normally referred to as self-esteem. In the HAM the term *self-sentiment* is used to refer to the aggregate of feelings about self. Self-empowerment strategies inevitably focus on self-concept and self-sentiment in order to modify not only self image but also to enhance the value attached to the individual as a person.

The interaction of the belief system and the motivation system is illustrated in Figure 1.3. This elaborates two of the systems which influence intention and which are shown in outline in Figure 1.2.

Its application can be illustrated by referring again to the example of teenage contraception choice mentioned earlier. While it is undoubtedly essential to have developed accurate cause-effect beliefs and to have accepted one's susceptibility to pregnancy, it would also be rash in the extreme not to recognize the power of the sex drive! Clearly strong moral values relating to sexual behaviour may override the sex drive or lead to avoidance of risk situations; however since 46 per cent of first experiences of intercourse were unprotected (Farrell, 1978), it would be wise not to bank on this! Less predictable perhaps might be the feelings of embarrassment and guilt associated with the prospect of a girl taking responsibility

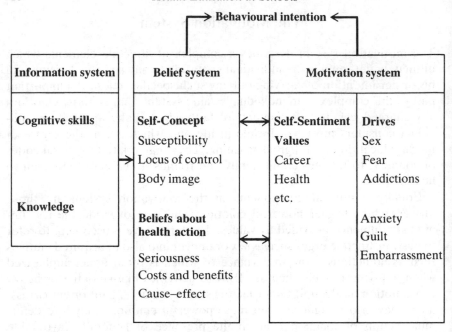

Figure 1.3 The health action model: interaction of belief and motivation systems

for contraception on this first occasion. As Farrell (1978) amongst others points out, this guilt would be associated with the double standard relating to male and female sexual roles.

The Normative System

The normative system within HAM refers to the different kinds of social pressure exerted on the individual's decision-making. An individual's behaviours will in part be influenced by his or her 'personal' beliefs about the health action, but will also be affected by beliefs about what is normal and acceptable behaviour – and, very importantly, by beliefs about how 'significant others' will react to the anticipated decision which the individual is contemplating. These latter beliefs are usually called *normative beliefs*. However, just as these 'personal' beliefs are only as influential as the values to which they relate, normative beliefs will have an impact only if the individual is motivated to conform with norms or comply with the wishes of significant others.

Three important normative elements are shown in Figure 1.4. These are considered to exert different degrees of pressure. For instance the power of

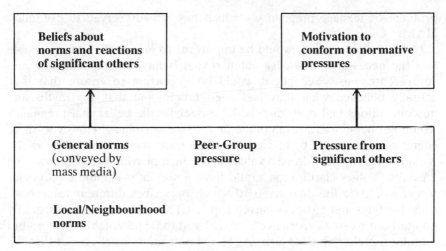

Figure 1.4 Three important normative elements

general norms (typically conveyed by mass media) would be less than the power of local neighbourhood norms (experienced by direct observation). Again, the pressure exerted by a highly significant individual – such as parent or girlfriend – would normally be much greater. The potential effect of a teenage peer group and the power of its sanctions has been well-recognized and needs no further comment here. Figure 1.4 complements Figure 1.3 above and describes the third system affecting intention in Figure 1.2.

The Health Action Model: Implications for Education

The health action model provides a kind of blueprint for educational action. The nature of such intervention will of course depend on the kind of health-education approach which is considered ethical and appropriate. Clearly a 'preventive approach' will want to provide inputs which result in the student making an approved and 'responsible' healthy choice. An 'educational' approach will seek to facilitate choice among alternatives. However, bearing in mind that genuinely free choice is difficult if not impossible in the absence of certain 'personality factors', a self-empowerment approach will want to develop those personal attributes which make such choice truly voluntaristic. A radical approach would want to draw attention to the structural and environmental 'facilitating and inhibiting factors'. The use of HAM as a planning tool can be illustrated by summarizing the kinds of educational input which might be provided to handle the problem of teenage pregnancy – which has already served to exemplify HAM.

In the first instance it would be important to ensure that young people had the necessary *knowledge* about sexual behaviour, reproduction and contraceptive use. Second, it would be important to ensure that they actually believed what they had been taught and that any myths and misconceptions had been dispelled – especially the belief that pregnancy would not happen as a result of the first sexual encounter! However, these cognitive goals would be less important than the focus provided by affect-ive teaching which addressed values and which provided self-empowering lifeskills. Values clarification would have a special place and a particular target would be the dual standard which prescribes different value posi-tions for boys and girls. As Farrell (op. cit.) and others have consistently pointed out, sexual experience is considered to be acceptable for boys but morally reprehensible for girls. As HAM indicated, a girl's belief that she would be viewed as calculating and promiscuous if she is seen to contem-plate contraception might well lead to sexual risk-taking.

While value *clarification* is an important element in this sex education programme, values *promotion* must also figure prominently and the damaging effects of unwanted pregnancy would of course receive empha-sis. The process of values teaching is discussed later but it is worth noting at this point that developing feelings of concern for other people may not be the easiest of tasks. On the other hand it is very tempting to consider 'plugging in' directly to the motivating system by generating a fear drive which might deter sexual experimentation. The prospect is very gratifying – especially for those who are irritated by the blatantly irresponsible behaviour of the young. However these temptations should be resisted! The theoretical principle is fine; however – even if it is considered ethical to create anxiety – it is extremely difficult in practice to generate just the right amount of fear for each individual. As research clearly demonstrates (Levanthal and Cleary, 1980) fear appeal can be not only a blunt instru-ment but a double-edged weapon; if it has an impact on one person it is just as likely to create defensive avoidance in a second and rebound totally on a third who will be more determined to take risks after the misguided threats than he or she was beforehand!

Lifeskills teaching, as part of a general self-empowerment strategy, has a central part to play in minimizing the risk of unwanted pregnancy – both generally and specifically. Its general function is the by now familiar one of increasing the capacity for autonomous decision-making and enhancing self-esteem. The more specific function relates to the facilitating factors which are interposed in the HAM between intention and action. In particular the social interaction skill of assertiveness facilitates the intention to refuse unprotected sexual intercourse. However, what of the general inhibiting effect of the social environment? The question of access to contraception has already been mentioned; less apparent is the more indirect effect of social climate in restricting access. For instance a recent international study by the Guttmacher Institute (Jones *et al.*, 1985) of rates of abortion and illegitimacy in developed countries revealed that the highest incidence was to be found where there were high levels of poverty and disadvantage, a general prevalence of 'religiosity' and narrow-mindedness and inadequate sex-education programmes. The implications would therefore seem to be that a programme of sex education should go hand-in-hand with social measures designed to deal with inequality and disadvantage, in other words, a broad health-promotion approach incorporating radical health education.

Teaching Decision-Making Skills

Reference has already been made to the current emphasis placed on informed decision-making in health education – indeed, as we have seen, it is at the very heart of the educational and self-empowerment models. We have also seen how even preventive-model projects such as 'My Body' seek to promote decision-making capabilities. The implication of all this is clear: young people need some kind of competence, or even specific skills, before they can make efficient decisions. The nature of these capabilities can be clarified by identifying the factors contributing to decision-making. This has, of course, been done: the health action model has shown how beliefs, motives, social pressures and various facilitating factors contribute to making health choices. We have also briefly commented on its application to a health-education programme designed to facilitate 'responsible' or even 'irresponsible' choices in relation to making decisions about unprotected sexual intercourse. The major processes involved in this programme are outlined in Figure 1.5.

Apart from an input of information providing the factual basis on which decisions might be made, beliefs must be examined and related to one's value system. This process of values clarification will also involve a timely reminder of certain values which are not open to discussion but are merely to be promoted (an issue which will receive further consideration). However, education purportedly designed to facilitate choice will be a sham unless the individual has been 'self-empowered' and believes that he or she is capable of choice and that it is worthwhile doing so. Similarly unless a broader health promotion programme has ensured that the physical and

Promoting decision-making

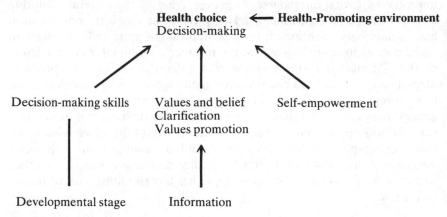

Figure 1.5 Promoting decision-making

social environment is conducive to decision-making, no genuine decision-making will be possible. What remains is the typically ill-defined specific skill associated with decision-making. Dorn (1977), in the context of drug education, defines this skill as 'the ability to anticipate and discuss "choice situations" in which teenagers may find they have access to drugs for the first time and ability to apply knowledge in such situations'. Psychologists specializing in the study of decision-making would, on the other hand, have a more sophisticated view. For instance, Janis and Mann (1979) emphasize the centrality of cognitive processes. They list seven criteria of efficient decision-making:

1. Thoroughly canvasses a wide range of alternative courses of action.
2. Surveys the full range of objectives to be fulfilled and the values implicated by the choice.
3. Considers positive and negative consequences of each alternative.
4. Searches for new information relevant to further evaluation of the alternatives.
5. Takes account of and correctly assimilates any new information even when this does not support the course of action he [or she] initially prefers.
6. Re-examines positive and negative consequences of all known alternatives, including those initially regarded as unacceptable, before making a final choice.
7. Makes provision for carrying out chosen course of action. Gives special attention to contingency plans which might be needed if known risks materialized.

A detailed discussion of decision-making is beyond the scope of this chapter. However, it is clear that if the subject is to be addressed seriously by teachers, they should recognize the complexity of the task. For example, as Cowley (1978) points out, both the cognitive and affective aspects depend on developmental stage. Cowley cites Kohlberg and Turiel (1971) who observe that in a group of young people aged 14–15 only 3 per cent of boys and 6 per cent of girls might be expected to handle the 'formal operational thinking' needed to indulge in 'vigilant decision-making'. Very careful thought, therefore, must be given to designing teaching methods which will provide decision-making skills and wean children from passive followers of authority to autonomous decision-makers.

In relation to HAM, decision-making skills would form part of the cognitive skills in the information system and would to all intents and purposes make a direct input to the process of calculating the costs and benefits of particular courses of action. Let us now turn our attention to the motivation system and examine the contribution of values teaching to the making of health choices.

VALUES CLARIFICATION, VALUES PROMOTION AND THE NATURE OF CONTROVERSY

Values teaching is central to PSE and health education. Of particular interest, in connection with the goal of informed choice, is the relationship between the *clarification* of values and the *promotion* of values. The promotion of certain values might well be regarded as moralizing – especially where such values are relatively narrow. On the other hand merely to encourage the clarification of values might be considered irresponsible. My view is that value clarification should be reserved for controversial issues – although this does, of course, beg the question of how controversy should be defined. In part this can be regarded as a matter of fashion almost: certainly the values goals of health education change in accordance with normative and political climates. For the present, however, let us consider the notion of values clarification which enjoyed cult status in the USA in the 1960s and early 1970s.

Values Clarification

The rationale for values clarification (VC) is simple enough: we live in a pluralistic society in which the only certainty is the certainty of change. Since no simple guidelines for the 'good life' receive universal acclamation, young people must be helped to make up their own minds and formulate their own code of values. Moreover they should be helped to reassess continually and revitalize conventional moralities. Raths (1978), a pioneer of values clarification, quotes Gardner (1964) who justifies this latter point of view in the following way, 'Instead of giving young people the impression that their task is to stand a dreary watch over the ancient values, we should be telling them the firm but bracing truth that it is their task to recreate those values continuously in their own time.'

As Simon – one of the chief proponents of values clarification – says, 'The values clarification approach does not aim to instil one particular set of values' (Simon *et al.*, 1972). However, it would be naïve to assume that this approach is values-free. As Simon (1974) points out, 'too often the important choices in life are made on the basis of peer pressure, unthinking submission to authority or the power of propaganda'. However, as a result of values clarification, 'students become . . . less apathetic, less flighty, less conforming, less over-dissenting. They are more zestful and energetic, more critical in their thinking and are more likely to follow through on decisions'. These characteristics are obviously highly prized!

Simon identifies the VC process as a hierarchy of seven stages or steps: (1) prizing and cherishing; (2) publicly affirming, when appropriate; (3) choosing from alternatives; (4) choosing after consideration of consequences; (5) choosing freely; (6) acting; (7) acting with a pattern, consistency and repetition. The implication of this procedure might at first sight seem to be that it does not really matter what you do so long as you have worked out the consequences of the act and related these to a value system. Success would be measured not so much by the nature of the choice but by whether or not people acted with commitment and consistency. Forcinelli (1974) took exception to the apparent amorality of the approach, pointing out that 'an educational system can produce a dishonest and potentially dysfunctional product and then merely say these are legitimate expressions of individual values. It is possible to conceive of one going through (VC processes) and deciding that he values intolerance or thieving.' Goodlett (1976) adopts a similar stance and argues for the inclusion of 'responsibility' in the VC equation as follows:

> In order to make personally satisfying and *socially responsible* decisions . . . [students] . . . must have a good understanding of self; what one values; what *society values*; the valuing process; the effects of peer pressure; risk taking behaviours; the strategies used in making decisions; the necessary information and the ability to identify alternatives and the consequences of behavior [author's italics].

The relevance of these activities for teaching decision-making and the parallel with the HAM elements is hopefully apparent.

Values Development by Design

Dalis and Strasser (1981) provide a rapid review of the development of school health education in the United States. They list the following 'milestones': 'ca. 1900 – Anatomy/Physiology; ca. 1920 – Health Habits; ca. 1940 – Health Knowledge; ca. 1960 – Health Concepts; ca. 1970 – Health Values Clarification/Awareness'. They then move us on beyond VC to what they call 'values development by design'. In short they describe a strategy to actually *promote* values. They recognize – as we need to do now – that certain values need clarifying while others need, at the very least, our active endorsement. They caution that developing values which are actively supported by the community will be labelled 'good teaching' while promoting values about which there may be disagreement will be called 'brainwashing'! It is thus important to try and distinguish those values which are controversial and those which enjoy the general acclaim – or acquiescence – of the public.

The Considerate Way of Life

Examination of recent reports from Her Majesty's Inspectorate reveals an official view of values to be promoted. For example, the curriculum document 11–16 (DES, 1977) mentions such goals as self-esteem, tolerance and health. There would be little challenge to such views although it might be argued that since health consists of mental, physical and social components which are on occasion mutually incompatible, it is inappropriate to seek to pontificate about particular health values. The argument for a short life and a merry one has been well rehearsed over the ages! However, the argument that a firm values-foundation is that of a 'broad assent to political democracy' is hard to challenge. In fact, the position adopted here is that health involves a state of equilibrium between self-actualization and responsibility – a kind of compromise involving a determined effort to develop individual capabilities while at the same time minimizing the chance that any individual damages the right of other people to grow and prosper. The notion of self-actualization has been thoroughly developed by Maslow (1968) and neatly operationalized by the Scottish Health Education Group in their catchphrase 'Be All You Can Be'. The notion of social responsibility has been popularly encapsulated in McPhail's term 'The Considerate Way of Life' and expressed not only in Moral Education

Projects such as 'Lifeline' (McPhail *et al.*, 1972), and 'Startline' (McPhail *et al.*, 1978), but also the health education project 'Living Well' (McPhail, 1977). All seek to 'help young people . . . adopt a considerate style of life . . . to take other people's needs and feelings into account as well as their own' (McPhail *et al.*, 1972).

The Nature of Controversy

By definition, those values which are not to be promoted are to be clarified because they are controversial. Fraser (cited in Stenhouse, 1969b) defines a controversial issue thus:

> A controversial issue involves a problem about which different individuals and groups urge conflicting courses of action. It is an issue for which society has not found a solution that can be universally or almost universally accepted. It is an issue of sufficient significance that each of the proposed ways of dealing with it is objectionable to some section of the citizenry and arouses protest. The protest may result from a feeling that a cherished belief, an economic interest, or a basic principle is threatened. It may come because the welfare of organisations or groups seems at stake.

It is clear that many health issues would be considered controversial in the light of the preceding definition. Two areas in particular were included in Stenhouse's Humanities Curriculum Project (Schools Council, 1970) – The Family and Relationship between the Sexes. This project was established in 1967 to offer, 'stimulus, support and materials appropriate to enquiry-based courses which cross the traditional boundaries between English, History, Geography, Religious Knowledge and Social Studies'. It is of special interest to PSE and health education – not merely because it handles controversial health issues but because it emphasizes the importance of non-formal teaching methods in facilitating decision-making.

Authority, Decision-Making and Non-Formal Teaching Methods

The humanities curriculum project (HCP) exemplifies the values-clarification process in pure form. Stenhouse argues that if the teacher is serious about promoting decision-making then the student must be not only helped to think and enquire but made to feel that the process was worthwhile because his or her viewpoint mattered. The very nature of the teacher's authority role, he argues, militates against the development of independent thought – especially in the context of the relatively authoritarian structure of most schools. Even where discussion and inquiry-based learning were used, there was a danger that discussion might degenerate into 'a guessing game about the mind of the teacher'. A guessing game is merely disguised instruction (Stenhouse, 1969a). The HCP solution was to use group discussion in which the teacher adopted the role of 'neutral and impartial chairman and resource consultant': even providing a point of view with full disclaimer that the students' ideas were worth just as much as the teachers' was sufficient in Stenhouse's opinion to contaminate proceedings with authority.

The HCP approach has been criticized of course; White (1969) for instance challenged the notion of neutrality pointing out that bias was inevitable since the 'chairman' chose which pieces of 'evidence' to feed into the discussion and when. McPhail feels it is unethical for the teacher not to respond to a pupil's request to know where he or she stands on a particular moral issue. However, perhaps the major problem with the HCP is that it is difficult to use – especially with the average and less-than-average ability students for whom it was originally intended. Moreover, developments in PSE and lifeskills teaching have provided more manageable structured learning experiences which incorporate elements of values clarification but also recognize the importance of providing social intervention skills for young people as a means of fostering personal development and providing competence in making decisions. The relationship between PSE and health education will now be considered.

PSE AND HEALTH EDUCATION:
A SYMBIOTIC RELATIONSHIP

The problematic relationship between health education and PSE was referred to at the beginning of this chapter in terms of a possible barrier to the adoption of coherent health-education programmes in schools. At times it seems as if the two terms are used interchangeably; on other occasions it would seem that health education is part of PSE or, alternatively, that PSE is part of health education. David's (1983) clear analysis of PSE in secondary schools includes health as part of the 'map of the territory' along with personal relationships, morality, social awareness, religion, philosophies of life and specific aspects of development in the context of occupation, politics, the law, the community and the environment.

PSE is manifestly charged with promoting satisfactory personal and social development – which, to all intents and purposes, satisfies the classic WHO definition of health as not merely the absence of disease but also mental, physical and social well-being. If this is the case what is health education's peculiar contribution? The value offered here is that, since PSE can legitimately lay claim to promoting health in its broader and more positive sense, health education's *main* role is to contribute directly or indirectly, in the short or long term, to the prevention of disease and disability at primary, secondary or tertiary levels and to promote the development and utilization of health services. This does not of course mean that it should adopt a 'victim-blaming' approach. Indeed, one of its major functions would be to raise awareness of the social origins of disease and seek, for example, to foster political action to remedy gross inequalities in health. However, to do this effectively, the support of PSE in general and lifeskills training and social education in particular is essential (Tones, 1982; 1986b).

Lifeskills Teaching and Social Education

The importance of self-empowerment has already been mentioned and the contribution of lifeskills teaching has been well-documented elsewhere (Hopson and Scally, 1981). It is, however, important to note a criticism levelled at lifeskills teaching which, because it allegedly fails to take account of the major social and environmental barriers to free choice, has been labelled a new, albeit more sophisticated, form of 'victim-blaming'. The problem is that the term has become debased – mainly due to the activities of organizations such as the Manpower Services Commission which apparently· seek to use lifeskills training as a form of social control ('One of the aims of Life Skills Training will be to adjust trainees to normal working conditions', MSC, 1973). Davies (1979) attacks this kind of approach in his advocacy of genuine social education for young people. His perception of the role of social education is:

> the more recent definitions of social-education-as-political-education require that the results be seen, not just in the form of young people's *personal* growth, of *self*-realisation, of *self*-determination. Rather, they assume that a major outcome will be that young people will *act together* in more self-conscious and organised ways – that they will form or join pressure groups, trade unions, political parties and so on.

And so, a combination of social education and lifeskills teaching will not only enhance general well-being and foster personal and social growth, it will also facilitate self-empowered decision-making about preventive health issues. The kind of social education defined by Davies will manifestly facilitate a 'radical' model of health education through critical-consciousness-raising about ill health and its social determinants. It will, presumably, encourage individuals to take the kind of collective action to which Freudenberg (1981) referred. Lifeskills teaching will provide the assertiveness and political skills needed to complement the newly created awareness of the issues. As indicated earlier *specific* health-related lifeskills teaching – for instance directed at the prevention of substance abuse (Botvin, Eng and Williams, 1980) – will presumably be more effective against a background of general social and lifeskills teaching.

TEACHING METHODS IN HEALTH EDUCATION

A detailed discussion of the kinds of teaching method which must be used if affective education is to be successful is beyond the scope of this chapter. Apart from the overlapping concerns of PSE and health education, which were mentioned earlier, it is well-accepted that these two complex areas of the curriculum share a common methodology. They are in short concerned to use informal techniques rather than traditional didactic methods. The teachers must possess the face-to-face social interaction and 'demystified' counselling skills which they will also hope to provide for the students. They will need to master not only one group technique but several. The HCP group with neutral leader has already been mentioned; Button's (1974) *Developmental Group Work* and the related tactics of *Active Tutorial Work* (Baldwin and Wells, 1979) require different approaches. The use of simulation and gaming; role-play and structured-skills training – all find a place in most if not all current developments. The challenge to the teacher should not be underestimated!

THE SCHOOL AS A
HEALTH-PROMOTING ENVIRONMENT

No discussion of the state-of-the-art of health and social education is complete without some consideration of the ways in which the broad notion of health promotion might be applied to the school. As indicated at the start of this chapter, health is now considered to result from more than just the personal decisions and choices made by individuals. Health is very much determined by the social and physical environment in which we live and work. Health promotion seeks not only to influence individual choices but to foster environmental change through legal, fiscal, economic and political action. The goal is often said to be that of 'making the healthy choice the easy choice'. The lessons for the school environment are self-evident. The benefits of good PSE teaching may be vitiated by an unhealthy hidden curriculum. A glance at the nutrition career reminds us of the potentially negative effect of tuck-shop and school meals – and as some have suggested – even examinations which reward decorative cookery skills at the expense of nutritious content! The effect of a squalid, unhygienic environment may militate against well-being: a school ethos dominated by competition and poor relationships certainly will! As HMI observe in their review of secondary education in England and Wales (DES, 1979):

> All aspects of the school and of the educational process, for example, the formal curricular programme, the formal teaching and learning, the character and the quality of experiences associated with learning, the attitudes and expectations of the teachers, the underlying assumptions, are factors which influence the ethos of the school and the development of individual pupils.

Many of the factors which contribute to an unhealthy ethos and environment may appear to be beyond the control of teachers – let alone pupils. Perhaps lessons should be learned from the political wing of PSE. Given the new emphasis nationally on working with parents, the critical-consciousness-raising function of health and social education should be directed towards the local community with a view of developing not only pupil power but parent power!

REFERENCES

Aronson, E. and Mettee, D. (1968) Dishonest behavior as a function of different levels of self-esteem, *Journal of Personality and Social Psychology*, Vol. 9, pp. 121–7.

Baldwin, J. and Wells, H. (1979) *Active Tutorial Work*, Basil Blackwell, Oxford.

Becker, M. H. (1974) The health belief model and personal health behavior, *Health Education Monographs*, Vol. 2, No. 4.

Botvin, G. J., Eng, A. and Williams, C. L. (1980) Preventing the onset of cigarette smoking through life skills training, *Preventive Medicine*, Vol. 9, pp. 135–43.

British Broadcasting Corporation (1983) *Understanding Cancer*, BBC Broadcasting Research, London.

Button, L. (1974) *Development Group Work with Adolescents*, Hodder & Stoughton, Sevenoaks, Kent.

Cataldo, J. K. (1985) Obesity: a new perspective on an old problem, *Health Education Journal*, Vol. 44, No. 1, pp. 213–16.

Coopersmith, S. (1967) *The Antecedents of Self-Esteem*. W. H. Freeman, Oxford.

Cowley, J. C. P. (1978) Decision-making skills – can they be taught? *Monitor*, No. 50.

Dabbs, J. M. and Kirscht, J. P. (1971) Internal control and the taking of influenza shots, *Psychological Reports*, Vol. 28, pp. 959–62.

Dalis, G. T. and Strasser, B. B. (1981) Teaching values in health education, in Russell, R. D. (ed.) *Education in the 80's: Health Education*, National Education Association of the United States, Washington DC.

David, K. (1983) *Personal and Social Education in Secondary Schools: Report of the Schools Council Working Party on Personal and Social Education*, Longman, York.

Davies, B. (1979) *In Whose Interests? Occasional Paper 19*, National Youth Bureau, Leicester.

Department of Education and Science (1977) *Curriculum 11–16* (Health Education), HMSO, London.

Department of Education and Science (1979) *Aspects of Secondary Education in England: A Survey by HM Inspectors of Schools*, Chapter 9, HMSO, London.

Department of Education and Science (1980) *A View of the Curriculum*, HMSO, London.

Dorn, N. (1982) *Facts and Feelings about Drugs but Decisions about Situations*, ISDD, Research and Development Unit, London.

Farrell, C. (1978) *My Mother Said*, Routledge & Kegan Paul, London.

Forcinelli, O. (1974) Values education in the public school, *Thrust*, March.

Freire, P. (1972) *Pedagogy of the Oppressed*, Penguin, Harmondsworth.

Freudenberg, N. (1981) Health education for social change: a strategy for public health in the US, *International Journal of Health Education*, Vol. 24, No. 3, pp. 1–8.

Freudenberg, N. (1984) Training health educators for social change, *International Quarterly of Community Health Education*, Vol. 5, pp. 37–51.

Gardner, J. W. (1964) *Self Renewal*, Harper & Row, New York.

Goldstein, M. (1975) Defining and studying health at the college level, *International Journal of Health Education*, Vol. 18, No. 4, pp. 241–53.

Goodlett, D. E. (1976) Values clarification – where does it belong? *Health Education*, Vol. 7, No. 2, March–April.

Green, L. W., Kreuter, M. W., Deeds, S. G. and Partridge, K. B. (1980) *Health Education Planning: A Diagnostic Approach*, Mayfield, Palo Alto, CA.

Hamachek, D. E. (1971) *Encounters with the Self*, Holt, Rinehart & Winston, London.

Harfouche, J. K. (1965) *Infant Health in Lebanon: Customs and Taboos*, Khayats, Beirut.

Harfouche, J. K. (1970) The importance of breast-feeding, *Journal of Tropical Paediatrics*, Vol. 16, Monograph 10, pp. 133–75.

Hargreaves, D. (1967) *Social Relations in a Secondary School*, Routledge & Kegan Paul, London.

Health Education Council (1982) *Schools Health Education Project 5–13: A Training Manual*, HEC, London.

Health Education Council (1983a) *My Body*, Heinemann, London.

Health Education Council (1983b) *A Discussion Paper on Proposals for Nutritional Guidelines for Health Education in Britain* (The NACNE Report), HEC, London.

Hirst, P. (1969) The logic of the curriculum, *Journal of Curriculum Studies*, Vol. 1, No. 2, pp. 142.

Holt, M. (1983) *Curriculum Workshop: An Introduction to Whole Curriculum Planning*, Routledge & Kegan Paul, London.

Hopson, B. and Scally, M. (1981) *Lifeskills Teaching*, McGraw-Hill, Maidenhead.

Illich, I. (1977) *The Limits of Medicine*, Calder & Boyars, London.

James, W. H., Woodruff, A. B. and Werner, W. (1965) Effect of internal and external control upon changes in smoking behaviour, *Journal of Consulting Psychology*, Vol. 29, pp. 184–6.

Janis, I. L. and Mann, L. (1979) *Decision Making*, Collier-Macmillan, London.

Jeffrey, D. B. and Christensen, E. R. (1972) *The Relative Efficacy of Behavior Therapy, Will-Power and Non-treatment Control Procedures for Weight Loss.* Association for the Advancement of Behavior Therapy, New York.

Jones, E. F. *et al.* (1985) Teenage pregnancy in developed countries: determinants and policy implications, *Family Planning Perspectives*, Vol. 17, No. 2, pp. 53–63.

Kerr, M. and Charles, N. (1983) *Attitudes to the Feeding and Nutrition of Young Children*, HEC, London.

Kindervatter, S. (1979) *Nonformal Education as an Empowering Process.* Center for International Education, University of Massachusetts, Boston.

Kohlberg, L. and Turiel, E. (1971) Moral development and moral education, in Lesser, G. (ed.) *Psychology and Educational Practice*, Scott Foresman, Chicago.

Levanthal, H. and Cleary, P. D. (1980) The smoking problem: a review of the research and theory in behavioral risk modification, *Psychological Bulletin*, Vol. 88, No. 2.

Lundy, J. R. (1972) Some personality correlates of contraceptive use among unmarried female college students, *Journal of Personality*, Vol. 80, pp. 9–14.

Manpower Services Commission (MSC) (1973) *Instructional Guide to Social and Life Skills Training*, MSC, London.

Maslow, A. H. (1968) *Toward a Psychology of Being*, Van Nostrand Reinhold, New York.

McKeown, T. (1976) *The Role of Medicine: Dream, Mirage or Nemesis?*, Nuffield Provincial Hospitals Trust, London.

McKinlay, J. B. (1979) A case for refocussing upstream: the political economy of illness, in E. G. Jaco (ed.) *Patients, Physicians and Illness* (3rd edn), Collier-Macmillan, London.

McPhail, P. (1977) *Living Well*, Health Education Council Project 12–18, Cambridge University Press.

McPhail, P., Ungoed-Thomas, J. R. and Chapman, H. (1972) *Moral Education in the Secondary School*, Longman, London.

McPhail, P., Ungoed-Thomas, J. R. and Chapman, H. (1978) *Startline: Moral Education in the Middle Years*, Longman, London.

Orbach, S. (1978) *Fat Is a Feminist Issue*, Paddington Press, London.

Phares, E. J. (1976) *Locus of Control in Personality*, Bordett, Englewood Cliffs, NJ.

Raths, L. E., Merrill, H. and Simon, B. S. (1978) *Values and Teaching*, Merrill, Columbus, Ohio.

Reid, D. and Massey, D. E. (1986) Can school health education be more effective? *Health Education Journal*, Vol. 45, No. 1, pp. 7–14.

Rotter, J. B. (1966) Generalised expectancies for internal versus external control of reinforcement, *Psychological Monographs*, Vol. 80, No. 1.

Samuels, S. C. (1977) *Enhancing Self-Concepts in Early Childhood*, Human Sciences Press, New York.
Schools Council (1970) *Humanities Curriculum Project*, Heinemann, London.
Schools Council (1977) *Schools Council Health Education Project (SCHEP) 5–13*, Nelson, London.
Scottish Education Department (1974) *Health Education in Schools*, Curriculum Paper 14, HMSO, London.
Seeman, M. and Evans, J. W. (1962) Alienation and learning in a hospital setting, *American Sociological Review*, Vol. 27, pp. 772–83.
Seligman, M. E. P. (1975) *Helplessness*, W. H. Freeman, San Francisco.
Simon, S. B. (1974) *Meeting Yourself Halfway*, Argos, Niles, Ill.
Simon, S. B., Howe, W. L. and Kirschenbaum, H. (1972) *Values Clarification: A Handbook of Practical Strategies for Teachers and Students*, Hart, New York.
Society for Public Health Education (USA) (1976) *Code of Ethics*, SOPHE, San Francisco.
Stenhouse, L. (1969a) Open-minded teaching, *New Society*, 24 July.
Stenhouse, L. (1969b) Handling controversial issues in the classroom, *Education Canada*, December.
Strickland, B. R. (1973) *Locus of Control: Where Have We Been and Where Are We Going?* American Psychological Association, Montreal.
Sutherland, I. (1979) History and background, in Sutherland, I. (ed.) *Health Education: Perspectives and Choices*, Allen & Unwin, London.
Tones, B. K. (1981) Health education: prevention or subversion?, *Journal of Royal Society of Health*, Vol. 3, pp. 114–17.
Tones, B. K. (1982) Health education in schools: the affective domain, *Journal of the Institute of Health Education*, Vol. 20, No. 2, pp. 27–30.
Tones, B. K. (1983) Nutrition, diet and the concept of health career: implications for health education. Paper presented at Scottish Health Education Group Conference, Aberdeen, September.
Tones, B. K. (1985) The school, health education and the prevention of smoking, in Peers, I. S. (ed.) *Smoking and Education*, TACADE, Manchester.
Tones, B. K. (1986a) Health education and the ideology of health promotion, *Health Education Research: Theory and Practice*, Vol. 1, No. 1.
Tones, B. K. (1986b) Promoting the health of young people: the role of personal and social education in achieving preventive outcomes, *Health Education Journal*, Vol. 45, No. 1, pp. 14–18.
Townsend, P. and Davidson, N. (1982) *Inequalities in Health*, Penguin, Harmondsworth.
Vuori, H. (1980) The medical model and the objectives of health education, *International Journal of Health Education*, Vol. 23, No. 1, pp. 1–8.
Wallston, K. A. and Wallston, B. S. (eds) (1978) Health locus of control, *Health Education Monographs*, Vol. 6, No. 2.
White, J. (1969) Open minded society, *New Society*, 31 July.
Wikler, D. I. (1978) Coercive measures in health promotion: can they be justified?, *Health Education Monographs*, Vol. 6, No. 2, pp. 223–41.
Wilkinson, R. G. (1977) *Socioeconomic Differentials in Mortality – the Importance of Diet*, Van den Berghs and Jurgens, London.
Williams, A. F. (1972) Factors associated with seat belt use in families, *Journal of Safety Research*, Vol. 4, No. 3, pp. 133–8.

Williams, T. and Roberts, J. (1985) *Health Education in Schools and Teacher Education Institutions*. University of Southampton Dept of Health Education.

World Health Organization (1984) *Health Promotion: A Discussion Document of the Concept and Principles*, WHO, Copenhagen.

THE SCHOOL CONTEXT

INTRODUCTION TO PART 2

The past five years has seen considerable headway being made in the development of school health education. A national survey of schools conducted in the early 1980s showed that they generally felt responsibility for promoting a realistic programme of health education for their pupils. Primary schools generally were shown to be, nonetheless, lacking in strategies for overall planning – a criticism confirmed by the various HMI surveys that have taken place recently. It is particularly good therefore to welcome the work, outlined by Noreen Wetton and Alysoun Moon, which is intended to provide a sound but flexible curriculum framework for primary schools. One of the important points they make is of the need for teachers to clarify what pupils themselves bring to the classroom in terms of knowledge, attitudes and values before health teaching begins. Noreen Wetton was herself a well-known head of a primary school before moving on to teacher training: she has devised many ways of successfully exploring children's perceptions of the world around them and is also part-author of a new reading scheme for young children. Alysoun Moon has a nursing background, having qualified and practised as an SRN before training to be a primary-school teacher. Alysoun is, amongst other professional interests, concerned to clarify the role of the school nurse in school health education. Noreen is currently Deputy Director and Alysoun Research Fellow on the Health Education Council Project: Health Education in Primary Schools.

The secondary schools, labouring against the constraints of examinations, the recent initiatives presented by CPVE and TVEI, difficulties presented by youth unemployment and falling school roles, present a different set of problems to those found in the primary school. Trefor Williams discusses ways in which health education can play a more important role in the secondary school. From his discussion emerges the need for the careful preparation of a school co-ordinator for the many tasks involved in what should be viewed as school-based curriculum development, and an investment in professional training.

Ten years' teaching in secondary schools, four years as an area health education officer, seven years' teaching in a college of education and three years as head of the school of studies in community care in a college of higher education, have provided Trefor Williams with a considerable and varied background of experience in health and social education. From 1973 to 1980 he was director of the Schools Council Health Education Projects 5–13 and 13–18 and currently is director of the HEC Health Education Unit at the University of Southampton. He has acted as adviser, since 1973, to the successful television series *Good Health* which is broadcast to junior schools.

Often schools find difficulty in catering for the needs of children with physical, mental and other handicaps and, as the Warnock Report suggested, these comprise about one fifth of all schoolchildren. Jill Coombs and Ann Craft outline some of the strategies which might be employed to match health education more closely to the special needs of these children. Of particular interest are the strategies they are employing to forge closer links between school, home and community – strategies which will be of benefit to a much wider audience. Ann Craft trained as a social worker and worked for ten years in a mental handicap hospital where she developed health education, sex education and counselling programmes for adult residents. Ann also produced health education teaching slides for use with students who have mental handicaps. Jill Coombs worked for a time in schools with children with severe hearing difficulties. She went on to work for three years on a research project at Keele University, working in local special schools, to study the drinking patterns and beliefs of children with mild and moderate drinking difficulties and the implications for health education. Ann and Jill are presently part of the team working on the HEC Health Education for Slow Learners Project based at the University of Bath.

2

HEALTH EDUCATION IN PRIMARY SCHOOLS

Noreen Wetton and Alysoun Moon

By health I mean . . . I want to be all that I am capable of becoming.
(Katherine Mansfield)

INTRODUCTION

The problem with Mansfield's definition of health is that while full of meaning for each of us it is not of any immediate use in planning a health-education programme and putting it into practice. Its very width can work against it, making it difficult for a teacher to know where to begin. Questions which primary-school teachers ask about health education tend to focus on the reality of today's classroom with all its demands and pressures rather than on definitions.

The difficulties of planning a health education programme for children in the primary-school age stem as much from the nature of the curriculum itself as from the health-education component. The ethic of the primary school is one of wholeness, of the integration of subject matter, time, space and resources. Groups are formed and re-formed, teachers work in co-operative situations, and barriers between groups and curriculum areas are relaxed. Much of early learning is seen to be achieved through activity and experience with emphasis on individual pace and direction. Children are asked increasingly to take on some of the responsibility for their own learning and this way of learning may be difficult to describe, chart and evaluate.

Putting a strong coherent health education strand into such a network can be problematic since health education itself, being both integrated and integrative is difficult to pin down, describe and evaluate. It does not fit into any one curriculum area and to teach it as a separate subject is to deny its very nature; to integrate it into the whole primary-school curriculum must be the answer. But there is such a wide range of topics to plan for, each competing for a place. Some topics may be supported by a wide range of materials while others will have little or nothing in the way of available resources. There is no set body of content in health education, no accepted body of facts. Health education is a dynamic area of the curriculum always changing and being changed. It deals with the person, with each child in the totality of his or her lifestyle of which school may be only one part. Health education in school cannot be separated from the child's home, family and community, and beliefs, needs and pleasures. It is an area of concern where the ownership of the curriculum may be hotly disputed, where different groups, parents, community leaders, governors, the local authority and health professionals may have priorities or points of view which are not always in accord. Then too there are those in the community who see health education as dealing with low status common-sense knowledge, with little claim to any real priority in an already crowded curriculum, one where literacy and numeracy should be the first consideration.

HEALTH EDUCATION –
A DILEMMA FOR THE SCHOOL

Parents may see health education as:
  Our job – you get on and do yours – which is to teach them
  Our job – except for the sensitive areas which we prefer you to do
  Your job – apart from the sensitive areas which we prefer to do
    ourselves
  Doing more harm than good through teaching about certain dangerous
    topics
  The responsibility of trained specialists brought in from the outside
  A shared task – we'd like to know what you are doing so that we can
    help you
  Parents may see health education as including or excluding:
  Exercise and fitness programmes
  Hygiene and first aid
  Safety education
  How the body works and changes
  Sex education
  Moral and religious education
  Antismoking and drug-abuse education
  No one is able to tell the parents exactly what health education is and so views are bound to differ. It is interesting to note that this is an area of the

curriculum in which parents feel strongly that they have a right to be involved. We might ask ourselves why. Is it because health education has a special status related to the child's whole development, to home and family life, traditions and culture – an area which parents feel is, by right, theirs?

Health professionals such as the school nurses, health visitors, health-education officers and dental-health educators will have their individual views of what should be the focus of health education. Some may see it as part of their role, others as an extension of it. Undoubtedly, they will have the kind of priorities which will reflect their background, training and previous specializations.

There are many different kinds of specialist organizations and groups, both local and national, supplying research findings and fact sheets or offering speakers, visits and materials. Each group will have its own priorities in health and safety education according to the work it is doing.

Teachers may see health education as:

A body of factual content to be put across in specific curricular areas, for example science

Part of day-to-day good habits and practice, about which children need to be reminded

A preventive task with its focus on present and future dangers and diseases

Part of the 'hidden' curriculum concerned with the development of a strong self-concept, good personal relationships and informed decision-making

The responsibility of someone else, for example parents, health professionals

Yet another pressure on curriculum time

Traditionally of low status, as a curriculum priority, it has been seen as common sense and part of the day-to-day work of the caring class teacher, an accepted part of a school's responsibility to the children in its care.

Health education has been around for a long time but the past 15 years or so has seen a turn in the tide of health education as public awareness of matters to do with health and well-being has increased. Within schools the way for change was paved by a number of education reports in the 1960s which highlighted the need for education to embrace all aspects of a child's development and include in a balanced curriculum a recognition of the physical, personal, social, emotional and health needs of children. School health education was further promoted by the formation of the Health Education Council in 1968. The Council established a network of Health Education Units around Britain which were to become the responsibility of the local health authorities. Health-education officers (HEOs) – more recently some with a specific brief for schools – have consistently provided teachers with help and support. Their provision of leaflets, packs and audiovisual aids has been an additional resource for school health education. In 1977 the publication of a discussion document, *Health Education in Schools*, by the Department of Education and Science prompted LEAs all over Britain to look at their policy guidelines for health education and the provision of resources and in-service training. Many developed their own initiatives in response to DES requirements and recommendations, producing materials for teachers which met their own particular needs and concerns.

Health education – as in no other part of the primary curriculum – is seen as an extension of the parental role. The DES has constantly urged parental consultation as a prerequisite to planning and while some schools have consulted with their parents this has generally only taken place when sensitive areas such as sex education are being considered. Such consultation now needs to be broadened to include a parental view and involvement in all areas of health education.

The first national curriculum development project in health education was 'Health Education 5–13' (1977) commissioned by the Schools Council in 1973 as part of a wider movement concerned with change and reform in the schools curriculum. SCHEP 5–13 helped to introduce a planned curriculum for primary-school health education and gave it some structure. Its aim was to establish health education as an integral part of education, not as an area of concern to be set apart or dealt with separately. The Health Education Council gave its support and helped to fund the dissemination of SCHEP 5–13.

Since then there have been a number of projects for primary schools which have sought to promote health education within the curriculum. Major projects include the 'My Body' project, adapted from the American Berkeley Project and 'Jimmy on the Road to Super Health', which is produced by the Scottish Health Education Group. There have also been a number of smaller project packs and resources which have been produced by both national organizations, for example RoSPA and small local bodies.

The 'Good Health' series from Central TV has also played an important part in highlighting current health concerns and raising awareness about health needs and issues in the primary school.

THE HEALTH EDUCATION
CURRICULUM – CONTENT AND ORGANIZATION

Teachers in primary schools are under great pressure to promote and develop health education in a way that will take account of society's current needs and concerns and the shift towards individual responsibility for one's own health. The schools are being bombarded by curriculum requirements in health education and resources which suggest starting points, content and methodology, differing emphases and changing concerns.

Some of the material available, however, which in theory encourages teachers to be adaptive fails to leave room for consideration of what the children bring to the topic, how they explain it and the language in which they do this. There may be a mismatch between the children's conceptual development and the demands of the material.

There is a need for a flexible, national framework to allow teachers to plan their health-education programmes to take account of children's unique contribution.

For many adults health education presents one major dilemma, that of preserving childhood innocence and delight while protecting the children from both immediate and long-term hazards and dangers. Primary teachers themselves may be faced with this conflict and look for guidelines, for a framework for planning which takes account of it and which enables them to make and justify curricular decisions. Such guidelines and such a framework have not been generally available. What then do teachers do?

A survey in 1982/83 revealed that while over 90 per cent of primary-school teachers wished to have or already had health education in their schools, more than 80 per cent had no coherent structure or framework within which to plan (Williams and Roberts, 1983). While pockets of good practice were seen to exist, the general approach appeared to be fragmented. Many teachers, especially in the early years, in nursery, infant, first schools or departments saw schools themselves as dealing with health-related topics in an incidental way; when a need arose, a visit or visitor was made available through outside agencies or sparked off by the arrival of a new package of resource materials. While such an approach can be spontaneous, rewarding and demanding, it can deal with health education simply on an *ad hoc* basis, one which lacks coherence, progression and sequence. Children may be presented with the same materials in successive years. Material may be used which dictates progression in a highly prescriptive way.

Further investigation across the primary-school age range reveals that teachers are using one or more of a range of approaches and that these differ from classroom to classroom according to the age of the children, the teacher's view of health education and the degree of consultation and co-ordination within the school.

Some depend almost entirely on input provided by visits from health and safety professionals, for example road safety officer, the school nurse, or visits to locations where these people might be seen in action. The extent of the preparation and follow-up in terms of health related learning activity varies.

Some allocate a specific time to health education. This varies from a regular lesson in which a different health education topic is discussed, to the allocation of a block of time when a particular topic is pursued and explored.

Some place health education firmly in one area of the curriculum, for example science, and pursue it in a scientific way. This is found particularly in the upper primary-school age range where material with a scientific base is more readily available.

Some include aspects of health education as a strand in a thematic approach, a topic or project which may be explored by all or only some of the children.

Some take a health education topic as the starting point for a thematic approach and move outward from the health-related focus to other facts, historical, scientific and environmental.

Much of the early years curriculum can be seen to relate to health, being concerned with healthy growth and development, social skills, personal relationships and interpersonal skills. Teachers are involved in an overlap and extension of the parental role and decisions have to be made about what to include and what can be left out.

Such a variety of teaching models and approaches depends to some extent on the unique skills and interests of individual teachers and the particular constraints on the curriculum within a school but such diversity, however, is both a strength and a weakness. Its strength lies in the variety, its weakness in a lack of coherence and structure and the absence of a framework to ensure continuity and progression.

The development of a health education curriculum will inevitably be linked to a consideration of the realities which face children outside the school as well as within it.

Healthy Lifestyles – a Progressive Course of Learning

It would be too easy to think of health education in the primary school as concerned with just one stage of children's learning. Schools can be organized in many ways as nursery/infant, nursery/first, infant, junior, middle or primary schools. Children may be moved from one school to another at different ages.

The organization of the schools themselves will differ. One school may separate its children into age bands, another will put them into mixed age groups. Some teachers may be found working in very individualistic ways in their own classrooms, while others will be working in teams or in co-operative settings. A whole range of adult helpers, paid and working voluntarily, will be found. Each school will be part of a community unique in its contribution and needs and in its social, environmental, cultural and home backgrounds and degrees of stability. This will be reflected in the quality of the relationships between the school and its community and in the quality of the learning and teaching.

A health-education programme must take account of those six and seven years of primary-school life during which children, leaving behind them their babyhood move to the threshold of adolescence. During this time, their perceptions and explanations of their own and other's health and health-related behaviours, their views and values of themselves and others will constantly be adapting, sometimes slowly, other times rapidly. With changes in physical growth come new physical competencies and concerns. With conceptual growth come new skills of organizing information, generalizing and reflecting on cause and effect. Perceptions of relationships, of feelings, of the role and responsibility of families, adults and peers change and are re-formed.

The primary school has the task of developing a health-education curriculum for these years, one which takes account of this great change and makes the transition smooth and positive. This is a unique opportunity to enable children to become all they are capable of. This stage in children's life is characterized not only by growth and change but by energy and enthusiasm, a desire to know and a pleasure in acquiring and practising skills.

The primary-school curriculum has the great advantage that it is not constrained by examinations or by the need for children to move from room to room to specialist teachers at given times in the day. There is freedom and flexibility of timetable which enables a teacher to use an integrated approach, to allocate blocks of time for a range of activities.

Children will work for the most part with their own teachers or team of teachers in their own classrooms or base areas. Barriers between traditional subject areas can be relaxed or removed. Group and individual work can develop at its own pace and be allowed to take its own direction. Health-education topics can be taken up, extended and reinforced across the curriculum in play, physical activities, music, movement, drama, creative activities and literature.

Parental involvement in the primary school has its own special quality not found again in secondary or further education. Parents can be found working in and around the primary school, gaining insights into their children's education and contributing to it in an increasingly important way.

But if the primary school has unique opportunities for developing a dynamic health-education programme and putting it into day-to-day practice, it also has a great responsibility. Much of the later lifestyle of the children will have its roots in early learning; attitudes, beliefs, values and behaviour are established in some measure in the social and educational climate of the primary school. The extent to which health messages and behaviours have been internalized at this stage will have its impact on the children's later health career.

Young children need to have knowledge as well as experiences and activity; knowledge about themselves, their bodies and the world into which they are moving in order to make important decisions which relate or will relate to their health. If health-related knowledge is presented to them too soon they will deal with it in idiosyncratic ways. They may ignore it, manipulate it to fit in with what they know already to look for fantasy explanations unrelated to health. If the language in which knowledge is presented or if the materials are inappropriate, they can and will get hold of 'the wrong end of the stick', and find themselves confused by seeming contradictions. If knowledge is too long withheld or presented inappropriately, failing to take account of how children perceive and explain the world of health, then they will make their own, seemingly logical explanations or again resort to fantasy as an answer. Their trust in adults and adult knowledge may suffer because of this and their own invented explanations may resist change.

Primary-school teachers are often expected to be experts in every subject or curriculum area, and health education is one of these. They need the support of a flexible framework for health education which enables them to maximize the potential for development in the primary school, to plan a relevant coherent programme which does not discount their own intuitive knowledge and classroom skills.

The number of topics which might be included under the umbrella of health education is so vast that teachers could be overwhelmed by the thought of planning even a percentage of them into the programme. One way of dealing with this would be to group topics under major headings. For younger children these headings might be: 'Knowing about myself'; 'Looking after myself'; 'Knowing about other people'; 'Looking after the place I live in'; 'Being looked after'. For older children the programmes could be based round three foundation stones: 'Looking after myself'; 'Personal relationships'; 'Community and environment'.

A CURRICULUM FRAMEWORK
FOR HEALTHY LIVING

A planning framework must offer teachers more than guidance in making relevant content choices. Teachers will want answers to questions such as: How do children internalize health messages? Through what classroom activities is this best approached so that there is real input on what children understand and do?

Recent research indicates that one-off activities, visits, visitors, talks, television programmes, have only short-term impact unless developed as a coherent strand in on-going learning. Other research suggests very strongly that activities such as colouring in of outline pictures, copying over or under print, completing sentences by filling a gap with a predetermined word or labelling diagrams all have little impact on children's learning and little transfer in terms of their content to everyday behaviour. Much of the children's focus is on completing the task in terms of language skills rather than on hearing the health message. Perhaps it is necessary for teachers to remember this when looking at available materials or devising their own work sheets. Many children in the primary school will be struggling with listening and speaking skills and working through the complex tasks of becoming readers and writers. All will be experiencing the demands of being members of groups, classes, of a school community much of which will be explained to them in unfamiliar language. Children do not learn about health and internalize health behaviours by being told what they should or should not do, what is good or bad for them. They learn from experience, through active participation, reflection and discussion and from role models around them. They learn more about their own health when they handle the language of a particular topic confidently. They learn in an unthreatening trusting class-and-school atmosphere. Everything they say, do, enact, illustrate and write about has to stem from their active involvement not from an adult view of what they should be told.

A HEALTH EDUCATION COUNCIL INITIATIVE

The Health Education Council Primary School Project, which started in 1984, began in response to a growing awareness of the need for this kind of broad-based health-education programme for primary schools. HMI reports confirmed the need for a planned progressive framework for health education with clearly defined links with other curricular areas and activities.

An as yet unpublished national survey of schools in 11 LEAs in England,

Wales and Northern Ireland took place during the first year of the project involving 13,020 children aged 7–13, 9,583 children aged 4–8, 15,743 parents, 1,148 teachers, and a number of health professionals.

A health education topics list was used, inviting adults to comment on the timing and importance of 43 topics. Children over the age of 8 were asked to consider the same 43 topics in terms of how interested they might be in them.

A new classroom research tool, 'Draw and Write Technique', was developed for use with the children under the age of 8. This illuminated something of the children's unprompted perceptions of what they believed they did to make and keep themselves healthy.

This national survey provided a broad picture of opinions, interests and perceptions. From the data a number of key areas were identified:

Keeping safe

Healthy eating

Relationships

Use and misuse of drugs

Exercise and fitness

These areas were then explored in greater depth using a development of the 'Draw and Write' investigation technique across the whole primary age range 4–13.

The analysis of each of these revealed:

A spiral of changing perceptions and growth of understanding

A spiral of developmental skills which significantly influenced children's learning

A clear indication of the kind of language that children themselves use at different stages

The added illumination of what their illustrations revealed

From this a spiral curriculum was developed in each of the key areas. The notion of a spiral of learning is particularly suited to health education. All that children are learning today will always have its roots in previous learning. The more this can be built on, revisited, reworked and extended the more stable the new learning will be.

The Framework

A framework and planning guide in the age ranges 4–7, 8–10, 11–13, set out each of the spirals and provided teachers with:

Simple classroom techniques for discovering and analysing where children are in their thinking

Key messages from the children

Critical concepts and skills at each age, and matching these with relevant
content, strategies and materials

Ways in which learning might best be achieved in different classroom
situations and appropriate methodology for helping children to make
wise choices and decisions about their own health and health behaviour

Ways of consulting and negotiating with parents and the community to
identify priorities and support

Curriculum models for planning with emphasis on cross-curricular links
and reinforcement

Ways of grouping topics

Ways of drawing on local and national networks of support

Classroom-based evaluation strategies

CONCLUSION

A central theme of the project has been the development of schools as
health-promoting communities. The framework was designed to provide
opportunities for the interaction between professional bodies, the home
and the community essential to achieving this.

Children's health education does not develop solely in school. No child
comes to his or her education in health empty-handed. This education will
have begun at birth and be subject to countless influences from home, the
community, the media and peer groups.

Health decisions are made for the child. When the opportunity comes
for the child to make his or her own, what he or she is learning at school
has to compete with other pressures and expectations.

Where the ethos and policies of the school, the relationships among the
adults and children, the role models that are presented and the day-to-day
health practices support what is taught in health education there is a
greater chance of the health messages having real impact.

A partnership between school and parents can make the overall effect
more productive and positive.

Similarly a partnership which draws together schools, parents and health
professionals reinforces and supports the school as a health-promoting
institution.

If the school sees itself in this central role it has a unique opportunity to
become a potent force for health within the community, responding to the
changing health needs of modern society.

The all-embracing nature of school-based health education does present
problems for teachers who wish to develop a curriculum programme. The
promotion of mental health, for instance, through building self-worth and

self-confidence is to do with achievement, recognition, mutual support and praise and opportunities for these are to be found in every area of the curriculum. The health of its members is promoted or undermined by the ethos of the school.

REFERENCES

Department of Education and Science (1977) *Health Education in Schools*, discussion document, DES, London.

Health Education Council (IIEC) (1983) *My Body*, Heinemann, London.

Schools Council (1977) *Health Education Project 5–13* (SCHEP), Nelson, Surrey.

Williams, T. and Roberts, J. (1983) *Health Education in Schools and Teacher Education Institutes*, Health Education Unit, University of Southampton.

3

HEALTH EDUCATION IN SECONDARY SCHOOLS

Trefor Williams

INTRODUCTION

The prayer of Roman poet Juvenal has reverberated down the centuries to become firmly enmeshed in the rationale and philosophy of the British educational scene. 'Mens sana in corpore sana' is a familiar and recurring theme for educators from Locke to the present time. Each time it surfaces after a period of dormancy, it remains as urgent and as relevant a message as ever. While the basic message remains the same, however, its interpretation has particular relevance for the time.

In Victorian times it was received, in the state schools, as a prescription to halt the declining state of the physical health of children and young people, which resulted (Interdepartmental Committee, 1904; 1905) in the provision of school meals, a school medical service, and the beginnings of the teaching of physical training, domestic science and health education. Today the message is interpreted differently as a need to provide for children a measure of self-empowerment, involving the ability to make choices and decisions concerning their health behaviour.

Very broadly the development of Juvenal's 'sound mind in a sound body' is very much still a proclaimed aim of the British secondary school – and always has been the true purpose of school health education. On the surface, therefore, it seems that the aims of school and that of school health education are congruent and in sympathy with each other. Indeed a $12\frac{1}{2}$ per cent random sample survey of secondary schools (Williams and Roberts, 1986) in England and Wales in 1981–83 revealed that 98 per cent of the respondents (head teachers and senior staff) agreed that schools had a responsibility to teach health education. Further information from this survey also revealed that

1. 95 per cent of the secondary schools included some health education in the curriculum.
2. Nearly 70 per cent of secondary schools had a planned programme of health education.
3. Well over 30 per cent of secondary schools had a staff member (co-ordinator) responsible for health education.

For school health education these glimpses of what schools say and believe are immensely encouraging – but, more pragmatically, it is what schools do that really matters. Do they match good intentions with good practice? There is reason to believe that they do – indeed if a similar survey were to be conducted now it would unquestionably reveal much greater activity, largely stimulated by the national concern shown for the rise in drug and substance abuse amongst young people. This concern manifests itself in several ways, chief of which is through the appointment, by each of the 101 Local Education Authorities (LEAs) in England and Wales, of Drug Education Co-ordinators, all of whom will be in post by the end of 1986. The Drug Education Co-ordinators will have the responsibility for the management and development of drug education for children and young people. It is particularly heartening, therefore, to know that most LEAs perceive drug education to be an important element within a more broadly based programme of school health education. In this sense the appointment of the Drug Education Co-ordinators will be of immense benefit to the general development of the school health education movement (Hodgson, 1985).

The arrival of the Drug Education Co-ordinators will unquestionably boost the status of school health education but will also highlight the need for clear policy and planning in school health education. Many LEAs have already, through a process of committees and working parties, produced guidelines and framework for schools, and it is to be expected that such products will become an important and increasingly necessary task for LEAs in the future. Experience shows that, where LEAs are able to work in harmony with District Health Authorities and, more particularly, with their health education services, schools benefit enormously. The skill and knowledge of the experienced health education officer, together with the human and material resources to which they have access, provides an enviable support to both LEA and to schools.

School Policy and Planning

While it is important for LEAs to develop a policy concerning school health education, it is the schools themselves that must bear the brunt of the planning and implementation of relevant programmes. While a school policy is vitally important, because it denotes a will to provide a programme, it is the planning itself which requires the energy, skill, ingenuity, diplomacy and perseverance. What, then, are the issues central to school health education and how might the process be started? Because each school is unique in terms of its ambience, organization, staffing, environment and pupils, there can be no definitive and all embracing blueprint for guaranteed success. There are, however, well tried and tested guidelines which provide opportunities for schools to think through their own programmes, tailored to their particular needs. The areas worthy of some consideration are listed briefly here, but receive more detailed consideration later under separate headings.

1. The nature of health education – its purpose
2. The 'content' of health education and its organization
3. The spiral curriculum – its meaning and purpose
4. Co-ordination of teaching across and within the curriculum
5. Materials and methods appropriate to health education
6. The school as a health-promoting community
7. Evaluation of the school programme

THE NATURE OF SCHOOL HEALTH EDUCATION

It is possible to identify two general views of school health education, each with perspectives so different that they might be thought of as opposite poles of a continuum of practice. For convenience we can label them as the *preventive model* and the *educational model* respectively. The former is primarily concerned with the prevention of illness and disease (and is sometimes referred to as the *medical model*), and attempts to achieve this end by deliberately influencing and changing the attitudes and behaviour of target groups in some defined way or to some predetermined end. The other model is more concerned with the development of personal autonomy than with specific behavioural outcomes.

The major difference between the two perceptions of health education is that while the preventive model is primarily concerned with the outcomes of a process of health education, the educational model is as much concerned with the *quality of the process*, involving decision-making itself. The former view would emphasize the urgency of helping young people accept and adopt certain modes of behaviour in the interest of their good health, while the latter view would urge that individual behaviour should be based upon informed decision-making.

If we decide that health education is concerned with more than just the prevention of disease to include, for example, notions of emotional well-being, we are immediately concerning ourselves with value judgments about what makes human life attractive and worthwhile. Once we set considerations of health matters in the broad context of human values then our perception of health education is affected. Baelz (1979) develops this theme further, pointing out that when we deal with human values there are no professionals or experts, we are all ordinary men and women sharing our experiences and insights. In this context teachers are often troubled by the notion of changing pupils' attitudes to conform to some norm or other. Baelz's comments on this matter are worth noting:

> It is sometimes said that changing people's attitudes is incompatible with respecting the individual's freedom of choice. There is a measure of truth in this, especially if the methods of change are manipulative. The difference between education and manipulation is not that the manipulator is all the time influencing his pupils while the educator is not influencing him at all. The difference rather lies in their respective aims. The educator encourages his pupil to develop the capacity to think for himself, while the indoctrinator wishes to make it impossible for his pupil ever to question the doctrine that he has been taught.

There is the possibility then of ambiguity and misunderstanding in the way in which the term *health education* is used, an ambiguity which needs to be picked over and clarified as thoroughly as is possible. As caring teachers we would all wish for young people to make decisions about their health so that they become and remain healthy in every sense of the word. In our eagerness and at times anxiety for the 'right' choice, however, we might be tempted to sacrifice our ethical qualms for the immediate gains of manipulation. Such immediate gains are very likely built upon the shifting sands of half-truths, rhetoric and false claims; the aims of health education, and indeed of education itself, rest more firmly upon individual autonomy resulting from decision-making skills and a democratic process. Unless schools develop a clear and shared view of what health education is about, further decisions concerning how it should be taught and evaluated become impossible to make. While not wishing to overtax this issue it is worth repeating and re-emphasizing the need to explore and discuss the purpose of health education fully as it will provide an essential baseline for future development. There is sufficient medical, biological and social evidence for teachers to confidently support the behaviour which might be reflected in a healthy lifestyle. The manner in which they can best do this, however, needs to be carefully assessed.

CO-ORDINATION –
ITS PURPOSE AND ORGANIZATION

The notion of co-ordination and the tasks associated with it provides the main focus of the Schools Health Education Project (SHEP) 13–18 in its work with schools. It became patently clear early in its work with schools, however, that although much of the work associated with developing a co-ordinated health education programme demanded a team approach, it was essential to have one member who would act as leader. This person, referred to as a co-ordinator, was the focus of the in-service work developed by the project. The co-ordinator is necessarily a key figure in the development of a school programme and requires considerable tact, skill and background knowledge concerning both curriculum development and health education. The project evaluations provided an interesting range of characteristics which an effective co-ordinator might need:

A senior member of staff

Sympathetic to the aims of health education

Open to the idea of curriculum development

Have leadership skills

Be sensitive to the views of other colleagues

Have training skills

Have relevant teaching experience

Commitment to see the process through

Reference has already been made to the importance of discussion and debate about health education amongst staff, and the experience of recent curriculum developments in schools confirms the need for frank and open discussion if they are to take root and flourish. In a narrower sense, however, it is important for a school co-ordinator to have the support of a team of colleagues as it is well nigh impossible for one person alone to think through and come successfully to grips with the many and varied tasks associated with this role. Experience and expediency dictate the desirability and indeed the advantage of forming a team of teachers, preferably from across the curriculum boundaries, who are chosen to provide a balance of experience, enthusiasm, skill and willingness to undertake the extra tasks associated with planning and implementing a programme of health education. It is important that members of the team be given the opportunity of thinking through issues and decisions together and, for this purpose, time for meetings has to be set aside either during or out of school hours. The cut and thrust of debate in a structured but common experience helps to provide a bonding and camaraderie which is essential to the well-being and health of the team. When discussing the tasks associated with the role of co-ordinator, therefore, it is necessary to see the team as an extension of the co-ordinator's role. The criteria which a school might employ to choose a team are discussed in more detail elsewhere (School Council, 1984) but generally speaking a co-ordinator needs to think not only of the experience, enthusiasm and skills which team members bring with them but also of the potential which the opportunity provides for the personal and professional development of the staff members themselves.

Co-ordination – in Practice

The term *co-ordinator* implies the wish to co-ordinate some aspect of school-based work which is already in existence or which might be brought into existence by a conscious decision of the staff. An early task associated with the role, therefore, would logically be to discover what health-education teaching is actually being attempted in the school. To accomplish this task a team will need to have arrived at a consensus view of at least the content areas of health education. Using such a content list as a baseline it is possible to discover which of the content areas are already being taught in the various subjects across the curriculum.

It is possible, for example, to construct a grid or checklist (Schools Council, 1984) based upon the main content areas of health education and then to invite heads of department and their colleagues to indicate whether they are included in the teaching of specific year groups. When the results of such an inquiry are assembled together on to a master grid for the whole school, they offer a picture of what is being taught by whom and to whom. It is for the co-ordinator and the team to decide upon the level of inquiry needed to give a clear picture of which health topics are covered and when. It is probable that two levels of investigation are needed; one at the initial and surface level to give a general picture of what is happening, and a second to provide a more detailed account and clarification of the depth of teaching and methods used.

When assembled with care a master grid gives a reasonable picture of what health education is being taught in a school and provides an excellent baseline for further and future developments. It provides, for example, an opportunity for spotting gaps, weaknesses, overlaps and major omissions. From it a team will be able to see what particular health topics are covered in any one year group and also in which particular subject area such teaching is concentrated. Further scrutiny will enable a team to see whether specific groups of pupils in any one year group are missing out on health education. Many schools are surprised by the amount of health education being taught across the curriculum, but many are also disturbed by the haphazard and piecemeal approach to the subject. Health education is often scattered across the curriculum of any one year group with little consideration of time or co-ordination. Frequently certain topics, for example sex education, are repeated with, for the pupils at least, monotonous regularity within different subject areas and with no apparent reference to each other. At the very least co-ordination of the teaching could offer a more rational and coherent approach. Teachers are sometimes worried by the apparent duplication of health topics which an investigation such as this reveals. It is worth remembering, however, that individual subjects bring their own distinctive perspective to bear on a topic which undoubtedly complements and expands the pupil's understanding of it. Co-ordination should attempt to bring together these contributions in such a way as to be coherent, intelligible and relevant to the lives of the pupils and not just as unrelated bits from three or four subject syllabuses with no clear overall focus. Successful co-ordination should add up to much more than the sum of the individual parts from subject contributions.

When a particular topic has been or is being taught to a particular year group, it can sometimes carry with it the force of tradition so that it continues year after year to be part of the curriculum. The fact that a health topic already exists in the curriculum for a particular year group is no valid reason for it to continue to be there. The master grid provides a useful opportunity for questioning such existing health-education teaching. Perhaps what is taught is there because it fits, in a subsidiary role, with other subject teaching or for other reasons not specifically related to health education or the personal and social development of young people. In this way some health-related teaching might be occurring with impressive frequency across the curriculum but with little regard to any order of priority associated with the needs of young people. The co-ordinator and team will need to satisfy themselves that what exists in the health-education curriculum exists for the right reasons and not because of the machinations of the syllabuses of other subject areas. In order to satisfy themselves on this account, school teams will need to consider how best to plan a programme for young people ranging from ages 11 to 16 or 18 which successfully caters for their various needs.

PLANNING FOR A
HEALTH EDUCATION PROGRAMME

It is not uncommon for schools to plan their health education in response to what they see as health crises in the lives of their pupils. For example, teaching about drugs, smoking, alcohol, sex, sexually transmitted diseases and other matters is often made a focus of attention when the problems associated with these topics appear to manifest themselves in the behaviour of young people. Judgements about what needs to be taught can sometimes be based upon erroneous assumptions, eye-catching media reports, half-digested and not clearly understood reports or upon personal observations of a small number of young people. Clearly a planned programme of health education will need to be based upon firmer foundations than these. For successful programme planning there is need for at least three important criteria:

1. An understanding of the content and processes of health education and promotion
2. An understanding of curriculum innovation and how health education might be organized within and alongside a school curriculum
3. An understanding of the potential of the school as a health-promoting community and of the school's place in the setting of the wider community

The Content and Process of Health Education

The health career and the spiral curriculum

An inherent difficulty of many of our contemporary health problems lies in the fact that they are embedded in the social and cultural lives of people. The social experiences of children and young people in their families and in the wider community provide a background against which new ideas, concepts and knowledge are placed. With little learning in the formal sense young people develop many attitudes, values, beliefs and behaviours directly or indirectly associated with their health. The notion of a health career line (Schools Council, 1979) is important in understanding how children and young people are exposed to and often adopt the values and attitudes of individuals who are particularly significant to them, such as parents, older siblings and, later, peers. Generally the career line approach to health behaviour focuses attention upon the social and other factors which might influence the development of health-related behaviour.

Teachers who are doubtful about the effects of such influences are referred to the work of Jahoda and Crammond (1972) who show that by about the age of eight groups of children in Glasgow have attained what is referred to as 'a mastery of the concepts of alcohol' to an exceptional degree. Their major conclusion is that attitudes towards alcohol and drinking are taking shape during the years from 6 to 10. Bewley *et al.*

(1979) in a study associated with cigarette smoking amongst pre-adolescent children, confirm that permissiveness towards smoking by parents, the influence of older siblings who smoke and the desire to conform with peer group behaviour all combine to shape the attitudes of young children. This point is again emphasized by the Goldmans (1982) in their study related to children's attitudes to and knowledge about sexuality. In this way an early health knowledge is the product of a socialization within a specific family or community culture. Such experiences provide a distinct frame of reference in which new health knowledge is received and interpreted (see also Campbell, 1984).

The concept of the health career is then an important concept to be taken into account in the planning of a programme of health education since it highlights the need to consider more carefully the scope and sequence of health education. It also exposes the 'response to crisis' approach which characterized school health education in the late 1960s and early 1970s and which still lingers on in some of our schools.

The truth of the matter is that young people do not come to school *tabula rasa* but come possessing knowledge, values, attitudes and behaviours closely or directly associated with health education. It behoves the educator to find out what these might be and to take them into account when planning a school programme. Within a class of 30 pupils there will be different perspectives, values, and behaviour; in fact 30 different health careers, some of which will resemble each other, others of which will be so radically different as to challenge the adoption of a bland 'universal' approach to health education.

Key Areas and a Sequential Programme

We have become increasingly aware that the 'one off' type of lesson has a limited and depressingly short-term effect upon pupils. Several studies in the UK and the USA (ASHA, 1985) demonstrate what we have suspected for a long time – that to be effective, teaching related to a specific topic, subject or area of work must be revisited several times during the school life of children. Each revisitation, however, needs to bring a new perspective, new knowledge and perhaps a different approach or strategy in accordance with the needs and levels of understanding of particular developmental stages or age groups.

Because of the limitations of time available for health education in the curriculum of secondary schools, a sequential approach to key areas of health education provides an obvious answer – while presenting the planners with the problem of having to decide what the key areas might be.

THE AREAS OF HEALTH EDUCATION

Inevitably a sampling of the views of staff colleagues about health education would reveal a range of opinions reflecting not only their perception of health education but the nature of education itself. At one level of understanding health education might be considered to be a list of content areas ranging from, for example, smoking to sex education, and, with the exception of a few topics, there is little difficulty in establishing general agreement on them in a school. Such a content list is important in helping to define the extent of health education across the curriculum, and sets a visible agenda for its operation in schools. In this way a content list of health education provides an agreed and concrete starting point for discussion and negotiation between staff members. A content list, as shown in Table 3.1, was found to be a most useful tool by the SCHEP 13–18 team in its work with schools, although the experience of the project would emphasize the need to use it as a staging post for further clarification and development, rather than as an end in itself.

A slightly different way in which content areas might be arranged is that currently being used in the context of the HEC Projects in Initial Teacher Education (began in 1982) and in Primary Schools (began in 1984). This means of organizing health content takes the view that because of the formidable number of health topics clammering for attention in the school curriculum there is a need for a relatively simple curriculum framework which allows response to local and national need without having to change its basic structure. The framework uses a three 'cornerstone' model as illustrated in Figure 3.1, and is intended to provide a means of clarifying the important health issues related to any developmental group of children.

It can provide a simplified tool which teachers can apply to their own curriculum and ask relatively non-threatening questions. What am I providing in my curriculum which helps children/young people look after their own health; helps them develop and cope with relationships at different levels and helps them understand the need for a harmonious and healthy community set in a well-cared for physical environment. It is likely that the latter form of organization suits better a health-education programme which is developed as an integral part of a personal and social education programme.

It is probably best for schools to identify a realistic number of priority strands of health education which it can develop as a sequential programme from year 1 to 5 and beyond if necessary. This could then become the 'heart' of the health-education programme which allows for responses to specific crisis needs which will inevitably occur.

Table 3.1   Health education in schools/colleges

Main content area	Examples of items for study within each main content area
	The working of body systems
Personal health, body management and human biology	Adaptation to environment, e.g. physical and mental stress
	Exercise – need for and effect of
	Health habits and personal hygiene
	Effects on body of alcohol, drugs and tobacco
	Common infectious diseases those sexually transmitted
Food selection	Nutritional needs of the body
	Nutrition and health, e.g. slimming, obesity, stress and anxiety, etc.
	Eating patterns of individuals and community
Growth and development from childhood through adolescence to adulthood	Body changes at puberty including individual differences and sexual development
	Emotional and social development accompanying physical change
Relationships	Parents and adult authority
	Peers
	Sexual relationships – with other and same sex
	Marriages and/or other long-term relationships
	Learning to cope with loss and separation
	With mentally ill and physically handicapped
	As situations for smoking, alcohol and drug activities
Education for parenthood	Growth, development and needs of young children
	Family roles and structures including one parent families, etc.
	Helping young children to cope with loss and separation
Community health	The National Health Service and alternatives
	Roles and relationships with doctors and hospital staff
	National and community health issues such as contraception, abortion, immunization, fluoride, etc.
	Attitudes to physical and mental illness and handicap
	Voluntary organizations and clinics, etc., e.g. Marriage Guidance Council, Samaritans, Brook Advisory Clinic
The environment in which we live	Litter, pollution including noise
	Meeting the needs of the community or living space, leisure and mobility
	Effect of the environment on physical and mental health
	Health issues such as sewage processing, refuse collection, etc.

Table 3.1 (*cont'd*)

Safety and first aid   Road-traffic education and driver education, etc.
Home
School and work
Leisure
Principles of first aid

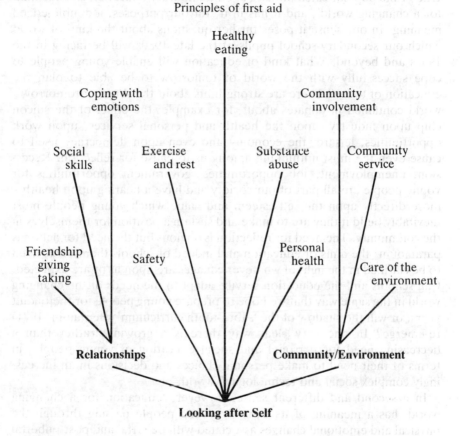

Figure 3.1 A curriculum framework based upon three 'foundation stones', outlining some suggested 'key areas'

Developmental Needs

Understanding how young people grow and develop as a basis for deciding 'priorities' or 'key' areas

One of the popular catch phrases of contemporary education is 'education for a changing world', and it has in it, for our purposes, a double-edged meaning. In one sense it poses further questions about the kind of world which our secondary school pupils of the late 1980s will be facing in the 1990s and beyond. What kind of education will enable young people to cope successfully with the world of tomorrow to be able to plan the education of today? There are strong hints about the shape of tomorrow's world contained in debates about, for example, the effect of the silicon chip upon industry, upon the health and personal services, upon work opportunities, leisure, the economy and even upon democracy itself to cause even the most unthinking among us to pause for reflection. Recession, unemployment, job opportunities, government opportunities for young people are all part of our society and have a bearing upon health – more directly upon the self-esteem and value which young people must inevitably build if they are to make and sustain a position for themselves in the community. The need for reflection is obvious but the need for action is paramount; the aims of education and indeed of schools themselves need to be clarified in the light of whatever changes are upon us or are expected. Can schools and the education service adapt to the needs of the changing world in the same way that we hope to prepare young people for their adult years, or will the shadow of the 'sabre-tooth curriculum' (Benjamin, 1971) re-emerge? In one very clear way there is a growing, rather than a decreasing need for personal and social education of young people, in terms of their need to make personal choices and decisions in an increasingly complex social and technological world.

In a second and different sense, however, 'education for a changing world' has a meaning of its own for young people passing through the physical and emotional changes associated with pubertal and post-pubertal growth. This meaning has more direct relevance to young people because they are experiencing their changes now, and there is nothing like the immediacy of the present to demonstrate how relevant to their lives health education is and can be.

Pubertal changes mark the beginning of a secondary phase of socialization which brings young people from childhood through to a mature adulthood. It is a time for learning and practising to be an adult, in the widest sense of the word, and, in a very direct and purposeful way, of working through important 'developmental tasks', the experience of which provides a basis for their very adulthood. Such developmental tasks are intimately interrelated with the physical, cognitive, moral and social growth of young people at this time and provide a context within which self-esteem and self-identity can re-emerge eventually into an adult figure and role.

The notion of 'developmental tasks of adolescence' will of course be familiar to many teachers, but Havighurst's (1972) original listing of them is still worthy of consideration, particularly within the context of planning a health education programme for young people.

Development Tasks of Adolescence
  (a) Achieving new and more mature relations with age mates of both sexes.
  (b) Achieving a masculine or feminine role.
  (c) Accepting one's physique and using the body effectively.
  (d) Achieving emotional independence of parents and other adults.
  (e) Preparing for marriage, for long-term relationships and for family life.
  (f) Preparing for an economic career.
  (g) Acquiring a set of values and an ethical system as a guide to behavior – developing an ideology.
  (h) Desiring and achieving socially responsible behavior.

Havighurst deals more fully with each of the developmental tasks, and interested readers are directed towards his work and that of Monaster (1977) for a more detailed consideration and further clarification of these tasks. In planning a programme for school-based work, therefore, it is vital to take into account the development needs of young people which are made more explicit through the notion of 'developmental tasks'.

Adolescent Health Needs

Now and in the future

A school health-education programme must present a balance between the present and future health needs of the pupils but there is an overwhelming need to ensure that whatever is included is seen by young people as relevant to their present situations. Social and other influences must be taken into account together with an understanding of the trends in adolescent health. For this purpose school teams will need to consult with medical colleagues and other sources. Much information exists in national and international reports and the personnel of the school health service are important allies because they have access to more detailed local knowledge which will help shape a health-education programme. The World Health Organization has also concerned itself with the health needs of adolescents and has published an excellent short report (1978) which provides much valuable and useful information.

Generally, reports concerning the health of a community show the incidence of death and morbidity (illness) related to age, sex and perhaps social class. For example, in the age group 10–19 accidents of one kind or another are the main cause of death in all European countries including the United Kingdom. This fact should influence the shaping of a health-education programme considerably, particularly if more detailed information relating the type of accident to sex and age group were available. At 16 young people are legally entitled to ride motorcycles and it is all too painfully obvious to the observer that the number of motorcycle accidents is appallingly high amongst adolescent boys. Similarly there is a fairly dramatic rise in the incidence of sexually transmitted diseases amongst older teenagers, a fact related to increased interest in the opposite sex and consequential sexual behaviour.

However, mortality and morbidity during adolescence should not be the only basis upon which to plan a health-education programme. It is necessary to remind ourselves of the health-career concept and what it implies for adolescent learning and behaviour. Adolescence is the period in which much health-related behaviour is initiated or where the continuation of already adopted behaviours are confirmed and hardened or rejected. The danger implicit in some of these behaviours becomes explicit only later in life during early, middle or late adulthood. Much heart disease amongst middle-aged and elderly adults, for example, is believed to be caused by an inappropriate lifestyle characterized by a diet heavy in animal fats and sugar, cigarette smoking and lack of physical exercise.

Emotional and mental breakdown is associated with an inability to cope with a wide range of personal relationships and situations which lead to overwhelming feelings of anxiety, depression and stress of many kinds. These are all patterns of behaviour which were learned and adopted much earlier in life. The huge number of deaths of both men and women, which are related to cigarette smoking – lung cancer, bronchitis, heart disease – is largely due to a habit begun during the adolescent years. If we were to concentrate upon those health problems which only manifest themselves during adolescence, our health education programme would be inadequate and probably educationally inept.

Methods of Teaching Health Education

The various methods of teaching health education are more than adequately dealt with elsewhere in this book; but nevertheless some comment is needed here as they play an important part in the development of an overall programme. The methods used by teachers tend to reflect the perceptions which they themselves have of this area of work. As previously discussed, at the extremes they might be represented as *persuasion* versus *autonomy*. The danger of using this kind of shorthand in attempting to illuminate the issues are obvious but if it helps to provoke thought and promote discussion it will be justified.

Do schools follow through their declared aims and objectives to think about the methodologies necessary in order to bring them to fruition? I have little doubt that those following roughly in the path of persuasion do employ materials and methodologies which attempt to persuade. This can largely be accomplished by careful selection of the facts, by a presentation of them in such a manner as to imply that they represent the whole truth or at least the part that really matters.

But what of those following the signpost *autonomy?* What methodologies do they use; what processes or procedures do they employ? Put bluntly, do schools have the stamina and determination to accommodate ideas such as 'decision-making', 'responsible and informed choices' and 'democratic processes' which are inherent in this view of health education. Is it possible for teachers to adopt a rational/neutral style of teaching when issues of deep personal and social concern are involved? Is it possible for teachers not to influence pupils in some involuntary manner? If teachers wish to opt for a style of teaching in health education which places emphasis upon the 'autonomy of the individual' then how can we help them manage the processes implied by such teaching within the context of a normal classroom? Can such processes be managed within the parameters set by traditional styles of teaching or must they employ different styles and strategies? How threatening might this be? It might be that schools generally do not have such clear views about health education that they are so discerning about methods. This lack of clarity is often compounded by feelings of protective paternalism which unconsciously lead teachers to influence young people 'for the best' – an unconscious sentiment with which most teachers consciously identify. This way we get the best of both worlds – by perhaps paying lip service to the notion of autonomy while practising subtle modes of persuasion – perhaps a cynical view?

The rational decision-making model of health education is, however, referred to more and more as the preferred if not the ideal mode of operation in schools. Health education is now generally seen as a process by which people can learn to protect and promote their own health and that of the community in which they live. What, however, is meant by process and how might it take place in the context of the classroom and school environment? One version of 'process' is seen as comprising activities – perhaps sequential in nature – involving: the acquisition of new knowledge related to health topics; the clarification of present attitudes and values; and their relationship to behaviour – (decision-making).

A Version of 'Process' in School Health Education

Knowledge

New knowledge is interpreted in the light of present knowledge, attitudes, values and present behaviour.

New knowledge

Perceptions	What does the message mean for me?	What do I do about the message?	Reject it?
Values	Is it relevant?		Reinforce my present behaviour?
Attitudes	Is it appropriate?		Store away for future reference or to forget?
Present behaviour	Does it conflict with or agree with my present knowledge, attitudes and behaviour?		Change or adapt present behaviour?

It is clear that in formulating the way in which the new knowledge might be structured and delivered it would be a good idea to find out what the pupils already know, feel and do; a sample of pupils' opinion would therefore provide a useful and relevant starting point for teachers.

In thinking of the possible stages of the process, therefore, we might consider some of the following questions:
1. What do pupils already know about the topic?
2. What do pupils feel about the topic?
   (a) Are they interested?
   (b) Do they feel involved?
   (c) Is it relevant to their lives?
3. What 'new knowledge' is appropriate and relevant to them and to their lives?

4. What will we ask the pupils to do with this 'new knowledge'?
   (a) *Learn* and understand its meaning
   (b) *Clarify* their attitudes/feelings about it
       (i) Are they interested; do they feel it important to them or to their community?
       (ii) Does it conflict with their present feelings? Why?
   (c) *Use it* in some way
       (i) Make decisions or solve problems for other people or themselves.
       (ii) Clarify how they might adapt or change present behaviour in the light of the new knowledge
       (iii) What motivations might be appropriate?
       (iv) How can we provide opportunities for practice in real life?
       (v) What skills need to be developed or reinforced?

Adopting a 'process' orientation to school health education has major implications then for how it might be managed in the classroom – and in the school. It implies an involvement with the pupils in several different ways and, of necessity, goes beyond the traditional view of teaching to embrace the best of current classroom practices which can be summarized by the new three R's – relationships, relevance, and responsibility.

Relationship means the importance of the relationships which exist within a classroom between teacher and those taught based upon an understanding by the teacher of human developmental need and of health education.

Relevance is vital to the motivation of pupils in terms of importance within their values, expectations and actual behaviour.

Responsibility is a key word in clarifying for pupils their own responsibility for personal and community health in terms of their own behaviour and also their participation in community decisions and activities.

It is highly likely that the majority of teachers will first come to health education through the materials which are available and therefore such resources need to represent the educational and ideological thought which has been developing in this area slowly.

The importance of this point can so easily be underestimated – materials are important both in their own right and as a form of initiation into the nature and purpose of health education itself. We are fortunate to have a reservoir of good materials from the various projects developed in the past few years and by LEAs and schools themselves. Indeed the *writing* of materials can provide teachers and schools with a useful means of working through the many issues involved in health education. Perhaps indeed it is the only real way by which the issues can become personally relevant to a school, individual teachers or pupils.

Organization within the School

Health education is still something of a Cinderella amongst other areas of the curriculum, a status which it shares with other areas of the 'soft underbelly' of the curriculum (Background Paper, 1984). There are, of course, many influences upon decisions on how a programme might be organized which have to do with the traditional view of the curriculum and the predominance of the examination-orientated subjects. Let us for the moment, however, focus upon a narrower theme.

Recent experience shows that broadly there are two ways in which programmes might be organized:
1. As a *course* within a school in much the same way as the traditional subjects are organized
2. As a cross-curricular activity.

One can refer to the former, no. 1, as a 'high rise' and the latter, no. 2, as a 'Manhattan' to make simple analogies with town-planning silhouettes. Each has its advantages as well as disadvantages. Each also has many possible variations and perhaps to cloud the issue even further one can possibly grow out of the other. An important question to ask is which suits individual schools best?

The high rise

Let us look briefly at the 'high rise' model. The essential point about such courses is that they are taught usually by a small group of two or three teachers (sometimes even by a single teacher). The subject areas or topics concerned are fairly clearly defined, the programme has timetabled space and is organized by an identifiable teacher. The small number of teachers involved makes its management comparatively easy, decisions concerning content and methodologies are easily dispensed with. The course can be organized with a minumum of fuss and inconvenience to the rest of the curriculum once curriculum space has been established.

It is possible for health education to appear as a 'course' in its own right or as an important aspect of a personal and social education course (PSE). In either case, however, it can be organized as a distinct and separate course.

A second variation of the 'high rise' occurs if health education becomes part of the 'tutorial time': in which the form tutors provide a health education programme to coincide with the curriculum time available to them – 'active tutorial work'. This will need careful preparation because of the considerable number of 'form tutors' involved and usually requires consultations and in-service training.

The Manhattan

The key to understanding this model lies in seeing health education itself as an eclectic area of study having roots in several subject areas. Its content and methodologies (depending upon one's own clarification) might stem from the (physical and human) sciences; the arts; social sciences; home economics; physical education; moral education and environmental issues. Indeed depending upon one's own viewpoint so health education is perceived. This is not to lay claim, on behalf of health education, to the vast territories of the whole curriculum but rather to emphasize and to underline its eclectic and cross-curriculum composition. In the absence of teachers specifically trained and equipped to teach health education – and it might be timely to ask parenthetically here whether this is the ideal for which to aim – it could be argued that a health-education programme should attempt to utilize the rich and varied talents of the staff as a whole. Indeed it is not too difficult to locate strands of health education within many subject areas – the real difficulty is in co-ordinating their respective contributions in such a manner that it becomes a coherent learning experience for the pupils themselves. It is so easy for such co-ordination to live only in the minds of teachers. How can this best be accomplished? Perhaps by providing a focal point, let's call it a 'core' – but with several important co-ordinated contributions from other subject areas. So our Manhattan model emerges!

A recent investigation (Jones, 1986) undertaken in 35 LEAs revealed a diversity of organizational methods. There is a growing trend, however, for health education to be more firmly located in a personal and social education programme following the timely comments and suggestions of HM Inspectors of Schools in their secondary schools survey (DES, 1979).

The School as a Health-Promoting Community

The notion of the health-promoting school rests upon the assumption that schools have concerns which go beyond the academic and intellectual development of their pupils which includes responsibility for their personal, social and physical welfare. If the skeleton of the school is its taught curriculum then its flesh is built out of the ethos which it develops and which arises naturally out of the concern of the headteacher and staff for the full and rounded development of each of its pupils – intellectually, physically, socially, morally and, if need be, spiritually. The reality of practice, however, is that schools tend to place greater emphasis upon the academic and intellectual development of their pupils than upon their healthy physical and emotional development.

There is a tendency to polarize thinking so that intellectual development is often seen as the obverse side of the personal and social development of pupils, but in truth they are inextricably linked together. Intellectual, academic and cognitive growth is part of personal growth; it should be seen as part of the growth towards the development of a realistic assessment of oneself, towards a self-identity, self-esteem and a growing sense of responsibility for oneself and one's actions – an ideal to which the democratic process aspires.

Of course schools vary dramatically in their ratings as health-promoting communities: some are excellent; some are poor; most are mediocre. If schools are to become communities where the 'health' of pupils is to be taken seriously and actively promoted, then there are important issues relating to school policy and practice which need to be clarified, elaborated and discussed openly between staff. Perhaps the most important issue relates to the need for congruence between what is taught in the health or personal and social curriculum and the 'hidden' messages which emanate from the policies, organization and values implicit in the way in which a school is organized and run.

An oft-quoted example of such incongruences stems from the differences which pupils recognize between what is taught about nutrition and their experiences in school tuck shops and school meals. Other inconsistencies are readily obvious on reflection – such as the teaching related to the use of tobacco which sits uneasily with the smoking behaviour of staff on school premises.

Generally the major emphasis is still placed upon the development of the health-education curriculum with little thought about how what is taught in the classroom might be supported and reinforced through the values and attitudes implicit in the organization, structure and staffing of schools.

It would be too much to expect schools to become fully operational health-promoting communities overnight but there are many ways in which small changes and adjustments can be made providing there is a willingness to discuss the central issues concerned. A small group of European school health educators recently discussed some of these central issues and the results (Williams and de Panafieu, 1985) are outlined in Table 3.2.

One further ingredient needs, however, to be mentioned in the context of the health-promoting school and this is the dimension of links between school, family and community. Health education which remains only school-focused is in danger of being irrelevant to the lives which pupils live outside school. Indeed experiences in the United States leads to the belief

Table 3.2 The health-promoting school

Aims for the school itself	Aims for school health education
To provide a healthful environment with regard to, e.g. safety, meals, hygiene, building and grounds	To promote a sense of responsibility in respect of the individual, the family's and the community's health
To provide exercise and leisure facilities	To encourage a healthy way of life and to present a realistic range of health choices
To provide a positive social environment	To enable the learner to fulfil his or her physical, psychological and social potential and to improve self-knowledge and self-esteem
To support the health-education curriculum	To provide and develop capacities and skills, e.g. to make choices and decisions; to manage stress; to handle conflictual situations related to health
To support the school health services and to develop further its relevance to the health education of pupils	To provide a health-knowledge base and skill in handling (i.e. obtaining, interpreting, using) information related to health

that health-education issues such as those presented by drug abuse can only be successfully tackled within a broad front of school, home and community. This poses some problems because of the reluctance of schools to teach concepts, values and knowledge which might conflict with those of the parent. This is more an apparent fear than real, however, as recent research (Joint Universities Project, 1987) amongst the parents of primary school children has helped to clarify. Other attempts across Europe (Campbell, 1984) continue to illuminate how schools, family and community can combine together to provide a total community which not only supports but positively promotes the health of children.

Evaluation of School Programmes and Assessment of Pupils

A general view of the purpose of evaluation is that it should demonstrate whether an activity has been successful or to what degree it has failed to achieve some stated aims. In this particular sense it could be interpreted as the 'counting of heads'; a quantifying and interpretation of data followed by presentation of results in some meaningful way. If on the other hand evaluation has to contend with matters of a more qualitative nature such as, for example, values and beliefs and their relationships to a range of behavioural options in response to proferred choices, then gathering data, interpretation and presentation becomes profoundly more difficult an evaluative task. More particularly if the aims of the teaching/learning activity are more concerned with the quality of the methodological process than their outcomes, traditional methods of evaluation might be severely challenged.

Some would argue that the evaluation of a programme which concerns itself with processes such as value clarification and decision-making as well as hard facts is too difficult a task to contemplate because of the bewildering array of variables which would need to be considered. Another view would wish to emphasize the need for sound longitudinal evaluative studies, spanning many years, as the only means by which to demonstrate whether the processes of decision-making or the acquisition of relevant knowledge make any difference in helping individuals choose healthier lifestyles. Whatever the aims of the style of teaching adopted, however, there are probably evaluative procedures to accommodate them. Very broadly there are two kinds of evaluation: formative and summative.

Formative

Formative evaluation is that in which assessment of progress – for example of a school health-education programme – is monitored so as to enable changes to be made, if necessary, to its content or to the methods employed. The evaluation helps to clarify, *if* changes are necessary and *what* they should comprise. In this way the formative evaluation would represent a sequential and accumulative description of the course – perhaps from the pupil's perspective and also that of the teachers. This data would then form the basis of decisions related to the organization and content of the course, thus helping to provide a course more fitted to the needs and desires of both teachers and pupils.

Summative

Summative evaluation, as the name implies, is concerned with finding out how successful the pupil or the course was in meeting the aims or the goals set. Teachers will be familiar with this form of evaluation as end of year or public examination, which provides a picture of to what degree the pupil or course was successful.

In teaching and evaluating health education, however, there are three elements which need to be considered:
1. Knowledge and understanding
2. Attitudes and values
3. Behaviour and decision-making

While strategies of evaluation/assessment involving knowledge and understanding are reasonably well-understood, those related to attitudes, values, behaviour and decision-making, however, pose difficulties for teachers. There is a clear need for help in this particular field which is not currently being met, although a recent report (Jones and Hill, 1986) offers some guidelines for the development of strategies of pupil assessment in health education. This report surveyed the assessment procedures in health education in 39 schools and provides some insight of the problems and how they are being tackled. Twenty of the 39 schools did undertake some form of assessment in health education, while 19 schools did not and, for a variety of reasons, ranging over 'lack of expertise', 'a belief that assessment should not, for ethical reasons, take place', 'lack of time' and 'lack of personnel'.

Suffice to say that the evaluation and assessment of school health education is not a well-researched or resourced area of concern. The standing and status of health education in the context of the school and its curriculum and also in the eyes of parents and school administration depends somewhat, however, on justifying its place in terms of its effectiveness. In a growing atmosphere of accountability in public expenditure, evaluation and assessment need to be taken much more seriously than it presently is.

POSTSCRIPT – A PRAGMATIC VIEWPOINT

Everything else said, the bottom line of school health education is in inviting teachers to become involved. Success is not only measured by a successful and fully integrated school health-education curriculum supported by a health promoting school and supportive parents. Success can be viewed, in a more pragmatic sense, by the work of one teacher who interacts successfully with one or more pupil in a small area of health concern. If one views school health education as a continuum ranging from the effect that one teacher might have upon one pupil at one end to the fully effective health-promoting school at the other it becomes a more tenable and realistic ideal. Presenting school health education in this way provides goals which might be achieved by every school and every teacher and is much less intimidating than the 'all or nothing' perspective. We know that the well-co-ordinated, sequentially planned programme, set within the context of a caring school and supported by family and community is much more likely to promote healthy lifestyles – but every little bit helps.

84   *Health Education in Schools*

REFERENCES

American School Health Association (1985) *Journal of School Health*, October issue.
Background Paper (1984) Personal and social education development in the curriculum, pp. 58–69, in *Developing Health Education: A Coordinator's Guide*, Faber, London.
Baelz, P. R. (1979) Philosophy of health education, in Sutherland, I. (ed.) *Health Education: Perspectives and Choices*, Allen & Unwin, London.
Benjamin, H. (1971) The sabre tooth curriculum, in Hooper (ed.) *The Curriculum: Contact Design and Development*, Oliver and Boyd, Edinburgh.
Bewley, B. R. *et al.* (1979) Factors associated with the starting of cigarette smoking in primary school children, *British Journal of Preventative Medicine*, Vol. 28, pp. 37–44.
Campbell, G. (ed.) (1984) *Health Education and Youth, A Review of Research and Development*, Falmer Press, London.
Department of Education and Science (1979) *Aspects of Secondary Education in England*, A survey by HM Inspectors of Schools, HMSO, London.
Goldman, R. and Goldman, J. (1982) *Children's Sexual Thinking*, Routledge & Kegan Paul, London.
Havighurst, R. J. (1972) *Development Tasks and Education*, McKay, New York.
Health Education Council (1982–8) *Health Education in Initial Teacher Education*, HEC Health Education Unit, University of Southampton.
Health Education Council (1984–) *Health Education in Primary Schools*, HEC Health Education Unit, University of Southampton.
Hodgson, A. (1985) *LEA Policies and Practices Relating to Drugs, Education and Drug Misuses*, NFER, Windsor.
Interdepartmental Committee (1904) *Interdepartmental Committee on Physical Deterioration*, HMSO, London.
Interdepartmental Committee (1905) *Interdepartmental Committee on Medical Inspections and Feeding of Children Attending Public Elementary Schools*, HMSO, London.
Jahoda, G. and Crammond, J. (1972) *Children and Alcohol: A Developmental Study in Glasgow*, HMSO, London.
Joint University of Southampton and University of Exeter Project (1987) *Health Education in Primary Schools*.
Jones, A. (1986) *SHEP 13–18: Some Years On*, C Report, Health Education Unit, University of Southampton.
Jones, A. and Hill, F. (1986) *Assessment of Pupil Achievement in Health Education*, HEC Health Education Unit, University of Southampton.
Monaster, J. (1977) *Adolescent Development and the Life Tasks*, Allyn & Bacon, Boston, MA.
Schools Council (1979) *Think Well*, Health Education 5–13, Thomas Nelson, Sunbury-on-Thames, Middx.
Schools Council (1984) *Developing Health Education: a Coordination Study*, Health Education Council, Forbes, London.
Williams, T. and de Panafieu, C. (1985) *School Health Education in Europe, Profiles of 15 European Countries*, Health Education Unit, University of Southampton.

Williams, T. and Roberts, J. (1986) *Health Education in Schools and Teacher Education Institution*, Health Education Unit, University of Southampton.
World Health Organization (1978) *The Health Needs of Adolescents*, Technical Report No. 609, WHO, Geneva.

4

HEALTH EDUCATION
FOR CHILDREN WITH SPECIAL NEEDS

Jill Coombs and Ann Craft

INTRODUCTION

The Warnock Report (DES, 1978) suggests that about one fifth of all schoolchildren have special educational needs. These needs have important implications for the teaching of health education. Only a small minority of these children are to be found in specialized educational settings, such as a special school or a unit in a mainstream school, the majority receives ordinary mainstream education. The issues which arise in relation to health education and children with special educational needs are therefore relevant to *all* teachers.

Inevitably this chapter reflects the very patchy and uneven progress in the field to date. From the literature reviewed later in this chapter, it appears that for some groups of children with specific handicaps, the account taken of their handicaps in health education is limited to sex education. No doubt individual teachers and schools are further on in their work, but this progress and practice has yet to be disseminated more widely.

Throughout this chapter, most frequent reference is made to children with mild and moderate learning difficulties. Not only is this group of children the largest with special educational needs, but there has also been considerably more work on their health-education needs than for other groups of children. Aspects of both past and present work* (some of it

---

* SCHEP 5–13 (1977) *Special Education Extension – Slow Learners 1979–1981*, Schools Council/HEC. *Training and Aftercare Phase of the Health Education for Slow Learners Project*, scheduled for 1982–5, ended 1983, HEC, *Health Education for Slow Learners Project 1984–1987*. The three main areas of this work are the evaluation of teaching materials; the development and evaluation of in-service training for teachers; and the

unpublished) are drawn on. Despite the fact that the very different causes of learning difficulties for individual children have different and particular implications for the teaching of health education, there are common issues and common ground which can help teachers to reflect on and improve their own classroom teaching for children with special educational needs. This chapter explores a number of these issues.

In the first half of the chapter, classroom practice in teaching health education to children with special educational needs is examined. This centres on considering the selection of appropriate resources and teaching methods, the influences of different educational settings, the purpose and content of health education and the special needs of particular groups of children. In the second half, issues in making links in health education between the school, the home and the wider community are examined. This includes considering why parents might be beneficially involved, differences in perceptions between parents and teachers and schools, practical issues in developing parental involvement, examples of how schools have involved parents in health education, and making links with the wider community.

CLASSROOM PRACTICE

What goes to make up good classroom practice in teaching health education with children who have mild and moderate learning difficulties? What are the issues and the problems relevant to this? In an attempt to answer these questions this section considers: selecting appropriate resources; teaching methods; the influences of different educational settings; the purpose and content of health education; and the special needs of particular groups of children.

Resources

'I don't know who designs these materials but they hardly ever seem to think about the less able children in the class.'

Teachers bemoaning the inadequacies of resources are common in all schools, but the provision of suitable health-education materials for children with mild and moderate learning difficulties does seem to be one area of particular neglect. Of course most teachers do adapt and make do with

development of home-school-community links in health education. Further details of this Project for the period 1984–7, can be obtained by writing for Newsletters to: HEC: Health Education for Slow Learners Project, School of Education, University of Bath, Bath BA2 7AY.

whatever is available, but this can be particularly difficult in health education, where many of the published resources seem to need a great deal of adapting for this particular group of children. The crucial problem hinges on the difference between educational and social development that exists for many slow learners. This is well-illustrated by the following quotes, which have been taken from a national questionnaire on health education for slow learners (unpublished) carried out as part of the work of the HEC: Health Education for Slow Learners Project. Teachers were asked to comment on the features that resources should have to make them suitable for using with slow learners:

> Simple, clear approach, but appealing to older children.
> Clear text, but relevant to the age group – not patronizing.
> Pitched at an interest level of the age group, and understanding level of primary children.
> Mature approach, but simple language.

The problem is that much of health education is about personal and social issues, and as many slow learners are no different from other children in these aspects of their development it is often quite inappropriate to use resources designed for younger children – although these may be at a suitable educational level, they are likely to come across as either 'too young', 'patronizing' or 'irrelevant'.

There has in fact been only one major teaching pack produced on health education specifically designed to be both socially and educationally appropriate for children with mild and moderate learning difficulties. *Fit for Life* (McNaughton, 1983) is a teaching pack consisting of pupil worksheets and activities alongside materials for teachers with suggestions about classroom use. The pack was written in collaboration with teachers of slow learners and is now in use in many mainstream and special schools. In a short evaluation project in 1983–4, teachers were asked to comment on why they liked *Fit for Life* (HEC, 1984). Comments by two teachers point out further important criteria used in selecting resources, which are considered in more detail in this section:

> We like the uncluttered drawings and that there are no labels on the illustrations, so we can use appropriate names for particular age groups.
> At the moment I'm finding that the worksheets that I choose to use are superb, they are very clear, very good for using as talking points.

What then, are the criteria that experienced teachers in health education use to select resources which are suitable for children with mild and moderate learning difficulties? It is useful at this stage to make a distinction between the detailed structure and format of a resource, and its overall ethos. In considering these in more detail, quotes have been drawn from the Project's national questionnaire on health education to illustrate teachers' concerns about these issues.

The detailed features of resources

'The trouble with most resources presently available is that they are too complicated for slow learners.'

The key to making resources suitable for pupils with mild and moderate learning difficulties is simplicity – without compromising on accuracy, interest value and relevance to chronological age. How this rule of simplicity is put into practice will vary with each class of children, but at the heart of it is a desire to minimize the difficulties which many pupils experience with their reading and writing. Comments which teachers frequently make about written resources for pupils are summarized in Table 4.1. The important features seem to be a balance between attractive, colourful and clear illustrations and the text, which should be easy to read and understand, using a minimum of technical language, clear and fairly large print, and an uncluttered layout. Much of this applies also to audiovisual resources (Table 4.2), where features of the commentary are particularly important, along with the length of time taken to show the resource (or whether parts can be selected out, as appropriate).

As many pupils with mild and moderate learning difficulties experience such difficulties with reading, writing and comprehension and as they spend much of their time at school trying to improve these skills, there is a good case for using alternative approaches in health education, which rely less on written and audiovisual resources. Alternatives such as the use of active and participatory teaching methods are considered in a later section. However, it is worth pointing out that these methods not only encourage pupils to be more successful, because they rely less on reading and writing skills, but are also appropriate methods for examining attitudes and values, and practising decision-making skills, which are important elements in health education.

The ethos of resources

The overall ethos of a resource is as important as its detailed content, structure and format – selecting a resource with the right ethos for a particular group of children should help to engage their interest and so encourage learning. But what exactly is meant by ethos and how can it be judged to be right or wrong? Experienced teachers make these kinds of

Table 4.1 Written resources

Features	What the teachers had to say
	Simple and attractive books with a minimum of reading
Format	Lots of pictures and easy to read
	Material needs to be essentially visual
	Illustrative material, simply set out with only a little reading matter
	Plenty of illustrations to support main points
Layout	Not too much on a page
	Only one large, clear picture per page
Text	Simple, short words, paragraphs and sentences
	Simple vocabulary at an appropriate reading level
	Clear, concise written material that is easy to understand – much of it (which is available) is too wordy
	Simple text, but not babyish
	Large, clear print
	Important words in large, bold print
	Simple explanations at ability level of 7–9-year-olds (for teenage slow learners
	Very basic vocabulary without very technical terms
Illustrations	Clear, simple pictures in bright colours
	Large, clear diagrams, drawings
	Illustrations with low language level
Approach	Uncluttered
	Repetitive
	Step-by-step approach
	Small segments of information
	Information accurate but not too complicated

judgements daily. Often it seems intuitive, but at the heart of these judgements lies their relationship with and knowledge of the children they teach. As health is so closely bound up with personal experience, the first rule of health education is *relevance*. For health education to have any chance of an impact on children, it must interest and engage them through being relevant to their own health-related experiences. Thus, two teachers commented that they would like to see in resources: 'Situations with a story pupils can identify with and then discuss.' 'Clear presentation of facts with relationship to the pupils' experiences.'

What then are the experiences of children with mild and moderate learning difficulties, and in particular their health-related experiences which resources need to reflect? This is arguably one of the most important questions for any teacher to ask, since the answers will fundamentally

Table 4.2 Audiovisual resources (films, videos, slides)

Features	What the teachers had to say Colour
Visual features	Clear, large, simple diagrams Labelling large, printed but not in block capitals
Commentary	Clear, unhurried commentary Simple, language would make it easier for our pupils to understand the main points Simple dialogue Understandable commentary Summarizes as it progresses
Overall	Films available give too much information too quickly Although there seem to be a lot of films available, they are too complex and detailed for the very slow learners; they seem to include too many aspects in one film and use complex language Not too long, e.g. 15 minutes maximum

influence their health education teaching. Although the answers are inevitably unique for each child and each class, there are a number of points worth raising.

Firstly, it is important to be critically aware of biases which may exist in health-education resources. The three most obvious biases are about race, sex and class; the dominant experiences reflected in many resources seem to be those of a rather stereotypical middle-class, white, male person. Other biases which are considered less often and which are often biases of omission are to do with age, sexual orientation and disability. The issue of social class bias seems to be particularly important to teachers of slow learners, which is a concern reflected in the following quotes about the kinds of resources teachers would like to see developed in the future (from the project's national survey about health education resources):

More working-class situations: most of our youngsters come from poor areas and deprived homes.

A sample range of easy-to-cook meals – no middle-class fantasy cooking!

Realistic everyday working-class situations. Need more emphasis on low incomes than usual. Most books and films rather middle class in outlook and seem to assume more affluence than is realistic today.

To make slow learners think – most books and films show a family with car, house, garden, etc. Need something to show struggles of loneliness, one-parent families, life in a high rise block of flats.

More multicultural resources – most material available does not cater for a multicultural society.

In passing, it is interesting to note that in this survey, comments about class bias were far more common than about racial bias, while there were no comments at all about sex bias.

The middle-class bias of many health-education resources is particularly important to teachers of children with mild and moderate learning difficulties since very many of their pupils come from working-class backgrounds* – this is particularly so for these children in special schools, where recent surveys have found between 89 per cent and 100 per cent of pupils to be from working-class homes (Combes, 1984a).

It is important then, that resources portray working-class experiences which reflect the home backgrounds of very many slow learners. However, this assertion immediately raises two questions: what is working-class experience and how can it be portrayed; should teachers be in the business of effectively restricting pupils' views of the world by selecting materials which relate primarily to the pupils' own experiences?

Both questions are important and deserve some discussion. Although it is useful to use class labels when talking about detecting bias in resources, there is a real danger of this leading simply to replacing middle-class stereotypes with working-class stereotypes. Inevitably there is a great range and variety in working-class environments and health-related experiences. Being mindful of such range and variety is the key to the second question also: whilst it is important to provide resources to which children can relate their own experiences, most teachers would want also to extend children's thinking beyond their own limited experiences. By offering and validating a variety of experiences in health education, it is possible both to endorse children's personal experiences, and to encourage them to develop a greater awareness and understanding of a wider variety of lifestyles and experiences. In this way, children's personal experiences are neither invalidated nor undermined, while at the same time they are placed within a wider social context. There are further implications of working-class health experiences for health education beyond this issue of the selection of appropriate resources, which are returned to later in the next section.

So where does this leave the classroom teachers faced with selecting

---

* Most surveys use parental occupation to distinguish between working-class and middle-class. Working-class occupations, as defined by the Registrar General for purposes of the national census, are primarily *manual* occupations. In the surveys of special schools for children with mild and moderate learning difficulties, very many of the pupils' parents (40–93%) have been in socio-economic groups 4 and 5 (semi-skilled or unskilled manual occupations). For an overview of these surveys, including other features of home background, see Combes, 1984a, 1984b.

appropriate resources for their pupils?* Although a few resources quite obviously show a restricted range of values and lifestyles, many contain rather more subtle forms of bias (both by commission and omission) which may not become apparent until the resource is used with particular groups of children. In this case, it can be instructive to highlight the biases as they emerge, with pupils, as one way of encouraging pupils to question the authority of written or visual materials.

Alternatively, it is useful to have a short checklist of questions to run through when selecting resources. The checklist in Table 4.3 is by no means exhaustive. It can be particularly useful and informative to go through the process of devising your own checklist with teaching colleagues, as this will enable the checklist to be pertinent to the needs of the children in your own school.

Teaching Methods

Many of the ideas around for classroom health education involve teachers and children in active and participatory methods of learning, which are particularly suitable for practising certain skills such as decision-making and exploring attitudes to health. For many pupils with mild and moderate learning difficulties health education may provide an important and rare opportunity to get away from reading- and writing-based teaching, which many find so problematic.

Ideas about active teaching methods which teachers have found to be suitable for use in health education, include quizzes, role play, simulations, project work, improvised drama, and games to promote decision-making and role play. There are quite a number of books which give detailed ideas, suggestions and advice on active methods which are applicable to health education, such as, *Using Role Play and Simulations* (COIC, 1985), *Gamesters' Handbook* (Brandes and Phillips, 1978).

---

* There are a number of recently published health education resources which portray a wide variety of urban and inner-city environments which are more relevant to pupils from working-class backgrounds than many other currently available resources, e.g. *Family Lifestyles* (Braun & Eisenstadt, 1985); *Values, Cultures and Kids* (Bovey, 1983); *Roles, Relationships and Responsibilities* (pack of drawings ILEA, 1985). However, none of these was designed with children with mild and moderate learning difficulties in mind and may therefore need some adaptations.

Table 4.3 Checklist: detecting the ethos of health education resources

Key areas	Questions
Race	Does the resource reflect the multiracial nature of society?
	Is the portrayal of ethnic minorities tokenistic? – e.g. illustrations tinkered with to show various races.
	Is the portrayal of ethnic minorities stereotypical? – e.g. ascribing certain health behaviours or problems to particular groups.
	Are important health-related experiences for particular ethnic minorities excluded?
Class	Are working-class values and lifestyles portrayed, and in relevant and realistic ways?
	Do the materials acknowledge limits to personal choices related to health? – e.g. arising from low income, housing.
Sex	Are sex role stereotypes perpetuated?
Family groupings	Does the 'happy nuclear family' prevail or are other family groupings included? – e.g. one-parent or step-families.
Environment	Are a variety of types of housing and local environments portrayed? – e.g. to include high-rise flats, council housing, inner-city terraces.
Lifestyles and values	Is a range of values and lifestyles portrayed?
	Are these appropriate for the children I teach?
	Are there implicit or explicit criticisms of some lifestyles and, if so, are these valid?

For examples of other checklists, see:
Health Care in Multiracial Britain (Mares, Henley and Baxter, 1958, chapter 15).
'Pour out the Cocoa Janet': Sexism in Children's Books (Stones, 1983, chapter 4).
The Analysis of Curriculum Materials (Eraut, Goad and Smith, 1975).
Challenging Unhealthy Stereotypes – A Guide to Analysing Health Education Materials (Oxfordshire Health Education Unit, 1986).
Hidden Messages? – Activities for Exploring Bias (Development Education Centre, 1986).

One commonly heard objection to using active learning methods is that they are all very well for high-achieving children, but using them with low achievers is very difficult. It is indeed important to acknowledge the difficulties there can be with these methods, difficulties which arise mostly from the fact that they are not very familiar to either teachers or children. There is a very real need for many teachers to learn about these techniques and to have the opportunity to practise them before trying them out in the classroom. Likewise, children need time and opportunities to learn the 'rules' of these new methods, to learn what is expected of them and what responses are valued. In many senses, some of the traditional classroom 'rules' are reversed, with value being put on discussion and self-expression, instead of a quiet and ordered classroom. This lies at the root of the comment that these active methods are all very well, but colleagues often comment disparagingly about noise and apparent lack of order in a classroom.

The success of active learning methods hinges on the relationship between the teacher and the class. Children will need to feel safe to embark on role play or discussions where they might reveal important things about themselves. It is essential at the outset to establish some ground rules, such as emphasizing that everyone has a choice about how much they reveal about themselves, respecting confidentiality, or that direct personal questions are not allowed. Finally it is also important to be aware of the potential power of some methods to evoke strong emotional responses or reveal problems for some children that will need very careful handling in a group, or may require following up later by the teacher.

Influences of Different Educational Settings

One of the most important influences on teaching health education to children with mild and moderate learning difficulties is the educational setting in which it takes place. These settings affect the application of much of what has been discussed in relation to using resources and teaching methods. It is therefore important to highlight the main influences of three common settings: special schools, special units in mainstream schools and mixed ability mainstream classes.

Only a small minority of children who have mild and moderate learning difficulties attend special schools. According to the criteria laid down in the Warnock Report (DES, 1978) and with moves towards integration, it is likely that there will be fewer special schools in the future. However, special schools at present appear to provide a positive environment for teaching health education. Many special schools have strong and well-established patterns of health education that are in advance of many mainstream school traditions. In the absence of exam pressures special schools have been freer to design a curriculum geared to the particular needs of their pupils. A fundamental aim is often to educate pupils for independent living, of which an important part is health and social education.

The structures of many special schools are also conducive to well-developed health education. In general, pupils spend much of their time with their class teacher, which brings opportunities for both building up a good relationship with pupils and acquiring detailed knowledge about children's home backgrounds. The relatively small size of classes, and of schools as a whole, also encourages closer relationships between pupils and teachers than may be practically possible in larger mainstream schools. Small class size also helps to make the use of active learning methods easier.

In contrast, teachers in mainstream schools and particularly in secondary schools have fewer opportunities to get to know the children they teach quite so well, because of larger class size and subject specialisms which reduce contact time with particular groups. In addition, exam considerations often mean that health education has considerably lower priority than in many special schools. Exactly how much health education comes the way of an individual pupil with learning difficulties may vary considerably and depend on a number of factors. For instance, many children with mild and moderate learning difficulties may not take subjects, such as science, which have a health-education component, or they may miss such lessons in order to have extra tuition with reading or writing. On the other hand, some subjects such as childcare or cookery are seen as suitable for the less able children, so that pupils may end up having more in this area of health education than some of their peers.

The structure of the special educational provision is also important. Special units where children spend most of their day, are more likely to be geared to meet the needs of the pupils in relation to health education. However, in many schools pupils with special educational needs spend most of their time in mainstream classes, withdrawing to the special unit for only a small number of classes, which rarely include health education.

Many schools also have a policy of mixed ability groupings for non-exam classes where health education may be taught, for example in tutorial periods. It is probable, therefore, that many children with learning difficulties in secondary schools and also in primary schools have health education in mixed ability settings. This raises the important question of how their needs can be met in this setting. Although materials and methods will need adapting for pupils with learning difficulties, this is rarely easy to put into practice in a mixed-ability class. It is perhaps understandable that in such circumstances, many teachers aim primarily at the children in the middle of the ability range. However, the potential for meeting diverse needs within a mixed-ability class is greater when using some active teaching methods, for example project-based discovery learning for groups or individuals, or small peer-led discussion groups. Mori (1981) suggests also that the teacher should capitalize on the strengths of individual children with special educational needs, by selecting methods in health education which will lead to success. The learning environment can also be maximized by reducing extraneous stimuli, so that the children with special educational needs are, for instance, seated away from windows and doors where distractions occur.

The Purpose and Content of Health Education

The starting point for this section is to return to the earlier question which arose out of teachers' comments about the need for health education to be relevant to children's experiences. This question has two parts: what are the health-related experiences of children with mild and moderate learning difficulties and what implications do these have for the purpose and content of their health education?

As noted earlier, a number of studies over the past 10 to 15 years have consistently found that very many children with mild and moderate learning difficulties come from families which are both working-class and disadvantaged (Birch *et al.*, 1970; Gillies, 1978; Pappenheim, 1982; Combes, 1984a; ILEA, 1984). This is particularly so for children attending special schools, many of whom come from families in socioeconomic groups 4 and 5. The kinds of disadvantages they experience arise from interrelated factors such as parental unemployment or low income, large family size, overcrowded housing, single-parent or changing family structures (Combes 1984a; 1984b). These factors may operate, together with socioeconomic status, to be significant indicators of increased risks of ill health and premature death. There is a wealth of evidence for this and, in particular, for the links between ill health and low socioeconomic status, much of it referred to in the 1981 Black Report from the DHSS (see Townsend and Davidson, 1982, for a summary of the issues and evidence).

Although there is much debate about how and why socioeconomic status is so strong an indicator of increased risks of ill health and premature death, it is clear that at least some of the causes lie within the social, economic and political structures which influence health, and which may not be subject to much personal control. This has very important implications for health education taught in schools. Perhaps the most obvious, important and the most controversial of these implications is that health needs to be taught about within its social, economic, cultural and political contexts. So how can this be translated into classroom practice? First, health education needs to be broader than its often traditional focus on individual responsibility for health, in order to encompass the responsibilities of local communities and services and national government for promoting health. This may mean, for instance, including on the health education curriculum the influences of housing on health (respiratory problems associated with damp housing) and how individuals or groups could go about improving such housing conditions within their local context – part of the *Health Skills Manual* which is currently being produced at CCDU in Leeds, will look at providing children with the opportunity to develop skills of relevance to improving health within their local communities (personal communication).

Second, in the more traditional areas of personal health choices, it is essential to remember that many children have quite limited choices not only because they are children but also because of their social or economic circumstances. For instance, parental income is a crucial factor in talking about food choices and healthy eating. Similarly some children may have very limited access to 'healthy' foods because of the location of shops in relation to where they live. Pupils may be restricted or find it hard to use health services because of a combination of the location of services, not having access to a car and expensive or irregular local public transport. Third, it is also important to set health education about individual health choices within the social and cultural contexts relevant to pupils. *Health Careers* (Dorn and Nortoft, 1983) is one health-education pack which explicitly sets out both to be relevant to working-class children and to explore the links between individual health choices and the economic, cultural and physical influences of paid and unpaid work on health.

These are just a few examples of how the *content* of health education for children with mild and moderate learning difficulties should be influenced to reflect children's health-related experiences. At this point it is worth noting two related issues: firstly to repeat that children's experiences inevitably vary between schools, classes and within classes. It is therefore essential that teachers use the process of listening to what pupils say about their lives outside school, providing an opportunity for them to express their health-related interests and of using both these to inform their teaching. Secondly, this listening is particularly important where there is a big difference between pupils and teachers in their health-related experiences. It can be all too easy to teach health education unthinkingly in a way which reflects the teacher's experiences and values rather than those of the pupils, because health education is so much about personal experiences. Many teachers are from middle-class backgrounds and have lifestyles which are in sharp contrast to those of their working-class pupils. This makes the process of listening to children and involving them in a dialogue about health, essential.

This also raises some questions about the *purpose* of health education. It might be tempting to think that a working-class health education is being advocated for working-class children. This is not the case. Health education for *all* children must include the wider political aspects of health and be sensitive to children's particular social and cultural contexts. Within this, health education can then offer choice, portraying a range of values and lifestyles, which not only include those relevant to children's present experiences but which also offer an opportunity for children to extend their thinking, understanding and choices.

The Special Needs of Particular Groups

Although the general aims of health are the same for all children, pupils with disabilities have to have their special needs addressed if they are to practise health-enhancing lifestyles now and in the future (Mori, 1981). Concepts such as positive self-esteem, self-confidence and informed decision making broadly underpin health education, but give rise to quite specific issues when pupils have had much reinforcement for views of themselves as individuals who always receive care, who do not take decisions, who are not going to be self-determining adults.

Studies done on the self-concept of children with handicaps suggest that such pupils tend to have poor self-esteem largely as a result of past experiences of failure and unfavourable reactions from significant others. These experiences may contribute to emotional adjustment problems, poor social interaction skills and intellectual functioning below potential (Cutforth, 1983). It is particularly important to structure perceivable success into educational tasks, so that the child can use newly found confidence to generate increased competencies. In physical education, for example, several authors describe programmes for both children with learning difficulties and with physical handicaps which have had beneficial effects on the total functioning of individuals. Besides developing motor skills, body awareness, and offering ways of constructively using leisure the programmes helped children to exercise choice and take more responsibility for mastering skills, to increasingly exercise self-discipline, to develop increased concentration spans, to persevere longer at learning tasks and to acquire improved social skills (Edgeley, 1981; Owens, 1981; Gallagher, 1984; Cutforth, 1986).

Assurances to children with physical or sensory impairments that they are 'like anyone else' can appear as not credible or inaccurate when they are confronted daily by their own limitations. Such statements need a context and a balance in health-education lessons which emphasize the similarities and differences among *all* children. Sensitively led discussions can lead to increased tolerance and understanding of handicap (Levenson and Cooper, 1984).

Some health-education topic areas need to include particular slants, for example in road safety, pupils with sensory or physical impairments need special teaching, and children with moderate and severe learning difficulties may be helped by a behavioural approach which breaks down the task of safely crossing a road into very small steps (Taylor and Robinson, 1979). For children who are regularly taking medication emphasis needs to be placed on careful adherence to medical instructions and on the dangers of mixing prescribed medication with alcohol or with unprescribed drugs. For children with behaviour problems who also have difficulties in relating to others, much work can be done in a health education setting. As one teacher in a special boarding school commented:

> Some life skills are more important than others. In our staff meetings we spend far more time discussing the problems a girl has in her relationships with peers and family, than ever we do discussing her academic abilities.

Personal hygiene and self-care skills need special emphasis, particularly as they have a strong bearing on social acceptability (Salend and Mahoney, 1982). Both incidental teaching (for example, making sure enough time is allowed for showers after physical education periods) and formal, planned approaches are used to help children assume responsibility for their hygiene and appearance. When pupils with severe mental or physical handicaps have always had parents or staff to look after their body care they require programmes to help them internalize the need for such skills. Actual practice can be reinforced by visual aids (for example, for students with moderate and severe learning difficulties see Holt and Randell, 1975; Craft, 1978; ESN(S) Consortium). In schools for children with physical handicaps teachers usually work closely in conjunction with school nurses on aspects of individual self-care such as assuming as much personal responsibility as possible for catheters, colostomy bags, cleaning out bowels and response to signs of urinary infection.

Sex Education

The whole area of sex education needs particularly sensitive handling. Not only will there be normal adolescent concerns, individual needs specific to conditions, and frequent mismatches between emotional maturity and chronological age, but there is also likely to be great parental anxiety which may be expressed as overprotection or a denial that the child is a sexual being. Many studies indicate that youngsters (and adults) with sensory, physical or mental handicaps have significantly less knowledge about sexual behaviour and response (Fitz-Gerald and Fitz-Gerald, 1978; Watson and Rogers, 1980; Stewart, 1982; Craft, 1983a; Baugh, 1984). Ignorance leaves individuals vulnerable to exploitation and denies them entry into adult status (Brown, 1983). All humans have sexual needs, feelings and drives and Baugh's (1984) comment with regard to sensory handicaps is universally applicable: 'Being impaired only interferes with the ability to gain the information and skills required to cope with these drives; it does not eliminate them.' Teachers in health education have a very important role to play in helping children understand the emotional and physical strands of sexuality in the context of loving and caring relationships.

'Accidental' cues provide much early information on sexuality for non-handicapped children, but sensory impairments seriously interfere with the picking up of such cues. For the child with hearing impairment confusion can arise because he or she does not hear the innuendos and taboos regarding sex. Poor language development makes the understanding of abstract concepts such as motherhood, relationship, maleness very difficult (Fitz-Gerald and Fitz-Gerald, 1978). Sign language about sexual behaviour is graphic and embarrassment may be experienced by student and teacher as anyone within visual range can 'overhear' (Baugh, 1984). The Fitz-Geralds (1978) give an indication of what is needed for deaf students:

> Sex education for the deaf requires highly visual materials supported with simple language. For example, the statement 'boys become men' entails the necessity of determining that the three word concepts are understood, that the plural is understood, and that the deaf person has a visual image of the meaning of the written concept.

Thus, pictures, films, slides, photographs, role playing, games are important aids in making concepts about sexuality understood.

Children with visual handicaps cannot satisfy their natural sexual curiosity through visual stimuli, which makes them more prone to developing misconceptions about sexuality. While the child is able to feel the reality of his or her own body, the concept of the body of someone of the opposite sex is not easily formed. Exploring the world by touch is generally encouraged, but there are social taboos about touching certain parts of other people's bodies. The rapid pubertal growth changes can create additional difficulties as the youngster with a visual handicap cannot readily be reassured by comparing himself or herself with peers or by looking at pictures (Smigielski and Steinmann, 1981). Mobility may be restricted so the opportunity to experience a variety of social environments is limited. Appropriate body language and posture may need to be taught as a social skill. The use of anatomical models has some value, but it must not be assumed that these models will always be accurately interpreted – they tend to be hard and cold! Unfortunately the more lifelike ones are expensive. In Sweden sex education classes for students with visual handicaps include volunteer live models for the students to explore tactilely. Smigielski and Steinmann (1981) suggest a sex-education teaching plan for blind adolescents which emphasizes using other senses to compensate for the lack of visual input.

The sociosexual education of children with severe learning difficulties may pose a special challenge to teachers, but the task has been approached in a number of imaginative ways. Goal-planning is particularly important in clarifying what a pupil is expected to *understand* and what he or she is expected to *do*. It is useful to distinguish between the two. For example, many people do not understand in any detail how their car engine works. But that lack of understanding does not stop them driving thousands of miles each year, and acting appropriately by observing the rules of the road, periodically checking oil, tyre pressure and petrol, filling up when necessary. The *understanding* component is very small compared to the behaviour or *doing* component.

Similarly, what would we want a young girl with severe learning difficulties to understand/do about menstruation? She may never be able to understand more than the very minimum – that having a period is a normal event, that she has not been dirty, that she is not bleeding to death. The only way she achieves this understanding may be the calm and matter-of-fact response of her mother or staff member, demonstrating by caring action and voice tone that there is nothing to be afraid of, acceptance, and that this is a common bond she shares with all women. However the *do* component is wider. With help and training she may be able to change her own sanitary towel and appropriately dispose of the soiled one (Richman *et al.*, 1984). She can learn to behave modestly, that is, not lifting up her dress to show others her sanitary towel, not leaving soiled towels in bathroom or bedroom. Lack of understanding need not be a barrier to appropriate behaviour, but inappropriate behaviour can lessen an individual's opportunities to leading an ordinary social life.

There are several examples of checklists which may be helpful in breaking down learning into sequenced steps (Bender, Valletutti and Bender, 1986; Cabon and Scott, 1980; Rectory Paddock, 1981). For a discussion on the use of checklists see Craft (1983b). Whelan and Speake (1979) outline a systematic approach which can be used to substitute inappropriate sexual behaviour with socially acceptable behaviour. Hamre-Nietupski and Ford (1981) report on an American programme for severely handicapped students, and Ware (in press) gives details of the development of a moral and ethics curriculum at an English school for children with severe learning difficulties. For suggestions of audiovisual resources see Craft (1982); SPOD (1982); FPA (1985).

Many schools for children with moderate learning difficulties have well-planned sex-education programmes in the general context of health or personal and social education. For examples of structure and resource suggestions see Craft *et al.* (1983) and McNaughton (1983).

Pupils with physical handicaps will need quite specific information on the sexual implications of their particular condition. This may best be done on an individual basis and by a recognized professional. However, teachers need at least background information and access to reference material, such as *Not Made of Stone* (Heslinga *et al.*, 1974); *The Sexual Side of Handicap* (Stewart, 1979) and *Sexuality and Disability* (Davies, 1986). SPOD, the organization concerned with the sexual needs of people with handicaps, produced notes and resource lists to help teachers (Davies, 1985). There are also books written for teenagers with physical handicaps which deal in a very straightforward way with the sexual effects of particular conditions, for example *Sex for Young People with Spina Bifida or Cerebral Palsy* (Stewart, 1983).

The opportunity in a health education context for getting factual information in an atmosphere which is largely free from emotional overtones may be the first time that pupils feel comfortable and secure enough to ask that taboo question 'Why am I like I am?' Brown (1983) found that her multiply handicapped students used discussion on the development of a fetus and birth to make sense of their own conditions and to explore realistically personal limitations and possibilities.

Although not all teachers have special training or the experience to answer condition-specific questions from students with handicaps or their classmates, they have a vital role to play in creating an atmosphere where such questions can be raised, and in helping pupils and parents to get in touch with appropriate professionals and services. In-service training courses run by the Family Planning Association (FPA) Education Unit and SPOD are available to help teachers explore their own attitudes and to examine ways and means of giving their students positive sex education.

The Warnock Report (DES, 1978) comments on the generally poor handling of sex education and counselling for young people with severe disabilities and recommends that sexual counselling, advice on contraception and genetic counselling should be more readily available to such young people and their parents.

HOME-SCHOOL-COMMUNITY
LINKS IN HEALTH EDUCATION

Children's experiences at home and in their local communities have an important influence on their health and their attitudes to many health issues. Indeed, a lot of time in health education is spent on topics to do with children's lives outside the school gates. There is therefore potentially a lot to be gained by involving both parents and the wider community in school health education, not least in increasing its relevance to children's lives outside school. However, despite this ideal, there is often a very big gap between the ideal and the practice. The aims of this section are to try and answer the question of why it is often so difficult to involve parents, to give some ideas of how to overcome the problems and to share ideas that have worked in various schools.

Involving Parents

Most of the parents of these children, they're just not interested in what we're trying to do at school – I mean you should see how few we get at parents' evenings. I sometimes wonder if some of them care at all about their own children – no, there's certainly no point in even *talking* about parental involvement in this school. It's a non-starter.

(Teacher at a special school)

We went up the school when Sarah first started there – the Head seemed quite nice, he explained all the arrangements, like for getting the school bus in the mornings and bringing in dinner money, and we had a look around the classrooms. I've been a few times since, when there's been a fuss with Sarah. They have evenings there sometimes when you can talk to the teachers, but we don't really go much as its a long way for us – my husband works evenings so I'd be leaving Sarah with the younger ones. Besides they let us know when Sarah's in any trouble so there's no real need to go, and the rest of it, like the reading and that, well it's best left to the teachers really, isn't it?

(Parent of special-school pupil)

These two quotes tell a familiar story, if a little in the extreme: of teachers who find parents unresponsive to their efforts to involve them actively in the school; of parents who see their role as limited to co-operation with the school's requests and helping to sort out trouble with their child, and who anyway often experience practical difficulties in getting to the school.

So how do some schools come to have parents actively involved in health education while others find even a parents' evening problematic? It is firstly important not to underestimate the practical difficulties involved, particularly for special schools with their large catchment areas. But there are also some important wider issues about how teachers and parents perceive one another, and what the roles of both should or can be. These wider issues need considering before going on to the practicalities of involving parents.

Why involve parents in health education?

As health education has as its concern the whole life of the child, parents *are* inevitably involved, although not always in ways which teachers perceive to be positive. Because health education looks at the needs of the whole child it can serve as a bridge which links parents and school in a common concern. For some parents it may be a way into the school which they would not otherwise have found. In their contributions to a handbook* giving details of parental involvement in health education, teachers have mentioned a wide variety of benefits accruing to school, parents and pupils. Most are perceived as mutual advantages. For example, an activity such as a Health Week draws in parents to see the work their particular child and his or her class have produced. It opens up the school and improves home-school relationships generally and it can also stimulate parent-child discussion at home on health topics which helps the child to understand that health education is not just another school subject to be left behind when the lesson period ends.

Particular examples of parental involvement are given later in this chapter. In broad terms good reasons for involving parents may be summarized under four headings. Firstly, it encourages consistency of approach, both for health education in general, and for particular programmes, for example, specific step-by-step hygiene skills for a youngster with severe learning difficulties. If parents are aware of what is happening at school they are better prepared to deal with questions, anxieties or misunderstandings. Secondly, many schools have found it valuable to consult parents about the health-education curriculum, both in terms of content and timing. After such a validating process, confidence in the programme has increased. Thirdly, the school may usefully serve parents in a facilitating role. This may be in terms of providing information about particular health services such as the school medical service, or genetic

* *The Handbook on Parental and Community Involvement in Health Education* is currently in preparation for publication in 1987 as part of the HEC; Health Education for Slow Learners Project.

counselling; it can also be by encouraging parents as a group to seek out information which is particularly relevant for them and their children.

Last, but by no means least, schools see the involvement of parents in health education as having important implications for the whole work and ethos of the school. Parents get used to coming into the school buildings and familiarity helps to increase confidence. This is particularly helpful to parents whose past pattern of involvement has centred on problem-prompted visits. Meeting teachers on a less formal basis builds up trust, and an informal setting such as a home economics room may help the parent to raise an anxiety, or ask a question which might have remained unspoken at a parents' evening. Such a context also gives teachers direct and easy contact and with it the possibility of discussing short and long term aims for a particular child. Teachers also gain insight into family dynamics. Parents who sit in on lessons or who discuss approaches and material with teachers may get a better understanding of unfamiliar teaching techniques. The comment 'He says all he does in your lesson is just talk' may not be repeated if the parent has actually joined in a class discussion and seen the learning that can go on in 'just talk'. Thus, there can be advantages to schools, parents and pupils in good home-school links established through health education.

Parents', schools' and teachers' perceptions of one another

If parents and teachers are to work well with one another on promoting children's education, it is essential to establish common understanding and good communication. Often at the heart of the 'problem' of involving parents is a difference between parents and teachers in their perceptions of one another and the roles of the school and the home in children's education. Although each parent and each teacher has a unique set of feelings and perceptions, some common factors have emerged from our conversations with both parents and teachers as part of our research.

Parent's perceptions of school depend on the interplay of three different factors: their own childhood experiences of school; their experiences of their own child's school; and their feelings about their child's educational achievements. For most parents it will be 20, 30 or more years since they were pupils at school and inevitably schools have changed somewhat, in both what is taught and the methods used in classrooms. Parents' own experiences at school will be important and often powerful influences on how they approach their own children's schools. Many may genuinely be a little in the dark about what goes on at school, or bewildered by the range and variety of activities, many of which do not fit the pattern of 'learning' in quite the same way as when they were at school.

Parents' ideas about what schools are like *now* will often be based on quite limited experiences of their own child's school such as collecting children from school, notes home, parents' evenings, open days, fetes, concerts and social activities. Most parents get a feel about a school which is based as much on how it looks, and how they are received when they visit, as on the quality of education it offers their children. In other words, the size of the welcome on the school mat is extremely important. In this context it is impossible to overestimate the impact which the once frequent notice 'No Parents Beyond This Point' must have had on parent-school relations.

Many parents of children with special educational needs are particularly sensitive about what they see as their children's failure at school. These powerful feelings may be sufficient to keep them from having more than the minimum contact with the school. For some parents, going to their child's school may evoke powerful memories of their own failure at school and generate antagonism towards a system that systematically fails a large number of children (this may be particularly so for parents of children at special schools, although some do see special schools as offering an education much better suited to their child's needs than a mainstream school).

In addition to these general perceptions of schools, parents' perceptions of teachers are also important. From our research, it seems that many parents of children with mild and moderate learning difficulties see teachers as very different from themselves: not only may the teachers be seen as the experts, the professionals who are responsible for their child's education, but there is also very often a cultural or class difference between teachers and parents. Parents may quite understandably focus on the differences between themselves and teachers, often resulting in barriers, when in fact very many teachers have much in common with parents, being parents themselves.

Teachers' perceptions of parents on the other hand also contribute to the equation. A commonly heard comment among teachers in special schools is that many parents of slow learners are not interested in their child's education, and in some instances are a source of counter-productive influence, which undermines the efforts of the school. This is particularly so when children are seen to come from homes where very different standards of behaviour, personal cleanliness and diet prevail. All these areas of course have important implications for health education.

Some teachers may not feel comfortable with the general trend towards increased parental involvement, recognizing factors such as the possible tension between the very personal interest the parent naturally has in his/her own child and the teacher's professional appreciation of that particular pupil *and* the rest of the children in the class. As an extension to this, teachers may have anxieties about involving parents in curriculum development where the strongly expressed views of a minority of parents may be in direct opposition to professional judgment of educational need. Topics such as sex education and drug education may be particularly sensitive to such pressures.

Given these differences in perceptions between schools, parents and teachers it is hardly surprising that initiatives to involve parents in schools are often unsuccessful or fraught with problems and slow to develop. It is important, however, to remember that the majority of both teachers and parents share a basic concern for the well-being of the children in their care. The problems seem to arise because parents and teachers may put this into practice in different ways. Failure to take this into account can lead to the writing off of a teacher or a parent as uncaring when in fact it is the form or expression of their caring which is misunderstood. Finally, it is worth pointing out that teachers' views of links with parents do not necessarily coincide with parents' views. In a recent report by the National Consumer Council (1986), parents and teachers in the same schools were found to have very different views about the school's practices on parental involvement: despite the school's views that they offered many and varied opportunities for parental involvement, many parents found that their opportunities for involvement were quite restricted.

Practical issues

Having considered some of the wider issues on parental involvement, there are also important practical issues to consider, which if ignored can equally contribute to disappointing outcomes to initiatives to involve parents. There are firstly some very real difficulties in involving parents arising from the large catchment areas of many special schools. Transport to school is problematic for parents, both during the day and in the evening, with some parents living 15 or more miles away from school. For parents relying on public transport, the journey to school may involve travel on two different buses. One important decision when planning to involve parents will therefore be whether the school can provide transport. Although many schools will have a minibus, collecting parents from a wide geographical area will be time-consuming and may need to depend on a volunteer driver. An alternative is to arrange for parents to travel to school with their child on the morning transport, space permitting, leaving parents to make their own way home unless the event lasts all day. Given transport difficulties, it may make more sense to hold a series of small local meetings for parents in different parts of the school's catchment area. Parents then would have less distance to travel, and there may be the bonus of meeting on more neutral premises, which may already be familiar to many parents.

A second aspect to the large catchment area of special schools is that many parents are isolated from parents of other children at the same school. One result may be that parents will arrive at school knowing few, if any, other parents present. It may be possible to reduce the deterrent effect of this by arranging for parents who live reasonably near to one another to come to school or school meetings together.

Another important question to address is whether to provide a crèche, since this may be an important deciding factor for parents considering going to school in the daytime. It may be difficult for some mothers to leave younger children with relatives or friends, particularly if the school is a long distance away and the parent expects to be absent for quite a time. The arrangement of a crèche could be eased by involving pupils, as part of their health education or childcare course, although insurance provisions and supervision for this will need checking.

The timing of a meeting or event may also interfere with other family commitments, such as taking or collecting other children from school. Evening meetings can present difficulties for single-parent families or those on shift work, while being more convenient for parents in full-time employment. Evening meetings or daytime meetings will prove impossible for different groups of parents, and schools therefore need to consider carefully the timing of their meetings (National Consumer Council, 1986).

When planning a meeting or event for parents it may be useful to consider the following questions:

How far will parents have to travel?

How many have their own transport?

For those with no transport, could a lift be arranged; with a neighbouring family; with the school transport; with the school minibus?

What time do the local bus services arrive and leave the school in relation to the timing of the event?

Are bus fares prohibitive for some parents (if so, could these parents have priority for school transport)?

Could small local meetings be arranged instead?

What is the best time to meet?

Will the school provide a crèche?

Are there any other practical difficulties which might prevent parents coming to school and if so how could they be minimized? (NB: It might be useful to consider this question in relation to the parents the school sees least often.)

Examples of how schools involve parents in health education

There are a great many ways in which different schools have involved parents in health education. The examples in this section are simply a selection, and by no means a definitive statement on parental involvement. They are taken from *The Handbook on Parental and Community Involvement in Health Education* (see footnote on page 105). This handbook will develop the issues highlighted in this section, and include a series of reports from schools giving details of how they have involved parents, and the difficulties and benefits experienced. These reports will include a contact name and address so that schools planning a similar initiative can get firsthand advice.

1. Consulting parents about the curriculum
Questionnaires for parents to prioritize topics which could be dealt with in health education. This could be followed up by a meeting to clarify and discuss the results and to feedback similar information from staff and pupils.
Consulting individual parents about the selection of appropriate health education modules for their child.
Meetings to canvass parental preferences for a range of audiovisual and written-health education resources.
2. Information about health education
Letter to parents outlining purpose and content of health education curriculum, and possibly also inviting comments.
Meeting to view resources to be used in the classroom, so parents can provide support at home (a common practice in dealing with sex education).
Class open days for parents to view work done in health education.
3. Parents in the classroom
Parents work alongside children in the health education lessons, maybe acting as a group discussion leader or providing support for the children in various activities.
Parents invited to home-economics lessons, for children to practise hospitality skills or for parents to sample food prepared by children in lesson.
Pregnant mother and/or mother and baby talk and demonstrate in child-care lesson.
Variety of parent talks about hobbies or professional activities related to health.
4. Health-education activities at home
Parents help children keep diaries on health-related topics, for example diet, exercise habits.

Parents collaborate with children on activities continued from the classroom, for example project work to collect information on safety, health
habits, parents' and relatives' opinions about health, historical perspectives on health and health services.
5. Workshops for parents
A great variety of workshops are possible, covering all areas of the school
curriculum, plus parents' own health interests. Groups may vary on the
degree of autonomy exercised over the content of workshops. Discussion of children's health education curriculum.
Follow OU Course on 'Parents and Teenagers'.
Invite a range of health professionals to talk about topics and services.
Parents explore own attitudes to and knowledge about health.
Parents and pupils together in 'quit smoking' groups.
6. Special events
Parents' group writes a 'children's health handbook' on common childhood
ailments, problems and tips for coping.
Parents make video on health topics, for example safety in the home, sex
education, for use in school or at parents' group.
Parents work as voluntary home-school-link workers, liaising between
school and parents.

Involving the Wider Community

Most schools probably involve outside community agencies in health education in a variety of ways. Visitors from and visits to outside agencies are
potentially beneficial, in introducing children to many services they may
use in later life. For instance, some schools have childcare courses run at
the local health centre, maximizing the relevance of the course by holding
it in the situation where pupils will attend if they themselves have children
in the future. The children thus become more familiar with the people and
procedures they are likely to meet there. There are, however, a few notes of
caution to be sounded, when involving outsiders either in the classroom or
in health education located in community settings. Visiting speakers will
need to be briefed carefully about the abilities of the children and about
the wider health-education context within which a talk or a visit may occur.
It may also happen that there is a conflict in approach between outside
agencies and the school, which will need to be explored prior to involvement with a class. There is an almost endless list of possible visitors or
visits, which could be included in health education:

Classroom visitors

Health education officer	Marriage guidance
School nurse or doctor	Family planning clinic
Dentist	Alcohol and drug agencies
Health visitor	Mental health agencies
Dietician	Community police officer
Social worker	Fire brigade
Psychiatrist	Road safety officers
Hairdresser	St John's Ambulance

Representatives from commercial firms, for example sanitary product firms, community theatre group (health theme to play)

Visits and community placements

Work experience in local community settings, for example old people's home or club/nursery-playgroup/family homes (to help with running home/childcare).

Visits to health centre, hospital, family planning clinic, antenatal, etc.

Link into courses at local technical college, for example first-aid course.

SUMMARY

This chapter has considered some of the key issues in the health education of children with special educational needs. Although there are many common requirements for *all* children in relation to health education, pupils with special educational needs have additional and particular needs. These range from very specific health-related problems experienced by some children with sensory or physical handicaps to the more generalized need for the teacher to use teaching materials, methods and approaches which take account of children's learning difficulties.

In looking at classroom practice the selection and use of resources were considered in detail, along with the content and purpose of health education, the influences which different educational settings have on children's health education, and the special needs of particular groups of children.

Health education is one aspect of the curriculum which benefits from good home-school-community links, since health is so bound up with children's experiences outside school. The reasons for and possible difficulties in involving parents were discussed, along with examples of the ways schools have developed to work with both parents and the wider community in health education with children with special educational needs.

ACKNOWLEDGEMENTS

The authors would like to acknowledge the Health Education Council for funding the Health Education for Slow Learners Project. The views expressed in this chapter do not necessarily represent those of the Health Education Council or of the Project.

REFERENCES

Baugh, R. J. (1984) Sexuality education for the visually and hearing impaired child in the regular classroom, *Journal of School Health*, Vol. 54, No. 10, pp. 407–9.
Bender, M., Valletutti, P. J. and Bender, R. (1976) *Teaching the Moderately and Severely Handicapped*, Vol. 2, University Park Press, Baltimore, MD.
Birch, H. G., Richardson, S. A., Baird, D., Horobin, G. and Illsley, R. (1970) *Mental Subnormality in the Community: A Clinical and Epidemiologic Study*. Williams & Wilkins, Baltimore, MD.
Bovey, M. (1983) *Values, Cultures and Kids*, Development Education Centre, Birmingham.
Brandes, D. and Phillips, H. (1978) *Gamesters' Handbook*, Hutchinson, London.
Braun, D. and Eisenstadt, N. (1985) *Family Lifestyles*, Open University, Milton Keynes.
Brown, H. (1983) Why is it such a big secret? Sex education for handicapped young adults. In A. Craft and M. Craft (eds) *Sex Education and Counselling for Mentally Handicapped People*, Costello Press, Tunbridge Wells.
Cabon, S. and Scott, L. (1980) *A Health Education Checklist*, Ickburgh ESNS School, ILEA, London.
COIC (1985) *Role Play and Simulation*. Careers and Occupational Information Centre, Moorfoot, Sheffield S1 4PQ.
Combes, G. (1984a) Drinking patterns and beliefs among ESN(M) school children, and their implications for alcohol education, Unpublished PhD thesis, Keele University.
Combes, G. (1984b) Drinking patterns among slow-learning schoolchildren and their implications for alcohol education. Unpublished report to the Alcohol Education Research Council.
Craft, A. (1978) *Behave Yourself!* and *The Picture of Health*. Teaching slides in the series *Educating Mentally Handicapped People*. Camera Talks Ltd, Oxford.
Craft, A. (1982) *Health, Hygiene and Sex Education for Mentally Handicapped Children, Adolescents and Adults: A Review of Audiovisual Resources*, HEC, London.
Craft, A. (1983a) Sexuality and mental retardation: a review of the literature, in Craft, A. and Craft M. (eds) *Sex Education and Counselling for Mentally Handicapped People*, Costello Press, Tunbridge Wells, Kent.
Craft, A. (1983b) Teaching programmes and training techniques, in Craft, A. and Craft, M. (eds) *Sex Education and Counselling for Mentally Handicapped People*, Costello Press, Tunbridge Wells, Kent.
Craft, A., Davies, J., Williams, M. and Williams, M. (1983) A health and sex education programme: curriculum and resources, in Craft, A. and Craft, M.

(eds) *Sex Education and Counselling for Mentally Handicapped People*, Costello Press, Tunbridge Wells, Kent.

Cutforth, N. J. (1983) Self-concept of the handicapped child in integrated physical education settings, *British Journal of Physical Education*, Vol. 14, No. 4, p. 5.

Cutforth, N. J. (1986) A movement programme for children with special needs in a comprehensive school, *British Journal of Physical Education*, Vol. 17, No. 2, pp. 69–70.

Davies, M. (1985) *Sex Education for Young People with a Physical Disability: A Guide for Teachers and Parents*, SPOD, 286 Camden Road, London N7 0BJ.

Davies, M. (1986) *Sexuality and Disability*, Tape-slide programme and notes, Graves Medical Audiovisual Library, Holly House, 220 New London Road, Chelmsford, Essex CM2 9BJ.

Department of Education and Science (1978) *Special Educational Needs*. Report of the Committee of Enquiry into the Education of Handicapped Children and Young People (Warnock), Cmnd 7212, HMSO, London.

Development Education Centre (1986) *Hidden Messages? – Activities for Exploring Bias*, DEC, Birmingham.

Dorn, N. and Nortoft, B. (1983) *Health Careers*, ISDD, London.

Edgeley, J. (1981) The way forward, *British Journal of Physical Education*, Vol. 12, No. 1, pp. 7–8.

Eraut, M., Goad, L. and Smith, G. (1975) *The Analysis of Curriculum Materials*, University of Sussex Occasional Paper 2.

ESN(S) Consortium. *Self Care*: 1. Cleaning my teeth. 2. Coping with my period. 3. Washing my hands. Laminated photos and worksheets. ILEA ESN(S) Consortium, Jack Tizard School, Finlay Street, London SW6 6HB.

Fitz-Gerald, D. and Fitz-Gerald, M. (1978) Sexual implications of deafness, *Sexuality and Disability*, Vol. 1, No. 1, pp. 57–69.

FPA (1985) *Bodies*. A game and body puzzles devised by A. Leyin and M. Dicks, FPA Education Unit, London.

Gallagher, M. (1984) Children with special needs in the area of motor development, *British Journal of Physical Education*, Vol. 15, No. 3, pp. 91–3.

Gillies, P. (1978) A study of mildly subnormal adolescents in Nottingham: Their characteristics and health knowledge, accompanied by a survey of parental and teacher attitudes towards health education, Unpublished MSc thesis, Nottingham University.

Hamre-Nietupski, S. and Ford, A. (1981) Sex education and related skills: a series of programs implemented with severely handicapped students, *Sexuality and Disability*, Vol. 4, No. 3, pp. 179–93.

HEC (1984) Report of evaluator's visit to schools that have purchased 'Fit for Life', HEC internal document, London.

Heslinga, K. *et al.* (1974) *Not Made of Stone*, Staflen's Scientific Publishing Company, Leyden, Netherlands.

Holt, A. and Randell, J. (1975) *Come Clean*, CUP, Cambridge.

ILEA (1984) *Characteristics of Pupils in Special Schools*, ILEA Research and Statistics, London.

ILEA (1985) *Roles, Relationships and Responsibilities* (pack of drawings), Learning Materials Service.

Levenson, P. M. and Cooper, M. (1984) School health education for the chronically impaired individual, *Journal of School Health*, Vol. 54, No. 11, pp. 446–8.

Mares, P., Henley, A. and Baxter, C. (1985) *Health Care in Multiracial Britain*, HEC/National Extension College, Cambridge.

McNaughton, J. (1983) *Fit for Life*, Schools Council, Macmillan Educational, Basingstoke, Hants.

Mori, A. A. (1981) Mildly handicapped children in the mainstream – implications for the health educator, *Journal of School Health*, Vol. 51, pp. 119–22.

National Consumer Council (1986) *The Missing Links between Home and School: A Consumer View*, NCC, London.

Owens, M. F. (1981) Mainstreaming in the every child a winner program, *Journal of Physical Education, Recreation and Dance*, Vol. 52, No. 7, pp. 16–18.

Oxfordshire Health Education Unit (1986) *Challenging Unhealthy Stereotypes – A Guide to Analysing Health Education and Materials*, Oxfordshire Health Education Unit, Ferry Hinksey Road, Oxford OX2 0BY.

Pappenheim, K. (ed.) (1982) *Special School Leavers: the Value of Further Education in their Transition to the Adult World*, Greater London Association for the Disabled, London.

Rectory Paddock School (1981) *In Search of a Curriculum*, Robin Wren Publications, Sidcup, Kent.

Richman, G. S., Reiss, M. L., Baumnan, K. E. and Bailey, J. S. (1984) Teaching menstrual care to mentally retarded women, *Journal of Applied Behavioral Analysis*, Vol. 17, No. 4, pp. 441–51.

Salend, S. J. and Mahoney, S. (1982) Teaching proper health habits to mainstreamed students through positive reinforcement, *Journal of School Health*, Vol. 52, No. 9, pp. 539–42.

Smigielski, P. A. and Steinmann, M. J. (1981) Teaching sex education to multiply handicapped adolescents, *Journal of School Health*, Vol. 51, No. 4, pp. 238–41.

SPOD (1982) *Sex Education for Mentally Handicapped People: A Teaching Aid*, Notes and teaching cards. SPOD, 286 Camden Road, London N7 0BJ.

Stewart, W. F. R. (1979) *The Sexual Side of Handicap*, Woodhead-Faulkner, Cambridge.

Stewart, W. F. R. (1982) *Sex Education for the Physically Handicapped*, Disabilities Study Unit, Wildhanger, Amberley, W. Sussex.

Stewart, W. F. R. (1983) *Sex for Young People with Spina Bifida or Cerebral Palsy*, Association for Spina Bifida and Hydrocephalus with the co-operation of the Spastics Society and SPOD, London.

Stones, R. (1983) *'Pour out the Cocoa, Janet': Sexism in Children's Books*. Longman for Schools Council, York.

Taylor, P. and Robinson, P. (1979) *Crossing the Road*, British Institute of Mental Handicap, Kidderminster.

Townsend, P. and Davidson, N. (eds) (1982) *Inequalities in Health: The Black Report*, Penguin, London.

Ware, J. (in press) The development of a moral and ethical curriculum for students with severe learning difficulties, in Craft, A. (ed.) *Mental Handicap and Sexuality: Issues and Perspectives*, Costello Press, Tunbridge Wells, Kent.

Watson, G. and Rogers, R. S. (1980) Sexual instruction for the mildly retarded and normal adolescent: a comparison of educational approaches, parental expectations and pupil knowledge and attitude, *Health Education Journal*, Vol. 39, No. 3, pp. 88–95.

Whelan, E. and Speake, B. (1979) *Learning to Cope*, Souvenir Press, London.

PART 3

A Co-ordinated Approach

INTRODUCTION TO PART 3

Most health attitudes of children are profoundly affected by parental and home influences, where health education takes place constantly, recognized or unrecognized. The child's peer group also exerts influence, and the power of media advertising is obvious. School may come last on the list of those who shape a youngster's attitudes, skills and knowledge of health matters. While a child's lifestyle may be largely shaped outside school, the influence of individual teachers and the cumulative influence of a well-run school may be considerable, and may be vitally important for some. It is an underestimated truth that teachers influence children's lives rather more than teachers themselves acknowledge, and much of that influence is channelled through subject teaching and pastoral care.

Co-ordination of the work done by different subject areas within a secondary school or within the varied work of a primary school must improve the effectiveness and influence of a school, adding to the effect of individual teachers' personalities on the lives of pupils. The concept of a school as a gathering of talented individual teachers all offering individual approaches to realms of knowledge, with the school as an intuitive and loosely managed collegiate system sounds splendid but is less successful in practice. Too many schools are in fact without clear leadership which aims to produce an agreed co-ordinated approach to a subject area such as health education, where all the individual talents and care of teachers develop not by personal whim but towards an agreed goal and purpose.

Such co-ordinated approaches require clear management and imagination and a team approach to the purpose of the school. Professionalism in primary and secondary schools lies not in individual inspiration but in joint and planned learning schemes, where each teacher complements others to re-inforce agreed areas of knowledge, methodology, skills, behaviour, attitudes and values.

In health education or personal and social education schemes this means selecting topics appropriate to each stage of a child's life, and having these topics dealt with in complementary ways in different teaching areas, re-inforced by tutorial or other pastoral-care systems, and bonded further by the informal curriculum and liaison with parents, as well as by recognition of the influence of the school's 'hidden curriculum'.

Tim Hull has a challenging task in viewing how science in general contributes to health education, extending his chapter on biology education in the first edition. After graduating from London University and obtaining an MSc from Southampton, he taught biology in secondary schools, lectured at a college of education, worked on the Schools' Council Health Education Project 13–18, and is now a senior lecturer in health education at an institute of higher education.

Len Almond is a lecturer in physical education and sports science at Loughborough, and he and his colleague Fiona Dowling consider the relationship of physical education and health education. Peter Farley taught English in Birmingham and Devon, and was then linked for some years with the Schools' Council Health Education Projects. Now working for Exeter Health Authority as a health promotion officer he considers the partnership of English with health education.

Kenneth David was a tutor-adviser in education for personal relationships in Gloucestershire, and a county adviser in Lancashire for nine years, with special responsibility for personal relationships. He has written and lectured widely in the fields of health education and pastoral care, and contributes a revised chapter on pastoral care and health education.

5

SCIENCE AND HEALTH EDUCATION
Tim Hull

INTRODUCTION

Some aspects of science, particularly biology have long been seen as having close links with health education. Indeed the growth of biology as a school subject between the two world wars was due in part to those groups and individuals who stressed the personal and social significance of science. For example, the British Social Hygiene Council (a forerunner of the Health Education Council) promoted the teaching of biology because an adequate biological knowledge among the general public was considered to be necessary for health education to be effective (Jenkins, 1979). It was the British Social Hygiene Council which organized the 1932 conference on 'The Place of Biology in Education'. In his introduction to the published proceedings of this conference Crowther (1933) stressed both the cultural and utilitarian value of biological education. He not only pointed out the more obvious applications of biological knowledge for healthy living, but suggested that man could not 'understand what he is and how he came to be as he is, without appreciating himself as a biological entity'.

Today it is not difficult to point to links between science and health education. Biology and integrated science syllabuses invariably include some reference to health and social issues. The following extract comes from a GCSE biology syllabus (Midland Examining Group, 1986):

> Heart attacks . . . and the possible influences of smoking and diet. . . . Beneficial effects of exercise. . . . Dental hygiene and care of teeth. Fluoride controversy.

Also the work of the Schools Council Project: *Health Education 13–18*

(1980) shows that many science teachers, especially biology teachers, are involved in health education, for example:

> science teachers formed the largest group of health education co-ordinators in project schools;
> the curriculum review undertaken by each project school illustrated that, at least in terms of content, science made a substantial contribution.

It would be misleading, however, to suggest that shared content was a satisfactory way of illustrating the relationship between science and health education. Health education is no longer seen merely as the transmission of information and advice about health issues. Beattie (1984) suggests that a 'biomedical' model of health education 'emphasizing individual health risks and how to avoid them' has only a modest record of 'success'. He describes alternative models of health education and argues that science teaching as currently practised has little contribution to make. Even if knowledge and understanding of topics such as diet, sexually transmitted infections, and the like are seen as important dimensions of health education, their inclusion in science is no guarantee that the work is appropriate. Indeed Hirst (1976) suggests:

> the understanding relevant to teenagers' problems of sex and drugs that actually emerges from biology lessons is often very limited and dangerous in its partiality.

Beattie (1984) goes further in arguing that too often 'scientific knowledge' is:

> employed as 'health propaganda' in which 'doctor's orders' (or their biological equivalent) are imposed in an authoritarian and directive way on vulnerable individuals. . . . It also too often takes it for granted that the responsibility for avoiding risks to health lies with the individual, which may in fact be simply 'blaming the victim'.

Clearly there are reservations about the contribution of science to health education, but science itself should not be just a body of knowledge. Considerable emphasis is placed on both the process of science and the relevance of science to the daily lives of young people (DES, 1985a). Bentley (1984), in responding to Beattie's criticism that science teachers 'are often ill-equipped or unsuited to the demands of contemporary health education' (Beattie, 1984), suggests that one could also argue that science teachers 'may often be ill-equipped or unsuited for the demands of contemporary science education'. The relationship between science and health education will depend in part on what we understand by science education and this may well vary from institution to institution. Let us examine this relationship by considering: the nature and purpose of science education as reflected by general trends and developments; the extent to which this view of science is compatible with the aims of health education; science education in practice; and the potential for developing the links between science and health education.

THE NATURE AND PURPOSE OF SCIENCE EDUCATION

Despite attempts in the 1920s and 1930s to liberalize the teaching of science, by 1960 it remained narrow and academic, at least in the grammar and public schools. The specialist science courses in biology, chemistry and physics were geared to those pupils intending to study science in the sixth form. Other pupils took one science, or general science, or even no science and for them, as Ingle and Jennings (1981) point out:

> the reality was still a long way from the ideals of science as an essential part of liberal education that had inspired the originators of the general science movement forty years before.

The establishment of the Nuffield Science Teaching Project in 1961/62 marked the start of a major phase of curriculum development. One of the principal aims of this project was to foster a critical approach to science with an emphasis on experimentation and inquiry rather than on mere factual assimilation. In other words science as a process was seen as important.

The first of the Nuffield materials were in the separate sciences and for pupils taking O-level. Although there was an emphasis on process the work was very demanding intellectually, especially in the lower years of secondary schooling (Ingle and Jennings, 1981). Further criticisms of these projects identified by Ingle and Jennings (1981) were that they were highly specialized and 'did not go very far in illustrating the social relevance of science'. In the second edition of the biology project (Nuffield, 1975) rather more material is concerned with 'the usefulness and social implications of biology to man's everyday needs, e.g. food and health'. For example, in Text 3 Living Things and Their Environments there is a section 'Natural selection in man today – survival in the urban environment' in which there is some attempt to relate the work to the lives of the pupils themselves.

Other science projects which followed, like Nuffield *Junior Science, Combined Science* and *Secondary Science* and the Schools Council Projects, *Science 5–13* and *Integrated Science* maintained this emphasis on science as a process. At the primary school level, both Nuffield *Junior Science* (Nuffield, 1967) and *Science 5–13* (Schools Council, 1972) stressed the importance of children identifying and solving problems. In *Science 5–13* (Schools Council, 1972), for instance, it was suggested that

In general children work best when trying to find answers to problems which they have themselves chosen to investigate. These problems are best drawn from their own environment and tackled largely by practical investigations.

Both these primary science projects produced teachers' guides rather than pupil material, to promote the teaching of open ended science. In *Science 5–13* eight broad aims were identified in order to develop 'an enquiring mind and a scientific approach to problems'. These are listed in Figure 5.1. Such aims not only reflect an open-ended approach to science but illustrate how closely science relates to other aspects of a child-centred primary curriculum. They also represent a model of science education which has much in common with health education. There is no agreed content to primary science, but the *Science 5–13* Project has produced a teachers' book called *Ourselves* (Schools Council, 1975). The authors suggest that children are interested in finding out about themselves. They also suggest that it is important that children do learn something about themselves and 'gain an understanding of biological variation'.

The Schools Council Projects *Progress in Learning Science* (1977) and *Learning through Science* (1981) go further in identifying the content of primary science. They describe a number of basic concepts or principles which children should build up while learning to explore and experiment scientifically. These include several which I believe are important in health education; they are a concept of:

Life cycle

Change

Interdependence of living things

Adaptation of living things

Other primary science materials, for example *Look* and *A First Look* (Gilbert and Matthews, 1981; 1982), include work which encourages children to find out about themselves including their feelings.

Since the late 1960s and early 1970s the content of secondary-school science has usually been organized in relation to key concepts or principles.

Figure 5.1 The aims of the Schools Council Science Project 5–13

On the biological side, for example, they might include:
  Variation within and between organisms
  Maintenance of the organism
  Homeostasis
  Growth and development; adaptability; evolution
  Interdependence of living things; ecological balance
  Despite this focus on concepts secondary-school science is frequently dominated by a large body of factual information which is remote from everyday life (ASE, 1979; DES, 1985a). In *Science 5–16: A Statement of Policy* (DES, 1985a) it is suggested that

> if science is to be taught to convey understanding, and confidence in the use of the knowledge gained . . . then the factual and theoretical content of many existing courses will need to be sharply pruned.

If the factual and theoretical content of science courses are to be reduced, how does one decide what to include? There seems to be widespread agreement that there should be some sort of balance in science education (ASE, 1973; 1979; 1981a; DES, 1977; 1985a; 1985b). Balance is important not only between process and content but between the main concepts of science and the personal, social and technological significance of science. In the HMI Working Paper *Curriculum 11–16* (DES, 1977) it is suggested that science should have three components:

> Science for the enquiring mind – underlying principles, the disciplines of the subject.
> Science for action – use and applications of those principles.
> Science for citizenship – concerns the role of science in personal and collective decision-making.

More recently the Secondary Science Curriculum Review (1983) identified a range of aims which it suggests reflect a broad and balanced view of science. Besides aims related to the process of science, underlying concepts or principles and the application of these principles, the review includes aims which touch on the personal and cultural dimension of science, for example:

> Pupils should have opportunities to:
> study those aspects of science that are essential to an understanding of oneself, and of one's personal well being;
> discuss, reflect upon and evaluate their own personal understanding of key scientific concepts, theories and generalisations;
> explore topics or themes which exemplify the limitations of scientific knowledge as an explanation of the human condition.

In Nuffield *Secondary Science* (1971) choice of content is based on the criteria of significance. The project is intended for pupils not taking O-level and it consists of a series of resource guides from which teachers select. In order to give significance to science it is suggested that

> each new aspect should develop from the pupil's immediate experience, and in this way pupils may be gradually introduced to fundamental issues which are likely to have considerable significance for them within a year or two.

The strategy of developing work from pupils' immediate experience reduces the gap between 'subject knowledge' and 'real life knowledge' or in Barnes's (1976) terms between 'school knowledge' and 'action knowledge'. For example, while most general or integrated science syllabuses for

13- to 16-year-olds would include something on variation and inheritance, Theme 2: 'The continuity of life' has a section entitled 'Why I am like I am' in which 'the significance of the pupil's own variation is developed'.

In many respects Nuffield Secondary Science reflects what Ingle and Jennings (1981) describe as the ideals of the general science movement which developed between the two world wars, that 'it should form an essential part of the general education of all young people . . . humanistic as well as scientific in scope, broad rather than deep in content'. This project certainly recognizes that in making science relevant to the lives of pupils, the personal, social and moral implications will need to be faced and that this is a legitimate part of science education: 'Social and moral issues can arise in the course of any scientific study, but they are likely to be particularly apparent in the work related to the human life cycle' (Nuffield Secondary Science, 1971).

The Schools Council *Integrated Science Project* (SCISP) (1973) is another project which not only emphasized the process of science but recognized science as a human activity and attempted to get to grips with its personal and social aspects. It is intended for pupils taking O-levels and its aims include:

> understanding the significance, including the limitations, of science in relation to technical, social and economic development. . . .
> Pupils should:
> . . . (a) be sceptical about suggested patterns yet (b) be willing to search for and to test for patterns, be concerned for the application of scientific knowledge within the community.

The material includes a unit 'Science and Decision-making' in which case studies illustrate the work of scientists and the way science is used. Pupils are encouraged to consider the decisions which have to be taken, very often when 'all the relevant data is not available and . . . science is only one of the many components which will influence the judgments made'.

It is suggested that '(more relevant) local issues' can also be discussed. Other examples which illustrate the way in which the material addresses personal and social issues include:

Changes in behaviour

Attitudes

Do you have strong attitudes?

When do attitudes become prejudices?

In what ways are people prejudiced in this country?

What can be done to overcome these prejudices?

Should anything be done?
Advertising and its influence
Reducing car accidents
The politics of 'the bomb'

Nuffield Secondary Science and SCISP clearly do not reflect the view that science is neutral and value free. Yet Layton (1986) suggests 'curriculum endorsements of value-free science are common place'. He suggests, for example, that 'the recent (1981) policy statement on the aims of science education by the influential ASE contain little which could be said to be value-related'.

Ambivalence about the place of values in science education is reflected in other ways. The GCSE National Criteria (DES, 1985b) for science subjects recognize that the personal, social, economic and technological applications of science are important. In 1983, however, when it was proposed that 'science examination criteria should in fact embrace social and economic issues' (Layton, 1986), the Secretaries of State for Education and for Wales expressed the view that the inclusion of such issues 'might make it difficult to avoid tendentiousness in the teaching of science subjects' a risk which was 'best avoided'.

An interest in personal and social issues in science may have contributed to the growth in human and social biology courses, but such courses are sometimes criticized for their 'poor science'. Indeed it was concern over the implications of the growing popularity of human biology as a school subject which led to a joint committee of the Royal Society and Institute of Biology on *The Teaching of Human Biology* (Royal Society, 1978). Of particular concern was the suggestion that for some pupils human biology was the only science studied and it was frequently taught in a non-experimental fashion. The main conclusion of the joint committee was that 'the study of human biology by pupils aged 13–16 can give a satisfactory introduction to biological science provided that it is experimentally and scientifically based'.

It may well be that some human biology and social biology courses are not experimentally and scientifically based. Although such courses cannot claim to be satisfactory as far as the scientific development of pupils is concerned, they may make an important contribution to their personal and social development. Indeed other courses and materials have been developed which are not science courses in their own right, but represent attempts to counter-balance the emphasis in many courses on 'science for the enquiring mind'. Examples of such materials include *Science in Society* (ASE, 1981b) and *Science in the Social Context* (ASE, 1982). *Science in*

Society is a separate course for lower sixth formers and one of its aims is that pupils should be able:

> To understand the need for, and to develop the ability to make reasoned decisions which take account of all relevant constraints; and to recognise that moral considerations are involved in all decisions.

The material includes decision-making simulation exercises on a variety of topics including fluoridation of the public-water supplies. Although the *Science in Society* project has been widely criticized as being 'ethically biased in favour of the maintenance of the status quo' (Gibson, 1985), it does represent one of the first attempts to ensure that ethical and moral issues form an explicit part of science teaching.

The stipulation in the GCSE National Criteria: Science (DES, 1985b) that

> At least 15 per cent of the total marks are to be allocated to assessment(s) relating to technological applications and social, economic and environmental issues, which should pervade all parts of the examination,

should ensure that the personal and social aspects of science are not neglected and that all science courses reflect a balance between science for
   The enquiring mind
   Action
   Citizenship

It is encouraging that the Association for Science Education: *Science and Technology in Society* Project (ASE, 1986) is developing units aimed at showing the social and technological relevance of science taught in GCSE. Also the Secondary Science Curriculum Review (1983) initiated curriculum development which is not only broadly based but has health education as an appropriate context for developing work in science.

THE RELATIONSHIP BETWEEN SCIENCE EDUCATION AND HEALTH EDUCATION

Having argued that science education is concerned with:
   Skills and processes (a scientific approach)
   Content chosen not only for its relationship to key concepts but for 'its value in living' (Black and Ogborn, 1981), its relevance or significance to the lives of young people
   Personal and collective decision-making which also involves economic, moral and social considerations
what is its relationship to health education?

A widely recognized aim of health education is to help people 'make choices and decisions about their own health' (Schools Council, 1984). Indeed Beattie (1984) in describing key features of his 'personal growth' model of health education included: 'to build self-esteem in the learner; to encourage the development of skills in life review and in personal problem solving and decision making'.

The approach to science advocated by *Science 5–13* (Schools Council, 1972) which not only stresses the skills and attitudes of an inquiring mind and scientific approach to problems but also encourages children to identify and investigate questions of their own choosing, is likely to enhance children's self-esteem as well as developing problem-solving and decision-making skills. I am not arguing that this approach to science provides an adequate programme of health education, merely that it is compatible and complementary, particularly when so many of the topics included in the primary curriculum, for example Ourselves, Food, Growth, Change and the like are relevant to both science and health education. For example, some children might become interested in the effects of exercise on their bodies as a result of work in PE. Using pulse rate as an indicator they might investigate the effects of exercise programmes of various types and durations.

As well as introducing ideas and concepts to do with exercise, fitness and training, this work could also explore individual differences and thereby promote an appreciation of the uniqueness of the individual and enhance self-esteem. Children could also be encouraged to consider:

Their own attitudes to exercise, including likes and dislikes

The opportunities for, and constraints on, taking exercise

The relationship between fitness and health and the like

There are many possibilities for topic work in the primary school which both are 'scientific' and make an important contribution to health education, although realizing their potential makes substantial demands of teachers.

The *My Body* project (HEC, 1983) illustrates how a topic can provide the basis for both science and health education, although it is very much teacher-directed and content-based and reflects different models of science and health education from those already described.

An approach to science which emphasizes process and encourages questioning and open-mindedness should be welcome from the health education point of view. Beattie (1984) is critical of the way science teachers too often use 'scientific knowledge' as 'health propaganda'. Clearly such an approach to science is neither 'good' health education nor 'good' science. The aims of the Schools Council *Integrated Science Project* (1973) suggest that pupils should be 'sceptical about suggested patterns', while in *Science 5–16: A Statement of Policy* (DES, 1985a) it is stated that science should encourage 'curiosity and health scepticism . . . the critical evaluation of evidence'. In making decisions about their health individuals will need to be able to interpret and evaluate evidence. It may not be the only skill necessary, but it is important in an age when knowledge is growing rapidly and new ideas are frequently proposed.

The relationship between diet and health is a good example of an area in which it is important to be able to weigh up the evidence and consider it with the many other factors which influence food choices. We are constantly being bombarded with information, often conflicting, about issues like possible links between salt and high blood pressure or the hazards/benefits of additives. How can we make informed decisions if we are unable to make some assessment of the strength of the evidence or do not appreciate that explanations of data are often very tentative, certainly an association between two factors is not necessarily one of cause and effect.

In the past the links between health education and science have been seen largely in terms of shared content. While I hope I have already gone some way towards illustrating this is not the case today I do feel it is unfortunate that 'content' has almost become *persona non grata* in some 'health education circles'. It is understandable in so far that content is sometimes seen as synonymous with the provision of information and health propaganda. Beattie (1984) suggests that providing information about bodily function, health risks, and how to avoid them, is not effective in bringing about specific behaviour changes to maintain health. Certainly this approach is not appropriate to health education for 'personal growth' although I believe that certain scientific/biological concepts are of underlying importance.

An understanding of health itself is dependent on such concepts. As discussed in Chapter 1, there is no universally agreed meaning of *health*, but it is widely accepted to be more than the absence of disease and to embrace the idea of 'balanced relationships within and between mind, body, society and environment' (European Communities Biologists Association, 1984). Dubos (1965) coined the phrase 'man adapting' to describe health as a dynamic interaction between a developing individual and their changing physical and social environment. Essentially *adapting* in this context is a biological concept which rests on further scientific/biological concepts. School science is not the only context in which children learn to understand these ideas, but it is an important one.

An understanding of scientific/biological concepts also provide a background against which decisions are made. Information about the effects of smoking on the body may not be a major consideration when youngsters decide whether or not to smoke, but some understanding of the multifactorial aetiology of heart disease and the notion of risk factors may be important when individuals consider the personal significance of evidence or advice which appears in the media, perhaps about the benefits of exercise or the relationship between heart disease and the contraceptive pill.

A few years ago a report suggesting that in some countries there appears to be no connection between smoking and coronary heart disease made the headlines. In Britain it seems that smokers are 1.5–3.5 times more likely to die from heart disease than non-smokers (Royal College of Physicians, 1977). This apparently conflicting information may raise the question of whether smoking really is a factor in the occurrence of heart disease. Only when the interdependence of physiological processes is appreciated can we begin to understand the complex interaction of the various risk factors, for example heredity, high blood cholesterol, smoking, and the like. In those countries where there seems to be little or no connection between smoking and coronary heart disease, it may be because of such favourable factors as low blood cholesterol.

This discussion is not meant to imply that there should be an emphasis on disease and ill-health. McKeown (1979) suggests that a preoccupation with disease can develop when undue emphasis is placed on its precursors. He sees no disadvantage in suggesting, for example, that physical exercise and control of weight promote the quality of life, but when people are

> also encouraged to monitor their weight, pulse and blood pressure, we are in some danger of crossing the delicate line which divides quiet confidence in health from a morbid preoccupation with its loss.

Science teaching, by looking at health issues within the broader content of biological concepts or principles and the natural phenomena of life, has an important role in promoting a positive view of health and health education. It should certainly avoid both 'a morbid preoccupation' with ill-health and the implication that responsibility for avoiding risks to health lies entirely with the individual and lead to 'victim-blaming' (Crawford, 1977).

If scientific/biological concepts are to be 'useful' and the gap between 'school knowledge' and 'action knowledge' (Barnes, 1976) reduced, they need to be related to the everyday experiences of pupils. In this way the link between science and health education can be made. Indeed it is suggested in *Curriculum 11–16: Health Education in the Secondary School Curriculum* (DES, 1978) that

> When an opportunity is provided for pupils to consider how a subject

impinges on their own lives their own behaviour or aspirations and how these affect their health and that of others then this is health education.

Much has been said about the importance of making science education relevant to the everyday experience of pupils. Some materials like Nuffield *Secondary Science* (Nuffield, 1971) have long reflected this philosophy and it includes many sections which relate very closely to health education, particularly in 'Theme 2: the continuity of life' and 'Theme 3: biology of man'. In Theme 3, for instance, there is an extensive section on the human life cycle in which it is suggested that the needs and wishes of pupils should not be overlooked and guidance is given about ways of exploring personal, social and moral issues.

Another way of making science more relevant and strengthening the links between science and health education is to use health education issues and concerns as a context for teaching science. The Secondary Science Curriculum Review (1983) has been developing ways of doing this. For example, while most biology and science courses in secondary schools include work on the composition of food, the importance of the various nutrients and the need for a balanced diet, the digestive process, feeding relationships and energy flow, and hopefully relate such work to the eating behaviour of pupils themselves, one of the SSCR groups (Secondary Science Curriculum Review, 1985) has developed an exercise to examine school meals. It involves pupils, catering staff and teachers in setting up a team to investigate the nutrition provided by school dinners, and, within the joint frameworks of economics, pupil preferences and health requirements, to change the school dinners for a trial period.

The link between science and health education is dependent on not just the choice of content or context, teaching methods are also important. The significance of the approach to primary science in which children investigate problems of their own choosing has already been mentioned and it is encouraging that the SSCR (1983) is looking at the application of primary methods to secondary science.

If opportunities are to be provided for pupils to consider how issues impinge on their own lives and their health, and if the gap between 'school knowledge' and 'action knowledge' is to be reduced then methods which encourage their active participation are essential. Some of these methods, like discussion, project work, simulations and decision-making exercises are already seen as a legitimate part of science education and examples from Nuffield *Secondary Science* (Nuffield, 1971), *SCISP* (Schools Council, 1973) and *Science and Society* (ASE, 1981b) have been mentioned. It is also accepted that in adopting these approaches that the boundaries of science become blurred and that personal, social and moral issues will be inescapable. It also underlines the importance of establishing links between science and other aspects of the curriculum.

An approach to science in which the personal perceptions of children provide the starting point recently received a boost from the Children's Learning in Science project (Brook, Briggs and Driver, 1984) and the *Learning in Science* project in New Zealand (Osborne and Freyberg, 1985). The former project states: 'Learning cannot be viewed as a passive process of absorbing knowledge, but as one of modifying and restructuring of ideas by pupils.' It is suggested that part of this process involves pupils talking about their own ideas in small groups, exploring alternatives, clarifying their views and so on. In other words approaches which 'value' the contributions of pupils and thereby enhance their self-esteem.

The relationship between science and health education seems considerable. There is not only a large element of shared content but a strong desire to ensure that this is related to the everyday experience of pupils. This can only strengthen the links between science and health education. Perhaps most importantly the methods advocated in science education can make a substantial contribution to the self-esteem of the learner and the promotion of individual autonomy, which are central strands of both 'education for personal growth' and 'education for community action in health' (Beattie, 1984).

SCIENCE AND HEALTH EDUCATION IN PRACTICE

In theory there is much common ground between science and health education. To what extent is this reflected in practice? Despite the emphasis in most recent reports and some materials, on process, concepts and principles, and relevance to the everyday experiences of pupils, there seems to be widespread agreement that we have some way to go before we have a broadly based science programme for all pupils (DES, 1985a). Certainly projects like Nuffield *Secondary Science* and *SCISP* had low uptake (Ingle and Jennings, 1981).

It is hoped that the further stimulus provided by the SSCR (1983), *Science 5–16: A Statement of Policy* (DES, 1985a) and the introduction of the national criteria for GCSE (DES, 1985b) will be more effective than initiatives in the past.

There is also undoubtedly a gap between the ideal and current practice as far as the specific relationship between science and health education goes. Work by Bamborough (1985) suggests that many science teachers see health education as content-based, are unfamiliar with informal teaching methods and do not appear to want the personal involvement with pupils implied by holistic health education.

As mentioned already there is considerable development under the auspices of the SSCR which is very encouraging. Unfortunately *Science 5–16: A Statement of Policy* and *The National Criteria* for science (DES, 1985a; 1985b) do not mention health education specifically and I sense some ambivalence towards the personal and social aspects of science in statements such as:

> The social and economic implications of scientific and technological activity also have a place, always provided that the teaching is essentially concerned to foster education in science itself.   (DES, 1985a).

Despite possible shortcomings in the way science is taught it is still important to consider the relationship between science and health education in school. Science has a content and method which relates in one way or another to health education. It is important to look at the contribution of science in relation to that of other aspects of the formal and hidden curriculum if a coherent approach to health education is to be achieved. This is true even if it is argued as Beattie (1984) has done that 'the biological and medical sciences have only a subordinate contribution to make to the theory and practice of health education'.

THE WAY FORWARD:
A CO-ORDINATED APPROACH TO
HEALTH EDUCATION

Much has been said about the need for some sort of co-ordination, not just for health education but all those aspects of the curriculum which contribute to the personal and social development of pupils (DES, 1979; Schools Council, 1984). But what is meant by co-ordination? It is certainly more than putting together elements of the existing curriculum. A report by the Scottish Education Department (1979) suggests it involves 'a synthesis of contributions in a way that has meaning and relevance to the present and as far as possible to the future lives of pupils'. Co-ordination also embraces both the formal and the hidden curriculum. Sometimes the term 'whole-school policy' is used.

One way of considering the part which might be played by science in a co-ordinated approach to health education is to look first at the sorts of health-education priorities a school might identify. Examples of possible priorities are given below for the first year of an 11–16 or 11–18 school.

They are based on two considerations which seem particularly significant for pupils in the first year, namely:

The change to the new school and the new relationships and opportunities which this presents

The onset of puberty around this time

The priorities themselves are likely to vary from school to school and time to time depending on need.

Health education priorities for Year 1

Getting to know the group/class. Getting to know oneself in the group. Fostering a sense of community. Establishing good group work and creating the opportunity to ask questions.

Adapting to the physical, emotional and social changes occurring around this time. An emphasis on individual uniqueness.

Developing an understanding and appreciation of their body and its functions.

Promoting decision-making using one or two areas which seem significant for pupils of this age, for example food and smoking.

Science teaching in the first two years of secondary school often involves pupils working together in twos and threes to carry out investigations. Ideally it involves pupils discussing the purpose of the investigation, sharing ideas and relating them to their everyday experiences. Such approaches not only have much in common with methods used in health education with its onus on good group work but are important strategies in science if the mismatch between teacher intention and pupils' actual involvement is to be reduced (Tasker and Freyberg, 1985). Even if the content of science teaching is not relevant to health education it is increasingly recognized that methods which are characteristic of 'effective' science teaching have much in common with those of health education. This will be particularly true if the use of primary methods in secondary science SSCR (1983) becomes widespread. It may lead to some shift in the control of learning in science from teacher to pupil.

As for the content of science in the first year of secondary school, it often includes work on growth and development (for example Nuffield *Combined Science* [Nuffield, 1970], *Science 2000* [Mee, Boyd and Richie, 1981] and the like). There is scope here for developing the contribution to health education and strengthening the links with other subject contributions. For example looking at human growth and development might provide a more interesting and relevant starting point. It could include measurement of their own height. If separate histograms are produced for boys and girls it may raise questions about differences in the growth of boys and girls as well as reinforcing ideas about individual variation and the uniqueness of the individual.

Nuffield *Combined Science* includes material on human reproduction which also introduces puberty and menstruation. Social and emotional changes could also be discussed in science, perhaps using some of the *Living and Growing* series (Grampian TV, 1985) as a stimulus. It is often questioned whether science is the best place for work of this sort which from the health-education point of view should provide opportunities for pupils to explore and understand their own feelings and those of other people, to be reassured about the changes and so on. Schools may decide to make provision for this sort of work elsewhere in the curriculum, but it is important not to ignore the science contribution. Even if the work in science is concerned with helping pupils understand the physiology of reproduction a sensitive and caring teacher can create a climate in which children might resolve some of their own worries and develop a more open and less embarrassed attitude towards sex and sexuality.

From a health-education perspective the first year seems a good time to include some work on the body systems in general. It could provide a balanced view of the body as a whole rather than the reproductive system in isolation, it could foster positive attitudes towards the body at a time when pupils are coping with the changes of puberty, as well as contributing to the 'usable understanding of his own body and its functioning' which was seen as important to the HMI Working Paper *Curriculum 11–16* Science (DES, 1978). Unfortunately such work does not seem to feature very strongly in lower-school science. It may be seen as providing few opportunities for experimental work, although this is certainly not true of the respiratory, circulatory and muscle systems. Indeed the growth in the health-related fitness components of PE programmes suggests that some link between science and PE is important in this area.

A focus on decision-making in lower-school health education also has implications for science. For instance decisions about eating could provide the context in which pupils investigate the composition of foods, the needs of the body, and the like. It could give work on food which often occurs in lower school science (although not usually Year 1) much more significance without compromising the 'scientific' nature of the work. The fact that home economics is also concerned with food again underlines the importance of some cross-curricular planning or co-ordination.

In theory it is not difficult to relate science to health education and other areas of the curriculum in the lower school (Years 1–3 or S1 and S2 in Scotland). In the upper school the issue is complicated by options and public examination syllabuses. However, even in the lower school there is a limit to the number of subjects which can be closely co-ordinated and maybe it is better to think of co-ordination as a process which includes:

Increasing awareness of what is included across the curriculum

Helping subject teachers appreciate how their work relates to health education

Enabling teachers to identify ways of strengthening these links with health education while avoiding unnecessary duplication

Co-ordination in this sense is as much concerned with methods and general school ethos as it is with content.

Science in relation to other areas of the curriculum poses additional problems in the upper part of the school. The extensive option system and inflexible examination syllabuses seem to have lead almost all schools to introduce an additional course which includes not only health education but many other aspects of personal and social education. Little if any attention is paid to the contributions from other aspects of the curriculum including those discussed for science. The problem is likely to be exacerbated by GCSE developments because of the increased emphasis on application and relevance. This is likely to lead to a greater emphasis on health-related issues not only in science but in subjects like home economics. It serves to underline the importance not only of co-ordination but of looking much more carefully at the curriculum as a whole. The Munn and Dunning reports (Scottish Education Department, 1977) initiated some work in this direction in Scotland, but there is still a long way to go.

CONCLUSION

Science will inevitably make a contribution to health education. The quality and extent of that contribution will vary from school to school, although if science teaching matches the ideals as reflected by recent reports and some projects the contribution will be considerable. It is widely recognized that science has an important role to play in the personal and social development of all pupils. It is suggested that science can contribute to health education through

The processes of science which not only encourage critical thinking but promote self-esteem and autonomy

The development of concepts fundamental to an understanding of health and health choices

The development of self-awareness and an understanding of the uniqueness of the individual

The application of scientific skills and concepts in personal and collective decision-making

However, if this potential is to be realized it will require changes in the way science is often taught and much more thought to be given to the way in which science relates to other areas of the curriculum.

REFERENCES

Association for Science Education (1973) *Science for the 13–16 Age Group*, ASE, London.

Association for Science Education (1979) *Alternatives for Science Education*, ASE, London.

Association for Science Education (1981a) *Education through Science*, ASE, London.

Association for Science Education (1981b) *Science in Society*, Heinemann, London.

Association for Science Education (1982) *Science in the Social Context (SISCON) in Schools Project*, Basil Blackwell, Oxford.

Association for Science Education (1986) *Science and Technology in Society Project (SATIS)*, ASE, London.

Bamborough, H. (1985) What do science teachers really think about health education? in *Health*, SSCR, London.

Barnes, D. (1976) *From Communication to Curriculum*, Penguin, London.

Beattie, A. (1984) Health education and the science teacher, *Education and Health*, Vol. 2, No. 1, p. 9.

Bentley, D. (1984) Science teaching and health education: the challenge accepted! *Education and Health*, Vol. 2, No. 4, p. 78.

Black, P. and Ogborn, J. (1981) Science in the school curriculum, in *No, Minister*. A criticism of the DES paper *The School Curriculum*, Bedford Way Papers, No. 4, University of London Institute of Education.

Brook, A., Briggs, H. and Driver, R. (1984) *Aspects of Secondary Students Understanding of the Particulate Nature of Matter*, Children's Learning in Science Project, University of Leeds.

Crawford, R. (1977) You can damage your health: the ideology of victim-blaming, *International Journal of Health Services*, Vol. 7, pp. 663–78.

Crowther, J. G. (1933) *Biology in Education*, London, Heinemann.

Department of Education and Science (1977) *Curriculum 11–16*, HM Inspectorate Working Paper, HMSO, London.

Department of Education and Science (1978) *Curriculum 11–16: Health Education in the Secondary School Curriculum*, HM Inspectorate Working Paper, HMSO, London.

Department of Education and Science (1979) *Aspects of Secondary Education in England*, HMSO, London.

Department of Education and Science (1985a) *Science 5–16: A Statement of Policy*, HMSO, London.

Department of Education and Science (1985b) *General Certificate of Secondary Education: The National Criteria*, HMSO, London.

Dubos, R. (1965) *Man Adapting*, Yale University Press, New Haven CT.

European Communities Biologists Association (1984) *Health Education and School Biology*, Institute of Biology, London.
Gibson, M. (1985) The teaching of ethics within school science, *The School Science Review*, Vol. 67, No. 239, pp. 270–6.
Gilbert, C. and Matthews, P. (1981) *Look*, Addison-Wesley, London.
Gilbert, C. and Matthews, P. (1982) *First Look*, London, Addison-Wesley, London.
Grampian Television (1985) *Living and Growing*, series.
Health Education Council (1983) *My Body*, Heinemann, London.
Hirst, D. H. (1976) *Moral Education in a Secular Society*, Hodder & Stoughton, London.
Ingle, R. and Jennings, A. (1981) *Science in Schools – Which Way Now?* Studies in Education 8, University of London Institute of Education.
Jenkins, E. W. (1979) *From Armstrong to Nuffield: Studies in Twentieth-Century Science Education in England and Wales*, John Murray, London.
Layton, D. (1986) Revaluing science education in Tomlinson, P. and Quinton, M. (eds) *Values across the Curriculum*, Falmer Press, London.
Midland Examining Group (1986) *GCSE Biology Syllabus*.
McKeown, T. (1979) *The Role of Medicine*, Blackwell, Oxford.
Mee, A. J., Boyd, P. and Richie, D. (1981) *Science 2000*, Heinemann, London.
Nuffield Foundation (1967) *Junior Science Project*, Collins, London.
Nuffield Foundation (1970) *Combined Science Series*, Longman/Penguin, London.
Nuffield Foundation (1971) *Secondary Science Series*, Longman, London.
Nuffield Foundation (1975) *O Level Biology Project* (2nd edn), Longman, London.
Osborne, R. and Freyberg, P. (1985) *Learning in Science*, Heinemann, NZ.
Royal College of Physicians (1977) *Smoking or Health*, Pitman Medical, London.
Royal Society: Biological Education Committee (1978) *The Teaching of Human Biology*, The Royal Society/Institute of Biology, London.
Schools Council (1972) *Science 5–13 Project*, MacDonald Educational, London.
Schools Council (1973) *Integrated Science Project*, Longman/Penguin, London.
Schools Council (1975) *Science 5–13 Project: Ourselves*, Macdonald Educational, London.
Schools Council (1977) *Progress in Learning Science: Match and Mismatch*, Oliver and Boyd, Edinburgh.
Schools Council (1980) *Health Education Project 13–18: Evaluation Report*, Schools Council, London.
Schools Council (1981) *Learning through Science*, MacDonald Educational, London.
Schools Council (1984) *Health Education 13–18: Developing Health Education*, Forbes, London.
Scottish Education Department (1977) *The Structure of the Curriculum in the Third and Fourth Years of the Scottish Secondary School*, HMSO, London.
Scottish Education Department (1979) *Health Education in Primary, Secondary and Special Schools in Scotland*, HMSO, London.
Secondary Science Curriculum Review (1983) *Science 11–16: Proposals for Action and Consultation*, SSCR, London.
Secondary Science Curriculum Review (1985) *Health*, SSCR, London.
Tasker, R. and Freyberg, P. (1985) Facing the mismatches in the classroom, in Osborne, R. and Freyberg, P. (eds) *Learning in Science*, Heinemann, NZ.

6

PHYSICAL EDUCATION
AND HEALTH EDUCATION
Len Almond with Fiona Dowling

INTRODUCTION

In this chapter we examine the context in which the first major funded project in physical education attempts to change the practice of teachers to incorporate a health focus in their work. This is followed by a description of the aspirations of the project and their implications in practice.

THE PE CURRICULUM

The historical role of health and fitness in physical education has been clearly identified in the literature (McIntosh, 1968; Smith, 1974; McNair, 1985), and The Physical Education Association of Great Britain and Northern Ireland proclaims that the objectives of the Association include:

> to promote the scientific approach to the improvement of the physical health of the community through physical education, health education and recreation. . . .
> to educate and instruct specialist teachers in physical education, health education and recreation, in teaching methods, in current theory and practice . . . and the best methods of improving the physical health of the community.

As part of a curriculum investigation in five local education authorities in 1977 teachers were asked about the role of health and fitness in physical education; 95 per cent of the respondents suggested that it had an important part to play in the curriculum. Recently, in a major survey of teachers and students, carried out by the Health Education Council's Initial

Teacher Education Project at Southampton University it was shown that over 90 per cent of both groups believed that physical education departments should be engaged in teaching about health.

However, a vocal interest in health and fitness together with rhetorical statements contained in a department's aims and objectives are far removed from the reality of what is being taught in schools. If one examines the surveys of the physical education curriculum (Hill, 1986; Williamson, 1981) it is difficult to identify precisely what the contribution of physical education in its present form is to a health focus. In Table 6.1 we can see the pattern of activities in a physical education programme. This clearly shows the dominance of competition-focused activities and little evidence of a direct concern for health and fitness.

Table 6.1   Pattern of activities in a PE programme

	Boys	Girls
Games	61.1	53.4
Gymnastics	12.7	16.2
Athletics	14.6	15.7
Cross-country	5.4	2.8
Dance	0.5	7.7
Swimming	1.6	1.2

This pattern is typical in many local education authority schools (Hill, 1986). In discussions with teachers about these results and in response to the question 'can you identify ways in which you encourage a concern for health and fitness in your programmes?', the replies showed that teachers saw fitness as their main concern but it was a spin-off from the normal programme; though cross-country running, popmobility and circuit training were used by some teachers for 'fitness work'. Health was seen as mainly hygiene, with diet as a topic for general discussion.

The mismatch between rhetoric and practice in schools is brought into sharp focus when we consider a study undertaken by Dickenson (1986) which shows that 72 per cent of young people between the ages of 11 and 16 undertook no physical activity outside of their school physical education programme, and 83 per cent did less than five minutes a day. This was a small sample (n = 500), but subsequently schools which have used the same survey are finding similar results.

There is little real evidence available on adult populations in this country about their physical activity patterns, but in Australia the Better Health Commission recently reported that only 35 per cent of men and 27 per cent of women engaged in any vigorous exercise in the fortnight before they were interviewed. Only 1 in 10 men and 1 in 20 women exercised vigorously three or more times a week during this period which is the minimum average level recommended by the National Heart Foundation to maintain adequate heart, lung and muscle fitness. Similar results have been reported in Canada where 85 per cent of adults failed to meet international accepted standards of physical fitness.

This would suggest that there is a problem in the adult population and a distinct hint that a similar pattern exists within the school population. Though a gap may appear between rhetoric and practice, there does appear to be a lot of interest amongst teachers for changing the focus of physical education and introducing a health and fitness component.

Drawing upon a survey of local education authority advisers (Booth, 1986), an analysis of written material provided by teachers for health and fitness courses, and an examination of the content of local authority health and fitness conferences, it is possible to build up a picture of the current state of development in health and physical education. It seems likely that about 600 schools are involved in developing specific units devoted to health and fitness within a physical education programme, though there are many others trying out and exploring ideas without a commitment to a major innovation. This probably reflects the growth of interest shown by local authority advisers as more and more courses are introduced into the INSET programme, starting from 1982, and the number of articles on health and fitness appearing in professional journals.

However, many of these courses emphasize fitness testing as a principal component of course content and this can be seen in written material produced by teachers. It is interesting to note that many teachers have been influenced by American literature, in particular books by Corbin and Lindsay (1985). Some teachers have developed a health education course within the physical education programme without any reference to other subject areas of the curriculum.

Booth's survey (1986) drew attention to the kinds of support identified by teachers as being necessary for the development of ideas. These centred on the need for resources to use as teaching material, more urgent local and national courses to update their knowledge base on fitness and health issues (particularly testing and correct exercises) and help to plan courses to fit into the usual physical education programme. No mention was made of the need for a rationale to identify a direction for health and fitness courses in schools.

HEALTH AND PHYSICAL EDUCATION PROJECT

It is in this context that the Health Education Council (HEC) in conjunction with the Physical Education Association (PEA) have provided funds for a two year project on health and physical education based at Loughborough University.

The aspirations of the project team are:

1. To establish the case for health-based programmes of physical education within the physical education curriculum
2. To sensitize representatives of the physical education profession to the role of health-based physical education in schools
3. To develop resources for use in schools

A Health Focus in Physical Education

The first of these aspirations is far from easy because as Haskell, Montoye and Orenstein (1985) show the relationship between health and fitness is not always a clear one and the effects of exercise on a person's health or fitness are not always the same. They make three important points in their attempt to make a distinction between health and fitness.

They argue that a high level of physical fitness is usually associated with good health, but improving fitness does not necessarily increase the resistance to disease. Also, they go on to argue that some patients with a disease, for example emphysema, can significantly increase their physical fitness without changing the severity of the disease or medical prognosis. Their third point centres on the fact that though physical activity may improve physical fitness and clinical health status at the same time, the improvement in health may be due to biological changes which are different from those responsible for the improvement in physical fitness. They argue that although endurance training may increase aerobic capacity which is due to an increase in oxygen transportation and utilization capacity, a reduction in coronary heart disease may be the result of alterations in lipoprotein metabolism or fibrinolytic mechanisms. Thus, though improvement in health and fitness may occur simultaneously, the exercise-induced stimulus for each may be different.

Balkamm (1985) in a teleological analysis of fitness sees health 'as a congruence between human purposes and the purposes implicit in how our bodies are designed and function'. For him, physiological integrity and absence of disease or injury are necessary conditions for health, but health is not given, it is an achievement brought about by sufficient and appropriate use of the body's organs. Health can only be achieved by intelligently choosing behaviours compatible with the purposes built into our bodies. The end of health is the harmonious state of being, resulting from the mind choosing purposes expressed in behaviour that are consistent with the purposes inherent in bodily function. The enjoyment of this state is what we are concerned with in discussions of health.

He goes on to speak of fitness and health not only as a difference in degree, but also in kind. Thus, a fit person is not someone who is merely further down the continuum of bodily function than a person solely concerned with his or her health; the fit person may be able to run ten miles in an hour as opposed to the healthy person who can only jog five miles in an hour. For Balkamm (1985) health is a state of enjoying the realization of potencies implicit in bodily design and function whereas fitness has some extrinsic goal, usually a performance as its object. This makes the body and its condition a means to an end.

Another difference between health and fitness concerns the specificity of fitness for something; thus fitness for rowing will be very different from fitness for rhythmic gymnastics. Also, the person aspiring towards fitness is concerned with striving for constant improvement, whereas the person concerned with health is usually more interested in maintaining a certain level of functioning.

Thus, in establishing a case for health and fitness within physical education there is a need to be aware of a number of conceptual issues that are far from clear. However, the value of exercise appears to be very strong. In a comprehensive review of the literature, Fentem and Bassey (1981) conclude, 'It is clear that physical activity is of considerable benefit to everyone both physically and mentally and should be seen as a necessary element in the pattern of daily living at all ages'. At a later date, Haskell, Montoye and Orenstein (1985) make a significant point when they say

> whereas definitive evidence of a cause-and-effect relationship between an increase in habitual physical activity or exercise and many specific health benefits is still lacking, there is sufficient evidence of a positive relationship to warrant advising a physically active lifestyle in conjunction with other positive health behaviours.

They go on to say

> the physical activity that appears to provide the most diverse health benefits consists of dynamic, rhythmical contractions of large muscles that transport the body over distance or against gravity at a moderate

intensity relative to capacity for extended periods of time during which 200 to 400 kilocalories are expended.

A Sensitizing Role

The second aspiration centres on the process of making people aware of the way a physical education programme can have a health focus and is heavily dependent on the accomplishment of the first aspiration. However, there is a prior concern which cannot be neglected. Before the physical education profession can examine what a health focus entails, they need to scrutinize carefully the existing programme in schools and to identify what is being accomplished, and ask if these aspirations are 'in practice' appropriate?

The recent debate in the media (see Hardy, 1986) about the role of physical education shows clearly that there is a considerable lobby for a strong competitive element. As Hill (1986) shows, the programme in schools reveals a heavy emphasis on activities in which competition is an essential element. Sparkes (1985) argues strongly that 'many physical educationists due to their socialisation within sport accept the competitive experience as a "taken for granted reality" .' He goes on to warn us that undue emphasis on the competitive element has dangers for a health-related fitness programme and states,

> if children are continuously placed in competitive contexts in which their incentive needs cannot be met, then their enthusiasm and interest is likely to wane rapidly, the end result for many will be to cease participation in any sort of physical activity.

This problem is complicated further by the demands of a health focus on teaching strategies.

Pain (1986) in a discussion on health-education initiatives in schools stresses the role of decision-making skills which require involvement by the students in their own learning, and a context where individual contributions from students are valued. He goes on to raise questions about the subsequent demand on teachers for a repertoire of teaching strategies to organize learning. In physical education this may prove to be a major problem, because Spackman (1986) shows that male and female teachers of physical education display a penchant for a prescriptive approach to learning and a preference for addressing a whole class where there is little opportunity for feedback from students.

Rose (1986) and Knott and Almond (1986) show similar results when they examine the tasks set by teachers in curriculum guidelines for primary physical education. Thus, the apparent requirements of involvement by students in their own learning in health education, where individual contributions are valued, may create a barrier for a profession which uses predominately a didactic teaching approach and pupil feedback is rarely encouraged.

In this scenario the sensitizing role of the project will need to take into account the demands that will be expected of teachers in making major adjustments to both their perceptions of physical education and their approach to learning if they are to take on board the idea of a health focus in their programmes.

The Use of Resource Materials

The third aspiration concerns the production of resources where very little exist. Booth (1986) in her analysis of Local Education Authority (LEA) initiatives in health and fitness informs us that almost every respondent in the survey identified this as a priority. Suggestions included computer software, handbooks and information packs on fitness tests, visual aids, guidelines for schemes of work, simple experiments, and sample materials of ideas currently in use. In addition, the respondents requested national and county courses to support resources so that the message of health and fitness could be spread effectively. It is interesting to note that little mention was made of the need for a rationale underpinning such resources.

For many teachers, however, the use of resource materials will involve a radical shift in thinking because they have argued that they are a practical element in the curriculum. The use of resources will require a different way of organizing their teaching and this will have repercussions on pupils who are used to a particular way of working in physical education.

There is another critical element involved in the use of resource materials which cannot be ignored. The resource provision will have a rationale underlining its implementation in schools, and if there is a mismatch with the teachers' value structures and perceptions of what a health focus is, the likely outcome will be the translation of a different message under the guise of a common framework. In addition, the teachers will not have been involved in the construction of the framework for the resources, therefore the process of thinking involved in the transformation of an idea will be denied to them.

This highlights the need for in-service courses as a prerequisite for the use of resources in schools. In order to capture the process by which an idea is translated into practice and to match aspirations with the reality of day-to-day teaching, careful thought will be needed to devise appropriate learning strategies for the teachers involved in innovation. The 'training of trainers' approach to innovation involves a translation of a message to others and a further translation down the line in conjunction with 'active learning' techniques. This approach may have many advantages but it does mean that the success of the innovation is dependent upon the successful accurate translation of a message down the line.

Another approach may be that teachers need to examine their own practices, explore different ways of obtaining feedback from pupils and build up a picture of the impact of their current programme on pupils. The opportunity to discuss within their department problematic issues concerning physical education, for example competition, and explore their own feelings about the issue may encourage a more reflective attitude. If this is supported by the opportunity to examine evidence about children's activity patterns or similar problems, they may begin to see the need for change of practice or, at least, examine the case for changing existing practices.

The support of resource materials as a starting point for exploring an idea may be an important crutch that teachers need, but they need to be seen as resources which challenge teachers to try out ideas and learn from the experience. Thus, resources need to be tied to in-service courses prior to teaching, but also afterwards during the process of trying out ideas, so that teachers have the opportunity of learning from each other. This approach will require the support of advisers in local authorities so that the innovation is seen as a way of helping teachers understand the implications of change on their own thinking about the potential of physical education.

The period before the production of resources was seen as an important phase for the project because it provided the opportunity to encourage teachers working with the project to engage in a number of curriculum exercises. The rationale for this initiative came from the project team's belief that teachers need to see the classroom and their teaching as problematic. In an earlier study by Almond (1986) on games teaching, teachers did not see their teaching as problematic in any sense until they engaged in a number of exercises which promoted reflection about their practices and discussion with their colleagues in other schools. Thus, the need for reflection and an examination of current practices was seen as an important first step in the project. This was achieved by asking the teachers to analyse their curricula and highlight where their major emphasis lay, to seek feedback from pupils about physical education and their experiences within lessons, and finally to find out how active young people were outside of the school physical education programme. These exercises were discussed within the school department and with colleagues from other schools engaged in the same enterprise.

148   *Health Education in Schools*

These reflective exercises were an attempt to make the teacher a 'stranger' in his or her classroom (Greene, 1973; Sparkes, 1985) in such a way that everyday classroom practices were seen with new eyes. Thus, as Ruddock (1985) suggests:

> The everyday eyes of teachers have two weaknesses: because of the dominance of habit and routine, teachers are only selectively attentive to the phenomena of their classrooms. In a sense they are constantly reconstructing the world that they are familiar with in order to maintain regularities and routines. Secondly, because of their business, their eyes tend only to transcribe the surface realities of classroom interaction.

Besides the idea of a stranger in one's own classroom, the exercises served as a device for teachers to recognize the need for rethinking, and possibly a change of practice. In such a position, the teacher becomes receptive to considering alternative interpretations of the physical education curriculum and hopefully is prepared to explore alternatives. At this stage, the project team believes that the teachers working with the project will be prepared to take a critical stance and scrutinize the resources prepared by the project with a reflective disposition as opposed to passively absorbing the materials and simply trying them out and completing an evaluation booklet.

This procedure is modelled on Stenhouse's (1970) notion of schools working within a project as 'experimental' schools where resources are seen as an invitation to explore ideas and contribute to our understanding of what a health focus entails in physical education. The materials are seen as procedural devices for teachers to explore the implications of their teaching and to contribute to the development of ideas in practice. In this way, it is hoped that the teachers and how they perceive their own situation, and the problems inherent within it, will be central to the development of understanding about an innovation and the role it plays within physical education.

REFERENCES

Almond, L. (1986) Research based teaching in games, in Evans, J. (ed.) *Sociological Issues in Physical Education*, Falmer Press, Brighton, pp. 155–65.
Balkamm, C. (1985) Teleology and fitness: an Aristotelian analysis, in Kleinman, S. (ed.) *Mind and Body: East Meets West*, Human Kinetics, Champaign, IL, pp. 31–7.
Booth, S. (1986) Survey of Local Education Authority initiatives in health and fitness. Unpublished report of the Health and Physical Education Project, University of Technology, Loughborough.

Corbin, C. B. and Lindsay, R. (1985) Concepts in Physical Fitness, Wm C. Brown, Dubuque, IA.

Dickenson, B. (1986) A survey of the activity patterns of young people and their attitudes and perceptions of physical activity and physical education in a Local Education Authority. Unpublished MPhil dissertation, University of Technology, Loughborough.

Fentem, P. H. and Bassey, E. J. (1981) *Exercise: The 'Facts'*, Oxford University Press.

Greene, M. (1973) *Teacher as Stranger*, Wadsworth Publishing Co., Belmont, CA.

Hardy, C. (1986) Competitive team sport and schools. *Health and Physical Education Newsletter*, No. 3, March.

Haskell, W. L., Montoye, H. J. and Orenstein, D. (1985) Physical activity and exercise to achieve health-related physical fitness components, *Public Health Reports*, Vol. 100, No. 2, pp. 202–11.

Hill, C. (1986) An analysis of the Physical Education Curriculum (11 14 years) in a Local Education Authority. Unpublished MPhil dissertation, University of Technology, Loughborough.

Knott, D. J. and Almond, L. (1986) An analysis of task setting in infant guidelines, *Bulletin of Physical Education*, Vol. 22, No. 3.

McIntosh, P. C. (1968) *Physical Education in England since 1800*, G. Bell, London.

McNair, D. (1985) The historical concept of health and fitness: a review, in Nichols, A. (ed.) *Health Related Fitness*, Proceedings of BUPEA Annual Conference, Belfast, pp. 99–119.

Pain, S. (1986) Current issues in physical education and health in schools in the United Kingdom, in S. N. Donald (ed.) *Trends and Developments in Physical Education*, E. & F. N. Spon, London.

Rose, C. (1986) Task setting in physical education, Paper presented at the annual meeting of the Teaching Research Unit at Birmingham University, 14–15 April.

Ruddock, J. (1985) The improvement of the art of teaching through research, *Cambridge Journal of Education*, Vol. 15, No. 3, pp. 123–7.

Smith, W. D. (1974) *Stretching their Bodies*, David and Charles, London.

Spackman, L. (1986) The systematic observation of teacher behaviour in physical education: the design of an instrument. Unpublished PhD dissertation, University of Technology, Loughborough.

Sparkes, A. (1985) The competitive mythology – a questioning of assumptions, *Health and Physical Education Newsletter*, No. 3, March.

Stenhouse, L. (1970) *The Humanities Project: An Introduction*, Heinemann, London.

Williamson, T. (1981) Balance in the secondary school physical education programme. Paper presented at the BAALPE Annual Conference 'Balance in Education and Physical Education'.

7

ENGLISH AND HEALTH EDUCATION

Peter Farley

INTRODUCTION

This chapter offers a brief survey of the main concerns of current teaching in English and shows how these relate to health education. At the outset however, is the problem of knowing what is meant by 'English'. The principal aim here is to consider English as a subject in the school curriculum, but there is a second and wider meaning which we should keep in mind. Language and learning are inextricably related, to the extent that educational success is often primarily a matter of linguistic success. In England, at any rate, the English language will be the vehicle for virtually all health education. Consideration of language for learning is not confined to that slot on the timetable generally called English. In this sense, English, like health education, crosses conventional curriculum boundaries with its concern for process and language/learning situations. There is a similar cross-curricular concern in that neither English nor health education has easily demarcated content boundaries. Indeed both could be described in the same way as John Dixon (1975) describes English: 'a quicksilver among metals – mobile, living and elusive'.

English in the secondary school curriculum can seem to be impossibly diverse and diffused. Depending on the school the timetable may show English, media studies, literature, language, communications, film and theatre and so on. Abbs (1986) argues that the discipline has become 'amorphous, spread out and weakened by an excess of conflicting conceptual claims and by narrowing instrumental pressures'. Teachers and others familiar with curriculum development in health may well recognize such a state of affairs.

As with any subject in the curriculum, emphases change not only from place to place but also over time. For our present purpose, it will suffice to say that there are essentially three strands in English as a subject – personal growth, skills and literature and cultural concerns. These are not mutually exclusive and together they provide the framework on which the fabric of English in a particular school is stretched. In the 1970s, it was possible to assert the idea of personal growth as informing current work generally, giving cohesion to the other strands. From the perspective of the late 1980s a more instrumental view of the curriculum generally and English in particular may be discerned, for which the drivers may be as diverse as the Technical–Vocational Education Initiative (TVEI) and developments in applied linguistics.

The concern for personal growth as a major strand in the teaching of English implies an emphasis on the needs and experiences of the learner. The primacy of content is lessened in favour of an attention to educational process, reflecting and enhancing the personal process of becoming which this approach seeks to nurture in the learner.

The concern with personal growth is, of course, shared by health education in schools. Health education is concerned with fostering and developing an understanding of growth and development, with the idea of health as the ability to function actively in the world, with preparation for parenthood, with personal relationships and with the exploration and understanding of the feelings, attitudes and values of oneself and others. English is concerned with the acquisition of personal language and the development of language behaviour and skills without which it becomes impossible to function positively and with personal control in the world. Language cannot operate meaningfully in isolation and the very use and existence of language implies relationships of various sorts. Through language, and especially through the experience of literature, we are able to understand ourselves more fully and to extend that understanding in order to enter into the lives of others.

Creative writing at its best represents the struggle for personal control and meaning. Further than that, I suggest that the values of personal space and privacy in writing have a part to play beyond the confines of the English lesson. The more personal modes of writing offer the means to relate knowledge to experience, attitudes, feelings and values – a central concern of the health-education process.

In considering skills in English, we should see that we are dealing with language skills generally. The basic skills are:
1. Adjusting intelligently to the great variety of communication situations one finds oneself in, each of which requires some different approach, there being no such thing as a correct English suitable for all occasions (and age groups).

2. Working out meaning for utterances in such situations, whether one is the author or the audience of the utterance. This involves:
   (a) Understanding of content or subject matter
   (b) Application of thought processes to it.

3. Generating wording to express that meaning
   (a) With vocabulary indicating the content
   (b) And vocabulary and syntax indicating the thought processes.

4. Processing the wording in the complex acts of listening, speaking, reading and writing (CCAE, 1978).

It will not be possible to pursue each of these, nor is it necessary. Instead, I propose to concentrate on the broad areas of speaking, writing and reading. As I have suggested, personal growth is seen to inform these for the most part. Normally our concern would be with the pupil's own growth and development in language competence, but there is no reason why that process itself should not be the subject of work in English as well as an aim. With preparation for parenthood in mind, some consideration of how people, especially young children, come to acquire language would be a valuable part of exploring language in English. After all it is the one school subject in which, by far, the greater part of learning occurs before school is even reached.

There seems to be general agreement that spoken language is the most neglected of English skills. This is ironic in that language is primarily a matter of speech and the most representative of all ways of using language is the situation in which two or three people talk to each other face to face. Language implies relationships, and spoken language implies the most immediate ones. The capacity to talk well in a variety of situations, to respond sensitively to other people and to understand what is really being said is necessary for social health, to make successful relationships and to learning as a whole. English has much to contribute to health education in this area, both within its own subject and in drama, and to the curriculum in general. It is difficult to organize exploratory talk and to provide experience of a variety of talk from the formal to the informal, but it is the case that group work provides the means of achieving a more effective situation for active language than the class discussion. Group work poses questions of classroom management, teacher direction and intervention and this is not the place to resolve them. Indeed the whole question of talk in the classroom raises issues well beyond the reach of this chapter and some of the suggested further reading at the end may help to resolve them. Nevertheless the contribution of the English teacher can be a crucial one for health education. I am thinking now not only of a classroom contribution but that he or she could well act as a kind of consultant, whether for the staff as a whole or in the setting of a health-education team.

With the advent of the General Certificate of Secondary Education (GCSE, 1986) it will no longer be possible to ignore the claims of spoken language skills – 'The course should seek to develop the ability to . . . communicate accurately, appropriately and effectively in speech and writing.' The importance given to spoken language in the new examination represents one of its most notable innovations, and may be seen as one of the major consequences of the Bullock Report on English, *A Language for Life* (DES, 1975). Who I am and how I speak are so inextricably linked that 'to criticise a person's speech may be an attack on his self-esteem' (Bullock).

With writing we again come up against the question of language use across the curriculum. By far the greatest number of writing tasks in schools (some estimates indicate 90 per cent) relate to the recall of information and the representational use of language. A further problem is that of audience so that by and large the only person addressed in school writing is the teacher in his or her role as examiner. The English teacher can provide a wider audience, both by carrying out his or her own role of sympathetic adult, with concerns which are wider than those of simply examining for accuracy, and by fostering fellow pupils as a trusted audience.

Reading is not simply a matter of decoding a text. Rather, the reader engages in critical and creative thinking in order to relate what he or she reads to what he or she already knows. Indeed, the response to a text involves intellectual and affective processes, and it was once well said that we do not so much read a book as a book reads us. The development of reading brings a development in personal confidence, an increase in control over language and a decrease in the control of other people's language over us as we recognize how they operate. The potential gains for our self-knowledge and knowledge of others are obvious. This alone relates to health education by way of personal development, but within the context of the English teacher developing reading there are more pragmatic considerations for health education. There is no reason why, for example, health-related material should not be used when considering the language of advertising. Similarly, the development of skills in finding out information and assessing its value and effect can be health-related.

Literature is the ground of the more social and cultural concerns of English. The range of possible connections with health education is vast and, of course, not unrelated to the way English teachers already make use of literature in their work. There are a number of possible starting points and these would include developing a health theme in a course of reading or simply being more alert to the health-related aspects of current work.

It is hard to imagine a serious reading of the English Romantic poets, for example, which did acknowledge the interplay between opium addiction and the imagination. Coleridge's lines in *Kubla Khan* say it all:

And all should cry, Beware! Beware!
His flashing eyes, his floating hair!
Weave a circle round him thrice,
And close your eyes with holy dread,
For he on honey-dew hath fed,
And drank the milk of Paradise.

There is a view common among English specialists that literature is some- how diminished by being used as ready-made resource material (extracts, case studies and so on) in a more general kind of humanities teaching. An alternative view is that far from being trivialized, literature enriches the endeavour it is enlisted to support or complements other modes of dis- course with its own particular resonance. A good example of this is the process whereby an excerpt from the journal of Katherine Mansfield, written shortly before her death, has appeared in a variety of health- related publications over the last 20 years or so, expressing with consider- able power a view of health with which health educators seem to identify and by which they may be inspired. The extract is usually printed in a shortened form, but I want to use it in full and for two reasons. By its sheer energy it challenges the often bland or arid language so often encountered in professional discourse in health education and it illustrates a central contribution to English. Personal experience is extended and access given to that of others from all ages and places in answer to the question 'What does it mean to be alive?'

Now, Katherine, what do you mean by health? And what do you want it for?
Answer: By health I mean the power to live a full, adult, living, breathing life in close contact with what I love – the earth and the wonders thereof – the sea – the sun. All that we mean when we speak of the external world. I want to enter into it, to be part of it, to live in it, to learn from it, to lose all that is superficial and acquired in me and to become a conscious, direct human being. I want to be all that I am capable of becoming so that I may be . . . a child of the sun.
(Stead, 1977)

The contribution of English to health education, then, can be viewed in a number of different ways. As a subject in schools it shares common concerns with health education. The normal range of English work complements health education and contributes to it in a number of respects. Equally the health-education perspective can serve to sharpen and refine work in English. Last, but by no means least, English in the wider sense can offer support to health education across the curriculum, in terms of method and in terms of the relationship between language and learning.

'Language', according to William von Humboldt, 'intervenes between man and nature acting upon him internally and externally.' Health education attempts to do precisely that.

SUMMARY

As a subject in schools, English shares common concerns with health education and the normal range of English work complements health education and contributes to it in a number of respects, particularly in the area of personal growth.

The health-education perspective can serve to sharpen and refine work in English. English in the widest sense can offer support to health education in terms of methods and the relationship between language and learning.

REFERENCES

Abbs, P. (1986) English as art, *Words*, Vol. 1, No. 8, January.

Canberra College of Advanced Education (CCAE) (1978) *Material on Language.*

Department of Education and Science (1975) *A Language for Life*, The Bullock Report, HMSO, London.

Dixon, J. (1975) *Growth through English: Set in the Perspective of the Seventies*, Oxford University Press.

General Certificate of Secondary Education (1986) *National Criteria for English*, para. 1.1.1.

Stead, C. K. (ed.) (1977) *The Letters and Journals of Katherine Mansfield*, Allen Lane, London. (Quoted, for example, in *Man Adapting* by René Dubos [1965]; *Health and School*, Devon LEA [1978] and Health Education 13–18 *Introductory Handbook* [1981].)

Suggested Further Reading

Barnes, D. (1976) *From Communication to Curriculum*, Penguin, Harmondsworth.

Health Education 13–18 (1984) *Developing Health Education – A Co-ordinator's Guide*, Forbes, London. (Contains a guide to discussion methods and management.)

Postman, N. and Weingartner, C. (1971) *Teaching as a Subversive Activity*, Penguin, Harmondsworth.

8

HEALTH EDUCATION AND THE PASTORAL SYSTEM

Kenneth David

INTRODUCTION

Since the first edition of this book in 1981 there have been many pressures, financial and otherwise, on the developing range of pastoral care in secondary schools, and critical traditionalists have murmured, 'the band wagon has finally stopped'.

In fact the 'band wagon' of more generous development and training in pastoral care has paid large dividends in establishing general attitudes and practices which have had the strength to withstand recent economy measures and troubled educational politics. There is now only limited dispute about the essential nature of good pastoral systems, of improved and more demanding tutorial work, and of the obvious strong links between learning and pastoral care. Falling school rolls and a reduction in pastoral responsibility posts have returned pastoral care in better shape to the class teachers and tutors where it has always been truly based.

Our changed society and the difficulties of motivating questioning youngsters appear finally to have established modern pastoral care views as an inherent partner of intellectual achievement rather than as an apologetic poor relation. The establishing and rapid success of the National Association for Pastoral Care in Education is some evidence of this. With this legitimization and partnership has gone a firmer relationship with health education and the so-called 'pastoral curriculum'. Terms such as 'pastoral curriculum' and 'personal and social education' (PSE) are widely used to describe the work done by secondary schools in affective education, in education for personal relationships and family life, and even in careers education and study skills.

Some of this area is also accepted as a modern and wider view of health education, and in fact the title of health education is used by many schools as an umbrella term for part of their curriculum planning and co-ordination.

This view of health education has one disadvantage; it means that the subject area is diffuse and extends throughout a school's curriculum and activities. It is difficult to encapsulate neatly in the timetable when it is a general umbrella term for many topics and approaches, and since health education co-ordination is difficult in its early planning it can be patchily dealt with in many schools.

PRIMARY SCHOOLS

In primary schools a co-ordinated approach to pastoral care and health education ought to be comparatively easy, for the class teacher has considerable freedom in controlling the planning of most of the work of a class of children throughout the year. Given guidance and enthusiasm by the headteacher, and given the easy personal relationships and pleasing family atmosphere of most primary schools, the integration of health education and a professional approach to pastoral care ought to be commonplace, and it is in fact generally so regarded.

Yet the considerable interest in and acceptance of better pastoral care systems and co-ordination of PSE/health education in secondary schools is not always matched in the primary-school world. There can be too great a reliance on an intuitive and loosely planned approach.

Everything done in secondary schools has its roots in primary schools, and one wonders why primary teachers often appear to be exempted from the professional challenges of secondary education in the caring and personal development roles. There can be an undue contentment in this area of work, even though primary teachers face the same demanding social and personal problems among their pupils that are seen at later stages. The generalist primary teacher seems to have negligible initial training preparation, few in-service courses provided, little educational literature, and very limited advisory interest in a more professional approach to their pastoral roles and to the health/PSE curriculum.

In considering better preparation in these roles the following requirements have been suggested (David and Charlton, 1987).
1. A need to advocate more clearly a wider socializing task in primary education, in preparing for children's future lives in a difficult and rapidly changing modern society

2. A re-examination of the effect of pastoral attitudes, of the curriculum, of teaching methods, and of welfare provision, in order to sharpen and professionalize what is sometimes only intuitive
3. To seek advice and support in developing practical and theoretical viewpoints on how primary teachers can organize curriculum, teaching strategies, and administration to achieve a wider socializing role
4. To revise and emphasize information on the health, welfare and counselling aspects of primary schools
5. To emphasize and study the appropriate 'pastoral curriculum' for a school, for PSE/health education has a practical curriculum content, requiring a clear co-ordinating purpose.

The immediate implications of this critical viewpoint could lead to two courses of action in a primary school seeking improvement in these roles. First, the effect of the school as an institution on its pupils and staff must be studied at depth by the whole staff. Administration, rituals and customs provide a 'hidden curriculum' which has obvious pastoral effects, and the school's place and part in its environment needs to be viewed carefully. Second, much deliberation must be given to selecting the PSE/heath-education curriculum topics which are seen as necessary for that school. Parents and children may be involved, and the value of different commercial schemes will be balanced with local needs.

Further discussion then follows, some details of which are explored elsewhere in this book. This may include such topics as appropriate visual aids and books, the regular use of visitors, appropriate recording and evaluation systems, the best kind of groups for discussion work, the possibility of using computers, careful liaison with parents and govenors, and most importantly what in-service needs are there for the teachers.

The personal and social development of children, using curriculum materials in areas such as health education, and with more planned and professional pastoral care, is of equal importance with their intellectual development, in fact each depends on the other. If the lamentable lack of true liaison and partnership between the primary and secondary sectors were altered, then perhaps secondary schools could learn to seek the attractive atmosphere and ethos of good primary schools, and primary schools could make more professional their pastoral care and curriculum co-ordination by adopting good secondary practices.

SECONDARY SCHOOL CO-ORDINATION

In secondary schools a director of studies may co-ordinate the personal and health education through academic subject departments, or a head of PE, home economics or science may have this responsibility. As schools put cognitive and examination matters into better perspective, so a managed, co-ordinated and professional approach to health may develop. A frequent lead for such co-ordination has come from the pastoral care staff, often pastoral heads, for the education in personal relationships courses, the welfare and counselling matters, and the constant attention on individual pupils are clearly appropriate links in a wide view of health. This pastoral co-ordinator, often a senior head of year, or a deputy head, will have certain questions to consider, and every school will have varying answers to suit their circumstances and staffing.

What system of meetings and consultations has to be set up, to ensure that there is efficient liaison with each academic department and pastoral head? Many schools are reducing the number of separate academic and pastoral-team meetings held under different deputy heads, and are wisely attempting a more integrated approach.

How are health matters to be introduced into the teaching? This may be by occasional courses, in which departments join in teaching to a theme – perhaps third-year sessions on alcohol and drugs, a day on parentcraft during the fourth year, and so on. These sessions would be paralleled by arranged teaching on other themes in specified departments. An alternative would be to deal with major relationships themes at whatever residential courses the school organizes, though this may mean limiting valued work to those who pay for some residential experience. Some schools have a series of visiting speakers, or members of staff, who give extensive lead talks on major health themes, with discussion in tutorials during the following week.

The best method of all will probably have a mixture of many approaches, suiting the teachers' personalities and reinforcing their different methods in a flexible but carefully guided scheme. Then each academic department and all aspects of the guidance and pastoral-care system will feel that they contribute equally and in a balanced and continuous pattern.

Her Majesty's Inspectors comment, 'In general, schools placed much greater emphasis on fostering the personal development of their pupils through pastoral care than through their curriculum' (DES, 1979, p. 208). Members of staff teach a great deal about social and moral issues, good relationships, responsibility, and other topics during ordinary subject teaching, and this must be integrated into the overall planning of the personal development of pupils.

One comprehensive high school set about planning a better approach to pastoral care and the pastoral curriculum as follows:

1. Senior staff debated the need to improve pastoral care (and better

academic achievement incidentally) and then led a series of discussions involving all staff, including certain ancillary staff, in pastoral teams. This school, by the way, had an ancillary staff member who was immensely popular and valued as a counsellor by senior pupils and who attended pastoral teams' meetings as a helpful school colleague.

2. The headteacher discussed ideas with the Governors, and conferred with contributory primary-school Heads.

3. A topic list of what might be included in a PSE/health-education curriculum was drawn up by a deputy head and contributions and criticisms were then invited from Governors, staff and some pupils. Pupils were asked to discuss the preliminary plans with their parents, and a letter to parents explained the project. The school's adviser was a regular partner in the staff discussions.

4. This topic list was eventually circulated to all departmental heads who responded with information as to when they dealt with any of the topics, with which classes or sets, and at what depth.

5. The results were displayed in colourful form around the walls of the deputy head's office, and a series of discussions were held, mostly informally with most of the staff, over a period of some weeks. Suggestions were taken as to how best the gaps in the topic list, not dealt with adequately in subject teaching, could be dealt with in special courses and by varying departmental setting and planning.

6. Tutorial teams met under pastoral heads to see how tutorial discussion time could use selected items from the topic list. Some six to eight topics were eventually chosen for each year to be developed in morning tutorial time, and in assemblies. Much thought was given to where co-ordination was possible at appropriate times of the year with topics being dealt with in subject departments.

7. Considerable bartering and discussion took place in departmental meetings to see where examination demands could be amended to match the school's growing PSE/heath-education topic list. Children were involved at times.

8. A one-day staff in-service training day was held on tutorial work and study skills. Primary school staff and Governors attended.

9. A series of meetings, partly in school time and partly after school, were held to work on better assessment and recording systems, counselling courses were considered, liaison with health education officers (HEOs) continued, and study skills were added to the agenda of departmental and pastoral-team meetings.

This was a good school in a far from easy neighbourhood, with excellent staff relationships, and the demanding project preparations paid dividends.

Guidance Periods

An increasingly popular way in which the pastoral staff can contribute to a school's efficiency is by having a timetabled weekly tutorial period, of the same length of time and with the same status as subject periods. This period, called 'guidance', 'tutorial', 'personal development' and various other titles, is then timetabled in such a way that a year-group of children, a group of staff responsible for the tutorial work of that year and a number of classrooms are available. The year head will then be responsible for a varied and flexible programme of work during the year. This can include large groups attending lectures on careers and health themes, small groups in discussion settings, an opportunity for regular interviewing and educational guidance of individuals and groups of pupils, and for personal counselling when needed. The school will need to plan carefully; staff will be invited to attend courses, so that the skills of counselling and group work are available in the team, and those staff skilled in careers education will be allocated to each year team, perhaps after the first year. Someone in the team, not necessarily the year head, will have experience with health education themes and will be able to guide his colleagues. Headteachers may choose to ensure that selected and prepared staff are available in each tutorial team to lead discussions in more controversial areas such as sex education.

A number of schools have also linked some therapeutic group work with this tutorial period. Whilst one is properly suspicious of the word *therapy* in a school setting, the average school does have a proportion of difficult or immature pupils who need specialist attention. Such attention from psychologists and others is often difficult to arrange, and a staff member skilled in developmental group work and counselling may lead a supportive group, intended to help with problem personalities, perhaps under the general guidance of an educational psychologist. If there is a flexible system of groups in the tutorial period, varying needs of individuals and groups can be met in a very natural way; but care must be taken that group work of a therapeutic nature is not undertaken by enthusiastic volunteers of an emotional or sentimental nature who may see themselves as amateur psychiatrists.

Of particular value to all types of tutorial work is interviewing visitors. Through preparation of questions beforehand, practice in social care in meeting and looking after the visitor and discussing the occasion afterwards, pupils can learn a great deal. They can learn how different people, such as the headteacher, a policeman, the caretaker, a clergyman, a health visitor, a young mother, view life, and they can learn many facts about society. If people are seen as individuals with their own feelings, cares and sensitivities, this usually has the valuable result of reducing stereotyping.

This tutorial cohort approach has many advantages. It is easily managed once the initial timetable and staff planning is done, it is comprehensible to pupils and it links health with a range of preparations for work and family life in a natural way. The major difficulty, of course, is the priority decision to allocate one of the week's teaching periods, in competition with the constant demands for more time in academic teaching departments. The demands of examinations appear so paramount, and the questionable feeling that health and guidance can be dealt with in normal teaching contacts is so easy to adopt, that we forget that good guidance tutorials make all the other work of a school more efficient and effective. We also forget that it is as important to be prepared for relationships in work and family, and to have a healthy life, in a satisfying job, as it is to be well-qualified in examinations. Unfortunately, success in examinations for some groups of pupils is easy to assess and publicize, and success in preparation for life for the majority can seldom be measured. Since learning and success in school are so closely linked with the motivation and happy personal development of a pupil, it seems sad that more priority is not given to such well-planned guidance periods.

Examinations are perhaps slowly being made more relevant and useful as part of the successful personal development of young people, rather than as an insistent record of their failings. The CSE failed despite its excellent innovations because educationalists failed to sell it well, and because GCE won on social and traditional points. GCSE may yet enrich our assessment procedures and show that achievement can have many forms, and that a changing and difficult future may value a variety of different personal skills and potentials. Profiling and pupils' personal records can clearly help in motivating pupils and in showing that learning is inevitably a joint contract and process between teachers and pupils. Form tutors can use their personal understanding and knowledge of their tutorial groups, and their informal relationships with their pupils, to give an important basis and lead in setting up profiling systems.

Morning Tutorial Time

A demand more commonly met by pastoral co-ordinators is to incorporate elements of health and personal relationships work into a regular morning tutorial time taken by class tutors. Most schools have such morning tutorial time, with basic pastoral groups and a regular tutor. The planning of such groups will have been carefully done at the time of their entry to the school, based on various factors such as friendship groups, ability mix and personalities, and it is unusual to have many changes as the group moves through the school. One has regretfully seen schools in which tutor groups are reformed each year and based on ability in examinations, which seems a recipe for alienation and discipline troubles in the school. One also sees the very successful use of well-planned tutor groups as a firm and contented base from which different abilities will develop in sets and option groups, with several subjects taught in the basic mixed-ability groups. Games and social events can be based on such groups, and much learning and preparation for life can then develop with sensible tutorial leadership.

Such teacher-leaders may remain with a group throughout their time in the school, or there may be changes after lower-school or middle-school years. Some teachers manage younger or older children better, and some develop particular expertise in dealing with the affairs of entry or leaving classes so that they are best kept with a particular section of the school. It can be argued that pupils have to learn to deal with different adults at work, and that changes of tutors at least in the senior-school help in this school preparation. The more timid and less confident pupils may need continuing contact with one adult.

Registration time is frequently a wasteful session. To take a register takes two or three minutes, and the remainder of the morning ten-minute tutorial time is frequently used then for an untidy package of tasks.

I recall with dismay visiting a comprehensive school once and joining a senior member of staff for her tutorial time. Nothing was prepared, pupils came and went freely, the teacher hurriedly prepared for her next 'proper' lesson, and the children left noisily for the next lesson, having totally wasted 20 minutes of school time. Confusion and lack of purpose are often the norm. Perhaps this is because many headteachers have not seen this time as anything other than a brief introduction to the day, and few demands have been made on staff.

There have been improvements recently in many schools, for a more purposeful content to the tutorial time is seen as setting the tone for the day's work in school, and is an opportunity for the tutor to get to know pupils and their work better. Many permutations of the time are possible: sometimes an assembly time is added to registration time to give a 20- or even 30-minute period, which gives an opportunity for more positive work; there may be a case for reducing registration time on some mornings to make a more worthwhile period of tutorial work on another day; pastoral teams may meet to plan work while pupils are at an assembly; groups may be put together to give one teacher a chance to take a discussion session, while the other teacher deals with individuals and with administration. A very satisfactory pattern in many high schools is where each form group has two 25-minute morning tutorial periods in a week, with brief 5-minute registration times on the three other mornings when assemblies are held. Forms are thus withdrawn from assembly time for their tutorial period.

A large comprehensive school of my experience actually reduced the amount of time devoted to tutorial work quite considerably. By then insisting on better preparation, and on entries in the Record of Work as with academic subjects, a far more purposeful use was made of time.

THE TUTOR'S TASK

We can now consider what the form tutor's task should be, and how this is linked with health and education for personal relationships. The following aspects of the tutor's task have been discussed in detail at many school in-service training sessions.

1. The tutorial period can represent the essence of the job of a good schoolmaster or schoolmistress, and represents the nature of good teaching. To know pupils well and to develop good relationships means that learning will flourish, with competent teaching.
2. These good relationships involve talking with and listening to children in a less formal setting and on a reasonably personal level.
3. He or she builds a family-type atmosphere in the group, using simple group work skills, as well as the effect of his or her personality.
4. The form tutor gathers and records relevant information about the pupils and ensures that administrative and welfare matters are dealt with properly. He or she will normally be the best informed member of the staff as far as knowledge of his or her group of pupils is concerned.
5. The tutor will learn to observe the pupils carefully, noting signs of ill health, of changing friendships, of hardship, attendance patterns and other matters.
6. He or she will support and enforce good order and discipline, for the two roles of counsellor and disciplinarian are compatible if a teacher is well-respected.
7. Parents of the tutor's pupils will know that he or she is available to them, and he or she should endeavour to meet them on occasions.
8. He or she will monitor general standards of work, individual progress in different academic subjects and homework.
9. The tutorial period will be carefully planned and positively used. (In considering item 9 one can now make certain assumptions):
    (a) There is co-ordination of health education in the school, including its social and moral implications

(b) The majority of this work is dealt with in subject teaching, or in special courses
(c) The tutorial groups have discussion time available to follow a limited and planned series of themes, which link with and support the work done in subject classes
(d) This planned approach to tutorial time is flexible enough to allow themes of immediate interest to pupils to be raised, or for particular worries and anxieties to be ventilated by the pupils, even if planned work is postponed
(e) There is guidance, support and in-service training for staff in tutorial work.

Tutorial Discussion

The tutorial time should not be just another teaching period; it is a time for some factual teaching but mostly it is a time for discussion and an exchange of views. Pupils develop their attitudes to human behaviour and positive health largely from their home experience and partly from their environment, by observing, listening and talking about their feelings, and thus slowly forming their own style of living. Teachers in tutorial time can help by providing evidence and opportunity for discussion in a particularly acceptable and friendly setting.

Discussion is difficult with groups of 30 children, and too often the majority of pupils listen passively to an exchange between the teacher and a few articulate children. Such listening can, of course, be useful, if minds are busy comparing and reflecting. It is better, however, to have more children contributing, for to put thoughts and feelings into words is to clarify them. If the room allows it, a class can be broken up into groups of 4–6 pupils discussing, commenting and reporting back to the class later; a panel of pupils can be used to report to the class on what has been debated in groups; half a class can discuss themes, while half do other work, and there can be a sharing of teachers' tasks in this, with a year head taking some pupils to allow a tutor a smaller discussion group. Interviews are part of the pattern also. Each child in a tutor group should have a personal interview with their year head and class tutor at intervals, perhaps whilst the class is involved in small groups or while some are working with task cards on written or oral work. The use of task cards for small group work is helpful, with cartoons, newspaper cuttings, photographs, questions and case studies stuck on cards and renewed periodically. There is ample published material as well, particularly from publications from the

Teachers' Advisory Council for Alcohol and Drug Education (TACADE) and from the Health Education Council (HEC) or from local Health Education Offices.

Developing human relationships and health matters – smoking advertisements, car accidents caused by drink, household accidents, work incidents – all provide good discussion themes. A well-trained class will regularly settle to small group work as a matter of routine, if some re-arrangement of desks is possible, or if pupils can 'clump' together somewhere. This can be fitted into a minimum of about 25 minutes, even allowing for registration and for a brief consolidation by the teacher at the end.

Lancashire teachers have devised a co-ordinated course in health, personal development, careers education and study skills for secondary years 1 to 6 (Baldwin and Wells, 1979–83). Leslie Button's (1981–2) *Group Tutoring for the Form Tutor* is another approach.

Tutorial Topics

So by teaching and discussion in class, as informally as possible, by personal interviews with individuals and pairs of pupils, and by small group work the tutor will introduce a wide variety of topics for discussion. Some topics will arise from the pupils' day-by-day concerns, some will be planned for oral work, and some will be factual and needing teaching.

One must debate, of course, how important facts and information are in PSE/health education, and how much more important are the attitudes and feelings that group work can develop under reasonably skilled leadership. So much knowledge is available that an instant dedication to memorizing discrete parts of it can seem futile at times, especially as apparent facts can change several times in a lifetime. The skills of locating, processing, assessing and controlling the use of vast areas of information may at times seem more useful. The twentieth-century Renaissance man knows how to manage infinite knowledge, not how to digest it.

Managing facts then perhaps indicates that discussion on attitudes and prejudices, feeling and experience, may be more important than a traditional teaching of facts about health, morality, social responsibility, and the wide variety of other tutorial topics that are relevant. There is a balance in these things which experienced teachers understand, though one wishes for a little more courage and boldness in tackling major social issues. The following kinds of topic may arise:

Values and morals in our lives – family rules
Learning and motivation – study skills
Family lifestyles – parenthood and childcare
Adolescence and health – maturity difficulties and moods
Authority and responsibilities – rights and duties
Society and communities – vandalism
Sexuality – boy/girl friendships
Friends and acquaintances – peer-group pressures, smoking and drinking
Personality and identity – emotions and individual differences
Communication and sociability – the language of feelings
The multicultural society – different attitudes and customs
Employment, unemployment and leisure

The tutorial discussion may offer an opportunity for pupils to discuss points heard in other lessons in a smaller group and with greater freedom, and it will be a time for further digestion of certain themes that the school deems important for living.

The following themes may be very testing for tutors in such discussion work and will need care, if indeed they are to be dealt with at all in tutorial time:

Aggression and violence
Sexually transmitted diseases and AIDS
Homosexuality and lesbianism
Deviance and abnormalities
Mental illness
Sex education (contraception, abortion, sensuality and other aspects)
Drugs and alcohol

Some schools choose to have selected tutors dealing with these themes with different groups in turn, so that some greater experience and confidence with questions will be apparent. This destroys the point of the tutor's family-group relationship, but may be necessary in some settings. The general knowledge of each tutor in a year team will almost certainly be limited where several of these themes are concerned, and pastoral heads and headteachers have to consider the quality and experience of their colleagues, and the need for more specialized work by prepared staff. This careful view of controversial subjects may inhibit the work of some staff, but may be more acceptable to parents, and to the local education authority (LEA) who have to deal with unwelcome complaints and publicity at times.

The following more traditional health themes are often dealt with poorly, or not at all, and may need to be dealt with in small groups by one tutor from a team experienced in this area of work or in occasional courses or subject teaching:

Smoking	Common ailments and illnesses
Home safety	Obesity and diet
Child development	The handicapped
Parentcraft	Community health
Suitable clothing	First aid
Cancer	Bereavement

Alternatively a lead talk can be given to all the year group by one prepared member of the team or by a teacher from a particular subject discipline, and followed up in tutorial discussion. Visiting experts may sometimes be asked to deal with a lead talk, or with visits to a series of tutorial groups or class lessons. Health visitors and health education officers are particularly helpful in this.

Discussion Methods

In such group work there will probably be questions by pupils and these must be considered with care, for mistakes can be made. A number of simple discussion techniques can be noted and Chapter 9 in this book is concerned with group work.

1. An informal setting is helpful, so that pupils can see each other as they speak. A group of 15 or 18 pupils is quite manageable, but a group of 8 or 10 often provides the best discussion opportunity.
2. Do not always interrupt when you disagree with a pupil's viewpoint, and do not attempt to answer every point raised. Members of the group will often do your answering for you.
3. Judge the right moment for intervening in discussion with your own experience, a question or a reminder of facts.
4. Do not be too provocative in order to liven up the discussion, and only give your own opinions at an appropriate moment, preferably when invited to do so by the group.
5. Help to clarify the discussion at intervals, by summarizing what has been said and what is being questioned.
6. Help shy members to contribute and restrain the over-talkative, by your interventions and by the way you look around the group.
7. Do not immediately present a group with a problem to discuss; ask them if there is a problem.
8. Keep good suggestions in the discussion by questions such as 'How would that work out . . . .?'. Do not hasten your choice of answer by

accepting the first good lead and emphasizing your agreement too quickly. Recognize all suggestions, and tolerate the irrelevant at times.

9. Fill awkward gaps by phrases such as 'Someone was asking the other day . . .' and 'John, you were saying . . .'.
10. If response is slow, consider case studies, role play, question sheets and written work.
11. Sum up at the end of a discussion going over the main points and pointing out agreements and disagreements. Finish while interest is still lively, perhaps ending with a question.

In serious discussion work with pupils many moral issues will certainly be raised and ideally the main questions will be debated by the staff themselves before they start a discussion theme with their groups. Some year heads circulate handouts to their colleagues with a summary of views, for example on boy/girl friendship or family stress, and others invite colleagues to agree on general attitudes in response to testing questions from pupils. The school's aims and objectives may be the starting point for these discussions, and while there will inevitably be widely differing personal viewpoints, a general moral response can usually be agreed. Pupils know that life is controversial and some divergence in response from teachers is not too difficult a matter.

One recalls a teacher of radical political views taking a humanities lesson and dealing with the subject of possible pupil participation in protest over chemical environmental pollution. A worried headteacher heard of this and expected complaints. In actual fact the down-to-earth common sense of a lively fifth-year class produced a first-class discussion on participation and citizenship. Pupils who had an affection for their teacher but who disagreed with some of his views argued alternative views with vigour and humour. The Head and I had underestimated the class and the teacher in fact: authority can be unduly afraid of controversy in school, yet normal life is full of controversy.

PLANNING

The introduction of improved tutorial practices, co-ordinated health education and better discussion techniques with children needs very careful planning and preparation. It is better to postpone such plans than to set off too ambitiously with ill-prepared and reluctant staff, and cynical youngsters sensing an imposed innovation.

One notes the HMI comment 'There were schools, however, of all types in which there was little evidence of substantial staff discussion about the school curriculum as a whole.' (DES, 1979, p. 210). Perhaps the climate in schools has changed since 1979? Meetings and discussions on co-ordinated programmes of work in any subject area are essential, especially in the PSE/health area, and programmes must if necessary be delayed until staff have had sufficient time to digest and debate ideas fully.

Many schools start such improvements in the lower-secondary classes, with voluntary teacher participation in a selected and keen team. This can then develop gradually through the school, involving more staff each year, and with a cohort of children accustomed to discussion work as they move up through the school. In other schools where there are few enthusiasts among the staff there can be some pilot schemes with keen voluntary teachers and selected groups of children. If the work is done well, and is seen to be useful, the idea will spread in time, if the school's leadership is positive and supportive. Critical attitudes by some staff may have to be faced, but one has seen many examples of the gradual reduction of criticism or even cynicism by a combination of careful development and preparation and accumulating evidence that such work is practical and effective.

A measure of what can be judged as effective may be the effect on learning and achievement. All pastoral care and tutorial work should contribute to an efficient school in which first-class classroom learning is the prime factor, and in which examination successes are properly valued as a part of education. So in introducing such work we should lay emphasis on the fact that a school's efficiency and its learning should be safeguarded and improved. After that we can illustrate how the ideas of positive health, personal development and other concepts follow and permeate the work, gradually proving that positive attitudes to health have a productivity measure in pupils' traditional learning and qualifications. Staff can also be shown that life is more pleasant and teacher stress reduced by careful health education and pastoral care with pupils.

When the time is appropriate in a school's development of such work, an in-service session with all the staff is useful, and such a session may be held in school time. Various devices can be used to arrange such conferences. Half the staff can be brought together for an afternoon with classes following a special timetable with the other teachers, and the process repeated on a further afternoon with a change of half the staff. Or the school may close earlier, and the staff invited to remain after the normal closing time as well. One has met many instances of both these methods being accepted and valued by staff. Teachers at the in-service session can then hear evidence from their colleagues, from visiting speakers, and even from pupils perhaps, can discuss plans, methods and materials, and develop support for and confidence in each other's work. In this way, by gradually involving more staff we can move from a simple tutorial system with few but clear demands on a few teachers to more purposeful group work by many staff, and from a tentative and simple co-ordination of health topics to a more interrelated and thematic approach, whilst still preserving academic rigour.

One school devoted two days to staff in-service work, with a quarter of the large staff freed for a morning or afternoon in turn, working on tutorial and study skills with a visiting adviser. A very difficult neighbourhood and school discipline troubles had led a small group of staff to be very cynical of in-service training, but the feelings were eased considerably through very open and frank discussions. Teachers under pressure can sometimes feel very isolated and vulnerable, and planned discussion time with their colleagues is essential.

PARENTS

The final word should be on parents. They have brought up their children in their own style of life, and most parents are caring and responsible. They must be kept informed of all our tutorial work and health education. For the children of parents who are not caring and responsible the school has a clear duty to prepare them for life in positive health and with an understanding of human behaviour as well as on cognitive matters. Other children need teachers to complement the words and actions of their parents. At a time of adolescence the family normally needs teachers not only to teach facts but also to set adult examples and to provide evidence of how people live in a difficult society where health and relationships are vitally important matters. The staff of a school, whether as class teachers or form tutors, are models to their pupils, whether they like it or not, and our professional approach is infinitely more worthwhile and enjoyable if we acknowledge this.

SUMMARY

This chapter emphasizes the wide-ranging nature of health education in schools, and relates responsibilities in this field to the pastoral system and tutorial work, this being seen as entirely complementary to the work done in classroom teaching. Appropriate methods and materials are reviewed, and particular attention is paid to the detailed work and responsibilities of the form tutor. Problem topics are discussed, and emphasis is laid on the total co-ordinated approach of a school to the personal development, both cognitive and affective, of young people.

REFERENCES AND FURTHER READING
Baldwin, J. and Wells, H. (1979–83) *Active Tutorial Work*, Basil Blackwell, Oxford.

Blackburn, K. (1983) *The Tutor*, Heinemann, London.

Button, L. (1981–2) *Group Tutoring for the Form Tutor*, Hodder & Stoughton, Sevenoaks, Kent.

David, K. (1982) *Personal and Social Education in Secondary Schools*, Longmans, London.

David, K. and Charlton, A. (1987) *The Caring Role of the Primary School* (In preparation), Macmillan, Basingstoke.

David, K. and Cowley, J. (1980) *Pastoral Care in Schools and Colleges*, Edward Arnold, London.

Department of Education and Science (1979) *Aspects of Secondary Education in England*, HMI survey, HMSO, London.

Department of Education and Science (1986) *Health Education from 5 to 16*, HMSO, London.

Hamblin, D. (1978) *The Teacher and Pastoral Care*, Basil Blackwell, Oxford.

Hamblin, D. (1984) *Pastoral Care – A Training Manual*, Basil Blackwell, Oxford.

McGuiness, J. B. (1983) *Planned Pastoral Care*, McGraw-Hill, Maidenhead.

Settle, D. and Wise, C. (1986) *Choices: Materials and Methods for PSE*, Blackwell, Oxford.

TACADE The Teachers Advisory Council on Alcohol and Drug Education, 3rd Floor, Furness House, Trafford Road, Salford M5 2XJ.

PART 4

TEACHING APPROACHES

INTRODUCTION TO PART 4

The content of what we teach has to be important, but the methods we use in the classroom can be of equal importance, for they frequently reveal our beliefs in and attitudes to that content. If we aim to influence children in their health careers, in their habits and attitudes to their personal health choices, then it is as well to discuss their own experiences of life and what they feel and fear and hope, rather than expecting only to tell them what they ought to feel and fear and hope. Health choices are as much about feelings as about information. Choosing not to smoke or experiment with drugs may have to be a lonely decision for a child or young person. An understanding of how difficult such decisions can be is as important as knowledge of the effects of smoking or experimenting with drugs; social conditions and peer pressures jostle with facts for priority.

The Teachers Advisory Council on Alcohol and Drug Education has been an influential organization in health education for many years, and has been in the forefront of informal educational methods, with many successful publications and with an excellent record of training conferences with teachers and health workers. William Rice is an executive officer in TACADE and has a national reputation as a trainer. A successful teacher, he puts his considerable experience to use in his chapter on informal methods and group work. He offers a view of the important area of methodology in health education, which in turn is part of new and more informal approaches in education generally.

Charles Wise is another experienced teacher who has worked in the health education field with the Schools Council Health Education Projects for some years before entering advisory work. He and Kenneth David have combined their views on sex education as a particular part of health education.

This area of health education often produces a wearisome reaction at times, as though sex education was some imposed subject which provokes the child population to excesses, and as though sex education was health education. Prejudiced views on sex education do an injustice to the many good teachers who respond to their pupils' needs and present balanced and careful views on sex as part of everyone's life. Health education is an infinitely wider area of education than its sex-education component.

9

WHY INFORMAL METHODS?

William Rice

PURPOSE AND PRACTICE

Voices were raised, fingers were stabbing the air, bodies were shifting in their seats, papers were being shuffled around and to any but the most unobservant, those concerned were clearly very much caught up in what they were doing.

The setting was an ordinary British Rail carriage and the topic, a smoker had lit up in a non-smoking compartment! Adopting a 'fly on the wall' role enabled me to listen and observe; to pick up the subtle and not so subtle words and gestures of those who had something to say and postures to strike. Strangely enough I linked the railway incident to a scene I had witnessed involving young people doing role play. There was the same animation and intensity, more or less the same apparent lack of involvement on the part of some of those present, roughly similar strong feelings being expressed by the leading players. Was it a case of life imitating art or vice versa? Or was I being reminded yet again of a compelling rationale for using a situationally based, informal approach to personal and social education (PSE); that is, the fairly close similarity of the learning process and context to the ordinary events of life?

The reader may well ask 'Where is the learning in such a make-believe classroom incident?' It is after all, only a piece of drama, nothing more.

Before reaching any judgements, let us return to the classroom to follow up on the role play mentioned earlier. At the conclusion of the role play, the players and observers gathered round to 'debrief' on the feelings and the facts as they were experienced by the group. The leader guided the group through an analysis of what had happened, and recorded many suggestions aimed at better resolving matters should it (the incident) perhaps occur again – in real life. What the classroom activity had attempted to do was to provide the students with a rehearsal, a chance to learn before the events actually occur. In other words, a preparation for life. In that respect the intentions are not all that different from other types of teaching although the methods certainly do differ from more traditional approaches.

I feel, therefore, that the general aims and objectives behind informal teaching methods should be readily understood. In more specific terms advocates of informal methods wish to improve students' listening and discussion skills, promote effective ways of decision-making and problem-solving, and encourage in students a sense of 'empowerment' and autonomy.

Such objectives require to be worked at through a variety of appropriate learning activities. Many of the more recent informal teaching packages contain work specially designed to contribute to the achievement of the aforementioned objectives, and others are on the way. But before discussing some of those learning activities, it may be useful to consider the views of some of those who regularly employ informal teaching methods. Their comments relate to some of the major preoccupations within the informal methods field.

Over recent years my working contact with the teaching profession (and others with an educational role) has tended to confirm a claim made by teachers themselves that informal methods are both widely known and in fairly common use. This is what one would expect given the popularity of such projects as *Active Tutorial Work* (Baldwin and Wells, 1979–83); Schools Council (1982) *Health Education Project, Life Skills Associates Materials* (Hopson and Scally, 1981) and TACADE's *Free to Choose* and *Alcohol Education Syllabus* teaching packs.

These relatively large-scale projects have been complemented by a number of handbooks which provide ideas for classroom activities and advice on methods and organization (Rice, 1981; Simnet and Ewles, 1985). Subjects other than health and personal education have also received attention from the advocates of informal methods and this widening of the front has raised awareness in the staffroom and elsewhere (DES, 1985).

During the course of my in-service work, I have often asked serving teachers to state their reasons for using or at least being favourably disposed towards informal approaches. Their replies have been most interesting and have been of much help to me in clarifying my thinking and in raising technical problems which need resolving.

CLASSROOM CLIMATE

One common reason put forward is the need somehow to create a particular type of classroom climate appropriate to the sometimes intimate and always personal tone of the topics dealt with during the teaching. It is entirely obvious that issues related to health in its broadest context are about people. Sometimes the people element gets overwhelmed by statistics, especially when they are embedded in the shorthand of the scientists: sample populations, target groups, smokers and non-smokers.

Treated in such a way, it is possible to operate on a more or less intellectual plane in which the reality somehow fails to arouse any feelings in either students or teachers. But when the teaching seeks to personalize the learning in order to look at the individuals, you and me and all the rest of the human family, it is possible that a different set of feelings and emotions begins to inform classroom activities. In those circumstances there needs to be a caring, concerned and supportive atmosphere, an atmosphere which cannot be imposed but is drawn out and nurtured from within the group (Abercrombie and Terry, 1978, pp. 4 and 5).

The Need To Share

An element of some importance in creating and sustaining a conducive climate, and one recognized by many teachers, is the need for the learning group to tap into its collective reservoir of knowledge and experience. Unless it is a most exceptional one, every group is a mixture of personalities and their differing experiences. In most learning environments there is at least one person, the teacher, who is somewhat older than the others, with all the implications of that important difference on one's point of view, sense of responsibility, maturity of judgement and so on. Even when the group appears to be homogeneous, one can sometimes find quite surprising variations in knowledge, especially in worldly wisdom; what we now refer to as 'street-wise'.

The real variety in groups can go untapped, perhaps most readily by teaching methods and styles which implicitly or explicitly hint at 'preferred' answers to problem-solving or analytical-type exercises. In such a 'closed-end' situation only the very assured or very confident student will risk disapproval or at least, misunderstanding, by honestly stating a personal and differing point of view.

In the more open (but not unstructured) methods favoured by some teachers, students are encouraged to share their convictions knowing that they will be given a hearing, quite often in an organized, systematic way.

The knowledge that one's arguments may well be (a) laughed at (b) disagreed with, and yet (c) sympathetically appraised can be an inducement for students to be their own person in the classroom, and one hopes, subsequently in the world outside. The ability to contribute to and take from a pool of human experience is a major expectation of those who engage in the more informal approaches to teaching.

Self-Regulating

Teachers frequently mention the development of a kind of *esprit de corps* among the members of a group. Some groups bring elements of such a spirit with them from the outside into the classroom (Blumberg and Golembiewski, 1976; Douglas, 1978, pp 37–41). It is highly likely that any school group will share time and interests together outside school and such ties can be very powerful and transfer readily into the classroom. It is also the case that some students may be outside the cliques, ignored at best, rejected at worst. Formal and informal methods alike require a minimum of cohesion if classroom work is to progress, but informal approaches, if they are to be successful, require a feeling of unity of purpose and the development of effective affiliations among students and attendant staff. If 'getting' from a learning environment is to be accompanied by 'giving' to that situation, if furthermore that give-and-take is to be in an atmosphere of tolerance, acceptance and care, it demands a leaving aside, at least for a time, of those allegiances which claim our loyalty in other circumstances. The effective teacher realizes the importance of co-operation in the furtherance of learning objectives and will prepare himself or herself with strategies which encourage group cohesion. Freed from competitive demands by accepting agreed classroom ground rules, students can become much more self-regulating in matters of common goal-setting and, when required, in appropriate forms of disciplining those who have wilfully disrupted the learning process (McMaster, 1982a, pp. 127–30).

Self-Directing

The agenda of any teaching programme is determined by any number of factors including, of course, examinations. In the domain of health and personal and social education, there are a great many topics of greater or lesser scale which call for attention. However, given the varying needs of young people as the result of differences in age, lifestyle, general and specific environments especially in a pluralist society, considerable care needs to be given to ways in which useful curricula are formulated. Teachers have reported on their experiences and in the best of cases seem to create a teaching programme which is a combination of self-choice (on the part of the students) and guided choice (the contribution from the staff). The notion of a needs-related teaching programme arouses a wide range of responses, from the eager, 'it's the only way to do it' teacher to those who genuinely feel that to hand the decision of what should be taught over to students is an abdication of responsibility.

In the case of quite specific subject areas such as mathematics, sciences and the humanities, trained minds and professional judgements properly lie at the heart of choices concerning curricula. However, health and PSE topics are not hidden mysteries, remote and unexplored by students. All of us have daily, indeed hourly and minute-by-minute experiences which can be reflected upon and used as bases for new learning. Because of this, many teachers have no difficulty in inviting students to be part of the process of formulating a learning programme (Kime, Schlaadt and Tritsch, 1977, pp. 10–12).

Inviting students to so join in is the easy part, having them accept the opportunity may be more difficult. It would seem that what might clinch the matter is to convince students that there are real personal gains to be made in a well-organized, competently executed health and PSE programme. There should be a utility about such schemes; an obvious practicality whose benefits are in the present as well as for the future. Learning, by definition, is a here-and-now operation but sometimes the awareness of that truth is not apparent to the learner and often the manifest outcomes of such learning lie in future phases in one's life. Informal topics and methods do have that future value but must, if they are to be taken seriously, produce present changes, however small, recognizable to and usable by the learner. Skill-based learning tends to have these characteristics. If one is to become proficient in a skill, there must be immediate feedback. This feedback is an important element in promoting motivation which in turn tends to encourage a self-directing element in the learning programme. In summary, the crucial elements are: a needs-related base, a teaching strategy aimed at meeting those needs, and learning activities which yield immediate feedback (Wiseman and Pidgeon, 1977, p. 62).

SITUATIONAL RELEVANCE

The search for relevance in teaching can produce some distorted perspectives. In the preceding section, attention was drawn to the vitally necessary 'filling in' role of the teacher in the process of developing a needs-related programme. Relevance is a transient phenomenon, not a fixed character-istic. Some needs may be very immediate, pressing and relevant, but in the larger context may justify only a modest amount of attention. Such deci-sions require a wider knowledge of human beings and life in general than is likely to be held by even late adolescents and are, in my view, the purview of the teacher.

That said, there is an obvious need to ensure that teaching which seeks to keep the whole child in mind embraces as many departments of life as is reasonable, given the many competing demands on time and resources, to say nothing about the very finite reservoirs of energy and motivation of both teachers and taught. Being reminded of the severe limitations imposed by busy timetables strongly suggests that decisions as to which aspects of life should be selected for examination must be particularly well chosen. One simply has not the luxury of adequate time in which to cover both the mundane, everyday issues *and* the esoteric, more attention-arousing circumstances which feature so prominently in *Dynasty* and in the pages of many books read by young and old! Teachers report that given the persistent concern about adolescent drug-taking, it is difficult not to overdo the time and attention given to that issue. In more general terms there is a tendency to look to the problem areas of life as sources in which one will find the desired relevant situations.

The combined pressures of adult concern (especially parents), media attention and the genuine concern of teachers to prepare young people to cope with the problems of life can, if not checked, result in an unbalanced 'diet' in which some topics such as mental health, loss and bereavement are very undertreated. Therefore in searching out a range of life situations to place under close scrutiny, care must be taken to not be overwhelmed by the problem of the moment (TACADE, 1986, pp. 10–11; SCHEP, 1982).

A BASIC STRUCTURE

All the foregoing relate to a particular basic structure that is by now fairly well-known and seems to have stood the test of time; I refer to the 'knowing, feeling and doing' formula.

Knowing is about factual information and knowledge, loosely but not very accurately identified with the cognitive aspects of learning.

A special note here is the idea of a 'core' of essentially usable knowledge about health matters, such as sexual and drug-related behaviour.

Feeling refers to the elusive world of emotions, attitudes and values. These are sometimes referred to as affective elements. Of special interest here is the growing acceptance of self-esteem as a determinant in health-related matters.

Doing is a general reference to a range of activities which include social skills. The particular point here is the current interest in and promotion of lifeskills, a wide-ranging category embracing the social skills mentioned and others such as problem-solving, and management of time and money.

This trio lies at the heart of some teaching programmes although it is seldom the case that the separate elements are clearly attached to the various exercises which constitute teaching schemes (DES, 1985, pp. 10–11). One must look closely at the component parts to identify which sections relate to one or other of the three elements in the basic formula.

Some Examples

Case studies

A useful example of how all three of the basic elements can appear in a single learning exercise may be found in a typical case study and its associated follow-up work (TACADE, 1984). Think of the usual format of case studies. There is a piece of shorter or longer prose, more or less packed with descriptions of character and behaviour, with some information about background environment thrown in for good measure. Let us say we decide to focus on the influences on the person's life. It is likely that the resulting list will consist of factual elements, some will relate to feelings, and others will hint at common skills, even if they are noticeably absent.

Follow-up work could:

Identify facts from among the other types of influences present and go on to score them as true or false understandings.

Separate positive and negative influences.

List the short- and long-term influences.

Pick up on those which relate to people as distinct from places and objects.

Identify those feelings which originate from within in contrast to those invoked by outside sources.

Focus on those influences which demand certain skills in controlling them, and so on.

The entire activity makes use of discussion, analysis, diagnostic skills, problem-solving, and with some imagination could merge into role play.

Problem-solving
Another example is the use of simple but effective co-operative problem-solving tasks. A popular version has five steps beginning with identification of the problem, clarification of the issues, collection and review of possible solutions, decisions about the most likely strategies, and finally a 'second thoughts' choice aimed at solving the problem with the least cost to all concerned; the so-called 'win-win' approach (TACADE, 1986, pp. 246–7).

As the activity is a shared one, in twos and possibly then in larger subgroups, co-operation and communication skills are foremost, in addition to those skills which are exercised in anticipating outcomes. The actual process will engage the students in presenting and, if needed, defending their case to others, perhaps in a semi-public way, in the presence of their peers. If the proposals are challenged, students will get a flavour of a particular kind of peer pressure.

In many cases problem-solving exercises will at least touch on factual knowledge, arouse a range of feelings, bring to the surface certain attitudes and possibly underlying values, and most certainly provide an opportunity to develop some very necessary skills, not the least seeking out and managing the help and advice of others. It will be up to the teacher, with knowledge of the students, to decide which aspects will receive varying degrees of attention.

Role play
How often have we heard someone say 'I wish you could see things from my point of view?' Role play is, at least on some occasions, a way of helping people to change role in order to have a new, if brief, viewpoint on life. The hope is that the insights gained through 'walking in another's shoes' will encourage among other things better understanding of people and the problems of life (Gahagan, 1978, pp. 14–16; McMaster, 1982b, p. 30).

A more specific objective is that students can try out a number of alternative strategies as part of a problem-solving exercise. An interesting example is the coping with peer-group pressures. By working through the various likely responses *in a non-threatening context*, weighing up the costs and benefits of the chosen strategies and generally settling on the most effective ones, students should be in a better position to act when the 'real thing' occurs.

Simulations, those longer and more structured role-play incidents, by reason of their greater complexity and carefully chosen built-in rules and constraints, enable participants to experience more fully the difficulties and frustrations often encountered in trying to cope with life's situations. Learning to cope with frustrations whilst continuing to find ways to manage situations are potentially useful skills for old and young alike and are difficult to develop and refine other than in the 'hands on' type of experience found in role play and simulations.

Among the important differences between 'real life' and role play/ simulations is the opportunity to rerun the incident as often as time and interest allow, searching for the most effective responses. Another is the crucial follow-on activity called *debriefing*. Debriefing is a diagnostic process during which the whys and wherefores are discussed and, very importantly, participants are encouraged to express their thoughts and feelings. Debriefing is not only diagnostic in nature, it should also assist participants to look ahead, to predict outcomes rather than simply responding after the event.

Above all, role play and simulations are methods by which certain skills are developed. In addition to those skills which relate to problem-solving and decision-making, estimating risks, making informed choices and so on, role play/simulations engage the participants in sometimes very intense social interaction in which listening and talking skills are of prime importance. Role play/simulations are valuable adjuncts to those methods which aim to assist cognitive development, and as such, can bring realism into what might otherwise be a dry-bones learning experience.

Using film

The use of the film (and video) medium is far from new. Secondary teachers were among the first to make use of what were then educational innovations. A proportion of films are intended to convey messages the acceptance of which is the reason for showing them to students. Some teachers, whilst endorsing the message of a film, may wish to use the opportunity to explore with students the methods used in the film to put forward the message. Right away then, two possible applications of film can be seen; the implicit/explicit purpose of the film, and an analysis of the persuasive techniques employed. By ensuring that the latter is attended to the possible gains from the use of visual media are increased (DHSS, 1986).

In recent years a quite different type of educational film has appeared, the so-called 'trigger' films. These are open-ended in that no firm conclusion is reached. The film does not terminate with an ending, it just fades out, leaving the viewers to provide their own ending. The value of this format is obvious. Whereas the film with an endpiece may still be subjected to analyses of both content and methods as well as a critical appraisal of the message, it requires more effort emotionally to involve the viewers. Triggers, if reasonably adequate examples of the genre, just ask for the viewers to follow through the action and add their own conclusion.

The format of trigger films is such that a fairly short film (usually no longer than ten minutes) with a simple story line, can assume a variety of meanings when added to by the creative imagination of a group of students. By the very same token, trigger films need thoughtful handling. The absence of a clear message can, for some viewers, be confusing. Others may interpret the apparent lack of conclusiveness as indicating an absence of firm knowledge concerning the subject matter of the film. Care must be taken to anticipate such perceptions, and students encouraged to understand both the content matter of a trigger film *and* the reason for its particular format. All of these suggestions clearly indicate a need for careful planning and preparation, and adequate time set aside for the best use of the medium.

Learning games

Space does not permit more than a brief mention of what some people regard, mistakenly, as the newest addition to informal methods. Learning games are, in fact, among the oldest methods. The games played by children often contain, in implicit forms, elements commonly found in aspects of everyday life. Games often touch on themes such as co-operation and competition, support and isolation, giving and getting; the list is really extensive.

Sometimes games can be used to engage students usefully in an exploration of issues too sensitive or difficult to tackle by more conventional approaches. Two fairly common examples should highlight the preceding points.

'Ice-breakers' are usually quite brief episodes used to break down those natural barriers found in new or recently formed social groups. The reason for seeking to break down those barriers is to speed up the 'gelling' process necessary for groups to work effectively to achieve common aims. There is nothing to prevent the teacher simply asking the group to set aside consciously their initially somewhat defensive posture but that might result in a stiffening of that defensiveness.

By engaging in an appropriate ice-breaker, the members immediately find themselves in a shared experience whose purpose may be a bit obscure. Any resistance feelings tend to be directed towards the instigator of the exercise and not at the group. During the debriefing all is revealed, that is, the purpose and rationale of the ice-breaker are openly discussed. The end result is usually a loosening up among the group and residual feelings of annoyance about the activity itself tends to diminish within a short time.

The game 'Broken Squares' provides an example of another set of learning experiences. The game consists of small groups working together to complete a number of squares using small, irregularly shaped pieces of paper. When correctly fitted together the pieces form a square. The problem is that all negotiations among the group members must be carried out without talking, signing or doing drawings. The game is about co-operation with a strong likelihood of competition creeping in.

To say it is about co-operation is to run the risk of missing out a range of important secondary themes such as leadership styles and perhaps less complimentary, non-leader styles. As with the Ice-breaker, the teacher could be quite direct and open about the purposes of Broken Squares but we have to ask what effect would that openness have on a typical group. How many people would more or less publicly respond to questions about one's leadership qualities or apparent lack of them? Again, the 'game' element comes to our aid. We can join in an activity with a serious purpose in a fun way, a quality which somehow protects our feelings whilst allowing us to learn if we choose to do so.

Scope for imagination

Probably all of the qualities mentioned in connection with the preceding methods are found in other informal methods. Puppetry of all kinds, mime, art forms, 'construction' activities in which certain provided items are juxtaposed to provide environments which in turn become the context for situations and events; all are capable of providing opportunities for creative thought and learning that is rich in insights.

Although these are unconventional methods, they should nevertheless be subjected to all the rules and principles applied to more familiar approaches. We should still be able to ask (and answer) questions about aims and objectives, evaluation and review. Conventional and unconventional methods alike should 'fit' the needs of students and be within the competence of the teacher. Apart from these considerations, your creative imagination is at a premium in the search for effective informal teaching methods.

A Practical Example

One school known to me made excellent use of its extracurricular 'clubs', the music, drama and the cine/video clubs, to supplement the health-education programme. It began when the health-education team concluded that the visual material on drug-taking then available was not really what was needed for their purposes. Someone had the idea of arranging a round-table discussion on this lack of resources. Arising out of that first meeting came the collaboration of the two groups mentioned with background support from the science and English departments. A script was prepared (checked and rechecked by the language specialists!) and subsequently dramatized and rehearsed by the drama group. In due course the playlet was put on tape, complete with incidental music. Quite apart from all the benefits accumulated during the various phases of planning, developing and finally, filming, the finished article had a 'feel' to it, an immediacy and indeed, sincerity that was very appealing. The end-product consisted of a short video and a series of suggested follow-up questions and activities, some of the latter also featured on video, a story within a story format.

From the onlooker's point of view, one could see practical problem-solving in action; how the interest of the students was fired; the encouraging way in which time outside the school day was given by staff and students to the project; and the way in which the thinking of the students concerning drugs was built into the script and the visual treatment.

The theme of the video is of some interest. It was about the way in which the promised and expected benefits of drug-taking often prove not only illusory but are quite the opposite of what can actually happen.

There is no need here to include a list of teaching/learning methods used during the project outlined, but the list is long and every item of proven educational worth. It might be an interesting diversion for readers to think about what methods and related activities might have been used during the preparation of the project.

EVALUATION

Recently, I came across the following statement preceding a learning activity: 'Objective (of the activity): I can see that different people have different points of view.' This must surely be a difficult objective to evaluate and, more importantly, therefore of little help to the teacher who wants to know whether the teaching is of benefit to the pupils, and if so, what form that 'benefit' takes.

The subject of evaluation, perhaps particularly in health education, is complex and, in parts, highly controversial. Given the limits of this chapter, one can only hope to offer the briefest of comment in the simplest of terms and to do so from a personal standpoint. The basic definition adopted by me is: 'Evaluation is a systematic process of determining the extent to which education objectives are achieved by pupils' (Grunland, 1971, p. 8).

There appears to be an evaluation continuum; at one end there are those who wish to evaluate everything done under the name of education, and at the other extreme are those who argue for the importance of process in education and are less concerned with outcomes. My stance is somewhere near the middle of that continuum.

My starting point is the desire/need to be as certain as possible that scarce time and resources are used in ways most likely to bring benefit to the learners. To reach such conclusions we need to be able in some way to evaluate what is being done. One can go further and say that parents, pupils and teachers alike have a right to expect utility and relevance in education and in informal educational methods that these qualities should be open to evaluation and assessment by appropriate means.

Arising out of that viewpoint and, on a purely practical level, is the question of framing one's objectives. Assuming that by some sound means one has determined the needs of pupils, generated a range of appropriate objectives and set about creating a curriculum likely to assist pupils to achieve those objectives. So far so good. This is the point where we began: the importance of somehow expressing objectives in clear and assessable terms.

In the 1930s, Ralph Tyler promoted a concept which ever afterwards influenced evaluation studies. Tyler stated that 'One can define an objective with sufficient clarity if he can describe or illustrate the kind of behavior the student is expected to acquire so that one could recognize such behavior if he saw it' (Tyler, 1949, p. 59–60).

The person who framed the objective quoted earlier obviously did not use Tyler's thinking to guide him. Those teachers who work hard at transposing objectives into behavioural versions of the same, make use of *action verbs*. A list of such verbs is likely to include:

   identify, recognize, define, recall, explain, list, assemble, estimate,
      match, select, create.

For most people these terms have a concrete feel about them and as such provide an important and yet often overlooked factor in evaluation, a consensus among those concerned; in brief, sharing a common terminology. Evaluation, being the process of determining the worth of something, must make use at some point of measurements. Measurements in evaluation are concerned with defining dimensions, extent and capacity of something. For measurements to be useful, they must be valid, reliable and practical in their application.

Returning briefly to an earlier reference to the 'knowing, feeling and doing' components of PSE curricula, one is reminded of the many problems to be faced in measuring achievement in those domains so exhaustively researched by Bloom, whose typologies remain with us today: cognitive, affective and psychomotor (Bloom, 1956).

Because of the great likelihood of variability in the learners, and in the context of PSE especially in the latter two categories, measurements of pupil achievement are based on some suitable agreed criteria rather than on a bench mark of what is claimed to be a norm of achievement. To construct a criterion-referenced measurement as part of an evaluation is not easy, but it is made more manageable when teachers know their pupils in the fullest sense of the term (Dick and Carey, 1978, pp. 78–80).

However, the nature of PSE work means that at the present time there are some important objectives that are not assessable. For example, teaching and learning about attitudes, and especially where shifts in attitudes are the hoped-for objectives, may be a long time in reaching fruition, if at all. We could just accept the situation, do our best, and hope!

Another approach would be to look for behaviours, currently assessable, which could be predictors of the long-term objectives. Evaluating by proxy, as it were, may be the best we can do in certain circumstances (Hamilton *et al.*, 1977, p. 57).

Experience tells us that there remain certain goals which are so long-term in relation to school, that evaluation by proxy is either simply not possible or, at best, speculative. The practicalities of teaching strongly force upon us the acceptance that *all* objectives need not be behavioural and open to assessment. However, unless the majority of our chosen objectives are capable of being evaluated we will find ourselves forever trying to defend what may be, if we could actually know it, the indefensible. Worse still, if the non-assessable objectives are dominant, that is, in the majority, we may not even know in which direction we are pointing our pupils.

One other aspect needs some comment, I refer to the desirability of evaluating any creative work of our own. In my view there is reason to believe that a proportion of those who teach PSE in its various forms and topic areas tend to adapt materials rather than closely follow the exact format of published programmes.

This is to be applauded but one should recognize that a cost could be a loss of some effectiveness. To explain this statement, mention must be made to the now common practice of writers of new materials to carry out field-testing, sometimes of an extensive kind. Too radical a departure from the prepared version, especially when prompted by expediency (and other, less worthy motives), may result in a less effective format (possibly due to the return of old errors which may have been removed during the trials).

Therefore, the innovative teacher should, from time to time, set up his or her own evaluation procedure. What follows is by way of a simple set of suggested procedures. The suggestions assume that teachers will wish to make use of a formative type evaluation; the 'while it's happening' type as distinct from summative evaluation, the 'after it's happened' format.

First Step: One-to-one evaluation. The teacher selects one or two pupils who are typical of the larger audience and personally observes the pupils at work on the trial material. Using this approach, teachers can pick up more readily on errors of commission and omission, time taken, unclear instructions and so on. Students may also give you a report on their *feelings* during the process. One-to-one exercises could also involve an outsider, for example, a teacher colleague or an outside expert, say on content.

Second Step: Small-group evaluation. As a result of the first evaluation, you may feel that you have an effective learning activity. You wish to refine it further before 'going public'. Select a small group (number should be in proportion to the total class size) of representative pupils. Care should be taken to ensure the truly representative character of those selected. 'Small-group' here refers to the number and not necessarily to the setting. If the materials are intended to form part of homework assignments, or project work, which would not ordinarily be conducted in a small-group format, then, clearly, those are the conditions under which the evaluation should take place. One-to-One and Small-Group evaluations should be carried out as close to 'real' settings as possible – if otherwise, why bother?

Third Step: Field evaluation. By now you are even more convinced of the potential of the materials and/or methods. You now wish to do a full-size trial with a class-sized group in the appropriate setting. As before selecting the group is of crucial importance. It is so easy to 'trial' new materials encompassing newer methods with students familiar with the genre – and so you may get a biased, if encouraging, evaluation report. Similarly, trialling new and say, informal, approaches with pupils familiar only with formal methods could well lead to a faulty read-out. The motto is 'Choose with care'.

The Next Step: Throw caution to the winds! If your work, which at each successive stage has been revamped to a greater or lesser extent, continues to impress you (and, by now, others), you should be in a position to open up the materials for others to use. If you are fortunate, someone will come along to carry out a summative evaluation, with all the paraphernalia of pre- and post-tests, arguments about validity and reliability and so forth. You may, at that stage, say to yourself 'I've cracked it' or, it may be a case of 'Back to the drawing-board'.

A TAILPIECE

By way of an ending, another little classroom vignette:

A group of third year girls had just finished testing a new drug-education board game – which had not worked too well – so the mood was not euphoric.

In answer to the question 'What, if anything, do you like about this particular group?' back came the swift response from one girl, 'They listen to you. We have arguments (smiles and titters) but you matter.'

The questioner could only nod to show his understanding, and his approval.

REFERENCES

Abercrombie, M. L. J. (1960) *The Anatomy of Judgement*, Penguin, Harmondsworth.

Abercrombie, M. L. J. and Terry, P. M. (1978) *Talking To Learn*, Society for Research into Higher Education, University of Surrey, Guildford.

Baldwin, J. and Wells, H. (1979–83) *Active Tutorial Work*, Blackwell, Oxford.

Bloom, B. S. (ed.) (1956) *Taxonomy of Educational Objectives*, Longmans, Harlow.

Blumberg, A. and Golembiewski, R. T. (1976) *Learning and Change in Groups*, Penguin, Harmondsworth.

Department of Education and Science (1985) *The Curriculum from 5 to 16*, HMSO, London.

Department of Health and Social Services (1986) *Double Take* videos and their accompanying teaching notes provide useful examples of how film material may be used in the classroom. Available from CFL Vision and TACADE.

Dick, W. and Carey, L. (1978) *The Systematic Design of Instruction*, Scott Foresman & Co., Glenview IL.

Douglas, T. (1978) *Basic Groupwork*, Tavistock, London.

Gahagan, J. (1978) *Interpersonal and Group Behaviour*, Essential Psychology Series, Methuen, London.

Grunland, N. (1971) *Measurement and Evaluation in Teaching*, 2nd edn, Macmillan, New York.

Hamilton, D., Jenkins, D., King, C., McDonald, B. and Parlett, M. (eds) (1977) *Beyond the Numbers Game*, Macmillan Education, Basingstoke.

Hopson, B. and Scally, M. (1981) *Lifeskills Teaching*, McGraw-Hill, Maidenhead.

Kime, R. E., Schlaadt, R. G. and Tritsch, L. E. (1977) *Health Instruction: An Actional Approach*, Prentice-Hall, Englewood Cliffs, NJ.

McMaster, Mc. J. (ed.) (1982a) *Methods in Social and Educational Caring*, Gower, Aldershot.

McMaster, Mc. J. (ed.) (1982b) *Skills in Social and Educational Caring*, Gower, Aldershot.

Rice, W. (1981) *Informal Methods in Health and Social Education*, TACADE, Salford.

Schools Councils (SCHEP) (1982) *Health Education 13–18, Introductory Handbook*, Forbes, London.

Simnet, I. and Ewles, L. (1985) *Promoting Health: A Practical Guide to Health Education*, John Wiley, Chichester.

TACADE (1984) *Free to Choose, Unit 3. The Story of Carol. PM. 2*, TACADE, Salford.

TACADE (1986) *Skills for Adolescence, Teachers' Manual*, TACADE, Salford.

Tyler, R. W. (1949) *Basic Principles of Curriculum and Instruction*, University of Chicago Press.

Wiseman, S. and Pidgeon, D. (1977) Project Evaluation, in Hamilton, D. *et al.* (eds), op. cit.

CHALLENGES FOR SEX EDUCATION IN SCHOOLS

Kenneth David and Charles Wise

INTRODUCTION

The label 'sex education' sometimes arouses high emotions, particularly in terms of personal and communal rights and responsibilities. Whilst the family has a major potential to offer advice, guidance and support to young people in sexual matters, schools clearly have their part to play, in our opinion. This can lead to critical argument about the way teachers approach sex education, and this we consider in this chapter.

Young people are sexual beings, and there can be a mythology which presumes that sexual feelings cannot exist or should be suppressed until it is convenient for the adult world to accept them. If one adopts this stance of 'adults know best', young people may as they get older, reject the messages which are being offered 'in their best interest'. This conventional adult-imposed teaching of sex may, at best, be ineffectual and, at worst, be detrimental to a young person's healthy development. One has to accept the freedom of choice which young people have on a range of sexual matters, but encourage them to make responsible informed decisions that are in the best interest of themselves and others. We are concerned with education, not with indoctrination, therefore the 'right' answer may be neither available nor desirable. This sentiment may be viewed as an abdication of responsibility on the part of the teacher, but those who are successful in this aspect of education are likely to have made a positive contribution in highlighting the importance of caring sexual relationships.

Sex is not a curse but one of the exciting and fulfilling experiences of life. Sometimes adults express their anxiety about teenage sexuality in such a way as to convey the view that growing up although inevitable is somewhat inconvenient to them. The notion of 'deferred gratification' dominates the view of some adults who fail to acknowledge the growing sexual awareness of adolescence and who merely wish young people to 'wait until they are older' (for what is sometimes not discussed).

We are concerned with values rather than rules, with discussion as much as teaching, with implications rather than conclusions; and ideally there will be a partnership between the family and the school.

The Department of Education and Science draft circular *Sex Education at School* (DES, 1986a) has been widely debated at the time of writing in an emotional and sometimes exaggerated manner. In Parliament and in media comment one would imagine that sex education was a major and dramatic extra subject. In fact, in the majority of schools in our experience it is a normal part of wider personal and social education or health education programmes, taught in an undramatic way by concerned and caring teachers. A minority of teachers and local education authorities (as in other professions and organizations, perhaps) have taken extreme views on elements of sex education, and have been quoted as though their views and methods were general practice, which is unfortunate.

There is little that most teachers would disagree with in the draft circular. We commend sex education being subsumed in a broader programme of personal and social education or health education. We agree that schools should not challenge or seek to undermine family relationships. The importance of personal integrity and the significance of moral values should be recognized, as should the risks of sexual promiscuity. Matters about which many people have strong and deeply held views, such as sexually transmitted diseases (including AIDS), abortion, homosexuality and the issues raised by contraception, should not be avoided.

The recently announced (1986) programme of publicity about AIDS makes explicit many matters which teachers have for a long time recognized as a growing concern for young people in society. Teachers must suffer having their experienced and common-sense attitude to sex education invested with a new political originality at times.

LOCATING THE TERRITORY

The Family, Sex and Sexuality

Sex education is not a singular crusade undertaken solely by those with a calling, but happens all the time, both within and outside family life, as the result of accidental, incidental and planned experiences. The way that people behave within a family, and their attitudes to sex, must obviously affect the attitudes of their children. Families shape their children in so many ways: sex roles can be learned by a child from the masculinity and femininity of parents; emotional responsiveness can be developed by the amount of touching of children that takes place in a loving family. Loving is a demonstrative action, and one often learns to love through seeing people who are loving, and being loved gives one some ability to give back love.

The caring family – despite the obvious 'failings' which occur from time to time – lays the foundation for a child to be able to cope with new situations as they arise; the uncaring family may give rise to a young person who is overdemanding, in need of constant reassurance or has doubts and fears about sexual matters.

Aims and Objectives

Some 40 years ago, Bibby (1945) writing about the aims of sex education argued

> that our people should grow up learning the appropriate facts in the best possible way; that their general attitude to sex should be a completely healthy one; that they should draw up for themselves a code of conduct after careful consideration of all the issues involved and should endeavour to behave according to this rationally determined code; and that they should react to the behaviour of others with sympathy, tolerance and charity, but without spineless acquiescence in a code inferior to their own.

This all-embracing statement expresses a clear moral message about the way one should conduct one's life, but the teacher will need to translate the words in more specific aims.

Over the years, individual schools and local education and health authorities have produced guidelines or statements relating to the purpose of planned school sex education. One LEA expressed its aims for sex education for first-year secondary-school pupils (11–12-year-olds) as:
1. To give a simple account of the facts of reproduction, in a setting of family life or of caring relationships
2. To prepare pupils for the changes of puberty so that they will appreciate that what is happening to them is perfectly normal
3. To encourage a sense of wonder in the creation of a new life, and to help them to develop a proper attitude towards reproduction
4. To satisfy the natural curiosity of pupils as far as it can be done at this age, and to give reassurance by emphasizing normality

One school expressed its sex-education programme for fourth-year pupils (14–15-year-olds) as:

1. The physical structure of our bodies with particular reference to the reproductive and glandular systems
2. A simple view of genetics
3. Intercourse, the growth of the embryo and fetus, birth, and some understanding of prenatal and antenatal care
4. An understanding of the physical and social implications of contraception; world population studies
5. The paramount importance of parental care, or of enduring adult models
6. Child growth and development, adolescence and puberty, and the link with adult maturity
7. Boy-girl relationships and courtship
8. Sex roles in our society and the sexual aspects of marriage

It should be emphasized that although there may be pressure for prescriptive or definitive statements relating to the teaching of sex education, each individual and group within a school has its own distinctive and unique needs and interests. Cultural, ethnic and religious differences within a group may be apparent or well-known, but the teacher should also show respect for personal circumstances, for example, family situations, maturation and friendship groups.

The Components of Human Sexuality

In common parlance, the word *sex* may be viewed as concerned solely with a physical act, but it represents a part of the totality of human sexuality. Perhaps the word *sexuality* is more apt because it indicates the various dimensions of one's life. Some aspects of sexuality are inherited whilst others are related to the environment in which one grows, for example, sex roles are learned from peers, parents, other adults and through the media.

Bruess and Greenberg (1981) suggest that there is no one way to define the complex concept of human sexuality but offer a framework of four interrelated components (Figure 10.1). The *social* component of sexuality is the sum of cultural influences upon our thoughts and actions, and social influences provide powerful messages for a child's growing view of maleness and femaleness.

The *psychological* component represents the learned aspects of sexuality from birth to death, whilst the *moral* component is associated with notions of 'right' and 'wrong' underpinned by humanistic or religious belief. The *biological* component contains labels which are viewed by some people as dominating human sexuality. However, to view these components as a

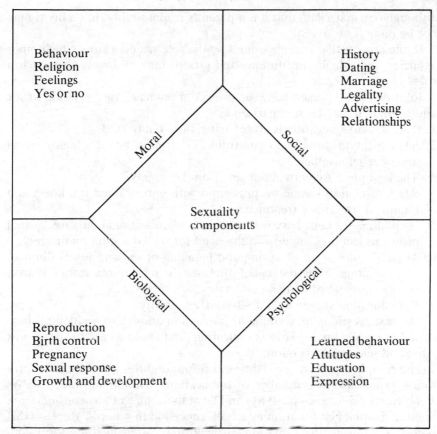

Figure 10.1 Four major components of human sexuality (from Bruess and Greenberg, 1981)

hierarchy would be wrong as together they must represent a more complete view of human sexuality.

Sex Education as a Shared Responsibility

The debate as to whether the sex education of children is the sole responsibility of parents has been a long and tortuous one. One could argue that even if the proposition were desirable it is not feasible, for young people are exposed to influences beyond the home over which parents have little or no control. Furthermore, some parents do not wish to be formally involved as sex educators with their children; such an arrangement may or may not suit either party (Lawton, 1985). For whatever reason, the proportion of children who receive no formal sex education at home is high, and although one may claim that it is a parent's responsibility, in reality it may not be done (Lee, 1983).

If one accepts that parents cannot be the sole sex educators which other agencies, individuals, institutions and groups may be involved in such a role?

Johnson (1968) presented seven prevalent points of view relating to sex education that may be summarized as:

1. The best sex education is no sex education of any kind.
2. Sex education should be quite frank, but it must be on a highly moral and/or religious plane.
3. The best place to learn about sex is on the streets.
4. Sex information should be presented with unrestrained frankness and bluntness (the shock treatment).
5. If children are kept busy with healthy and educational pursuits, sexual problems can be avoided and the need for sex education minimized.
6. There should be an accepting and blending of sex and love in human life, resulting from the belief that sex is a foremost rather than a rearmost aspect of human personality.
7. Sex education should be a do-it-yourself activity.

These suggestions may stimulate discussion about the accidental, incidental or planned nature of sex education, and about a case for or against adult and school intervention.

The complexity of whose rights and responsibilities are legitimate have found expression in a number of publications (Dominian, 1977; NCW, 1984; Responsible Society, 1981) and lie at the centre of any consideration regarding a planned programme of sex education in schools. Recent HMI reports relating to the provision of health education in some local education authorities comment upon the need for a partnership between parents, the community and the school.

Sex Education as a Concern of the School

In recent years, a number of government department publications have indicated that sex education may be considered as part of the school curriculum, although there are no mandatory powers to enforce its inclusion (DES, 1981a; 1986b).

Under Section 8 of the Education Act 1980 parents have the right to know the context and manner in which a school deals with sexual matters, but they are not offered the right to withdraw their children (DES, 1981b). However, the involvement of parents is encouraged to reduce unnecessary conflict and respond positively to the perceived needs and interests of young people. It is clearly difficult to gain total parental agreement on what should or should not be included as 'sex education' in view of the widely different family backgrounds found in any one school.

One of the potential strengths of the school's involvement is that it can provide a trusting environment in which children learn to respect and tolerate differences and to recognize and perhaps understand many human aspirations and fears, and the challenge for the school may be to develop an agenda which complements and supplements the family-based advice, guidance and instruction, and compensates for omissions.

Whilst Reid (1982) reports an increase in formal sex education in schools during recent years, there is little reliable evidence of the quality of learning and teaching provided by schools. There remain, of course, counter-arguments which object to the school's intervention (Hayton, 1985). One of the greatest challenges for the teacher may be to decide *whose* attitudes, beliefs and values, and behaviours represent an acceptable view to a range of interested parties as to what constitutes 'sex education'. If one accepts that there is no universal code of sexual behaviour, what position does the teacher take?

The diversity of family backgrounds in a school or community cannot be reflected in any one family, so the school may have an important role to play in providing a forum in which tolerance and sharing of experience may be promoted in a multicultural society.

ISSUES FOR RESOLUTION

If the school wishes to evaluate its current provision or to start the preparation of a planned programme, the following issues can provide points for consideration.

It is relatively easy to talk about sex education in the abstract, but with time as a scarce resource, teachers and trainers may use these statements to trigger discussion and as an aid to planning an agenda. The statements (which do not necessarily reflect our standpoint) may also provide stimulus material for student debate.

Sex Education Is More than the Transmission of Biological Facts

To equate sex education solely with factual information is like viewing geography in terms of national boundaries, history as a chronology of battle dates, and drama as the reading of playscripts. Whilst each represents a part of the whole, in themselves they represent an incomplete view of the whole. Bibby (1945) states that:

> A study of ancient or contemporary history, or even a superficial knowledge of the lives of one's acquaintances, will rapidly dispel any illusion that there is necessarily a close correlation between the extent of an individual's biological knowledge, and the excellence of his actions.

More recently Reid (1982) indicated that the transmission of factual information is unlikely *in itself* to have a positive effect upon sexual behaviour. The occurrence of unwanted teenage pregnancies, does not necessarily result from lack of knowledge but may be more closely allied to attitudes, beliefs, and values, personal motivation and the context in which one finds onself.

However, biological facts are important as they provide an important element in informed decision-making. To withhold facts from young people may be an expression of neglect rather than care in the hope that ignorance and innocence are in some way related.

If the school claims to be a caring and health-promoting institution, one owes it to young people to dispel myths, eradicate 'old wives tales' and to reduce the anxiety induced by doubt and uncertainty.

> DES, DHSS, local education authorities and FPA policy statements all advocate providing sex education within the context of personal relationships, as opposed to dispensing purely biological information.
>
> (FPA, 1984 Fact Sheet D3)

Sex Education May Appear in Many Places Within the Curriculum

In terms of location, planned sex education may be found in one or more of the following places within the curriculum
1. Sex education within one subject area, for example biology
2. Sex education within a group of subject areas or faculty, for example geography, history, and religious education, or the humanities
3. Sex education within a health-education course or programme
4. Sex education within a careers, health, moral, political and social education course or programme
5. Sex education as a series of short courses or 'one-off' events
6. Sex education as an integral part of all subject areas or faculties
7. Sex education within the tutorial provision or pastoral curriculum
   One or more of these patterns may be provided for one or more years in a school. Sex education will be provided through not only the formal

curriculum but the hidden curriculum. In some schools sex education appears under such labels as 'Family Life Education', 'Preparation for Parenthood', 'Design for Living', or other descriptions.

Gordon (1981) believes that sex education should more appropriately be entitled 'Family Life Education' and must include the following principles:
1. Enhancing the self-concept
2. Preparation for marriage and parenthood
3. Understanding love
4. Preparation for making responsible decisions
5. Helping people understand the need for equal opportunities
6. Helping people develop tolerance and appreciation for people
7. Contributing to knowledge and understanding of the sexual dimension of our lives

Pugh (1980) and Whitfield (1980) advocate the inclusion of Family Life Education in the curriculum of all children. The concepts used should fall within the experience of young people rather than be viewed as an area of academic study. In any scheme of sex education one has to guard against the temptation to give complicated explanations for which young people are not ready.

Sex Education Is a Continuous Process Throughout School

Sex education may be formally introduced in the primary school, for this may be the best place to lay the foundations of sexual knowledge and when basic knowledge can be put over in the same way that so much other knowledge is given.

It is often the case that girls reach puberty whilst still in the junior school, and it is necessary for boys and girls of this age to have a simple understanding of the body changes at puberty. There are junior classes where girls experience their first menstruation without any preparation from parents. Again with sensible attitudes and safeguarding a sense of privacy, teachers can help pupils to accept this bodily development as part of the normal process of growing up.

It is advisable that parents be invited to enter into partnership with the school and an explanation of proposals for planned sex education is offered. A PTA or parents' meeting may be an ideal occasion on which to display one's outline plans, to exhibit booklets or written materials and to show any films, slides and video which one proposes to use. The Schools Radio and Television programmes provide excellent materials which with the use of a video facility may be incorporated into a planned scheme of work. It is, however, particularly important that audiovisual aids are not seen as the sole teaching medium as there are other rich resources within and outside the school, for example, family albums, books, magazine articles, newspaper cuttings, photographs and the young person's own experience.

In secondary schools sex education can be part of a general programme of health education or personal and social education (PSE). It is better if the sex education section of the PSE programme is dealt with as soon as possible after children enter the secondary school. They are coming into a different setting, more formal and structured than in the primary school, and with the influence of older children who may have a robust view on sexual matters. If, in the first term, one can give short courses, children at a formative stage will have a knowledge of how the adult community can put into perspective the muddled knowledge of sex which children will be absorbing from many sources. One need not set this at too high a level of sophistication, though children in the first year of secondary school are already asking questions and sometimes have adult attitudes and views. It is better to relate all that is done to a family-life setting, and some in-service training in how to do this will be helpful for all teachers who take such courses.

It is helpful to consider carefully the way in which one is to work with young people. The teacher will aim to create an atmosphere in which all those present feel secure and contribute willingly to discussion, showing respect for the feelings of others.

It is reasonable to relate sexual information to maternal, paternal and protective feelings. All the time one should endeavour to give children a feeling that sex is important and human, and involves caring, and relate scientific information to human feelings and family relationships.

Children are naturally curious and may ask questions about abnormalities and disasters, as well as about healthy development. Two tension points in the teaching are often sexual intercourse and birth, and teachers will usually lead up to these points gradually and make them logical conclusions of sexual and caring relationships. One has to remember pupils' inexperience in emotional and relationship terms, though it is surprising how many 11- and 12-year-olds have already seen or sensed depths of sexual experience in their families; in the same class may be pupils who have had a very sheltered upbringing. The teacher has to aim to help children in both situations without either boring one or frightening the other.

One should encourage humour and laughter at appropriate moments for this can often be a good break in tension; and most teachers will anticipate those parts of the work which may produce sniggers or embarrassment by taking care to emphasize normality, giving children the feeling that sexual matters are proper and adult themes which people can discuss rationally.

The work done in sex education in the first year may be reiterated in subsequent years of secondary education, but should reflect the growing independence of the adolescent. Increasingly young people will ask more demanding questions and expect an adult response. No questions should be avoided, *but* where these impinge upon the teacher's or another person's private world, the occasion should be used to clarify the boundaries between everyone's private and public world. The reasons for not answering all questions can in itself be the subject of discussion.

Sex Education Should Not Cause Personal Hurt or Offence

In any class, it is possible that some members have fantasies and misinformation relating to human sexuality. Also, whatever the age group, there will be some children with personal problems in their homes. Thus the view that the teacher may have about what constitutes 'normal' family life may be put to the test by those before him or her.

One's aim is not to offer an unattainable ideal in family life, but all the time to offer the best of models, emphasizing respect for parents who do not reach these models. A child may have knowledge of ugly and exploitive behaviour in a family setting; the teacher, in speaking of difficult matters may not condemn, but will offer alternatives and offer explanations of why humans fail to reach high standards of behaviour. There are many different kinds of family values, and sexual behaviour is essentially a private matter with standards that are set in each marriage partnership; this need not stop us talking of caring behaviour and common values.

Sensitive teachers will not avoid issues and the way they deal with them can in itself give security; sensitive children may be given additional individual advice, counselling or support.

In the early stages of group life, it may be useful to have a box for anonymous questions for those pupils who have worries or queries which they do not wish to reveal publicly. The teacher will be able to consider the response beforehand and avoid any indications as to the possible source.

Sex Education Is for Boys and Girls Irrespective of their Academic Ability

In a coeducational school, the case for or against the separateness of boys and girls for sex education lessons may be of lesser importance than whether or not both sexes participate in a school programme.

In some schools, the least able girls in the upper school through their curricular option choice, experience a plethora of sex education-related modules or units through childcare and development, human or social biology and home economics. Perhaps there is an assumption that this category is more vulnerable to unwanted teenage pregnancies than others. To consider sex education in terms of the prevention of pregnancy is yet another incomplete way of assessing needs and the sexist and academic overtones are clearly apparent!

Many, if not all, of the issues relating to human sexuality demand the attention of both sexes. Sex education may include consideration of the theory and practice of the Sex Discrimination Act (1975) upon the lives of young people in terms of advertising, employment, education, the provision of housing, facilities and services, family life, and taxation. The Equal Opportunities Commission, established in response to the Act, may supply some interesting insights into potential and real discriminatory practices. The school through its curricular provision may transmit powerful messages to boys and girls as do the day-to-day administrative and organizational arrangements.

Sex Education Emphasizes the Likelihood that Young People Will Experience Differing Rates of Physiological, Psychological and Social Development

Within any age group there are likely to be physical differences in terms of appearance and behaviours. For some young people there is an acceptance of this situation but in others there is an unease which may range from bewilderment to self-destructive introspection. To reassure them that their uniqueness is to be highly valued and to offer support for those who remain unconvinced may be one of the greatest kindnesses that any individual and groups can offer.

A glance in the mirror and comparison with peers may evoke the question 'Am I normal?'. It may be helpful to encourage the notion of 'normality of difference' (Settle and Wise, 1986), where the individual recognizes and values the uniqueness of himself or herself and others.

The age of consent is unlikely to accommodate the desires, drives and impulses of all those concerned, but is an example of where a legal system tries to protect the sexuality of young people by treating an age group in a similar way.

There are indications that aspects of sex education are dealt with too late (FPA, 1984, Fact Sheet D2), but there are a number of issues of an ethical, moral and religious nature that influence teachers as to whether they should include some aspects of sex education in a school programme. Apart from these issues, the teacher's view of a child's conceptual development may influence the course of study; for example an eight-year-old may not be able to conceptualize aspects of birth control.

Sex Education Should Be Responsive to the Felt Needs of Young People

An overdependence upon adult experience may bore the young learner and may not accurately reflect his or her current experience. The teacher who provides lucid accounts of the way things 'are' may be indulging in a dangerous form of self-delusion.

One of the primary sources of sex information and misinformation are peers (Barnard, 1968; Thornberg, 1981; Schofield, 1964) and it may be within this context that the teacher finds his or her role. Balding (1983) found in a survey of over 1,000 young people in Cornwall that only 1 in 10 boys claimed that the classroom was where they learned the facts of life. Even fewer girls found the classroom to be the main site for such information. Friends were the primary source and thus if misinformation is being transmitted then the school, with its captive audience, seems to have an important corrective function to play.

As stated earlier, however, sex education should go beyond cognitive-intellectual development. Sex education should not be viewed as something that is done 'to' or 'for' young people, but something that is done 'by' and 'with' them. It may be, for example, that some children in a group take major responsibilities for the rearing of siblings in the absence of one parent, so we could use this experience to enhance the learning of others.

Risk-taking is a feature of the young person which may require particular attention in sex-education lessons as the consequences of inappropriate sexual behaviour may have considerable negative effects, and consequences on a youngster's personal, family, community and social well-being. As Eden (1985) stated:

> In spite of claiming to know all about sex, most teenagers who engage in sexual intercourse do not use contraceptives and may have a complete misconception about sex. The most difficult lesson to teach is the motivation to say 'No'.

Young people should be encouraged to view themselves as controllers of their own destiny rather than 'straws in the wind' or victims of the expediency of others. There are good reasons for adhering to family and society norms that enhance healthy living, but little sense in succumbing to the fashion or short-term inclinations of a subculture bent on the creation of anxiety in oneself and others.

Sex Education Should Be Based upon an Appreciation of the Influences upon Young People's Sexual Behaviour

The influences upon one's sexual behaviour are many and varied (Figure 10.2) but notably no two people are affected in the same way by similar stimuli. For example, whilst housing may be a factor for particular individuals, it is not necessarily a reliable predictor of behaviour.

Some influences may be so strong that they are beyond the control of the individual. It is unlikely that school sex education will be able to eradicate social deprivation, for example, and political action may be necessary if one wishes to remove major impediments to healthy sexual development.

The widely divergent beliefs and customs within various cultural and religious groupings may be found within one classroom and present particular tensions for young people and teacher particularly if an environment in which respect for differences is absent. Opinions about arranged marriages, birth control, fertility and premarital sexual activity may find expression in daily exchanges outside the classroom. One of the most disconcerting features of today's British society is the way in which human sexuality is exploited and portrayed through the media for entertainment

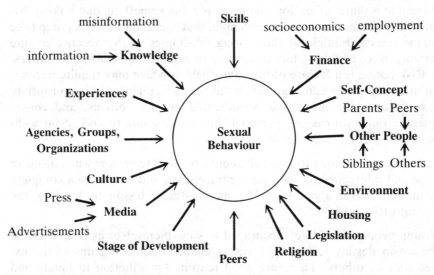

Figure 10.2 Influences upon sexual behaviour

and financial gain. Negative images projected by adults do little to encourage youthful responsibility; where are the adult models of virtuous behaviour which are so highly valued by some parents, pressure groups and others?

Sex Education May Be Viewed as a Response to Crisis, Pressure and Statistics

The intervention of the school in response to crisis may be totally inappropriate and even counter-productive. Initially, one may have to determine what constitutes a 'crisis' and who decides that intervention is likely to rectify the situation or prevent further occurrences?

Perhaps one of the primary sources for crisis identification is made in response to the real or perceived pressures of individuals, groups and communities beyond the school gates.

In the United States, political and religious groups have attempted to influence teaching about evolution, women's rights, sex and the events of recent history. In the religious context, fundamentalist groups have exerted pressure through the courts, Bruce (1983) notes that

> The courts see themselves as the defenders of the national interest against local particular interests. The fundamentalists see themselves as the defenders of the family, God, America, patriotism, free enterprise and all other traditional values.

Pressure groups are also a feature of British life and some have attempted to act as guardians of the nation's moral well-being. Apart from the strength of moral arguments, some individuals and groups cite statistical evidence in support of their concern. The examples of anecdotal evidence are legion as are snippets of data plucked from 'authoritative' papers that are used overtly to stimulate (or discourage) a school response. The incidences of sexually transmitted diseases and unwanted teenage pregnancies seem to be particular targets of concern.

If statistics are used as a primary source, it raises the issue of whose figures are to be accepted as a basis for further action. The following examples have been taken out of context to illustrate the potential danger of incongruence in figures taken from differing sources. Whilst all examples have something to say about teenage pregnancies, they do not offer, in combination, a coherent view of the situation.

> Fewer than three out of every 100 teenage girls gave birth in 1982, compared with five ten years earlier.

> (FPA, 1984, Fact Sheet F1)

Legal abortions performed on 15 year old mothers rose steeply after the 1967 Abortion Act (from 2.63 per 1,000 in 1969 to 6.50 in 1973) with the increased availability of the operation, but since then have fluctuated between narrow bands of 6.5 and 7.5 per 1,000 15 year old girls. The birth rate, on the other hand, has fallen in this age group from 3.90 per 1,000 in 1973 to 2.42 in 1982.

(FPA, 1984, Fact Sheet F2)

Young teenage mothers have increased 700 per cent over the last twenty years.

(Eden, 1985)

Between 1974 and 1978 in England and Wales, 18,881 girls aged 15 became pregnant, and 12,873 of these pregnancies were legally terminated under the new Abortion Act, 1967.

(Russell, 1981)

Russell (1981) stated that his own studies and a national survey involving over 300 schools in England and Wales show that half of the girls who are below the statutory school-leaving age at the time of the birth fail to return to school, in spite of the widespread willingness of schools to be helpful and supportive.

The school should not necessarily interpret singular localized incidents as an indication of the general situation or believe that national and/or regional statistics relate unequivocally to the behaviour of its children. It is vital that sex education is based upon the teacher's knowledge of his or her pupils rather than some belief that is impossible to substantiate.

Sex Education May Be Expressed in Terms of 'Do' and 'Don't'

Sex education can vary between two extremes. On the one hand there is an imposed form of moral education in which there is little discussion, perhaps little opportunity for questioning, and an atmosphere in which an adult attempts to 'inoculate' the young against moral tragedies. At the other extreme is simple reproductive education which is comparatively easy to teach, impersonal and without any specific overt moral or social context. In this approach, it is presumed that an individual's understanding of sexuality can come from a biological study of the reproduction of the dog, fish or rabbit. Both these extremes must be criticized, and it is suggested that there is a middle ground in which sexual knowledge is given to young people in a setting which is moral in a wide sense of the word.

A checklist of dos and don'ts may fail to influence sexual behaviour if young people are not motivated to care for themselves and others. Adults do have to indicate where they stand and should not abdicate their responsibility to assist young people to make decisions concerning the expression of sexuality; a *laissez-faire* attitude towards casual sexual relationships with its attendant health hazards is difficult to justify in a mature being.

Sex Education Should Be Taught by Experts

Bruess and Greenberg (1981) state that

> In some respects everyone is a sex educator, but the person working in a formal sex education program in particular must be comfortable interacting with others about sexuality as well as with personal feelings about his or her own sexuality!

The message is that one should 'know thyself' prior to and during work with young people and Kirendall and Calderwood (1967) emphasize the special relationship which the pupil may have with the teacher.

> Parents, students and educators alike recognize that the teacher is all-important in sex education. Efforts to substitute this crucial teacher-pupil relationship by assembly-type programs, a series of talks by outside experts or reliance on visual aids alone have proved ineffective. The burden of good sex education rests on the individual classroom teacher.

The involvement of outside agencies in the classrooms offers a rich potential for young people, but an unplanned session that 'provides answers to questions that children don't ask' may be a wasted opportunity. It may be a more profitable learning experience for young people to use the 'visitor technique' (Lancashire, 1980; Button, 1982) whereby they prepare an agenda for entertaining and interviewing people of their choice; through this process, people from the community provide a valuable resource.

Experts are not necessarily those with a medical background. Parents, community workers, teachers, religious leaders and representatives of statutory and voluntary organizations are amongst those who may contribute to sex education.

Over the years, local education and health authorities have provided training for teachers and at a national and regional level, the Family Planning Association and Marriage Guidance Council have made excellent contributions.

Bruess and Greenberg (1981, pp. 188–95) stipulate certain rules for the sex education which may be summarized as follows:

Language – socially acceptable terminology to be used at all times

Disclosure – no one may be asked to disclose or to be encouraged to show off

Questions – No question is stupid if the person asking is sincere

Topics – Certain topics are beyond the scope of this course

Availability – Teacher may be available to discuss issues requiring follow-up

Feelings – All feelings expressed will be accepted. Not all behaviour can be expressed, nor will it be accepted

Thoughts – May be shared if volunteered

Input – Broadly based, researched offering

Humour – Used sensitively, it may release tensions in individuals and groups

For someone to be designated an 'expert', one may suggest that in addition to his or her knowledge on sexual matters, he or she would follow these rules of interaction with young people.

In some schools, teachers engage outsiders to conduct sensitive aspects relating to sexuality. The expert may work with the group whilst the teacher is out of the room; this arrangement presents difficulties for development opportunities and may indicate to the class the teacher's insecurity or lack of interest. As a general rule, teachers, pupils and those subcontracted to act as leaders or experts should negotiate the basis of their work together (this is part of the totality of the learning experience).

Sex Education may be Effectively Promoted through the Use of Less Didactic Teaching Approaches

A range of teaching materials have been developed by major national health and social curriculum development projects which require the active participation of the learner (Button, 1982; Lancashire, 1980; McNaughton, 1983; SCHEP, 1977; SCHEP, 1982). If one is to move from sex instruction with its heavy moral overtone to sex education, the involvement of the learner is of paramount importance. To enact the popular educational expression 'to start from where children are' will require the teacher faced with a class of 20 or more pupils to resist the temptation to lecture and in so doing treat them all the same.

Teacher-directed inputs of short duration may be used to stimulate discussion and other developmental activity; the use of the trigger film has great potential for many aspects of health education.

Sex Education Suffers from Language Difficulties

A contentious issue, and one which may support or undermine the implementation of sex education, is the acceptability of the language used to describe aspects of human sexuality. Bibby (1943) has expressed preference for 'scientific terminology'; Kilander (1968) for 'socially acceptable terminology' and Lee (1983) went to the heart of the matter when she said,

> Finding a common language for sex is a concern not confined to the classroom. To work out an approved way of communicating the subject which does not offend, alienate or cause misunderstanding is a problem which perplexes the people who formulate school curricula as much as it does the teachers and pupils.

The language used in classroom work needs consideration; we feel it questionable for the teacher to use vernacular sexual terms, but there is no need to be overzealous in avoiding reference to them by pupils. Children will know a variety of such terms, and this should be discussed quite openly. The teacher can say that the proper names and descriptions will be more helpful to most people and that this is the normal language in discussion of relationships.

Sex Education as a List of Topics

Many schools express their intentions for sex education in terms of content. Sometimes there are brief statements relating to aims and objectives, audiovisual resources, reference books, but almost without exception there is a list of topics to be covered. What is often absent is a clear indication of the links between these seemingly disparate labels, the way in which they are to be considered and the modes of interaction to be offered.

If one considers such a list (in alphabetical form), one may find it difficult to see how the items are related to each other and to the needs and interests of young people at various stages of development.

Abortion	Genetics
Birth control	Homosexuality
Boy–girl relationships	Human reproductive system
Childbirth	Legality
Childcare and development	Loving
Courtship	Marriage
Divorce	Masturbation
Emotional relationships	Menstruation
Family life	Parenting

Pregnancy

Puberty

Role of mother

Role of father

Separation

Sex roles

Sexual intercourse

Sexually transmitted diseases

From such a list, the teacher may be tempted to study 'puberty' yesterday, 'birth control' today and 'sex roles' tomorrow and fail to emphasize the relationship of sexuality to positive human relationships and personal feelings.

The use of such topic lists as a checklist, to aid in a co-ordinated and planned approach throughout the primary and secondary school years, however, may be useful. Linking topics to particular age groups, varying them with the needs and interests of children as they arise, and developing and exploring issues in different years is a skilful and important task, and one way of helping young people to consider some of the major issues in family life and society.

CONCLUSION

Sex education *may* reduce the incidence of sexually transmitted diseases and unwanted pregnancies, but it is unlikely that one will be able to attribute this position to a school's intervention. One should see a programme not as a 'cure-all' recipe but as an aid to the promotion of personal and social development. As Bibby (1945) states,

> To expect by sex education alone to wipe out prostitution and casual promiscuity, to make all marriages successful and all divorces disappear, to abolish adultery and prevent all fornication, is to be hopelessly unrealistic. Many and deep seated are the sexual ills of society, and education unaided will not eradicate them. Economic and political changes and a new social and spiritual vision are needed too.

Gordon (1981) believes that unless society can reduce racism, sexism, poverty and individual vulnerability one should not expect sex-education programmes to have a major impact. This statement highlights the context in which the teacher in the school works as a sex educator and the inference may be that one should set realistic aims prior to embarking upon any planned intervention.

The challenges are many and varied, but we, the authors, believe that the caring school does have an important role to play in the healthy sexual development of young people.

REFERENCES AND BIBLIOGRAPHY

Balding, J. (1983) Co-ordination between schools: the role of the HEO, *Education and Health*, Journal of the Schools Health Education Unit, University of Exeter, Vol. 1, No. 2.

Barnard, D. (1968) How to teach sex, *New Society*, 4 April.

Bibby, C. (1943) Sex education in the school, *Health Education Journal*, Vol. 1, No. 2.

Bibby, C. (1945) Sex education: aims, possibilities and plans, reprinted from *Nature*, Vol. 156, 6 October, p. 413 and 13 October, p. 438 (© Macmillan Journals Ltd).

Bruce, S. (1983) Goodbye Mr. Darwin, *Times Educational Supplement*, 2 September.

Bruess, C. E. and Greenberg, J. S. (1981) *Sex Education: Theory and Practice*, Wadsworth Publishing, Belmont, CA.

Button, L. (1982) *Group Tutoring for the Form Teacher*, Hodder & Stoughton, Sevenoaks, Kent.

Department of Education and Science (1981a) *The School Curriculum*, HMSO, London.

Department of Education and Science (1981b) *The Education (School Information) Regulations*, Statutory instruments, Schedule 2, No. 630, HMSO, London.

Department of Education and Science (1986a) Draft circular on *Sex Education at School*, HMSO, London.

Department of Education and Science (1986b) *Health Education from 5 to 16*, Curriculum Matters 6, HMSO, London.

Dominian, J. (1977) *Proposals for a New Sexual Ethic*, Darton Longman & Todd, London.

Eden, P. J. (1985) Conception, misconception or contraception, *Health Education Journal*, Vol. 44, No. 2.

Family Planning Association (1984) *Fact Sheets*, July, D3.

Goldman, R. and Goldman, J. (1983) *Children's Sexual Thinking*, Routledge & Kegan Paul, London.

Gordon, S. (1981) The case for a moral sex education in the schools, *Journal of School Health*, Journal of the American School Health Association, special edition, April.

Hayton, P. (1985) The rationale for sex education in the school curriculum, *Health Education Journal*, Vol. 44, No. 2.

Johnson, W. R. (1968) *Human Sexual Behavior and Sex Education*, Lea and Febiger, Philadelphia.

Kilander, H. F. (1968) *Sex Education in the Schools*, Macmillan, Toronto.

Kirendall, L. A. and Calderwood, D. (1967) Basic issues in sex education, *Californian School Health Journal*, Vol. 3, No. 1.

Lancashire County Council (1979–82) *Active Tutorial Work*, Basil Blackwell, Oxford.

Lawton, A. (1985) *Parents and Teenagers*, Unwin, London.

Lee, C. (1983) *The Ostrich Position*, Writers and Readers Publishing Co-operative Society Ltd, London.

McNaughton, J. (1983) *Fit for Life*, Macmillan, Basingstoke.

National Council of Women of Great Britain (1984) *Sex Education: Whose Responsibility?* NCW, London.

Pugh, G. (1980) *Preparation for Parenthood*, National Children's Bureau, London.
Reid, D. (1982) School sex education and the causes of unintended teenage pregnancies, *Health Education Journal*, Vol. 41, No. 2.
Responsible Society (1981) *Sex Education in Schools – What Every Parent Should Know*, Responsible Society, Wicken.
Russell, J. K. (1981) No joy in the youth club, *Guardian*, 1 September.
Schofield, M. (1964) *The Sexual Behaviour of Young People*, Penguin, Harmondsworth.
Schools Council Health Education Project (1977) (SCHEP) *Think Well*, Nelson, Sunbury-on-Thames.
Schools Health Education Project (1982) (SCHEP) *Health Education 13–18*, Forbes, London.
Settle, D. and Wise, C. (1986) *Choices: Materials and Methods for Personal and Social Education*, Blackwell, Oxford.
Thornberg, H. D. (1981) Adolescent sources of information on sex, *Journal of School Health*, special edition, April.
Whitfield, R. (1980) *Education for Family Life*, Hodder & Stoughton, Sevenoaks, Kent.

Useful Books for Teachers

Dixon, H. and Mullinar, G. (eds.) (1985) *Taught Not Caught: Strategies for Sex Education*, Learning Development Aids, Wisbech.
Lee, C. (1986) *The Ostrich Position*, Allen & Unwin, London.
Went, D. (1985) *Sex Education: Some Guidelines for Teachers*, Bell & Hyman, London.
Fact Sheets are available from: Family Planning Association, 27–35 Mortimer Street, London W1N 7RJ.
Whittey, Carole (1985) *Sex Education in Multi-Ethnic Schools*, National Organization for Initiatives in Social Education.

PART 5

FURTHER DEVELOPMENTS

INTRODUCTION

A recent national survey has illuminated the extent to which outside agencies are used by teachers in the context of health education. Those visitors who are interviewed by pupils, help to plan work with pupils and are used as classroom teachers, speakers or advisers can add to the quality of health teaching in schools. Whilst the major work of health education in schools must inevitably lie with the teachers the development of extensive co-operation with other professional workers is essential to a proper understanding of how school-based work relates to life and work in the community.

Ian McCafferty taught for ten years in a comprehensive school and a college of technology. He then worked as deputy director of the Schools Council Health Education Project 5–13 for three years before becoming area health education officer for Nottinghamshire. He has been extensively involved in local dissemination and training related to various school health-education curriculum projects at primary and secondary level and is currently in a senior management position in the county. He is in an extremely good position to review the use of visitors and other resources from a wide range of perspectives, having worked both inside and outside schools. He is assisted in this presentation by colleagues from his department.

The 16+ age range has been badly neglected by health education – most of the efforts of the past ten years having been focused on the 5- to 16-year-olds. There have been several recent initiatives started, however, which attempt to redress this imbalance, and Gay Gray outlines for us some of the issues involved in these. Gay Gray, herself a former secondary-school teacher, gained valuable experience, writing material and evaluation strategies for TACADE before working on the 12 to 19 project which she now jointly directs.

11

HEALTH EDUCATION UNITS AND THE USE OF VISITORS IN THE CLASSROOM

Ian McCafferty with colleagues Anne Moore, Jean Hildreth and Nancy Beecroft

INTRODUCTION

The issue of using visitors in schools to contribute to health education programmes is an interesting one, for attitudes over the past ten years have shifted considerably. In our early experience many schools did little but bring in visitors for 'one-off' health-education sessions. Too often these were of the 'shock horror' variety and directed at large numbers of children. As time progressed there was a reaction to that situation suggesting that only teachers should teach, for they alone knew the children and their circumstances, or had the requisite skills. By 1986 the position seems to have stabilized. The vast amount of health-education curriculum materials that have been produced over the last ten years could, if used to the full, virtually fill the whole school timetable. Teachers now need not lack the knowledge or the resources or, with the training available, the skills to teach health education. At the same time, however, more effort is being made to look at the preventive educational role of many other professionals in the various public services. Schools are seen as a legitimate target for their preventive work, and it is therefore logical to establish what role such visitors can play, and what training they need.

The visitors are many and various. In 1985, for the Commission of the European Communities, a paper was produced outlining the potential links between school and community on health issues (McCafferty, 1985). One of the immediate findings was that in a brief survey no fewer than 25 agencies were discovered who made some input to secondary school health education, either through representatives of those agencies going into schools, or through visits (see Figure 11.1). The numbers identified for primary schools and nurseries were of course fewer, and less varied, but none the less a substantial potential input (see Figures 11.2 and 11.3).

What this amounts to is a very significant group of agencies interested in health who could, and do, contribute to health education in schools. This chapter will look at some of these agencies, at how the schools perceive their help, and at how they see themselves being used in schools. There will be a section on the training of National Health Service (NHS) staff who wish to carry out work in schools and the chapter will conclude with a summary of the drawbacks and advantages of visitors in health-education programmes.

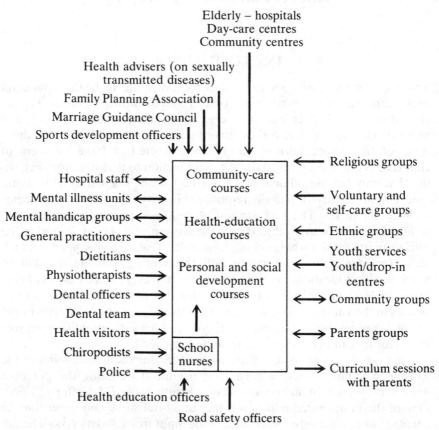

Figure 11.1 School and community links (11+)

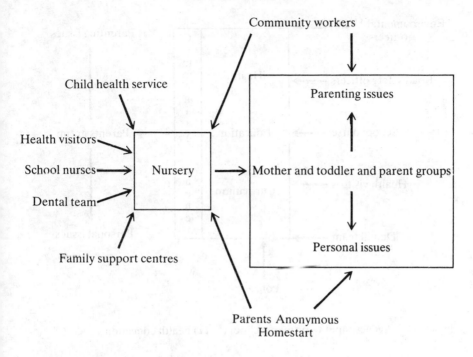

Figure 11.2 Agency input to nursery-school (pre-5) health education

HEALTH EDUCATION UNITS

Health education units (HEUs) can make a major contribution to school health education. This section looks at what these units are, what health education officers (HEOs) do in general and their potential value to schools. Health education units are part of the NHS. It is worth saying this at an early stage because many people think they are branches of the Health Education Council (HEC) or that they are part of the local authority, particularly the education authority. In fact they are almost entirely funded by their district health authorities (DHAs), the local bodies who run the hospitals and community health services. In spite of a government compulsion to reorganize the NHS at any point at which it looks as though it may be successfully organizing itself, health education has made progress since it became an NHS responsibility in 1974. The concept of preventing ill-health rather than curing it has become more prominent, with the result that many health authorities now have policies designed to assist in the

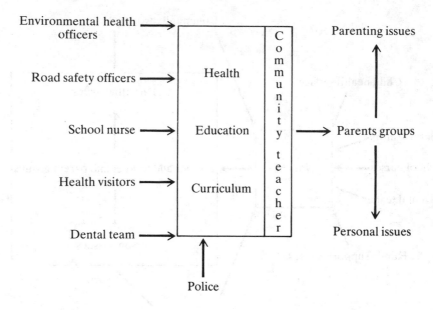

Figure 11.3 Agency input to primary-school (5–11) health education

prevention of ill health or the promotion of good health. Several authorities, for example, have developed policies on issues such as smoking, diet,
exercise, alcohol and vaccination. One result of this increased emphasis on
prevention is that HEU may have become better staffed and equipped to
assist those who wish to carry out health education. The health education
officers came from a fairly wide professional or graduate background, a
substantial number from teaching or nursing, some from social work and
community development, some from environmental health. Many of them,
from both graduate and professional backgrounds will have taken the one-
year post-graduate diploma in health education.

General Functions

Health education units differ in their organization but a broad concensus
would be that they advise, support, and train those who wish to carry out
health education. A HEU therefore may endeavour to assist doctors,
nurses, teachers, social workers, environmental health officers, the media,
occupational health services, community workers, voluntary groups and

the vast number of other groups and professions who meet the public and could be permitted to educate people about their health.

A glance at Figure 11.4 indicates how one such unit uses its specialist team of HEOs and targets them at specific professional and voluntary groups. Clearly, smaller units will not have the range of specialisms, others may group them differently or organize on the basis of health issues, for example heart disease, drugs, alcohol, exercise, and the like. Virtually every unit will be different, but all will wish to help.

Schools

Most health education units expect to work with schools, and for many it is a major priority. The problem sometimes may be to distinguish the different roles of an LEA inspection and advisory service and the HEU. Clearly, any LEA which has an inspector or adviser who is designated solely for health education or which has created a joint appointment with the DHA will have clear ideas as to the role it expects to play in developing health education. Many LEAs do not have such a post, however, or they have posts with multiple functions such as personal and social education (PSE) which include responsibility for health education, or they attach health education to subject areas such as science, PE or home economics. In the majority of districts therefore the relatioship between LEA and DHA for the provision of health-education services is a matter of local negotiation.

There are, however, some well-defined areas of practice. Most HEUs carry a wide range of resources for the teaching of health education, be they films, videos or slides. They will also stock printed materials such as booklets, leaflets and posters, many of which are provided by the HEC. This is a useful baseline service, for it provides health information and a means of setting up a health education programme for a teacher who is unfamiliar with the work.

Another key area is advice and training. Teachers will be at many different levels in their perception and skills in teaching health education. The function of an HEU is to be aware of these levels and provide advice and training commensurate with them. Teachers in the initial stages of providing health education may be uncertain about some of the content, be it to do with sex education, for example, or drugs or even diet. There should be regular access to such information initially to inform or later to keep teachers up to date. Quite soon teachers will perceive the need for careful planning throughout the various years and within year groups. They may then need help with co-ordinating these programmes and the appropriate resources. Many HEUs could, and do, provide such advice

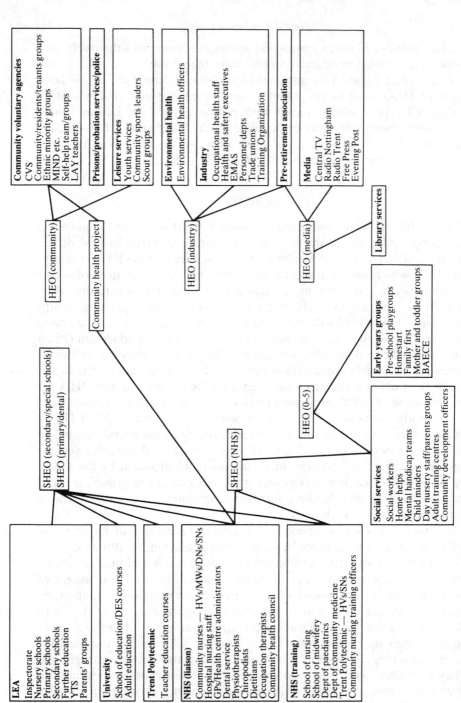

Figure 11.4 Local agencies/networks carrying out health education with health education unit resources/advice/training

and training, in the best of all possible worlds with the active co-operation of the LEA.

The issue of method in health education takes the process a stage further. Here the lines between health education and what may well be provided by the LEA in terms of training for pastoral care and social education become less obvious. Many of the teaching skills required for good health education, such as group skills and the encouragement of participation, the development of the self-concept and the like are shared with many other subject areas. The similarity of styles in the training applied to personal and social education, active tutorial work, careers education and health education are quite obvious. Close liaison in the provision of such courses is necessary, and the function of health-education training in that context should be clearly delineated. Health education is not simply an application of personal and social skills work. The NHS has responsibility for the prevention of ill health and the promotion of good health. It must therefore have targets, and criteria for judging whether those targets are being achieved. To say therefore that health education is simply an element of social-skills training is to ignore the potential behavioural outcomes on specific health issues. This element has to be discussed and come to terms with in any planned training.

One further obvious training function of an HEU is in conjunction with the many schools health education projects (SHEP) supported by the HEC and TACADE. There can be very few remaining age groups, or curriculum areas not covered by their projects, with over 20 such still receiving funding at the present time. Each HEU will almost certainly carry this material and can provide at the very least some basic advice as to its application. The great majority will have disseminated some of the work through local courses or conferences. In this respect and in the provision of teaching resources and baseline information, a unit probably has more time and resources available to help teachers than many advisers are able to offer with their multifarious functions. In the best of all worlds, the LEA and the HEU will operate a partnership with the LEA promoting and endorsing health education in the curriculum, providing support and collaborative training with the DHA, and being willing to refer teachers to the unit and to grant free access to its schools for HEOs. Such partnerships should prove fruitful.

Policies

As has already been stated, many DHAs have developed policies on such issues as smoking, diet, alcohol, exercise and so forth, in pursuance of preventive goals. Many LEAs over the past 20 years or more have already set out to establish health education in the curriculum through the development of policies or guidelines for schools. The present climate within education contains elements of criticism of 'top down' LEA policies which tell schools what they should do. Such policies are criticized chiefly on the grounds of their ineffectiveness in bringing about real change in the curriculum and in teaching methods. It is suggested that change only really takes place from within an institution which is itself committed to that change, and that few schools will react so positively to imposed guidelines.

There is undoubtedly considerable truth in this view, and teacher reaction to the plethora of policies and guidelines on everything from computers to multiracial education, from special needs to health education, is particularly clear to those who have been involved in their dissemination. There are, however, virtues in these policies, for they provide official endorsement of the view that health education has a clear role to play in the school curriculum. This view is not always accepted within institutions or among colleagues. The existence of policy documents together with dissemination and training, gives a very positive support to those wishing to establish or develop programmes. If an LEA does consider that health education has a role to play, then its statement of that view in the form of a policy has a long-term effect, not always obvious through immediate change. Certainly where an LEA and DHA have jointly developed such policies, then the function of the HEU in training, supporting and advising schools is made clear and this in itself is another very positive virtue of such policies.

Of all visitors to schools therefore HEO have the most clearly delineated and catalytic function. They can provide assistance themselves, provide a clearing-house for assistance from other sources, and offer help to train those other visitors who can contribute to the schools health-education programme.

The remainder of this chapter looks at the function those visitors can perform and the ways in which schools perceive and utilize them.

VISITORS TO SCHOOLS – THE HEALTH SERVICE VIEW

The Problems They Encounter

We obviously cannot individually describe the characteristics, virtues and possible shortcomings of all those who visit schools. We have chosen to concentrate particularly on health professionals who make up a majority of such visitors, knowing that most of their advantages and disadvantages are shared by others.

The main anxiety expressed by school visitors is their lack of teaching skills and experience. Some have a limited amount of information about teaching obtained from within their professional training, but many feel it is inadequate and does not equip them with the necessary skills for school health education. Many take part in health education in schools without any knowledge of teaching skills – some enjoy their participation, others would hope never to repeat the experience! This is unfair to them, and to the pupils who expect a high standard of teaching and who may quickly take advantage of anyone faltering or failing to maintain interest and attention.

Many visitors expect to have to cope with discipline in the classroom, not realizing that teachers are responsible for this and should always be present during a visitor's contribution to school health education. Some are fearful of awkward or personal questions, which they may be unable or unwilling to answer satisfactorily. They feel this would result in a reduction of their credibility by pupils and teachers. There is thus, for many, a degree of tension before the process actually begins.

Health professionals use medical terms freely among themselves but sometimes also in the classroom, resulting in elements of their input being unsuitable or incomprehensible to the pupils. Unfortunately, some visitors are unaware of this problem and leave pupils confused. Hopefully visitors are, to some extent, aware of pupils' different backgrounds before speaking with them and many health professionals realize that they may get involved in discussing delicate issues which could disturb or offend some children, for example, fostering and adoption. A few visitors will admit that they have definite biases which could affect their presentation of some information and be in direct opposition to the philosophy of the school, family planning for under-16 girls is often mentioned by visitors as a problem issue in schools of particular religious or ethnic balance.

Most visitors have a limited time only to give to school health education. Their statutory duties must take precedence and although they realize that working with small groups is preferable to speaking with a large year group, they are often unable to visit the school several times to repeat their contribution. They may also have to cover statutory work for colleagues at short notice and perhaps fail to turn up for the lesson. Some health service managers consider health education to be a minor and relatively unimportant part of their staff's caring role and although not actively discouraging school health-education participation, can prevent it taking place by failing to provide cover for the individuals concerned. It is not always easy therefore for visitors to carry out their teaching functions and occasionally allowances have to be made. Preparation time is also required and many visitors find themselves preparing work at home.

It is not always easy for visitors to say no to a request. Some are asked to participate in school health-education topics which teachers could quite easily teach without the help of health professionals, such as relationships or basic anatomy. Others are asked to undertake topics which are beyond their capabilities, genetics being a prime example. Refusing for any reason presents problems and may cause friction between the visitor and the school. A few visitors have experienced unwelcoming staff and an abrupt or casual manner can cause a nervous or inexperienced visitor to view the whole experience with considerable anxiety. Sometimes sessions are changed by the school, or the number of pupils in the group is increased; this can upset the visitor and affect the teaching session. In short, visitors should be treated in schools very much as though they were teachers in training, with thought given to their nervousness, to discipline, to a welcoming environment, and to the fact that they have probably had to prepare much of what they are going to say in their own time. More thought is now being given to their training, especially in the health service, in the police force and in environmental health departments in order to prepare visitors better. None the less, they will never be teachers *per se*, and a degree of nurturing would never come amiss.

Recognizing Their Needs

In Nottinghamshire County, 1980, a study was carried out to ascertain the training needs of school nurses who were increasingly being required to participate in school health education (Moore, 1981). They were asked by questionnaire about their interest in health education, their involvement at that time, their anxieties and problems and their own expectations regarding health education. They were asked for their perceived training needs for school health education and the health topics about which they felt most confident and able to use with pupils. There was a high response rate and the study has proved useful in programme planning.

Some multi-disciplinary courses for NHS staff had been held prior to 1980, and it was hoped to continue these with similar and further health-education information for specific groups. It was found that comprehensive school nurses participated in school health education to a greater extent than the peripatetic nurses. Most nurses preferred working with small groups or using 'one to one' counselling methods, giving practical demonstrations, and answering questions during teaching sessions. Short talks with visual aids and formal lecture-type sessions were occasionally undertaken but generally disliked and avoided. Their comments regarding training needs included requests for knowledge of teaching skills and methods, counselling and communication skills, health-topic information, use of equipment and visual aids and preparation and planning for teaching.

For the visit to be successful the visitor needs some information to plan effectively. The following list which is issued as a 'pro forma' for planning to health professionals on our training courses may seem very basic, but, with personal experience, this information is very rarely offered to a visitor.

1. The age and ability span of the group
2. Number in the group
3. Subject being covered
4. What course is this a part of
5. The time the group meets
6. The exact time for you
7. Aim for the group
8. Your objective
9. Previous knowledge of your topic
10. Your requirements

The pro forma can be taken by the visitor to the planning meeting and completed, or as a last resort completed over the telephone, and with the information gathered the visitor then has at least some basic knowledge of the group upon which to begin preparation. Any teacher involved in inviting a number of different visitors to their group may well consider it worthwhile to prepare a similar pro forma for the use of visitors. Ideally a visit to the group and the opportunity to sit in on a lesson to get the 'feel' of the group and the level of communication would make a better introduction.

Health Education Courses

Several health education courses have been held during the last five years, each consisting of five one-day sessions, now increased to six days. Sixteen health service staff, from the same profession, are accepted on each course, every person having more than two years experience in their post and having a proven interest in health education teaching. The courses are run by two senior HEOs in health-education rooms at local health centres.

On completion of the course the group members are expected to be able to plan and prepare group sessions and lead and support different types of groups in formal and informal situations. They should be able to communicate effectively with pupils and adults of varying abilities and ages.

Outline programme

1. *Theory and practice of health education*
   Includes aspects of health and prevention; health choices; aims; approaches and major areas; methods; availability and rationale for health education; the structure and services of HEUs, liaison between units, the HEC and the DHSS.
2. *Approach to schools*
   Guidelines to a professional and effective approach to schools and further education colleges, as to classroom involvement
3. *Preparation for teaching*
   Definition of aims and objectives, contributions to school health-education courses, lesson planning and tutorials
4. *Group work*
   Investigates the theory and practice of group work, strategies for teaching and working with groups of varying ages and abilities and situations, including choice of suitable topics
5. *Visual aids and resources*
   The value, choice and effective use of suitable resources; presentation methods; practical sessions including use of equipment, for example film, overhead and slide projectors; creation of visual aids for use with 'micro' teaching sessions; availability of resources, use of other professional contacts for schools; liaising with HEU
6. *Teaching methods*
   Acceptable and suitable methods of teaching health education
7. *Communication skills*
   Listening skills, verbal and non-verbal communication; practical communication exercises
8. *Counselling*
   Health-professional involvement; counselling qualities; skills and methods; confidentiality; limitations and boundaries
9. *Topic information*
   Up-to-date health-education information on resources, including new teaching material suitable for schools and other groups
10. *Teaching session*
    A ten-minute teaching session by all group members based on the lesson plan prepared during the course. The method, visual aid and

topic are chosen by each individual. The courses are held for health visitors, school nurses and chiropodists. Dieticians and midwives are now also interested in taking part. Evaluation by course members has been positive and valuable links are made among health-service staff, schools in their areas of work and members of the HEU.

Positive Contributions Made

Having catalogued earlier some of the problems visitors face, it is important to look at what motivates them and what they bring to schools. Visitors feel they have positive contributions to make to school health education. Many health staff are known to the pupils and teachers and some visitors have a knowledge of the pupils' health and background. Pupils are generally co-operative with visitors, especially if they are encouraged to be so by their teachers, and they usually recognize their visitors' expertise and experience of health issues. The visitors' information is usually up to date and their health knowledge is wider than that of teachers, particularly in relation to present preventive measures and the care and treatment of certain conditions or health problems.

Visitors often form useful links between school and the community and can give important information to pupils and teachers about health issues and local services. Visitors also say that they learn more about school life and appreciate the school health education which is undertaken by teachers. Although the visitors' background and lifestyle may be different from that of the pupils, many have a high degree of understanding and empathy, and the skills and aptitude to adapt their approach and language to the individual or groups whom they meet in schools. Their expertise need not necessarily impede their ability to communicate. The visitors' contribution to school health education need not, and possibly should not, be in the form of formal classroom teaching. Many feel, and are, unqualified to teach formally; they believe that teachers are the experts and are able to teach about many health issues very effectively. Visitors are able to liaise and co-operate with the class teacher by being present for question and answer sessions, to lead small groups, to give practical demonstrations alongside the teacher or to present a short section of a session. Health education on a one-to-one basis too can often take place in quiet surroundings, such as during health-appraisal sessions which are carried out by school nurses.

Visiting health professionals can be an invaluable reference point for a school other than simply in the classroom. They, in common with other professionals, know all about their own organizations and the services they provide. They can explain why a service operates in a particular way, and what the functions are of various people within it. Those kinds of insights can be helpful and can often reduce tension and misunderstanding between groups of professionals. In terms of health issues, advice and information about common childhood illnesses can be given to pupils and teachers. Specialist information on topics such as asthma, epilepsy, diabetes and adolescent problems can be provided individually or to groups of teachers or parents who need to know of the care necessary for some pupils. That kind of helpful liaison can be extremely useful in the long-term development of co-operation between the school and the health service.

There are particular areas, however, where health professionals feel they have a special contribution to make in the classroom. Such subjects as personal care, diet and nutrition, sex education (contraception, menstruation, sexually transmitted diseases), first aid, home safety, drug education (alcohol, solvent abuse, smoking and illegal drugs) and specific health topics such as rubella and measles often benefit from a contribution from a health professional.

Many visitors are enthusiastic about their involvement in school health education and if they are suitable to be involved and encouraged by teaching staff, they will willingly promote positive health attitudes and practices with pupils and teachers. As the Court Report (1976) states: 'Health staff are required to be the representatives of health in the everyday life of the school.' The correct use of visitors is too good an opportunity to be missed.

VISITORS AS A TEAM –
A DENTAL-HEALTH MODEL

The previous section described ways in which training was provided for a variety of health professionals to help their work in schools. Here we describe another approach, where a special team has been set up and trained to deal with a specific health-education target in schools, dental health.

Dental disease has been one of the most common kinds of illness, one causing a great deal of pain and misery, costing the NHS in the region of £500 million a year and yet is a condition that can be prevented. It has also been an area fraught with misconceptions and diverse messages that served only to confuse the public, a large proportion of which were convinced that the loss of some, if not all, permanent teeth in adulthood was inevitable. It seemed important then to dispel misapprehension and to use more adequately community dental staff, whose clinic commitment was reducing, in a systematic unified approach to dental-health education. In 1980, the area dental officer therefore initiated a team approach to dental-health education in Nottinghamshire, with staff of the community dental service, that is, dental therapists, dental hygienists and dental surgery assistants delivering the dental-health message to nearly all sections of the community, particularly to schools. A senior HEO based in the HEU and senior dental officer were given responsibility for training, advising and co-ordinating the work of the team. A full account of the development of the team appears in 'Developing Dental Health Education' (Hildreth, 1982).

In 1986 the Nottinghamshire dental-health education team is 15 strong. The membership ranges from staff who have been involved for almost all of the six years of its development to those who have only a few months' experience.

The number of team members fluctuates as the individuals tend to be of an age when marriage and pregnancy are likely. This is an advantage in that new blood can revitalize the team, but it is also a disadvantage in that the training needs of individuals are always at different stages. Occasionally it is possible to recruit new members en bloc but it is more likely that individuals join the team singly.

Each member is responsible for a number of schools in Nottinghamshire, this tends to be in the region of 40 and includes all educational establishments. Their weekly commitment to dental health education varies from a half to one day depending on their clinical work. This is flexible, but the need for the programming of the whole of the community dental-service staff requires that the team members organize their work in advance and keep where possible to their allocated time and day.

Team meetings, which all members are expected to attend, are held about once a term. The meetings last usually for a whole day and are considered essential for the development of dental-health education. On a general basis the meetings help to give cohesion to the team, because the diverse location of the dental clinics in the county means that many team members would otherwise have no opportunity to meet. Members gain reassurance and encouragement from discussion about other people's experiences, including ideas for visual aids and how they may have coped in difficult situations. More specifically the team meetings are training sessions, aimed at furthering the knowledge and expertise of the group. Here again much can be gained from interaction within the group, newer members not only drawing on the experience of more established members, but bringing new approaches to liven up old messages.

The Training of a Dental Team

The overall training in many respects covers those areas mentioned in the previous section concerning other health professionals, but because of the more extensive nature of the programme the emphasis is somewhat different.

The dental-health education message

The basic message was established early on in the life of the team, because as stated previously the confusion centred on dental care and left the public cynical about the whole area, therefore it was essential that the team should be unified in what they were saying. It is necessary, however, to be brought up to date as new research appears and the team meeting is a forum for members to raise issues they have encountered in their work.

Also, as part of the strategic plan for the health authority the senior dental officer and senior HEO have been required to put forward objectives for dental-health education over a ten-year span. These cover some 14 programme areas throughout the community with strategies for implementation. An essential part of this implementation rests with the ability of the team to work towards the objectives, and the expertise of their managers to ensure that the team's training is adequate to do this. With regard to schools especially, efforts are made to review school-screening results wherever possible, so that the dental-health message can be more specific, that is, if oral hygiene appears to be the problem then plaque control would be emphasized rather than the giving of a general talk.

Review and assessment of resources

Perhaps above all other topics in the health-education field, dental audiovisual aids are the most prolific. This seems to be one reason why it is chosen by school nurses, health visitors and students when they are training in schools. Not all of these resources, even the most up-to-date, are consistent in what they are trying to say, especially those for younger children. Messages often become distorted in the effort to simplify. It is important therefore that the team know what is available and how best it can be used, if at all. A development from this was the production by the team of a dental-information book, a project pack for schools, leaflets dealing with dental care in pregnancy and leaflets for the parents of young children.

Approaches to teaching

Teaching approaches form a large part of the training programme. New team members are expected to spend time in schools observing teachers working with different age groups and team members generally are encouraged to be aware of what is happening around them in the schools they visit. In a more structured way, sessions at team meetings have covered lesson planning, school and classroom organization and group work skills. This forms an important part of team training together with experiences brought back to the group for discussion. Many team members have built good relationships with teachers in their schools, but not all individuals are able to do this easily; the training process and team effort does to a degree help these members. It is important that team members have a professional approach to their work, that they see themselves as part of the wide field of health education and that they work towards becoming involved at this level.

One major problem in the earlier stages of team development was the inability of team members to be aware of the intricacies of school organization and the possibilities of such events as of staff absences disrupting their lessons. It is quite easy to understand why someone who has put a great deal of effort into preparation can be disgruntled if 'things' are not quite what they expected, but it is also a fact that visitors to schools have to learn to accept. At the same time, it takes some courage on the part of a team member when confronted by 80 children instead of the 30 expected to decline to take the session if the school has inadequate reasons for changing the arrangements. To help to allay this happening, a booking form was designed by the team members which they fill in when arranging their talk (Appendix 11.1) giving a copy to the school. Not all members use this, but those who do find it a very useful aid should the situation be different from what they expected; it also helps them to ensure that a member of staff stays with them in the classroom.

Liaison with allied professionals

Dental-health education has not become an isolated part of the health-education field, because the senior HEO responsible for team training is based within the Nottingham Health Education Unit. Liaison within the unit remains high and the team are trained to be part of the unit and to see dental health with a wider view.

Associated with this is the regard for other professionals and what they are trying to achieve, for example dieticians. Because attention to sugar in the diet and the choice of alternative sugar-free foods is an important part of the dental message, it is essential that information from both dieticians and the dental team does not conflict. Part of team training therefore involves meetings with such professionals and liaison continues at team management level so that contact and awareness are maintained.

Evaluation

Evaluating this team approach to dental-health education is not easy. Over the past 12 years the decay rate of children's teeth has fallen locally, but this is also true nationally, and there appear to be multifactoral reasons for this, such as fluoride toothpaste, fluoridation of water supplies as well as dental education. More subjectively, team members have noted, because of their contact with the same schools over a number of years, that improvements in dental care, knowledge and attitudes have occurred.

The training which the team receives seems to have implications for individual professional development. When asked to consider what, if anything, they had gained personally from being involved in the team, members were able to specify areas in which they saw improvements in themselves which helped them in the clinical setting. They felt that their increase in knowledge and communication skills helped them to deal with patients more adequately and that they had become a resource for other members of the community dental service. Generally team members seem to see team involvement giving them greater job satisfaction, more responsibility and independence as well as confidence and an opportunity to meet more people.

Some Problem Areas

There are some drawbacks to this type of work which have to be recognized. The basic problem is one shared by a number of professions, where some members are given time to go into schools and teach. Not all dental officers or dental surgery assistants or, indeed, health visitors, environmental health officers or the like are convinced of the value of health education. To them, sessions given to other staff to carry out such teaching may be a waste of time, and something that throws an added workload on to themselves. It may be that some levels of management are also less than convinced, and in that case the problem is obviously compounded, particularly for younger or less experienced team members.

The work also carries its own burden of preparation time, finding locations, writing reports, missing lunch hours and a general disruption to the working day which would be much more straightforward if they carried out normal duties. The value of a team approach here is that such problems can be shared, ways found to solve difficulties and a general sense of belonging to a group where at least everyone there is trying to achieve the same end. From the schools' point of view they seem on the whole to value the team involvement in school activities, the majority of team members have as many dental-health education sessions as they can cope with. There is still the danger of them being used for the one-off talk, but the more experienced they become the more able they are to judge when this is likely to happen and so plan their work accordingly. In many instances the team see themselves, and are seen by school staff to be a resource and a personal adviser. The discussion that takes place in staff rooms before or after the classroom involvement is therefore of vital importance.

VISITORS – THE SCHOOLS' VIEW

Teachers have indicated two main reasons for asking specialist visitors to come into school. The first centres on expertise, the idea being that very few teachers have received training in health education and that there are therefore areas of knowledge that would best be dealt with by a specialist. That situation has changed somewhat in the last ten years, for there are now large quantities of curriculum materials available to teachers, and the view has certainly developed that health education is more about process and skills than it is about knowledge. It would also be true to say that at primary level and in most areas of secondary school health education any adequately prepared teacher knows quite enough to teach what is required.

The second reason remains more valid. It suggests that there is a case for bringing representatives into school from a variety of agencies that the children may have to know about and deal with in later life. These people may indeed have interesting expert knowledge to share, particularly from the caring professions, so that the school may get the best of both worlds.

It would be well to recognize the impact of interesting visitors in both the primary and the secondary sector. In a primary school a visit from 'Valerie Vole', a suitably attired representative from the Water Authority, may do a great deal of good by re-inforcing messages about playing near rivers, streams or ponds. Teachers will almost certainly already teach about safety but the message will perhaps be remembered better if it is associated with an interesting visit. Similarly a visit from an ambulance crew with their ambulance and its equipment can allay fears and perhaps inculcate a more responsible attitude to using and calling for an ambulance in an emergency.

At an older level family-planning nurses can prove invaluable, providing expertise in a very necessary area, and perhaps being asked, and giving answers to questions that pupils may feel unable to ask a teacher. Many of us who have given talks in schools will recall being asked some fairly fundamental and important questions on this topic, often when the 'official' talk and question time is finished. Many years ago in Nottingham it was decided to train health advisers (or contact tracers) to go into schools to talk not just about sexually transmitted diseases but about the importance of immediately visiting the clinic if the person thought that he or she might have a problem. By talking about how the clinic worked and about its confidentiality, and by demonstrating that the people who worked there were nice, friendly, unshockable human beings, they helped to dispel some of the fear and suspicion that are often endemic to such clinics. The health advisers themselves are of the opinion that this has helped to stem the spread of sexually transmitted diseases because young people refer themselves earlier and thus reduce further contacts from an infected person.

The object of the exercise with visitors therefore is to use their time effectively, both for the benefit of the school and also for the visitors themselves. There has to be some 'pay off' for both. As in the preceding case, pupils may use the services provided more effectively, or in more general terms the visitors should feel that their sessions will contribute to a better-informed and perhaps healthier population.

There are ways of maximizing these events for the benefit of all: the pupils; the teacher; the visitor; the wider community and the service or profession from which the visitor comes and to that end a few 'ground rules' are offered.

Criteria for Using Visitors

1. Are they offering something which the teacher can not?
2. Is the information or expertise on offer something special?
3. Could the teacher do this easily?
4. Will the experience be of value to the pupils?

In our training courses for health visitors, school nurses and chiropodists, apart from giving them confidence to work in schools if invited, they are given the preceding criteria to work to, and if the answers to 1, 2, and 4 are in the affirmative and to 3 the answer is No, then they accept the visit. To give an example, a teacher who has not been a nurse will not know what work a nurse does, or why he or she does it, but may have sufficient knowledge for the pupils' purpose at that particular time. Only the teacher and the nurse can decide that together. If the work of a nurse is an integral part of the project the pupils are engaged in, then only a nurse can fulfil those criteria.

Teachers will often say the pupils appreciate seeing someone new in the classroom, and that may be so, but if the purpose of inviting someone in, is merely to entertain in that capacity then there will be no pay-off for the visitor. There is much literature published whose aim is to inform about professions, their work, and the part they play in the community. The teacher needs to ask 'Will the information in the literature be sufficient for the pupils, together with some other discovery learning?' that is, asking questions in the community, or 'Has the visitor an essential part to play in that learning process?'

What Can the School Expect of Visitors?

If the preceding criteria have been met, and it has been decided to proceed with an invitation there are a few issues the teacher needs to consider about the visitor before issuing that invitation:

The visitor is not a teacher and may not have a teacher's skills.

How well will the visitor therefore communicate with the pupils?

What form will the pupils interaction take?

Will the teaching situation be what the visitor expects?

People coming into school are very often overawed by the situation and those who have been excellent speakers in the village hall or in their own domain are often disappointing in a school. We all have memories of school and perhaps these get in the way and visitors who are at ease speaking to adults or in other locations are often stilted in the classroom The language used or level of the communication may not be correct for the pupils for, as mentioned earlier in the chapter, people in the medical and nursing profession, for example, use medical terminology in their work and it is difficult for them to leave that behind when speaking to children.

Many adults remembering their own schooldays will recall the teacher at the front of the class with the pupils in rows facing the 'lecturing' teacher, and this is often the way visitors expect to approach their visit to the classroom, with very little interaction with the pupils except for a few questions at the end of the talk. There is a lot to be said therefore for the suggestion that visitors should go to a school beforehand to absorb the house style.

What Information Does the Teacher Need?

What exactly will the visitor expect to do?

For how long?

What preparation is needed beforehand, by the pupils?

What follow-up work can be prepared?

Will the visitor expect the children to do anything?
Will the visitor need any audiovisual aids?
Will the visitor bring any equipment?

When a visit is being arranged, for convenience and to save time, most communication is usually done either by letter or by telephone, but for a visit to be successful it is advisable for the visitor to come to school for a pre visit to meet the pupils and the teacher. There can then be a full explanation of what is expected of the visitor and for the visitor to assess the situation.

The teacher will want to know what the visitor will do and say to enable the pupils to be prepared for the visit and to make preparations for any follow-up work. The visitor may want to do some kind of activity with the pupils, bring various aids or equipment. This should be encouraged and the teacher will need to fit these activities into the preparation.

Will It Be Worthwhile?

The main reason for using visitors in the classroom is that they are an invaluable teaching aid, but the experience for the visitor, the pupils and the teacher should be interesting, educationally worthwhile and be part of a logical sequence of events. One main outcome should be enjoyment for all. If the visitor feels the experience was something they would rather not repeat, then it may be that they simply do not have the skills required to communicate with children; there is no shame in that, for by definition teaching is not their chosen profession. It may be, however, that they were insufficiently briefed, or that the school situation was different from what they expected, or that the pupils had not been prepared sufficiently to respond or make best use of their time. All these issues are preventable, and any teachers who have initiative enough to arrange for suitable visitors would clearly be wise to invest further time in such preparation.

Active Tutorial Work – Receiving a Visitor

Active Tutorial Work (Baldwin and Wells, 1979–83) is probably the most widely used material exploring the pastoral and tutorial roles of schools. One of its most successful strategies is the organizing of a visit to the school. This involves inviting and receiving a visitor in the classroom by the pupils themselves. All the elements of what has gone before in this chapter are there. Who would be a suitable visitor? What would they have to tell us? How should they be invited? What will they need when they come? How can we make them welcome? What questions will we ask? How can we thank them?

Teachers who have used this material are most invariably enthusiastic about the process, with the pupils taking responsibility themselves, and of equal importance putting themselves in the visitors' shoes and thinking about their needs. Such principles could be admirably applied to visitors who come to talk about health, by both staff and pupils alike.

CONCLUSION

There seems to be a good case for using visitors in a health-education programme. If schools select the right kind of expertise for the right reasons the experience is one which is beneficial to both visitors and school. Training visitors seems to be a useful process, giving them skill, understanding and confidence, albeit in the last case sometimes to say No. It is significant that the health-education element has grown substantially in the training of nurses, particularly community nurses. The professionals allied to medicine, such as dieticians and chiropodists and environmental health officers are also keen to develop these skills and many undertake the certificate in health education. Dental staff have their own diploma in dental-health education and at the time of writing the police force are reviewing their teaching/liaison role in schools.

In our experience there seems to be an equally good case for helping the people in these professions who want to teach, by giving them the support of working as a team. Agreement over exactly what message should be given to whom, when and by what means, is fairly fundamental, yet such policies are not that common. Bearing in mind that many health authorities are now producing preventive policies on such issues as diet, smoking, exercise and alcohol, a cohesive approach to those messages by people going into schools would seem desirable. Prevention of ill health and the promotion of good health is undoubtedly of increasing importance and status. One way to develop that in schools is to help and train the teachers themselves, the other is to equip and co-ordinate the visitors they increasingly use.

REFERENCES

Baldwin, J. and Wells, H. (1979–83) *Active Tutorial Work*, Blackwell, Oxford.
Court Committee (1976) Report of the Committee on Child Health Services, *Fit for the Future*, HMSO, London.
Hildreth, J. (1982) Developing dental health education, *Nottingham Practical Papers in Health Education*, No. 4, Nottingham HEU/Nottingham University and Adult Education Department.

McCafferty, I. (1985) Health education – the potential for links between school and community, in International Symposium *The Role of the Teacher in Health Education*, Commission of the European Communities, Luxembourg.

Moore, E. A. (1981) School nursing and health education, Diploma in Health Education thesis, University of Leeds.

APPENDIX 11.1   DENTAL HEALTH EDUCATION

This is to confirm the arrangements made with .... on
....

Speaker:
Address and Telephone No:

Venue of talk:
Telephone No:

Date: Time from: To:

Age range of group/s: Number:

Person/s who will be present during talk/s*:

Additional information:

Any other work done or planned in health education:

Arrangements for follow-up:

NB In the case of schools, a member of staff is required to be present during the talk.

12
THE '16 TO 19' AGE GROUP
Gay Gray

The other day a friend gave me a ballpoint pen, in the hope that it would put 'some sparkle' into my writing. The body of the pen is transparent, full of liquid and tiny, coloured, sparkling dots, and as I tilt it, the pattern and sparkle change constantly. You may well be asking yourself what this has to do with health education for the 16–19 age groups. It occurred to me, as I sat twiddling the pen, wondering where to begin, that it would almost be easier to describe the changing kaleidoscope of coloured dots in the pen than to describe the educational scene as it relates to the 16–19 age group. In a recent review of 16–19 education, the point was made that the scene is shifting constantly with every month seeming to bring a fresh initiative (Pratley, 1985).

In order to bring a semblance of stability into this potentially confusing area, and to give this chapter some coherence, I have decided to focus on some of the issues, which we have had to address, in developing health-education materials for the 16–19 age group, as part of the Health Education Council's 12–19 project. The project was funded by the HEC for three years, from 1983–86 and was based in the Health Education Unit (HEU) at the University of Southampton. The main aim was to develop initiatives specifically for 16–19-year-olds. In the course of this work, the project team was faced with many questions. A number of these are likely to be relevant to anyone concerned with implementing health education for this older age group.

WHERE DO WE FIND 16–19-YEAR-OLDS?

One of the questions raised at the beginning of the project related to identifying the most appropriate education institutions for reaching this age group, in order to implement health education. If our aim was to reach the largest number, where could they best be contacted?

The predecessor to the project had been SHEP 13–18, funded jointly by the HEC and the Schools Council (in association with SHEG and the Transport and Road Research Laboratory). The main focus of SHEP 13–18 was to raise the profile of health education in secondary schools, and to encourage a co-ordinated approach to health education. To this end, in-service training programmes were run in more than 30 LEAs and two publications were produced, namely a guide for co-ordination and a set of classroom materials (Forbes Publications).

During the life of SHEP 13–18, the primary concern was secondary school education, and, with compulsory education ending at 16 years, there were obvious gaps in provision for the 16–19 age group.

The figures in Table 12.1 give an indication of the educational and economic activity of 16–18-year olds, as at January 1984. The proportion of 16-year olds attending school was then 31 per cent; however, only 3 per cent of 18-year olds were still at school, compared with 14 per cent who were in further education, 20 per cent who were unemployed and 62 per cent who were mainly in employment.

Figures for this age group are notoriously difficult to assess and predict, as it is not a static population. For example, in 1984, within a short space of time, a young person might have moved from school, to unemployment, to a youth training scheme (YTS). Figures tend to differ depending on the source from which they originate, understandably with youth unemployment being such a political issue.

Table 12.1   Educational and economic activity of 16–18-year olds, as at January 1984

Great Britain

	16-year olds	17-year olds	18-year olds	16–18-year olds
Numbers in age group	899,000	909,000	929,000	2,737,000
Percentage				
Full-time education	45%	31%	17%	31%
– School	31%	19%	3%	17%
– FE	14%	12%	14%	14%
YTS	25%	6%	–	10%
Unemployed	13%	17%	20%	17%
Other (mainly in employment outside of YTS)	18%	46%	62%	42%

Source: Department of Education and Science (1985) *Statistical Bulletin*, February. (Figures were not given in this source for 19-year olds.)

Moreover the figures for 1984 may be of little relevance in 1987, as the educational and employment situation is in a state of flux. For example, since January 1984, the YTS has been extended to two years, the certificate of pre-vocational education (CPVE) has been introduced (the first major pre-vocational initiative to be offered through both schools and colleges). There are no entry qualifications and it is available to all 16-year olds; the unemployment rate for those aged 18 to 24 has continued to rise; the status of young people between 16 and 21 has been affected by government legislation. Their choices, for example of whether to attend a certain college, leave home, go on a YTS course, or seek employment, will all be influenced by current regulations. In recent years, there has been political controversy over new board-and-lodging regulations (restricting the bene-fit that allows homeless young people to stay in temporary accommo-dation); over the awarding of grants; over the removal of young people under 21 from the protection of the Wages Council (which guarantees 1 in 5 a minimum wage of £45 to £56 a week); over supplementary benefit being reduced, if a 16-year old refuses a place on a YTS scheme. The extent to which unemployed 16–19-year olds can study and still claim benefit has similarly been subject to restrictions (the 12 and 21 hours study rules).

Educational opportunities vary from one LEA to the next, including school sixth forms, sixth-form colleges, further education colleges, skill centres and tertiary colleges. There has been a marked growth in the number of tertiary colleges which have been established in recent years. In some areas, such a Richmond upon Thames, there is a total break at 16, with the tertiary college the sole provider after that. In others, for example, Hampshire, the tertiary college exists alongside other arrangements.

Attendance by a young person in these settings is also disparate. It may be part-time, or full-time, of varying duration, as part of a full-time scheme which is mainly based elsewhere.

If the educational scene, pre-16, seems complex, it is a model of simpli-city compared with the entanglement of routes and courses on offer to the 16-plus age range. The choice includes A-level, CPVE, B/Tec (Business and Technician Education Council), CGLI (City and Guilds of London Institute), YTS and RSA (Royal Society of Arts), as well as those courses on offer to the pre-16 age group, for example GCSE and TVEI.

Although young people are being strongly encouraged to pursue some form of training or education after the compulsory school-leaving age, a significant number do not have any contact with formal education post-16. Are there any other settings concerned with the personal and social education of young people, where health education might be appropriate?

Important informal settings include youth clubs, unemployment drop-in centres, working with girls projects, youth community projects and youth custody centres.

Again there appear to be no certain figures concerning the numbers of 16–19s who can be reached through the Youth Service. A DES (1983) study offers some information concerning attendance at youth clubs, for example, that among the older age group there were more unemployed than employed attenders, but precise percentages according to age seem difficult to ascertain. Attendance at clubs may be erratic rather than regular and tend to depend on specific events, such as a disco or outing. Several practising youth members considered that many of their club members would cease regular attendance once they were old enough, or appeared old enough, to go to a pub! However, others commented that growing numbers of the older age group were turning to the Youth Service, owing to increasing unemployment.

Unfortunately (as perhaps was to be expected!), there seemed to be no easy answer as to where we could contact the greatest number of 16–19-year olds. This age group was relatively under-resourced in terms of health education materials, but there seemed no clear indication, in terms of attendance, that attention should be focused primarily on one type of setting.

WHAT ARE THE OPPORTUNITIES AND CONSTRAINTS ON HEALTH EDUCATION WITHIN DIFFERENT SETTINGS?

My next step was to explore the appropriateness of these various settings for health education. What opportunities were there for health education with the age group? What constraints were there?

During the first year of the project, staff and young people were interviewed in a variety of settings in the West District of Southampton. These included a sixth-form college, a technical college and various youth-service settings. In addition to those staff working in the actual settings, a number of other professionals were interviewed, for example, an adviser for Further Education and the Youth Service, a health education officer, a young people's advisory service doctor, and a Further Education curriculum development officer. One of the aims of the interviews was to ascertain some of the issues which affect the implementation of health education within different institutions or services.

This consultative process was continued in the second year of the project. A 'development' group was formed, consisting of staff, who worked with the age group, in both formal and informal educational settings, and from various parts of the country. The group met at monthly interviews from January to September 1985. On the agenda for the meetings was an appraisal of the issues raised by the research. To what extent did the perceptions and experiences of the people interviewed in Southampton tally with those in other parts of Britain?

In both the research and development phases, it was obvious that there were marked differences between the *raison d'être* of the formal and informal sectors which would affect the implementation of health education. An institution geared towards examinations and training offers a very different environment to that which has leisure activities as its base.

In a formal setting, staff have a captive audience. They can predict their likely contact with a group of young people – the number and length of sessions. However, in the informal sector, attendance is of a more voluntary, transitory and casual nature. Staff need to be prepared to seize opportunities for health education, to respond to situations which arise.

The following comments from two youth workers in the development group may help to illustrate this:

'The mobility of people you are working with is a problem – regarding floating membership'.
'It's got to be *that* evening'.

This is not to say that it is impossible to plan health education in the informal sector; health fairs, a residential away from the club, a group of young people who opt to meet on a regular basis, are among the possibilities for pro-action rather than reaction.

Staff in Further Education, sixth-form colleges and school sixth forms commented on the perceived low status of health education by both colleagues and students. (Students are attending to obtain qualifications.) Examination subjects take precedence over health or personal and social education. Pre-vocational training may be accepted as a necessary prerequisite to increasing employment opportunities, but the relevance of health education may be more difficult to grasp, especially if it is taught in a prescriptive, traditional way.

In informal settings, both staff and young people expressed the importance of distinguishing between youth-service provision and formal education. They perceived the youth service as offering leisure activities, as existing for young people. It was seen almost as a balance to formal education which was perceived as being imposed *on* young people. Again, comments from youth workers might best illustrate this:

'The club is their space, their territory, and they feel easier talking to each other on their home ground.'

'The young person's expectations are very different regarding your role. They want nothing to do with *education*!'

Some problems seem shared by both formal and informal settings. One of these is the lack of trained staff to implement health education. Another is time; in formal settings, time on the timetable, while in informal settings, the routine supervisory, organizational tasks may leave little time for actually talking with young people.

Other constraints identified included the low morale of the teaching profession (this particularly related to the teachers' action in 1985); the financial resources available (which seemed to differ tremendously from one site to another. In the formal sector, funding from the Manpower Service Commission had, in some instances, been a valuable resource for health education); the rooms available; the unclear boundaries of health education; and the fact that health education is still perceived by many people as 'blocks' of topics, such as smoking, alcohol, and contraception, rather than as an overall approach.

I am conscious of possibly painting an excessively gloomy picture! Perhaps I should redress the balance by mentioning some of the many opportunities identified for health education. It should perhaps be borne in mind that some of the items previously mentioned as constraints, will, for some, be opportunities (for example, rooms, money). Similarly, the introduction of educational initiatives, such as CPVE, can be a constraint, in terms of, for example, the added pressure on staff and the stress caused by any innovation, but, on the other hand, it can be a golden opportunity, when social and personal development is incorporated into the core curriculum and when an opportunity is afforded by increased funding for staff training in participatory methods.

Low levels of unemployment were seen by some as creating more opportunities for health education. There were increased numbers of young people staying in formal education and therefore more opportunity for contact. The likelihood of unemployment, after a scheme or course, could mean greater relevance being attached to non-vocational education. If the status or esteem conferred in our society to those in employment, is to be denied young people, educators need to place higher emphasis on helping them to feel valued and to value themselves. This means helping them not only to use and develop their own 'resources', to be as 'healthy' as possible at any moment but also to recognize the social issues affecting their health, over which they may have had little control.

In the Youth Service, the voluntary nature of young people's use of the settings, makes it imperative that they feel at ease, and places increasing emphasis on the need for youth workers to be able to relate to young people. This special relationship between staff and client, based on mutual respect rather than authority, is compatible with current health-education approaches of facilitating learning rather than a more traditional didactic approach.

Furthermore, there can be little doubt that the nature of youth work is in harmony with personal and social education. Both place emphasis on the importance of self-directed behaviour and aim to foster the active participation of young people in the planning and provision of activities. According to some of the staff from the Youth Service, in the development group, this can, however, sometimes be a hindrance in promoting health education; 'there is the complacent assumption that it is done', 'there is a lot of talk about participation . . . how much are they (the young people) involved in running their clubs? In making their rules?'.

HOW DO WE DECIDE ON THE CONTENT OF HEALTH EDUCATION FOR THIS AGE GROUP?

Perhaps the question that needs to be asked before this is 'Who should decide on the content of health education?' The philosophy underpinning much health education work is that of empowerment, of encouraging young people to take responsibility.

The majority of staff to whom I talked in the project believed that, if the aim was genuinely to empower young people, they must also be given the power to decide on the content of health education. The content should be based on young people's perceptions of their health needs. One youth worker gave us the following advice: 'I think the most important thing is that you should be starting with the young people themselves. We as adults can come up with an agenda for them, but you need to talk to them.'

There was also widespread agreement amongst young people that they wanted opportunities to talk, to question, to be listened to and to have questions answered fully and honestly. They definitely did not want to be told what to do.

However, we have also had to recognize the difficulties of adopting an approach which is based on respecting young people's choices. Does it mean that we ignore epidemiological data? Road safety was rarely mentioned by young people as a topic of importance in health education, yet the primary cause of death for 15–24-year olds is road accidents.

How important is the content, the choice of topics in health education? If the question 'What would you like to cover in health education?' is asked, the reply is likely to comprise a list of topics. Yet, if health education does indeed consist of three domains: cognitive, affective and skills, underpinning these topics may be common themes. For example, in road safety, a specific core of information (including knowledge of the highway code) might be identified, but also included would be themes such as self-image (for example does our image of ourselves affect our choice of car, motor bike, the way we drive), risk-taking, the effects of drugs on decision-making, an awareness of consequences, valuing oneself and others, coping with emotions, assertiveness, awareness of alternatives, environmental issues, the role of the government and manufacturers in health issues and the influence of the media.

These themes are likely to be equally relevant to nutrition education or to drug education. How important then is the choice of topic, or is the choice of 'themes' more relevant?

There seems to be a need to accept in health education, whether it concerns decisions on the content of a programme, or on the desired outcome of the programme, that there is a constant tension between wanting to say to young people, at one end of the continuum 'You choose!' and at the other 'Do this!'. Their choice will be affected by numerous factors: their awareness of the issues involved; their perception of the range of choices open to them; the social, environmental and economic constraints on their choices; their past experience – to name but a few. The following quotes from two students at a further education college typify the tendency for choices for this age group to be more influenced by what is happening here and now, than by consideration of the future:

I don't think most young people think about the future. When people get heart diseases when they're middle-aged – they think that's so far off. You *should* worry about it, but I don't think most people do. When you start to get about forty, you think, maybe I should be a bit careful!'
Most people just sort of take the days as they come – they don't sort of think about it, really. I mean, I don't know what I'm going to do next year. It seems so far away that you just don't think about it. Too occupied.

Staff may well see their role as increasing young people's awareness about the variety or nature of choices open to them. Similarly, the extent to which staff are inclined to be prescriptive will be influenced by the setting in which they are working, and by what they themselves are bringing to health education. Their own values, agendas and skills will affect the amount of freedom that they are willing to allow young people. They may feel tempted to utter 'Do this!' in certain areas rather than others.

It seems important to recognize that this continuum does exist and to be open with young people about any constraints on their choices. If they are to be actively involved in planning a health-education programme relevant to their needs, there is likely to be an element of negotiation, both between one another and with any member of staff concerned.

As a project, it seemed impossible to prescribe content for a mythical homogeneous group of 16–19-year olds, when defining their needs is likely to be dependent on such a wide variety of criteria, including social class, employment/unemployment status, race, residential location, gender, marital status, mental and physical handicaps, past and present health/ illness experiences. A more viable alternative was to suggest methods by which staff and young people could assess their own health needs and negotiate a programme appropriate to those needs. These methods include the use of photographs, quizzes, brain-storming, community activities, case studies, as well as 'just talking' with young people.

WHAT FORM SHOULD HEALTH EDUCATION TAKE?

Here there was little disagreement. High emphasis was placed by both staff and young people on the importance of participatory methods. One young person commented:

'There's nothing worse than being sat down and their saying, like, "this is a lesson: you should do this, this and not this".'

The way of working is seen to be of paramount importance. Methods are required which acknowledge the past and present experience of young people and which build on those experiences and help them to value themselves and others. Again and again it was stressed that what is fundamental to effective health education is a rapport between staff and young people, and a need to establish trusting, open relationships with individuals and within groups.

This is not to deny that the more traditional didactic styles are at times appropriate in health education. In order to make decisions related to their health, young people need certain information – and a lecture, a leaflet, a film may be the most appropriate way of giving them relevant facts. However, they also need an opportunity to explore their values and attitudes, to weigh up what is right for them, to develop the skills necessary to build relationships and communicate with others. This requires a style of leadership which involves talking with them, rather than at them; it involves skills of triggering discussion and encouraging participation.

As a project, we could offer a range of activities that might help in this process. We aimed to illustrate the transferability of the activities to different health areas, and to encourage staff and young people to adapt the materials according to their needs.

One difficulty encountered, which in a chapter of this length, we can only touch upon, is the complexity of developing health education materials for a multicultural society. If we are to build on the wealth of cultural backgrounds, we need to ensure that the illustrations (both visual and verbal) reflect those cultures. Furthermore, there is the difficulty that certain values which underpin the pack may at times be incompatible. Avoiding sexism sometimes sits uncomfortably alongside avoiding racism. Carole Whittey (1985) in a document on sex education in multi-ethnic schools, writes:

> The educator in a multi-ethnic situation, who addresses the task of improving the status of women by offering greater opportunity for independence in whatever sphere of her life – be it sexual, financial, social – runs the risk of being accused of devaluing cultures other than her/his own.

Furthermore, although the emphasis of the project's material was on process, on the adaptation of a way of working, that way of working may itself be culturally bound. Inviting a group of students to draw a line, representing their life and to plot significant health events upon it is an alien concept to certain cultures, for example the Chinese. The issues are complex, and can possibly only be resolved with increased representation of different ethnic groups in the development of health education initiatives.

A PROBLEM OR A SPARKLE?

I began this chapter with reference to a sparkle: a sparkle in a novelty pen. I would like to end with reference to another sparkle: the sparkle of young people. All too often 'youth' are depicted as problems in the media as 'hooligans'. The focus is on their 'irresponsible' behaviour – their drug-taking, violence and sexual 'immorality'. At the World Health Organization conference on 'School as a health-promoting community', May 1986, Wadad Haddad (Regional Officer for Family Planning, WHO), presented a paper which closed with the following words; I can think of no better ending:

> We must stop seeing adolescents as problems – adolescents are wonderful with their energy, idealism, flexibility and creativity. They are a great

resource and hope for the future. The more we acknowledge and set out to meet their needs, the better place the world will be, for us, for them and for generations to come.

REFERENCES

Department of Education and Science (1983) *Young People in the Eighties*, HMSO, London.

Haddad, Wadad (1986) *Adolescent Sexuality: A Growing Concern for Parents and Governments*, Report No. 8021F, Regional Office for Europe, WHO, Geneva.

Pratley, B. (1985) *Signposts '85*, Further Education Unit, London.

Whittey, Carole (1985) *Sex Education in Multi-Ethnic Schools*, National Organization for Initiatives in Social Education.

Appendix I
AGENCIES OFFERING
RESOURCES FOR HEALTH EDUCATION

We acknowledge additional help from Tracey Collins of Gloucestershire Health Education Services.

Alcohol Concern
305 Gray's Inn Road, London WC1X 8QF
Tel: 01-833 3471

National charity with three main aims: to raise public awareness of the problems alcohol can cause, to try to improve services for people who are drinking too much and to promote preventive action at a local and national level.

ASH – Action on Smoking and Health
5–11 Mortimer Street, London W1N 7RH
Tel: 01-637 9843
9 Queen Street, Edinburgh EH2 1JQ
Tel: 031-225 4725
40 Eglantine Avenue, Belfast BT9 6DX
Tel: 0232 663281

Publishes quarterly newsletter.

Boulton-Hawker Films Limited
Hadleigh, Ipswich, Suffolk IP7 5BG
Tel: 0473 822235

Have been producing and distributing 16mm educational films for schools since 1946. Current free catalogue lists over 200 films including 50 titles dealing with health education. Video cassettes also available.

BBC Education
London W5 2PA
Tel: 01-991 8031

BBC radio and television programmes, reflecting continuing commitment to health education, are designed to support and enrich school and college activities. Details of series and supporting publications distributed to all schools annually in March/April.

British Dental Health Foundation
88 Gurnards Avenue, Fishermead, Milton Keynes, Bucks
Tel: 0908 567614/567639

British Heart Foundation
102 Gloucester Place, London W1II 4DH
Tel: 01-935 0185

British Institute of Traffic Education Research
Kent House, Kent Street, Birmingham B5 6QF
Tel: 021-622 2402

Provides traffic-education materials for primary and secondary schools and further education establishments. Resources catalogue available.

British Life Assurance Trust for Heath Education (BLAT)
BMA House, Tavistock Square, London WC1H 9JP
Tel: 01-388 7976

Exists to promote the further education of the medical profession and the general public in the field of preventive medicine and health. Resources include publications, learning materials, film library, information library, recording and duplicating service.

British Nutrition Foundation
15 Belgrave Square, London SW1X 8PS
Tel: 01-235 4904

Publishes background papers for professionals working in or teaching nutrition, plus books and leaflets. Catalogue (including audio-visual materials) available.

British Red Cross Society
9 Grosvenor Crescent, London SW1X 7EJ
Tel: 01-235 5454

An independent voluntary organization. Main aims are training and voluntary service to the community, within the fields of first aid, nursing and welfare, and support for the International Red Cross.

British Temperance Society
Stanborough Park, Watford WD2 6JP
Tel: 0923 672251

British Universities Film and Video Council
55 Greek Street, London W1V 5LR
Tel: 01-734 3687

Brook Advisory Centre
153A East Street, London SE17 2SD
Tel: 01-708 1390/1234

Branches throughout England and Scotland provide help and advice about birth control, pregnancy testing, counselling and referral and help with emotional and sexual difficulties to young people. Education and Publications Unit, 10 Albert Street, Birmingham B4 7UD (Tel: 021-643 1554) provide free catalogue of education material.

Camera Talks Limited
197 Botley Road, Oxford OX2 0HE
Tel: 0865 726625

Has produced a large number of programmes for health education in schools, colleges and universities. Slide-tape programmes with printed commentaries; the cassetted tapes are in pulse and synchronization with the slides. Videos also available.

Cancer Research Campaign Education and Child Studies Research Group Department of Epidemiology and Social Oncology, University of Manchester, Kinnaird Road, Manchester M20 9QL
Tel: 061-434 7721

Aims to provide a range of effective materials and advice for teachers and lecturers on the subject of cancer. Interest from schools and colleges is welcome.

Catholic Marriage Advisory Council (CMAC)
15 Lansdowne Road, London W11 3AJ
Tel: 01-727 0141
18 Park Circus, Glasgow G3 6BE
Tel: 041-332 4914

The experience of those counsellors who regularly visit schools to talk with pupils about sex, love and personal relationships is made available to teachers through the CMAC service for teachers. Resource list available.

CFL Vision
Chalfont Grove, Gerrards Cross, Bucks SL9 8TN
Tel: 02407 4433

Major distributor of documentary films and video cassettes on education, training, health subjects and general interest. Free catalogue.

Concord Film and Video Council Ltd
201 Felixstowe Road, Ipswich, Suffolk IP3 9BJ
Tel: 0473 76012

Registered charity operating a library of video cassettes and films. Specializes in material concerning contemporary social issues and health-education topics. Distributor for material produced by many organizations including the Health Education Council. Bi-annual catalogue.

DHSS Information Division
PO Box 21, Canons Park, Honeypot Lane, Stanmore HA7 1AY
Tel: 01-952 2311

Disabled Living Foundation
Information Service, 380–384 Harrow Road, London W9 2HU
Tel: 01-289 6111

Family Planning Association (FPA)
27–35 Mortimer Street, London W1A 4QM
Tel: 01-636 7866
4 Clifton Street, Glasgow
Tel: 041-333 9696

Free inquiry service. Publications. Free leaflets, posters and factsheets. Mail order book service. Education unit has range of courses and educational/training resources.

General Dental Council
37 Wimpole Street, London W1M 8DQ
Tel: 01-486 2171

Dental health education programme for schools and colleges of education. Posters, leaflets, films, slides and models. Catalogue available.

Gibbs Oral Hygiene Service
Dental Health Education Consultants, Hesketh House, Portman Square, London W1A 1DY
Tel: 01-486 1200

Dental health education service. Publications, project kits, films, videos, models, lecture service. Free catalogue.

Guild Sound and Vision Ltd
6 Royce Road, Peterborough PE1 5YB
Tel: 0733 315315

Major distributor of educational, sponsored and training films and videos. Preview service and off-air recording scheme.

Health Education Bureau
34 Upper Mount Street, Dublin 2, Ireland
Tel: 01-761116/766640

Set up in 1975 as an Irish government body with responsibility for health education. Its work in schools has essentially been in the areas of teacher training and developing resource materials for teachers. Education, training, research and library services.

Health Education Council (HEC)
78 New Oxford Street, London WC1A 1AH
Tel: 01-631 0930

Schools Section, set up in 1972, has now become the Young People's Programme; caters for young people aged 4–19. Resources Centre, 71–75 New Oxford Street, incorporates audiovisual and other multi-media materials, library and information service. Leaflet available.

Health Education Index
124 Belgrave Road, London SW1V 2BL
Tel: 01-631 0930

The most complete resource reference in health education. Lists more than 9,000 items including leaflets, booklets, film strips, slides, tapes, cassettes, videos, models, wall charts, teaching kits and posters. Revised every two years.

Help for Health
Wessex Regional Library Unit, South Academic Block, Southampton General Hospital, Southampton SO9 4XY
Tel: 0703 777222 (ext. 3753)
    0703 779091 (24-hour Ansaphone)

Self-help groups and voluntary organizations. Publications on health, illness and disability. Sources of practical help in the community.

HMSO Publications Centre
PO Box 276, London SW8 5DT
(Mail and telephone orders only)
Telephone orders: 01-622 3316
General inquiries: 01-211 5616

Catalogues available on: medicine and health; mother and childcare.

Independent Broadcasting Authority (IBA)
70 Brompton Road, London SW3 1EY
Tel: 01-584 7011

Health-education series together with appropriate back-up materials produced every year. Details of current programming and publications for schools and of free liaison and in-service support activities available to schools and LEAs from: David Lee, Education Officer (Liaison), Independent Broadcasting Authority (above address).

Institute of Alcohol Studies
Alliance House, 12 Caxton Street, London SW1H 0QS
Tel: 01-222 4001/5880

Institute of Environmental Health Officers
Chadwick House, Rushworth Street, London SE1 0RB
Tel: 01-928 6006

International Planned Parenthood Federation (IPPF)
18–20 Lower Regent Street, London SW17 4PW
Tel: 01-839 2911

ISDD (Institute for the Study of Drug Dependence)
1–4 Hatton Place, Hatton Garden, London EC1N 8ND
Tel: 01-430 1991

Library and information service about drug misuse. Publishes material about drugs and sells publications for other organizations. List of publications available.

Institute of Health Education
14 High Elm Road, Hale Barns, Cheshire
Tel: 061-980 8276/8696

Members exchange information and views. Comprehensive information service on medicine, teaching and education, nursing, community medicine, public and environmental health.

Kraft Kitchen
Kraft Foods Ltd, St George's House, Bayshill Road, Cheltenham, Glos GL50 3AE
Tel: 0242 36101

Full-colour recipe cards, including nutritional information. Recipe booklets also available.

London Food Commission
PO Box 291, London N5 1DU
Tel: 01-633 5782

Registered charity whose objects are to relieve sickness, ill health and disease in Greater London and to advance public education in nutrition and diet. Advice and information service.

MENCAP (Royal Society for Mentally Handicapped Children and Adults)
123 Golden Lane, London EC1Y 0RT
Tel: 01-253 9433

Founded in 1946 as the Association of Parents of Backward Children. Provides services through divisional offices around the country: welfare and legal advice, counselling, education and training, employment service.

Mental Health Film Council
380 Harrow Road, London W9 2HU
Tel: 01-286 2346

Consultancy and advice on mental health and appropriate media. Catalogue, quarterly newsletter, information service.

National Childbirth Trust (Education for Parenthood)
9 Queensborough Terrace, Bayswater, London W2 3TB
Tel: 01-221 3833

Organizes classes for preparation for childbirth; branches all over the country. Trains antenatal teachers, promotes breast-feeding and organizes postnatal support for new parents. Encourages birth education by provision of resource lists of books and visual aids, and study days for teachers.

National Confederation of Parent–Teacher Associations (NCPTA)
43 Stonebridge Road, Northfleet, Gravesend, Kent DA11 9DS
Tel: 0474 60618

Exists to help schools of all kinds to establish happy relationships between home and school.

National Deaf Children's Society
45 Hereford Road, London W2 5AH
Tel: 01-229 9272/4

Network of about 140 voluntary groups over the UK. Provides advice on welfare and education, plus services and information for deaf children and their families. Free information sheets and booklets.

National Association for Maternal and Child Welfare
1 South Audley Street, London W1Y 6JS
Tel: 01-491 2772

Aims to further education in matters connected with maternal and child welfare. Resources include: publications and suggested syllabuses for use in schools and colleges; advisory service; parentcraft education. List of publications available.

National Marriage Guidance Council
Herbert Gray College, Little Church Street, Rugby, Warwickshire CV21 3AP
Tel: 0788 73241

Runs courses, and regional and local training events for teachers and others. Bookshop. Free catalogues.

National Society for the Prevention of Cruelty to Children (NSPCC)
Young League, 67 Saffron Hill, London EC1N 8RS
Tel: 01-242 1626

Set of information sheets for students aged 15+. Speakers and film shows for groups of students in parenthood and allied subjects. List of films included in information pack, plus publications and publicity material.

National Youth Bureau
17–23 Albion Street, Leicester LE1 6GD
Tel: 0533 554775

Resource centre for youth work policy-makers and practitioners. Information service, books and pamphlets, training advice and materials, research. Catalogue available.

Nursing and Health Visiting
United Kingdom Central Council for Nursing, Midwifery and Health Visiting (UKCC)
23 Portland Place, London W1N 3AF
Tel: 01-637 7181

The English National Board for Nursing, Midwifery and Health Visiting (ENB)
170 Tottenham Court Road, London W1P 0HA
Tel: 01-388 3131

The Welsh National Board for Nursing, Midwifery and Health Visiting (WNB)
Floor 13, Pearl Assurance House, Greyfriars Road, Cardiff CF1 3RT
Tel: 0222 395535

The National Board for Nursing, Midwifery and Health Visiting for Scotland (NBS)
22 Queen Street, Edinburgh EH2 1JX
Tel: 031-226 7371

The National Board for Nursing, Midwifery and Health Visiting in Northern Ireland (NBNI)
RAC House, 79 Chichester Street, Belfast BT1 4JE
Tel: 0232 760831

The responsibility for education and training of health visitors and school nurses passed in 1983 to the five statutory bodies listed above. The National Boards publish the syllabus for health-visiting courses which includes a study of the principles of learning and teaching, and some teaching practice in preparation for health education activities.

Office of Health Economics
12 Whitehall, London SW1A 2DY
Tel: 01-930 9203

OPCS Monitor
These information sheets supply the statistical background on which many reports on health education are based. Available from: Information Branch (Dept. M), Office of Population Censuses & Surveys, St Catherines House, 10 Kingsway, London WC2B 6JP

Project Icarus Ltd
Raglan House, 4 Clarence Parade, Southsea, Hants PO5 3NU
Tel: 0705 827460

Registered charity producing visual aids for health education. Subjects range from birth control to alcoholism.

Royal Society for the Prevention of Accidents (RoSPA)
Cannon House, The Priory, Queensway, Birmingham B4 6BS
Tel: 021-233 2461

The largest and most comprehensive safety organization in Europe. List of publications, posters, films, etc., available.

SCODA (The Standing Conference on Drug Abuse)
1–4 Hatton Place, Hatton Garden, London EC1N 8ND
Tel: 01-430 2341

National co-ordinating organization for services for people with drug problems. Lists available of specialist services throughout the country.

The Scottish Health Education Group
Woodburn House, Canaan Lane, Edinburgh EH10 4SG
Tel: 031-447 8044

The Spastics Society
12 Park Crescent, London W1N 4EQ
Tel: 01-636 5020

World's leading organization for the care, treatment, training and education of children and adults with cerebral palsy (spasticity). Leaflet available. Information service.

Sports Council Information Centre
16 Upper Woburn Place, London WC1H 0QP
Tel: 01-388 1277

Teachers Advisory Council on Alcohol and Drug Education (TACADE)
3rd Floor, Furness House, Trafford Road, Salford M5 2XJ
Tel: 061-848 0351/2
Southern office: 202 Holdenhurst Road, Bournemouth BH8 8AS
Tel: 0202 295874

National educational organization. Develops in-service teacher training courses in health education. Classroom course material, back-up resources for teachers, speakers, and a reference/study facility in Salford. Termly bulletin and other publications.

Tenovus Cancer Information Centre
11 Whitchurch Road, Cardiff CF4 3JN
Tel: 0222 42851

Publications include surveys of opinion and attitudes of the public and of GPs on cancer, and leaflets and posters on smoking and advice on the early detection of women's cancers. Cancer Information Pack for Schools. Film library and lecture service. Resource lists and catalogue available.

Viewtech Audio Visual Media
161 Winchester Road, Brislington, Bristol BS4 3NJ
Tel: 0272 773422

Films, videos, filmstrips, learning packs, audio-visual equipment. Incorporates the Gateway and the Rank educational film libraries. Free catalogue.

Appendix II

SCHOOL HEALTH EDUCATION IN EUROPE

Trefor Williams

There are difficulties and dangers in attempting to sketch an overview of school health education in Europe. Within the thirty-two or so countries there is a diversity of approaches and developments which cannot be addressed in any other than the very broadest of terms. There is, in addition, certain to be as great a diversity of approach within each country as there is between the countries themselves. This diversity becomes clearer when we learn that some countries, for example the Netherlands and Italy, now have legislation concerning the inclusion of health education in the school curricula; others such as the United Kingdom (where several important school projects are under way) rely upon policy and discussion documents; while yet other countries, such as Greece, Spain and Portugal, are just beginning to feel their way forward.

School health education in Europe can best be described as in the process of evolution. However, the phases of an evolutionary process are often so blurred that they are difficult to identify with clarity until the process is complete. If we were to visualize an evolutionary continuum, it is likely that each country would occupy a wide spread over parts of it (see Figure II.1). It is therefore more helpful to think in terms of national trends within such an evolutionary continuum, and it is possible to identify at least five phases through which school health education has passed or is presently passing in Europe.

THE EVOLUTION OF
SCHOOL HEALTH EDUCATION

Phase 1: Teaching Materials

The development of classroom materials, teaching packs, posters, leaflets, etc., is usually the first response and the first phase of the evolutionary

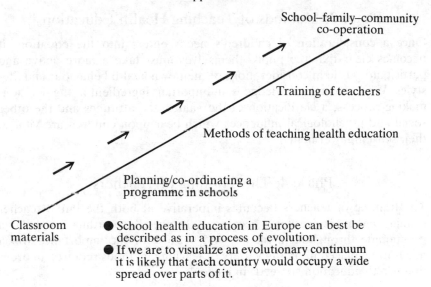

Figure II.1 The evolution of school health education in Europe: a continuum

spiral. All European countries have produced packs of materials of various kinds, sometimes in response to crisis concerns such as 'drugs' or 'tobacco', and at other times by interest or pressure groups resulting in 'dental health', 'healthy eating' or 'safety education' packs. Not infrequently these packs become effectively the health education curriculum, but they also pose problems for schools which want to know where in the general curriculum they might be placed, how they might be used to best advantage and who amongst the staff is to be responsible for them. These questions lead inevitably and naturally to the following phases.

Phase 2: Planning and Co-ordinating a Programme in Schools

The *ad hoc* nature of the 'health education pack' syndrome gives way generally to a desire, and sometimes the will, to think about planning a more effective programme. This often leads to a closer analysis of what the needs of the pupils might be at different stages of schooling and a consideration of the many different ways in which these needs might be met or co-ordinated through the various areas of the existing curriculum.

Phase 3: Methods of Teaching Health Education

Once a consideration of children's needs enters into the equation, it becomes clear that the pupils themselves must take a more active and participatory role in considerations of their own health behaviour and life-styles. While factual knowledge is an important ingredient in the decision-making process, a clarification of the values, the attitudes and the other social and psychological influences which bear upon children are vital to their self-empowerment.

Phase 4: The Training of Teachers

The training of teachers becomes imperative at both the initial teacher training and in-service stages because of the need to co-ordinate and plan a programme throughout a school, and because of the importance which needs to be placed upon the variety of teaching methods required in order that health education succeeds in its goals.

Phase 5: Family and Community

The recognition of the important part parents and the family group play in the successful implementation of school health education is now wide-spread throughout Europe. Parents and the wider community are import-ant partners with the school, and without such a partnership a coherent, meaningful and lasting programme would be hamstrung. Education auth-orities are generally aware of the fundamental importance of placing programmes such as drug education firmly within a school–family–commu-nity dimension.

The difficulty of placing a particular European country on this continuum is compounded by the fact that – due to international conferences, work-shops and working parties – there is now a clear awareness and acceptance of what needs to be done. However, this awareness is not easily translated into practice because the tradition of schools, particularly as they bear upon curriculum matters and teaching styles, is not easily changed.

  Perhaps the base line for action on school health education in Europe was laid in 1980 by a seminar 'Constraints in the Education for Health of Schoolchildren' organized by the WHO (Europe) and held in Gent, Bel-gium, under the chairmanship of Professor Veelsteek of Gent University. The report of this seminar, which considered in some detail the viability and pathways forward for school health education, emerged at roughly the same time as the WHO Regional Office for Europe produced its Regional Strategy for Attaining Health for All by the Year 2000. The two reports complemented each other in many ways, emphasizing the need for:

- a reappraisal of the objectives of health education in general and the need for a more dynamic approach to the promotion of health;
- the importance of the promotion of health to children and young people, and their involvement in decision-making related to both personal and community health.

There has followed, at intervals, a succession of international events which have succeeded in enhancing the status of school health education/ promotion to a point where national governments now view it generally with approval and support. Such governmental favour has been brought about partly by the problems of drug abuse, cancer and, more recently, by AIDS: problems which education in the broad sense can help to contain and perhaps help to solve.

In outline the history of the European school health education movement since 1980 can be summarized as follows:

1980

WHO European Office: 'Constraints in the Education for Health of Schoolchildren and Parents', Gent, Belgium; a reappraisal of where school health education was in terms of its underlying principles and in terms of its practice in European countries.

1981

(a) International Union for Health Education (European Office): 'Preparing for Healthy Lifestyles in Society', a European Seminar, Halle, GDR; a consideration of the materials and frameworks for school health education.

(b) Health Education Unit, Department of Education, University of Southampton: 'New Directions in Health Education'; a seminar which considered several important issues, such as (1) a framework for a health education curriculum; (2) the school/community interface, and the development of a practical partnership between school, family and community.

1982

International Union for Health Education (European Office): 'Educating Young People to Avoid Smoking and Alcohol Abuse', Vienna, Austria; an attempt to consider the medical issues, health education principles, school programmes and relevant research into abiding health issues facing Western societies.

1983

WHO and German Youth Services: 'Perspectives of Health Promotion for Youth in the European Region', Spitzinsee, FDR; an attempt to perceive health education from a distinctly social-scientific viewpoint. Confirmation of the need for health education to consider social, psychological and political influences upon young people in the shaping of their health behaviour.

1984

WHO and the Health Education Unit, Department of Education, University of Southampton: 'School Health Education in the European Region', Burley, Hampshire, UK; a workshop based upon the shared perception of colleagues from twelve European states concerning the status of school health education in their respective countries. Arising out of this seminar was published *School Health Education in Europe*, a monograph offering profiles of school health education in fifteen European countries. Also arising out of this seminar was the holistic concept of the 'health-promoting school'.

1984–5

Council of Europe: select committee of experts on the role of teaching staff and their basic and in-service training in education for health, Strasbourg; the discussion ranged over the main issues facing the implementation and development of school health education in schools, which are summarized in the final report.

1985

Commission of the EEC: 'The Role of the Teacher in Health Education', a seminar for the member countries of the European Economic Community, Luxembourg; an exchange and discussion of ideas relating to three main

Health Education Council (1983) *My Body*, Heinemann, London.

Health Education Council (1983) *A Discussion Paper on Proposals for National Guidelines for Health Education in Britain*, The NACNE Report, HEC, London.

Hodgson, A. (1985) *LEA Policies and Practices Relating to Drugs, Education and Drug Misuses*, NFER, Windsor.

Holt, J. (1983) *Curriculum Workshop: An Introduction to Whole Curriculum Planning*, Routledge & Kegan Paul, London.

Jones, N. D. (1982) *Understanding Child Abuse*, Hodder & Stoughton, Sevenoaks, Kent.

Maslow, A. H. (1968) *Towards A Psychology of Being*, 2nd edn, Van Nostrand, Princeton, NJ.

Monaster, J. (1977) *Adolescent Development and the Life Tasks*, Allyn and Bacon, Boston, MA.

Nash, W., Thruston, M. and Baly, M. (1985) *Health at School – Caring for the Whole Child*, Heinemann Nursing, London.

Open University (1979) *The Pre-School Child*, Open University Press, Milton Keynes.

Pring, R. (1984) *Personal and Social Education in the Curriculum*, Hodder & Stoughton, Sevenoaks, Kent.

Profitt, R. (1983) *Hand in Hand Assembly Book*, Longman, Harlow.

Reid, D. and Massey, D. (1986) Can school health education be more effective? *Health Educational Journal*, Vol. 45, No. 1.

Ross, H. and Mico, P. (1980) *Theory and Practice in Health Education*, Mayfield Publishing Co., Palo Alto, CA.

Schools Council (1977) *Schools Council: Health Education Project 5–13*, Thomas Nelson, London.

Schools Council (1983) *Fit for Life*, Books 1, 2 and 3, MacMillan Educational, Basingstoke.

Schools Council (1984) *Developing Health Education – A Coordinators' Guide*, Forbes, London.

Settle, D. and Wise, C. (1987) *Choices, Materials and Methods for Personal and Social Education*, Basil Blackwell, Oxford.

Strchlow, M. (1983) *Education for Health*, Harper & Row, London.

Tones, B. K. (1986) Promoting the health of young people: the role of personal and social education in achieving preventive outcomes, *Health Education Journal*, Vol. 45.

Townsend, P. and Davidson, N. (eds) (1982) *Inequalities in Health: The Black Report*, Penguin, London.

Went, D. (1985) *Sex Education – Some Guidelines for Teachers*, Bell Hyman, London.

Williams, T. and De Panafieu, C. (1985) *School Health Education in Europe: Profiles of 15 European Countries*, HEC Health Education Unit, Department of Education, University of Southampton.

Williams, T. and Roberts, J. (1985) *Health Education in Schools and Teacher Education Institutions*, HEC Health Education Unit, Department of Education, University of Southampton.

World Health Organization European Office Copenhagen (1984) *Health Promotion: A Discussion Document of the Concept and Principles*, WHO, Copenhagen.

themes: (a) the health-promoting school; (b) training of teachers; (c) major health issues facing society. The report provides a summary of the main conclusions and recommendations to the EEC.

1986

WHO/Scottish Health Education Group: 'The Health-Promoting School', Peebles, Scotland; a dynamic workshop conference based largely upon small group work and considering each of the (by now) well-known important issues facing school health education, such as: (a) the school's role in the promotion of health; (b) the health education curriculum; (c) the health-promoting school – a working model; (d) methods in school health education; (e) training teachers.

1986

The Commission of the EEC in collaboration with WHO (European Office) and the Council of Europe: 'Health Education in the Pre-Service Training of Teachers', Luxembourg; a conference which for the first time drew together three of the main international organizations concerned with the promotion of health in schools. The conference confirmed the generally growing belief that health education should be included in the pre-service training of teachers primarily as a sensitizer to the health issues facing their future pupils.

The last-mentioned seminar augers well for future collaboration between international organizations and there is now the likelihood of a jointly supported feasibility study for a European school health education project starting some time in 1987. The European school health education movement can only gain from properly conducted and constructed exchanges of ideas, materials and, perhaps more importantly, experiences between countries. There is in Europe a great deal of experience and creativity available which can be channelled for the common good and it is possible that this will come about sooner than later.

REFERENCES

Council of Europe: Publications Office, Council of Europe, Strasbourg.

EEC: Directorita General, Social Affairs and Education, Batiment Jean monef, Plateau du Kischberg h-2920- Luxembourg.

International Union for Health Education: European Officer, Professor Maria Modello, University of Perugia, Perugia, Italy.

University of Southampton: Health Education Unit, Department of Education,
University of Southampton, Southampton, England.
WHO-sponsored: WHO European Office, Copenhagan, Denmark.

SELECT BIBLIOGRAPHY

Anderson, D. (1979) *Health Education in Practice*, Croom Helm, London.
Baldwin, J. and Wells, H. (1979) *Active Tutorial Work* (Books 1–4), Basil Black-well, Oxford.
Barnes, D. (1976) *From Communication to Curriculum*, Penguin, Harmondsworth.
Bates, I. J. and Winder, A. (1984) *Introduction to Health Education*, Mayfield, Palo Alto, CA.
Brandling, R. (1983) *All for Assembly*, Cambridge University Press.
Braun, D. and Eisenstadt, N. (1985) *Family Lifestyles*, Open University Press, Milton Keynes.
Brennan, W. (1982) *Changing Special Education*, Open University Press, Milton Keynes.
Burns, R. (1982) *Self-Concept Development and Education*, Holt, Rinehart and Winston, New York.
Button, L. (1974) *Development Group Work with Adolescents*, Hodder & Stough-ton, Sevenoaks, Kent.
Campbell, G. (1985) *New Directions in Health Education*, Falmer Press, London.
Campbell, G. (ed.) (1986) *Health Education, Youth and Community*, Falmer Press, London.
Craft, A. and Craft, M. (1983) *Sex Education and Counselling for Mentally Handicapped People*, Costello Press, Tunbridge Wells.
David, K. (1983) *Personal and Social Education in Secondary Schools: Report of the Schools Council Working Party on Personal and Social Education*, Longman, York.
David, K. and Charlton, A. (1987) *The Caring Role of the Primary School*, Macmillan, Basingstoke.
Dubos, R. (1967) *Man Adapting*, York University Press.
Engs, R. and Wantz, M. (1978) *Teaching Health Education in the Elementary School*, Houghton Mifflin Co., Boston, MA.
Fogelman, K. (ed.) (1983) *Growing Up in Great Britain*, MacMillan for the National Children's Bureau, London.
Ford, B. (1977) *Health Education a Source Book for Teaching*, Pergamon Press, Oxford.
Goldman, J. and Goldman, R. (1982) *Children's Sexual Thinking*, Routledge & Kegan Paul, London.
Green, L. W., Krenter, M. W., Deeds, S. G. and Partridge, K. B. (1980) *Health Education Planning: A Diagnostic Approach*, Mayfield, Palo Alto, CA.
Hamblin, D. (1983) *Guidance 16–19*, Basil Blackwell, Oxford.
Health Education Council/University of Southampton (1986) *The Health Education Awareness Day*. Materials for mounting a health education experience for initial teacher education institutions, Health Education Unit, Department of Education, University of Southampton.

INDEX

Abbreviations: HE health education; PSE personal and social education;
PE physical education.

Health action model (HAM), 22 ff.;
categories in, 23–4; decision-making,
22–3; decision-making skills, 31–3;
and health actions, 26; and health
beliefs, 25–6; health belief model
(HBM), 25–7; implications, 29–31;
interactions within, 28; and
motivation system, 27–8
health belief model (HAM), 25–7
health education: agencies, 222;
barriers to implementation, 4–5;
boundaries, 2; central areas, 62;
central government pressure, 5;
collective action, 11–12; content,
69–70, 97–103, 246–9; co-ordination,
65–7, 134–7; courses, 227–9;
evaluation, 81–3, 187–91; in guidance
periods, 161; and HEOs, 50, 217 ff.;
marginal status, 3–4; materials, 77,
87–93; nature, 3–4, 62–3, 97–100;
organization of, 66–8, 78–81;
teachers' perceptions, 50; planning,
66–8, 169–71; in primary schools,
51–6, 157–8; priorities, 135; and
'process', 76–7; 'refocussing
upstream', 11; *The School
Curriculum* (1981), 15; major aim of
SCHEP, 9; and science, 120 ff.,
128–33; in secondary schools, 63 ff.,
158–60; and special education, 86 ff.;
specialist topic emphasis, 100; the
spiral curriculum, 67–9; surveys,
60–1; in tutorial work, 166–8;
umbrella term, 157; and WHO, 38;
and the 16–19 age group, 241 ff.
Health Education Council (HEC),
50–1, 113, 120, 166, 219; and 16–19
age group, 241 ff.; *My Body* project,
22, 51, 129; Initial Teacher Training
Project, 69, 141; and PE, 140–1, 143;
Primary School Project, 56–8;
SCHEP manual, 8; and special needs,
86 ff.
Health Education 5–16 (1986), 198
Health Education Officers (HEOs), 50,
112, 160, 219 ff., 222, 244
health education units (HEU), 50,
219 ff., 241
health-promoting schools, 39–40

heart disease, 7
Her Majesty's Inspectors (HMI) *see*
Department of Education and
Science
hidden curriculum, 15, 22, 50, 80
'high rise' model of HE, 78
homosexuality, 167, 211
Humanities Curriculum Project (HCP),
36–7, 39, 148
hygiene, 49, 105, 141

'ice breakers', 185
influences on the young, 206–7
informal methods, 5, 93–5, 176–7; *see
also* discussion methods, group work,
methods
Initial Teacher Education Project, 69,
141
initial training of teachers, 69
in-service training, 142, 146–8, 169–71,
226 ff., 242, 266
Integrated Science (1973), 123, 126–7,
129–30, 132–3

Junior Science (1967), 123

knowledge, 76

language: and relationships, 151, 211;
skills, 151–2
learning: and pastoral care, 156, 162,
164, 167, 170; games, 185–6
Learning through Science (1981), 123
life skills, 38–9, 100, 177; and families,
14; and self-empowerment, 12, 26, 30
literature and HE, 153–4

'Manhattan' model of HE, 79
Manpower Services Commission
(MSC), 38, 246
marriage guidance *see* National
Marriage Guidance Council
mass media, 16–17, 21, 58, 150, 222, 248
medical model of HE, 6–8, 62
menstruation, 102
mental handicap, 10, 100, 167
methods of teaching HE, 39, 75–7,
93–4, 249–50; decision-making, 22–4,
31–2, 75; discussion methods, 168–9;

themes: (a) the health-promoting school; (b) training of teachers; (c) major health issues facing society. The report provides a summary of the main conclusions and recommendations to the EEC.

1986

WHO/Scottish Health Education Group: 'The Health-Promoting School', Peebles, Scotland; a dynamic workshop conference based largely upon small group work and considering each of the (by now) well-known important issues facing school health education, such as: (a) the school's role in the promotion of health; (b) the health education curriculum; (c) the health-promoting school – a working model; (d) methods in school health education; (e) training teachers.

1986

The Commission of the EEC in collaboration with WHO (European Office) and the Council of Europe: 'Health Education in the Pre-Service Training of Teachers', Luxembourg; a conference which for the first time drew together three of the main international organizations concerned with the promotion of health in schools. The conference confirmed the generally growing belief that health education should be included in the pre-service training of teachers primarily as a sensitizer to the health issues facing their future pupils.

The last-mentioned seminar augers well for future collaboration between international organizations and there is now the likelihood of a jointly supported feasibility study for a European school health education project starting some time in 1987. The European school health education movement can only gain from properly conducted and constructed exchanges of ideas, materials and, perhaps more importantly, experiences between countries. There is in Europe a great deal of experience and creativity available which can be channelled for the common good and it is possible that this will come about sooner than later.

REFERENCES

Council of Europe: Publications Office, Council of Europe, Strasbourg.
EEC: Directorita General, Social Affairs and Education, Batiment Jean monef, Plateau du Kischberg h-2920- Luxembourg.
International Union for Health Education: European Officer, Professor Maria Modello, University of Perugia, Perugia, Italy.

University of Southampton: Health Education Unit, Department of Education, University of Southampton, Southampton, England.
WHO-sponsored: WHO European Office, Copenhagan, Denmark.

SELECT BIBLIOGRAPHY

Anderson, D. (1979) *Health Education in Practice*, Croom Helm, London.
Baldwin, J. and Wells, H. (1979) *Active Tutorial Work* (Books 1–4), Basil Black-
well, Oxford.
Barnes, D. (1976) *From Communication to Curriculum*, Penguin, Harmondsworth.
Bates, I. J. and Winder, A. (1984) *Introduction to Health Education*, Mayfield,
Palo Alto, CA.
Brandling, R. (1983) *All for Assembly*, Cambridge University Press.
Braun, D. and Eisenstadt, N. (1985) *Family Lifestyles*, Open University Press,
Milton Keynes.
Brennan, W. (1982) *Changing Special Education*, Open University Press, Milton
Keynes.
Burns, R. (1982) *Self-Concept Development and Education*, Holt, Rinehart and
Winston, New York.
Button, L. (1974) *Development Group Work with Adolescents*, Hodder & Stough-
ton, Sevenoaks, Kent.
Campbell, G. (1985) *New Directions in Health Education*, Falmer Press, London.
Campbell, G. (ed.) (1986) *Health Education, Youth and Community*, Falmer Press,
London.
Craft, A. and Craft, M. (1983) *Sex Education and Counselling for Mentally
Handicapped People*, Costello Press, Tunbridge Wells.
David, K. (1983) *Personal and Social Education in Secondary Schools: Report of
the Schools Council Working Party on Personal and Social Education*, Longman,
York.
David, K. and Charlton, A. (1987) *The Caring Role of the Primary School*,
Macmillan, Basingstoke.
Dubos, R. (1967) *Man Adapting*, York University Press.
Engs, R. and Wantz, M. (1978) *Teaching Health Education in the Elementary
School*, Houghton Mifflin Co., Boston, MA.
Fogelman, K. (ed.) (1983) *Growing Up in Great Britain*, MacMillan for the
National Children's Bureau, London.
Ford, B. (1977) *Health Education a Source Book for Teaching*, Pergamon Press,
Oxford.
Goldman, J. and Goldman, R. (1982) *Children's Sexual Thinking*, Routledge &
Kegan Paul, London.
Green, L. W., Krenter, M. W., Deeds, S. G. and Partridge, K. B. (1980) *Health
Education Planning: A Diagnostic Approach*, Mayfield, Palo Alto, CA.
Hamblin, D. (1983) *Guidance 16–19*, Basil Blackwell, Oxford.
Health Education Council/University of Southampton (1986) *The Health Edu-
cation Awareness Day*. Materials for mounting a health education experience for
initial teacher education institutions, Health Education Unit, Department of
Education, University of Southampton.

Health Education Council (1983) *My Body*, Heinemann, London.

Health Education Council (1983) *A Discussion Paper on Proposals for National Guidelines for Health Education in Britain*, The NACNE Report, HEC, London.

Hodgson, A. (1985) *LEA Policies and Practices Relating to Drugs, Education and Drug Misuses*, NFER, Windsor.

Holt, J. (1983) *Curriculum Workshop: An Introduction to Whole Curriculum Planning*, Routledge & Kegan Paul, London.

Jones, N. D. (1982) *Understanding Child Abuse*, Hodder & Stoughton, Sevenoaks, Kent.

Maslow, A. H. (1968) *Towards A Psychology of Being*, 2nd edn, Van Nostrand, Princeton, NJ.

Monaster, J. (1977) *Adolescent Development and the Life Tasks*, Allyn and Bacon, Boston, MA.

Nash, W., Thruston, M. and Baly, M. (1985) *Health at School – Caring for the Whole Child*, Heinemann Nursing, London.

Open University (1979) *The Pre-School Child*, Open University Press, Milton Keynes.

Pring, R. (1984) *Personal and Social Education in the Curriculum*, Hodder & Stoughton, Sevenoaks, Kent.

Profitt, R. (1983) *Hand in Hand Assembly Book*, Longman, Harlow.

Reid, D. and Massey, D. (1986) Can school health education be more effective? *Health Educational Journal*, Vol. 45, No. 1.

Ross, H. and Mico, P. (1980) *Theory and Practice in Health Education*, Mayfield Publishing Co., Palo Alto, CA.

Schools Council (1977) *Schools Council: Health Education Project 5–13*, Thomas Nelson, London.

Schools Council (1983) *Fit for Life*, Books 1, 2 and 3, MacMillan Educational, Basingstoke.

Schools Council (1984) *Developing Health Education – A Coordinators' Guide*, Forbes, London.

Settle, D. and Wise, C. (1987) *Choices, Materials and Methods for Personal and Social Education*, Basil Blackwell, Oxford.

Strehlow, M. (1983) *Education for Health*, Harper & Row, London.

Tones, B. K. (1986) Promoting the health of young people: the role of personal and social education in achieving preventive outcomes, *Health Education Journal*, Vol. 45.

Townsend, P. and Davidson, N. (eds) (1982) *Inequalities in Health: The Black Report*, Penguin, London.

Went, D. (1985) *Sex Education – Some Guidelines for Teachers*, Bell Hyman, London.

Williams, T. and De Panafieu, C. (1985) *School Health Education in Europe: Profiles of 15 European Countries*, HEC Health Education Unit, Department of Education, University of Southampton.

Williams, T. and Roberts, J. (1985) *Health Education in Schools and Teacher Education Institutions*, HEC Health Education Unit, Department of Education, University of Southampton.

World Health Organization European Office Copenhagan (1984) *Health Promotion: A Discussion Document of the Concept and Principles*, WHO, Copenhagen.